A Thomas the Falconer
Mystery

D1062393

WITHDRAWN

A RUINOUS WIND

The Thomas the Falconer Series

THE RUFFLER'S CHILD
A RUINOUS WIND

A RUINOUS WIND

A Thomas the Falconer Mystery

John Pilkington

This first world edition published in Great Britain 2003 by
SEVERN HOUSE PUBLISHERS LTD of
9–15 High Street, Sutton, Surrey SM1 1DF.
This first world edition published in the USA 2004 by
SEVERN HOUSE PUBLISHERS INC of
595 Madison Avenue, New York, N.Y. 10022.

British Library Cataloguing in Publication Data

Pilkington, John, 1948-
    A ruinous wind. - (A Thomas the falconer mystery)
    1.   Great Britain - History - Elizabeth, 1558-1603 - Fiction
    2.   Detective and mystery stories
    I.   Title
    823.9'14 [F]

    ISBN 0-7278-6031-3

Typeset by Hewer Text Ltd.,
Edinburgh, Scotland.
Printed and bound in Great Britain by
MPG Books Ltd., Bodmin, Cornwall.

Acknowledgements

M y grateful thanks are due to: Sheila Ashcroft, assistant librarian of the Surrey Archaeological Society; the staff of Exeter Central Library; Grant Taylor and Geoff Pearson, falconers; Doctor Philip Evans; and as always my family for withstanding the worst that the wind could do.

For my father

Prologue

J ost van Rijssen's wife heard the Factor arrive at the end of a cloudy afternoon in late August, two days after the news had broken that the Spanish fleet was scattered. The threat of invasion, it seemed, was passed, and all of London was rejoicing. The bonfires that lit yesternight's sky still smouldered, the nearest at East Smithfield a stone's throw away, while in the City a mood of high excitement still prevailed. Otherwise, life in the parish of St-Katharine's-by-the-Tower, was unchanged: 500 households, many of them immigrants, crammed into a ragged trapezium of smelly, smoky tenements between Wapping in the east, the Tower in the west, East Smithfield on the north and the River to the south. A district of many trades, and of countless breweries, in which the narrow-fronted house of the merchant Jost van Rijssen looked no different to any other. Within the house, likewise all was unchanged. The baby howled, the older children ran wild, and the servants were insolent. Especially Tacy. Red-haired Tacy, the youngest and prettiest maidservant, had given Jost's wife cause for grief from the moment she arrived. But this evening, though neither of them yet knew it, all of that was about to end.

The Factor's task was to visit certain premises and collect the small but regular payments made to the Venturers. All she needed to know about the Venturers, Jost had told his wife, was that they were a group of merchants and speculators with varied interests, of whom he was proud to call himself an associate. This spoke of the success he had made of his life, since coming to England twenty years ago as a very young man, when those with the means and the foresight to flee the Low Countries had begun to do so before their land was overrun by

1

the Spanish. Jost, along with others of his fellow countrymen, had indeed prospered in London. Downstairs, the ground floor of the house was a treasure trove: bales of fine cloth from Flanders, rolls of Genoa velvet, Venice silk and soft sarcenet were stacked ceiling high. Cypress chests filled with plate and pottery stood against the walls. Sacks of spices, brought off the great ocean-going ships to the wharves upriver, filled the house at times with a heady perfume. Upstairs, where the household crowded into two airless, noise-filled floors, things were considerably less ordered. It gave Jost's wife cause for wry amusement to know that the well-dressed clients who came to do business with her husband, who took a glass of sack at his beechwood table before striking their bargains, had little inkling of the chaos that prevailed a few feet above their heads.

Jost was downstairs now, having dismissed both his prentices and bidden the last customer of the day a polite farewell. His wife was listening at the head of the stairs. It was past five of the clock and normally the next sound would be that of the key in its heavy lock, as Jost closed up shop for the night. But this night, she knew, he was awaiting the Factor.

She heard him come in, heard his low voice. Her husband, who habitually adopted the tone and modulation of his clients' speech, spoke softly in turn. She heard Jost go to the bargaining table. She thought there was the clink of coins, but this could have been mere fancy. It scarcely mattered, because she knew what would happen next – and it did not concern the Factor. She heard him go, heard the door close. Then came Jost's heavy footfall on the stairs, and the call she was expecting.

'Sophia!'

She had taken a few steps back along the passage. Now she waited a moment before coming forwards to answer.

'*Ja, ik ben boven.*'

'Speak English,' her husband ordered. The only time they seemed to speak Dutch nowadays was in bed. And since the birth of the last child, such moments of intimacy had become rare indeed.

'I am here,' Sophia answered, and came down at last, her wide hips brushing the narrow stairwell on either side.

2

Jost stood on the bottom step, his blond, bushy beard pointing up at her. He was looking more portly than ever, she thought, in his new padded doublet.

'Send Tacy down now. I want her to help me with the tally.'

She willed herself to meet his eye and hold it, and took a sliver of comfort as he lowered his gaze. When he spoke, his tone was harsh to conceal the shame that lay beneath the words.

'Hurry! And bid her bring a seed cake and a jug of Rhenish.'

'Your supper . . .' she began, and saw his mouth twitch with impatience.

'It will wait. Do as I say!'

She turned away and went back up the stairs.

A few minutes later Tacy came from the scullery bearing a tray with the wine and cake. At the head of the stairs she turned towards Sophia, and threw her a smirk of such brazen defiance that it was all her mistress could do not to strike her. Then Tacy descended and Sophia closed the passage door behind her, a little too loudly. She would not stay to listen to what followed, she told herself – then stopped suddenly, tears starting from her eyes. She berated herself: had this not happened often enough before? As she knew only too well, Jost was a choleric man, with needs which must be answered. The girl was but a simpering country wench when all was said and done, a mere vessel for his lust . . . and yet, Sophia knew she had been a good wife! How was she to blame, if she was now bloated and weary from child bearing, her skin blotched and dry, so that Jost had turned cruelly from her and sought release elsewhere?

Then she heard the scream.

For a moment she thought it was a cry of passion: her husband, she knew full well, was fumbling and foining Tacy among the bales, as he had done many times of late. But then came another scream, of pure terror. And in an instant Sophia was wrenching open the door and clattering down the stairs in her pattens, hair flying, for she knew that something terrible was happening.

It had happened already.

First she noticed that the door, which she thought locked,

3

was open. Then Tacy screamed again. Sophia ran across the rush-strewn floor towards the noise, and halted.

Her husband lay motionless, his back towards her, his breeches about his ankles, atop the writhing, screaming form of Tacy, spreadeagled on a cushion of bales, her skirts around her waist. Her apron had been pulled up to cover her head, but she had torn it aside and lay howling in fear, pinned down by Jost's bulk, all colour drained from her face.

And Jost . . .

Sophia saw the patch of blood at the base of his skull, matting his thick blond hair, and felt her heart stop. Dazed, she watched as Tacy with all her strength pushed Jost's limp body off her, scrambled aside and, screeching as only the distracted can, sank heavily to the floor. Her eyes rolled, and spittle ran down her chin.

Sophia paid no more attention to her, only looked down at the body of her husband, his sightless eyes staring upwards. Vaguely, she wondered if he had died before consummating his lust.

And still Tacy's howls filled the room . . . filled the street, if not the whole parish. The door creaked suddenly on its hinges, as if a blast of air had disturbed it; like the first flurry of an unforeseen tempest, which promises nothing but destruction.

One

T he militiamen returned to Petbury at sunset on a Friday, having spent another fruitless afternoon standing to on the Wantage road, in readiness for the call which never came. Instead, a sweating messenger on a lathered horse had come past, reining in just long enough to shout that the great Armada had been set alight by fireships, and victory was with the English. Some of the younger Petbury men had cheered while others looked sceptical, but nobody argued when someone suggested that in the absence of any orders, they might as well head for home. In the days that followed, however, the sceptics felt they had won the day, as rumour sped in upon rumour. The wildest ones, it seemed, were the fleetest: the Spaniards, far from being defeated, had landed on the South Coast and, reinforced by the Duke of Parma's forces, were even now marching on London. Nay, said the next one – London had fallen already, the Queen was captured and on her way to Rome, to stand before Pope Sixtus as a penitent. Then, after an anxious night in which nobody slept, came a messenger from the Lord Lieutenant of Berkshire to say that the Queen, far from being a prisoner, had gone downriver from London to Tilbury to rally her troops. Later the news broke that the Spanish fleet was indeed in disarray, being driven eastwards by high winds and out into the North Sea where, without powder and shot or even adequate food and water, they had no chance of regrouping for an attack. Then it was that the beacon on Lambourn Down burst into flame once again as it had done almost three weeks back, though whether it was as a signal this time, or merely fired in celebration by some jubilant spirit, nobody was certain.

All through Harvest Time, since the signal fires had sprung up on that fateful Tuesday, the second day of August, the manor of Petbury, like every other village, farm and homestead in southern England, had remained in a state of anxiety, if not in readiness. Even Thomas Finbow the falconer, ever a man for the quiet life, had been obliged to shoulder a pike and undergo rudimentary muster training alongside his fellows. Now at last it seemed the danger really had passed, though nobody was sure what would happen next. But there was no mistaking the wave of relief which swept through the country in the latter days of that windy, rainy August, as young and old alike hurried to get the harvest in. Despite the foulest summer weather most could remember, it was a good harvest, and the face of Sir Robert Vicary glowed with satisfaction as he rode about his tenant farms to watch the wheat, oats and rye stowed safely in the barns.

On the evening of the last day of August, a Wednesday, Thomas walked back to the falcons' mews with a hooded falcon on his wrist, one which he was still training at the lure. The new bird, brought from St Botolph fair in far-off Lincolnshire, was a swift flyer and showed great promise. Sir Robert was, as ever, eager to try her on the Downs, but recent activities had prevented such sport, which afforded his falconer no small relief as the bird was far from ready. While doing muster duty along with the other men of Petbury, Thomas had had little enough time to spend with his falcons. Now that the autumn migration was beginning, he had hoped to catch a pair of wild soar hawks, barely a few months old, ripe for training. Instead, he found himself tied to the manor while events in the English Channel decided his fate.

He placed the hawk on a perch, slipped off the hood and loosed the jesses from her legs, noting with satisfaction that Eleanor had placed food and fresh water close by. Seeing that all the birds were quiet, he walked the few yards to his cottage, lifted the latch and stepped inside.

The fire was banked, there was bread and cheese on the table and a jug of beer, but no sign of Eleanor. He frowned. Of late, his thirteen-year-old daughter had been giving him cause for concern. At first it had amounted to little more than a giggle when she noticed the heads of the stable lads turn as she walked past. Then the giggling gave way to a smile at the farrier's son, who was fourteen years old and already a lusty youth. Thomas had sighed inwardly, only too aware how pretty the girl was – was she not the image of her late mother, whom as a young man he had trailed after with the same hangdog look he now saw on the face of the gangling farrier's boy?

The sound of the latch startled him from his reverie, and he turned quickly as Eleanor came in. There was a glow in her cheeks, as if she had been running. He tried to fix her with a stern expression.

'I thought you'd be at table before me.'

She took off her worn cloak and hung it on a peg. 'Lady Margaret had further duties for me. She's tricked up in her finest.'

Thomas raised an eyebrow. If guests were expected to dine at the great house tonight, it probably meant a hawking party tomorrow. He had better be ready.

When they sat down to eat, however, he soon learned the cause of Eleanor's suppressed excitement. She was only too eager to speak of it.

'Catherine's with child again.'

He nodded. Lady Margaret's servant Catherine had married James the groom two years back, and had already given birth to her first child. A second was not unexpected.

'You'll be taking over her tasks, then.'

'More than that.'

He caught the gleam in her eye, and waited.

'I'm to be my lady's new maid. She wants me to move into her chamber. Sleep in a trundle bed beside hers.'

He considered, chewing on a hard crust of bread, then saw her break into a wide smile.

'She says I can have her sea-green gown, now that I'm near tall enough to wear it. And I shall have care of her jewels, even the Roman pearls and the gold chain with the agates!'

Thomas kept a straight face. 'So your father must needs get his own supper, after a hard day's toil.'

7

She levelled a knowing gaze at him. 'You can eat with the kitchen folk. Nell was asking after you only this morning.'

Watching his expression, she laughed outright. Talk of Nell, the new cook, never failed to embarrass him. There had been much mirth about Petbury since someone first noticed Nell's tendency to flush and fumble with her ladles whenever the tall falconer dropped by the kitchen with a clutch of birds for the supper table.

'Never mind that,' he grunted. 'Lady Margaret ought to have spoken with me first. You're still young to be a ladies' maid.'

She pouted, then caught the look on his face and stopped herself.

'But then, I suppose she knew I'd be hard-pressed to stop you.'

She grinned and poured more beer. And her joy was such that he could not help but return the smile, and be happy for her.

The next morning, thinking of Eleanor while he went about his work, Thomas received news which took the grin off his face at a stroke.

'Epsom Downs?' he muttered, waiting cap in hand before Sir Robert in the stable yard, where he had been summoned only minutes before.

His master nodded, standing tall in his new riding boots while grooms scurried about readying his favourite hawking horse. He was in good humour this morning, which after the strain of recent weeks was no bad thing, perhaps. But the task he was laying upon Thomas spoke of a long journey, and much work at the end of it.

'I am invited by the Earl of Reigate to his great house of Barrowhill, which is in Surrey. Near the village of Tadworth. Fine hawking country, Thomas. The Earl has his own falconer, but I have a mind to take you along. There will be many noble guests – rich pickings for you, if you work well!'

Thomas was silent. He disliked travelling long distances to great men's houses, where both the country and the company were unfamiliar. But, if Sir Robert wished it . . .

8

'Come now, don't sour the air with your long face,' Sir Robert boomed, turning to nod with approval as his horse was led forward. 'The Earl is one of the wealthiest men in the southern counties – his house is famous throughout England. You will see sights you never dreamed of. The Countess is a Lady of the Queen's Bedchamber.' He dropped his voice, bent his head closer. 'Plenty of female company at Barrowhill. You'll not turn your nose up at that? A man who's been widowed as long as you have?'

Thomas struggled to prevent the flush rising on his face. Sir Robert's guffaw told him he had lost the battle.

'Time you found yourself a new wife, Thomas,' the knight said, prompting a snigger from James the groom, who stood by with face averted. 'How many years is it now?'

'Nigh on five, sir,' Thomas answered, making a silent vow to clip James's ear at the earliest opportunity.

'Long as that?' Sir Robert mused, and stepped on to the mounting block. 'Well then – the matter's settled. We shall leave for Surrey at first light on Saturday. Prepare a carrying cage for the hawks.'

He gripped the pommel and swung his large bulk expertly into the saddle. 'It's three days' ride at the least. Pick yourself out a good mount – and be sure to take your best hawking gear. I scarcely know the Earl, but I hear he's a man who takes his pleasures seriously.'

'Very well, Sir Robert,' Thomas answered, resigning himself to the task. Then as his master shook the reins, touched heels to his horse and rode off towards the falcons' mews, he was obliged to follow at a run, jamming his cap on his head as he went.

So it was that two days later Sir Robert Vicary, accompanied by his falconer and a single manservant, rode out of the gates of Petbury and took the road running south from Wantage.

Thomas had made his farewell to Eleanor and delivered a short but, to his mind, necessary sermon on her behaviour while he was absent. On the ten-mile ride to Newbury, he had ample time in which to reflect that the words had passed as mere shadows through his daughter's mind, to be forgotten as soon as he was gone. She had waved him off, then turned to walk cheerfully to the house and to her new duties. Lady Margaret, it was noticed, did not come down in the early morning to bid Sir Robert goodbye. Though few spoke of it, there was a general acceptance at the manor that relations between the master and his wife were at best cordial, at worst indifferent. It was thought that he took his pleasures elsewhere, especially in London which he had begun to visit more frequently in the past year. He had even been seen at Court, and was mixing more with men and women of exalted station than the country squires and other hawking and hunting friends with whom he had always associated. The invitation from the Earl of Reigate was testimony to this new state of affairs.

After a short rest and a bit of dinner at Newbury the three men pressed on apace, reaching Tadley by mid-afternoon. Simon, Sir Robert's ageing manservant, was unaccustomed to riding and began to complain of soreness in his limbs, but his master was insistent that they reach Finchampstead by nightfall. Luckily the rain held off and the road was fair, so that at the end of a hard day in the saddle they reached the village as lights began to appear. The inn was neither large nor sumptuous, but they were all too tired to care.

That night, as Thomas climbed the stairs to the room he would share with other travellers, including an exhausted Simon, who was already abed, the door of the best chamber opened above him, and Sir Robert called out his name.

When he entered the room the knight was reclining on the bed in his shirt and breeches, his head propped against feather pillows. In his hand was a goblet of claret.

'Will you join me?' Sir Robert asked, and gestured to a flagon on a nearby chest.

'Nay, I'm for my bed, Sir Robert,' Thomas smiled. 'I've grown unused to long riding these past years.'

Sir Robert said nothing, but took a long pull from the goblet and wiped his mouth. 'What I told you, some days ago,' he began, then paused to belch. 'It . . . wasn't quite the truth.'

Thomas's body ached for sleep, but he waited.

'The Lady Felice . . . the Countess of Reigate,' Sir Robert said, almost in the manner of someone stating an oath, 'is not a Lady of the Queen's Bedchamber. Not any more.'

Thomas raised an eyebrow politely.

'She was, until recent times,' the knight went on, 'until she was dismissed by Her Majesty, for . . .' he trailed off. 'For some small indiscretion that need not concern you.'

'Very good, Sir Robert,' Thomas muttered, wondering where all this was leading.

'The Earl and his wife, Thomas, are Epicureans,' Sir Robert said, and smiled suddenly. 'They are people of a high mounting spirit, that care little for worldly trifles. That is why men of quality and wit flock to their court. For a court it is,' he nodded emphatically. 'Little more than twenty miles from London, and but a few miles from the Queen's palace of Nonsuch, which is one of the fairest sights of the realm . . . yet even Nonsuch, I hear, pales beside the Earl's seat of Barrowhill.'

Sir Robert stared absently at the coverlet on which he sprawled, then seemed to recollect himself. He took another drink, and swung his gaze on to his falconer.

'What I mean to say, Thomas,' he continued, 'is that you, as always, enjoy my trust. I am confident therefore, that I may count on your discretion in . . . in the days ahead.'

At last, thought Thomas, he comes to the nub of it. He was merely being told to turn a blind eye to whatever his master got up to in the halls of this pleasure-loving Earl.

'Be assured of it, Sir Robert,' Thomas answered. 'I ask only that you allow me to keep myself busy.'

Sir Robert seemed content. He tipped his goblet, drained it at a gulp, then waved it in Thomas' direction.

'You will have a pleasant time of it, have no fears on that score,' he said. His features twisted into a huge yawn. 'Now I'd best let you go to your bed. We've more hard travel tomorrow.'

Thomas made his slight bow and went out to the passage. Behind him, another loud belch rang out in his master's chamber.

*   *   *

The next morning Sir Robert and Simon the manservant both overslept, so that Thomas had not only time to take his pint of porridge in peace, but an hour in which to exercise the two falcons he had brought. Both the female – Sir Robert's favourite, Clorinda – and the tercel were restless when he entered the stables, so that he was glad to take them out of the cage and into a nearby field where they could soar.

Today, Sunday, the cloud had thinned and sunbeams poked through. Within the hour horses were saddled and ready, and a bad-tempered Sir Robert came out followed by a stiff-legged Simon. Wordlessly the three men mounted up and clattered out of the inn yard, taking the road for Bagshot.

The road led through the great forest of Windsor, a royal park, but there were no hunting parties this morning. Indeed, all the countryside through which they rode seemed oddly quiet. It was plain to see how the invasion scare had left its mark upon the land, with militiamen pressed into service from every village, and many folk, it was said, having gone to the coast to watch the great sea battle, even though it had ended weeks ago. An odd time, Thomas thought as he rode, to be having revels; what kind of man was this Epicurean Earl with his private court?

The thought faded as another long day's riding began to take its toll on his body. By mid-day they had passed through the parish of Bagshot, cleared the forest and reached Woking, which stood in fair meadows near a river. The rolling county of Surrey, a patchwork of arable, emerald-green pasture and woodland, stretched away southwards towards the low hills of Guildford.

Past Woking they forded the river Wey, then at the little hamlet of Ripley struck the straight road running north-east to Cobham, where Sir Robert intended to pass the night. So at last, after a ride of more than thirty miles, they forded the wide river Mole and pulled wearily into the village, with the welcome smoke from chimneys hanging in the air, and a peal of bells sounding for evensong.

After supper in the inn, Sir Robert and Simon having gone early to their beds, Thomas went to the stables to check that the horses were well cared for, and fed the birds. Coming out into the dusk he sniffed the air, frowning slightly as he felt the wind, rising from the south-west. It spoke of more gales. Tomorrow they would reach the Downlands of Leatherhead and Epsom – but high winds meant there would be small opportunity for hawking. If there was one thing he loathed, it was having time on his hands with nothing to fill it.

To shake off the feeling of foreboding, he walked into the taproom and called for a mug. The place was almost empty. Perhaps the Cobham folk were strict observers of the sabbath, he thought vaguely as he took a stool near the fire. Finding the ale good, he took a long draught from his mug, then lowered it to find himself staring into a pair of the shiftiest eyes he had ever seen, barely a yard in front of him.

The eyes belonged to a spindle-thin, tousled-haired man in travel-stained clothes, with an unkempt beard and a face seamed with grime. On the floor beside him was a lumpy pack, patched and bound up with hempen rope. But oddest of all, to Thomas' mind, was not the roll of parchment tied around the man's neck, arresting though it was, but the manner in which he had taken the facing seat so subtly, without Thomas being aware of him.

For a moment neither of them spoke. The man's eyes, however, did service for both of them. In a very short time Thomas had the feeling that he had been thoroughly assessed and dismissed as a harmless artisan passing *en route* to nowhere of importance.

'Wind's getting up,' the tousled-haired man said with a bland smile, as if to emphasize that this was merely the chaff of conversation.

'True enough,' Thomas said, allowing his own eyes to survey the fellow in return. The man had no mug, but clasped an old leather bottle such as horsemen often carried.

'Bound for London?' he asked, in a way that suggested he knew perfectly well Thomas was not.

Though noted on the Berkshire Downs as a shrewd judge of character, Thomas found himself hard-pressed to gain some point of reference here. For now, he merely shook his head.

'I'm named Tobias,' the man said suddenly. 'Licensed to beg in the county of Surrey. Want to look?'

He held up the parchment. With a brief shrug Thomas declined the invitation. Though he could read as well as any Petbury man who had endured a few short years at Doctor Scambler's tiny village school, he had the feeling that a perusal of the crabbed handwriting on that dog-eared paper would tell him nothing.

'A penny would buy me a drop of small beer,' Tobias said, with a sideways shift of his eyes towards the bottle.

Thomas sighed, brought forth the coin and held it out, but the beggar hesitated a moment before taking it. Then he leaned back and favoured him with a wider smile than before.

'I thank you, master falconer.'

Thomas must have showed his surprise too readily for, to his consternation, Tobias gave a snort of laughter.

'I'm no moonman, nor a witch, master,' he said, and sniffed loudly. 'You're a servant to his lordship in the best chamber above, is't not so? And those are your hawks in the stable.'

Thomas took a drink from his mug, and kept silent.

'You'll be for the Downs, by Leatherhead,' the beggar added, more as a statement than a question. When Thomas still refrained from comment, he went on: 'It's the best country for falconing. No secret, that.'

Maybe there was no harm in the man after all, Thomas thought. Though for a beggar, licensed or no, he was too clever by half.

'I'm falconer to Sir Robert Vicary,' he said, stifling a yawn. 'He's visiting his friends—' he stopped himself.

'At Barrowhill?' came the swift reply. The eyes were suddenly alert. 'What company be there now, do you know?'

Thomas stiffened inwardly and tried to meet Tobias's stare, but now he saw the eyes slide across the taproom towards the doorway. The next moment, he realized why.

'Oi – you!' came a deep-throated shout. Thomas turned to see the drawer, a fat man in a filthy apron, bearing down on them.

In a moment Tobias was on his feet, and had assumed the shambling, fawning demeanour of beggars the world over.

'Mercy, goodman,' he whined, grabbing his pack with his free hand while he held the leather bottle forward with the other. 'I'm poor Tobias, licensed to beg in the county—'

'Shut your foul mouth,' the drawer growled, clapping a broad hand round Tobias' neck. 'We don't serve thieves and vagabonds here – get your arse outside!'

And poor Tobias was promptly shoved across the floor, through the open door and out into the night. Perhaps it was a trick of the firelight, but as the beggar disappeared, whining pitifully the whole time, Thomas thought he caught the hint of a gleam in one rolling eye, which was directed at him, and him alone. *You see that this is my part*, the eye seemed to say, *and I must play it to the hilt.*

Then the interlude was over. The few other drinkers in the room chuckled, turned back to their ale and resumed their gossip.

Thomas drained his mug, rose and left them to it.

On the following afternoon, with the breeze blowing at their backs, Sir Robert and his two servants rode the last twenty miles from Cobham, through Leatherhead and past Willmore Pond to Epsom, where the rolling Downs opened above and about them. Passing the tiny hamlet of Burghouse, they rode south-east to Tadworth. From here, Sir Robert had been told to leave the track where it bent around a marking post, and strike due east.

For another quarter hour they rode in silence, Sir Robert cantering ahead now in his eagerness, while Thomas and Simon trotted behind. Larks twittered above, and still the Downs rose, until presently a grassy ridge appeared ahead of them, stark against the skyline. With a shout Sir Robert spurred his horse forward, his cloak flying, then reined in as he reached the summit. Thomas and Simon rode up on either side of him and halted. Grey-headed Simon, a simple Berkshire Downland man, could not refrain from letting out a gasp. For his part, Sir Robert took in a great gulp of sweet air, and smiled in anticipation.

15

But Thomas could only gaze in silence at the gleaming domes with their fluttering pennants, the many-sided towers and high, decorated walls of the splendid palace that dominated the wide escarpment beyond.

They had reached Barrowhill.

Two

I n the lengthening shadows of late afternoon, Sir Robert's party splashed through a shallow stream and climbed the slopes of the long hill. Passing through a gateway in the outer wall, which was of solid red brick, and into an inner park where deer scattered at their approach, they found themselves beneath the plastered and stuccoed walls of the massive house itself. It was indeed a palace, a 'prodigy house' such as powerful men had been building in recent years to demonstrate their wealth as well as their taste. Pinnacles and turrets with mullioned windows towered above a vast, imposing entrance with gilded plasterwork and stone sculptures above. Beyond the house, its stables and outbuildings, Thomas glimpsed elaborate gardens with trellised walks, groves and flower beds – and further off, a wide lake that had no doubt been dug by the labour of many men. It was an enchanted place, an oasis of luxury in the midst of these treeless hills, across which drifted low, milk-white clouds.

As the horsemen clattered through a side archway into a broad courtyard there were shouts, and grooms hurried out to take their mounts. A grey-haired man in a sober gown and black doublet appeared, and bowed low as they reined in before him.

'I bid you welcome to Barrowhill, Sir Robert. I am John Broad, steward to the Earl of Reigate.'

Sir Robert got down stiffly, nodding to the steward. Thomas and Simon were in the act of dismounting when suddenly there rang out a blast of trumpets which startled both men and horses. Peering upwards, they saw three trumpeters in scarlet livery, sounding their fanfare from an exposed gallery high above. Whoever ruled here, had notions of grandeur indeed.

As the trumpets ceased, there came a shout of delight, and here came the host, hurrying down a flight of steps from a door at the end of the courtyard. Maybe the sennet, thought Thomas, had not been for their welcome at all, but to announce the entrance of the Earl himself. His next thought, as the Earl reached the bottom stair, was that the man needed such trumpery to give himself the stature he lacked. He was well below average height, though handsome enough, with a neatly trimmed beard and blond curls tumbling from beneath a tall, richly decorated hat. His doublet was likewise embroidered with golden thread and with jewels, his wide breeches of peach-coloured satin, the shoes heavy with gold buckles. The word 'dandy' was barely adequate to describe the lord of Barrowhill.

'Sir Robert!' cried the Earl, clasping his hands about his guest's and kissing him on the cheek. 'What times we shall have! Tonight a banquet – tomorrow, hawking and hunting! The company has awaited your arrival with such impatience, I've had to stuff them with strawberries and ply them with my best charneco!'

Smiling broadly, Sir Robert murmured how delighted he was, then raised his eyes to the walls about him. 'Your magnificent house, my Lord – such descriptions I've heard, fail dismally to do it justice. Even Nonsuch cannot match it!'

The Earl almost squealed. 'Nonsuch was built by Henry the Eighth in imitation of the Château of Chambord on the Loire – my Barrowhill has more rooms even than Chambord!'

Sir Robert nodded politely and, somewhat lost for words, gestured to Thomas, who doffed his cap and stepped forward.

'My falconer, Thomas Finbow.'

'Splendid!' trilled the Earl, and turned to his steward, who stood by, maintaining a grave expression. 'Send him to Will Holland at once.'

The steward bowed and turned to Thomas. Simon, busy unpacking Sir Robert's gear, was ordered to follow another servant to chambers already prepared.

The grooms stood by, waiting to unsaddle the horses, so

Thomas quickly united his own pack and the cage with the hawks. As the Earl ushered Sir Robert away, he heard his master enquire after the Lady Felice, which prompted another squeal from his host.

'God's knees and knuckles, she's sitting for her damned portrait again! There's a Dutch painter in the house, eating my pork and quaffing my beer, and neither of them in the slightest hurry to finish! Tell me, how shall I bear it?!'

Then the two nobles were striding up the steps, their servants quickly forgotten. As his master disappeared inside the house, John Broad relaxed visibly and favoured Thomas with a shrewd smile.

'You'll grow accustomed to Lord Edmund. Come, let me take you to the falconer. He has lodgings prepared, and a supper for you if I'm not mistaken.'

With a nod to the old steward, Thomas picked up the cage and followed him through an arch towards the rear of the great house. Past stables and kennels they walked, skirting a paddock where horses grazed, and up a slope to a tiny hut beside a copse of small oaks, no doubt planted by the builders of Barrowhill. Against the wall of the hut, sheltered from the wind, was the open lean-to, a falcons' mews similar to the one Thomas had built at Petbury. The sight of the familiar lifted his spirits.

Will Holland was a quietly spoken man with a dark beard and deep brown eyes which met Thomas's gaze steadily, the two falconers at ease with each other within minutes of their meeting. John Broad left them, bidding Will be ready for a lively hawking party in the morning. The Earl was anxious to show off his birds to his guests, especially Sir Robert.

'I hear your master's always been a hawking man,' Will mused, as he and Thomas took a pathway up on to the Downs. Each carried a bird on the wrist.

'All his life,' Thomas answered. 'I've trained many a soar hawk for him, and for the Lady Margaret. Not to mention the pair of gyrfalcons – the master's pride.'

Will nodded. Loosing the leash from his hawk, a magnificent bird with a great hooked beak and richly speckled down on its chest, he slipped off the hood and held his arm aloft. At once

19

the bird spread its wings, lifted itself and climbed in a steady spiral until it was little more than a speck high above their heads. Thomas followed suit, letting the smaller tercel speed away, to hover at lower altitude. Both birds were eager to hunt.

The falconers watched their charges as evening fell, and a breeze sang through the long grass. A moment of unspoken understanding passed between them: this was their world, the open Downland and the sky, and a falcon hanging above, floating on the current as if part of the very fabric of the air.

With a half-smile, Will voiced the thought for both of them.

'A pity we've to serve our betters all of tomorrow.'

Thomas nodded.

'Have you a wife, children?' Will Holland asked.

'A daughter,' Thomas answered. 'My wife died of a fever, five years back.'

'And you've not remarried?'

Thomas threw him a rueful smile. 'You as well? My master chides me about it, without mercy.'

'You'll lodge with me,' Will said. 'I've neither wife nor child, so there's room enough.' He threw Thomas a sly look. 'And if you're looking for womanly company while you're at Barrow-hill, I can point you in the right direction.'

Thomas gave a slight shrug. 'I take what comes my way.'

'Tadworth's three miles south-east, towards Walton,' Will said. 'The Red Bull inn has good cheer, of an evening.' Having passed on this piece of information, he grew businesslike. 'But then, you'll likely be fit for naught but to fall into your bed like a corpse, by tomorrow night. My Lord works us till we drop when he's guests he wants to outdo.'

'The other guests . . .?' Thomas enquired, and saw Will's mouth tighten with disapproval.

'Company I like not,' he said. In his eyes, a frank gaze which said: I speak to you as a fellow, of the brotherhood of falconers. Thomas returned the gaze expectantly.

'A party from London,' Will said. 'Came down two days ago. Some are but hangers-on. Others – there's Sir George Brunning . . . a man I'd not cross for a purse of angels. He's said to have killed men in duels. Too handy with his sword-arm, not to

20

mention his tongue. Another . . .' he trailed off, gave a slight shake of his head. Thomas waited.

'If you thought my Lord was a man of high fashion,' Will continued, 'you'd best clap eyes on Sir Thomas Wilkes. They say he spent three hundred pounds on new clothes and horse trappings, just for this visit.'

Thomas frowned. 'I've not heard of either of them.'

'The sons of jumped-up gentry,' Will told him. 'Projectors, I hear they're called – such as make their fortunes where they may. My master has fingers in many pies.'

He shaded his eyes, peered upwards as his hawk dropped like a stone and sank its talons into a hapless crow that had strayed into its vision. A gust of wind lifted both men's collars.

Will sighed and clapped Thomas on the shoulder. 'I grow tedious. Come, let's go to our supper.'

He raised his arm and gave a sharp, keening cry, so that the mighty hawk wheeled and carried its prey obediently towards them.

Supper in the small cottage was a simple affair of pottage, bread and mutton from the kitchens, washed down with beer brewed of the second malting. But there was plenty of it, so that at the end Thomas sat back with a grateful smile at his host.

'As good as a banquet,' he said. 'I shall need to step outside and walk it off.'

Will gave him a sober look. 'Best have a care where you walk,' he said. 'The Earl has traps set about the park.' He lowered his voice. 'A poacher was caught last year . . . master's dogs tore him to pieces.'

Thomas frowned.

'They're the law here,' Will went on. 'Lord Edmund, and especially her – Lady Felice. They answer to no one – save the Queen when she's down at Nonsuch, which bain't too often.'

'I hear the Countess was sent away from Court,' Thomas said, though as always, gossip came unwillingly to his tongue. Will seemed to sense that, and favoured him with a wry look.

'She's got a reputation, you might say,' he allowed. 'I

wouldn't enquire too closely into any of the goings-on at Barrowhill, if I were you.'

He was not smiling. Thomas drained his mug and set it down on the board. 'Good advice, I'd guess.'

They rose then, to see to the falcons. As they stepped outside darkness was falling. From the vast shadow of Barrowhill lights burned at many windows, and the faint sound of hautboys, shawms and viols was carried towards them on the wind.

'The Earl has his own music-makers,' Will said. 'And keeps a tame poet in his house in London, so I hear. He lacks for nothing in the realms of pleasure.'

The cloud had thinned, and there was a three-quarter moon to aid them as they walked round to the lean-to. The falcons roused at their approach. As they put out fresh water for the birds, there came a roar of distant laughter.

'The Great Chamber stretches almost the full length of the house,' Will said. 'Round to the right, there are steps down to the gardens and the maze. Master don't like us to go there, but if you want to stroll, it's the place you're least likely to be noticed.'

Despite his tiredness, Thomas was curious to explore. 'I'd like to take an hour before I go to my bed,' he said.

'Remember – have a care where you walk,' Will warned him.

Thomas nodded and walked off down the slope, towards the gardens of Barrowhill.

Rounding the corner of the great house, he saw that flickering torches had been placed on iron stands, illuminating the wide steps that led down to lawns, flower beds and, in the distance, what he took to be the maze. The noise from the Great Chamber was louder here, but there was nobody outdoors, and none to challenge him as he walked freely among the well-kept beds and vine-covered walks. The perfume of late summer roses, and of flowers he did not know, filled his nostrils. As he quickened pace to put some distance between himself and the house, the darkness closed about him, but there was enough moonlight for him to pick his way. Still the gardens stretched away, paths winding between walls, box hedges and arched bowers, with marble statues at many corners. From somewhere came the noise of falling water: there must be a stream, or even fountains. He paused to take a deep draught of night air. The manifestation of such enormous wealth, beside which even his master's large but plain house appeared almost humble, made him uneasy.

He turned a corner, and was diverted to see how the hedge had been cut into some fantastic shape, that of a winged creature he did not recognize. At its base it was fashioned into an alcove where a stone seat was placed, offering privacy from three sides . . . and from whence, all at once, came sounds: a muffled oath, a gasp and a rustle of silk or satin. And Thomas halted, cursing silently. Believing himself alone, he had grown careless. The seat was occupied by two people, in an act of unmistakeable intimacy.

Swiftly he averted his gaze and turned to walk away, but it was too late. From behind came an angry male voice which stopped him in his tracks.

'Stand still, you devil!'

There was a hurried exchange of low voices behind him, and then a silence. Biting his lip, Thomas waited. To his surprise, there came laughter: a woman's laugh, low and musical, even languid.

Then, a man's footfall.

'Turn about, damn you!'

Thomas turned, found himself looking at a tall, muscular man in a white rouched shirt and breeches of some gold-embroidered material that shone in the moonlight. The man was hatless, his hair awry. He glared at Thomas, looking him up and down, then noting the plainness of his simple garb, began to relax somewhat.

'Who are you, rogue? How dare you trespass?'

'Forgive me, sir,' Thomas said mildly. 'I'm falconer to Sir Robert Vicary. I'm new to the country – I was caring for my hawks, and lost my way.'

The man sniffed, visibly regaining status as he perceived the threat diminishing. 'Servants aren't permitted here,' he snapped. 'I could have you dismissed for spying, man!'

'I can only ask pardon, sir,' Thomas replied. 'As for spying, I've seen nothing. If you'll allow me, I'll go to my lodging.'

The man still glowered. From the seat behind him, dimly visible in the shadow of the bower, came a low chuckle. The man bristled and half-turned, tense with embarrassment.

'God in heaven, madam . . .' he began, then stopped himself as if realizing the situation was beyond saving. With a stifled oath he took a step into the shadows, caught up some items of clothing, and turned back to Thomas.

'If you knew me,' he said quietly, 'you would know how close you came to oblivion, falconer.'

Thomas met his eyes, and saw the cold fury that suffused them. It was no idle boast. With a half-glance behind him, the man strode quickly away in the direction of the house.

Now followed a moment which seemed to last an eternity as Thomas stood his ground, at a loss whether to go or stay. He could but thank his maker for the dimness of the light, as his face would likely have shown up crimson.

Finally there came another rustle of clothing, and a pale shape materialized from the shadows of the bower to raise itself before him. As she came forward, clouded in voluminous skirts of silver and blue, Thomas realized that he had somehow known from the beginning that he was in the presence of the Lady Felice, Countess of Reigate. As if it too would serve her, the moon slid from behind a cloud at that moment and shone full on her face.

Thomas swallowed audibly. She seemed to glitter, which he soon understood was because of the wealth of jewels that hung about her: dangling from her ears, round her neck, on her gown, her fingers and about her wrists. Her black hair was dressed in a caul of tiny pearls. The dark eyes peered archly at him from an oval face, which even in the dim light Thomas could see was heavily painted. Below the neck, he was aware that her gown was cut so low, her breasts were all but exposed. Her pale skin showed beneath a gleaming necklace of many-coloured stones.

'So you are Sir Robert's falconer,' she said gently. 'Do you have a name?'

'Thomas Finbow, my Lady.'

She displayed not the least sign of embarrassment. Rather, she still seemed amused by the whole episode.

24

'Well, Thomas Finbow, see what you get from poking about in private gardens of a night-time.'

'Indeed, my Lady, it was foolish of me,' Thomas answered, praying silently that she would simply let him go. He vowed he would never set foot in the garden again.

She surveyed him from head to toe, rather as if she were looking over a new horse for purchase.

'Do you like being a falconer?' she asked suddenly, and smiled. She was indeed a beautiful woman. Small wonder that the Earl would have her portrait painted.

'It suits me well enough, my Lady,' Thomas told her. 'I want no other work.'

Unable to stop himself, he gazed at Lady Felice . . . until she gave a yawn, and the spell was broken abruptly. What was he to her, after all, but a servant in leather and fustian?

But she was not done with him yet. She made a sudden movement, pulling at her wrist. There was a faint chink of metal. Extending one pale hand she proffered a silver pendant. Its value, Thomas guessed, was equal to half of his yearly wage.

'Well, take it,' Lady Felice said, as if irritated that he should need instruction. 'As a little token of my gratitude, for your seeing nothing.'

'Nay, my Lady,' Thomas said, 'I need no payment.'

'You defy me?' came the reply. There was a slight edge to her voice. 'Then you are either a very bold falconer, or a very stupid one.'

'It is too grand a prize for me,' Thomas said. 'If you'll permit me, I'll be on my way, and not presume upon your ladyship's privacy again.'

There was a faint intake of breath from Lady Felice. 'You *do* defy me,' she said, as if in wonder at such behaviour. 'Do you make so free with your master – or indeed, with your mistress?'

At this, Thomas felt his stomach tighten. His brief, dangerous indiscretion with the Lady Margaret, two years ago in London, was a memory he kept hidden away in a corner of his mind – a secret known only, he believed, to the two of them. But then, he had never been entirely certain, and never would be.

He bit his lip and dismissed the notion, lowering his gaze to rest on the silver shoes of Lady Felice.

'A man who cannot be bought,' she continued coolly, 'may be a danger to some – but most of all perhaps, to himself. You strayed from your path, falconer. Such imprudence is not tolerated here at Barrowhill. Do you mark that?'

Thomas took a breath, and nodded.

'You will speak of this,' Lady Felice said, 'to no one. Else –' and here she leaned forward slightly, so that he saw her chest heave – 'the consequences will be very grave; the price far too high. Do not mistake me.'

He forced himself to meet her gaze, and almost shivered. There sat a demon in those eyes, beside which the angry threats of her lover (was he her lover, or merely a man with whom she had dallied this once?) counted as nothing.

'I do not mistake, my Lady,' Thomas answered. 'May I leave you now?'

She did not answer, but peered into his face as if to satisfy herself that there was no vestige of a threat. In the far distance, borne on a sudden breeze, came once again the sounds of high revelry from the Great Chamber.

Then the Lady Felice dismissed him with the curtest of nods and he turned abruptly, his heart pounding with mixed emotions, and walked away from her into the welcome gloom of the gardens.

Three

T he next morning as Thomas, Will Holland and other men from the Earl's estate were readying their birds, the best-attired hawking party he had ever seen rode out of the gates of Barrowhill.

He and Will had been up since dawn preparing for the day's sport. Grooms and cottagers with some hawking knowledge had joined them, at Will's request, because of the size of the party. The Earl's train was so grand that not only noble guests would ride to hawk, but the better of his servants who were gentlemen themselves, men like John Broad and the usher of the Earl's Great Chamber, a weasel-faced man named Henry Barnard. These two rode out before the main group, and reined in near the mews where the falconers waited.

'You have instructed Sir Robert's servant thoroughly, I hope?' Barnard asked, looking haughtily down at Will.

'Thomas needs little instruction from me, sir,' Holland replied, and busied himself with the jesses on his bird's legs. Thomas sensed his friend's resentment. Indeed, he took an instant dislike to Barnard himself.

'The Earl will wander where the mood takes him,' Barnard said, frowning at Thomas. 'You may find yourselves over the Kent border by evening. You'll have to make your own way back.'

'Are we not to have mounts, then?' Thomas asked. Barnard's contemptuous snort gave him his answer. Clearly he, Will and the other men were expected to spend the entire day on foot.

John Broad, who seemed a kindly man, favoured Thomas with an indulgent smile. 'Do not fret, falconer. If the Earl is pleased there'll be a goodly purse for you at the close of the day.'

Most of the Barrowhill men seemed cheered by his words. Thomas and Will, each taking a bird on the wrist, saw that the other falcons were hooded and ready – not before time, because a loud fanfare of trumpets sounded, and all eyes turned to see the splendid procession that emerged from the house.

It fell little short of a royal progress. The Earl and Countess led the party, attired in colourful riding clothes, Lady Felice in a tall hat ornamented with bows. Behind them came several noblemen including Sir Robert Vicary, and as many ladies on throughbred mounts. Garish padded doublets, velvet cloaks, feathered hats and richly embroidered gloves were everywhere. Prominent among the men, Thomas noted with a tightening of his gullet, was the one he had encountered last night in the gardens, and whom he now learned was Sir Thomas Wilkes. Today Wilkes kept some distance between himself and Lady Felice, paying close attention to one of the younger ladies, who seemed highly flattered by it.

'That's Sir George Brunning behind Wilkes,' Will murmured. Thomas saw a shorter, stockier man on a very frisky horse, who seemed to be permanently on the alert. Others were more at ease, taking their cue from the chattering Earl, eager to enjoy the day. The younger men, tricked up like peacocks, rode beside the Countess's ladies-in-waiting, flirting openly and vying with each other for attention. All of this pageant was familiar enough to Thomas, steward of countless hawking parties throughout his years of service to Sir Robert. But he was soon to see sights that were somewhat stranger to him.

The first was a dwarf in a brightly coloured suit, mounted on a little piebald pony which struggled to keep up with the party. As the riders fanned out and reined in before the falconers, there were hoots and insults from some of the men when the dwarf trotted up – but the fellow seemed not to mind, indeed he encouraged the attention. There was now much milling about, snorting of horses and rattling of harnesses. Laughter rang out in the morning air. Today there was a breeze, and both falconers looked anxious. If the wind increased, it would make their day's work difficult.

'Who's the stunted fellow?' Thomas asked Will, as they walked forward to hand birds up to their masters.

'The Earl's fool,' Will answered quickly. 'Whatever you do, don't offend him. He's more dangerous then he looks.'

Thomas threw Will a glance and saw that he was in earnest. In fact, he had begun to realize that Will Holland never made jokes. Years of service at Barrowhill seemed to have given him an air of melancholy that jarred with his obvious contentment in his work.

But there was no time for idle ruminations, because Sir Robert was leaning down from his horse, wearing a broad smile.

'Half asleep, Thomas?' the knight asked. 'A run across the Downs will shake you up.'

'That it will, Sir Robert,' Thomas replied, and handed him the mighty Clorinda. Sir Robert held his favourite peregrine aloft, showing her off to all and sundry. Indeed, showing off seemed not merely acceptable in this company, but compulsory.

The other member of the party that caught Thomas's attention was the portrait painter, for he stood out like a songthrush in a flock of parrots. This man was clean-shaven, wearing plain dun-coloured riding clothes topped off with a large cap from which his long brown hair hung loosely. He said little, remaining for the most part close by Lady Felice. But when he urged his gelding forward to receive a hawk, Thomas saw a pair of bright eyes regarding him with frank curiosity from beneath the cap.

'Will you take the tercel, sir?' Thomas asked. He had placed a small bird on his wrist, for he sensed that this was no hawking man, but one who was merely along for the ride.

The fellow's mouth shaped itself into a bleak smile. 'One you can afford to lose, is't not so?' he enquired.

Thomas shook his head. 'You will not lose him, sir. If he carried off, he would merely return home when ready.'

The man held his gauntleted wrist out and allowed Thomas to settle the bird on it. He then gazed at it for some moments. 'A splendid creature,' he muttered.

Thomas, too busy to indulge in conversation, was turning to ready a small saker for one of the Countess's ladies who had ridden forward and sat waiting, wearing an amused smile.

'Surely such a bird is too plain for your palette, master Kessel,' the young lady said in an ironic tone.

'Not so, lady,' the other replied mildly. 'I would spend all my days getting the likeness of birds and beasts on to canvas, could they but pay me for my time.'

'Is it merely payment that drives you?' the lady countered. 'I had thought it was the beauty of your subject.'

'Beauty is all about, for the eye that sees,' the painter replied, in an accent which Thomas found strange. 'A worm may look beautiful, if the light sit fair upon it.'

He turned back to Thomas. 'Yours is a calling I envy,' he said, and turned his horse away.

Thomas came forward with the little falcon in its embroidered hood and held it up to the young lady in-waiting, but she made no movement to take it. Instead she looked down at him.

'I have not seen you before.'

'No, my lady,' Thomas replied. 'I am Sir Robert's falconer.'

'Are you indeed,' came the reply. And still no arm was offered to take the bird. Thomas waited patiently, and finally had no choice but to meet the cornflower-blue eyes which gazed into his.

'Then you know no one,' the lady said in a tone of mock sympathy, as if she would help him overcome this disadvantage.

The little saker was restless. She shifted on the gauntlet, so that Thomas lowered his arm and stroked her back lightly with his finger. She quietened at once.

'I do not need to know names to do my work, madam,' he said in a calm voice. Though he had small doubt that the young woman had a mind to toy with him a while yet.

'And is it the only work you can do?' came the sudden question, spoken low enough for just the two of them to hear.

Thomas managed a polite smile. 'Indeed, madam, I have no time for any other,' he answered.

'You poor fellow,' the young woman purred. 'If I found you

of a night-time in the Earl's labyrinth, I would find sweeter work for you, and better payment than you have dared imagine.'

Thomas kept his smile in place. 'Your ladyship is kind. But I am a poor servant, who must keep his place.'

There followed a pause, but most of the party had birds on their wrists now and were already moving off, starting their mounts for the open Downs. There were excited shouts. The young lady glanced round, then at last offered her wrist so that Thomas could place the saker upon her bejewelled gauntlet. She took it, then peered down at him again, and now her voice was hard.

'I am Lady Deverell, ward to the Earl and Countess. If I choose to ride on the Downs, which I may, I will ask your master to bid you accompany me. You would be wise not to thwart me.'

And even if Thomas had words of reply, they would have been redundant, as Lady Deverell pulled sharply on the rein, so that her mare jerked its head back and whinnied. Then holding the saker close to her body she wheeled and cantered off.

Thomas sighed and was turning to Will when a loud voice called out from close by. Sir George Brunning had ridden up and sat glaring about, while his horse shifted restlessly beneath him.

'Where the devil's my hawk?' he demanded.

Will Holland stepped forward quickly with a large, spirited bird at the ready. He held it aloft, but instead of offering his wrist Brunning merely scowled. 'You kept me waiting last time, falconer,' he snapped. 'I warned you then, I am not a patient man.'

'Your pardon sir,' Will answered quietly, and held the hawk out. Brunning sniffed and leaned forward, but at that moment the restless bird lifted a leg and bated from the fist.

'Careful, you fool!' Brunning shouted, and thrust his arm against Will's. The hawk, startled beneath the hood, flapped its wings. By now the other men had ceased their tasks, and all eyes were on Will.

'Take hold of the leash, Sir George,' he warned. 'She is too eager.'

31

Brunning breathed in sharply. 'You dare instruct me?' he shot back, letting the reins fall from his hand. But at that his horse stamped nervously, which obliged him to catch hold of them again. Otherwise to Thomas' mind – and the faces of those about him told him he was not mistaken – the man looked as if he were on the point of striking Will with the back of his hand.

But instead, Brunning exhaled, controlling his temper, and allowed Will to settle the bird on his gauntlet. All the while, the falconer had been whispering soothing words to her. There was an audible sigh from the watching men as Brunning quickly raised his arm, which obliged the hawk to dig her talons into his thick gauntlet.

The tension had eased, but as Brunning touched heels to his mount, he turned in the saddle and shot a savage look at Will. Then he muttered under his breath, and rode away.

Thomas turned to his companion, who merely shrugged and returned his gaze in silence.

It was a long day for the falconers; a day of bagging up larks, snipe and plovers, with the occasional heron or crane, as the hawks soared, stooped and brought in their catch. The party roamed at a leisurely pace across the wide downlands of East Surrey, splitting up into small groups so that Will, Thomas and the men of Barrowhill were hard pressed at times to follow. None of this land was as yet enclosed, and settlements were sparse. They were barely twenty miles from London, yet it was wild country, closer in nature to the western counties of Berkshire and Wiltshire that Thomas knew. This was his work, and he was in no hurry to return to Barrowhill. He had begun to think that despite its magnificence, there was something unwholesome about the place.

Around midday, he and Will snatched a moment to eat their bit of dinner from the pack they had brought. In the distance nobles and their ladies were riding together in twos and threes, splashes of colour against the rolling green plain. The Earl and Sir Robert were nowhere in sight.

'Are they not hungry?' Thomas mused, sitting on a tussock

and stretching out his long legs. 'There's no banqueting chamber out here.'

'You're wrong, Thomas,' Will answered, and pointed. Following his extended arm Thomas saw a horseman trotting towards them through the long grass. Soon he made out the sharp features of Henry Barnard, the Earl's usher.

Will got to his feet as Barnard reined in and quickly handed him the falcon from his wrist. He had a brisk air about him.

'This spot will do as well as any,' he said. 'The carts will be here shortly. You can help set up the trestles.' He looked disapprovingly down at Thomas, who was still seated on the grass.

'Stir yourself, man!' he snapped.

Thomas got slowly to his feet. As he did so he heard shouts and the creaking of wheels, and was surprised to see the horned heads of a pair of oxen appear over the brow of a hill. There came the crack of a whip, and the cries of drovers, and soon a small train of carts lumbered into view, ambling in their direction.

Barnard wheeled his horse and rode towards the leading cart, gesturing to the driver. In a few minutes they had reached the flat area where Will and Thomas stood, and the man was sawing hard on the reins. Grudgingly the huge oxen slowed to a halt, and stood blowing steam from their nostrils.

Now there was different work for the falconers, as they were recruited as servingmen. From the carts, stools and trestle tables were unloaded, followed by silver plate, jugs, dishes and baskets, and in a short time a banquet did indeed appear upon the Downs. And as if at a signal, members of the hawking party began arriving from all directions, dismounting and throwing themselves eagerly on the grass, without ceasing their chatter and laughter. The Earl, Thomas had to admit, knew how to entertain his guests in style.

Last of all came the Earl himself, at the head of the largest party which included Sir Robert and Sir Thomas Wilkes, with the Countess and her ladies close behind. Soon Thomas, Will and other Barrowhill men had their hands full, as birds were handed down to be hooded, leashed and perched on cadges, the wicker frames which Will had seen fit to have ferried out on the carts.

'You didn't tell me this was usual practice,' Thomas muttered to him under his breath, as they worked quickly to settle and water the hawks, some of which were overexcited from the hunt.

'It's a French custom, I hear,' Will answered. 'Does your master not entertain his guests in such fashion?'

Thomas shook his head. 'He lives a simpler life than yours, thank the Lord.'

'You wouldn't change places with me, then?'

Thomas glanced at him. 'You're not content in the Earl's service?'

'Tarry here a while, and you'll not wonder at it,' Will said.

There came a chorus of hoots and a gale of laughter from the party seated near the trestles, barely a dozen yards away. Thomas looked up and frowned, not liking what he saw.

The Earl's dwarf had clambered up on a table and was reciting some rhyme, now and then kicking his short legs out in a grotesque parody of a country dance. Some of the watchers laughed, others merely shouted insults. Like the falconers, the fool was earning his keep, maintaining his act as several of the younger gallants threw fruit rinds at him. Far from desisting however, the fellow seemed to redouble his efforts, as if desperate to please. Which, Thomas thought wryly, was very likely the case.

Then, as he was turning away to resume his work, events took a darker turn.

The fool was capering about at the end of the Earl's table, dangerously close to its edge, and now singing a lively ballad in a surprisingly fine baritone voice. Mercifully the throwing of missiles seemed to have ceased, though it was clear that some of the guests cared little for the song and wanted more knock-about fare. One young man, already half drunk, got to his feet and with a sudden movement threw the contents of his goblet into the fool's face.

There were cries of 'Shame!' but they were half-hearted, and tempered with laughter. The fool spluttered, shook himself like

34

a dog, then made an ironic bow of thanks. But before he could continue his song, his assailant leaned forward and gave him a violent shove which sent him toppling off the end of the table, to land hard on his back in the grass.

The laughter died away somewhat, as one or two people rose, craning their necks to see if he was hurt. But such a fall was as nothing to the fool, who had no doubt suffered worse in the past. He scrambled to his feet, then went into a defiant crouch and stuck out his tongue at the man who had pushed him. There followed a general hoot of laughter, and scattered applause.

It, however, was a misjudgement. The young gallant, realizing in his fuddled fashion that he was losing the game, stepped forward and smacked the fool smartly across the face. The fool staggered back, stunned, and sat down heavily on the turf.

Thomas stood breathing evenly, forcing himself to remain at his place, though he wanted to walk over, help the fool to his feet and deliver a word of rebuke to the boorish gallant, who stood hand on hip, glaring contemptuously about. Beside him, Will was watching in silence.

Now all eyes turned as if for guidance to the Earl, the undisputed Master of the Revels, who sat on a stool by the table. He himself had paid little attention to the entertainment, being engaged in conversation with Sir Thomas Wilkes. The Countess, seated on his right, wore a look that suggested she was long used to such goings-on and utterly bored by them. Now, they were both obliged to take notice.

'God's heart and thighs, master Spencer,' called the Earl, 'Have a care! Do you not know what a good fool costs me?'

The young man sniffed, seemed to collect himself, and made an elaborate bow in the Earl's direction.

'I crave pardon, my Lord,' he called back. 'Your claret is so fine, I've made too free with it!'

'Well then, make free with your hand, and help my man to his feet,' the Earl retorted, irritated by the sober atmosphere that had fallen upon the party.

Spencer bridled, then assumed a resigned air and reached down to help the fool up. The fool, who appeared unhurt, took

35

his hand, smiled and yanked him forward with such force that he fell flat upon his face.

There was a gasp from the onlookers. Whereupon the fool sprang up, dusted off his hands, stuck out his rear and broke wind.

The effect was instantaneous: a loud roar of laughter that shattered the tension at once, followed by wild applause and shouts of approval. The Earl joined in delightedly, screaming with laughter and banging the table with his fists.

Only now did Thomas relax, realizing that he had sorely underestimated the resilience of the diminutive fool. He watched the fellow walk round to the Earl's side, where he received a pat on the head like a naughty puppy. For his part the foolish Spencer, red-faced with rage, could only get to his feet and walk towards the tethered horses, no doubt intending to ride off and lick his wounds in some far corner of the Downs.

Will Holland had moved aside and was busying himself with the hawks. Before joining him, Thomas allowed his gaze to wander over the company. The Earl, the Countess and their guests had resumed their chatter, their eating and drinking as if nothing had happened. On the grass, where sat lesser members of the assembly, Thomas noted some who were not smiling. One was the steward, John Broad. Another, who gazed long at the Earl without any discernible expression, was the painter, Lukas Kessel.

Thomas turned to his birds. A moment later, from some distance away, came a shout. He looked up, as did others, and saw Spencer, the humiliated gallant who had only just ridden off, spurring his horse back towards the party. He shouted again, then gestured wildly. Something in his manner unsettled both Thomas and Will, who without a word began walking towards him. Others did the same, and a ripple of alarm spread among the company as men got to their feet, peering at the agitated figure of Spencer, who still sat on his horse, waving his arms.

When Thomas and Will reached him he turned his horse quickly, cantered to the edge of the flat hillock which had

36

served as the banqueting hall, and down the slope beyond. The falconers followed.

As they began to descend, they saw the dark shape in the grass.

Only then did Thomas register – and seemingly nobody else had paid the matter any attention – that Sir George Brunning had not been at dinner. Now, they discovered why. Spencer had dismounted and stood in shocked silence, staring down at the bulky figure. Thomas, then Will Holland, came up at a run, and halted. There were shouts behind them as others descended the slope, but neither of them turned, their gaze being held by the motionless body of Sir George Brunning, on his side with blood about his neck, eyes open in an expression of pure amazement. Strangest of all, was the scrap of parchment pinned to his doublet, with some writing upon it.

The first to reach the bottom of the slope, for some reason, was Sir Thomas Wilkes. The falconers stood aside as the tall man, tense with distaste, knelt down to examine the body. With a muttered oath he tore the paper from Brunning's clothing and peered at it. His mouth was tight as he turned to the others.

'How's your Latin, master Spencer?' he asked in a harsh voice. 'It reads "*Perite Scelesti*".'

Looking pale, the young man swallowed and said: 'I believe it would translate best, as: "So perish the wicked".'

Four

W hat unsettled Thomas most in those first days at Barrowhill was not the killing of Sir George Brunning, but the manner in which the Earl and Countess disposed of the matter.

At first there was alarm, followed by incredulity. Sir George was dead, but a stone's throw from the feast, and nobody had seen or heard anything. His horse was soon found beyond the next hill, grazing contentedly. Nobody, it transpired, remembered seeing him ride in to dinner. For that matter, nobody remembered with any certainty which party he had last hunted with. Which raised one rather unimportant, but nevertheless pertinent question.

'His hawk,' Will muttered, standing with the other men in a group about the body. 'What's become of his hawk?'

The Earl, who stood nearby with Sir Thomas Wilkes, rounded on his falconer in a rage. 'Is that all you can think of?' he cried. 'Damn you and your carelessness – you should have kept an eye out for him! He's a city man, unused to the Downs. Why else would he have fallen?'

There was a silence before John Broad, who stood silently among the other Barrowhill servants, voiced the thought harboured by many of them. 'My Lord, this was no fall. See where the blood—'

'The blood,' a cold voice interrupted, 'is about his neck, where it was broken. He fell from his horse. Is it not plain enough?'

The voice was Sir Thomas Wilkes', which prompted another silence. Thomas glanced round at the strained faces. From the hill above, out of sight, came raised voices. The Earl's first instruction on being told of the discovery was to Henry Barnard, to keep the ladies away from sight of the body. Now it seemed they clamoured to know what was happening.

'An accident, of course!' cried the Earl. 'A most dreadful tragedy – he was a dear friend.' He turned in an agitated manner to Wilkes, and to a tight-lipped Sir Robert who stood near. 'The Countess will be distraught . . . my friends, you must help us in our distress, for I cannot bear it!'

And to the embarrassment of many, tears sprang from his eyes and rolled down his cheeks. With a sob he turned and hurried away across the grass.

It was Wilkes who took charge.

After ordering John Broad to attend his master, he issued swift instructions to the other men. The house guests were to return to the ladies, see them horsed and accompany them back to Barrowhill at once. Servants were soon scurrying off to dismantle the tables and load the carts, while the falconers had enough to do caring for the birds. Two men were singled out to wrap Brunning's body and fashion a makeshift horse-litter on which to drag it back to the house, once the company had departed. Nobody, it seemed, must have sight of it. And nobody, it seemed to Thomas, must mention the parchment which he, Will and young Spencer had seen Wilkes take from the body.

As he was walking away to prepare the falcons for the journey back, Sir Robert called him over.

'I would speak with you this evening, at the house,' he said in a low voice.

Thomas was about to speak, but his master cut him short. 'At the house,' Sir Robert repeated. 'Till then, you talk of this to no one.'

Thomas nodded and went off to his work.

The afternoon passed rapidly, the servants of Barrowhill seemingly glad to keep themselves busy. Little was said, and in a very few hours no trace remained of the party on the Downs apart from meat-bones, fruit rinds and trampled grass. Hawks were hooded and taken back to the mews, where Thomas and

Will watered them after their day's sport. Meanwhile the corpse of Sir George Brunning was brought to Barrowhill by a round-about route – to be placed, not in any chapel, but in the brewhouse.

Thomas learned of it when he and Will entered the falconer's hut and cast themselves down, wearied by the day's events. He frowned. 'Why the brewhouse?'

Will was taking a long, welcome pull of beer from a mug. He sighed, wiped his mouth and handed it to Thomas.

' 'Tis farthest from the great house,' he answered.

Thomas took the beer, eying him grimly. 'The man was murdered, Will. You know it as well as I.'

Will looked levelly at him and said nothing.

'So, what's to be done?' persisted Thomas.

'Done?' Will seemed oddly subdued about the whole matter. 'What can you or I do?'

Thomas waited until Will lowered his gaze. When he spoke, his tone was more surprised than indignant. 'Perhaps your place matters more to you than you let me believe.'

Will looked up sharply then. 'What d'ye mean?'

'I mean if your master wishes to conceal this killing, pass it off as an accident, you won't be the one to open your mouth.'

Will started to speak, checked himself, then looked away.

'No, I won't be the one. And if you've your wits about you, you won't either.' He got up, took a few paces about the floor, then turned to face Thomas.

'Have you wondered why a man of my age has never married?' he asked abruptly.

Thomas gave a slight shake of his head.

'There's a woman in Tadworth I'd marry at the drop of a hat,' Will told him, 'and think myself the happiest man in England.' He gazed out of the tiny window, watching the evening draw in. 'Except that I'd not bring her here, to live at Barrowhill. Not for a thousand crowns.'

Thomas waited.

'Twelve years since I came from the village, to be the Earl's falconer,' Will went on. 'I always had a way with hawks – John Broad knew of it, and got me my place. I counted myself the

40

luckiest lad on the Downs. Now . . .' he trailed off. 'There's times I wish I'd never set eyes on this house.'

He moved to where Thomas sat watching him, and lowered himself on to a rickety stool. 'I told you they were the law,' he said. 'Believe it, Thomas, there's none here would dare go against them. Do your work and keep your own counsel, and soon you'll return safe to Berkshire, and your daughter. Speak out, and . . .' He waved a hand vaguely, then looked away again. 'You think me a coward.'

But Thomas shook his head. 'Nay, I'm no judge of men's souls.'

At that moment both of them were startled by a shout from outside the hut. A man was calling Thomas by name.

'It's my master,' Thomas said with a frown, getting to his feet. Only then did he remember that Sir Robert had said he'd want to speak with him. Quickly he went to the door and threw it open.

Sir Robert stood alone, some distance from the hut, the breeze blowing his cloak about him. As Thomas appeared he called out: 'Come with me, now.' As Will Holland stepped out beside Thomas, Sir Robert said: 'You, falconer, are to attend your master within the hour, in the withdrawing chamber.'

Will bowed respectfully. With a glance at him, Thomas followed Sir Robert, who was striding briskly away.

They walked in silence past the stables, the dovecote and the gardeners' huts to a squat half-timbered building from which came an unmistakeable reek. Without hesitation Sir Robert shoved the door open and the two of them entered.

The brewhouse was deserted, but lit by a couple of smoky tallow lamps. Here amid the stench of malted barley and stale beer, the covered body of Sir George Brunning had been placed on a board across two barrels.

Questions rose in Thomas's mind, but he kept silent as Sir Robert walked forward and drew back the cover. Without looking round, he beckoned. Coming up beside him, Thomas looked down at the pale, lifeless face. Its peaceful aspect jarred with his memory from that morning: of the florid-faced man who had spoken so harshly to the falconers. Now, Sir Robert's instruction took him by surprise.

'Help me turn him over.'

Thomas blinked, but the other had already seized the heavy corpse and was struggling to turn it. Taking hold of the lower torso he added his strength to his master's, and between them they rolled the body on to its front, steadying it with some difficulty when it threatened to slide off on to the floor. Sir Robert then stepped to one side, picked up one of the lamps and held it above Brunning's head.

'There!' he breathed. 'What do you see?'

Thomas peered closely at the back of the neck. Someone had made an effort to wipe the blood away, but it appeared now that there had never been much of it in the first place. What was clearly visible was a small, deep wound at the base of the skull, between that and the first vertebra. Thomas took a breath, then answered.

'A single thrust, Sir Robert. One that can kill with little effort, but great speed.'

Sir Robert looked grim. 'An assassin's blow, then.'

Thomas nodded. 'A difficult one.' He hesitated, then: 'I've seen it before. It was the work of an Irish kern.'

He looked round and pointed to a slim, dagger-like blade which was stuck into a barrel-head beside the wall. 'The kerns – the poor foot-soldiers – use a long narrow dagger, somewhat like that . . . like a brewer's bung-knife. But a poniard, if sharp on both edges and in the right hands, could have done this.'

Sir Robert nodded and straightened himself.

'It's murder, sir,' Thomas said.

But Sir Robert's only reply was: 'We must turn him over again.'

Between them they rolled the body back to its first position, then covered it. Only when Sir Robert turned to face him did Thomas see how tense his master was.

'You will tell no one,' he began, then noting the expression on Thomas' face, added quickly, '– for the present! You must trust me in this, Thomas.'

After a moment Thomas nodded. 'If you wish it, Sir Robert.'

'I do,' Sir Robert answered. 'And while we are here, as guests of the Earl, I would urge you to keep your keen eyes open.'

Thomas nodded.

'Let's get outside,' the other said, wrinkling his nose. 'This place will make me retch.'

Thomas followed his master out into the sweet evening air. Some way off, from the direction of the kitchens, could be heard shouts and the clatter of plates.

'I had forgotten,' Sir Robert said. 'You are to attend on the Earl, along with master Holland, as I shall myself. You had better make yourself ready.'

Then, leaving Thomas to his own devices, the knight walked off quickly towards the house. Candlelight shone brilliantly from the tall, traceried windows of the Great Chamber.

Half an hour later Thomas and Will Holland stood in the Earl's withdrawing chamber, on the first floor of the house.

It was the first time Thomas had been inside Barrowhill, and the splendour of the rooms sobered him. In this smaller chamber, which opened off a long gallery lined with pictures, wall hangings were suspended from floor to ceiling, depicting scenes from the history of the ancients. Around the walls were chests, padded chairs and a carved oak dresser, on which was displayed a set of gold plate. And on the floor was spread a Turkish carpet of red and green, such as were brought from the Levant by merchantmen. In the centre of the carpet stood an oak table with candles, silver flagons and goblets upon it. Seated behind were the Earl and Countess, along with Sir Thomas Wilkes and Sir Robert Vicary. John Broad the steward stood stiffly to one side, holding his staff of office as if to ward off potential attackers.

The Earl, who appeared to have been fortifying himself from a flagon close at hand, eyed the two falconers with some distaste, as if nettled at having to deal with them in this way. He opened his mouth, then coughed and closed it again.

And once again, it was Wilkes was seemed to take charge. After looking hard at each man in turn, he spoke to Will.

'We would speak about what happened on the Downs.'

Will remained silent. Beside him Thomas shot a swift glance at Sir Robert, but the knight refused to meet his eye.

'The news will reach London tomorrow,' Wilkes told them, 'that Sir George Brunning died in a hunting accident. An unfortunate fall from his horse. You both saw, as did we all, how frisky and intemperate the animal was this morning.'

He waited, daring either man to offer a challenge. When none came he continued in a businesslike tone. 'There will be no inquest . . .'

At this John Broad stirred slightly. The tension in the room was palpable. But as Wilkes cocked his head almost imperceptively in his direction, the steward merely cleared his throat and gazed at the floor.

'There will be no inquest here,' Wilkes continued. 'Sir George has kinsmen in London who will wish to deal privately with the matter.' He paused, then levelled a deliberate gaze at Thomas, as if to remind him of what had passed between them only the night before. Thomas met his eye without expression.

'My Lord the Earl, and her ladyship the Countess – indeed all of us,' Wilkes said, 'are glad of your loyal service in the matter. It shall not be overlooked.' He paused, looking in turn at both falconers. 'There's nothing further, is there?'

Try as he might, Thomas could not help but speak.

'Is master Spencer not here, sir?' he asked innocently.

There was a chill moment. Irritated by Thomas' boldness, Wilkes opened his mouth, whereupon there came a faint sound from his left. The Countess, who had sat in dignified silence throughout, now spoke.

'Master Spencer has had to return to London suddenly,' she said softly, though there was no mistaking the steeliness of her gaze. 'I fear the day's excitements have upset him greatly. He is but a young man.'

Thomas met her eyes, and read the truth behind them. Spencer had been packed off, perhaps with a handsome purse for his silence. The falconers were naturally expected to follow his example and keep their mouths firmly shut. From the corner of his eye, Thomas could see Sir Robert signalling furiously with his eyebrows, commanding him to hold his tongue. But for some reason, he felt uncharacteristically rebellious. The whole business was beginning to annoy him.

'And the parchment,' he enquired. 'With the Latin upon it – has that also disappeared?'

Now he had overreached himself, and everyone knew it, which meant they had to act. Beside him Thomas could sense Will Holland imploring him silently to desist. He swallowed, readying himself for the rebuke that would surely come. And of course, it must come from his master, Sir Robert.

'How dare you speak to her ladyship in such fashion!' Sir Robert shouted. 'I've a mind to have you flogged and cast out of my service!'

The others relaxed somewhat, in the safe knowledge that the knight would deal firmly with his own servant, as they would any of theirs. For his part, thinking of what had passed between the two of them less than an hour before, Thomas knew that his master was but play-acting. Well – he too must do his part.

'I crave pardon, sir,' he said, suddenly contrite. 'I did forget myself – the shock of stumbling upon the body . . .'

But the next moment he knew he had underestimated Lady Felice, who was not fooled for one moment. Taking a breath, the Countess fixed him again with her gaze, and said: 'There was no parchment, falconer. Do you mark that?'

'Yes, my Lady,' Thomas replied in a neutral tone. 'Mayhap I was confused for a moment.'

'And is there any other matter about which you are confused?'

'I think not, my Lady,' Thomas answered, and dropped his eyes, letting them feast on the bold colours of the carpet. Beside him, he heard Will let out a long sigh.

'Then you may go,' the Countess said, and half-turned to the Earl at her side. 'Unless, my Lord, there is anything you wish to add?'

Thomas realized then that he had almost forgotten the Earl, who was muttering under his breath in between taking frequent pulls from his goblet. Now, the master of Barrowhill – who it was becoming clear, was in truth no master at all – spoke up.

'God's liver and lights, haven't we put an end to the matter?

Send them away now, and let's to supper . . . where are my music-makers?'

He got clumsily to his feet, and Wilkes and the Countess followed suit with evident relief. Sir Robert was the last to rise, throwing Thomas a swift glance in which were both irritation and approval. John Broad, at a word from the Countess, came forward to usher the falconers away.

They were glad to be outdoors. Not until they were striding uphill towards the falcons' mews did Will make a move to speak. Whereupon, fully expecting an argument, Thomas was taken aback when the other turned to him with an amused expression, and shook his head.

'By the Lord, Thomas, you try your luck mightily.'

Thomas said nothing. He had the feeling that the matter was far from over. But at least with Will he was at his ease, and felt no need to dissemble.

'I'd a mind to poke you in the ribs while we stood there,' the other went on, 'save that someone would have seen me. You don't know how close you came to digging yourself a very deep pit.'

'I do know,' Thomas replied. 'And I'd be glad to forget about it, for the present.'

Will stopped and faced him. 'Would you, now,' he said. 'Well mayhap I've the remedy.' He glanced up at the sky. 'We shan't be needed again today, and the night's not too far advanced . . . are your legs rested enough for an hour's walk into Tadworth?'

Thomas managed a smile. 'I believe they are, at that.'

'Good. It strikes me we've earned ourselves a good supper and a little female company – let me get my purse.'

An hour later, with the Downland breeze lessening behind them, the two falconers descended a hill and struck the road that led south from Epsom to Tadworth. Within minutes, they turned a bend in the road, which now climbed slightly, and lights appeared ahead. Village dogs began to bark. Then came the squeak of a sign on rusty hinges, and there was the welcome sight of the Red Bull inn, set back a little from the way. A moment later they entered, to a blast of warm, fetid air and a general shout of welcome.

'It's the hawkman!' called out a fellow in a canvas jerkin and wide-brimmed hat. 'Come in, you pelting rogue!'

The interior of the inn glowed with firelight, diffused through a pall of smoke from tobacco pipes, lamps and a few cheap candles. There was a fair-sized crowd of village folk, giving off the familiar smell of ale and unwashed clothing. Will, being a local man, was recognized at once and greeted like a long-lost son. Peering about, Thomas saw that every table seemed to be occupied, but a couple of empty stools soon appeared and the two of them sat down, glad to ease the weight from their limbs.

'Been a week or two, hasn't it, Will?' a female voice enquired. Thomas turned to see a pretty fair-haired woman in a plain hood, wearing a knowing smile. Will stumbled to his feet, his face glowing, quickly confirming the impression that this was the woman he would marry at the drop of a hat. Or a feather. In a moment he was busy swiping a stool from a nearby drinker and setting it down for his lady-love. And all the while, he smiled like a fool, so that Thomas marvelled at the change in him.

Seated opposite was the man who had called out in welcome, and who now raised his mug to Will in mock salute.

'The Earl let you out for the night, has he?'

Will turned absently, gesturing to Thomas. 'Here's my friend Thomas Finbow – another falconer. This is Ben Mallam, the jingler.'

Thomas nodded to the man, who surveyed him shrewdly before he spoke. 'And where are you from, master falconer?'

'Berkshire, the manor of Petbury,' Thomas answered.

'I believe I've passed by there,' Ben Mallam said. 'I was bound for the horse fair at Wantage.'

Thomas eyed him warily. Jinglers, or horse-coursers, were notorious rogues who bought broken-down or diseased nags and then used a variety of cunning methods to make them look good enough for purchase. Just then a drawer appeared, apparently at Will's behest, and set down two full tankards of ale. Thomas turned to give his friend thanks, but saw he was fully occupied with his fair-haired lady. Indeed, she was now on his lap.

He turned back to the jingler. 'I wouldn't have thought there was much in the way of horseflesh to bring you here,' he said.

The man smiled, a very crafty smile indeed. 'You'd be surprised, my friend.'

He felt a hand on his shoulder then, and turned to see that Will was eager to present his lady.

'Here's my good friend Thomas,' he told her. 'Thomas, this is my Doreth. Her father's the smith here in Tadworth.'

Thomas smiled at Doreth, who caught him off guard by promptly leaning forward and kissing him on the cheek.

There was a chuckle from across the table. Thomas turned back to Ben Mallam.

'I find you falconers much alike,' he said, not unkindly. 'More at ease with your hawks than with people.'

Thomas took a draught of ale, which was passable and quite strong, then lowered his mug. 'As with you and horses, perhaps,' he replied.

The jingler shook his head. 'Nay, you're mistaken. 'Tis the ways of men that such as me must learn, if we will earn our bread. The horse is but the merchandise. No different to kickshaws, or costards.'

Thomas shrugged and took another drink. As the noise of loud laughter and conversation filled his ears, he reflected that the man was probably right. He spent far more of his time in the company of winged creatures than he did with two-legged ones.

There came a sudden shout of merriment, and he looked round to see a woman in a tattered red perriwig and a faded taffeta gown standing nearby, gulping from a mug. Urged on by a group of half-drunken young men, she tilted the mug back, held it upside down to show that it was emptied, then slapped it down into the hand of a man who sat watching – clearly the one who had paid for the drink. There was another roar of laughter at his expression of bemused helplessness.

'Hold on to your purse,' Ben Mallam muttered, leaning closer to Thomas. 'And your jockam, too.'

Sure enough, the woman swung her eyes across the room,

48

and fixed at once on the unfamiliar face of Thomas. He groaned inwardly – too late. Next moment she had crossed the floor and plumped herself uninvited in his lap.

'You want to treat me, master?' she asked, breathing beer fumes in his face. 'You can walk me home after, if you will.' Then she whispered in his ear: 'Or in the yard out back. It's a fair night for cunny-catching.'

She gave a throaty chuckle. Close to, Thomas saw that her cracked lips were painted with sheep-reddle, her face pitted with pock-marks. Somewhere behind him, Will Holland was stifling a laugh. It seemed he was at the mercy of the village trull.

'I thank you,' he said with a smile, 'but I'm weary, and—'

'And he don't want a dose of the French Marbles,' Ben Mallam finished. Thomas glanced up and caught his eye, which carried a clear warning despite the grin on his face.

The woman glared. 'Anyone ask you to pipe up, horse-prigger?' she demanded. 'I wouldn't serve you for a fistful of crowns.'

Ben Mallam laughed. 'When did you ever set eyes on a fistful of crowns?' he crowed. 'There isn't a swadder in Surrey hasn't foined you in the ditch – for a packet of pins at that!'

A few drinkers close by heard and guffawed. The woman took a sharp breath and opened her mouth, and instinctively Thomas raised a hand to stop his ear against the expected flood of abuse. But instead, from behind him came a female voice, one of unmistakeable authority.

'Madge Clapperdaw! On your feet and out that door – now!'

The room quietened, and Thomas swung round to see a tall, dark-haired woman in a good russet-coloured gown and a clean apron, standing by the taproom doorway.

In a trice Madge had heaved herself off his lap, and assumed a hangdog look. 'Lord, Moll, you know 'twas only sport—' she began, but the other would have none of it.

'I told you last time: you upset my customers again, I'll have the constable lay his switch across your back.'

A sulky look came over Madge, and her lower lip stuck out. ''Tis my place,' she retorted. 'I'm Tadworth-born, not like some!'

There were mutterings from a few of the drinkers, but still the landlady – for such she appeared to be – stood firm. Indeed, she took a pace towards Madge, who flinched away.

'Here,' Moll said and held out her hand, in which were a few coins. 'Will that serve for your night's wages?'

There was a pause, but Madge was no fool. She took the coins, pulled her gown about her shoulders and slouched out of the door.

The conversation rose again. Thomas threw an admiring look towards the tall woman, who was turning away. But then her glance fell upon Will Holland, and the effect was remarkable: a sunbeam through clouds. Doreth rose from Will's lap, so he could stand and greet Moll. Without thinking, Thomas also got to his feet.

'Cousin Will,' Moll smiled, and offered her cheek. Murmuring his greetings, Will kissed her, then turned to Thomas.

'Here's my friend master Finbow – falconer to one of the Earl's guests,' he said. To Thomas he said: 'Moll was married to my cousin, John Perrott. Now she's innkeeper in his place.'

'You are most welcome,' Moll said to Thomas. Then with a wan smile she added: 'You'll not mind Madge. She's a poor woman with none to keep her, and must earn her bread any way she can.'

Thomas was about to make some reply – until he met Moll's brown eyes, which locked on to his . . . and he knew that, whatever else happened, he was not going back to Barrowhill that night.

Five

Half an hour later, in Moll Perrott's back parlour which served as private dining chamber, Thomas sat down to the best supper he had eaten since leaving Berkshire. Will and Doreth were on one side of the board, he on the other. And when he learned that his unspoken hope – that Moll would likely join them later – would be fulfilled, he set to with a relish. For such a meal might not have disgraced his master's table back at Petbury.

There were capons, roasted larks and woodcock with a dish of cabbage and onions. There was loin of hare with a black sauce, and plenty of rye bread. For a dessert there were roasted pears and cheese. And all of it washed down not only with the best house ale, but with Alicant and Muscadine too. It was a feast which drove the events of that long day from his mind as it did Will Holland's, so that both grew merry in each other's company.

'Moll keeps a good table, does she not?' he asked Thomas, smiling as he scoured his trencher.

'That she does,' Thomas agreed. Through the open door to the taproom came laughter, then shouts. Some were calling for a song.

'How long since she was widowed?' he asked, trying to sound unconcerned. There was a chuckle from Doreth, who had finished her meal and was running a hand through Will's hair.

'Three years back,' she said. 'And no man's dared ask for her hand since.'

Thomas raised an eyebrow. 'Are they so afraid of her?'

Will shook his head. 'Don't pay this one any mind,' he said, with a look at Doreth. 'Moll's a woman of business, cleverer than most men I know. There's several have asked, only she keeps 'em guessing, and waiting – and so they keep coming in the Red Bull, and drinking her ale . . .' He smiled and waved a hunk of bread at the doorway. 'Is it not a fair plot for a comedy?'

Thomas did not answer, but cocked an ear towards the open door. A hush had fallen, for a reason which soon became clear, as a woman's voice rose in song: softly at first, then louder, and every ear was bent towards it. The song was one he had not heard before, made long ago by the Downland folk. It told a simple, ageless tale of lost love – but it was not the verses that held him – rather the sweet voice of the singer. When she had finished, to loud cheering and much banging on tables, he looked at Will and at Doreth, saw that they too were moved almost to tears. Doreth sniffed, and put her head on Will's shoulder.

'That was Moll, was it not?' Thomas asked.

Will nodded.

To Thomas' disappointment Moll did not come to the supper table in the parlour after all, but stayed among her customers, instructing the drawer to keep her guests well attended, and sending the kitchen wench in to clear the table. So that quite soon Thomas, feeling his presence surplus to present needs, rose and said he would go back into the taproom for a final mug.

Will stood up too, clapped him on the shoulder and said in a voice slurred with drink: 'You'll have guessed I'm not going back to that poky hut tonight, Thomas. Can you find your own way?'

'Don't fret about me,' Thomas told him. 'You've more important matters afoot.'

Will turned to Doreth, who was getting to her feet, yawning. She favoured Thomas with a sleepy grin.

'You come in to Tadworth again, we'll make you welcome.'

'You already have,' he replied, but already the two of them were stumbling through the kitchen door, arms about each other.

The inn was still crowded, the air thick with smoke and

fumes. The clamour of drink-sodden voices filled Thomas's ears as he found himself a seat near the chimney corner. As he perched on the edge of a bench, a figure detached itself from the throng and approached him. Though the face was familiar, for a moment he could not recall who it belonged to – until the man spoke, with the distinctive accent that he had first heard that same morning. It was the portrait painter from Barrowhill.

'You seek a change of surrounding, master falconer,' he said. 'I also.'

Thomas, his body stuffed with good food and his mind clouded with ale and wine, struggled in vain to remember the man's name. As if in answer, the painter provided it.

'Lukas Kessel,' he said, with a stiff bow. 'And not, as our friends at Barrowhill would have it, a Dutchman. I am Flemish.'

'Thomas Finbow . . . you want to join me in a mug?' Thomas asked, though there was clearly nowhere to sit, and in any case he felt disinclined to converse with the man. But Kessel gave a slight smile, and shook his head.

'No, I do not stay. I have a borrowed horse outside who will not wait. The Earl's horsemaster is most covetous of his master's steeds – he keeps a range of colts of the new Arabian breed.'

Thomas stifled a yawn, and cared little that Kessel saw it.

There was a pause, then Kessel said: 'You are a man of keen sight, I think. Like your hawks, no?' When Thomas made no reply he went on: 'My eyes are my living. But today, they saw things they did not like. Since I came here, to Lord Edmund's palace, I see many things . . . some I know not how to speak of.'

In spite of himself Thomas found that the man's gentle voice, which he strained to hear above the din, had caught his attention. He met his eye. 'What manner of things, master?'

The painter hesitated, as if deciding whether to trust Thomas or not. Finally he shook his head. 'Another time, perhaps.'

Thomas opened his mouth, then closed it again and looked round, because the laughter and hubbub had once again diminished in readiness for a song – only this time, to his disappointment, Moll was not the singer. Instead, a cheerful male voice rang out, launching into the first verse of a bawdy song of sheep-stealing. And the performer was none other than the jingler, Ben Mallam.

Thomas listened until the end of the verse, which prompted a roar of laughter and was followed by a deafening, off-key chorus as the whole company joined in with the refrain. With a smile he turned back to Kessel – but the painter had gone. Peering through the haze, he saw the back of a dark cloak disappearing in the direction of the door. With a sigh, he picked up his mug.

The next moment he felt something akin to a shiver pass through his whole body, as a very different figure materialized and sat down beside him on the bench that by some act of conjuration had suddenly become vacant.

'Enjoying yourself, master?' Moll Perrott asked.

'I am now, mistress,' Thomas said, and smiled.

Moll smiled in return, and Ben Mallam's strident voice seemed to fade away, while the entire room melted into a colourless backdrop; as if she were a portrait.

The drinkers had staggered home, and the fire was low. The drawer had hung up his apron and gone, the serving wench snored on her pallet in the kitchen – and still Thomas and Moll sat, in the owlhoot hours, and talked.

They talked of small things, none of much consequence. And when they had talked enough with their voices they talked with their eyes, then their mouths. And finally Moll blew out the candles and they walked together through the dark kitchen and up a narrow stair to her bedroom above the inn, and climbed into her bed, both of them too tired to do anything but wrap themselves close and fall asleep.

In the raw dawn, when the birdsong woke them, they peeled back the sheets and fell upon one another, each as hot as the other, wordless and breathless, working hands and mouths over one another's bodies and finally cleaving in a sweating, bucking act that rose to a fast, furious pace, drawing cries from both . . . until the bed knocked against the wall, shaking dust from the ceiling and waking the poor kitchen wench below, who screamed in alarm. Then Moll threw back her head with its mass of walnut-brown hair and gave a shout of laughter, which drew a similar sound from Thomas. And spent, as if from a foot-race, the two of them lay back on Moll's soaking bolster and sighed in unison.

'Poor Nan's afraid of her own shadow,' she said presently. 'She'll calm down once she shakes herself awake.'

'Is she unused to hearing such sounds from above?' Thomas asked in a casual tone that did not fool Moll for an instant.

'You think I take a man to my bed every night?' she enquired, then gave a low laugh when he looked abashed. 'I'm not Madge Clapperdaw, master Thomas. I can pick and choose.'

'I don't doubt that,' he said, and kissed her tenderly on the mouth. 'And I count myself a lucky fellow.'

Then he rubbed his eyes and sat up. 'But soon I must leave you. Will Holland and I have our hawks to tend, and they'll not wait.'

Moll sighed, stretched her arms wide, and gave a long yawn. 'And I have an inn to keep,' she said. 'Nor will that wait.'

They dressed and went down to the kitchen, where sleepy-eyed Nan was already raking out the embers. She stole such a sheepish, sidelong look at Thomas and Moll that both of them laughed.

'Heat some milk up, soon as you can,' Moll instructed her. 'We'll have porridge and a bit of bread.'

But Thomas, who had sat down on a stool to pull on his boots, shook his head. 'I must be on my way,' he said, with a look of regret. 'Will's likely home already.'

'Not if I know Doreth,' Moll told him. 'She'll not set him free till she's done with him.'

In the end he accepted a bowl of lukewarm milk, drinking it standing in the doorway as he watched the sun climb steadily up over the Downs. Somewhere nearby a cock crowed. A few fleecy clouds scudded in at speed, which gave him cause for relief. High winds meant there would likely be no hawking today.

Then the events of yesterday rose in his mind, and he grew

sombre. A footfall behind made him turn around. Moll came to him with a smile, and he brightened at once.

'How long will your master stay at Barrowhill?' she asked. He smiled at her. 'For a while yet, I hope.'

'Ah,' murmured Moll, keeping a serious face. 'You expect to have me on tap, to enjoy any night you can get to the village?'

He opened his mouth, saw the mockery in her eyes, and said: 'Just to sit and hear you sing would be joy enough for me.'

She arched her eyebrows. 'Well now. What breed of fair-voiced falconer are you?'

'One who sees now how lonely he is,' he answered, as if he had only lately come to understand it himself. When Moll said nothing he added: 'If I had my wish, I would take you back to Berkshire, where I'd have you on tap for the rest of my days.'

Moll met his eye. 'What makes you think I would go with you?'

He placed an arm about her. 'It's but my fancy. May I not have that to cheer me, while I go about my work?'

She leaned close, so that her hair brushed his cheek, and spoke softly. 'Come back when you can. I will be here.'

Then she kissed him and went off to her kitchen, calling to Nan to stoke up the fire.

Will Holland was not at the hut when Thomas returned little more than an hour later. Nor had he seen any sign of him on the Downs, though he looked back often on the path. At Barrowhill, men were already about, in the gardens and the stable yard, and smoke rose from the chimneys. Going straight to the mews, Thomas stiffened abruptly as he entered, his senses alert. Something was wrong.

Putting down the pail he moved slowly among the birds on their perches, looking closely at each. There had been some disturbance, for feathers lay on the ground where there had been none yesternight. At once, he saw the culprits: two of the tercels had been 'crabbing' – fighting when they stood too close together. One of them, clearly the loser in the fray, had been torn in several places, its feathers stained with blood. The other roused on its perch, very edgy.

Talking gently all the while, Thomas stooped to uncover a small barrel and picked out a piece of meat. Then he approached the jittery hawk and, holding out the morsel, coaxed it into bending forward. But instead of sinking its beak into the food, the bird flinched away, then gave a cough.

There was a sound behind, but Thomas did not turn. Only another falconer knew how to approach without startling the birds.

'Is he sick?' Will asked, coming up quietly beside him.

Thomas stooped and sniffed the muting – the hawk's dung – below the perch. 'A quinsy, I think. Have you any rangle?'

'Aye.' Will moved to a corner, found a small dish of fine gravel. 'This should cleanse his gorge.'

Setting the dish before the tercel, he began stroking its feathers. Thomas set water down, and at length the bird took a drink, and began to peck at the gravel.

With some relief, the two of them began their work. The injured tercel was taken out, cleaned and tended. The other birds were restless and eager for exercise. Within the hour, though the wind was a little strong, Thomas and Will had taken the two largest hawks up the path on to the Downs. Only then, when the birds had soared, did they begin to relax somewhat.

'I was a sluggard this morning,' Will said, by way of apology. 'I should have been up an hour sooner, walked over to the inn to fetch you. Only . . .' he threw Thomas a glance. 'Mayhap you'd not have thanked me for disturbing you.'

'Mayhap,' Thomas answered. 'How did you know I'd stayed there?'

Will gave him a sly smile. 'Because I know Moll.'

Thomas chose not to pursue that. 'By the same token, I thought it best not to come looking for you.'

'You'd have been hard put to find me,' Will told him. 'There's a place we go in secret. Doreth's father thinks she's home abed.'

Thomas faced him. 'Why don't you marry her, and have done with stealing about like a lovelorn youth?'

A slight frown creased Will's forehead. 'I told you why.'

Thomas sighed, and changed the subject. 'The painter, Kessel, was at the inn last night,' he said.

The other shrugged. 'He goes where he will. Her ladyship treats him as an equal, though he's but a servant like you or me.'

'He acted as if he wanted to talk,' Thomas went on. 'I think he was sorely disturbed by what happened on the Downs.'

Will looked sour, as if he did not like to be reminded of the business. 'He's a close fellow,' he muttered, then as an after-thought added: 'He was no friend of Brunning. But then, in truth, nor was any man. Even my lord the Earl, despite his tears—' He broke off, as if he had said too much. 'Though none that I know of would do . . . what was done.'

He looked up suddenly, shielding his eyes from the sun which poked through the ragged fleece of cloud. 'Thomas! Look there!'

Thomas looked, and saw a mighty peregrine – not one of those they had brought with them – floating high above their heads. As the two falconers gazed, it dropped like a stone upon a small bird, a plover perhaps, turned sharply in the air, clamped its huge talons about its prey, and carried it aloft.

Will turned to Thomas in surprise. 'I know that bird,' he said. 'It's Brunning's hawk!'

But the two of them could only watch as, bearing its limp prey beneath it, the great bird climbed to a great height and flew leisurely away from them, until it was lost to sight.

'Brunning's no longer,' Thomas said. 'She's masterless now, and will hunt for herself.' A thought struck him. 'It's as though she means to haunt Barrowhill – for as long as she likes.'

Then turning to Will he added: 'Or, mayhap, until her master's killer is found.'

Will stared back at him, not liking the notion at all.

The day passed off peacefully enough, as the two falconers tended and exercised their hawks. No order came to ready the birds for their masters. By evening their work was done and Will called Thomas to him, to walk over to the kitchens for supper.

In the vast kitchen at Barrowhill, there was near uproar. A

sweating, black-bearded cook in a greasy apron lorded it over half a dozen frantic lackeys and as many wenches, bellowing orders, cuffing them at the least provocation, seemingly satisfied with nothing. The room was filled with shouts and cries, punctuated by the clatter of cooking pots and ladles and the clang of plate. Servingmen dressed in the Earl's scarlet livery walked out with laden platters, heads held high, ready to be marshalled into line by the usher of the Great Chamber, then ran back in, wiping grease from their hands. At the huge fire, the heat of which could be felt a dozen feet away, a boy stood dripping with sweat, turning the spit on which half an ox was skewered. Tables groaned under the weight of dishes filled with everything from poultry to a stewed carp more than a yard long.

At a nod from the cook, who pointed to a couple of platters from which they could help themselves, Thomas and Will got a trencher and a mug each and retreated outside to the yard. Here, seated on upturned baskets before the wash-house, they could eat supper in peace, while yards away the din continued unabated.

'Must be a big party in the Great Chamber,' Thomas mused, his mouth half-full.

Will snorted. 'Nay – it's like this every night!'

'Do they never dine alone? My master and mistress do, often.'

For some reason, Will was in a mood to talk. 'There's always company. His lordship hates to be alone – and Lady Felice grew tired of him within the first month of their marriage.' He lowered his voice. 'Mayhap that's why they've no children.'

'Not a love-match, then,' Thomas observed with a wry smile.

Will gave another snort. 'More a money-match. She brought him lands in Hampshire and Kent, with a handful of tenant farms, not to mention six thousand crowns. West of here, round Oxted and Godstone, he's started enclosing the Downlands. A lot of folk hate him for it.'

Thomas nodded. 'I thought him the kind of man who'll please himself, whatever the consequences.'

Will Holland was growing unusually heated. 'You don't

59

know the half of it, Thomas,' he spat. 'To him the land's but a toy – a gaming-table. He's got iron mills in the Weald and a gunpowder mill on the stream at Godstone, turning it foul . . . why, this very house is but a monument to his vanity. His father's old manor wasn't near grand enough for him. He razed it and built again, only bigger. Brought the best stonemasons here, as well as Italians to fashion statues and lay out the gardens, so he could hoist his flag of hope. The hope that the Queen would wish to come here one day, on one of her Progresses. Then he could entertain her in high style, gain favours . . . I know not what.'

He reflected for a moment. 'Only now, with his wife dismissed from Court, it may never happen.' He gave a malicious chuckle. 'Maybe there's justice and retribution for all – do you mark me?'

Thomas nodded slowly. 'You've a shrewd eye, master.' And seizing the moment, as they sat in the cool evening mopping their trenchers with hunks of bread, he asked: 'Have you thought any more on Brunning's death?'

Will frowned. 'A little.'

'How does it appear to you, now?'

Will seemed not to understand. 'Why, no different to how it appeared yesterday.'

Thomas glanced in the direction of the brewhouse. 'Do you know if they've taken the body away?' he asked.

Will shook his head.

'Leave aside the harsh kind of man he was,' Thomas pressed him. 'Can you think of any reason why one would wish him dead?'

Will eyed him warily. 'Plenty! The way he has dealt with me, for a start. Is that the way your mind moves?'

Thomas shook his head quickly. 'No! In any case, you and I were together all day. Someone planned the deed, one who knew when and how to do it. Remember the parchment: "*So perish the wicked . . .*"'

Will was growing agitated. 'We'd best forget that, Thomas.'

'Listen to me.' Something in Thomas's voice made the other man turn sharply. 'I will trust you. My master wants me to see

60

what I can discover. He likes not the way the death is being concealed.'

Will hesitated. 'We're as brothers, you and I,' he said finally. 'And for that reason I warn you again, not to peer closely into this matter. If the Earl has reasons for concealment, he won't brook interference from a mere falconer.' He glanced curiously at Thomas. 'You are a deal closer to your master than I am to mine, that much is plain.'

Thomas shrugged. 'He trusts me.'

'And how deeply do you trust him?' asked Will.

Struck by his tone, Thomas answered: 'He has his faults, but he is not a bad man. He wishes no one ill.'

'But,' Will persisted, 'why is he here? Have you thought much upon that?'

Thomas realized that he had not thought much upon it at all. He was used to Sir Robert's hawking and hunting trips, and thought of this one as nothing more than another stay of pleasure. He recalled his remark back in the stable yard at Petbury, about the abundance of female company at Barrow-hill, which had indeed turned out to be true. The thought sobered him: which of those pretty ladies might be sharing his master's bed-chamber while he was here?

He glanced at Will, who was looking closely at him. 'Do you not see?' he asked quietly.

When Thomas remained silent he went on: 'Mistake it not: the Earl wants something of him. Mayhap to invest in one of his ventures, I know not . . . why else do you think he craves the company of a mere country knight, who's neither wit nor courtier, and of no real consequence in the land?'

It was true, and he should have seen it. While this thought sank home, he asked: 'And Wilkes, is he . . . ?'

Will was nodding. 'Wilkes, as was Brunning. Men like they have no need of friends – only partners in their projections.' He frowned again. 'Even his ward, Lady Deverell, is here not because the Earl wished to provide for her when she was orphaned, as he claims, but because of what she may inherit when she's of age. Else the Countess would never put up with such a wayward little trull.' He shook his head. 'Times are changing, Thomas. Thanks to the lawyers, money and property end up now in the hands of women.' He broke into a wry grin. 'As it has with Cousin Moll.'

Thomas nodded absently. Though he would have liked nothing better than to talk about Moll, and to dwell on the sweet pleasure she had given him, his mind was racing – towards which destination, he knew not. The thought struck him now that Sir Robert too might be in some danger.

Will slapped him on the shoulder. 'Come, let's look in on the birds and have a game of cards before we go to our beds. My purse won't bear another night in Tadworth for some days yet.'

He took the trencher and mug from Thomas, got up and walked off to return them to the kitchens. Thomas too stood up, feeling the breeze coming in off the Downs. The light was fading, and already candles glowed from the windows of Barrowhill. When Will returned, the two of them walked in silence up to the hut to see to their charges. For some reason, Thomas found himself recalling the knowing smile of the jingler, Ben Mallam. Perhaps he was right: it was the ways of men that one must learn to fathom, being far harder than those of beasts.

In the very early morning, he was awoken by the splashing of rain on the roof – and by something else: a distant cry, very faint, and not that of any bird or animal that he recognized.

Throwing off the covers, he rose from his pallet. On the other side of the room Will too was stirring. Stumbling about in the dark, Thomas crossed to the door, flung it open and froze.

From the dark bulk of Barrowhill, lights were showing on the upper floors. He scanned the windows.

And through the hard rain that fell, he heard it: a woman's scream that chilled him to the bone.

Six

The two falconers dressed hurriedly, then ran through the downpour towards the house. In the kitchens people were stirring, awoken by the scream and by shouting from above. There was general confusion, though some of the men were lighting lanterns, and talked of arming themselves and looking for intruders. Meanwhile scullery wenches and laundresses gathered in corners, trying not to show how much they were enjoying the excitement.

Thomas's instinct, as he and Will stood wiping the rainwater from their faces, was to go through to the passage and make for the stairs, but Will stayed him.

'Nay, only the higher servants and the ladies' maids are permitted upstairs.'

'My master . . .' Thomas muttered. He had a cold feeling in his stomach, borne from a terrible certainty – unthinkable though it seemed – that another murder had been committed. But even as the two of them hesitated, the door was opened suddenly and there was the usher, Henry Barnard, with a gown thrown hastily over his chemise and a face red with anger.

'What rabble is this?!' he shouted at the room in general, and at once a silence fell. 'Return to your beds! Dawn's almost upon us, and then you will fall to your duties – not before. Master Marmion!'

This was clearly the name of the black-bearded cook, who now came forward in his stockinged feet, his boots still in his hand.

'I look to you to restore some order here,' Barnard told him. The man nodded curtly – there was clearly little love between these two – and turned away, berating all and sundry for their foolishness. The fact that he had been the chief one calling for swords and bucklers a moment ago was quickly forgotten.

The servants began moving off. But as the falconers made to follow, Barnard placed an authoritative hand on Thomas's shoulder.

'I am commanded by Sir Robert to take you to him,' he said. 'Come with me.'

With a surprised glance at Will, Thomas followed the usher out.

They passed into a wide, flagged passage lit by torches, then gained the main staircase and strode up it. Barnard said not a word: clearly he disliked the order. On the first floor, there was an air of controlled panic. Ladies' maids hurried about from chamber to chamber, carrying trays and linen. From somewhere came the sound of a woman weeping hysterically. Ahead, the stooped figure of John Broad appeared briefly, looking like a man who had dressed in haste, then vanished again.

Then came a familiar voice, and Thomas breathed a quick sigh of relief.

'Thomas! Here!'

Sir Robert stood outside a closed door in his hose, a gown draped round his shoulders and a sword in his hand. Beside him was his manservant, Simon, an old cloak of his master's over his shift. He looked glad to see Thomas.

'Go now, see what help you can give,' Sir Robert ordered, and Simon hurried off. Then with a nod to Barnard, who at once turned on his heel and strode away, he gestured to Thomas to join him.

'We heard a scream, sir—' Thomas began, but his master shook his head impatiently. His face was pale in the half-light.

'Wilkes is dead.'

Thomas merely stared, but the other began to speak rapidly, as if to keep his own fear in check.

'And someone else has died along with him. The maid heard a noise and ran into the chamber – the scream you heard was hers. The Earl has been roused, and is dressing

64

now . . .' He broke off, glancing up and down the wide passage. 'I want you to go inside with me, before he arrives. We must move swiftly.'

Thomas nodded, whereupon his master turned the iron handle on the door and thrust it open. As soon as the two of them had entered the room he closed it behind them.

It was a grim sight.

At the far side of the luxuriously appointed chamber, with its gilt mirrors, carved chests and wall hangings, stood a massive four-poster bed. The heavy embroidered curtains were drawn back, so that the occupants – for there were two – could be clearly seen in the candlelight. One was Sir Thomas Wilkes, naked save for a rumpled shift, which was stained with blood. He was on his side, in a twisted, unnatural position – but there was no mistaking the dark patch of blood at the back of his neck.

The other occupant . . .

Thomas swallowed. 'Lady Deverell.'

'Do not speak of her!' Sir Robert's voice was sharp, so that Thomas turned to him in consternation.

'Listen to me now, Thomas,' said his master quickly. 'For I know what may follow. They will remove her body, and conceal it. Then, when the excitement has died, they will put it abroad that Lady Deverell has gone away – to Scotland, or the Continent, anywhere far enough. They daren't let it be known what has occurred, lest—' He broke off, but Thomas's mind raced ahead.

'Lest it damage her inheritance?'

If Sir Robert was surprised that Thomas knew of the matter, he did not show it, merely grew more urgent. 'Examine them both, swiftly, and tell me if I am right: that they have been killed in the same manner as Brunning.'

Thomas took a deep breath, nodded and walked over to the bed. First, though he knew it was fruitless, he felt for the great artery in the necks of both Wilkes and the woman, to assure himself that life had indeed gone from both. And in doing so, he could not help but look upon the body of Lady Deverell.

She wore a gossamer-thin chemise of finest lawn which had been pulled down to her waist, exposing her small breasts, the nipples painted with vermilion as though she were a Bankside callett. Her face too was painted, though her long hair was unbound. She lay half across Wilkes' body, her face set in a rictus of terror, one arm up as if to protect herself. There was little doubt that the two had been disturbed in the act of love. And yes: Wilkes had been stabbed at the base of the skull, exactly like Brunning. There was the deep wound, the blood newly congealed about it.

But Lady Deverell? Thomas's stomach heaved as he moved her body slightly to examine it, and saw the wash of blood. She had been stabbed, presumably with the same weapon – but not in the neck. Whoever had killed Wilkes, so cleanly and effi-ciently, had seemingly lost all control when it came to his paramour. A great welter of gore had spilled from the deep gashes in her heart and stomach, soaking her shift and the sheets beneath.

Trying to remain dispassionate, Thomas began trying to count the stab wounds, then as he reached ten, he paused and drew a deep breath. His master had come up silently beside him.

'It's as I thought?' Sir Robert murmured.

Thomas nodded. 'With Wilkes. But the other . . .'

'I see it plainly enough,' his master said, and laid a hand on his shoulder. 'Come away now.'

But as both men moved to leave the sickening sight, Thomas saw the parchment. When he froze, Sir Robert turned and saw it too. It had been placed around Wilkes' neck, on a length of twine, and tucked into his shift. Without being able to read the words upon it, Thomas guessed at their meaning.

Sir Robert let out an involuntary oath, gazing at the body of Lady Deverell. For there was another parchment: an irregularly shaped scrap, not neatly written and placed like the other, but seemingly torn from a corner of it, scrawled upon in haste and thrown down beside the body.

But now there were voices outside. Giving Thomas a shove towards the door, Sir Robert bent, plucked the parchment quickly from Wilkes' neck, grabbed the other one and stuffed them both hurriedly inside his gown. He had barely time to take two steps away from the bed himself before the door flew open, and several men crowded in.

First came Barnard, then three or four of the male house guests, all with drawn swords. At the sight of Sir Robert and his falconer in the room, there were expressions of surprise, followed by mutterings of suspicion.

'Come inside, sirs, and hurry,' called Sir Robert, a shade too readily. 'I have beheld a most fearful sight, that drains the courage from my body. See for yourselves!'

He gestured towards the bed. There were gasps, and not a few stifled oaths. One or two men turned away, white-faced. But Barnard was not one of them.

'May I enquire, Sir Robert, what you and your servant were doing here?' he asked, fixing the knight with a bland stare.

Sir Robert addressed him directly. 'As the Earl's friend, I wished to view the scene for myself – scarcely believing what the maids told me – and to discover what I could before his lordship arrives. He is a man of deep sensitivities, as you know. I would spare him the details, which might unnerve him.

Barnard said nothing, but walked forward and looked down at the bodies for himself. The other men stood aside in silence. His face had a sickly look on it as he turned away.

'You have disturbed nothing?' he asked.

Sir Robert shook his head.

'Then perhaps we should vacate the chamber, until . . .' Barnard seemed unusually lost for words. 'Until his lordship commands what shall be done.'

'Agreed,' Sir Robert said, and signed to Thomas to follow him out. The other men did the same. Barnard, the last to leave, closed the door behind him. In a chamber nearby, the hysterical maid was still being comforted by others.

'How in God's name . . .' Barnard muttered, then stopped himself as Sir Robert looked enquiringly at him. After a moment he went on: 'The room is inaccessible from outside, or from above . . . anyone coming in or out is easily seen – as

67

would be any who came by the stairs. Who could have done this?'

One of the younger men voiced his thoughts. 'Who – or what, if not some malignant spirit?'

They fell silent. Then an agitated, high-pitched and unmistakeable voice sounded from the far end of the passage, and every man turned. First John Broad appeared, then the Earl, walking towards them with rapid steps, fully dressed in feathered hat, buckled shoes and richly embroidered doublet.

Even a double murder, Thomas thought wryly, would not prevent the Lord of Barrowhill from looking his best.

An hour later, as the sun rose and the household servants set to their daily tasks, Thomas waited by the paddock, as he had been ordered. The rain had ceased, but the grass had already soaked his boots. On his gauntleted wrist was his master's falcon, Clorinda, quiet under her soft leather hood. To all outward appearances Sir Robert and his falconer – whether appropriately or not, given the circumstances – were setting off early for some sport on the Downs. But Thomas knew better: this was to be a conference, at which no other ears were required. So it was with surprise that he saw his master emerge from the house – not alone but in the company of the Earl's steward, John Broad.

Broad had a dog on a leash, a frisky hunting spaniel, eager to be exercised. But to Thomas's eyes it seemed this too was but a cover: Sir Robert had asked the steward to accompany them so they could talk freely, away from the eyes and ears of Barrowhill.

A moment later he had greeted both men with a respectful nod, and the three were walking briskly away up the path. Sir Robert did not speak until they were out of sight of the house, whereupon Broad, who had fallen behind, hailed him.

'For pity's sake, Sir Robert, have a thought for an old man's legs,' he cried. At once Thomas and his master turned and retraced their steps. As they approached, Sir Robert murmured his apologies.

'I believe we've come far enough,' Broad said, somewhat out

of breath, and stooped to untie his dog. With a bark, the animal raced away across the grass, startling several birds, which took flight at once. Sir Robert then unleashed his hawk, drew off the hood and raised his arm, whereupon the huge bird lifted herself and soared away.

After watching her climb to where she could drift on the warm air currents, the knight turned to the other two. His expression was grim.

'Master Broad wishes to know our minds, Thomas,' he said. 'I ask you to tell him what we have discovered.'

Thomas faced the old steward, found himself being shrewdly observed by a pair of owl-like eyes. To his surprise, he found that he was relieved to tell him all.

For half an hour the three men moved slowly about on the Downs, hardly noticing where they walked. John Broad, Thomas found, had a sharp mind which took in every piece of information. From time to time, he asked questions: how did Thomas know what kind of blade would make such a wound? Where had he been a soldier, and when? Had he told anyone else of his discovery?

Eventually, Thomas and Sir Robert having once again gone over the details of their brief examination of the bodies, Broad halted and held out his hand. 'Now, Sir Robert, I pray you let me look at these fearful messages.'

Sir Robert took the two pieces of parchment from his doublet and handed them to the steward. The one that had been around Wilkes' neck had been folded in quarters, then rolled up. When Broad opened it out, it was clear that the bottom right hand corner had been torn off, and there the other piece fitted. Both bore epigrams: on the larger piece, was once again the Latin motto '*Perite Scelesti*'.

'Thus perish the wicked', if I recall my Latin,' Sir Robert muttered.

'Nay – rather: "perish thus, ye wicked",' Broad countered. Then he pointed to two more words, further down the page.

'But this one is signed, where the one that was pinned to Sir George's doublet was not,' he said, and read aloud: ' "*Vindex Reginae*".'

Sir Robert looked thunderstruck. ' "Avenger of the Queen"?'

There was a silence. The steward's spaniel appeared, his tongue hanging out, and trotted towards the three men. Seeing them so preoccupied, he wandered away again.

After a moment Broad glanced at the other scrap of parchment, and lowered it at once. 'No Latin here,' he said somewhat thickly, and held it out so that both Sir Robert and his falconer could see the two words clearly enough.

They read simply: 'His Harlot.'

'So, master Broad, what must we do?' Sir Robert asked after a short silence.

Broad shook his head. For the first time that morning, Thomas thought, he looked as if his years sat heavy upon him. Presently he looked up from his reverie, put a hand to his mouth and whistled loudly. There was a distant bark, and the spaniel came bounding up. Without another word, the steward fastened the leash about his neck, and began to walk. The other two walked with him.

After a few minutes, Broad halted.

'What would you have me do, Sir Robert?'

Sir Robert's reply was firm. 'Let me tell the highest authority – the Privy Council. This is more than the murder of one man, some simple revenge killing . . . the same hand killed both Sir George and Sir Thomas. And mark the parchments. Which queen would anyone wish to avenge, but the Queen of Scots?'

Broad frowned. 'But neither Sir George nor Sir Thomas were part of the council – they neither tried nor condemned her. They are not men of policy. They have no power at Court – nor anywhere else, save in their business ventures—'

'Then there is some link,' Sir Robert interrupted. 'Someone who has lost money – a creditor with a grudge . . .' He trailed off, realizing how lame the theory sounded.

And now, choosing his moment, Thomas spoke. 'Sir, if I might make so bold, we are overlooking several things.'

Both men turned as if they had all but forgotten his presence. John Broad nodded to him.

'Speak, falconer.'

At Sir Robert's nod of assent, Thomas began to lay out the picture that had only now begun to form in his mind.

'I believe we should look not merely at how both men were killed, but where and when. Sir George on the Downs, almost within sight of the entire company . . . Sir Thomas in his chamber, with friends and servants within easy call . . .' He took a breath. 'The killer is close by. He knows how to pick his moment. He is clever, resourceful, and he is ruthless.' Then as an afterthought he added: 'Where he lost control was in the matter of Lady Deverell. The scrap of parchment was torn off then and there, and written on impulse, in that same chamber. I believe if we examined Sir Thomas's writing case we would see that the quill and the ink had been used.'

John Broad and Sir Robert said nothing. In the far distance came faint cries, then the blast of a horn.

Broad turned to the other men with a somewhat bitter smile. 'The Earl is hunting,' he explained. Seeing Sir Robert's expression he added: 'Her ladyship encouraged it. She fears he is unnerved by the events of the past days.'

Turning to Thomas, he urged: 'You see clearly, falconer. Please give vent to your thoughts.'

'Only a man – and a determined one at that – would know how to wield a poniard in such fashion,' Thomas said. 'This man's mind is deformed by hatred, yet he has some purpose – revenge perhaps, since there was no immediate gain to be had from killing either Sir George or Sir Thomas.'

They walked on apace, each one busy with his thoughts, until Thomas broke the silence again. 'And, I fear he is not yet done.'

Sir Robert looked at him sharply. 'You mean . . .?'

'Indeed, sir – I fear for your life too, as I do his lordship's,' Thomas answered. 'It looks plain to me: anyone who could gain access to Sir Thomas's privy chamber, and single out Sir George on the Downs, had ample opportunity to kill others. His targets are men of high station.'

Only now did it seem to occur to Sir Robert that he himself might be in danger. But when he turned towards John Broad, the steward seemed unsurprised.

71

'You reason well, falconer,' he said. 'And the same thought has already occurred both to the Earl and Countess. For which reason his lordship has taken steps. He has instructed me to send word to an old servant of his father's, a former man-at-arms. He will be here before nightfall, and a body of armed men with him. They will be housed at Barrowhill.'

Thomas and Sir Robert digested the news. Then Broad spoke again, in a tone that was almost apologetic.

'Sir Robert, if you wish to leave here, for your own safety, I would of course understand – as indeed would any man – and would hasten to assist your departure. Yet —' He broke off, as if seeking the right words. Sir Robert waited. 'I would beg you, for myself alone, not to go yet,' Broad said. 'I have need of you. And of your servant.'

This was a surprise. The other two looked at the old steward in silence. Absently, he leaned down to rub his spaniel about the neck, gazing at the distant shape of the great house, which was now fully in view.

'When his lordship succeeded to the title on the death of his father, he inherited me along with everything else,' he said, with a rather sad smile. 'Would that my old master were alive. He would have known how to deal with the matter.'

He turned a frank gaze toward both Sir Robert and Thomas. 'My master has enemies, I have little doubt on that score. The way he has lived this past dozen years, he could scarcely have avoided it.' He frowned. 'Indeed, we may need to look no further than his own household.'

Sir Robert spoke up urgently. 'Master Broad, if you have suspicions, speak freely – and in Thomas's hearing. I have absolute trust in him. Indeed,' he added, 'perhaps a falconer's eye is the one that will serve best, since our murderer seems able to go where he will – even fly in and out of windows.'

'Or mayhap, tunnel underground,' Broad replied. 'There are said to be ancient tombs beneath Barrowhill. A grim site for so fair a palace, do you not think?'

Sir Robert grimaced. 'Had you spoken those words but three days ago, I would have thought you mad. Now . . .' He waved a hand in the direction of the magnificent house, its domes gleaming in the morning sunlight.

Broad spoke again, more briskly. 'You ask of my suspicions. If you mean, is there one within the household I deem capable of doing . . . what has been done, I cannot say so. Yet there are those I do not trust.' He hesitated. 'The painter, for one.'

Thomas remained impassive, though his thoughts were leaping up like crickets.

'And Filbert,' Broad said, adding by way of explanation: 'The Earl's fool. He loved his old master – my master, as I did. And he professes love for his lordship. Yet . . .' He shook his head. 'There are times when I have glimpsed the anger in his eyes, and marvelled how he keeps it in check.'

'What of the house guests?' asked Sir Robert.

Broad shrugged. 'Some of them I scarcely know, it is true. Yet they are all as unnerved by events as the Earl, of that I am certain. Indeed, some are leaving today.' He turned to Sir Robert with a weary look. 'They have sworn not to speak of the matter until the Earl makes it known in his own fashion. Yet I fear, word will out soon enough. And those in high places—'

'Will also learn of the death of Lady Deverell,' Sir Robert broke in, prompting a sharp look from the steward. After a moment, he lowered his eyes.

'Indeed, even her ladyship will not be able to keep the lid on this scalding-pot,' Broad admitted. He turned to Thomas. 'I would be glad of any discovery you may make, falconer. You have carried arms yourself – hence I will make you known to master Jaggard when he arrives. Perhaps you may accomplish something between you.'

Then, suddenly agitated, he added: 'That is, of course, if you are still here – your pardon, Sir Robert—'

'No matter,' Sir Robert made a dismissive gesture. 'I will not leave yet, master Broad. I believe you wish to do what is right, as do I. And . . .' he lowered his voice, though there wasn't a soul within a hundred yards, 'I have my own reasons for wanting to see the matter resolved, come what may.'

Turning to his falconer he said: 'Thomas, have we not forgotten my Clorinda? I fear she has carried off, merely to spite me for paying her so little attention. How like a woman, eh?'

Thomas walked back up the hill, shading his eyes as he searched the sky for sign of the bird.

Seven

H ugh Jaggard rode in through the gates of Barrowhill at
dusk, a company of half a dozen men behind him. There
was no fanfare of trumpets, and no welcoming party save John
Broad standing in the torchlit stable yard, with Thomas beside
him.

Matters had not stood still, indeed it had been a long and
arduous day for all at Barrowhill. Despite pained protestations
from the Earl, several of the gentlemen and ladies who had
helped to make up so colourful a company had departed for
London and elsewhere, taking their servants with them along
with their opinions. The Countess, rather than join the Earl in
his attempts to remonstrate with his unhappy guests, merely
retreated to the chamber on the upper floor where she sat most
days for her portrait.

The bodies of Sir Thomas Wilkes and Lady Deverell had
been removed. Instead of being spirited away as Sir Robert had
feared, that of Emma Deverell, as a ward of the Earl and
Countess, was to be buried in the ornate tomb of the Meeres,
Earls of Reigate, some miles away near the site of the former
manor. Wilkes, like Brunning, Thomas learned, was to be taken
to London and turned over to relatives. Once again, there
would be no inquest. This manner of dealing with the business
was suspicious in itself. It was as if the murders had never taken
place, and the deaths were to be looked upon as some sort of
tragic accident. Unfortunately for the Earl, too many knew of
the discovery of the blood-soaked bodies in Wilkes' chamber
for that to be believed.

Thomas was still turning the events over in his mind as the
men-at-arms clattered into the cobbled yard. Soon the air was

filled with men's voices and the rattle of harness, the creak of leather and of joined armour. Jaggard himself, a heavily-built man with a thick blond beard flecked with silver, wore an old cuirass and helmet that looked as though they had seen service in many a campaign. As he dismounted and came forward, Thomas looked into the weather-beaten face and knew this was a strong man, who ploughed his own furrow and made sure everyone respected it.

'Master Jaggard. I trust you are in good health,' John Broad murmured, somewhat distantly, and turned to present Thomas. Jaggard pulled off his helmet, nodded at the steward, then focussed his bright blue eyes upon the other.

'So you've trailed a pike yourself, master Finbow?'

'Unwillingly,' Thomas smiled. 'And for but short duration.'

'No matter,' Jaggard replied. 'I may have need of you.' He gestured towards his men, who were dismounting and untying their packs, and lowered his voice. 'It's not the company I would have chosen, had I not been in haste. Some are old comrades-in-arms, but others I have recruited from the county militia – men I scarcely know.' He looked at John Broad. 'I will instruct them myself, but you must needs keep an eye out. I cannot vouch for their skill – or their manners.'

John Broad nodded, though his face showed some displeasure. 'I'll have a servant show you to the quarters we have prepared,' he began, but Jaggard shook his head.

'First, will you take me to the armoury? I need to see what weaponry is here.'

Broad hesitated, then turned to lead the way. Thomas, feeling this was not his domain, was about to walk away and find Will. He had barely seen him all day and was uneasy about leaving him to tend the falcons alone. But at once, Jaggard stayed him.

'Will you come with me? I would speak with you.'

Without waiting for an answer, he set off to accompany John Broad into the house. After a moment, Thomas followed.

On the ground floor, beside the kitchen storeroom, the three stopped outside the locked door of the armoury. For many years now, every English nobleman had been required by statute to keep a store of weapons and armour for the defence of the realm. Though the Earl, it transpired, had been somewhat lax in that area. This became apparent as soon as Broad had found the key, unlocked the heavy door and pushed it open, to the accompaniment of a loud squealing of hinges. Evidently the room had not been entered in years.

Thomas found a stub of torch and struck a light, so that Jaggard might examine the modest store of swords, pikes and bucklers. There were a few elaborately tooled suits of armour, clearly designed for the tiltyard and the tournament rather than for true combat. Against the far wall was a rack of dusty calivers. Jaggard turned, his face showing little emotion.

'May I have charge of the key, master steward?'

John Broad, who had remained by the door, made no answer at first. 'I am loth to part with it,' he said finally. 'It is my duty to retain all the keys of the house, save those that are in the charge of the usher of the Great Chamber.'

Jaggard regarded him calmly. 'And if your murderer struck again, tonight, and I wished to arm the men of the household at once, would your legs get you down here quick enough?'

A frown creased Broad's forehead. 'How many weapons might you need, to waylay one man?' he asked.

'You are certain there is but one?' Jaggard countered. 'From what I have heard—'

'What you have heard may amount to little more than rumour,' Broad interrupted. 'I would urge you to wait until master Barnard and I have acquainted you with the facts, as his lordship has charged us to do. Until then, the key remains on my chain.'

Jaggard shrugged. He looked like a man who was used to ruffling feathers, and expected few favours in return. 'Very well, master,' he replied. 'I will take counsel with you, if you will furnish a cup of wine to ease our discourse. Is that not fair?'

Broad nodded curtly and turned to lead the way. Thomas was struck by the difference in the steward's manner from the one he had displayed that morning on the Downs. He now appeared less like a kindly old retainer, and more like an officious chamberlain whose authority has been challenged.

Silently he followed the other two out into the passage, where Jaggard turned to him.

'I fear our talk must wait,' he said.

'No matter,' Thomas said. 'You may find me at the falconer's hut beyond the paddock, or on the Downs with my hawks.'

Then with a nod at John Broad, he left the torchlit interior and went outdoors, glad of the freshening breeze on his face.

Will Holland was not at the hut, but had fed and watered the birds. Seeing them contented, Thomas went to his bed as night came down fast beneath a cover of thickening cloud. Despite his weariness his mind was active, and he took a long while getting to sleep. So it was with some irritation that he was awoken in the silent hours by Will stumbling in drunk, and falling over the end of his pallet.

'Christ's blood, what . . .?' came the mumbled oath, as Thomas sat up with a start, seeing the swaying figure silhouetted against the dim light from the tiny window.

'Pardon, master Thomas . . .' Will said with mock formality, then sat down heavily to pull off his boots. 'I forgot you were here.'

Thomas yawned and shook himself. 'No need to ask where you've been,' he began, but Will wagged a finger at him.

'You misjudge me, sirrah,' he said in a solemn tone. 'I do confess I walked into Tadworth to find Doreth, but matters . . .' He belched, then continued in something closer to his normal voice. 'The matter is, she scorned to have me fumble with her . . . she has a harsh way, at times. Says there's all sorts of rumours about, and her father thinks if I do truly love her, I should have the courage to leave the Earl's household and seek service elsewhere. There, that's the nub of it.'

Thomas, wide awake now, spoke through the semi-darkness. 'What rumours are there about?'

Will sniffed loudly and threw his boots into a corner. 'They're simple folk, round here,' he said vaguely. 'Don't take much for them to start talking of evil things lurking at Barrowhill . . . as if we hadn't demons enough with a murderer on the loose.'

He pulled off his leather jerkin, threw that into another corner, then began taking off his shirt.

'Any man would think it were my doing, the way Doreth berated me . . . and half the Red Bull throng within hearing, all ready to enjoy the fray!'

'You had a brabble, in the inn?' Thomas asked.

'That we did,' Will said, 'and it fell to name-calling and worse. I was wrong to pick this night, for I believe it is that phase of the moon's cycle when women turn waspish . . . least, Doreth always does – here now, feel that!'

He thrust his shirt into Thomas's hands. It was wringing wet, and the stench of strong beer rose from it.

'What did she do, throw a pint pot over you?' Thomas asked, feeling inclined to laugh for the first time in days. But Will was not amused.

'A full mug!' he cried. 'And she'd have caught up another, save that one man stopped her. 'Twas then that Moll threw us both out. Her own cousin, too . . .'

Thomas was relieved that Will could not see his smile in the dark. 'Get to your bed,' he told him. 'The morrow will put a different aspect upon it. I'll stake my purse, if you go back with a bunch of posies and beg forgiveness of Doreth – and of Moll – you'll be restored to favour soon enough.'

But Will was unconsolable in his melancholy. 'I swear to you, Thomas,' he mumbled, 'the worst thing is, she is right. This is an unwholesome place, and I should find the courage to quit it.' He sniffed, as if close to tears. 'Then, who would care for my birds?'

Thomas sighed and made no answer. With another sniff Will got unsteadily to his feet, stumbled over to his own pallet and fell upon it. Thomas lay back and pulled up his blanket, expecting the sound of heavy snoring to fill the room very quickly. But instead Will's voice floated sleepily to him through the darkness.

'He was a queer sort of rogue, that beggar. The one who stopped Doreth from dousing me again, as if I weren't wet enough already . . . he was a mite too nosy for my taste.'

Thomas sat up, a bell of memory clanging in his head.

'What beggar?'

'Been wandering about the village all day, 'swhat I heard . . .' Will answered. He yawned long and loud. 'Name of Tobias. Poor Tobias . . .' he muttered sadly, and fell asleep.

The next day, Friday, dawned misty with a promise of sunshine. Despite a sore head Will roused himself, took a long draught of water and accompanied Thomas out to the falcons' mews. They were still at their work when there came a shout from the paddock below. Shading his eyes, Thomas saw the figure of Sir Robert, leading his horse. Leaving Will's side, he walked down the grassy hill at once to meet his master.

Their greeting was brief, for it was clear Sir Robert had a great deal on his mind. He came quickly to the point.

'Thomas, I fear you must leave the hawks to master Holland. I have other work for you.' With a glance towards the house – as if anyone could overhear from such a distance – he went on in a low voice: 'I like not this man Jaggard, any more than does John Broad. He is an insolent fool. Moreover, even if the truth be uncovered, I fear the Countess will stifle it before it is out.'

Thomas frowned. 'Master Broad – he has the parchments—'

'John Broad is an old man,' Sir Robert interrupted. 'I see now there is a struggle for supremacy within the household. Henry Barnard is a younger man, who covets the steward's place.'

Sir Robert fell silent, allowing Thomas time to mull over the matter. When he spoke again, his voice was heavy with irony.

'Do you know what Barnard has proposed? A lavish entertainment, on the lake, with music and fireworks, and a pageant and a mock battle, to celebrate our glorious victory over the Spaniard. Jaggard's men would play soldiers – literally.'

Thomas's face was such a blank that Sir Robert almost laughed. 'Do you not see?' he cried. 'It is a clever plan – one by which the Earl and Countess may restore their reputation. The Queen herself will be invited here, as will everyone of substance. If it proves grand enough, the Barrowhill Entertainment will be the talk of all England – perhaps even rivalling the

Earl of Leicester's magnificent Pleasures, thirteen years back . . .' He shook his head, stirred by the memory. 'A sight like that one does not easily forget, Thomas. The Earl and Countess would gain great admiration by it, not to mention much influence.'

Thomas gazed down at the grass, still wet with dew, and nodded slowly. 'And the murders will be forgotten.'

'That,' said Sir Robert, 'is why no pains must be spared to find the killer and apprehend him. And in this I need your help.'

Thomas waited. During their conversation Sir Robert had let his horse's reins drop, so that the animal could lower its head and graze a little. Now he caught them up again, and began stroking the neck of the sleek gelding, his favourite Barbary.

'You know what they say at Petbury?' he smiled. 'If a spoon be lost, or even a bodkin, send for Thomas. The eyes of the falconer are keenest.'

Thomas managed a wry smile. 'I have never tried to seek for a ghost – at least, not yet.'

'It is no ghost,' Sir Robert said grimly. 'A wicked man wielded that poniard, and I believe you were right that he is close by – maybe even within these grounds.'

He gazed in the direction of the house. From the highest point, a hexagonal tower, the Earl's pennant floated. 'Would that you were permitted to enter his lordship's Prospect Room,' he mused. 'They say you can see every part of the manor from there, and further. Three or four miles, in any direction.'

Absently he ran his gloved hand down the horse's withers, then straightened, his manner suddenly brisk. From his belt he took a full purse, shook it so that it jingled, and handed it to Thomas.

'You have my leave to go where you will,' he said. 'Find out all you can – not merely in Tadworth, but beyond. You can go where I cannot. For I am watched, while I am here.' Seeing Thomas's expression, he nodded. 'Subtly, of course . . .' his eyes wandered back to the Prospect Room, with its windows on every side. Thomas had the sudden notion that he too was being observed, then dismissed it as mere fancy. He eyed his master keenly.

'I will do what I can, Sir Robert.'

'I know it,' Sir Robert replied, then giving the reins a tug, began walking his horse towards the mews, with Thomas beside him. 'Now, if you will give me my Clorinda, I would like to go hawking – alone. And I have no need of any trumpets to sound me on my way.'

Though his master's charge lay heavy upon him, Thomas found that he was relieved to get away from Barrowhill. After Sir Robert had ridden away, he found Will Holland and told him what had transpired, swearing him to secrecy. Will, though still mournful this morning, took the news stoically.

'I'd ask in the village first,' he said. 'Though if there's been any strangers about, I haven't heard of them.'

'Save the wandering beggar,' Thomas said quietly.

Will frowned, then remembered. 'Oh, that one,' he muttered. 'Aye – ask Moll. There isn't much she don't get to hear about.'

Thomas nodded. 'I must leave the hawks in your good hands,' he said in an apologetic tone, but Will waved him away.

'Go on, leave me in peace. I've a tabor in my head playing a moorish rhythm.' But then the sly grin that occasionally graced his sober features poked out. 'If I remember aright, she was asking after you. Cousin Moll, that is.'

Thomas turned and walked off towards the Downs, in the direction of the Tadworth path.

What began as a disappointing morning turned into an eventful day.

Arriving in Tadworth with a powerful thirst, Thomas went at once to the Red Bull. The taproom was empty, most of the customers being those who worked the land, but the drawer recognized him and brought him a mug of best. To Thomas's enquiry, he replied that Moll had gone to the market at Walton. He did not expect her back before nightfall. Upon further enquiry he grew somewhat impatient, if not surly. No, there had been no strangers about that he knew of. And he had seen naught of any wandering beggar.

Thomas took his mug outside and sat on a huge elm log that

served as a bench. The morning was fair, the village street quiet. From the fields about came the distant sounds of husbandry: of sheep, and cattle . . . and closer, the rumble of wheels. He glanced around to see a horse with a laden cart in tow, turning the bend at the bottom of the village. The driver wore a wide-brimmed hat against the sun. And then Thomas received his first piece of luck; for walking beside the cart in casual conversation with its driver was the jingler, Ben Mallam.

As he drew level, Mallam bade the man farewell and started to walk towards the tavern. Seeing Thomas, he stopped.

'Master falconer,' he said with a smile. 'An odd time of day for you to be taking a mug.'

'I would gladly buy you one, master Mallam,' Thomas answered. 'Will you sit a while with me?'

Mallam's expression grew wary, but nevertheless he agreed. After the drawer had gone the two men sat side by side in silence, until Mallam decided he would break it.

'Well, sirrah,' he said, wiping his mouth with the back of his hand. 'If it's information about horses you seek, mayhap I am the man for you. For aught else. . .' He waved his hand.

'I heard there was a coil here last night,' Thomas said with a smile. 'My friend Will received a dousing from his sweetheart.'

'I heard so too,' Ben replied, and took another drink.

'I also learn there was one here that I met a while back. I was sorry not to renew acquaintance with him. He's named Tobias.'

Ben Mallam said nothing, but Thomas could almost hear wheels in motion behind his green eyes. Finally he asked: 'The beggar? What would you want with such as he?'

Thomas gave a shrug. But Mallam seemed intrigued, and Thomas saw now that he was one of those blessed – or perhaps saddled – with a keen sense of curiosity.

'Couldn't be you suspect, as do I, that he's a strange fellow for a licensed beggar?' Mallam asked, with a gleam in his eye. 'A little too clever, mayhap?'

Thomas merely raised an eyebrow.

'And much too eager to poke into other folks' business,' Ben added. Choosing to take Thomas's silence for assent, he went on: 'Or mayhap you guessed, as I did, that the licence was forged.'

Thomas blinked. 'How can you be certain?'

It was Mallam's turn to shrug, but in his case there was an air of triumph about it. 'Because I know who forged it.'

Thomas took a mouthful of ale to hide his growing excitement. He knew in his bones that Poor Tobias had some connection, however remote, with Barrowhill. Why else would he have been so interested, back in the inn at Cobham, in Thomas's visit?

'How came you to know that?' he asked.

'Come, master Finbow,' Ben said after a moment, as if tiring of the fencing bout. 'You may not have a hawk on the hand, but you are hunting, are you not?'

'Well,' Thomas answered, 'mayhap I am, at that.'

'I move about a deal, is all,' Mallam said. 'And use my ears. And anyone with as sharp an eye as mine may tell a fake seal from a true one: they are not neat enough, nor graven with hard steel, but picked out with a knife-point. But I return to my question: what do you want with the beggar – whether he be false or no?'

'Say that it touches on some business of my master's,' Thomas replied finally. 'And I have leave to reward those who help me.'

Ben Mallam considered. 'Perchance I could set you to him.'

'To the beggar?'

'Nay, I know not where he is. To the jarkman – the one who forged the licence.'

As Thomas turned to him, Ben tilted his mug back and drained it. Meeting his gaze, he said: 'Every county has at least one – London has a swarm of them. Scriveners who have ended up in the Counter for debt, failed schoolmasters, poor clerks fleeing shrewish wives . . . the man I have in mind came from Monmouth by way of Gloucester, then Oxford, where for a quart of cheap wine, some penniless scholar helped him with his meagre Latin. Now he works the county of Surrey – and one who knows where to look may find him in Leatherhead. It's but four miles away.'

'There's a shilling and a good dinner for you,' Thomas told him, 'if you bring me to this man.'

Mallam's eyes narrowed. 'What do you wish to do with him?'

Thomas was aware that he must tread carefully. A jingler was no friend of the law. Choosing his words, he answered: 'I seek the beggar, not the jarkman. I will pay him for his trouble, and leave him be.'

Ben Mallam stood up suddenly. Having made a decision, he was eager to be on the move. 'You are fortunate indeed, master,' he said, 'that your need sits well with mine. Tomorrow, I'm for the horse fair at Banstead. Today I will go with you to Leatherhead, and mayhap find a couple of nags to trade. I will announce you as one in urgent need of a passport. Can you play the part?'

'I believe so, so long as my Kendal Green does not betray me.'

'Then let's to the stable.' Seeing the puzzled look on Thomas's face, he gave a snort of laughter. 'Jesu, did you think we would go on foot? I'm no Downland hare. You can ride double, can you not?'

Thomas nodded, though he did not relish the thought of a bone-shaking ride along rough lanes, seated behind Ben Mallam on some broken-down jade fit only for the slaughterman's knife. Hence his relief when, a short time later, he found himself astride a small, wiry horse with a good brown coat and a thick mane, that responded well to the rein and to Ben's tongue-clicking commands. In a few minutes they had left the village and were trotting westward across the hills towards Leatherhead.

'He's a Spanish jennet,' Ben explained over his shoulder. 'I call him King Philip – and I'll not take less than fifty crowns for him.'

He did not speak again until they descended into the valley of the river Mole and came to Leatherhead. Here, as he and Thomas dismounted stiffly in the rutted street amid barking dogs and the stares of village folk, Ben gazed about, rubbed his stomach and said: 'It's close to midday. Shall we first seek that dinner you promised me?'

Thomas straightened his back and worked his shoulders. 'We will, presently. First, I ask you to take me to the jarkman.'

Ben shrugged. 'I hope you have a strong stomach.'

With Thomas striding beside him, Ben led his horse along the street, then turned down a narrow lane between timbered houses. Here a stench rose in their nostrils, for there were dunghills against the walls, and the drain was choked with rotted food and refuse. Ragged children ran out shouting and women appeared at doorways, but Ben Mallam merely grinned and picked his way through the mire, while King Philip stepped skilfully over loose stones. In a short time they reached the end of the lane, which opened on to wasteland with meadows beyond. Here they stopped outside the last cottage, a broken-down hovel with eaves that sagged almost to the ground. The door, of unfinished deal planks, was rotted at its base.

Keeping hold of the horse's reins with one hand, Ben put the other to his mouth and gave a sharp whistle, then another. Nothing happened, save a shriek from a kite that fluttered from somewhere behind the house and flew away across the rooftops.

Still they waited, until there came a muffled voice and at last the door was thrust open. From the gloom within a face poked out, as ruddy as that of a red-ochre man, framed by matted red hair and a wild beard of the same hue. There was a moment while the man surveyed his visitors in silence. Then Ben spoke.

'I do hear from a palliard, you're a bene-faker of gybes as well as of jarks, master,' he said with a knowing smile. 'Can you aid one who must leave the county within a week, if he may avoid the trining-chats?'

The red man's eyes were screwed up tightly, as if the outdoor light troubled him. Then they widened in recognition.

'I know you – you're the jingler.'

Ben nodded. 'How fare you, master Fludd?'

'Ask me nothing,' came the short reply, in a lilting accent which was unknown to Thomas. 'Only tie your nag to the corner post and come in.' Turning his rheumy eyes on Thomas, he demanded: 'Is this the cove? Has he two bords and a flag to pay me?'

Thomas nodded curtly, uneasy at the thought that he had no notion of how much Ben had just committed him to laying out. But in spite of himself, he felt a small surge of excitement. He was on a trail, of sorts: he could almost scent it. Though where it might lead, he had not the least idea.

Eight

Evan Fludd lived alone, and in considerable squalor. The interior of the hovel reeked of every imaginable kind of human neglect: rotten wood and dung, rancid grease and stale cabbage. The floor was of stamped earth, the walls were cracked and full of holes, the thatch full of vermin. Daylight showed in several places, and pails stood beneath to catch the rain. The only furniture was a straw pallet in one corner, raised off the damp floor on slabs of rough-hewn timber, and a joined stool beside the fireplace which served as the kitchen. But along one wall, where the only real light came in through a small window, was a workbench covered with sheets of parchment, broken knives, lumps of wax, scraps of copper and of pewter. On the rotting sill stood inkpots, quills and a sandbox. Here was the workplace of a jarkman: a professional forger and maker of false seals.

Ben Mallam had declined the invitation to enter. Instead he presented Thomas as his friend and said he would wait outside to mind his horse – which seemed a sensible enough step, given the circumstances. So Thomas, stooping lest he crack his head on a sagging beam, took the stool that was shoved towards him and sat himself down while Fludd rolled up the sleeve of his smelly, threadbare gown and stepped to the work table, every inch the man of business.

'Where is it you wish to go?' he asked.

Thomas hesitated, uneasy at pursuing the matter of a false passport. He had intended simply to ask for information about Tobias, pay something in return and leave. But Ben had handed him a plot, and he must now play it out.

'To Dover,' he answered. 'And beyond.'

Fludd turned his watery eyes towards him. 'I would see a little white money, before I proceed.'

Thomas found his purse, drew out a shilling and threw it on to the cluttered table. Immediately, Fludd picked it up and bit it.

'I'm no coiner,' Thomas said with an attempt at levity. 'The penalties are somewhat too severe for me.'

The other fixed him with a bleak stare. 'Know you not what risk I take?' he demanded. 'The penalty for faking such documents is imprisonment for life, with a terrible burning of the face!'

'I ask pardon,' Thomas replied. Then, an idea coming to mind, he added: 'I would have a licence somewhat like that you made for my friend Tobias.'

It was a mistake. Fludd's head snapped round at once, and with his red beard bobbing, he retorted: 'I ask no names! And you'll have what I will provide! Can such as you know the names of the Justices, or the correct terms of address, let alone the marks of the seals and the . . . ah!' To Thomas's alarm he broke into a fit of sudden coughing, his gorge so thick with flux that it appeared he might choke. He turned away and grabbed a cracked pot, into which he coughed horribly, leaning over the work table, his raddled body racked with the fearful attack, until mercifully it began to subside. After some minutes, it ceased.

There was a long pause while Fludd gathered his strength. His eyes were closed, which Thomas assumed was due to the coughing. But when the man faced him again, it was with a look of deep suspicion.

'First you wished for a passport to leave England . . . then you ask for a licence to beg. Know you not what it is you want?'

'The passport,' Thomas answered, his mind working rapidly. 'I may have need of a licence when I return – that can wait . . .'

But Fludd, though he showed no reaction, was a man who trusted nobody. So it was that Thomas was caught off guard when with remarkable speed the jarkman whipped a poniard from some hidden pocket of his gown and lunged forward, holding the point close to his eyes.

Thomas froze, then slowly allowed his gaze to meet the other man's. There was nothing there but a bitter hostility, along with a powerful instinct for self-preservation.

'You're no fugitive!' Fludd spat. 'What do you want here?'

From somewhere outside came a great din of snarling and yelping, followed by the shouts of children. Apparently two dogs were fighting. Whether Ben was in earshot or no, Thomas decided against calling out. Instead, he tried the simple truth.

'I'm seeking a murderer,' he said. 'And it may be that Tobias, for whom you made a licence, can help me to him.'

The red-faced man gasped aloud, and shook as if another bout of coughing threatened to undo him. With a trembling hand, he lowered the poniard a fraction so that it rested against Thomas's cheekbone, below his eyelid.

'I've naught to do with murder!' he cried. 'I'm a feeble old man . . . a poor scrivener . . .' His breath rattled in his chest. 'Ask me nothing, only state your business and get you gone!'

'Some plain intelligence, is all I desire,' Thomas answered quietly, adding: 'I tricked the jingler into bringing me here. He knows naught of my search—'

'And I wish to know naught of it!' Fludd snapped. 'I want you gone!'

'Then take the shilling,' Thomas said, keeping his control, 'and kindly lower your dagger.'

But Fludd shook his head. 'First tell me your station – who sent you?'

After a moment Thomas answered: 'I cannot say. I risk my own neck in saying as much as I have. Tell me of Tobias, and I will leave and not trouble you again.'

There was a pause. Then to his surprise, a moan of deep anguish came from Fludd's mouth. He dropped his hand, and the poniard with it.

'See what a fool I've become!' he cried woefully. 'I knew I should not have had dealings with such – he had the stink of the law about him, even though he'd kicked his heels in Newgate . . . runagate scab! By the Lord, I could . . .'

And while Thomas watched, the jarkman raised a shaking hand before him, screwing his fist up tightly in helpless rage.

The man's half mad, he thought with growing dismay. And hence, could anything he said be believed?

Unable to think of any other course, he fumbled for his purse and took out another coin. 'You have the shilling,' he said. 'Here's another sixpence, when you have told me all you know about Tobias. Then I will go.'

After a moment Fludd calmed himself, though his expression remained wary. But he appeared to have decided that Thomas was not a representative of the law. Or perhaps, a shilling and a half was merely too large an amount to forgo.

'Stokes,' he said, and quickly lowered his gaze. 'The true name of the one you seek is William Stokes. He wished for a licence to wander the county until Michaelmas. That is all I know.'

With some relief, for Fludd's words bore some stamp of truth, Thomas rose to his feet, breathing hard. The gloom and the stench were beginning to damp his spirits. But as he raised his hand to throw the sixpence on the table, he saw the suggestion of a crafty smile lurking beneath the man's tangled beard . . . and in a moment he knew that he was not the only one who had a part ready rehearsed. Nor was the man as mad as he pretended. His anger rising, he took a step forward, threw down the coin, then with sudden speed grabbed Fludd's wrist in a firm grip, so that he screeched and dropped the poniard. His other hand, Thomas placed tightly around his throat.

'You've tried my patience long enough, master,' he said. 'The truth now, or I'll ride to the Earl of Reigate and tell him all about you. It matters not to me how fearful a branding you get.'

And though Fludd gagged and squealed and writhed in his grasp, Thomas's grip was too strong, and the matter was settled quickly. For whatever else the wily jarkman was, he was nobody's fool, and he sensed that his only recourse was to tell what he knew.

'Enough!' he cried, tugging at Thomas's hand, which still held him firmly by the throat. 'I will tell you! Leave me be!'

There was a noise at the door. Without turning around, Thomas knew that Ben Mallam had heard the commotion and come in to investigate.

'Jesu, falconer,' he began, 'what the devil do you—'

'Wait outside!' Thomas called over his shoulder, in a tone that brooked no argument. Without a word, Ben Mallam went out.

'The beggar,' Thomas said, pushing his face closer to the jarkman's. 'I want to know all you know of him – now.'

'Mercy – my throat . . .' Fludd croaked, and fearing another coughing bout Thomas released him. But not before he had stooped quickly and picked the poniard up from the floor.

'The beggar,' he repeated.

Fludd stood panting, rubbing his throat with one hand, while the other flapped about in unfeigned agitation. 'Poole,' he mumbled. 'He goes by the name of Anthony Poole. The part about the licence is true. By Michaelmas, he said he would have settled his accompt – whatever that be, I know not. Save that . . .' He broke off, suddenly fearful. 'Swear by Christ you will not say I talked!'

'I have said already,' Thomas replied. 'It is between the two of us.'

'He is not what he seems!'

Thomas snorted, his patience spent. 'That much is plain even to a blind mule . . .' he began, but Fludd was shaking his head.

'Nay, nay . . . he is not what he seems – neither beggar, nor papist, as he claimed he was. I can smell a Romish fugitive from ten yards – have I not helped many across the Channel? Poole is of a different stamp – I know not what. And that,' Fludd declared, with the best he could muster in the way of dignity, 'is all that I know. He came once, then came again when I had made the licence, and was gone. Finis!'

After a moment Thomas tossed the poniard on to the pallet, then with a final glance at Fludd went outside. Here, even the stench of the lane was as perfume to his nose.

Then he looked around for Ben Mallam, knowing immediately that it was futile. Both the jingler and his Spanish jennet were gone.

It was a long walk back to Tadworth, and even the weather turned against him. After taking dinner in a cheap tavern, indifferent to the stares of Leatherhead folk, he left the village and took the lane by which he and Ben Mallam had ridden in, little more than an hour since. There was no sign of Ben, and Thomas regretted the manner of his dealing with him earlier – like the jarkman, the jingler would want nothing to do with another man's quest if it looked like leading to trouble. Now, matters weighed upon him as he resigned himself to the journey, with no firm plan beyond reaching Tadworth by evening. He could return to Barrowhill and tell Sir Robert about the false beggar – at least he had some information to show for his pains. And of course, he might see Moll; the thought cheered him considerably as he tramped the rutted way, then struck a Downland path that looked familiar. At least it led in the right direction. And then, the heavens opened.

He had seen the dark clouds looming from the west, and knew he was in for a soaking. He was hardly unused to such weather, at home on the Berkshire Downs, but even so the force of the downpour caught him unprepared. In a very few minutes, with no hope of shelter, he was drenched to the bone. And what had begun as a simple foot journey of about four miles, turned into an afternoon of wandering about the Surrey hills, each one alike in the blinding uniformity of the heavy rain. Finally he encountered a gloomy shepherd in a sodden cape who set him on the right path, and within the hour he found himself on the edge of Tadworth, its single street now a rivulet of mud.

It was evening already, and only now was the rain beginning to diminish. And when Thomas entered the Red Bull, with the welcome glow of its banked fire, the first person he saw was Ben Mallam, warming his feet on the hearth.

There was no greeting. Ben merely glanced at him, then turned back to the fire. He too had received a soaking, though less severe than the one Thomas had endured. His hair like a flat poultice against his skull, his clothes dripping and boots squelching, Thomas walked to the chimney corner and lowered his tired body on to the same oak settle where he had first sat and talked with Moll, three days earlier. It seemed like weeks ago.

It was Thomas's part to be contrite. While he tugged off his boots, seeking the right words, there came a subdued snort of laughter. He glanced up to see Ben regarding him without rancour.

'Found your way back, then,' he murmured. 'Was it not a sweet shower of rain?'

'Aye.' Thomas peeled off his jerkin, which was beginning to steam, then said: 'I owe you an apology, and a dinner. Will a supper serve instead?'

Ben merely stared into the fire. Then without taking his eyes from the leaping flames, he said: 'You shouldn't have played fast and loose with me, master Finbow.'

'I told you it was information I sought,' Thomas answered mildly. 'Fludd was the one played false – and stuck a poniard in my cheek. I dealt with him as he deserved.'

'Did you now?' Ben turned an unfriendly eye upon him. 'Looks to me as though you scared him witless so he'll pack up his jarks and move elsewhere. And so for a time, any man in need of his services will be hard pressed to find him. Time is precious to such men, falconer. Indeed to all those of us who have not a wage and a livery, and a safe place to lay our heads of a night-time.'

Thomas sighed. 'I ask your pardon. Let me buy you one of Moll's best suppers, and a jug of wine to sit beside it.'

Ben appeared to mull the matter over. But when he half-turned to Thomas, the gleam in his eye was back, along with the suggestion of a smile.

'I'll not be taking supper here,' he said. 'I'm expected elsewhere, come nightfall.'

Thomas waited.

'Yet, if you've a mind to settle the score between us, I've work for you. Indeed, it may sit well with your plans.'

Thomas regarded him with some surprise. 'Work?'

'At the horse fair tomorrow,' Ben replied. 'I'm for Banstead, at first light. I can use another pair of willing hands. And another voice.'

Thomas watched the steam rising from his breeches. 'I've little skill with horses,' he began, but Ben waved the objection aside.

'What I will ask of you is simple enough. Merely a matter of doing the part I set out for you. And, consider this: the fair draws folk of every sort, from all corners of the county – indeed, from London and beyond. Might not your wandering beggar be there?'

'He might,' Thomas allowed, seeing the wisdom of such a plan.

'Then you'll come with me?'

'I'll come.'

'Good!' Ben rose abruptly from his seat. 'Wait for me at the bottom of the village at sunrise – whether there be sun or no. It's a five-mile ride.' Seeing the look on Thomas's face, he laughed. 'Do not fret – you shall ride in style, as befits a 'prentice horse-courser. I've a jade for each of us.'

He clapped Thomas on the shoulder, then stooped and said in a low voice: 'Sunrise, remember – I'll not brook any delay, even though I may well understand the cause of it!'

With a chuckle he moved off towards the door. Thomas turned round, and saw the reason for his amusement. His face lighting up at once, he rose from his seat, because Moll had walked in.

When the last revellers had gone, singing raucously at the moon, and the door was bolted, Moll came to her bed. Thomas lay on his back asleep, as she had left him an hour since, bidding him take his rest and not wait for her. She herself was always so tired after an evening's business that she could do little but pull off her dress and crawl under the coverlet. But ever a light sleeper, he stirred, sensing her presence, and raised his head as she settled down beside him.

For a moment neither of them spoke. Then after he had leaned over and kissed her and drawn back, seeing the exhaustion in her eyes, she said: 'You should come to me on a Sunday, my duck, when I might find time for us to enjoy each other.'

He smiled. 'To lie beside you is joy enough. And besides, I must leave you at dawn once again.'

'For the horse fair?' She yawned deeply, and added: 'You must mark Ben Mallam. He's a rogue and a half – there are many he's cony-catched over the years would willingly take a knife to him if they see him. You're likely to find yourself embroiled in a quarrel.'

'Nay – I'm fleet of foot for a man of my age,' Thomas told her, to which Moll gave a snigger.

'Then mayhap we'll play at barley-brake, and chase each other round the fields and pretend we're young again,' she murmured.

Before he could think of a reply, she had closed her eyes and drifted at once into sleep.

When the first glimmer of morning showed, he managed to leave the bed without waking her, and tip-toed down the stairs in his stockinged feet. In the kitchen, Nan shifted on her pallet but did not wake. Lifting the latch, he stepped outside into the chill damp of early dawn, and sat on a barrelhead to pull on his boots. To the east, the low rooftops of the village stood black against the sky.

A short time later he had walked downhill to where the houses ended and the lane turned. At once there came a low whistle, and the stamp of hooves. Peering through the dim light, Thomas saw Ben Mallam astride his trusty Spanish jennet, holding a grey horse by a lead rein.

'Your breakfast,' called the jingler, and tossed him an apple. Within minutes they were riding across the Downs, northward towards Banstead. And very soon, the instruction began.

'Our first task,' Ben Mallam told him, 'is to sell that thing between your legs – I speak not of your pizzle, but of the jade. He must fetch ten nobles, with which we shall proceed to the other task: to whit, the purchase of four or five others which I will then drive to Smithfield market – but that part matters not to you, master Thomas. Yours is to be my goad, and help me conclude the sale.'

'What must I do?' Thomas asked, with a growing feeling that he was not going to like the answer.

'I will instruct you to the letter,' Ben smiled, and sniffed the early morning air deeply. He was a different Ben Mallam today:

cheerful in the certainty of one who is about the business he was born to do.

'First,' he said, 'you will do naught without my signal, and act only upon that. I may speak with many buyers before I scent the right one. Then when I rub my beard, so –' and here he demonstrated the innocent-looking action – 'you will step forward as one who is no friend of mine, but who knows the horse. And you will sing its praises: what a good continuer he is, how sweet-tempered, and so forth. How you have heard that one across the field will pay more, and you would advise our mark to snap up the jade while he may. As you see, my friend, 'tis naught to a clever man like you. Is that not plain?'

'Plain enough,' Thomas replied. 'Tell me but this: is the horse stolen, or so full of disease that he will drop dead before Friday next? Or is he merely old, but you have doctored his teeth with an iron so that he looks five years younger than he is?'

Ben frowned at him. 'Jesu, falconer. You must think me a very common forsworn villain.'

'We have horse fairs in Berkshire too,' Thomas told him.

'I know it,' Ben retorted, and could not resist a smirk. 'I believe I cozened your master's steward out of a nag one springtime, at Wantage.'

Thomas made a wry face. 'He was always too trusting, old Martin.'

'See now,' Ben resumed, clearly feeling they had strayed from the matter in hand. 'You agreed to aid me, not to pass judgement on my profession. Content yourself that whoever buys the grey deserves what he gets. 'Tis the other part of the day's work that should irk you: those we shall bargain with when we come to buy are men of my own fellowship. Then, we must have our wits sharpened to a needle's point, with scarce a moment to draw breath.'

'Do you have another part for me, then?' Thomas enquired.

The jingler grinned, and clicked his tongue to King Philip to trot a little faster.

'That I may, master falconer,' he said.

*　　*　　*

97

It was Saturday, a day of sunshine and cloud, of good luck and poor, of laughter and of savagery. But from the first, as he and Ben Mallam came off the Downs and rode into the fair-field at Banstead, Thomas knew that it was to be a day of events. He sensed it as they entered the meadow, the grass already trampled to mud underfoot. He smelt it in the heady mixture of ale and horse-dung, of boiled tripe and pigs' trotters from the stalls that were already setting up, and in the air of excitement that permeated the crowd which began to surge in. And soon, the shouts of the coursers were carrying above the hubbub.

Ben Mallam was tense now, even though he wore an easy smile and waved to some that greeted him by name. On every side, the business of buying and selling of horseflesh was beginning. And what a parcel of sun-burned rogues these jinglers were.

Most wore pinked leather jerkins and riding boots, some bareheaded, others in sweat-stained hats with bands and perhaps a feather or two. Some had a horse to sell, but most were buying: here at the country fairs, where folk were more readily gulled, they bought at low prices the strings of nags which they would then drive away to their own stables or to those of their fellows. Here they set about improving the looks and condition of the animals, by a hundred cunning methods, before taking them to Smithfield, where a broken-down jade bought for forty shillings now jetted proud, with a false star upon its forehead, its sores covered with paint, and sold for four times the price.

About the jinglers clustered a flock of willing lads, the skipjacks, whose part was to ride the nags up and down to demonstrate their worth. Each of these, like the jingler, had his part well studied, knowing which horse would leap in lively fashion when touched on the rump (because it had been well beaten the night before), which would not open its mouth to show its teeth (because its lips had been pricked with a nail), and which would not stand too much riding before it showed its age. It was a world of trickery and knavery, and a man must indeed have his wits well honed to make his way in it.

During the first part of the day's business, Thomas found that he had time to look about. Ben Mallam, quickly falling into conversation with one man after another, soon let him know that they were to ignore each other until he gave the signal. Potential buyers came and went: farmers, tradesmen and folk of humble station, with the occasional yeoman or gentleman's son looking for a workaday horse at a bargain price. There was also a parson in a dusty black gown, who wanted a nag to get about the parish. For a moment, from Ben's manner it appeared that this was a favoured buyer, but as Thomas drifted within earshot he gathered that the churchman was no fool, and was not impressed by Ben's praising of the grey's youth and vigour. Even Thomas could tell, had he not already ridden the horse for five miles and felt it tire beneath him, that it was far older than Ben claimed, with but a short life ahead of it.

Then about mid-morning, as the sun disappeared behind fleecy clouds, Ben struck lucky. A man and a woman, both slightly the worse for drink, walked up to the grey and began looking him over. Thomas, who had been moving about the fair but had seen no sign of Tobias, had grown bored with his lot, and was caught off guard when he saw Ben staring pointedly in his direction and frantically rubbing his beard. Hiding a smile, he sauntered over to the little group, ready to play his part.

'I'd not have him, at that price,' the grey-bearded man was saying with an attempt at authority, though it was soon clear who would be making the decision. His lady, an apple-cheeked matron with a spark in her eye that belied her years, was patting the grey's neck, apparently taken with his docile temper.

'I believe he would serve to get my herbs to market,' she said to Ben. 'Can he carry a pair of panniers for ten mile, and not fall to his knees?'

'Fall to his knees?' echoed Ben Mallam in a scornful tone, clearly at full tilt. 'He could carry ten panniers and your ladyship besides, seeing as you're but a sylph and would weigh no more than a spaniel. Am I near the mark?'

The lady snorted, but the spark in her eye grew brighter. If she is so easily gulled as that, Thomas thought to himself, his part would be simple after all. Catching Ben's eye, he spoke up.

'I hear the parson has offered you a good price for this horse, master,' he announced. 'Have you not sold him yet?'

Ben turned with an expression of contempt, and looked Thomas up and down. 'I know not who you are, sir,' he sneered, 'but if you think seven nobles a good price for a beast such as this, you know as much about horses as I know of the elephants of Afric.'

'I know a good continuer when I see one,' Thomas replied. 'I've a mind to bid for him myself.'

At this, the grey-bearded man bridled. 'See, fellow,' he said, 'Goodwife Brook and I were here before you. Be good enough to stand off and bide your turn.'

Thomas turned a blank gaze on the man. 'I'll wager my money's as good as yours, sir,' he countered. 'Indeed if I were to offer the courser nine nobles, I'd guess that were beyond your purse.'

The man blew his cheeks out in fierce indignation. 'How dare you presume in that, you rogue! I hire a dozen such as you every harvest time, you—'

'Peace, master.' Smiling, Ben Mallam moved forward smoothly and placed himself between Thomas and the customer. 'I know an honest man when I see one, and it's you and the goodwife I'd fain strike a bargain with, not this interloper.' To Thomas he said: 'Leave us to our business, and seek for a nag elsewhere.'

As Thomas turned away, he was hard pressed to keep a straight face, for he heard the apple-cheeked woman whisper to her friend: 'Offer ten nobles, and no more!'

A few minutes later, as he stood beside a stall selling bottled ale, Ben sauntered up and touched him on the shoulder.

'Not bad, for a 'prentice,' he murmured. 'Though you took a risk naming the parson. Those two might know him, and learn that he made no such offer.' But a grin was spreading across his face, and he added: 'Yet, you did well enough. Shall we slake our thirst? The real work's still ahead.'

They stood beside the stall watching the crowd, each with a bottle in his fist, apparently in idleness. But Ben Mallam was hard at work, his keen eyes everywhere, making a thorough survey of the cheapest horses, along with their faults. He noted the way the young skipjacks rode them, judging whether the horse was frisky by temperament or because of some jingler's remedy that would wear off by nightfall. From time to time he asked Thomas to walk casually up to one beast or another and listen to the talk of those who stood about. And it was while engaged in this task, that Thomas chanced to look across the field – and quickly turned away. He had seen someone he knew – but not the counterfeit beggar. It was the ex-soldier, Hugh Jaggard.

And he had turned too late; for Jaggard had seen and recognized him, and was starting towards him.

Nine

There was neither greeting nor courtesy. Though Jaggard wore no cuirass today, only a worn canvas jerkin and a leather cap, his manner was as forthright as when he had stepped down from his horse at Barrowhill, two days before. Striding up to Thomas, he demanded: 'What in God's name are you doing here?'

Thomas raised an eyebrow. 'I have leave of my master to go where I will.'

'To a horse fair?'

'Is there some reason I should not?'

Jaggard took a deep breath. 'The Earl has given me leave to order the movements of all servants at Barrowhill. Have you forgotten, we seek a murderer?'

'I am servant to Sir Robert Vicary, not the Earl,' Thomas told him calmly, though he resented the man's tone. 'Besides,' he added, 'I might ask what business *you* have here.'

'I owe you no answers!' the other shot back. 'I am a hired man, who has his task appointed.'

Thomas considered. Despite Jaggard's way, he had a mind to trust him. And to have someone to trust at Barrowhill, apart from melancholy Will Holland, seemed like a boon after all. A crushing remembrance of the grisly events of the past week, which he had managed to put from his mind of late, now came down upon him, so that he must have betrayed himself. For Jaggard, peering closely at him, asked quickly: 'What is it you are concealing from me? Speak!'

Standing in the muddy field, with the raucous voices of the horse-coursers and the hubbub all about him, Thomas made a decision. He needed this man, not as an enemy but as an ally.

Taking a step away from the edge of the throng, he signalled to Jaggard to follow. Then, when the man had drawn abreast, he said: 'I am seeking a false beggar, who calls himself Poor Tobias. I saw him a week past, in Cobham, and he was eager for news about Barrowhill. Since then he has been in Tadworth, and I have learned that his licence is forged. I spoke with the jarkman who forged it.'

The ensuing silence on Jaggard's part was long – too long for Thomas to feel comfortable. But he stood his ground and waited. He had a notion that this man could tell truth from lies readily enough. Finally, with some relief, he heard the other man say: 'You keep odd company, falconer.'

Thomas turned and indicated Ben Mallam, who was twenty yards away in conversation with another jingler about a pair of nags, one a spavined roan with a hangdog expression, the other a nutmeg-coloured gelding.

'The jingler there, helped me to the jarkman. He thought our friend the beggar might be here, at the fair.'

'He may well be,' Jaggard said.

Thomas looked sharply at him. 'You know this?'

'I know there are two beggars in the lock-up,' Jaggard answered. 'The marshall has leave to hold them while the fair lasts, which is until midnight.'

He paused, as if weighing up in his turn whether he should trust Thomas. 'We never did have our discourse,' he said finally.

'Do you truly relish old soldiers' tales?' Thomas asked. 'It's a part of my life I care not to think on.'

Jaggard eyed him. 'You think I am one of those boasts of his sword-play, and the corpses he has made, before he falls to drinking himself maudlin?' he asked.

'No,' Thomas replied. 'I think you are one whose service was long and harsh, so that he knows no other way to live now than by offering his sword-arm for hire.'

Jaggard paused, and an odd look came into his eye. 'You are sharp enough, falconer,' he muttered. But there was no softening of his gaze as he added: 'Hence you shall know that I'll kill any man who dares to thwart me.'

'I see that,' Thomas answered.

'Well,' came the rejoinder, after another pause. 'Do we go to the lock-up, and see if there lies your false beggar?'

Thomas looked round for Ben Mallam, but had lost sight of him in the throng, which was now at its thickest. Half of Surrey indeed seemed to be here. Hence, he reasoned, Ben would forgive him if he lost himself for a while. With a nod at Jaggard, he turned to follow him towards the gate.

The lock-up was no more than a pen surrounded by a wooden pale, open to the sky, and guarded by a fat man in a smock who had evidently been imbibing too freely from the flagon at his side. He looked nervous when two tall men bore down upon him and asked to see the prisoners within.

'By whose order?' he asked.

'That of the Earl of Reigate,' Jaggard answered. 'One of these men may be a fugitive we seek.'

The man was abashed, by Jaggard's obvious authority and by the fact that he had not the least idea how to proceed. 'Mayhap I should summon the marshall,' he mumbled, getting to his feet.

'Summon him if you will,' Jaggard told him. 'But if you'll let me question the beggars, it may be that our man is not one of them – hence we will be on our way.'

The man looked from Jaggard to Thomas before making up his mind to co-operate, which meant no more than unbolting the gate behind him and letting them walk in. But when he made as if to follow, Jaggard blocked his way, insisting that he must question the men in private. The fat man hesitated, until Jaggard dug in his purse and produced a silver tester. 'What say you go and refill your flagon, and let us do our work?' he asked.

Without a word, the man took the coin and departed.

The two prisoners were sitting on the grass with their backs to the rough fence, their hands and legs tied before them. One was a young man, emaciated and dirty, with dried blood on his face, perhaps the result of some affray which had brought him here.

The other was Tobias.

Thomas stiffened as he met the same pair of shifty eyes which

104

had first peered at him over his mug in the inn at Cobham. There too was the same pack at his feet – and the same fawning expression was upon the man's face, until suddenly the light of recognition dawned. And this reaction was all Jaggard needed.

'Get up,' he said, stepping forward. Before Tobias could offer any protest, he had gripped his arm, and with enormous strength yanked him up on his feet. Tobias blinked.

'Mercy, good master . . .' he began, in the whining tone that Thomas remembered. 'I'm Poor Tobias, licensed to beg in the—'

'No you're not,' Jaggard snapped, and thrust him against the fence, which shook alarmingly. 'Your licence was forged by a pelting jarkman, who has spilled news of you to this man here. Now talk to me, or I'll break your fingers – thus.' And he seized the man's right hand, which was still bound to the left, and gripped the forefinger in his fist with such a practised movement that Tobias dropped the act in an instant.

'Good Christ, I'll speak!' he cried, in a voice so different from his usual one that Thomas stared in surprise. 'Don't break it,' he added, looking Jaggard in the eye now, as one who knows that he has met his match, physically at least.

'What were you doing in Tadworth?' Jaggard asked him.

'Looking for someone,' was the reply, which did not please Jaggard at all. Half-turning to Thomas, he asked: 'What was his true name again?'

'Anthony Poole,' Thomas replied, moving closer. Looking keenly at the impostor, he asked: 'Why were you so interested in what company would be at Barrowhill?'

Poole said nothing, even when Jaggard fixed him with a hard stare. But remarkably, though his disguise was lost, the man was still calculating. Thomas saw it now, in the gleam of his eye, which was undimmed.

'Whatever business you think you have with me, sir, you are mistaken,' he said to Jaggard. His accent was that of a London man, born and bred.

'I'm not the one has business with you,' Jaggard told him. 'I'm taking you to his lordship the Earl of Reigate. He will decide what is to be done with you.'

Poole was breathing hard now, looking from one to the other and back again.

'What is it you think I've done?' he asked, but Jaggard was not prepared to waste more time. Stooping, he whipped out a knife and cut the man's bonds from his legs. Then, seizing him by the shoulders, he shoved him forward and marched him through the gate. Still seated against the fence, the other prisoner watched them depart with vacant eyes.

The turnkey was standing just outside. As the little group appeared he wiped his mouth nervously, then came forward to fasten the gate after them. 'See here, master,' he began, 'you asked only to question the man. I don't have power to release prisoners, 'tis the marshall of the fair that says so . . .'

But Jaggard barely checked his stride, saying: 'You may inform him that this man is a fugitive, taken by order of the Earl of Reigate to Barrowhill, where he will be dealt with by due process of law.'

Though that, Thomas suspected, was likely as much of a fiction as Poole's licence to beg in the county of Surrey.

As they walked their charge away from the makeshift gaol, one on either side of him, he could not refrain from asking Poole how he came to be locked up. But Poole, it seemed, had given up all notions of co-operating. He merely stared at the muddy ground, as if he had not heard.

Jaggard steered the prisoner through the crowds and out of the fair-field, oblivious to the curious stares of onlookers. In the lane, boys were looking after a large number of horses that were either not for sale or newly purchased. One of them saw Jaggard approaching and at once began untying a large chestnut horse from a hurdle. But now Thomas halted and said: 'I cannot ride back with you. Not only is the horse I came on sold, but I told the jingler I would help him purchase new mounts.'

Jaggard was impatient. 'It's no more than three miles to Barrowhill, across the Downs,' he said. 'The prisoner can walk while we take turns to ride my horse. We can be back before suppertime.'

Thomas considered. 'Well,' he said, 'will you wait a while, while I discharge my debt of gratitude?'

'To a jingler?' Jaggard looked askance.

'It's thanks to him that you have your prisoner.'

Jaggard sighed and looked about. From the field, the roar of the fair continued undiminished. 'It matters little at what hour we return,' he conceded finally. 'Your master and mine, and many of the household, are gone away to the funeral of Lady Deverell.'

Thomas frowned. He had almost forgotten about the impending burial. The fact that it was taking place quickly did not surprise him. At Barrowhill, the Earl and Countess's attempts to draw a veil over the murders no doubt continued in earnest.

'Give me an hour,' he said. 'And I will be ready.'

After a moment Jaggard nodded. 'You'll find me over by that oak,' he said, indicating a large tree beside the lane. 'I need something stout to tether this one by.'

His glance took in Poole, who had stood motionless throughout the discourse, though his manner fooled neither Thomas nor Jaggard. The first chance this man got, he would try to escape.

Thomas turned and walked back into the crowd.

It was afternoon, and the stalls had all but sold out of drink and victuals. Bargains had been struck, gulls cozened and double-dealers unmasked, and still the business of the horse fair flowed on, an unstoppable tide of barter, shouting and derisive laughter. Thomas found Ben Mallam at last, struggling to hold the horses he had seen earlier – the roan and the nutmeg gelding – while seemingly in heated negotiations for another. This horse, a stout Friesland, was in the charge of an evil-looking rogue in a patched coat, who was indifferent to Ben's bargaining skills.

'Jesu, I wondered where the devil you'd got to,' Ben snarled as Thomas walked up. 'I need you to hold these two while I take a proper look at this raddled old mule.'

'Your eyes are failing, Mallam,' the other growled, with a surly look at Thomas as he took up the reins. 'There's naught wrong with this nag that a week's good grazing won't cure.'

'Mayhap you think my wits are failing too,' cried Ben, 'if you think I don't know the glanders when I see it. Here!'

And stepping forward, he gripped the animal hard by the weasand-pipe, near the root of its tongue, so that it jerked its head and snorted. Still Ben held on, until presently it coughed – once, twice, and only then did he let go – whereupon the horse's jaws began working as though it were eating, and a thick, honey-coloured spittle appeared on its lip.

In triumph Ben turned on the seller and sneered: 'You tried to cog me before, you whoreson javel – you lost then, as you lose now! Take your sick jade off, and your dirty arse with it!'

With a muttered oath, the patch-coated man snatched up the Friesland's reins and jerked them savagely, so that the horse whinnied in pain and alarm, its jaws still flapping. As he went Thomas saw a dangerous look in the man's eye, and caught the whiff of strong sack on his breath.

'You'd best expect trouble from that one,' he warned. But Ben snorted and began looking about the field.

'I've no time to spend on him,' he said. 'The best deals have been struck, and I still lack two or three jades for Smithfield.' He looked hard at Thomas. 'What have you been about?'

Thomas shook his head. 'Better you know not,' he answered. 'But I have only an hour's more labour to offer you. Then I'm called back to my master's service.'

Ben grunted. 'Then we'd best make speed,' he said.

As things went, an hour was all Ben needed to conclude his purchases. After much hard talking, mutual scoffing, spreading of palms and scratching of heads, he and another jingler, a fellow who was well-known to him, struck a bargain for a pair of Galloway nags that, the seller swore, would not be separated as they were sworn bosom friends, and he would sell both together, or neither. So a short time later, a more cheerful Ben Mallam, leading two horses while Thomas followed with the others, headed towards the entrance.

No sooner had they cleared the gate and turned into the lane, than a storm broke upon them.

The first Thomas knew of it was when a large stone came hurtling past his head, and caught Ben Mallam hard on the shoulder. Ben grunted with pain and staggered, letting the horse reins fall from his hand. Thomas whirled about to see another stone flying towards him. He ducked instinctively, so that it smacked against the neck of one of the Galloway nags he was leading. The animal squealed and reared, but there was no time to look to any of the horses, because Thomas knew at once that they had a fierce fight on their hands. As he had half-expected, the patch-coated man that Ben had offended only a short time ago had been waiting for them in the lane, along with three other rogues to back him up. Quickly the quartet bore down upon them, two with heavy sticks in their hands, one with a knotted rope which he swung about his head, and their leader with a cudgel. And from the corner of his eye, Thomas was aware of the horse-holders in the meadow opposite leaving their charges and flocking to the lane to watch the fray. From the shouts of enthusiasm and encouragement it was clear they fully intended to enjoy the spectacle – free of charge, too.

If it was a short-lived interlude, it was a better match than anyone expected. For the assailants were surly from drink, and from having done poor business, merely glad of someone on whom they might vent their anger; while Thomas and Ben were sober, and perhaps fitter – and cleverer.

Ben was the first to feel the pain of assault, as one stick-swinging rogue caught him on the side of the head. But though dazed, the jingler dropped into a crouch and came up, fists flailing, and caught the man hard on the chin. His head snapped back, giving Ben time to seize the stick and wrench it from his hands. Thus armed, he was able to do sterling work against his first opponent, while ducking the rope which the second swung at his head.

Thomas, meanwhile, had not fared well. His first opponent was the leader himself, the patch-coated villain with the cudgel. Beside him was the second stick-wielder, half-crouching, seeking a chance to crack Thomas on the head so that his knees might buckle. If he went down he was doomed, for a beating would surely follow. So his first tactic had been to use his agility and dodge blows from both sides, while trying to seize the cudgel. This proved difficult, and both men managed to land blows on his arms, shoulders and the upper half of his body despite their poor aim and even poorer technique. Pain throbbed in his left arm, and he felt the wetness of blood through his jerkin, under his ribs.

As always, on the few occasions when Thomas found himself forced into violent confrontation, the memory would spring into his mind of a muddy field in the Low Countries, with the awful din of battle about him; the shouts and cries in half a dozen tongues – Spanish, Dutch, French, English, Scottish . . . an inferno of pain, terror and smoke . . . *I'm a falconer*, he had said to himself, almost in disbelief – *I have no wish to take up arms, nor to take men's lives* . . .

But he had done both, because he was given no choice in the matter, as now. Only half-aware of his actions, he lashed out, ignoring the stick which cracked down on his shoulder, and managed to catch the wielder by the throat. With a fierce strength he tightened his fingers, so that the man's eyes showed fear and his hands came up. Dropping his stick, he grabbed Thomas's wrist, and so began a trial of strength, each man aware that to let go would likely spell disaster.

However, there was still the matter of the rogue with the cudgel. Keeping hold of his opponent, Thomas tried to dodge the weapon when it came whistling past his head. The first time, the patch-coated man missed his target. The second time, though Thomas tried to duck again, the cudgel caught him on the neck and the ear, a thundercrack blow that knocked the lights out. The pain was intense and sickening, and signalled defeat. Helplessly Thomas felt his grip loosen, indeed all his muscles begin to fail him, and despite the voice in his head urging him to stay on his feet, his knees sagged. As he sank down on to the soft mud of the rutted lane, he knew he was not going to get up again.

But he had forgotten Hugh Jaggard.

Through a fog of dizziness, his strength seemingly leaching away into the ground, Thomas was dimly aware of a deep voice, distinct from the background chorus of cries, catcalls and raucous laughter that still came from the watching boys. Somewhere above him, whence he had expected kicks and blows, there came scuffling and angry shouts, and something heavy landed with a thud beside him. Then came a clash of steel, and a cry of agony.

Fighting the ringing in his ears and the pain that threatened to black out his senses, Thomas put his fists on the ground and got himself on to all fours. Blinking and breathless, he peered to one side and saw the man whose throat he had been holding only seconds ago, lying on his back as if asleep. Blood ran from a deep gash on his forehead. Trying to focus clearly, he grew aware of someone close by, stooping, and a voice he knew calling his name.

'Here . . .' he muttered foolishly. 'I'm here . . .'

Then two pairs of strong arms lifted him, and he was on his feet, and the mist was clearing. Ben Mallam, his face bruised and grim, was peering into his eyes. A little further off stood Hugh Jaggard, apparently unconcerned. Around them the four ruffians lay on the ground in various positions, all of them motionless.

'Jesu,' Ben said, sounding short of breath. 'We'd both been fit for naught but crowbait, if yon fellow hadn't come to our aid . . . friend of yours?'

Thomas caught Jaggard's eye, and saw a trace of amusement.

'I do believe he is,' he said.

It was evening by the time Thomas and Jaggard reached Barrowhill, with their silent prisoner in tow. They had hardly spoken on the journey back across the Downs. Ben Mallam, looking subdued, had muttered his thanks to Jaggard, who ignored him, and taken his string of horses away, with no greater hurt than a few cuts and bruises and a torn jerkin. Jaggard, after a rudimentary examination of Thomas's injuries, was eager to leave, insisting that Thomas rode his horse while he walked ahead holding Poole by a rope. So in this fashion the odd-looking party trudged by the brooding walls of the house and into the stable yard, coming to a halt under the watchful gaze of the Earl's usher, Henry Barnard.

'Who is this?' was Barnard's only greeting, as he looked disapprovingly at the ragged figure with the bound wrists. Poole, for his part, appeared to have retired into some private world, and was oblivious to the stares of those about him. Jaggard offered some words of explanation, which pleased Barnard not at all.

'The Earl and Countess are not yet returned,' he said. 'Nor is your master' – this with a perfunctory nod at Thomas. 'I know not what we should do with the man until then.'

'Lock him in a barn, or some secure place,' Jaggard told him shortly. 'When the Earl returns we may question him at leisure.'

'We?' Barnard was angry. 'You propose to appoint yourself inquisitor here?'

Jaggard looked him over calmly, though Thomas knew that the man was as tired and hungry as he was, and had not escaped the fray at Banstead without a few bruises of his own.

'I will do the Earl's bidding,' he replied, 'as will you. Now, which outhouse will serve best for a temporary gaol?'

It was Thomas who suggested the brewhouse, without mentioning that he had already been inside it. So, since neither of the others could think of a better choice, Poole was marched into the building and told to sit on the floor, while Jaggard fashioned makeshift shackles from rope.

Barnard left them to their task, saying he would report the matter to the Earl as soon as he returned. Thomas, after checking that the single window was nailed shut, could not help but feel a deal of pity for the prisoner. On the journey back, he had begun to harbour doubts about the whole enterprise. Though the beggar was clearly not all he seemed, neither had he the air of a wicked man, nor even a petty criminal.

But Jaggard was as flinty, close-mouthed and coolly efficient as if he relished the task. Perhaps he was pleased to have some result to show for his hire. As they headed for the door, Thomas looked down at the seated beggar, and suddenly remembered.

'His pack,' he said. 'We left it in the lock-up at the fair.'

Jaggard shrugged. 'I doubt there's aught but rags in it.'

'I will ride over to Banstead, when I can,' Thomas said, with a glance at Poole, 'and see if it's still there.'

'You'd be wasting your time,' Jaggard replied. 'I'll stake my

112

sword that it was torn open and picked through before we'd travelled a hundred yards.'

It was true. But whether the man was beggar or no, Thomas could not leave him in this fashion. At the door, he turned and said: 'I will bring him something from the kitchen.'

'The devil you will,' Jaggard replied. 'The rogue'll talk better on an empty stomach tomorrow. They always do.'

'Some water, then,' Thomas said. 'At least let him drink.'

Jaggard snorted. 'If you will have it so,' he said. 'Only make sure you bolt the door when you leave.'

A few minutes later, Thomas returned with a pitcher and bowl and set them down beside Poole, who did not appear to have moved a muscle since he had been left alone. After checking that the man could reach the bowl, even with his wrists bound, Thomas filled it with water, then rose and started to go. Looking down once more, he saw Poole regarding him steadily with that disconcerting gaze that seemed to convey a host of things. *I know that you know I am no murderer*, was one of them.

Though he wanted nothing more than food and drink and to tend his hurts, Thomas had many questions. He allowed himself one.

'Why did you not give some account of yourself at the fair?' he asked. 'You might have talked your way out of this.'

There was silence.

'You did not help yourself,' Thomas insisted. A thought struck him forcibly. 'Mayhap you wanted to be brought here.'

Poole surprised him by giving a short laugh. 'Mayhap I did a few days back,' he muttered. 'Only now I'm too late.'

'Too late for what?' Thomas asked.

Poole gave a sigh and, reaching out awkwardly with his cramped forearms, managed to pick up the bowl and raise it to his lips. He drank deeply, then put it down.

'I can tell you naught, master falconer,' he said after a moment. 'Though I am grateful for your kindness, it matters little. I'll die before I reveal anything of myself to that ruffling man-at-arms. I've been at the hands of worse than he.'

Thomas stared. 'You were afraid he'd break your fingers—' he began, but Poole was shaking his head.

113

'To buy a moment for thinking,' he said. 'Your man lacks the skill of a Spaniard or an Italian – and more, he takes not the pleasure in it that would achieve his ends. He'd break me at last, it's true, but I would be spent, my senses gone. In any case, he'd learn little of any value.'

'You would endure torture?' Thomas asked, gazing into Poole's face. 'Why? What is it that is so important?'

But the man merely shook his head, having said all he was prepared to say. Hence Thomas's surprise as he made to walk out of the door, when he heard the prisoner ask, 'Tell me this: is Brunning the only one?'

Thomas stopped in his tracks, turned to meet Poole's steady gaze again.

'The only one?' he echoed.

'Killed,' Poole said. 'Has any been killed, beside him?'

'How did—' Thomas began, then checked himself. He burned to speak to Sir Robert, to turn the matter over, so that between them they might come at some answer. As things stood, questions seemed to lead only to further questions.

'Sir Thomas Wilkes is dead,' he admitted, and wondered why he did so. To his consternation, Poole merely nodded.

'Now, you may perhaps answer the question I first asked you in the inn at Cobham,' he said. 'What other company is at Barrowhill that does not normally reside here?'

Wary now, Thomas shook his head, whereupon Poole snapped: 'No Dutchmen?'

Thomas stared. 'There's a portrait painter – master Kessel,' he said. 'They call him a Dutchman, though—'

'Then you'd best watch him,' Poole said. 'As keenly as one of your falcons watches.'

After which, he closed his eyes and lowered his head, as if he had fallen at once into a bottomless sleep.

Ten

T he Earl and Countess, along with Sir Robert and the rest of their party, had not yet returned to Barrowhill. So Thomas was relieved to go to Will Holland's hut, to wash himself and bind the cuts on his arm and his side, to take a drink of beer and a mouthful of bread. Though his ear still throbbed from the blow he had received, he counted himself lucky to have escaped the fray at Banstead with little more than minor hurts.

Will was not there, but on looking in the falcons' mews, Thomas saw that the birds had been fed and seemed content. In the hut he threw himself down on his pallet, intending to take a short rest before rising to wait upon his master. He wanted not merely to tell him all that had occurred, but to learn what was likely to happen to Anthony Poole. Try as he might, he could think of little else besides the prisoner's parting words. Whatever the man's business, he now felt certain of one thing: this was not the one who had killed Sir George Brunning and Sir Thomas Wilkes, let alone Lady Deverell.

He awoke with a start in pitch darkness, aware that he had been dreaming – of Eleanor. She was upset about something, but would not tell him what it was. Sitting up, he shook himself awake, listening for the night-birds and trying to guess the hour. Then he realized what had woken him: music.

He arose, opened the door and looked out. From the direction of the gardens a bright glow was visible, and on the wind drifted the strains of a galliard, beautifully played by a full consort of viols, hautboys, flutes and cornets, accompanied by a tabor. As Thomas listened, beneath the music he could discern the sound of raised voices, with now and then a peal of laughter. The Earl and Countess were entertaining again, this time out of doors.

Fastening his jerkin, he walked down the slope towards the house and turned the corner, recalling with some unease his one and only previous visit to the gardens. But the sight that now met his eyes put all other thoughts from his mind.

The lawns, terraces, and walks blazed with light. Torches stood in rows, leading off invitingly in all directions, as far as the lake which glittered in the distance. Before the house the orchestra was seated, eight or nine in number, playing with vigorous abandon. Close by were banquet tables crammed with dishes of sugared deceits, sweet wafers and candied fruit. Servingmen hurried about, while the brightly dressed company, some seated, others drifting here and there at leisure, were engaged in the serious business of enjoying themselves to the full.

Familiar figures were soon identifiable in the torchlight: the Earl, seated with silver goblet in hand, beating time to the music with a beringed hand; John Broad, standing stiffly to one side, every inch the man on duty; Henry Barnard, brusque in a smart blue doublet, keeping his minions at full pitch; and the Countess . . .

The Countess was dancing.

Wearing a full gown of red, gold and orange, her hair dressed in high bouffant, she pranced the lively steps of the galliard, fully aware that all eyes were upon her. Even from a distance, Thomas could see light reflected in the sheen of sweat on her exposed neck. As when he had first encountered her, emerging from the shadows of the bower, she shone. That was her part, Thomas saw: to outshine her husband, whom she ignored, saving her bright smile for her dancing partner, one of the prettier young gallants. The man smiled back at her in full knowledge of what he was about – which, Thomas guessed, was to wait until the Earl was sufficiently drunk not to notice when he and the Countess slipped away beyond the edges of the torchlight. It was the liveliest and most irreverent funeral feast Thomas had seen – if funeral feast it was. Perhaps its purpose was merely to erase the memories of an otherwise sombre day.

116

There were other servants, standing a respectful distance from the glittering company, listening to the music. Thomas moved to join them, attracting no more attention than a few nods of recognition. There was no sign of Will, which meant that his friend had most likely walked into Tadworth to repair relations with his Doreth. His gaze drifting across to the orchestra, Thomas now saw that it was Filbert, the Earl's fool, who provided the percussion. Standing beside the seated viol players, he seemed content to be engaged in lighter duties than usual, beating the tabor with consummate skill.

Then Thomas noticed Lukas Kessel, and remembered Poole's odd-sounding instruction: *watch the Dutchman*. The painter, in a dark woollen suit and without his soft cap, stood looking out at the brightly lit gardens. Though he sipped from his goblet, he was sober and somewhat removed from the party. Surely, Thomas reflected, Poole was not suggesting that Kessel was a murderer? A less likely suspect he could scarcely imagine.

With a long, drawn-out note, the music stopped, and the night air was full of laughter and voices, the clatter of trays and dishes as servingmen came and went. Thomas realized that he had not yet seen Sir Robert. As he scanned the assembled guests, some of whom were drifting off towards the gardens, he heard the Earl call out: 'My favourite, damn you! I'll have my favourite coranto – now!'

At once the orchestra, well rehearsed, broke into the 2/4 rhythm of a coranto, which for some reason prompted laughter and perfunctory applause. The Countess and her gentleman, with several other couples, at once formed a group and began to dance, the Countess's laugh clearly audible above the music. But her smile was wide, and it was for her partner alone. Watching the Earl, Thomas saw no sign of jealousy on his part, save that he drained his goblet and held it out to be refilled immediately by an attentive servant.

At last he saw Sir Robert, walking alone up the wide stone steps from the gardens, looking somewhat thoughtful. Thomas detached himself from the watchers so that his master saw him, and at once beckoned him forward. As he drew near, Sir Robert peered at him. 'Your ear is swollen,' he remarked. 'What brabble have you got yourself into now?'

'It was naught but a fairground scuffle, sir,' Thomas answered. Eager to unburden himself of his news, he quickly told his master what had happened at Leatherhead and at Banstead, ending with the clapping up of Anthony Poole in the brewhouse.

Sir Robert looked stunned, saying: 'I have not seen Jaggard since I returned. I know not whether he has told the Earl—' he drew breath suddenly. 'He has not! The man begged leave to speak with the Earl the moment we returned, but was refused. His lordship had more important matters in hand.' He gestured to take in the torchlit panorama. Thomas waited, suddenly aware of what was coming next.

'I will speak with this counterfeit beggar,' Sir Robert said. 'Now, in private. Come with me – and bring a light.'

'Are you sure it is wise, sir?' Thomas murmured, overstepping himself in his unease at his master's impetuosity. But since Sir Robert had already set off, he had little choice but to seize a torch from its sconce and follow.

'I asked you to trust me in this matter before, Thomas,' his master said, as they walked away from the sounds of revelry and rounded the corner of the house. 'If I may learn something of this before the Earl questions the man – let alone the Countess – it will help me . . .' He trailed off, frowning. 'You maintain that he is no murderer – though you cannot be certain.'

'No, sir,' Thomas admitted. 'Yet I would stake much on it.'

Sir Robert did not speak again until they had walked to the rear of the house, past the stables and approached the brewhouse. The yard was deserted. Taking the torch from Thomas, Sir Robert indicated that he should unbolt the door. As they entered there was a sound of hurried movement from within, and seconds later they were peering down at the subdued figure of Anthony Poole, still bound, blinking up at them in the flickering light.

Nobody spoke until Sir Robert handed the torch back to Thomas, stepped forward and said: 'I am Sir Robert Vicary. Be forthright with me – tell me what your interest is in Barrowhill, and in his lordship, and I will speak on your behalf. If you refuse, I cannot aid you. You are unlikely to leave here alive.'

There was a moment's silence, then Poole answered: 'I did not expect to.'

Seeing the expression on the man's face, Thomas's heart sank. He was fully prepared to die, and they would be no nearer to coming at the truth of the matter.

But Sir Robert was not done. Fixing Poole with a stern look, he said: 'My servant Thomas does not believe you are a murderer. Indeed, if you had carried out such savagery as has been done here, I myself would find it strange that you are still wandering the district, with a poorly forged licence at that. Did you truly wish to be caught?'

Poole merely shook his head.

'Yet you knew of the death of Sir George Brunning,' Sir Robert persisted, 'and showed no surprise at news of Sir Thomas Wilkes – you know something of this matter, a fool could see that!'

When Poole merely looked away, Sir Robert, reining in his impatience, added: 'I know of no other breed of man would behave as oddly as you have done, and refuse to speak even when threatened with torture.' He paused, as if hoping that his words might have greater impact, and finished: 'I believe you are an intelligencer, in the pay of the Crown.'

Poole met his eyes, but showed no reaction. Thomas, watching closely, thought he sensed a quickening of the man's pulse. Instinctively he knew that his master, not a man noted for the sharpness of his wits, had hit the nail squarely on the head.

'I will take your silence for assent,' Sir Robert said. And though it may have been merely the unsteady light of the torch, Thomas thought he detected a trace of the old gleam behind Poole's eyes. Then the prisoner spoke, as if determined to grind all such illusions to dust.

'You may take what you like, sir,' he said softly. 'You'll learn nothing from me.'

Sir Robert gazed at him for a moment, then grew brusque. 'As you wish,' he said. 'I will leave you to ponder your fate.'

He turned away, raising an eyebrow at Thomas, who made to follow. As they reached the door he threw a final glance at Anthony Poole, but the man refused to meet his eye.

Outside, as Thomas and Sir Robert walked away in silence, there came a clattering of hooves, and a bulky man on a fine sorrel horse rode past them. Seeing Sir Robert, he gave a respectful nod, raising his gloved hand in salute. Thomas caught a glimpse of a broad, dark-bearded face before the man disappeared into the stableyard.

'Jonas Reed, the Earl's horse-master,' Sir Robert said shortly. 'Mark how he's better mounted than I am!' Checking his stride, he added sourly: 'Here, even the servants are a law unto themselves.'

Then he dismissed Thomas ill-humouredly, saying he would speak with him on the morrow, and stamped off towards the distant strains of the Earl's favourite coranto. It seemed it was being played for the second or third time in succession.

In the hour before dawn, Thomas lay on his pallet, having given up all attempts at sleep. The music had ceased a short while ago, the torches had been extinguished, and the members of the household, both high-born and low, were gone to their beds. A silence lay over Barrowhill, broken only by the call of barn owls. From the adjacent mews beyond the thin wall of Will's hut, Thomas could hear the hawks stirring on their perches, sensing the approach of daylight. If only he might be left to his proper work, he thought for the twentieth time. *For a falconer*, Ben Mallam had said, *you keep odd company*.

He got up restlessly, pulled on his boots and jerkin and went outside. It was Sunday morning, and within a few hours the entire house would be expected at chapel. He sniffed the air and turned, feeling the wind. It had changed within the past hour, and now came from the south, bringing a faint salt whiff of the sea.

Then he saw the running man.

Only a falconer's eyes could have made out the figure, with but the starlight and the half-hidden moon to aid him. The man came from the direction of the stable yard, stumbling as if the ground were unfamiliar to him. Gaining the paddock, he climbed over the fence and stopped, half-crouching, his head twisting about. At once, Thomas knew: Anthony Poole had not only freed himself, but was about to steal a horse and make his escape.

In a moment Thomas was running downhill, his boots swishing through the grass. As he neared the paddock he heard the snicker of horses, and saw the Earl's precious Arabian colts milling about near the wattle fence. Their sound covered his approach, so that, ducking low, he was able to skirt the perimeter and come closer to the fugitive, who he now saw was working his way across the paddock, hoping to cut off the animals' retreat. A difficult task, he thought, then flung himself down flat in the grass, because Poole's head had swung quickly in his direction.

He was cursing himself for his foolishness. Had he really thought Poole would merely lie there and wait to be interrogated? Buying time, he had said earlier . . . time to work his bonds loose, or find something to cut them with – the earthenware bowl, of course. Its broken shards would be enough. Unwittingly Thomas had provided him with the means of escape.

But at least now he could act, because Poole had turned away, and was moving towards the horses again. Nervously the colts bunched closely together, stamping and tossing their heads. As Poole worked nearer they edged away, then as one they began to bolt – which was all the opportunity Thomas needed. He jumped up, vaulted the fence and had gained the middle of the paddock before the other saw him. At once he turned to run, but Thomas was quicker. In a trice he had launched himself forward, grabbed the man's spindly legs and pulled him to the ground.

Then, somewhat late, he learned that Poole had a knife.

The brewer's bung-knife, he thought vaguely, an innocent enough tool, now become a weapon . . . how could he, let alone Jaggard, have left it stuck in the barrelhead, even if it were beyond the prisoner's reach . . . all this, as he wrestled grimly with the man, each fighting desperately to turn the blade

121

towards the other, their breath coming in shorter and shorter bursts. As if from far away, Thomas imagined Ben Mallam's voice: *Jesu, falconer, you've been a mite careless this night, wouldn't you say?*

I would, he thought, as with relief he realized that he was the stronger, and his opponent was weakening fast. Gradually Thomas forced his hand down, then brought his knee up and pinned Poole's wrist flat. He gasped, let go the knife, then lashed out with his other fist, but Thomas caught that too, and bent it backwards. Finally, amid much panting from both of them, Poole's body went limp, and he sank on his back in the grass. Across the paddock, the colts snorted.

'Mayhap you've played the beggar so long,' Thomas said between breaths, 'that you are weak from malnourishment.'

Poole said nothing, though his breathing gradually slowed. Squinting in the feeble light, Thomas saw his eyes dull with defeat, though not with fear. Fear was something he seemed to lack entirely.

Thomas picked up the knife, intending to toss it aside, then a thought occurred to him. But even as he held it to Poole's neck, the other let out a harsh cry of laughter.

'You haven't the killer's eye, falconer,' he said. 'You'd make the poorest inquisitor I ever saw!'

Thomas sighed to himself, knowing it was true. 'Still,' he countered, 'I'm man enough to take you back to the brewhouse, and stand guard over you till dawn.'

Poole was silent, as if weighing his chances. The dullness had gone from his eyes, though there was no gleam of triumph there. Yet there was perhaps, a glimmer of hope.

'A bargain, falconer,' he said finally. 'You have earned that.'

Thomas kept his grip on the man, but his senses were racing along with his pulse, and Poole knew it. 'Decide quickly,' he muttered. 'Else I'll not have time, and you'll learn nothing.'

'Time?' Thomas echoed. 'You expect me to let you escape?'

'If you want to learn aught of value, you will,' Poole said, a note of urgency creeping into his voice.

Thomas shook his head slowly. 'I'll not trust you again.'

'You believe now that I am a murderer?' Poole asked at once.

Thomas hesitated, meeting the man's eye, which did not waver. 'No,' he said finally, 'Yet you are about something that stinks of death. You are too close to it to be truly innocent.'

Poole gave the briefest of nods. 'That I am,' he agreed. 'And more deaths than there have been at Barrowhill.'

Thomas read the hope in Poole's eyes, as if he were slowly drawing him into his snare. 'Are you so trusting of me?' he asked, 'that you think I will keep my end of the bargain?'

'Yes,' Poole answered, and waited.

Thomas was struggling. One voice told him to pull the man to his feet, take him back to the brewhouse and tie him up tightly. His master would approve; he might even be rewarded for his vigilance in foiling an escape. The other voice told him that here was an opportunity not to be squandered. Sir Robert would perhaps prefer that he find out something of what lay behind these terrible events. Furthermore – nobody would know that he had assisted Poole. The man's means of escape would quickly be discerned – but the one likely to be blamed was Jaggard.

The breeze was rising, and there came movement from the horses in the paddock behind him. He glanced up quickly, saw that dawn was approaching. With a heavier heart than he liked, he made his decision. 'Speak then,' he said, 'and if I believe you, I'll let you go. But on foot – no horses.'

Poole nodded quickly. 'Will you now free my arm?'

Warily Thomas raised his knee, then moved aside and sat in the grass, letting the other know plainly that he was watching his every movement. Poole sat up stiffly, rubbing his chafed wrists.

'I'll tell you what I can,' he said, fixing Thomas with a somewhat grim stare, 'which is not much. But first, I will say that I know not who killed those men. Nor, I believe, does anyone. Else, they would know who is *Vindex Reginae* – the scourge of the Dutch.'

Thomas caught his breath. 'Aye,' Poole nodded. 'I see that name is known to you too.'

A host of questions rose in Thomas's throat, but Poole shook his head as if to stay him.

'The same hand is at work here as in London,' he said. 'Yet that is not why I was sent.' He paused then, as if seeking ways of telling no more than he must. 'Listen, falconer, for I can say only this, and then you will let me go, or . . .' He swallowed, and added: 'I was ordered to follow Brunning, to delve into his actions, and discover his associates. That is why I came into Surrey. Now he is dead, and I can do naught.'

'Ordered, by whom . . .?' Thomas began, then seeing the look that came over Poole's face asked instead: 'What did you mean – the scourge of the Dutch?'

'I have said it,' Poole answered. 'Find the madman who is tearing the Dutchmen in tatters, and you will find who killed Brunning and Wilkes.'

'And Lady Deverell,' Thomas added, frowning to himself. 'Then why . . .?' he started to ask, but saw Poole was not listening.

'I will not say more,' he said flatly. 'Now free me, and we'll not meet again. Indeed, if you truly wish to help me, you will forget Poole and recall none but Poor Tobias, who has gone begging elsewhere – as far away as can be.'

'Go then,' Thomas said, and got to his feet. The other followed suit, somewhat stiffly. Seeing him thus, Thomas was struck by what a pitiful sight he made, with neither pack nor begging bottle – naught but the rags on his back.

'Wait,' Thomas said, though the man was already moving off, eager to be gone. 'If you come with me I'll give you money.'

Poole hesitated, but when the other walked across the paddock and climbed the fence he followed. Within minutes they were at the hut, Thomas had found his purse and was placing coins in Poole's grimy hand.

'Poor Tobias thanks you, kind master,' he said in his whining voice, though his smile conveyed more than mere gratitude. As he turned to go, Thomas tried a final question.

'Will you at least tell me if my master is in danger?'

Poole gave a quick shrug, and said: 'He may be – unless he is truly an honest man. And such is a mighty rare bird, falconer.'

Then with a nod at Thomas he was away, breaking into a trot

as he gained the narrow path up to the Downs. Thomas watched until the gloom swallowed him up.

At six o'clock, having done his best with his appearance, he joined the rest of the household as they entered the chapel for morning prayers. In the carved pews at the front sat his master and the other gentlefolk, some looking as though they had barely slept, which was likely the case. There was no sign of the Earl or the Countess. John Broad and Henry Barnard were in their allotted places, and for the first time since returning from the horse fair he saw Jaggard, staring ahead, with his men sitting about him in a stiff-necked body, clearly here under protest.

At the last moment, as the ageing parson made his entrance, Will Holland crept in at the back and slid into a seat beside Thomas. He was out of breath and stank of sweat.

'You succeeded in fighting her off this morning,' Thomas murmured.

Will half-turned to him. 'You're a bold one to speak of fighting,' he muttered. 'What happened to your ear?'

Thomas shook his head once, and asked: 'Do the Earl and Countess not attend prayers?'

Will gave a little snort. 'Never. Some folk say the Lord would smite them for their wickedness if they dared enter his house.' Then he yawned, and mumbled: 'Where's the Dutchman? He never misses a sermon, that one.'

Thomas started, and quickly scanned the assembled faces.

Will was right: Lukas Kessel was missing.

The moment Thomas filed out of the chapel with the others, his master appeared at his shoulder and ordered: 'Follow me, now.'

They walked into the house by the kitchen entrance, startling the servants, who bowed and bobbed as Sir Robert, in his best plum-coloured doublet, strode brusquely through to the hallway. Thomas followed, half-anxious, half-intrigued, until they were alone at the foot of the great staircase. Then, looking about him like a stage conspirator, his master halted and said: 'There was almost another killing last night – here in the house.'

'Almost?' Thomas repeated, his thoughts racing ahead.

'Kessel, the painter,' Sir Robert said. 'Only he's made of better stuff than I thought. Would you believe that he fought the fellow off?'

Thomas said nothing, but a very unpleasant notion floated up and lodged itself in the forefront of his mind, so that he had to draw breath to master it: Poole was the killer after all, and he had helped him . . . the next moment, he saw it made no sense. *Watch the Dutchman*, the man had warned him. Hence his relief was great when his master made matters clearer.

'It was the music and dancing that saved him,' he said. 'The villain had to wait until the house was quiet, which was just before dawn – Kessel was not yet asleep when he struck.'

'He is hurt . . .' Thomas began, and Sir Robert gave a nod.

'A glancing blow with the poniard, because he turned in time, and stayed the thrust. His hand is sorely cut.'

'Then he saw the man's face,' Thomas said, but Sir Robert grimaced.

'His chamber was too dark.'

Thomas grew calmer inside. It could not have been Poole: in the time before dawn, he was rolling about in the paddock with Thomas, fighting for possession of a brewer's bung-knife which would barely cut a round of cheese.

'At least we may be sure of one thing,' Sir Robert said as if reading his thoughts. 'Since yon counterfeit beggar was locked in the brewhouse, he is not our murderer. Your instinct was true.'

Thomas swallowed. 'Indeed, sir,' he muttered, then changed the subject. 'Has the Earl been told about—'

'Of course,' his master interrupted. Somewhat agitated now, he leaned closer and confided in his man as one who knows he has no one else to trust.

'Thomas, the Earl is distracted. He has fled to his Prospect Room at the top of the house, and swears he will not come out until the killer is caught. The Countess has ordered that the servants not be told – only Broad and Barnard are aware of the matter. And you must not speak of it.'

Thomas nodded.

'The tale is, that Kessel lost his footing in the night and cut himself,' Sir Robert continued. 'But you and I will go and speak with him, and when we have learned all we can, I will decide what to do.' He paused, and added in a bitter tone: 'I would dearly love to leave the whole business, take my hawks and return to Petbury. Yet I cannot!'

'Will you tell me why, Sir Robert?' Thomas asked. Poole's warning that his master may be in danger sprang into his mind.

'Because I too am now tainted,' his master replied, with a helpless look. 'I must see the matter through, or my own reputation will be in shreds.'

Thomas stared, but Sir Robert shrugged and said: 'Enough now. We will go to Kessel's chamber.'

Taking the stairs two at a time, he led the way to the upper floor, past the grand rooms and up another stair to the topmost storey. A servant was walking towards them bearing a bowl and cloths. Startled by Sir Robert's sudden appearance, he bowed low as the other strode past him and stopped outside a closed door.

The servant looked askance, then realized that both men were waiting for him to go and hurried off. Only then did Sir Robert open the door, gesturing to Thomas to follow. It brought to his mind a similar entrance some days ago, when he had been obliged to examine the bodies of Wilkes and Lady Deverell. Silently he offered thanks that yet another murder had been avoided.

The room was surprisingly large and airy, but it was the diffused light that he noticed, for they were on the north-facing side of the house, away from direct sunlight. Then he saw a fine upholstered chair on a dais, and before it a large object on a stand, covered with black velvet. This, of course, was the studio, where the Countess sat for her portrait. Against one wall, on a long paint-stained trestle, were scattered the tools of Kessel's trade: his brushes and palettes, bladders of colour, pots of linseed oil and glue. The smell was not unpleasant.

There was a sound, and Kessel appeared from an inner door that led to his bedroom. He was wearing only breeches and a

127

plain chemise, with a heavy bandage about his hand – but it was his distraught expression that stopped Thomas in his tracks, realization dawning on him. The painter stared at both men, as if in a trance.

'He has killed me too,' he said, '– for now I cannot paint.'

Eleven

The interview was short, for Kessel could tell them little about his attacker. He had been alone in his bed, unable to sleep – he was a poor sleeper, he said. He was lying on his front, and happened to stir – it was then he became aware that someone was in the room. Though he heard no footfall – nothing, until the figure loomed over him, and he caught the flash of a blade: a long narrow blade. He had raised his hand instinctively, and cried out when the poniard laid his palm open, a deep gash that bred profusely. His cry was enough to startle the man – he was certain it was a man, though he saw nothing but a shape – and something that glittered about his neck, like a jewel. He had lunged at him again, but Kessel had caught his arm and struggled with him briefly – the man was strong, he said. Then the intruder had seemingly lost his nerve, and turned to run. How he had gained entrance, Kessel had no idea. He believed he came in through the studio and left the same way, but no door had been forced. It was a *phenomenon*, he said, like the killings of Sir George and Sir Thomas . . . yet he was but a painter, a humble artisan. He had harmed no one. Why did the killer choose him?

He stood beside the covered portrait. Half-raising his bandaged hand, he said: 'They have sewn up the wound, yet it will be weeks before I can work. I fear the Countess will send me away and engage some other painter to finish her likeness.'

'I will speak with her,' Sir Robert told him. 'I believe she will keep you until you are well enough to resume. If not, I will commend you to a friend in London, who may be able to use you.'

Kessel made a formal bow of gratitude. 'I am your humble servant, Sir Robert,' he murmured.

'We will leave you to take some rest,' Sir Robert said. But Thomas, who had been glancing idly about, asked leave to examine the room. His master shrugged. 'If you will, though I know not what you expect to find – secret staircases, mayhap?'

He walked to the doorway, saying: 'When you have done, seek me in the chamber by the Long Gallery. There is more to discuss.'

Thomas nodded, and waited for Sir Robert to close the door behind him. Then he turned to Kessel, who was watching him without expression.

'When you spoke to me, in the Red Bull at Tadworth,' Thomas reminded him, 'you said there were things . . .' Then, seeing the man's expression, he stopped.

'Another time, master falconer,' Kessel said. 'I am tired and sore. In any case,' he added, 'I meant not things that touch on these deaths.' He gazed at the floor, as if the thought had only now become clear. 'I too, was to be slain . . . why is it so?'

Thomas shrugged. Thinking of Poole's words, he asked: 'Do you know aught of the murders among the Dutch in London?'

Kessel frowned, and shook his head slowly. 'I have not been in London for almost a year.' Then, his eyes widening, he asked: 'You mean, this attack was because people here believe I am Dutch?'

'It may be,' Thomas said. 'I know little of it. But if I can learn aught that may help uncover the matter . . .'

Kessel gestured vaguely. 'Look about, as you wish,' he said. 'I will lay myself down for a while.' And he went back into his chamber, pushing the door to behind him.

Unsure what he might be looking for, Thomas began to search the painter's studio. As expected, he found nothing untoward. The mullions were sound, the casements large and well made. Looking out, he doubted whether anyone could climb up here in any case: there was no ivy on the walls, no obvious foothold. He examined the ceiling, the walls, door-frame and floorboards. Finally, when he was on the point of

130

giving up, his glance fell on the open fireplace, in which it appeared no fire had burned for the entire summer. And here, he found something that interested him. For peering up the chimney, he saw a very faint glimmer of daylight.

It came not from directly above, but from one side, many feet up. With it came a slight draught of air, that lifted the dust he had stirred with his boots. Standing in the back of the hearth, squinting upwards, he tried to make out the size of the opening but could see little. So he went and found a stool, placed it under the shaft, and stooping under the chimney breast, climbed on to it. And now, his search bore fruit.

The intruder had climbed down the chimney.

The first obvious sign was streaks in the coating of soot in the shaft. Then to his surprise he found several shallow recesses in the brickwork, that had been made deliberately. For someone who knew where to place his feet it would not have been a difficult climb. Standing on tip-toe, he found the opening of the side shaft – or rather the tunnel, for such it was: leading off at a sharp angle to heaven knew where – and wide enough to admit a man.

He climbed down, went back into the studio and searched for something solid on which to raise the height of the stool, so that he might examine the shaft better. But there was nothing that would serve, and in any case it did not matter. He could easily return with a ladder and verify what he now knew to be plain: that the opening had been made by the builders of Barrowhill, for a purpose. He had little doubt that it connected with other chimneys in other rooms – perhaps in every room. Hence, anyone who knew the house intimately might move freely about without detection. This part of the puzzle, at least, was laid bare. Standing in the centre of the room, dusting off his jerkin, Thomas felt a sense of triumph: he could tell Sir Robert, if not of secret stairways, at least of secret chimney shafts.

From Kessel's chamber came the sound of snoring. Softly, Thomas moved across the floor of the studio and let himself out.

*　　*　　*

A few minutes later he stood in the Withdrawing Chamber, feeling a great deal less elated. For not only was Sir Robert present, but John Broad and Henry Barnard, both of them seemingly in poor tempers, and Hugh Jaggard, who looked almost choleric.

Sir Robert's face was grim. 'The prisoner Poole has escaped from the brewhouse,' he said.

Thomas took a deep breath, having made a decision whose consequences he dared not think on – not yet.

'I know, sir,' he replied. 'I aided him.'

The silence that fell was short-lived, before every man's mouth opened at once. Barnard, being the one with the loudest voice, managed to override the others.

'Then you will be arrested and clapped up in his place!' he shouted. 'But first you will tell us why—'

'Master Barnard.' It was John Broad who spoke, standing on his age and his dignity. With an oath that was almost audible, Barnard gave way to him.

'You had some purpose, I trust, falconer?' the steward asked, though his gaze was not kindly.

Thomas nodded. 'I did, master Broad. For though Poole is no murderer, I learned much from him about the killing of Sir George and Sir Thomas. And –' here he looked directly at Sir Robert – 'I know how the murderer came and went without being seen.'

There was another short silence. Glancing from one man to another, Thomas felt sure he had done right in confessing his deed, for now he might unburden himself fully and let matters take their course. The one burr in the flour sack was Jaggard. Noting the look on his face, Thomas felt not fear of what the man might do, but shame at the way he had betrayed him. Yet, how else could he have acted? He braced himself as Sir Robert spoke.

'When did you intend to tell me of this?' he asked quietly.

'This morning, sir,' Thomas replied swiftly, seeing the hurt in his master's eyes. 'Then you forestalled me by telling of the attempt on master Kessel's life. For a moment I doubted my own actions – yet after, I grew certain. For at the time the

132

intruder was in Kessel's room, Poole was with me in the paddock, where I caught him trying to steal a horse—'

'Enough!' It was Barnard again. 'Why should we believe a word of your testimony? You are the most impudent falconer I ever knew! First you neglect your duties to wander his Lordship's lands at will, then you go off for days and lie with whores in the village!' Seeing the light of anger in Thomas's eyes only encouraged him, for he went on: 'More, you turn up at a horse fair in wicked company – had master Jaggard not encountered you, how may we know what further deeds you had committed?' At that he stopped himself, for Sir Robert had risen from the carved chair in which he sat, with an expression of fury. Knowing his master's moods, Thomas expected an explosion – but none came. Making a supreme effort, his master looked at each man in turn.

'Master Finbow had my leave to go where he would,' he stated. 'Since the Earl has seemingly cast aside all concern, I wished to find the truth of the matter – as I do still. Then I will make matters known and call in the highest authority.'

There was a very different kind of silence now. Both Broad and Barnard, Thomas saw, looked ill at ease. Only Jaggard still wore an angry look, and it was directed at Thomas. He sighed, knowing there would have to be a reckoning.

For now he faced his master, trying to let him see that he would speak with him and explain himself. Sir Robert caught his eye and, seating himself again, said: 'Let Thomas tell his tale, that we may see the extent of the matter. After, I will speak with him alone.'

Nobody dared object, because they were not of Sir Robert's station, and moreover he was their master's guest. Yet, as he drew breath and began his account of Poole's escape, Thomas knew that he would not tell all to these men, but save some details for his master's ears alone. So he made no mention of *Vindex Reginae*, only told that there had apparently been some similar murders in London, and that Poole believed the same man was responsible. When he came to the matter of Kessel's studio, he realized that he would have to tell of the chimney shaft, for he had already said that he knew how the murderer came and went. Berating himself for blurting it out, he described what he had discovered, then stopped and waited for the response.

John Broad spoke first. In a somewhat tired voice, the old steward said: 'The tunnels that connect the chimney shafts are known to some of us – those who have been longest in his lordship's service.'

The weight of his remark was not lost on Barnard, whose eyes blazed. But before he could utter a word, Jaggard, who had stood impatiently throughout Thomas's account, added his voice.

'Then we'll have them searched from top to bottom, and stopped up with good stone and mortar,' he said. 'Hence if the villain means to try again, he must needs use a door like anyone else.'

'That is a matter for the Earl,' Sir Robert said, looking about briskly. 'Since he is not only master of Barrowhill, but the builder of it—' He broke off, as if regretting his words.

Barnard seized his chance. 'Do you suggest, Sir Robert, that his lordship, being privy to this means of ingress, knows full well how the murderer moved about the house, and hence—'

'I know not what to suggest, master Barnard,' Sir Robert replied. To signal that he had grown weary of the debate, he stood up abruptly. 'I will speak with the Earl and the Countess, and be guided by them,' he said pointedly. 'And I know that as their loyal servants you will act in the same manner.'

Nobody spoke, though a dozen questions now hung in the air. As if to show himself the man of deeds rather than words, Jaggard bowed to Sir Robert and headed for the door, saying he would muster his men and mount a full search of the house and its surroundings. Barnard, too, went off to his duties, with a parting glance at Broad. For his part the old steward remained until he was alone with Thomas and Sir Robert, then spoke up.

'I cannot help but say you have been rash, falconer. The Earl—' He stopped and said instead: 'I know the Lady Felice will be displeased. You should fear her wrath, as do all who serve her.'

134

Thomas inclined his head but kept his composure. Sir Robert said: 'I ask you to leave the Countess to me for the present, master Broad. I am going hawking, and she has already said she will accompany me.' Turning to Thomas, he asked: 'Will you ready my Clorinda, and meet me in an hour?'

It was but a small hawking party that took to the Downs that morning under a blanket of grey cloud. Will Holland, trying to appear alert, had hastily brought out the Countess's favourite lanner falcon in its richly embroidered hood, and set it on her hand. Thomas had similarly placed Sir Robert's Clorinda and, accompanied by two servants with hunting dogs, the group moved uphill and then down, so that the towers of Barrowhill were momentarily lost to sight. To Thomas, this disappearance always produced a feeling of some relief.

The Countess wore a deep-blue riding gown and hat, with gloves and long boots of soft leather. She appeared composed though somewhat distant, speaking little to the servants. When she unhooded the lanner and let it soar, with a tinkling of tiny silver bells, Sir Robert rode alongside her, murmuring his praises, though to Thomas's eye the bird was not exceptional. Walking beside Will, he watched with some satisfaction as his master and the Countess rode off a little way. Sir Robert, not without charm when it proved necessary, would speak privately with her, and hence some course of action might emerge. For, as he had long realized, the Countess was the real ruler of Barrowhill, though the entire household tied themselves in knots trying to maintain the picture that it were otherwise.

He told Will something of his tale as they walked at a fair pace, keeping the riders in sight. The dog handlers had hurried ahead to flush out small game, and larks, plovers and even snipe rose from the long grass. As Sir Robert released his hawk, Will said: 'Everyone knows the Earl has taken to his tower.'

After a moment, Thomas gave a nod. 'I would have guessed so.'

'It is his refuge,' Will went on. 'He often fears for his life – hence the man-traps, and now that whoreson Jaggard strutting about with his bullies at his back. If this murderer is not found soon, I fear his lordship will lose his reason.'

'I believe he will be found,' Thomas said, and as Will looked sharply at him, added: 'He tried to kill Kessel in the night, and failed. He is no spirit of the air, nor is he infallible.'

Will swallowed. 'He tried to kill the painter! Why?'

Thomas shook his head.

'Then . . .' Will looked suddenly nervous. 'If servants are also his intended victims, who might be safe?'

'You are, I think,' Thomas told him. 'Being such a plain target, up there in your shambles of a hut, he could have picked you off by now with small difficulty.'

'I might thank you, master Thomas . . .' Will began, then quickly assumed a respectful air, for Sir Robert was riding towards them. He reined in some yards away, and beckoned Thomas forward.

'I have talked somewhat with her ladyship,' he said in a low voice. 'No action will be taken against you. Indeed, she is more anxious than she may appear that this matter be resolved speedily. She fears for the Earl's life, and her own – as do we all. It seems the last of their house guests are departing this morning for London, in some haste.'

Thomas was about to speak, but Sir Robert half-raised a hand. 'Tell me now, those things you omitted to tell in front of Broad and Barnard.'

With relief, Thomas recounted all that Poole had told him: of the murders among the Dutch community in London, and that the name *Vindex Reginae* was known. 'I believe Kessel was also his target because though he is Flemish, most think of him as Dutch. And Poole was certain that, as he voiced it, the madman who is tearing the Dutch to tatters is the one who killed Brunning and Wilkes. He confessed that he had been sent to watch Brunning – though he would not say by whom.'

Sir Robert's reaction to this last piece of news was explosive. 'Good Christ! So their venture is being uncovered piecemeal . . . I was right to shy from it.' Eyeing Thomas, who did not understand, he said: 'I see one road to an answer. The Dutchman who sold me my gyrfalcons, two years back – you remember?'

Thomas managed a nod, his heart sinking as he guessed what was coming next. 'Henry van Velsen.'

'Van Velsen,' Sir Robert echoed. 'Is he not well placed among his folk? You must go to London and find out all you can, then return quickly. I will arrange a horse from the Earl's stable.'

Thomas said nothing.

'I know how you dislike the city, Thomas,' his master said, briskly but not unkindly. 'Yet once again, you may go where I cannot. You have already learned more than anyone, and done your sums aright – the link with the Dutch is a key, I am certain.'

'I feel sure of it too, sir,' Thomas admitted. And seeing there was little choice in the matter, he lowered his gaze to stare at a beetle crawling through the grass. *It must be a forest to him, he thought, as London was to me. No doubt it will be so again.*

He took the road that led due north, by Cheam and Sutton, and through good farmlands to Mitcham and Streatham. To his right, windmills on the hills south of Dulwich were turning in the breeze. Passing by Clapham village he forded the stream and rode into Newington. The river was to his left, though out of sight, yet already the familiar smell came to him, and already on this Monday morning the traffic was increasing as he drew nearer the roaring capital: carters, horsemen, countrymen and women carrying baskets and yokes of panniers. A swadder with a heavy pack called to him, thinking him a man of some station because of the mount he rode: a big Barbary horse from the Earl's stable. But Thomas barely heard him: his mind was forging ahead, as the church spire of St-Dunstans-in-the-East rose above the treetops, and finally the tower of St Mary Overies on Southwark shore, then the crowded rooftops, and the masts of the sailing ships riding at anchor below the bridge. Then the suburbs spread out on either side, and the road led straight ahead to London Bridge, and the noise from the north bank swirled across the water towards him. He was back in the capital.

First he must find a stable in Southwark where he might leave the horse. Agreeing a price with the ostler of the Half Moon Inn, he placed coins in the man's hand and walked off towards the bridge. On his way through Newington he had seen the ditches dug, seemingly against invasion, and been obliged to cross by a makeshift bridge. Militiamen watched him pass, though he was not challenged. Now he found a turnpike had been set up across the road, so that he had to give an account of himself to a pair of boys barely into their teens, sweating under half-rusted cuirasses and helmets. A poor defence they'd make against the Spaniards, he thought, realizing that even though the great Armada was said to be far away off the Scottish coast with the English navy in pursuit, the fear of an invading army had not passed. Indeed, as he walked up the wide thoroughfare to the crowded bridge, he believed he sensed a heightened atmosphere of fear and excitement, then thought better of it: it was but the hum of London once again that closed about him as it had done when he was last here, two years before.

Emerging into Bridge Street, he turned right along the crowded wharves, seeking the familiar turning to Botolph Key, where his old friend, the dealer in birds of every sort, had his shop. His spirits lifted when the Key opened to his left, then sank again as he pushed his way through the noisome crowd and stood dumbfounded, gazing at the entrance to what had once been Henry van Velsen's shop. There were no cages, no squawking birds, and no van Velsen. Instead there was a cloud of dust, and a din of saws and hammers, and men in labourers' aprons toiling on every side. His friend, it seemed, had moved away.

He took a deep breath, then looked towards the adjoining shop on the left, which seemed familiar. The open front was crammed with sacks and bales of wool, leaving only a narrow entry. Threading his way through, Thomas confronted a round-faced man in greasy clothes, who nodded and asked him if he could be of service.

'You were once before, master,' Thomas told him. 'A long while back. I'm a friend to Henry van Velsen, the dealer in birds. Can you tell me where he has gone?'

The man narrowed his eyes and peered, but clearly he did not recall Thomas, or did not wish to. His manner was more wary, and somewhat less patient, than Thomas remembered. He shrugged and said the dealer had gone several weeks back. The shop was now taken by a ship chandler, who was having it altered. No, he did not know where the Dutchman was now.

'These are dark times for the Hollanders,' the man said. 'They are banding together, protecting their own. As we all must do.'

He made as if to go, but Thomas tried to stay him. 'I have heard of some trouble among the Dutch,' he said quickly. 'That is why I am here, out of concern for my friend. I am eager to see him safe – can you not point me to him?'

The man shook his head and began to turn away, but seeing Thomas's face fall he seemed to relent, saying: 'There are many of his countrymen in Saint-Katharine's-by-the-Tower. If you ask there, I dare say you may have word of your friend.'

This much would serve; indeed it had to. Thomas thanked the man and went out into the narrow street.

It was almost midday and he was hungry, but a restlessness was upon him so that he began to walk downriver, past the Legal Keys with their myriad smells, past Billingsgate where the fishing boats landed their catch, until he found himself in Petty Wales, with the walls of the Tower looming above. Skirting the ditch, he walked to Great Tower Hill, and soon found himself in a throng trying to pass through the city wall by the narrow postern gate. When he got through at last, he realized he was part of the traffic for East Smithfield, which was ahead of him beyond Little Tower Hill. Now Thomas had little need to ask directions, for the tower of Saint Katharine's was clearly visible above the mass of rooftops. His pace quickening, he plunged into the crowded parish with its choked streets of narrow-fronted houses and shops, the smell of the river strong in his nostrils.

He stopped at a bakehouse, the powerful scent of new-baked loaves stirring his stomach, and asked for the shop of Henry van Velsen. The baker, sweating and streaked with flour dust, said that there was a dealer in birds two streets away, fronting the river. So at last, with a lighter heart,

Thomas emerged from a narrow alley and came to a quay where small ships were moored. From there he let his ears guide him, for the unmistakeable shrill and squawk of birds rose above the surrounding din, so that he passed a very few houses before stopping outside a small shop, its entrance cluttered with wicker cages. A moment later he was inside, a grin on his face, as an astonished Henry van Velsen emerged from a low door at the back.

'My friend!' he said, breaking into a slow smile of recognition. 'You are come to buy falcons?'

Thomas shook his head. 'Can I buy you a dinner instead?'

As it transpired Thomas's purse remained untouched, for van Velsen would not hear of his dining anywhere but above the shop, with himself and his wife. Thomas had not seen Maria van Velsen before and was struck by her distant manner, until when he was seated at the table his friend leaned across and said: 'My wife cannot speak, though she hears well enough.'

He nodded and gave Maria a smile as she placed a bowl of boiled chicken and leeks before him. There was coarse bread, and some cheese of a deep yellow, and a huge stein of ale with a hinged lid. She sat down beside her husband, and bowed her head while he said grace.

Van Velsen was greyer than when Thomas saw him last, the lines deeper about his eyes, though his manner was still open and direct. They talked as they ate, of everyday matters – not about the grim events of two years back, when Thomas and his friend had fought for their lives against a mob of bullies in the Bear Garden. Instead they spoke of their children – van Velsen's daughters were married and gone – and of their work, and the events of this Armada Summer . . . until van Velsen pushed his plate away, found his tobacco pipe and pouch, and fixed Thomas with a steady gaze.

'Now tell me why you have come.'

Leaving out some details, Thomas told of the murders at Barrowhill, which he believed were connected with others he had heard about in London. But when he came to this part the reactions of Henry and Maria van Velsen were such that he

140

stopped, aware that he had alarmed them. The next moment Maria had half-risen from her stool, a frightened look on her face.

Van Velsen broke the silence. 'You are very late, Thomas,' he murmured. 'And I think you will get no help, from anyone.'

Twelve

T homas looked hard at his friend, and saw the fear in the eyes of even this man, who possessed courage beyond that of almost anyone he knew. Watching his face, van Velsen merely nodded.

'You heard aright,' he said. 'There have been killings . . .' He broke off, for his wife was shaking her head vehemently at him.

After a glance at Thomas, he spoke some words to her in Dutch, at which she frowned and again shook her head. Seemingly not wanting to hear their conversation, she began taking away the bowls and platters. Van Velsen watched her for a moment, then turned back to Thomas.

'It is difficult to speak of. One of the dead was the husband of her close friend, Sophia van Rijssen.' Then after a moment's hesitation, the Dutchman embarked upon the longest speech Thomas had heard him make.

'You know of St Barnabas?' he asked. When Thomas shrugged, he continued: 'His symbol is the rake. We – the Nederlanders – call him Barnabas, for he is the Rake which gathers. To others he is the Factor. He came, and took – not for himself, but for those who employ him. Those men who swore they would protect the Nederlanders – and who have not done so!'

Now anger smouldered in his eyes. Thomas watched, showing no reaction.

'Some call me a fool,' van Velsen said. 'Because I would not pay, as others did, but defied their warnings . . . even when they said my shop would be burned and my birds killed, even when my wife begged me to pay and put an end to it . . . and my daughters begged me, and their husbands called me a madman for defying them – still, I would not pay. I and my prentices guarded the shop, armed with calivers, day and night . . . even when my friend the wine merchant was killed, stabbed in the back of the neck, I would not pay . . .' He stopped, seeing the look on Thomas's face.

It was time to tell all, to show his friend that he would help, if he could. '*Vindex Reginae*,' Thomas said quietly. 'The scourge of the Dutch. The same hand is at work where my master stays. I fear for his life too.'

Van Velsen's eyes widened. 'Then mayhap you have cause, if your master is one with them.' When Thomas frowned, he continued: 'I would not pay, even as the terror grew among our countrymen . . . you think we have spared a thought for the Armada of Spain, when our people have been slaughtered here in their beds, even as they slept, and not a soul saw who was the murderer?'

Maria van Velsen was carrying trenchers into her kitchen. There was a rattle, and a spoon fell to the floor. As she stooped to retrieve it, Thomas saw her terror. She shook with it.

'Forgive me,' he said, realizing he had blundered into something far worse than he imagined. 'I did not mean to stir your fears. Let me know what I might do. I owe you my life, remember –' and here he looked van Velsen in the eye – 'and like you, I pay my debts.'

There was a silence. Maria stood and without looking at either man went out, but he sensed a softening of her feeling towards him. Van Velsen merely shrugged.

'I know not what you might do – what any of us might do,' he said. 'No one knows where he may strike next.'

'This man,' Thomas began,' – the Factor . . .'

Van Velsen shook his head. 'Barnabas is not the scourge. Though some believed he was, at first, or linked to him . . . now he has ceased his work as the Rake, for he too is afraid. As any man who has dealings with the Dutch, is afraid.'

Thomas placed a hand on his friend's arm. 'Tell me the rest,' he implored. 'My master is wealthy, and not without powerful friends—'

He broke off, for van Velsen gave a snort. 'Those friends of the Earl you spoke of – Sir Someone and his friend – were they not powerful?'

Thomas nodded.

The Dutchman drew a deep breath. 'It began after the news came that the Spanish fleet was burned and sank,' he murmured. 'All of London rejoiced . . . then we learn it is neither burned nor sank, but blown away by the wind. Still the bells rang, and no army landed, and England is spared – but not the Nederlanders.' He struck a light and relit his pipe, puffing at it until the smoke came, then took a long draught. 'He cares not who they be – traders, merchants, some wealthy men, some not . . . I have a caliver in my chamber, and a knife in the bolster . . . when I sleep, that is.'

He paused, then: 'If you would seek this man, you are alone. The Venturers – the ones who sent the Rake, who took money from the Nederlanders – have failed us; the City Fathers care only for London's defence against the Spanish . . . the soldiers are all gone away . . . and besides, since no man knows what he looks like – this *Vindex* who leaves letters on the bodies of the dead – how may anyone pursue him?'

Thomas gazed down at the table, then asked: 'Why do you think he has made the Dutch his target?'

Van Velsen gave him a bleak look. 'Have not foreigners always been blamed, as the Jews were, for every ill? From spreading plague, to poisoning wells – or helping the nation's enemies?'

Thomas grimaced. 'You are certain nobody has seen him?'

The other hesitated. 'There was one – a servant to Jost van Rijssen, the merchant. But she is taken to St Mary of Bethlehem, for she is as a savage beast and must be constrained.'

'You mean, she has lost her reason?'

Van Velsen gave a nod. 'She will not speak of it – she cannot.'

Despite his friend's pessimism, Thomas felt a faint stirring of hope. 'Your wife's friend . . .'

'She was not in the room – she saw nothing,' van Velsen told him. 'Only heard her servant scream.' Seeing Thomas's expression he said somewhat sharply: 'Must I make a picture? Van

144

Rijssen was making free with the girl when he was killed. His wife had to lift his body off hers.'

Thomas said nothing, but he had formed his resolve. He would seek out the servant girl and try to question her. Had he not a way with beasts?

He opened his mouth, but van Velsen had anticipated his question. 'I will not go to that place,' he said in a low voice.

Thomas eyed him. 'Tell me the girl's name, and I will go.'

'Tacy,' came the reply. 'Tacy Pritchard. She has red hair. But you waste your time, my friend, for she is very mad.'

It was not a great distance, but his steps were heavy as he walked along the Minories with the city wall on his left, crossed the Whitechapel road before Aldgate and tramped the length of Houndsditch. Finally he stood before Bishopsgate with the Dolphin Inn on the corner, where he had once stood, two years before, trying to resolve a puzzle in his mind. Now he did so again, with some amazement at the way matters had turned to bring him back here to the same spot. His way seemed as full of shadows now as it had then.

Yet he had learned much from his friend, and a picture had arisen in his mind with some clarity. The Dutch community, he now knew, had been terrorized into making payments to a shadowy group – these Venturers – supposedly for their pro-tection. That Sir George Brunning and Sir Thomas Wilkes had been members of this group he had little doubt. That the Earl of Reigate was also one – perhaps even its instigator – seemed likely. What troubled Thomas most was that Sir Robert had seemingly been invited to Barrowhill to join this coterie of brutal men who cared nothing for the law, provided they reaped fat profits.

But into this profitable, if wicked, business, laying it raw with the deadly blade he wielded, had come a force that was utterly unforeseen: *Vindex Reginae*, the self-styled Queen's Avenger, bent on some fearful crusade of his own, who had set about murdering the Dutch and anyone who had dealings with them. And apart from Kessel, the only one who had set eyes on him was a mad girl confined to the insane hospital of St Mary of

Bethlehem – the notorious Bedlam, which now stood before Thomas, a little way along Bishopsgate: a modest two-storey building with barred windows. Summoning all his reserves, he crossed the lane at an angle and walked up to the entrance.

He was not alone, for it was afternoon, and visitors who paid a penny were welcome to enter and walk the long hallway on the ground floor, and gape at the spectacle: the permanent inmates in their twenty-one rooms. And Thomas, playing the sightseer along with the other half dozen, most of them scoffing young men come from the tavern, placed his coin in the porter's hand and was admitted. He had heard of this place, and tried to brace himself for the sights – but nothing had prepared him for the noise: the roaring, yelping, banging and rattling of manacles, the wild laughter and weeping that broke upon him like a sea wave as he entered the poorly lit, foul-smelling gallery.

He hung back, for he did not want to be a part of the group that strolled forward, pointing and laughing at the antics of the wretched individuals whose rooms gave off the hall on either side. Some were confined in chains, fierce and defiant, some very obviously a danger to anyone who ventured near. Others lay on filthy straw, or sat with their backs to the hall, or moved about distractedly, or stood motionless, staring at nothing.

His nerves taut as a bowstring, he stood near the entrance, unsure how to proceed. A large woman in a plain frock and apron came in the door then, carrying a heavy basket, which she set down, perspiring from what had evidently been a long walk. He turned to her with some relief.

'May I beg your help, mistress? I seek a red-haired girl named Tacy Pritchard . . .' he began, but the woman turned to the porter and began speaking urgently to him. After a moment Thomas realized that they were man and wife.

He waited until the discourse was over, whereupon the woman looked at him as if continuing her conversation, and said: 'She is in my charge, on the women's side. What do you want with her?'

'I am a friend to her family,' Thomas lied, 'and seldom in London – may I try to speak with her?'

'She seldom speaks, and only then to the gallery maids,' the

146

woman answered. 'You may try, but do not come near. She bites and scratches.'

He swallowed and, following the woman's extended finger, walked along the hall to an open doorway near the end. Stairs led to the upper floor, whence came more shrieking and wailing. A man's voice shouted: 'I'll hang you all, for I am the true hangman!'

He stopped at the doorway and looked inside.

Sitting upright on a mass of straw was a rather plump, pretty girl of no more than sixteen years, her long red hair dirty and tangled, her chemise stained and torn. She was holding something that Thomas could not see, working her fingers about it in a rubbing motion. Whether she saw him or not he was unable to tell for she gave no sign, only looked down at her hands, which never ceased their movement.

The porter's wife was passing behind Thomas, heading for the stairs. Quickly he turned to her, asking: 'Can you tell me aught of her condition, mistress? I will pay for your trouble.'

The woman stopped and set down her basket. 'Donations are sorely needed,' she said. 'We have but a small allowance from the city, and 'tis never enough. This one's family have sent not a groat for her keep. Yet she has her pottage and broken bread, and a little meat when we may, though she thank us not.'

Thomas noted the pointedness of her gaze, dug in his purse and found some silver, which the woman took without comment. Before she could pick up her basket and go, he asked: 'Who confined her here? The Dutch family who worked her?'

The porter's wife shook her head. 'She was sent from Bridewell, for she is not merely mad, but wicked – she will tell you so herself. No physic will work upon her, save the cross she had when she came, which is her only company.' And having said all she was willing to say, the woman caught up her basket and went.

Thomas turned – and froze, for Tacy was staring him full in the face, and now he saw what she held in her hand: a small crucifix.

He returned her gaze and smiled, and she did not react. So he took a step forward into the cell – for it merited no other

147

description – and said: 'Tacy, I am Thomas. I have spoken with your mistress . . .' Then seeing a look of faint bewilderment cross her face, he rejected that topic and said instead: 'I am come to speak with you, and help you if I may.'

She merely stared, then lost interest in him and looked down at her hands, which resumed their constant working.

He took another step and played his only card: a length of white ribbon he had bought on a whim from a fripperer's stall in Houndsditch. As he drew it out and held it, Tacy looked up.

'For your pretty red hair,' he murmured.

His hopes rose, for it seemed she had never been offered a gift before. With an odd look, she allowed him to lean forward and place the ribbon in her hand. Then she struck.

First her nails raked his cheek, missing his eye by a whisker. At the same time she spat, an incredibly large gobbet that landed on his lip. As he reeled back, startled, she broke into a cry, half triumph, half rage, and balling up the ribbon in her other hand, she threw it at him.

'Tacy's a whore,' she cried, 'and not pretty, so ye lie! And liars be sinners and sinners be cursed and soused in blood and all that lie between whores' legs will die where they lie!'

She leaped up, and he saw now the leg-irons, which had been hidden in the straw, fastened to a ring in the wall. He stepped back, putting his hand to his face and seeing it striped with blood, which seemed to enrage her further. The sad figure of the dumpling girl he had encountered a moment ago was transformed into a snarling, spitting harpy who merely wished to do him harm.

Yet, he told himself, this is who he must try to tame if he would find out anything at all. Wiping his face on his sleeve, he forced a smile, and said: 'Tacy is no whore, but a girl who is sad and far from home. And . . .' Here he weighed the risk, then said firmly: 'And I am looking for the man who killed your master – master van Rijssen. He must be caught, before—'

He broke off, regretting his rash words, for the change in Tacy was alarming. Her face assumed a look of pure terror, and throwing her head back, she gave a scream that shook the rafters.

'The wheezing man!' she yelled. 'His breath is a gust of poison – save Tacy from the wheezing man!' And at once she began beating the air with her hands, as if warding off a bee swarm, howling and wailing and dribbling at the mouth. And with sinking heart, Thomas realized too late that the noise had not only set off a chorus of shrieks from other inmates on all sides, but brought the sightseers to the cell in a body. They crowded behind him, laughing, mimicking Tacy's howls, some throwing in lewd comments and suggestions, so that Thomas turned savagely and thrust them aside, striding to the entrance while the howling of Bedlam filled his ears. He did not look about him again until the porter let him out into Bishopsgate, and the cloudy sky was above him, and he was walking swiftly along Houndsditch, his breath coming fast, oblivious to the folk on either side. And as he walked he cursed inside himself; for he had learned little, and done nothing but harm.

He found van Velsen in the shop with his prentice, a young Dutch boy who was mending cages with withies. One look at Thomas told his friend all he needed. Drawing him to the rear, he pointed to a sack of grain and told him to sit. Then with his own hands he cleaned the scratches on Thomas's face, finally pronouncing them shallow enough to heal without leaving any noticeable scar.

He asked nothing of his friend, not even at suppertime when, having accepted the invitation to stay the night, Thomas took a meal and a cup of sweet wine with his hosts. Maria, however, seemed to have mastered her earlier unease, and van Velsen told him that his wife would know what he had learned. So he spoke of Tacy and repeated her words, about the 'wheezing man'.

Maria shuddered and went off to her bed, leaving Thomas alone with his friend. After some thought van Velsen said: 'That wheezing breath minds me of those who work with hemp, or flax. After many years their breath is short, and comes loud – finally it rattles in their chests, and they are not far from death.'

Thomas stared. 'It may be that you have helped to track down this murderer,' he said.

Van Velsen met his gaze. 'If I have any part in finding him

out, then I will rest easier in my bed.' He stifled a yawn and stretched his broad shoulders. 'We say our farewell in the morning, my friend. And you will take our prayers with you.'

Barrowhill rose insolently above the waving grass, its decorated walls garish against the leaden sky, when Thomas rode back under its shadow on the Tuesday morning. The sweeter air of the Downs was as perfume to him after the stench of London, and the ride south through the Surrey hills had been pleasant. After stabling the horse he went at once to the falcons' mews, only too aware of how much he had neglected his hawks. Seeing that several were missing, including Sir Robert's favourite, he guessed that a party was out, which also explained Will Holland's absence. He examined the other birds, all of which needed exercise. Indeed, one or two roused on their perches and looked at him as if at a stranger. It would not do. So it was that, content to be about his own work again, he rounded the hut with a hooded falcon on his wrist, and walked straight into Hugh Jaggard.

'They told me you were returned,' he said at once. 'Why did you not report to me?'

Thomas sighed. 'Am I now one of your foot soldiers, who must stand ready to be counted and dismissed?'

'I am ordered to protect everyone – man, woman and child!' Jaggard snapped. 'How may I do that if none pays me any mind?'

Thomas stood still, stroking the hawk's back with his finger, and returned the other's gaze. 'Mayhap you should issue everyone with a suit of joined armour,' he suggested, with a half-smile. 'Then they might sleep easier of a night-time. Indeed, such a consort of clanking might scare an intruder out of his wits, and we could give thanks for our deliverance.'

Jaggard scowled and opened his mouth, then closed it again, and turned his head away abruptly, making a choking sound. Thomas's smile vanished: the thought struck him that Jaggard was under such strain, with his ill-defined and thankless duties, that he was weeping like a maid. The next moment his lips parted in surprise: the man was laughing.

'God's heart, only another ex-soldier could make me split my sides as you have done,' he mumbled, and began wiping tears from his eyes. 'Have I not felt as useful as a bucket with holes since the day I arrived?'

Thomas found himself laughing a little in turn, which surprised him. The events of recent days, he had thought, offered little scope for amusement. 'It gladdens me to see you thus,' he said. 'I had not forgot what I owe you – starting with an apology, for letting our prisoner go as I did . . .'

Jaggard was nodding, even as his laughter subsided. 'It was hard,' he allowed. 'Yet when I turned the matter over, I cannot swear I would have acted differently.' He fixed Thomas with a knowing look. 'And, I believe you did not tell all before those two priggish cuffins – I mean Broad and Barnard.'

Thomas raised an eyebrow. 'I serve my master, Sir Robert.' When Jaggard said nothing, he added: 'Let me repay you for your help at the horse fair, if naught else. Will you walk on the Downs with me, while I exercise the hawk?'

Jaggard nodded his approval. 'Gladly.'

They walked for an hour, and then another, until their stomachs growled in unison and drove them to the kitchens for their dinner. Relieved to share his knowledge, Thomas held little back from Jaggard, ending his tale with the visit to Bedlam and the howls of mad Tacy, which still rang in his ears. Jaggard was astounded: he had been able to discover nothing at Barrowhill, nor were the Earl and Countess disposed to confide in him. It was as if he were expected to pluck the murderer from the air and spirit him away with the least sign of disruption, so that the house might return to its normal function: serving the whims and desires of its noble occupants, for ever.

'Now I have the picture plain before me,' he said in a low voice, as they crossed the stable yard shoulder to shoulder. 'Our foe is no spirit, but a fanatic, like to the zealots of old who cared nothing for their own lives but were bent upon some higher cause: his cause is the weeding out of the Dutch and all who aid them – even, it seems, those who use them. He is swift and cunning, and without mercy, and he comes and goes through every cranny as he will – like the wind itself.'

Thomas nodded. 'I cannot draw it better than you have done.'

Jaggard exhaled deeply. 'But how in Christ's name may we come at such as he?'

'Would that I knew,' Thomas muttered. 'It is nigh enough to make a man despair.'

'No,' Jaggard replied. 'That I will not do. He is a mortal man, not a devil, and wields a weapon that we both recognize. If we can snare him, he may be taken, and brought before his betters.'

Turning to Thomas, he placed a hand on his shoulder. 'Now let's fill our bellies at the Earl's expense,' he said, 'and frighten the kitchen wenches with our farts.' Then abruptly he asked: 'Did you truly lie with whores in the village, as Barnard claimed?'

'Not with whores,' Thomas answered mildly, and thinking of Madge Clapperdaw added: 'Yet if you are not particular, there is one that will serve you well enough.'

Jaggard broke into a grin. 'Since when could a ruffling cove like me afford to be particular?'

Sir Robert returned soon after Thomas had eaten his dinner, and at once sent word for him. A moment later he stood before his master while he sat alone at the high table in the Great Chamber, with servingmen to bow to his every need, but no sign of host or hostess.

'The Countess dines alone in the Withdrawing Chamber, with her ladies,' he said with his mouth full. 'The Earl . . .' He waved his spoon to convey what was common knowledge: the Earl was still in his Prospect Room, and had not set foot beyond its door.

At his master's urging, Thomas told all that had befallen him in London, and added that he and Jaggard were now as one, and would work in consort to try and discover the killer. Yet, though his master voiced his approval, he was not cheered by the news.

'I am a plain hunting man,' he said, 'and I see no other course than to flush our quarry out. Only then may we mark him and draw the net tight.' He grimaced. 'I have tried to speak of it to the Earl, but he will admit no one unless they talk of matters he likes – music, say, or wine . . .'

Thomas said nothing, though a question was on his lips that was difficult to voice. To his relief, his master broached the matter himself. Glancing about to reassure himself that no servants were within earshot, he said in a low voice: 'Thomas – I think you have wondered at my dealings with the Earl and his friends.'

Thomas nodded slowly.

'I will tell you this,' Sir Robert continued, then paused and laid down his spoon as if his appetite had ebbed away. 'I have been a fool – a Berkshire Bumpkin, as I overheard one of those primping young eyases say to his smirking fellow. A fool, to think I was invited here for aught but my money.'

Touched by his master's candour, Thomas waited.

'They are powerful, Thomas,' Sir Robert said. 'And their purses are deep. There is no enterprise too bold, nor too foul, for their taste, so long as it promise a fair return on investment. Offering Dutch merchants protection from their enemies – for a price – is but one of their lesser ventures.'

'This much I have guessed,' Thomas said.

His master nodded and sighed. 'Hence you see why I must put an end to it, for I will not be drawn into the mire with them – whether I be bumpkin or no.'

'You have acted well from the beginning, Sir Robert,' Thomas murmured. 'There will be no stain on you—'

'Nay – you are mistaken,' the other interrupted. 'For if the Earl's honour is lost, all those who have sat at his table are tainted. Hence, while this murderer is loose, to leave now and go back to Petbury will look like no more than my fearing for my life, instead of rejecting the Earl's hand of friendship.'

Thomas could offer no reply, for it was true. Sir Robert sighed again and said: 'So, I am a kind of prisoner here myself. No pretty songbird in a wicker cage – rather a clumsy old haggard, in a gilded and painted aviary.'

He lowered his eyes, pushed his platter away and picked up his goblet of dark claret, staring at the huge silver salt-cellar that held sway from the centre of the table. Without a word, Thomas left him and walked out of the Great Chamber.

Thirteen

By evening the cloud had broken, and at sunset Thomas sat with Will Holland on the grass outside the falconer's hut and told his story once again. Will was phlegmatic, almost good-humoured – the reason for which was not long in coming.

'Doreth and I will be married,' he announced. 'As soon as the Earl will release me from his service.' His face dropped. 'Yet, none may see him. I have asked master Broad to speak up for me, but he swats me away like a fly on his horse's rump.'

Thomas offered Will words of congratulation, adding that he wished he might go to Tadworth and see Moll. 'Yet my master wants me near,' he said, 'and I fear to leave him.'

Will looked sober. 'Cousin Moll's a sly one at times. Mayhap you won't want to hear of it, but there was another from Barrowhill once, used to sneak out of a night-time to be with her.'

Thomas said nothing. His feelings for Moll he had put away of late, not knowing how long he was to remain here. Yet she was in his thoughts every day, and he entertained a strong sentiment that he was in hers.

'But then, it's not my place to speak of that,' Will said, somewhat hastily. 'Besides,' he added, 'why may we not both go tonight after curfew time, and lie with our lady-loves for an hour or two? Who is to know?'

'Curfew?' Thomas asked, frowning. 'Whose notion was that, Jaggard's?'

'Who else?' Will answered. 'Since he has accomplished naught, he must be seen to do something. Though to my mind, he'd catch a flittermouse before he caught a murderer.' He sat up, shading his eyes with his palm. A figure was walking past the paddock and ascending the slope in their direction. As the man drew near, both falconers got to their feet.

'Talk of the devil,' Will muttered. 'It's one of Jaggard's cut-rate soldiers.'

The man wore an old cuirass like Jaggard's and carried a short pike, but he was overweight and puffing even from the short climb. Stopping short of the hut, he called out: 'Master Finbow!'

'What is it?' Thomas called back.

'You are ordered to come to the house. Sergeant Jaggard will speak with you.'

'Why can't he come himself?' Thomas asked, but the man was already turning away.

'He is to take you to his lordship,' he said, and walked off.

Will and Thomas exchanged looks. 'So he is promoted to sergeant now,' Will said, snapping to attention. Seeing Thomas's absent expression, he added in a softer tone: 'I'll tell Moll you will be with her, as soon as you may.'

Thomas nodded and set off towards the house.

Jaggard was waiting for him in the great hallway below the stairs. As Thomas came up he said: 'We are to go to the Prospect Room, for the Earl will speak with us both – on a matter of great importance, he has said.'

Thomas frowned. 'Is my master with him?'

'I do not know. But those clowns Broad and Barnard are there.'

They walked in silence up the stairs, and were met on the upper floor by a liveried servant who said he would conduct them to the Earl. They followed him along the wide candlelit passages, then up a stair to the top floor where Kessel had his studio. This time Thomas found himself ascending a spiral stairway at the south-western corner of the house, which ended in a short passage blocked by a heavy oaken door. When the servant tapped it was opened immediately, and both Jaggard and Thomas blinked – not in surprise, but because of the brightness that blazed forth.

'Come inside – hurry!' It was the first time Thomas had heard the Earl's voice for many days. Stepping into the room, he felt himself entering a bowl of light. Some of it, he realized, was due to the last rays of the setting sun, streaming through a tall window. Indeed, the room, which was almost circular, had windows on every side, so that it seemed a miracle how its roof was supported by the narrow piers between. Inside, candles were set high and low, casting wild shadows on floor and ceiling.

The Earl was sat in a carved chair, his back to the sun. As his eyes adjusted, Thomas saw a table before him, spread with a profusion of books and papers. Close by stood John Broad, his back as straight as his staff of office, and Barnard opposite him. There were three other men: one in livery whom Thomas recognized as the leader of the Earl's orchestra, a viol player. Beside him stood another who, from his dress, appeared to be a humble artisan, ill at ease in this company. The third man, Thomas recalled, was the Earl's horse-master, Jonas Reed.

'Falconer!' The Earl's voice was even shriller than usual. 'You are honoured, for you are chosen to play a part in a Great Enterprise that is about to be hatched at Barrowhill. I have your master's sanction in drawing you into our little circle.'

He beamed, and Thomas's heart sank; for if he knew a hawk from a swan, he was about to hear something appalling.

'The next week,' the Earl cried, 'will see an act of creation such as these Downs have never beheld! A fortress shall rise beside the lake, crowned with battlements and towers. Men-at-arms shall garrison it – ' here he included Jaggard, who looked, Thomas thought, as uncomfortable as he was, – 'While on the lake itself,' the Earl went on, 'a little Armada, represented by a Spanish galley and an English man-of-war, shall do battle to the death.' His smile was broad and, Thomas thought, somewhat wild, as if he were almost distracted. 'Not in a literal sense of course,' he added,' – unless someone grow careless!'

There were murmurs from those assembled, though Thomas began to sense that he and Jaggard were not alone in feeling ill at ease. In fact, the only man who looked pleased was Barnard (for it was his scheme, Thomas remembered). John Broad, though he remained silent, was tense as a lute-string. Reed, who kept his eyes on the Earl, showed no emotion at all.

'The Barrowhill Entertainment,' proclaimed the Earl, 'will not merely rival the great entertainments of the last decade – it shall surpass them! Music, dancing, fireworks, feasting, and to crown all, a sea battle – and see now how you are honoured, for our great Sovereign herself is invited, with all her train!'

Thomas blinked. The Queen . . .?

'Master Barnard!' the Earl cried. 'Will you set forth in brief our little stratagem?'

'You are too modest, my lord,' Barnard murmured, 'for you are as always the sole artificer of your own Entertainments – as was his late majesty, King Henry.' And though the Earl dismissed such obvious flattery, he was clearly pleased by it, saying: 'Enough of your sugared words – show them the plot!'

Leaning over the table, Barnard spread out a large sheet of paper, on which were drawn scenes and devices which at first meant little to Thomas. But as the grand plan unfolded he began to discern its purpose, and even to see some merit in it.

'The lake, drawn to scale thus,' Barnard said, savouring his moment. 'On its western side, a castle of timber and boards, yet so cunningly wrought and painted as to seem like stone. Our carpenter, master Finch –' and here he nodded briefly in the direction of the dumbfounded artisan – 'shall have charge of its construction. Signor Mannizzi, a master mason who was much admired by his lordship's father, the late Earl, is coming from London to supervise. Here –' he indicated coloured drawings of a ship drawn by oars, and another under full sail – 'the Spanish and English vessels, for the building of which, shipwrights are being engaged. Sergeant Jaggard shall have charge of the soldiers, firing of ordinance and harquebuses, and execution of the battle. The music naturally falls under the domain of our own leader of the orchestra, as will direction of the masquerade . . .' As the Earl raised a hand, he quickly added, 'Subject of course to his lordship's approval.' He paused as if to ensure that he had forgotten nothing, then as if seeing Thomas for the first time, added: 'There will be other devices to delight the company – such as a giant figure of a steed, guided by men beneath its hide – master Reed here shall have a free rein, if you will forgive my jest, in devising it!'

When nobody laughed, Barnard continued: 'And, since it is well known how her royal majesty loves hawking, a great hawk, on wires, shall fly in and startle our guests before delivering a message from its beak. Master Finbow, the falconer, will oversee the rightness of the bird's construction.'

Thomas merely stared, which prompted a smirk from Barnard and a shriek of laughter from the Earl.

'Calm yourself, falconer!' he smiled. ' 'Tis no hard task for one of your experience. Holland shall have care of all the hawks while you attend the builders – it will be a holiday for you!'

Thomas opened his mouth, but a swift glance at the faces turned towards him told him there was no room for escape. The Earl would be obeyed; and besides, it seemed his master had already allowed it. He bowed, and managed a faint smile of acquiescence.

'Splendid! By the Lord, what celebrations we'll have!' cried the Earl. 'And if I know our glorious Eliza, she will hasten to Barrowhill before we are even ready!' He stood up and addressed the group in a tone that brooked no dissent. 'You have but one week, gentlemen and masters – you had best work day and night!'

'One week?' It was Jonas Reed who ventured to break the shocked silence. 'Nay, my Lord, that bain't near enough time.'

The man spoke in the thick accent of a north-country man. But at once he seemed to regret his words, for the Earl turned upon him with a wild look in his eye. 'If seven days was enough for God to create the world, master Reed, it shall be enough for a host of men to knock together a few devices of plain timber, wouldn't you say?'

Reed swallowed audibly and bowed, though Thomas sensed the man's pent-up resentment. But in that, he was not alone.

There was another short silence, which meant they were all dismissed. Jaggard, Thomas, Reed, Finch and the music-maker bowed and filed out, leaving the Earl alone with his gentlemen servants. Judging by the look on Broad's face, it was plain to

159

Thomas that words would be batted across the table the moment the door closed.

He and Jaggard did not speak until they were out in the stable yard, with its comforting smell of dung and straw. But when Thomas turned to the other, he was surprised to see him smiling.

'At least I'll get to put that whoreson troop of mine through their paces,' he snarled. 'By Christ, I'll make them sweat!' He raised an eyebrow at Thomas. 'Why so glum, my friend? This is what the Earl means by a matter of great importance. Three dead here, and another stabbed; a killer roaming the country, the nation barely saved from invasion – yet what concerns his lordship most is his Grand Entertainment!'

Thomas nodded ruefully. 'And you may play soldiers, while I play puppet-master.'

Jaggard guffawed and clapped him on the back. 'Not until tomorrow! The night is ours, and it isn't done yet. Will you walk with me into Tadworth, and point me at this market-price whore you told me of?'

Thomas, his spirits lifted by the old soldier's manner, broke into a smile. 'I will!'

That night, when Moll came to her bed in the Red Bull, she seemed to Thomas almost a stranger. Though she kissed and colled him and was eager for his strong body, she said little, even when at last they lay spent beneath her sheets in the silent hours, he with his arm about her bare shoulder.

He wanted to explain his absence, but she dismissed the matter saying: 'Ben Mallam was here, and told me of your adventures. And Cousin Will, before he went off to his Doreth.'

'You have been much in my thoughts,' Thomas said, and when she made no answer went on: 'Do I presume, if I think you have thought of me?'

'Nay,' Moll answered, and touched his cheek so that he winced. 'But now I wonder what fingernails made these scars.'

Seeing how the scratches made by Tacy might look, he told her something of the tale. But being obliged to leave out many details, he sensed the questions which rose to her lips, though she gave them no utterance.

'Did you think I had lain with some wild drab in London, and tried to cheat her out of her sixpence?' he asked.

She said nothing.

'You are more than enough for me,' he murmured. 'All that I spoke when we first cleaved to each other, I would say again now.'

'Thomas.' Something in her tone heralded an announcement – or perhaps a request. He drew breath, only stroking the hair which lay across her cheek while she spoke. 'You think I am as my dull Cousin Will has shown me to you. A teasing inn-keeper's widow . . . every woman's bosom friend, and every man's lusty wench, especially when he has drained his third mug of the night and commenced to licking his chops at sight of my paps.'

He frowned. 'Nay, I—'

'Let me speak.'

He returned to stroking her hair, which did not displease her, and waited.

'You have not played me false, nor I believe would you do so, for I have known many men. You guess, I know, that some have even lain in this bed, and others have fallen at my feet, even begged me to marry them. I never cared a fig for more than one, or two at most.'

He began to glimpse the path she was laying bare – until she brought him up with a jolt. 'He I have in mind was an Italian – and now I learn he is coming back to Barrowhill.'

'The mason . . . Manniss . . .?' he fumbled with the name.

'Mannizzi. Niccolo Mannizzi, from Spezia.' She pronounced the words with an accent, so that it was plain she had been taught how to say them. Thomas caught his breath.

'He works in stone,' she went on. 'The Earl employed him – much of the fine carving on that house is by his hand. Yet after a time they fell to quarreling – Niccolo and his lordship – because of the Countess. Naught he did was good enough to satisfy her ladyship, Niccolo said, nor would it ever be. One day he spoke his mind – for he was proud – and as you will know, such forthright ways are not permitted at Barrowhill. He was marched to the Earl's borders like a villain, and sent on his way.'

'You love him still,' Thomas said, shocked to find an emptiness inside him such as he had not felt for many years – perhaps not since Mary Finbow's death.

'I know not, until I see him,' Moll said.

'And you shall, for he is coming to help build the Earl's entertainment.' Then he saw it: 'Yet in truth, he comes back because of you.'

She gave a tiny movement of her head, which was enough.

'Well,' said Thomas after a moment. 'If I have a rival, so be it, for you are worthy of any struggle.'

She sighed. 'I want no men fighting over me – though it has happened more than once, here in this inn.'

'I do not doubt that,' he answered.

'Besides,' she murmured, 'there will be no brawling, for like you he is a man of gentle ways. His breath is short, so that he saves all his strength for his work. It is a sickness that comes often to those who toil with stone, and breathe its dust.'

Thomas started, so that she was alert at once. 'What is it, my duck?' she asked. 'Speak.'

'His breath – comes it so short, that he might be called a wheezing man?'

She hesitated. 'He may wheeze a little, at times . . . as when he is fatigued by some effort or other.'

And though she caught her lower lip, regretting her words, Thomas said nothing, for they rang true. And when she raised her head so that he might free his arm, each of them turned from the other with closed eyes, though neither slept.

So it was that the grounds of Barrowhill were transformed, in the days that followed, into a great beehive of activity. All the Earl's fear and caution, it seemed, was forgotten in his enthusiasm for the Entertainments, which now occupied his every waking hour. And among those whose work was made doubly hard, none complained louder than Jaggard.

'I am become like that monster of old tales – the many-headed hydra,' he told Thomas, as they stood beside the lake in the morning breeze. 'First I am sergeant of this catchpenny garrison – not only the rogues I came with, but a scratch company of auxiliaries: gardeners and grooms who can scarce hold a pike straight let alone fire a caliver. Yet they are to be dressed in fustian and armour, and expected to put on a show like the nation's finest. Also, I am chief gunner and master of ordinance, in charge of enough powder to blow the entire house to the Indies and back. And now I find I am Master of Fireworks, who must risk life and limb running about with a taper, surrounded by brimstone and saltpetre and the Good Christ knows what else . . . and still, I am bodyguard to his lordship, and must watch every man's move, lest some joiner or plasterer whip a poniard from his belt and show himself to be our murderer-at-large.' He blew out his cheeks and exhaled a long breath. 'Now tell me your task lies heavy upon you, and I'll slit your gizzard!'

Thomas was smiling, in spite of his dismay at finding himself overseeing the building of the massive hawk. Ten feet from beak to tail, with a wingspan of twenty-five, the preposterous bird was to be hidden under a false covert of green canvas and foliage, then at the crucial moment, brought forth and propelled on taut cables across the lake towards the royal pavilion, where the nobles and guests would be seated. Here it would stop before the throne, raised on a velvet-covered dais, and the Earl himself would pluck the parchment from its beak and read the oration (as official Poet of the Entertainments, he had composed it himself). It was, everyone said, a wondrous device, and there was great interest in its construction. Carpenters were already at work on the light wooden framework, which was to be covered with painted cloths, cunningly shaped to resemble plumage.

Other teams of workmen, meanwhile, were having their own difficulties. When the Earl was finally persuaded that it was impossible to build two ships in the space of a week, a couple of river boats were purchased from Thames Ditton and brought overland on carts, to be transformed by Finch's men into a Spanish galley and an English fighting vessel. Meanwhile the giant horse was taking shape under the watchful eye of Reed the horse-master, who it seemed was a stern overseer; his men could be heard quarreling among themselves each day from the far side of the lake. At the same time the ground beside its edge was found to be too soft to support the massive castle, and cartloads of broken stone had to be brought in to provide foundation. It was on the second day of such activity that Thomas saw a small group of men walking by the lake shore, stopping some yards away beside the castle plot. One was Henry Barnard, who waved to him, bidding him join them. As he walked up he saw among the assembled artisans a handsome, dark-complexioned man of middle height, with a clean-shaved chin and neat moustaches, wearing a mason's apron over his workaday clothes.

Barnard turned as Thomas approached, saying: 'Falconer, I am ordered to present Signor Mannizzi, who is come to oversee the building of the castle. Any assistance you may render each other will no doubt serve to speed our enterprise.'

The Italian smiled and gave a slight bow, which had a hint of mockery about it. Thomas nodded in return, meeting the eyes of his rival with veiled curiosity. At once, however, Mannizzi was caught up in Barnard's explanations, and was obliged to look away at the drawings from which he must work. But to Thomas's eyes, as he returned to his own tasks, the man seemed to be listening with only half an ear, and his eyes strayed at times to the great house two hundred yards away. Perhaps he wishes he were engaged on some real stonework, Thomas thought – or does his mind stray further, in the direction of Tadworth? Or, worse . . .

With a heavy heart, he walked back to the skeleton of his half-built hawk.

That afternoon, Sir Robert came riding up to Thomas and said he would go hawking, though it was clear he was making an opportunity for the two of them to talk. Relieved to see his master again and to get away from the flurry of construction work, Thomas walked beside the horse and told of his most recent discovery. When, haltingly, he voiced his suspicions about Mannizzi, Sir Robert was amazed.

'This man a murderer? That cannot be!' he exclaimed. 'He is respected throughout the country for his craft. He has a reputation.'

Thomas shrugged. 'And he is a Catholic.'

'An Italian, who has lived for many years in England,' Sir Robert countered. 'No lover of Spain – and no hater of anyone, I would venture, even the Dutch.' He paused, and shook his head. 'Mannizzi is not our *Vindex* – I would stake my life on it.'

Thomas levelled a steady gaze at his master. 'How many other strangers would know the house so well – let alone know of the chimney shafts, and the footholds in the brickwork?'

'He was not the builder,' Sir Robert objected, 'but a carver, who did the decorative stonework—'

'Until he was humiliated, and dismissed by his lordship.'

Sir Robert was frowning, eager to sweep aside what he preferred not to believe. 'But he was not here during the time of Sir George's and Sir Thomas's deaths – I hear he was at work on a statue commissioned by the Earl of Hertford.' He looked angrily at Thomas. 'You grow too hot in your accusations!'

Thomas said nothing, ashamed suddenly that his own emotions might be ruling his judgement. They had reached the falcons' mews and he began readying the bird, which was restless: Will had failed to exercise her. 'Lolling in Doreth's bed again . . .' Thomas muttered, as he walked back to Sir Robert with Clorinda on his wrist. His master was sitting motionless on his horse, gazing at the brooding walls of Barrowhill. When he leaned down to offer his gauntlet, Thomas saw the marks of strain about his eyes.

'Why not send word now to your friends in the Privy Council, Sir Robert?' he urged. 'Lest this matter drive us all to distraction before it is resolved.'

His master sighed, took his Clorinda and lifted her, his face relaxing into an expression of mingled pleasure and admiration.

'Is she not a princess among falcons?' he asked.

Thomas nodded. 'She is.'

'Then I will ride and let her hunt, and bring her back to the mews myself.' A hint of a smile lifted the corners of his mouth. 'You have more important matters to see to.'

Thomas met his eye. 'That was a cruel jest, sir, to put me in the Earl's service for this purpose . . .' he began, but his master shook his head.

'Nay – I had good reason. What better way for you to observe at close quarters the doings of the household, and all those that come and go?'

Thomas hesitated, then said: 'The one I have fixed upon, you dismiss out of hand.'

'It would take a great deal to convince me that Mannizzi could do such deeds as you and I have seen here,' his master answered.

'Would it take another murder?' Thomas asked, too late to rein in the thought. But instead of blowing hot as he expected, his master merely shook the reins, and holding the mighty hawk aloft, spurred his horse away towards the Downs.

That night Thomas took his supper in the kitchen while the Earl's servants snatched a morsel here and there, many of them standing up, before hastening off to some duty or other. Marmion, the cook, seemed not to eat at all, but existed on spleen and venom washed down with beer from a barrel in the corner. The talk was of the deluge of house guests expected for the Entertainment, and the added work it would mean for everyone. Extra cooks and servingmen were being hired from the village, along with washerwomen and maids. Listening absently, Thomas drained his mug and was about to rise from his stool when Jaggard strode in with his troop of exhausted regulars, demanding to be fed.

'God's arse, I wish I'd never set foot in this place,' the old soldier muttered as he sat down beside him. 'I've half a mind to train my culverin on yon pasteboard fort and blow the tripes out of that whoreson Italian.'

'What's he done to stir your wrath?' Thomas asked, trying to look as if he were merely amused.

'Enough,' Jaggard retorted. 'All I did was offer advice as to how the parapets must support my men – plain military sense – and he twitches his moustache and tells me to take myself off.'

He poured himself a draught of beer and gulped it, then

added: 'He's an odd cove, too: wanted naught to do with the Dutchman – that painter with the face like a sick mule.'

Thomas looked down at the table. 'I wonder why that should be,' he murmured.

Jaggard took a hunk of bread from a platter and shoved it into his mouth. 'I know not, Thomas,' he said between chews. 'It appears to me now that half of those here are fit for the madhouse.'

Thomas watched the cook break into a sudden rage, lunge at the turnspit boy and crack him across his pate. 'You may be right,' he muttered.

The rest of the troop had found a bench and pulled it up to the table. Clapping his hand briefly on Jaggard's shoulder, Thomas rose and went outside, the cool evening air like balm on his face after the heat of the kitchens. In the stable yard a groom was rubbing down Sir Robert's horse, which meant his master was returned and no doubt dining with the Earl. Strolling absently past the paddock, he thought of his struggle in the grass with Anthony Poole, only four days ago, and the way events had turned about since. As he walked up the grassy slope towards the falconer's hut, two riders appeared suddenly on the ridge above, cantering from the Downs at a leisurely pace. Presently he realized that neither had seen him, riding close together as they did, apparently in intimate conversation. He stopped by the corner of the paddock and waited until the pair drew closer . . . then stiffened as he recognized them.

One, sitting his horse in an ungainly manner, his bandaged hand clearly visible, was Lukas Kessel. The other figure was female, her full riding skirts swaying about the flanks of her thoroughbred mare – and she was laughing, a musical sound that Thomas knew at once. As he stood motionless beside the fence, he clearly saw the Lady Felice, Countess of Reigate, slide her hand along Kessel's thigh. Then leaning towards him, she offered her mouth to his kiss.

Fourteen

E arly the next morning – Friday, the sixteenth day of September – Will came home as Thomas was feeding the hawks. Not feeling inclined to indulge him, Thomas said nothing, even when he commenced a detailed account of last night's revels at the Red Bull. But when he came to the part that concerned Moll's visitor, Thomas stopped work and fixed him with a blank look.

'You seek to taunt me, or to make me jealous?' he demanded.

Will frowned. 'Nay – I sought to comfort you.'

'How so?'

'Because he – the Italian – did not spend the night with her. I know this.'

Thomas said nothing.

'It seemed to me Moll was somewhat cold towards him,' Will went on. 'Save when they sang.'

Thomas started. 'They sang together?'

The other nodded. 'As they used to, years back when he was working here. I thought this much you knew already.'

Thomas looked into Will's face, and read nothing there but friendship and concern. The man was incapable of guile. With a sigh, he said: 'I ask your pardon for my harshness. I am not myself this morning.'

Will put a hand on his shoulder. ' 'Tis Barrowhill, and its master and mistress, that do this to a man.'

'And now you have the care of all the hawks, by yourself.'

Will shrugged. 'It is no hardship. And if I have been lax of late, I will make amends. I will exercise all the birds today with the lure, and take your master's out on the Downs.'

Thomas nodded absently. The prospect of spending another

day on the false hawk, displeased him more than he liked to admit.

'Filbert was at the inn too,' Will said. He took up a besom and began sweeping up the hawks' pellets that lay scattered beneath the perches.

Thomas looked up. 'The fool? I thought he never left the Earl's quarters.'

Will grimaced. 'Mannizzi brought him. They're friends – always were. A stranger pair you never saw in your life. As for the Earl, he'd likely drunk himself to sleep.' He brightened suddenly. 'Now I recall, I've a message for you – from Mallam.'

'What does the rogue want with me now?'

'He said he would clap eyes on you soon – he comes here, to bring nags for the horse-master.'

At that, Thomas broke into a laugh. 'Then he'd best hire a brace of good horse doctors,' he said, 'and have them examine each jade from teeth to tail. Else every one will drop to its knees the moment Mallam's got his money and gone.'

No sooner had Thomas walked down to the lake, less than an hour later, than he found himself caught up in an atmosphere of gloom. A disaster had befallen those concerned with the pre- parations for the Entertainments – indeed, had befallen the entire household: the Queen, it seemed, would not be coming to Barrowhill. In fact, it was learned, she would not leave her rooms in St James's Palace, for she was in mourning for her close friend – some said, her first and only love – Robert Dudley, the Earl of Leicester.

Thomas stood among the motley group assembled by the lake shore, and heard John Broad deliver the news in sombre fashion. Leicester's death, from a fever, had occurred almost a fortnight ago but had gone unproclaimed and unnoticed by many, caught up as they were in the fear of invasion and the victory over the Armada. But Elizabeth was prostrate with grief and had shut herself away for days after, so that her servants had resorted to breaking down the door of her chamber.

Glancing about the company, Thomas saw that the darkest cloud rested on the face of Henry Barnard. All the gentleman

169

usher's plans, perhaps all his hopes, now looked as if they were about to be crushed. Thomas almost felt sympathy for the man at that moment, until the next announcement confounded everyone's expectations, even drawing gasps of astonishment.

'Yet we need not despair,' John Broad was saying, his voice raised to carry to the edges of the group, where Jaggard's men were arriving to see what the fuss was about. 'For though proper respect is due to my Lord of Leicester's memory, the nation still rejoices at our recent delivery, and merriment shall not be out of place. Hence the Entertainments will not be cancelled. His lordship will address us all in person, within the hour, as to how we are to proceed.'

There was consternation on all sides. Finch and his team of carpenters and joiners, Jonas Reed's men, Jaggard and his troop, the painters and plasterers, carters, labourers and groundsmen who had all toiled to build the great structures that were now taking shape beside the lake, began to talk among themselves. The show would go ahead, but without its royal guest – how was that to be?

The answer was not long in coming. Barely a few minutes later a small but colourful procession rode out of the stable yard, skirted the gardens and approached the lake from its south side, which was open to the fields and the Downs beyond. In the lead were the Earl's trumpeters, who blew a long blast and then a sennet as they drew near. Behind came the Earl himself, gorgeously attired and riding a fine Arabian stallion, and the Countess, mounted on the same chestnut horse Thomas had seen her ride the evening before. Close by her was Kessel, his hand still bandaged, in a formal suit of black, and then the Earl's fool on his pony, in a scarlet doublet and cap. Behind rode Sir Robert in his best cloak, a sword at his side.

The men at the lake made way, forming a deep crescent about the riders, who reined in with formal precision. Behind them, the half-built castle of plain boards was a mockery of such pomp, but the Earl paid it no attention. Instead he raised himself to his full height in the saddle and cried out: 'Good men of Barrowhill! Hear me, your lord!'

A silence fell. The Earl's voice was shrill, and though he

smiled there was the same feral look in his eyes that Thomas had seen three days ago, in the Prospect Room. And now, other eyes noticed that the stallion's reins shook in his hands, so that Henry Barnard strode forward to take the bridle and steady the high-spirited animal.

But the Earl appeared not to notice. 'You have been dismayed, as I have, by the news from London,' he called, 'no doubt thinking all your toil and devotion will come to naught. Well fear not, for the Barrowhill Pleasures, in celebration for our nation's glorious victory, shall go on as planned! Many distinguished guests are already invited, who would be grief-stricken if the Entertainment were postponed. So, let nothing slow your labours, nor diminish your joy, for all is as before!'

He paused, noticing for the first time some blank expressions on the upturned faces, then moistened his lips and cried: 'Our guests, ruled over by a noble and masked personage that ye may take as your Queen, will arrive in a body as arranged, to be welcomed by our heralds, before seating themselves for the games and the tilting, followed by feasting, music and masquing as evening draws in. At the last, our glorious climax: the sea battle, representing England's victory over Spain, will now take place at night – and let the stars gaze down in humility, for we shall outshine them!'

Jaggard's jaw dropped so sharply that those close by swore they heard it. Thomas could almost read the old soldier's thoughts: a mock battle with cannons and harquebuses was dangerous enough at the best of times, but in the dark . . .

'Moreover,' the Earl continued, 'we have been sick at heart, to learn that our subjects think badly of us for withdrawing from their company of late.'

Now, the tension in the air was palpable. Barnard, standing stiffly at the Earl's side holding his horse, kept his face impassive, as did John Broad. Jonas Reed, sitting motionless on his tall horse, turned away. But there was no mistaking the unease rippling through the small crowd of working men – not least because the Earl spoke as if he were not merely lord of Barrowhill, but its king.

'Again I say – fear not!' came the shrill command. 'For if any man dares threaten my life, let him come forward! I will hide no longer, but show myself for all to see, upon the dais beside my Queen! And let God's will be done!'

The silence that followed this climax was intense but brief, for Barnard suddenly let go the horse's bridle and began clapping his hands. Others followed swiftly, one or two even managing a cheer, and then everyone else joined in so that quickly the lakeside rang with loud applause, as no doubt the Earl expected. Filbert the fool, rising to the occasion, leapt up on his horse's saddle and executed a few shaky somersaults, then stood feet astride, beating his palms together. Only Sir Robert, who had sat his horse with eyes downcast, and Kessel and the Countess, remained still and silent.

'Wednesday shall be the first day of our Entertainment,' the Earl cried as the applause subsided. 'Hence, all must be in readiness by Monday next, when rehearsals take place. Each of you has his part – and I know none will fail us. God bless you all!'

And seizing the reins, he wheeled his horse abruptly and rode away, his trumpeters spurring their mounts forward to overtake him. The rest of the party followed behind in more stately fashion, Sir Robert bringing up the rear. The Countess, Thomas thought, had remained subdued throughout the entire business. There seemed little doubt that it was she who would pose on the dais as the substitute queen. He watched until they had rounded the garden wall and disappeared, then turned to look at the faces about him. Nobody spoke, but an air of dismay hung like mist over the lake, as each man began to return slowly to his appointed task. Soon the noise of sawing and hammering rose once again, followed by the clatter of Jaggard's pikemen drilling beside the castle. On the water, oars poked from the sides of the Spanish galley, which was almost ready for its first trials.

John Broad had stalked off, while Barnard at once became busy with his drawings, calling Finch over for another discourse about loopholes and embrasures. Thomas walked back to the site of the hawk's construction, and found Mannizzi there.

The mason must have been at the rear of the crowd, for he had seen no sign of him. The two men exchanged nods. When Thomas gazed at the huge skeleton, which was now nearing completion, Mannizzi broke the silence.

'You are fortunate, sir, to be but an adviser here, like me,' he murmured with a little smile. 'We need not dirty our hands.'

'I would rather dirty mine,' Thomas answered, 'and be about my proper work. I am too old for toys, no matter how splendid they may be.'

Mannizzi peered at the falconer with his dark eyes. 'You deem yourself above such frivolity,' he said.

'Nay – each to his craft,' Thomas replied. 'Mine is the care of hawks.'

An invisible spark passed between the two men, though quite what occasioned it was uncertain. Watching Mannizzi, Thomas saw no hint of jealousy in the man's eyes, and felt sure that Moll had told him nothing of their relations. There was, however, more than mere polite interest on the part of the mason.

'Any man who saw you while the Earl was making his speech, might read how you feel,' he said after a moment.

Thomas raised an eyebrow. 'And what is your feeling, master Mannizzi?'

'About what, signor?'

'About this fine enterprise on which we are engaged.'

The other gave a slight lift of his shoulder. 'I am a hired artisan, who must go where the purse is offered.'

'You mean to say you had no choice in the matter?' Thomas asked.

Mannizzi seemed to consider, before answering: 'A man always has choices, signor falconer.'

'Aye – so perhaps you had other reasons for returning to Barrowhill.'

Mannizzi was now looking intently at him. 'I had not thought we were at fencing,' he said gently. 'Yet I did feel your *stoccata* just then. Must I make with my *pararla*?'

Thomas did not react, but the other smiled and added: 'Perhaps even you are falling prey to the corrupting air of this place.'

'How is that so?'

Mannizzi's smile remained intact. 'Where I come from even a child may smell villainy, as he also learns the scent of death.'

Aware of the quickening of his heartbeat, Thomas said: 'And I wonder if you know more of what has taken place here than you may admit.'

Mannizzi frowned slightly. 'Now you make your *punta*,' he said, 'yet still I do not know why. You will understand if I take my leave, before I am obliged to meet your charging blow.'

He walked off unhurriedly towards the castle. Thomas watched him go, deep in thought, then became aware that a silence had fallen about him. Looking round, he saw that the joiners had stopped work on the hawk's skeleton and were watching him.

'Pay me no mind,' he said. 'I am out of humour this morning.'

One of the men snorted. 'Are not we all, falconer? Breaking our backs to be ready by Monday – and for what?'

Thomas shook his head.

Yet the preparations rolled on. The next day, Saturday, Thomas watched the two fighting ships being put through their paces. The Spanish galley was propelled by sixteen oars, and everyone from prentices and stable-boys to kitchen servants had been pressed into service as oarsmen. The English vessel, with its masts and sails, demanded a different range of skills for which only sailors were suited. So Jonas Reed, the best horseman in Barrowhill, had ridden hard to London the previous afternoon and returned late at night with half a dozen rogues from Limehouse and Wapping, eager not merely for the small purse that was offered but the chance to drink anything wet, steal anything portable and make lewd advances toward anything female. Jaggard's men gripped their pikes and stood on the shoreline, eyeing these sunburned interlopers grimly.

Meanwhile the hawk was nearing completion, as was the giant steed, almost twenty feet high. After the tilting and feats of horsemanship, the huge animal was to approach the nobles in the pavilion, lower its massive head and open its mouth, out of which would tumble sweets and comfits as well as gifts for the ladies. Beneath its caparison, a team of four men worked the cumbersome creature: one in the neck; the others below to move it along and guide it.

The grand pavilion for the seated guests, with a canopy against the weather and a raised dais at the forefront, was being built on the lake's eastern shore. It would be hung with cloths of arras and strewn with rushes. To the south, the sward was wide and flat enough for the tilting to take place, while further around the lake, to the south-west, stood the false covert from which the great hawk would fly across the water on its cables. On the west, directly opposite the spectators, was the castle, its walls painted grey and beginning at last to resemble stonework. Between the castle and the pavilion, the Spanish and English vessels would do battle on the lake, the English supported by caliver and cannon-fire from the fort, with many a flash of sulphur and brimstone. After a suitably stirring encounter the Spanish galley would lose the fight, and once its occupants had got safely away a small charge would be set off, blowing a hole in the vessel's hull so that she sank.

It was a bold undertaking, Thomas had to admit, and as the day drew to its close there was a growing sense of achievement, and of hope, that perhaps if things went well in the days to come the Earl might be restored to his former humour, and all might share somehow in the success of the enterprise. Already it had had the desired effect of pushing the fearful business of the murders out of mind, everyone from the Earl himself to the humblest kitchen boy being caught up in the excitement. Noble guests were expected from across the county as well as from London – among them many of those who had taken themselves away but a week ago, following the funeral of Lady Deverell. Most surprising of all, however, was the Earl's announcement that plain folk from the Downs and the farms about, and even from Tadworth village, would be allowed into Barrowhill on the evening of the Sea Battle, to share in the celebrations of England's glorious victory. Such a thing had not happened since the time of the Earl's father.

Among those who expressed unease at the Earl's blatant

courting of popularity, was Hugh Jaggard. 'I am not a hydra,' he growled, 'but a millipede, that must now run in ten directions at once!'

On Sunday, though morning prayers had taken place as usual, there was no sabbath respite for those at the lakeside. Jaggard, Thomas and others stood in the grey, windy morning, watching the sailors struggling to raise sail on the English man-of-war. From the Spanish galley came the muttering of oarsmen who would much rather be on dry land.

Reed, the horse-master, was riding past and heard Jaggard's remark. 'Mayhap you'd like to 'ave care of three score extra mounts,' he snorted, 'with 'alf your stable lads gone to be shipmen!'

'At least your horses don't bellyache from dawn till dusk,' Jaggard retorted, 'nor do they get soused and fall to fighting.' He glanced round at the company in general. 'I fear a battle of a different sort before Wednesday, with real heads broken.'

Reed, even more surly than usual this morning, jerked his reins and rode off. Finch, the mild-mannered carpenter, spoke up. 'It's not a brawl I fear, so much as accident. We've had too little time to build the castle and the steed, let alone ready the vessels. If some joint do split, or pin sheer off, who knows what may befall those engaged in a battle in the dark?'

Nobody had an answer to that. Just then, there came a shout from across the lake, and Thomas saw Sir Robert riding towards him. Leaving the other men, he walked around the south shore, glad of the opportunity to speak with his master again.

Sir Robert dismounted, and led his horse away towards the Downland path so that Thomas might walk beside him. Each had little in the way of news that was not already known to the other. But to Thomas's enquiry about the Countess playing the part of the Queen, his master responded with a bitter laugh.

'Is it not fitting? He to indulge his every whim, even pretending that the real sovereign has come to shower glory on his enterprise; she to play the part of a queen, when all about know her for a harlot!'

Thomas did not react. But if Sir Robert regretted speaking

176

his mind so forcibly this morning, he did not show it. Perhaps the Earl's proclamation of yesterday had sickened him, for suddenly he burst out: 'I am weary of them all – weary of this show, and of this place! I yearn for the tranquillity of Petbury.' He threw Thomas a glance. 'As no doubt, do you.'

Thomas nodded, and his master continued: 'This new-found courage of his lordship's, to offer himself freely as a target, is but a sham. He will be surrounded by guards, so that any who draw near him shall be marked.'

'I had guessed as much, sir,' Thomas replied. 'But may it not serve to flush out the killer, as you wished?'

Sir Robert lowered his gaze, saying: 'I fear that *Vindex Reginae* is long departed from here, and that the murders will never be solved.'

Thomas hesitated, then said: 'I still harbour doubts concerning Mannizzi.'

'You have spoken with him?'

'Aye, and found him close as a whelk in its shell. And I hear he dislikes Kessel – for what reason, I know not.'

At that, Sir Robert gave a snort. 'I would guess the reason, for it is easy enough. He despises the Countess, and hence all men who dally with her.'

Thomas showed his surprise. 'I had not thought it common knowledge—'

'Nothing that goes on at Barrowhill lies hidden for long,' Sir Robert interrupted. 'And the Lady Felice grows bold, caring little for discretion.' He frowned to himself. 'Meanwhile her husband lives in terror of every shadow. A servant lies in his chamber every night, armed with a caliver, and another sits outside the door. And before you ask, he has had the chimney shaft boarded, but not bricked up. He will not do so, for I learn that he was the artificer of the network of tunnels. It is his means of escape.'

'From what?' Thomas asked, but his master merely shrugged.

'A man with his hand in so many enterprises may have good cause to fear for his life.'

Thinking of the Dutch murders now, and all that van Velsen

177

had told him, Thomas said: 'For this reason if no other, I believe the killer is still at hand. Indeed, I feel it is so.'

Sir Robert glanced at him, then looked away. They stood near the falcons' mews, gazing down at the paddock, which held a growing number of horses by the day. Several of the Earl's closest neighbours had arrived early, in readiness for the Entertainments. Some would go hunting the next day and some hawking, Sir Robert told him, which caused Thomas to frown again.

'Tomorrow is the first day of rehearsal, when I am to help make the great hawk fly.'

His master's face softened, and bore the hint of a smile.

'Then you shall be excused your duties, for nothing must come in the way of the fledgling's first flight.'

Thomas sighed. Behind him the mews was quiet: Will was exercising falcons on the Downs. Gazing past the paddock towards the stable yard, he grew aware of a commotion: loud voices, hoofbeats, and dust rising above the rooftops. Sir Robert noticed it too, and said: 'I would guess the dealers have arrived, with the extra mounts Reed wanted.'

A figure appeared below the paddock in a rough jerkin and hat, leading a sturdy brown horse. As Thomas watched, another man pointed him towards the falconers' hut, at which the fellow peered upwards in Thomas's direction, then waved cheerfully.

Sir Robert threw him a questioning look, which Thomas answered with a wry expression. 'Mallam,' he muttered.

That night, against his better judgement, Thomas joined a group that set off across the Downs into Tadworth.

Jaggard and his 'regulars' were at the forefront, with Will Holland, Ben Mallam, Thomas and a handful of Barrowhill men behind. While Thomas and Will had other reasons for going to the Red Bull, the rest were bent on the drowning of sorrows and, perhaps, the settling of scores, for it was known that the sailors had disappeared immediately after sunset in search of similar diversions. What this Sunday night might bring, Thomas did not like to dwell on, save that there would likely be a number of sore heads in the morning for the grand rehearsal.

As they drew near the inn, Thomas found his heart thudding. He had little idea how warm, or otherwise, his welcome might be. For all he knew, Mannizzi was here already, for he had seen nothing of the man since suppertime. Indeed, there were now so many new faces at Barrowhill, drafted in to help with the Entertainment, that it was possible to take a meal surrounded by strangers. The kitchens, wash-house, buttery and brewery were overflowing with servants, while horsemen and grooms came and went between the stables and paddock. In this mêlée, keeping an eye peeled for anyone suspicious was impossible, and he felt some sympathy for Jaggard, who threw open the Red Bull's door and marched in, calling for the strongest ale in the house, and plenty of it.

As Thomas found a bench and lowered himself on to it, Moll appeared.

There was a brief, private smile between them, before she put on her innkeeper's face, bidding every man welcome and sending the drawer hurrying off. Will Holland had disappeared in search of Doreth, and Thomas found himself seated opposite Ben Mallam, as he had been once before . . . could it be less than a fortnight ago?

Yet, there are times for reflection, and times for merriment, and Thomas was glad to slake the thirst that the day's service at Barrowhill had given him. The first mug of ale barely touched the sides of his gullet. The second followed almost as fast. By the end of the third, he began to enjoy Mallam's tales of the jingler's art, and was calling for another jug.

'Jesu, Thomas,' Ben breathed, banging his mug down, 'the Earl's Pleasures are the talk of Surrey. Every knave with a spavined nag to sell is bent on doing business here. I envy not yon horse-master, even if he do have a prigger's tongue and a northman's stinginess, for he must needs double his wits to find out their tricks.'

Thomas grinned and took another drink. The noise of the crowd filled his ears, and the room swam a little. How long is it since I have been drunk? he asked himself . . . was it so far back

179

as his time in the Low Countries, when any man would drink himself into a stupor to blot out the horrors of battle?

He realized Mallam was addressing him.

'That whoreson Jaggard will have a fight on his hands before long,' the jingler said, with a smile of anticipation. 'Folk here are possessive of their women – even a cross-biting old stale like Madge. Does he think he's her only client?'

Thomas looked round to a table where Jaggard's men, already drunk, were cheering on one of their number who was engaged in arm-wrestling with a local man. Jaggard himself was balanced precariously on a rickety stool, a mug in one hand, the other fumbling at the skirts of Madge Clapperdaw, who sat on his lap.

'That's old soldiers for you,' Thomas said, then noticed three or four young village men, standing some feet away with hard expressions. 'Fools,' he muttered. 'They'll get naught for their pains but broken heads, if they tangle with him.'

Mallam grinned. 'Might be worth a wager, though. Are you in?'

Thomas shook his head and took another drink. A loud cheer rang out from the corner, followed by the beating of fists on tables: Jaggard's man had apparently won the bout. Thomas tilted his mug to the ceiling, then glanced around and saw that some minutes had passed, apparently without his knowledge, for both Jaggard and Madge had disappeared. So had the group of young men who were watching them. An alarm bell rang, somewhere in the back of his mind, but he was uncertain what it portended. He raised his mug and found it empty. Then he decided the feeling of urgency stemmed from his bladder, and got to his feet.

'The jakes,' he mumbled, but Ben Mallam was engaged in animated conversation with a man at his side, and did not hear.

His head swimming, Thomas pushed his way through the throng, found the door and got himself outside, where the cool night air hit him in the face like a douse of water. Unsteadily he walked round the side of the inn, seeking a spot where a man might make water in peace and comfort. Somewhere nearby, he heard the clatter of a horse's hooves, but paid it no mind. From

180

within, the din of the Red Bull crowd carried undiminished. He rounded the yard wall and walked past Moll's stable, fumbling with his breeches. There was a dungheap against the wall, its ammonia stench rising in his nostrils. He paused, blinking in the darkness, for there was something else against the wall, too: a pale shape, motionless, but with some momentum, or even memory of movement about it, as if it had only now fallen down, or . . .

He froze, sobering up as he stood. The clothing was torn, so that the pale torso was exposed. And even before the sickening smell rose in his gorge, overpowering even that of the dungheap, he saw the dark wash of blood that glittered in the starlight, almost covering the lower part of the body of Madge Clapperdaw.

Fifteen

The death would be concealed, of course: for nothing must overshadow the Barrowhill Pleasures. This much became clear in the hours that followed.

First Thomas had gone back into the inn and found Jaggard, sitting at the table with his men, mug in hand, the picture of innocence. But at sight of Thomas's face he was alert at once, rose immediately and followed him outside. When they reached the fearful sight in the yard he staggered, turned aside and retched.

'Good Christ, I was with her but a short while ago . . .' He swung his gaze sharply at Thomas. 'You think I did this?!'

Thomas's head was reeling. The faces of possible murderers danced before his eyes, only to be summarily dismissed: Mallam? He was in the inn, was he not? Jaggard's men, too. Will Holland? Incredible. Mannizzi? He shook his head, not wanting to confront that possibility yet. Which still left Jaggard – and the young men who had followed him and Madge out.

'Those village men . . .' he muttered, but Jaggard shook his head. 'I faced them down, smacked one about the ear. They took off – they were but boys.' He rested his hands on his knees, breathing heavily, then raised himself to his full height.

'Thomas: meet my eye, soldier to soldier, and tell me you think I am capable of this.'

Thomas looked, read the alarm in the other man's gaze – and something he had not seen before: fear. Even a man like Jaggard could be afraid. 'Nay,' he said at last. 'I do not think so.'

Jaggard exhaled deeply, took an unsteady step forward and peered down at the body. 'Poor old callett,' he muttered. 'She

did her last bit of business against that same wall, with me . . .'
He wiped a hand across his mouth. 'The whoreson must have
been watching! But who would rend her so – like a wild dog?!'

He turned away, but Thomas started suddenly, and bent
down to look. At first he had thought it merely a fold of Moll's
clothing – now he saw, and plucked it from about her neck: a
scrap of paper, with words dimly visible upon it – not written
with a quill, but scrawled, seemingly with a knifepoint, in her
blood.

Jaggard was staring. 'Another . . .!' He turned sharply and
slammed his first against the wall, grunting with the pain he
caused himself. 'Here, under our noses! God's heart, I'll find the
devil, and when I do . . .'

Thomas, cold sober now, grasped him by the shoulder.
'Enough! We must act. Borrow a horse and ride fast to Barrow-
hill, find my master . . . mayhap you'd better tell Broad, and
Barnard too.'

Jaggard nodded, breathing deeply. 'You . . .?'

'I'll stay with her,' Thomas answered. As an afterthought he
added: 'You'd better find mistress Moll first, and tell her . . .
bid her keep folk away from the yard.'

Glad to have some course of action, Jaggard nodded and
hurried off. In the minutes he was alone with the body, Thomas
steeled himself to look more closely at it. Little examination
was needed, however, to confirm his first impression: that
Madge had been savagely stabbed, many times, in the chest,
stomach and abdomen, with a sharp blade. Mercifully, she
appeared to have died quickly, perhaps from a deep wound to
the heart. He knelt down and felt the body: it was still
lukewarm.

A moment later came footsteps, and Moll rounded the inn
wall, walking quickly. Thomas moved to stay her, then stopped
in his tracks. Behind, walked Niccolo Mannizzi.

There was a short silence. Clearly nobody else knew what had
happened, for the noise from inside the inn continued unabated. Moll stared at Thomas, then caught sight of the blood-
drenched corpse, and put her hand to her mouth. Mannizzi
came forward, placing an arm about her.

'Master Jaggard . . .' Thomas began, then stopped: hoof-beats rang on the cobbles, then galloped off through the village.

'He has taken my horse,' Mannizzi said. His sharp eyes fell upon the paper in Thomas's hand, but he said nothing.

Thomas fixed him with a hard look. 'Where were you, in the past half hour?' he asked.

This time the silence was even shorter, and it was Moll who broke it. 'He was in my chamber,' she said.

Less than an hour later a terse discourse took place in the darkness, only a short way from the body, which was now covered with a horse blanket. Sir Robert, Jaggard, John Broad and Henry Barnard had ridden in together. Jaggard had called his men out, and they formed a none-too-sober but subdued guard some distance away, preventing access to the yard.

Briefly, Thomas gave an account of his discovery, remembering to mention that he had heard someone riding away a short time before. For his part, the disgraced Jaggard could add little except for admitting that he had been with the village whore only minutes before she was murdered.

'By the Lord, and you shall suffer for it!' It was Barnard's harsh voice that rang out. The man was furious: this was the last thing he, or anyone else, wanted to happen at such a time, with important guests flocking to Barrowhill for the Entertainment . . .

'Not now.' It was John Broad, wrapped in a heavy cloak against the night air, and looking like a feeble old man. 'We have work to do – the body must be removed for burial. The Earl—'

'The Earl must not hear of it!' Barnard snapped. 'We all know his lordship is unnerved by the earlier killings – in any case, this need have no link to the deaths of Sir George and Sir Thomas! The woman was a common drab—'

'Who has been stabbed in the same manner as Lady Deverell.'

All eyes turned to Sir Robert, who had been silent until now. Turning to Thomas, his master said: 'I believe you may have

184

found something on the body – something you chose not to mention?'

Thomas met his master's eye, and realized for some reason he had decided to take all of them into his confidence. With a brief nod, he produced the paper and held it out.

Sir Robert took it in his gloved hand. 'Have we taper, or tinder-box?' he enquired.

Jaggard struck a light and held it up. After a moment Broad stepped forward, peered at the poorly formed words and shuddered.

'"*Vindex Reginae*",' he said quietly.

'And the rest of the message?' Sir Robert's face was gaunt in the dim light.

'"*Perite Scelesti*" once again – "Perish, ye wicked". And . . .' Broad frowned. 'The other words are not Latin. They read: "She whored on the sabbath".'

There were intakes of breath, even muttered oaths, from the assembled men. Barnard, becoming aware that there were matters here which others understood better than he, looked if anything, even angrier. Jaggard hung his head. Only Sir Robert, and despite his frailty John Broad, would summon enough authority to take matters in hand.

'Who else knows of this?' Sir Robert asked Thomas.

'The innkeeper, mistress Perrott. And Mannizzi, the stone-mason. He was with her, and now comforts her.'

He kept emotion out of his voice, and when Sir Robert looked hard at him, merely added: 'I believe he was with her at the time this murder took place.'

There were mutterings. This time Jaggard spoke up. 'Half of Tadworth is in the inn, Sir Robert,' he murmured. 'Along with some from Barrowhill. Anyone might have slipped away, waited for . . . for me to leave, and . . .' He faltered, then drew breath: 'Even the painter was here earlier, so I heard . . .'

'Kessel?' Barnard glared at him. 'You seek to throw suspicion on him now – even though he was almost a victim himself?'

Jaggard opened his mouth to answer, but it was John Broad who cut him short. 'It is not the time to seek the culprit. As soon as I return, I will speak privately with her ladyship, who must

185

decide what will be done. In the meantime, wrap the body and put it on a horse, take it to Barrowhill and conceal it.'

He glanced around the company, his eyes resting on Sir Robert. 'Unless any man has a better course?'

Sir Robert shook his head. And so it seemed, for the present, the matter was settled. While Jaggard spoke quietly to his men, Broad and Barnard walked off to their horses with scarcely a glance at each other. Sir Robert walked to his, indicating to Thomas that he should draw close. When they stood beside the stirrup, Sir Robert murmured: 'It seems you were right – but not about Mannizzi.'

Thomas merely nodded, and watched his master climb into the saddle. The emptiness he felt inside he could not explain, even to Sir Robert. And it had little to do with the murder of poor Madge Clapperdaw, who had sat on his lap and pouted at him with her painted lips the first time he had set foot in the Red Bull.

Monday morning came, a day of cold drizzle – and the first day set aside for rehearsals.

Thomas had barely slept, turn about as he might, so that when Will roused him at dawn he walked heavily round to the back of the hut, took a pail and poured cold water over his head. To Will's wry comments about excess of ale, he merely nodded in acquiescence. It seemed that Moll had told no one about the murder, nor did Thomas wish to speak of it. Stuffing a hunk of stale bread in his mouth, he walked down to the lake.

There was much bustle, though little order, among the assembled men, and he was content to throw himself into the work, trying to drive last night's events from his thoughts. Already the sailors had rigged the man-of-war but were having difficulty hoisting sail from her narrow deck, while the stable-lads mustered in a sleepy-eyed group beside the moored galley, an unlikely bunch of fighting Spaniards. The giant steed, covered with rain-soaked sheets, stood lifeless beside the tilt-yard. The covert in which the great hawk was concealed had been completed the previous night, and rose some yards back from the waterside, an ungainly structure of poles and branches from which two heavy cables emerged. The cables extended across the edge of the lake towards the grand pavilion, where they ended fixed to two heavy posts sunk deep in the ground and strengthened with stanchions. When the time came for the hawk to fly, the covert would collapse at the cutting of several cords, and the exposed bird's huge wings, which were hinged and folded, would be spread out. Thomas and others would then guide the bird from beneath along cables greased with lard, to which it was fixed on hidden runners, and push it so that – in theory – it would glide smoothly over the water and halt in front of the pavilion. Theory, however, was found to be a fickle jade; for as soon as the hawk had broken free of its cover and spread its wings it moved but a few inches, then refused to move any further.

There was cursing and swearing, and much kicking at posts and shaking of cables, but still the bird hung motionless in the air, its carved wooden beak flapping open in mockery of the hapless artisans below. Thomas stood among them, heavy of heart, and did not even look round when a voice behind him said: 'She needs a prey to tempt her.'

'She needs a fire up her fundament,' said Sawyer, the under-gardener who had been put in charge of flying the hawk. 'For a farthing I'd set light to her myself.'

'That would be shame, for she looks very fine,' came the reply. Thomas turned about and saw Lukas Kessel, his bandaged hand half inside his doublet, watching from a few yards away.

The two men's eyes met. But whatever thoughts lay hidden behind the painter's slight smile, no man could read. With a gesture towards the suspended hawk, he said: 'May I offer assistance?'

Thomas shrugged, but Sawyer waved him forward. 'If there is aught you can do, master,' he said, 'we shall be in your debt.'

'It is a matter of balance, I think,' Kessel said. 'Too much weight on body and tail, not enough displaced to the wings. Tie something on to the pinions, and she will glide.'

Seeing the sense of his words, Thomas was nodding. Sawyer sent a boy running for lumps of broken stone from the castle plot, while others hunted around for lengths of cord. In a short time the hawk's wings were weighted, and men stood holding them on either side, ready for the signal.

'Why not take yourself round the lake, and see how she looks?' Sawyer suggested. Thomas turned to the painter.

'Will you walk with me, master Kessel?'

'Gladly,' came the reply, and both men set off around the lake shore. A few minutes later, having walked in silence, they approached the grand pavilion, its sides now brightly painted. There came a shout from Sawyer. Thomas halted and waved a hand to show he was ready.

There was now a growing sense of expectation, and men had stopped work at other points about the lake to watch. Heads appeared above the walls of the castle and at the sides of the fighting vessels riding at anchor. Despite the events of last night Thomas felt a rising of his spirits as he gazed at the mighty hawk, her magnificent wings spread wide, and took some pride in the fact that he had helped to shape her. From a distance, she was real.

Sawyer shouted a command, and his men started to run beneath the cables, arms aloft, heaving the great bird forward. There came a creak of timbers, and a hiss of greased rope in the horn runners. The hawk's wings shook, then drooped slightly, her body lifted . . . and a mighty cheer rose from all sides, as Sawyer's men halted by the edge of the lake and let go – for the hawk was in flight!

Steadily she glided out across the water, her fan-like tail splayed out, and slowly gained momentum, for the cables sagged in the middle before rising again as they approached the pavilion. Like some giant creature from ancient myth, wings vibrating, the hawk passed within a few yards of the delighted galley oarsmen, who waved their caps and shouted, as did the sailors on the man-of-war. On she flew towards the eastern shore, still gaining speed, so that a sense of alarm gripped the onlookers, fearing now that she was too heavy and would overshoot her target. But to palpable relief, the hawk began to slow as the cables rose again, until finally, to universal delight, she came to a halt before the dais, lurched slightly as the runners locked against the end stops, and hung suspended, her huge wings shuddering.

Thomas breathed a great sigh, and found that he was smiling. Beside him, Kessel, clearly moved by the event, was gazing in silence. All about the lake was cheering and shouting, while Sawyer's men could be seen in a jubilant group, engaged in mutual slapping of thighs and thumping of backs.

'Remarkable,' Kessel murmured, standing at Thomas's elbow. 'A man can be proud of this achievement.'

'I thank you,' Thomas answered. From the house came a sudden blast of trumpets. All eyes turned in the direction of the stable yard, and all hearts sank.

But this morning it was not the Earl who was come to view the rehearsals, but the Lady Felice, on a golden-brown horse, with several ladies riding alongside her. As the group rounded the pavilion the Countess saw Thomas and Kessel, and reined in some yards away. Both men plucked their caps off and bowed, then met the icy stare of their mistress, chief guest of honour of the Entertainments, and substitute queen.

'Here you are again, falconer,' the Countess said, ignoring Kessel and favouring Thomas with an indulgent smile. 'Indeed, it seems you are everywhere nowadays, does it not?'

Thomas swallowed, imagining that she had been told of last night's discoveries. Having no ready answer, he merely inclined his head, aware that she was staring at him pointedly and not at her portrait-painter. Shifting her gaze abruptly, she took in the mighty hawk on its cables, though remaining unimpressed.

'A pretty toy,' she murmured. 'Is it large enough, do you think, to lift a man and carry him off – for ever?'

Both men must have showed surprise, for she laughed, at which her ladies quickly followed suit: a high-pitched, musical chorus which drew the attention of every man about the lake, while Thomas and Kessel could only stand their ground. The moment went on too long, however – and now Thomas sensed an intent on the part of the Countess: she was humiliating Kessel. From the corner of his eye he saw the painter struggle to conceal his discomfort, while the ladies sat their horses and mocked him.

Finally, it was over. Without another glance at the two men, the Countess shook her reins and trotted away in the direction of the castle, pointing out the sights to her companions. Kessel watched her go, then dropped his gaze. When he looked up again, he met Thomas's eye, and winced.

'We never did have our talk about—' He broke off and nodded towards the distant bulk of Barrowhill. 'Now I think we never shall – for it has no meaning.' He took a deep breath. 'Nothing here has meaning, falconer. I came, and was imprisoned by its splendour, by its beauty . . . yet I was as a fool, who knows not when he is merely drunk. All is surface, and all is displayed but to flaunt its owner's wealth, for ultimate profit . . . in such a world, evil will always find entry. And then, no man can know what follows.'

He started to move away, then stopped short as if some thought had just struck him. When he turned and came back to Thomas, his face had relaxed.

'Indeed, I have been a great fool, to tarry here like a lapdog, performing antics for my supper while my hand is healing . . . soon I will paint again – yet not the portrait that lies covered in my chambers. Let some other lapdog finish it.'

He held out his left hand, and Thomas took it awkwardly, realizing the man had made an important decision. Their eyes met.

'I believe I have misjudged you, master Kessel,' he said.

Kessel smiled. 'If so, I did deserve it. Mayhap one day our ways will cross again, and I will paint your falcons, for they are less proud than their masters.'

Then he half-raised his bandaged hand and walked away, quickening his pace as he rounded the pavilion. He would be gone, Thomas knew, before nightfall.

That afternoon, spirits having risen considerably with the knowledge that the great hawk, at least, would not disappoint, attention turned to horses, in particular to the giant steed.

The tiltyard, a grassy rectangle on the south side of the lake below the pavilion, had now been cordoned off, and a wooden fence erected along its centre line. Though this was no full-

190

blown tournament – for nothing would rival the Queen's Accession Day tilts, held in November – there were enough young gallants among the guests to put on a good show, and interest was growing. After the nobles and gentry had jousted, medieval fashion (though these days no serious injury was expected), a quintain would be set up for humbler folk to try their luck. Some of the Barrowhill men agreed to take part, especially since wagers were in the offing.

Thomas took his dinner with Jaggard, then walked back to the lake, where a small crowd was gathering. The ex-soldier had kept himself busy during the morning, training his scratch gun crew while his more trusted corporals drilled the ragbag company of pikemen. Neither man spoke about last night, nor did Thomas ask where Madge's body had been hidden. It was almost as if, like the other, grander victims of *Vindex Reginae*, she had never existed.

As they arrived, grooms were riding mounts back and forth in the tiltyard, and watching them on horseback was Jonas Reed, the horse-master. Seeing Thomas and Jaggard, he rode forward, reined in and looked down at them from the saddle. 'I hear there was murder done last night,' he said. When neither man replied, he went on: 'The same devilish spirit that struck before, both here and on the Downs.'

Thomas said nothing. Finally, meeting the man's questioning glance, Jaggard answered: 'It's likely there was no connection. She was a village drab, that fell foul of some wicked cove and his twisted desires . . .'

Reed snorted. 'You do not believe that, goodman Jaggard, any more than I. You'll not treat me as a fool.'

Jaggard looked away, and Reed's gaze fell on Thomas. 'It appears to me, falconer,' he mused, 'that ye are privy to much that's known only to my master's high servants. A man might wonder what special parts you possess, to make you so popular.'

Thomas raised an eyebrow. 'I serve my master, Sir Robert Vicary, and do his bidding alone,' he answered.

Reed's lip puckered in a sneer. 'Then have a care, now that the Dutchman's fallen from grace, you are not bidden to serve another.' And seeing the double meaning was lost on neither man, the horse-master clicked his tongue and cantered off.

'God's heart, I'd like to take a tilt at that whoreson javel,' Jaggard muttered, then spat. 'Come to that, I'd take a tilt at anyone. Mayhap I should seek a means to vent my ill humour.' And straightening his shoulders, he marched off towards the castle, from where the barked commands of his corporals could be heard.

Having no further duties at the lake, Thomas thought of stealing away to look in on the falcons. But at that moment a group of riders appeared, trotting towards the tiltyard, his master among them.

For some reason Sir Robert was in a better humour than Thomas expected. He left the other men and drew close, saying: 'I hear the great hawk has made a wondrous flight. Did she lift your hopes along with her?'

'She did, sir,' Thomas replied. In a lower tone he added: 'I spoke with Kessel – he is leaving Barrowhill.'

When his master frowned slightly he added: 'He is no murderer, I am certain of it.'

Sir Robert's face cleared. 'I did not truly believe he was,' he replied. 'Yet I know we must consider no man above suspicion.' He sighed. 'Last night's bloody deed appears to me as wicked as any of them. What threat was that poor rivelled drab to anyone?'

Thomas shook his head, trying to ignore the feeling of gloom that came upon him. 'I fear the trail is cold,' he said. 'It appears now that *Vindex* does not merely stalk the Dutch and their allies, but sees himself as a champion of the sabbath.'

'Or a defender of chastity,' Sir Robert finished, with a wry look. 'Yet no Puritan would act as he has done: rather a Papist fanatic – one who saw the Spanish threat as a ray of hope.'

When Thomas frowned, his master added: 'Yet would even the most fanatical of Papists stoop to such blood-letting? It is the work of a diseased spirit – a savage.'

'A savage who writes Latin,' Thomas murmured.

Sir Robert looked away, shook the reins and rode off.

Thomas waited until he was out of sight, seeking a moment

to take his leave, when there came a great shouting and stirring from out on the lake: the Spanish galley and the English man-of-war were about to do battle.

Every eye turned in their direction: Jaggard's soldiers, the painters putting their last touches to the pavilion, Sawyer's men who had hauled the great hawk back to her covert, Reed's stable-lads struggling to manoeuvre the giant steed into position – all stopped work to watch. And the events that followed exceeded every man's expectations – even if they did not go entirely to plan.

The rehearsal started well. First there came a trumpet blast from the castle – one of the Earl's trumpeters being seconded for the purpose – followed by the loud report of Jaggard's culverin. At the signal, the 'Spaniards' began straining at their oars, even managing to whip up a small wake from their vessel's prow. The man-of-war, meanwhile, had hoisted sail and came proudly forward, her small cannon making a red flash as it fired its blank charge. There was shouting from both crews, and men stood on deck brandishing fake swords. It was a splendid sight: the English pennant floating in the breeze from the topmast of the man-of-war, while the galley sported a red-and-gold Spanish standard. And as watchers clustered eagerly along the lake shore, the two fighting ships joined in combat.

This much was planned, for the lake was neither deep nor wide, and neither vessel could build enough speed for any serious damage to occur. Nevertheless the collision came as a shock, the crack of timbers audible on every side. The man-of-war, her specially raised decks towering above the hapless galley, had the clear advantage, and along with the firing of blank rounds and rattling of swords and bucklers, now came the derisive laughter of the professional sailors, followed by a stream of insults. The 'Spaniards' retaliated in kind, and presently missiles began to fly between the two ships: first balls of wadding and rags, hastily dipped over the side and soaked, then sticks and chunks of wood – and finally a large stone, which flew from the man-of-war and caught one of the leading oarsmen on the shoulder. His cry of pain and surprise echoed across the water.

Thomas was watching intently, his heart beginning to quicken. Others shared his unease, and there was a growing restlessness along the shore. At the castle, Jaggard's soldiers came clattering down the wooden steps.

On the lake, things got rapidly out of hand. Both vessels were seemingly locked together, though whether by accident or design no one was certain. But the next moment, matters became clearer when a grappling hook soared through the air and lodged itself in the galley's hull with a thud. All movement on the man-of-war was now about her foredeck, where ropes quickly appeared. And at once the sailors' intentions were revealed: they were about to board the galley.

This was not part of the design. The first to react was Jaggard, who came to the lake shore, waving his arms. Jonas Reed rode his mount into the shallows, shouting at both crews to stop. All was in vain: out in the middle of the lake where no man could prevent them, the English and Spanish crews commenced to fight each other – and no semblance of play-acting remained. The sailors, unpopular from the start, had seemingly been saving their resentment until such time as they could give it free rein – and the time was now, with no Earl and Countess, noble guests or official spectators within sight. The Barrowhill landsmen, for their part, not one of whom had wanted to be a Spaniard in the first instance, vented their own anger on the ready-made foe.

Mercifully the battle was short-lived, but it was long enough to wreak havoc. The sailors swung themselves on to the galley, where their opponents struggled to defend themselves as the boat swayed from side to side. Now weapons, hitherto concealed, were quickly in view: spars, short cudgels, lengths of knotted rope. For their part the landsmen had to make do with oars, too long to wield effectively, and the wooden swords with which Jaggard had provided them for safety's sake. Soon the galley was rocking dangerously, while the air resounded with cracks, thuds and the cries of the injured. It was quickly evident, however, that the hardened sailors from the Thameside taverns, though heavily outnumbered, were well-prepared and well-armed, and had the advantage of balance. Splashes sounded across the lake as one by one the galley's crew either leaped, or were shoved into the water. Finally came a raucous cheer from the man-of-war's crew, who stood triumphant in the galley, tearing down its ensign.

One by one the crestfallen Spaniards swam, waded and staggered ashore nursing cuts and bruises, some holding their heads. But it was clear that no serious hurt had been done, as both watchers and participants gathered on the lakeside, chastened but relieved. Thomas was among those who helped drag some of the winded ones out of the water, where they lay gasping and dripping on the strand, flinging curses at their assailants.

Jaggard ambled towards him, half-angry, half-amused. 'True courage cannot be denied,' he called out. 'At least it was an English victory!'

At that moment, a shaft of sunlight was caught and reflected from one of the distant windows of Barrowhill, almost dazzling Thomas. Shading his eyes, he looked up and saw that it came from the all-seeing eye of the Earl's Prospect Room.

Sixteen

Tuesday, the final day of preparations, dawned grey and damp. There had been heated recriminations the previous night, during which a furious Henry Barnard had issued several ultimata – the chief one to the sailors, that any repetition of their outrageous behaviour would result in dismissal without further payment. The galley oarsmen, by contrast, had their pay doubled as an inducement to fight on the day of the Entertainment, to which most agreed provided they did not have to practise again. Thus the matter was settled, for other rehearsals had yet to take place, in particular those of the musicians, who would play in a boat on the lake at intervals throughout the great day.

Thomas took his bread and porridge with Will Holland early in the morning in the Barrowhill kitchen, which was already filled with activity. Neither had said much to the other of late, but once outside Will broached the subject of Madge's murder.

'Moll told me of it, yesternight,' he said haltingly. 'No one else knows – that is . . .'

'Save Mannizzi,' Thomas finished. When Will remained silent he added: 'You may save your sombre face – I know they are together. Indeed, I wonder now why they ever remained apart.'

Will sighed. 'She said his work took him away, to London and other places, to make statues and whatnot for rich men's houses. But it appears to me they parted so that both might search their hearts and decide what to do. She cannot marry him, for he is a Papist. And more, he . . . nay, I will not say more.'

196

He placed a hand on Thomas's shoulder, not meeting his eyes. 'I told you she was a sly one,' he said.

Thomas walked off through the stable yard, heading once again for the lake. In two days the Pleasures would be over, and perhaps at last he would be able to return to Petbury, to Eleanor and to his work. Then he might set about trying to forget. He was turning this thought over as he rounded the grand pavilion, and for want of anything better to do approached a group of men clustered about the giant steed. Among them was the diminutive figure of Filbert, the Earl's fool. Beside him stood Niccolo Mannizzi.

He returned Mannizzi's slight nod, then realized that he had interrupted a heated debate. Filbert, red in the face, was gesticulating towards the steed, which towered above. Facing him, equally red-faced, was the chief groom, in charge of working the creature from within.

'I think only of your safety, master,' the man said in an exasperated tone. 'If you were to topple from that height, you would break every bone in your frame.'

'You think that is the greatest height I've scaled?' demanded the fool, in a thick London accent. 'I once flew from the gallery of the Old Theatre in Shoreditch, and no man could see how! You but do your part from within the horse, and I will do mine!'

The man sighed. Sawyer, who stood by, turned to Thomas and muttered: 'He wishes to ride the great steed when it approaches his lordship. Some might wish he would break his back, and spare us his antics for the future.'

The argument raged on, but as Thomas and other men drifted away, one thing seemed clear: the Earl's fool, by nature of his position here, would get his way in the end.

Thereafter the morning passed peacefully enough. The steed was put through its paces, its hidden operators becoming more expert as time went on. Reed the horse-master arrived, sitting as always on his sleek sorrel horse, to watch the giant creature lumber towards the empty dais, open its mouth and let fall a shower of wood shavings, in lieu of the dainties that would be hidden there on the morrow. Meanwhile Jaggard's men, who would form the guard of honour when the guests arrived, were drilling with halberds on the tiltyard. Thomas joined the crew beside the false covert, where they practised the launching of the great hawk until they were tired of it. It was about midday, as the men about the lake paused to take a bite of dinner, that Thomas saw Mannizzi walking towards him.

'May I talk with you a little, master falconer?' he asked. Thomas nodded, and the two walked down to the lake shore.

'Now I understand why we were at fencing some days ago,' Mannizzi said after a short silence. When Thomas did not reply he went on: 'It is difficult for men, who find themselves in such a . . .' he paused, then: 'In my country, we say *uno triangolo*.'

Thomas shrugged slightly, showing that he understood.

'When we were young,' Mannizzi continued, 'we might settle it with our bare hands. But now . . .' He gave a wry smile.

And for the first time, in the relative tranquillity of the lakeside, Thomas heard the man's breath: even, but somewhat short, with a soughing beneath, like waves on pebbles. At once the phrase leaped to his mind: 'the wheezing man . . .'

He fought to keep his face impassive. *He cannot be Vindex Reginae, for he did not kill Madge*, he said to himself. Moll had told him the man was with her, and she would not lie.

Surely she would not lie – not to him . . .

Mannizzi was watching him closely. 'You are troubled,' he said quietly. 'I wish there were some way I might help.'

Thomas frowned. 'Why would you want to help me?' he asked.

The man did not reply, but seemed to be weighing things in his mind. 'Why would you?' Thomas repeated, somewhat sharply.

'Because they have laid a burden upon you that is heavy for one man,' Mannizzi answered. 'I see this now.' He lowered his eyes suddenly. 'How like them is that.'

Thomas watched him. 'I do not understand your meaning.'

'These *assassini* . . . the deaths that none wishes to speak of. The woman killed behind the inn – she was not the only one, yes?'

Thomas said nothing.

'Meanwhile,' Mannizzi went on, speaking slowly and evenly, 'Lord Edmund and his Countess ride to the hunt and dally with their toys, and leave the foul business of seeking murderers to a falconer. Mayhap they think you might soar like your birds and see all that lies below as a hawk does?'

Thomas stared into the other man's eyes, and saw . . .

Not the eyes of a killer. Instead, returning his gaze with remarkable calm, he saw a man who was close to death.

An unspoken current passed between them, as it had at their first meeting. But now, Thomas thought he understood it.

'Would that I always see as clearly as do my birds,' he said, after a while. 'For I find I have misjudged you, as I did another. My vision was clouded . . .' he broke off, then finished: 'By other matters.'

Mannizzi was nodding. 'Such a matter would cloud any man's vision – would she not?'

Thomas smiled faintly. 'Indeed she would.' Questions arose in his mind, though he knew not how to voice them. But somehow Mannizzi seemed to understand.

'Now, you think of the future,' he said. 'For it may be that yours is full, like the promise of good harvest. Mine is short, so that I must reap what I can, while I may.'

Thomas lowered his gaze, whereupon Mannizzi sighed. 'Now I will go to my rehearsal, for I am not yet finished here.' He pointed to the musicians' boat that was moored some distance away. 'I am to join the chorus that will sing the praises of our glorious Queen tomorrow.' He gave a little shrug. 'It is she I will think of when I sing – royal Eliza – rather than the one who sits in her place.'

He walked off around the lake: a huddled figure, drawing his collar about him against the light drizzle that was beginning to fall.

As the day drew to a close, a gathering took place in the tiltyard for all those concerned with making the Barrowhill Pleasures a success. More than a hundred people – sailors and soldiers, horsemen and music-makers, gardeners and grooms, clustered about a rostrum that had been quickly set up for

Henry Barnard, now styled Master of the Revels, to address them.

'You have all done well,' he began in a loud voice, 'and your efforts have not gone unnoticed. His lordship is greatly pleased by the preparations, and is moved to thank those who have taken such pains to do his bidding.' He paused for emphasis, then went on: 'I speak of a gold angel, for the officer having charge of each team – and a half angel for every man that does his part full proud!'

There were stirrings of interest: at least some reward would be forthcoming. Standing beside an exhausted Hugh Jaggard, Thomas heard him mutter: 'I'll piss that much against the brewhouse wall in a couple of hours.'

'Our day will begin at ten of the clock,' Barnard was saying, 'when the guests will ride in through the gates, to be met by our Lord and his followers.' He could not but help a slight smirk of satisfaction, quickly suppressed. 'The guard of honour will form, and his lordship will conduct the party to the pavilion. Our music-makers and singers will entertain after the great hawk has flown across the lake with the oration on its beak, which the Earl will read, a welcome for our noble sovereign. She will arrive in a great coach drawn by twenty horses. Let all men pay her due reverence!'

He looked about as if daring anyone to show dissent. Then he wished all well for the morrow, and ended the meeting abruptly.

As Thomas walked off he caught sight of a solitary figure sitting in the empty pavilion, watching impassively. When the man stood up to leave, he saw that it was John Broad.

And from the house, drifting faintly on the breeze, came a sound he had not heard in weeks: music and laughter, from the Great Chamber. The Earl and Countess were entertaining once again.

The day dawned fair and chill, with the first scent of autumn: the day of the Barrowhill Pleasures, that would become the talk of London and the Southern Counties for years to come.

Thomas and Will rose early and dressed themselves in the new livery which all men had been given: Will in the Earl's scarlet, Thomas in his falconer's green. After bread and cheese and a mug of small beer they joined the groups forming around the lake – even Will was required to serve today, leaving the birds to fend for themselves. He and Thomas made their way to the false covert, where Sawyer and the company stood, stamping about on the dew-soaked sward. Little was said, for all knew their parts, but the tension could be felt on every side. Soon, eyes began straying towards the house.

And suddenly it was time – and the time had been well chosen: for as the sun climbed above the copse of small oaks beside the falconer's hut its rays struck the decorated plasterwork of Barrowhill, which glittered like a band of jewels, and at once trumpets rang out loud from the upper storeys. These were followed by a great shout from beyond the gates, and men turned in wonder: for the noble guests had somehow got themselves cased and mounted early, and departed from the house's environs without being seen. Hooves sounded, as if a small regiment were drawing near, and Thomas noticed for the first time that Jaggard and his men were conspicuous by their absence. Along with others, he hurried round the lake to the edge of the stable yard, from where one might see the main gateway – just in time. For now a great company appeared in the park outside: thirty or forty gentlemen and ladies, richly dressed and well mounted, the gallants with their swords swinging – and all were wearing masks.

Even the masks were a sight in themselves: cunningly fashioned and richly coloured, many resembling birds or beasts, others fantastic creatures of myth and legend. Thus attired the party drew near to the gate . . . and now, a gasp went up from the onlookers: for a splendid coach came into view, drawn by two long lines of horses, guided by grooms in livery and escorted by Jaggard's men, their helmets amd cuirasses buffed to a shine and halberds over their shoulders. Inside the coach could be glimpsed a figure that, had anyone not known otherwise, might easily be taken for Queen Elizabeth herself: arrayed in a vast white cape with high collar, trimmed with ermine and covered with jewels, a silver coronet upon her head. A faint sound, almost a sigh, rose from the watchers: whatever might be said of her, there was no denying the Countess could stun men to silence when she chose.

But now came another blast of trumpets, and hoofbeats, and another, smaller party appeared from the stable yard and cantered towards the gate, as if to deny the splendid company access. In the lead was the Earl in red and gold, with a herald at his side bearing his standard. Behind rode Filbert on his pony, in his best suit and cap, then John Broad and Henry Barnard, and finally Jonas Reed with a small escort of mounted servants in livery. This group reined in just inside the gates, and both companies now halted facing each other. The herald's voice rang out, in some sort of challenge, to which the leader of the guest party replied in similar vein. Then came the Earl's voice, making some speech of welcome, which was followed by a cheer and loud laughter. The Lord of Barrowhill, some muttered, may have lost half his wits, but not his charm. He and his escort now moved aside, then joined the company as it filed through the gates in procession to the lakeside pleasure ground. As Thomas and others moved to their stations, he saw the Earl produce a mask from his cloak and pull it on. The others of his party did the same, so that all were now masked save for the servants. And so the laughing, chattering audience took their places in the grand pavilion, while Jaggard's men marched to the castle. On the lake, the music-makers were already in their boat. Servants appeared with baskets full of sweetmeats, while others carried trays with flagons of wine. Soon the strains of a galliard rang clear across the water. On the dais, the Earl and his 'queen' could be seen taking their seats along with their more important guests.

Thomas, Will and the other men exchanged glances: if the start were anything to go by, the day would mark more than a mere local event – it would be memorable indeed. But there was no time to waste, for now came the signal: the thud of Jaggard's culverin from the castle, followed by a volley of caliver fire – and the hawk's company sprang into action.

There was a twang of severed ropes, and the false covert collapsed, exactly as planned. A gasp of astonishment went up from the crowd in the pavilion, followed by one of wonder as the great hawk appeared. Quickly her wings were unfolded, and boys scurried about attaching weights while Thomas, Will and the others fanned out and steadied the bird above their heads. In a moment, she was ready.

'Behold, my Lord – yon winged messenger!' came a shout from the pavilion. Exactly who had uttered it no one was sure, but as a cue it was clear enough. At a word from Sawyer the hawk's crew leaped forward, pushed the massive creature along its cables, and ran to the lakeside, skidding to a halt with hearts in mouths.

She did not disappoint. Thomas and Will, with everyone else, watched the bird's magnificent flight, dipping and rising – and culminating in a perfect stop before the dais, drawing a cry of admiration from the onlookers, followed by wild applause. The Earl, all smiles, stood up, stretched his hand out and took the parchment which had been wedged in the hawk's beak. Turning to the assembled guests he unfolded it, and recited in a clear, melodic voice.

> *Let all assembled gentles now rejoice;*
> *For ye are bidden welcome to our feast.*
> *And here beneath our sovereign's bounteous gaze,*
> *Are wonders past the ken of man or beast.*
> *Such Pleasures scarcely seen beneath the sun,*
> *Shall swell the hearts of every soul alive;*
> *That men will ever talk of Barrowhill,*
> *And England's glory shall for ever thrive!*

The Earl lowered his paper and bowed, and at once a shout of approval went up, followed by the drumming of feet upon the boards of the pavilion, while his 'sovereign' inclined her head in acknowledgement of the fair sentiments expressed. Seizing a goblet from a proffered tray, the Earl raised it and drank a toast, in which others quickly joined. Cries of 'God preserve her royal majesty!' could be heard from far across the lake.

Now music began again, and the Earl seated himself as a song rose from the assembled chorus in the boat. Watching from the shore, Thomas saw Mannizzi among the four or five singers, his fine voice adding tenor to the sweet lilt of the soprano and contralto. What such exertions might be costing the man, he realized few were aware – certainly none of the gorgeously arrayed company in the pavilion. Nor, he thought to himself, would they have cared much . . . He moved away, to join Will and the other men beside the ruins of the hawk's covert.

So the morning passed, in music, games and feasting, under-scored by a growing excitement as the time for the tilting drew nearer. Thomas and Will, with the Barrowhill men, including the soldiers and sailors who would not be needed until nightfall, gathered about the barriers to watch. Several young gallants had by now appeared, well mounted and wearing glittering suits of armour, carrying lances with coronals attached so that no man's armour would be pierced. The Earl's trumpeters stood by, the herald on his horse beside them, while grooms hurried back and forth. Reed, the horse-master, now riding a fine Neapolitan courser, trotted forth to have last-minute words with the assembled jousters. It was then, while waiting for the grand assembly of men and banners, that Thomas heard a familiar voice close by and turned in surprise.

'Jesu, I thought you'd never look round,' Ben Mallam said. 'I'm offering a wager: that tubby fellow on the roan will fall on his first course.'

'How did you get in?' Thomas asked, then gave up, for the jingler's grin rendered all questions superfluous. 'If you're offering wagers you must know something no one else does,' Thomas said drily. 'Did you furnish the horse?'

Mallam shook his head, still grinning. But now came a flourish of trumpets, and a roar from the pavilion, where the crowd were obliged to crane their heads to gain a good view of the tiltyard. The dais was now empty, the Earl and Countess and their party having taken their seats on another raised platform outside the barrier. All eyes turned as the riders filed into the tiltyard in their finery to shouts from the onlookers. Round the arena they rode, acknowledging the praise, colours fluttering, with here and there a lady's scarf tied to a lance, as was the old custom. Then they rode out to make way for the first pair to joust, and a hush fell. The two men took positions at opposite ends of the ground, one on either side of the centre fence, and lowered their visors.

The herald called out their names, the Earl stood and let fall his baton, the two horses stamped nervously – and charged, full tilt. The riders thundered toward each other, gaining speed, borne on the surge of excitement from the crowd; lances were lowered to the horizontal, shields raised – and they engaged, in a blur of caparisoned horses, shining armour and flying plumes.

There came a loud crack and a splintering of wood, and the riders had passed each other, still horsed. A roar went up, for the man on the chestnut carried his lance intact, while the one on the roan . . .

The one on the roan swayed once, twice, then fell heavily from the saddle.

There came a gasp, and stewards hurried forward. Even the Earl was seen to rise from his seat, though not the Countess. Spectators held their breath – then a wave of relief swept over the ground, as the unhorsed 'knight' was helped to his feet and stood, winded but unhurt, still holding his splintered lance.

Thomas looked at Ben Mallam, and merely raised an eyebrow.

'It was no witchcraft,' Mallam said, his shoulders beginning to rise of their own accord. 'I saw yon fellow back in the stable yard before he got mounted. He's pickled as an eel.'

Thomas watched, and saw that the defeated man's stagger indeed owed as much to drink as it did to injury. He shook his head, then glanced back at Ben Mallam and saw that he was staring in wonder at the great steed.

'Jesu, what in heaven's name do they plan to do with that?'

'You'd better wait,' Thomas told him.

They waited until dinnertime, Mallam taking full advantage of the food that was brought out in baskets. To the mutterings of Will Holland, who told him he ought to make himself scarce before someone realized he was an interloper, Ben merely laughed and said that come nightfall, all of Tadworth would be here to watch the sea battle, and who would talk of interlopers then?

The tilting was over, without serious mishap; and in the afternoon the Earl and Countess returned to their seats on the dais. There was a different atmosphere about the grand pavilion now, as many of the guests had eaten and drunk to excess. Hoots of laughter could be heard, with some men clearly unable even to stay on their feet. A few had removed their masks, though most retained them, as did the Earl and Countess. For the first time that day, Thomas thought of his master: presumably Sir Robert was somewhere among the masked figures, though he could not identify him.

Now came a stirring about the great steed, which had been kept out of sight behind the pavilion. Ben Mallam, captivated by the creature, stood at a discreet distance behind Thomas while grooms crawled underneath its flapping sides and raised it into position. One man had climbed into the neck, for the net containing sweets and gifts was being lifted into the horse's mouth, ready to be released. Now its gigantic head rose, almost twenty feet above the ground, while the crew inside began to strain at their harnesses. The steed took a step, then halted.

There came a cry, and a tiny figure ran up, waving his arms. Ben Mallam gave a short laugh. 'Who's that little rabbit?'

Thomas did not reply, but watched Filbert berate those who stood by for proceeding without him. Perhaps they hoped he would change his mind, for there was a general unwillingness on the part of the grooms to help him up. Eventually, however, a ladder appeared and the Fool clambered up it, to perch himself precariously on the creature's broad back. Since there was no saddle, a couple of ropes were thrown, which he caught skilfully. One was made fast to the horse's bridle while the other was passed under its neck and its end thrown up to him on the other side. Thus secured, he sat triumphant, a figure of ridiculous proportions, having proved himself right – for there was some laughter from the men below; and hence there would be laughter from the revellers in the pavilion.

Slowly, the steed began to walk.

Watched by Thomas and the others, the huge creature's

human legs picked up pace, so that it lumbered around the pavilion, prompting screams from a few startled ladies who were the worse for drink. People turned to see the giant horsehead rise on its ropes to lour down upon them, jaw flapping and eyes rolling.

There were cries of admiration – then of surprise. For now the Fool was seen sitting on the steed's back, holding on to its mane of plaited cords, and grinning insolently down at everyone. Who are the little folk now? he seemed to say – and the joke was not lost on the crowd, who began laughing at once. The laughter grew, as every man pointed the fool out to his fellow, some guffawing, others applauding and shouting their approval. The masked figure of the Earl now rose, and though the fool's presence was as much a surprise to him as to anyone, he seemed to enter into the spirit of things with a benign wave of his hand. The Countess wore a faint smile, seemingly content that matters were going well – as indeed they had been all day, from the very beginning. Below, beside the tiltyard, Thomas, Will and Ben Mallam watched with others, as the fool enjoyed his moment of glory. Then the horse took another step, so that its enormous mouth was above the dais. Its jaws opened wide, and a shower of gifts and dainties rained down upon the guests.

Now there was uproar, mingled with shouts of pleasure. Gallants hurried forward, crowding on to the dais in their eagerness to grab the prizes for their ladies. The little cakes, marchpanes and comfits were quickly seized and thrust into mouths, while others jostled for the toys: handkerchiefs, combs, ribbons and lace were held aloft, while the luckier women delighted to find rings and jewel-boxes placed in their hands, or offered by some smiling gentleman on bended knee, once he had fought his way out of the fray. Those further back began to press forward, so that in little more than a minute a small crowd was milling about the dais . . . which, perhaps, should have been expected, but seemingly was not. For soon the Earl and Countess were being engulfed in a mêlée of stooping, pushing gentlemen, some of whom were growing heated.

'Jesu,' muttered Ben Mallam, at Thomas's side. ' 'Tis worse than the horse fair.'

But alarm was spreading. Jaggard and his soldiers were running towards the pavilion with their halberds. Other men began to hurry from about the lakeshore and the tiltyard, all eyes on the dais, which was become a sea of heaving bodies. Seats were overturned and hangings pulled loose, and now John Broad was seen, unmasked, clearing a path with his staff of office so that the Countess, in her enormous gown, could be helped clear of the throng. Mercifully, people moved back to let her pass, though there was a chorus still of indignant oaths and the cries of men who had slipped in the crush and been trodden on.

But Thomas found himself staring upwards, at Filbert.

The men beneath the horse, by now, had realized that matters were going askew, and red-faced figures began appearing from beneath its frame – which spelt disaster. For the steed's neck fell suddenly, and its back drooped – and there came a scream from several throats as the Fool lost his grip on the horse's mane . . . and fell headlong into the middle of the heaving mass.

This was serious. Jaggard and his men were shouting, pushing men back as they forced their way to the Earl, who was now lost in the mêlée. The Fool had disappeared – but then he emerged suddenly, screaming, his hands to his head in a gesture of wild despair. His screams were echoed from several female throats, and cries of dismay came from the men. Everyone fell back, as if at a command, so that a circle appeared on the dais, widening rapidly, and in its centre . . . in its centre was the masked, red-and-gold-clad body of the Earl, lying on his face.

Jaggard was first to reach him, swearing, thrusting men aside brutally. Thomas and Will followed with the soldiers as the crowd stood, silent now but for the sobbing of distraught women. From nowhere John Broad came hurrying, his white hair awry, to drop breathlessly on his knee beside his master.

There was no note, but there was blood on the hair and neck.

Cursing audibly, Jaggard crouched and turned the body over. Broad took the limp hand to feel for a pulse, though from his face, with little hope of finding one. Carefully Jaggard lifted the Earl's mask – that of a grinning wolf – and removed it.

There was a universal gasp. For it was not the Earl's lifeless face that stared upwards, but that of his usher, Henry Barnard.

Jaggard fell back as if struck. Slowly he got to his feet, breathing quickly, and turned as others did . . . to hear a voice that rocked them all to the core.

The Earl, mask in hand and hair dishevelled, had materialized from the crowd, and now came forward unsteadily. He made a sound, somewhere between laughter and weeping.

'See how loyalty is rewarded!' he cried. 'The faithful has rendered me immortal!' And with a shriek, he threw his arms wide and fled from them all, towards the safe haven of his house.

The fool leaped from the dais and ran headlong after him.

Seventeen

Barrowhill was in turmoil.

At first, with seemingly no one in control, guests and servants alike milled about in dismay, those who had taken a surfeit of drink sobering up rapidly. Soldiers and sailors alike were running to guard the pavilion, their feud forgotten in the excitement. Presently some of the gentlemen began calling for grooms, and horses were brought from the stables so that those most distressed by events could be escorted away. Gradually a semblance of order began to prevail, as John Broad, Jaggard and Jonas Reed ushered guests away from the lakeside towards the house.

Thomas stood by the body of Henry Barnard with a number of men: Will Holland, Sawyer and two of Jaggard's soldiers who had been ordered to guard it. Ben Mallam had made himself scarce as soon as matters got out of hand. All about, faces were numb with disbelief. Finally Sir Robert appeared, and called Thomas to his side.

Sir Robert's mask, which dangled from his wrist, was that of a black crow. With a gesture almost of despair, he tore it off and threw it aside. 'Within sight of us all!' he hissed, and Thomas saw the anguish on his face. 'How bold can this assassin become?'

Thomas shook his head, but his mind had been working rapidly. Somewhere in the crowd, masked like the guests, *Vindex Reginae* had waited for his chance. Somehow, in the confusion following Filbert's fall, he had taken that chance. Somehow . . .

His master was speaking. 'We will seal off the grounds – no man shall leave until he has been examined as to his whereabouts when the Earl . . .' he snorted at his own mistake: 'When Barnard fell. This is our chance – someone must have seen whoever wielded the knife!' He looked sharply at Thomas. 'Assuming it is the same hand . . .?'

Thomas nodded. He had had time for a cursory look at the body, which was enough. 'The same blade – I would swear to it.'

'Then he has overreached himself!' Sir Robert cried. 'For only those of high station were in the pavilion, and only those known to the Earl and Countess, and trusted by them, were hard by. At last, we may begin to close on him!'

Thomas hesitated, then asked: 'How many knew that Barnard had dressed in the Earl's likeness? It was a brave ploy . . .'

'And fatal! None knew, I suspect, but he and the Earl himself. They must have switched places when the company moved to the tiltyard, or even earlier . . .' Sir Robert clenched his gloved hand. 'Had I been near, instead of keeping my distance as I have for the past week . . .'

'None could have prevented it, sir,' Thomas murmured. 'For who would expect him to strike at such a time—'

But his master was afire. 'We all should!' he snapped. 'Broad, myself, Reed, that clod Jaggard – what use has he been? Do you realize what consequences there might be, had the Earl been slain as intended?' He looked once more towards the body, which had been covered with a cloak, then lowered his eyes.

'We have been outwitted, Thomas,' he said in a quieter voice. 'And yet I cannot rest, until . . .'

He broke off, for Jaggard was walking briskly towards them.

'Your pardon, Sir Robert,' he said, 'but the Countess begs you to attend her in the withdrawing chamber at once. Master Broad is there already.'

The old soldier kept himself stiffly to attention, but Thomas saw the strain that he bore. His future, indeed, now looked bleak.

Without replying, Sir Robert stalked off towards the house, calling over his shoulder: 'Thomas, come with me.'

Thomas glanced at Jaggard, then followed.

*   *   *

211

The room was very still, so that the candles that had been brought in against the dim afternoon light barely flickered. The Countess had changed her attire, and now wore a sky-blue gown trimmed with lace. Sitting behind the long table with a cup of wine at hand, she seemed to have shrunk: from a queen, to . . .

A lady-in-waiting. For, Thomas remembered now, that is what she had once been: close to the monarch as one could be, yet no monarch. Nor would she ever be so close again: each of the men who stood in silence – Broad, Jaggard, Reed, Thomas, and the seated Sir Robert – read it in her manner, if not in her face.

John Broad spoke, his own mask of dignity intact in spite of everything. 'Her ladyship has asked me, as her steward, to assume authority over her husband's seat of Barrowhill. His lordship . . .' he hesitated, gave a small cough, and continued: 'His lordship is unwell – the strain has been very great. His physician has been summoned. Hence we all must serve him as we may, to put matters in hand.'

Nobody moved a muscle, and Broad seemed to be waiting to see who would be first to break the silence.

It was Jonas Reed, looking remarkably calm, who spoke in his thick accent. 'I want leave to search house as well as grounds, master Broad. No one can get clear . . .' he broke off and threw a contemptuous look at Jaggard: 'So long as yon toy soldiers do their part, and man the gates.'

Jaggard stood stiff as a pike, staring at the wall hangings.

Broad glanced briefly at Sir Robert, who was nodding, and back to Reed, who marched out in his heavy riding boots.

Sir Robert slapped a hand on the table. 'The sea battle,' he said, 'will of course be called off—'

'No.'

All eyes turned to the Countess, who drew a deep breath, raised her silver cup and drank from it. When she put it down, Thomas saw her hand tremble.

'The sea battle shall go ahead, according to the Earl's design. He will watch from the Prospect Room.' She turned to Broad.

212

'Though the villagers and farm folk will not now be admitted. Will you see to that, master steward?'

Broad bowed his assent. When the other men exchanged glances the Countess, somewhat agitated, added: 'Indulge me, sirs, as you indulge him. For he has talked of nothing else, except his great battle on the lake . . . I fear if it were denied him, he might . . .'

She lowered her gaze, then half-turned to Sir Robert with a look almost of pleading. No man that saw could fail to be sobered by the change in the Lady Felice. It was as if her power had ebbed away, draining into the foundations of this vast palace that would become her prison. Now they understood: her husband had lost his nerve, and soon all England would know of it. Her hopes of restored favour and glory were gone.

Broad was signalling with a barely perceptible jerk of his head. Thomas and Jaggard bowed, and went out.

Night fell, the cannon on the castle thudded and the fireworks soared, sputtered and cascaded into myriad sparks. Balls of wildfire landed in the water, hissed loudly and went out. Watched not by hundreds, but by a handful of servants including Thomas and Will Holland, the English man-of-war did half-hearted battle with the Spanish galley in the middle of the lake. The grand pavilion was empty, the great steed was gone, the giant hawk had been taken down from her cables. And though the lake itself was surrounded by torches, beyond all was darkness save for a few lighted windows in the house. At the top of the south-west tower, no light showed from the Earl's Prospect Room, though some people fancied they saw a standing figure, caught momentarily in the flashes of fire from the lake.

Very quickly – much more quickly than it had before – the English vessel outmanoeuvered the Spanish galley, whose crew quickly abandoned her. There was no exchange of insults, and no boarding party. The last man to leave set the charge that blew the bottom out, then swam clear as the vessel sank in barely six feet of water. The fireworks roared and crackled once more in celebration of victory, and it was over.

Thomas and Will watched the last of the sparks die out, then walked away towards the falcons' mews. There would be no masque, and no celebratory feast as had been promised for all those who had worked on the Pleasures. Instead despair sat like an invisible cloud over Barrowhill, made flesh by Will Holland's gloomy countenance.

'I fear all that din will have unnerved the birds,' he said. 'We'll likely have work to do.'

'I'll sit out the night with them,' Thomas said. 'Sleep will likely give me the cold shoulder.'

In the end both of them sat up with the falcons, feeding them scraps of meat and talking soothingly to them, for Will was correct: all the birds were restless, fidgeting on their perches and bating. So it was with relief that the two falconers watched the first glimmer of dawn appear above the Downs. With it came a sharp breeze, rising from the east.

Others too had been up all night, for the calls of Jaggard's men patrolling the grounds like watchmen could be heard in the distance, along with the stamping of nervous horses in the paddock. Barrowhill itself was a grey, silent bulk, with the first wisp of smoke from the kitchen fire starting to rise.

At Will's urging, Thomas left him at the mews and went first to break his fast. As he entered the kitchen a figure rose at once from a corner trestle: Niccolo Mannizzi.

His face was drawn and pale in the morning light, as if he too had had no sleep. When Thomas sat down facing him he began speaking, quickly, as if he had been waiting to unburden himself.

'When you and I talked, two days ago,' he said, 'I did lament that none seemed able to help you in the hunt for this *assassino* . . . this demon who springs from the air, and disappears again.' Seeing Thomas's exhausted face, he caught his breath, and with an effort went on: 'Please hear me – for I have lain awake all the night, knowing something was fighting to get free of my thoughts . . . something I knew, yet feared to face.'

He coughed slightly. Watching him intently, Thomas felt a jolt. Mannizzi's eyes were afire: the man was struggling to control his emotions along with his breathing. Glancing about the room to see that no one was within earshot, he nodded in encouragement.

'Speak – I will listen.'

'*Bene* . . . for there is no other I can tell.' He leaned forward and said: 'I know who this man is.'

Thomas froze.

'There is one, whom I would see at times, in London,' Mannizzi said. 'One to whom I did confess much, when I was unhappy and had drunk too much wine . . . whose confidence I shared, for he despised this man that employed us both, as I did . . . though his reasons were different from mine, yet also the same. For like me, he is of an older faith – but unlike me, he holds it secret. Like the secret family he has, in a poor house in Cripplegate Ward by St Giles, where goes all his money. So that he must keep his place, as he keeps his hatred locked away inside his heart, a heart of molten stone like to the great volcano of Etna, that will one day burst forth and wreak fire and vengeance on all those within its reach.'

He sagged, his breath coming in rasps. Without knowing that he did so, Thomas reached out and grasped his wrist.

'Who is he?' he whispered. 'Tell me!'

'You know him!' Mannizzi wheezed. 'He is here, helping now with the search that he knows is fruitless, so that he laughs inside . . . who is the one that never walks, but only rides?'

Jonas Reed . . . Thomas let go his hold on Mannizzi, though the man had barely noticed it. They stared at each other.

'But – he is fiercely loyal to the Earl . . .'

'A sham,' Mannizzi hissed. 'He hates him, as he hates the Lady Felice – all those who sin yet see no need to confess it!'

Thomas spread his hands flat upon the table. Thoughts crowded in fast: could Mannizzi be certain? More important, could he be trusted . . . ?

'But the Dutch murders,' he muttered. 'What cause had he to turn upon them? It makes no sense.'

Mannizzi looked puzzled. 'Dutch? I know naught of this . . .'

'I will need more to take to my master,' Thomas said, his mouth dry as chaff. 'There is no proof . . .'

'No proof.' Mannizzi nodded vigorously. 'For he is too

clever. The cleverest man in Barrowhill. One who fought so bravely in Ireland – yet what he tells no one is, he fought for the other side. For the rebels!'

Thomas swallowed. In his mind's eye, the image of a long knife arose, such as the kerns use. *He fought with the Irish . . .*

He stood up. 'I must find my master.'

Mannizzi rose to follow, but Thomas stayed him with a raised hand. Across the kitchen, Marmion the cook watched with a surly expression as he walked towards the servingmen's door.

'Here, you can't go into the Great Hall – it's forbidden!'

'I must see Sir Robert,' Thomas threw back. 'And John Broad.'

'Master Broad's broken fast and gone out,' Marmion retorted.

Ignoring him, Thomas shoved the door wide. It banged behind him, but no one followed.

He walked swiftly, then broke into a trot, then found he was running. He ran past servants in the hallways who stopped and stared at him. One or two called out, but he paid no mind, only ran up the great staircase two steps at a time, gained the first floor and ran to the door of his master's chamber. He grasped the handle and thrust it open.

There was an oath, and Sir Robert sat up stark in his bed, his night-shift creased and soaked with sweat. Across the room a sleepy-eyed Simon was readying his master's clean hose. He jumped in surprise. 'By the Good Lord, Thomas, what're you about—?'

'It will not wait,' Thomas said. Sir Robert stared at him, then threw his coverlet aside and stood up.

'What has happened?'

In as few words as possible, Thomas told him.

Sir Robert listened, then sat down heavily on the bed. 'A Papist, at Barrowhill . . .?' He shook his head.

'It grows clearer to me by the minute, Sir Robert,' Thomas said. 'One who knows the house, and may have learned of the chimney shafts . . . who comes and goes as he pleases . . .'

'And rends women's bodies . . .?' Sir Robert was frowning. 'And murders Dutchmen all over London?'

Thomas gave a shrug. 'I understand it no better than you – yet I believe we must stay him and question him. If we are wrong . . .'

Sir Robert stood up again. 'Very well. Wait for me outside, by the stable. And find John Broad . . .'

Thomas was already hurrying off. But when he walked swiftly out through the kitchens and into the yard, he saw a small body of men marching towards him in determined fashion. At their head was Jaggard.

'Thomas, folk are swearing blind you've lost your reason,' he began. But instead of halting as he expected, Thomas strode up to him and said: 'We must speak now – alone.'

Jaggard looked at him once, then nodded. Together they took a few paces away from the men-at-arms, while Thomas talked urgently. There were others about in the yard, too: grooms, dairymaids, washerwomen – all of whom stopped their work, sensing a growing excitement.

Jaggard listened, then his jaw sagged. 'God's heart – but then we're too late!'

Thomas stared. 'How?'

'Reed – he's with the Earl,' Jaggard gulped. 'They've gone hawking.'

'So early . . .?' Thomas grabbed him by the shoulders. 'Where?'

'On the Downs, where else?' Jaggard shot back. His tongue came out and slid about his dry lips. 'Good Christ . . . he said he'd ride along to protect him!'

Thomas turned and ran for the paddock. Behind him, Jaggard was shouting to his men to get themselves horsed. As he ran, Thomas cursed as he had not cursed for years, while the picture formed in his mind: the Earl decides on a whim, after all that happened yesterday, to go hawking – and who would dare stay him? Rather they would encourage his taking the morning air as a healthy sign, to take his mind off matters . . . a ray of hope . . . perhaps even Will had felt it, as he placed a falcon on the Earl's gauntlet, knowing no better. Mayhap he had given Reed a bird too – knowing no better . . .

Indeed, perhaps someone had even suggested a little hawking

on this bright Thursday morning – Reed, say? he thought, as he vaulted the paddock fence. Though he, at least, knew better . . .

He rode bareback, for there were no saddles within reach. Past the falcons' mews he rode, slower than he liked, for the only mount he could catch was a dappled mare, past her youth. Will appeared at the door of the hut, surprised, and shouted as Thomas rode by without a word. Down at the paddock there was a flurry of movement: men were hurriedly saddling horses.

He topped the first ridge, and the Downs spread wide before him. There was no sign of man or beast. Down the slope he rode, slapping the little mare's rump in his haste. Up the next hill – and still nothing. Breathless, he pulled up, staring about.

He looked up, and saw the falcons.

They had both climbed to high mountee, and floated gently on the air currents – a great passage-hawk which he recognized at once, for it was the Earl's favourite; and another, a tercel. He dug his boot heels into the mare's sides and rode up a slope, then halted, blinking, as the rising sun smote him in the face.

Shading his eyes, he peered, and saw in the distance – not two riders, but three. The Earl was one; Reed, who always sat high in the saddle, was another. The third was a small figure on a pony.

He urged the mare downhill, beating her rump, forcing her into a gallop against her will. He gained the bottom of the slope, and as soon as he thought himself near enough, he shouted. But the riders were not only out of earshot – they were moving. As he watched in dismay, they cantered unhurriedly up the far slope and disappeared over the ridge, following the hawks.

He bellowed into the mare's ear, and slapped her again, so that she jerked her head in alarm and sprang forward. Across the valley bottom they sped, and up again, and atop another hill . . .

He was closer now. He shouted, saw the men draw rein and turn – too late. For Reed saw, and understood. To Thomas's horror the man reached out, yanked the reins from the Earl's hands and spurred his mount away, pulling the other's horse

218

with him.

Hanging grimly to her mane, Thomas raced the little mare for all she was worth, feeling her sides heaving beneath him with the effort. Up the far hill they galloped, and down again . . . and he slowed, breathless, looking from side to side.

He had lost them.

Then came a cry – of rage, or anguish, he knew not what – but it came from beyond a hill to his left, where the ground rose steeply. He urged the mare forward again, up the hill, and gained the summit, too slowly – far too slowly. Now he began to despair, for there were horses in the defile below him, but no riders.

Another cry, and he saw: a tangle of bodies in the grass. Kicking the mare's sides, he willed her forward, then leaped from her back and began to run.

But he was too late: for the Earl lay prostrate in the grass. Near him, a ridiculous spectacle: Reed, the tall horse-master, fighting with a dwarf.

But even as Thomas ran he checked himself, surprised. Will Holland's words sprang to his mind: *more dangerous than he looks* . . . he had given them no thought, until now. Now he saw Filbert fight for his life, and it was a creditable performance.

Reed had him pinned by the arm and had clearly struck him, for there was blood about the Fool's contorted mouth. But as Thomas watched, Filbert kicked out hard and caught the man in the thigh, so that he grunted and loosed his grip. Filbert kicked again, his puny legs wide, and caught Reed on the shins. Reed lashed out with a hand, but Filbert ducked nimbly, then came up, his small fists whirling, and caught the man in the throat.

Then it was, as Thomas drew close, seeking his chance to intervene, that he heard it: a great whistle of breath, like a creaking door: eerie and terrible, and barely human.

This time, there was no mistaking the Wheezing Man.

And now he saw, too, the stone-hard face of the horse-master as he reached into his doublet and drew out the long blade from its hidden sheath. Thomas shouted – but even as he did, Reed made his powerful thrust: not in the back of Filbert's neck, for

219

he had no time. He merely felt with one hand for the gap between the Fool's ribs, then fixed him through the heart and stood back, apparently calm, though the dreadful whine of his breath continued unabated.

It was a dance. Thomas watched aghast as the two men stood as if joined together: the Wheezing Man – who it seemed only wheezed at times of such passion – holding his terrible skene by its hilt, a good three feet taller than Filbert, who shuddered from head to foot yet remained upright, pinned like a butterfly. His stubby arms flailed the air, too short to reach the man who had killed him. Blood gushed from the wound, flowing down his doublet, and still the two held their pose. Staring at the fool's face, Thomas saw the look of utter helplessness that passed across it.

Then his life was over. Almost casually, Reed placed his riding boot on the little man's stomach and shoved him to the ground, at the same time drawing the narrow, dripping blade out of his body.

There was a moment; then Reed turned to face his new foe.

Neither man spoke, for there was nothing to be said. Thomas saw the icy look in the man's eyes . . . and once again, a mist seemed to rise about him. A muddy field . . . screams and shouts, the clashing of pikes . . .

He swallowed, crouched, and felt for his own knife at his belt. But it was then that he was aware of movement, away to his right. The Earl was not only alive . . .

'Murder!' he shrieked, and sat up unhurt. He had but fainted.

There came a harsh laugh, and it was Reed. 'Aye, murder,' he gasped, his breath still short, though he tried to master it. 'My wife and son ye have murdered . . . my hopes, ye have murdered!'

His head whipped aside, for there was a shout, and hoof-beats . . . Thomas spun round, and saw a horseman come charging over the ridge at full speed. He was aware of others behind, but they did not matter: for Reed had stepped back, a look of alarm on his face. The next moment the horseman had wrenched his mount to a violent halt so that it fell to its knees, jumped from the saddle, and was striding quickly forward. It was Jaggard.

There came a shriek of metal, and the old soldier's sword glittered in the sunlight. Reed backed away, but Jaggard came on, looking neither to right nor left, a smouldering fire in his eye. Reed raised his long knife, and Jaggard's sword swept it aside with a clang, so that it flew into the air. Then he drew back his arm . . .

Thomas turned away, saw far above the two falcons still hanging like specks in the sky. He heard the scream and forced himself to look back to where Reed sat slumped on the grass, blood running from his vitals.

Jaggard stood leaning on his sword, breathing deeply. Slowly he turned to face Thomas, the anger draining from his face.

'He has paid.'

Thomas walked over to the Earl and reached down to help him to his feet, then paused.

The Earl was still sitting up in the grass, staring. Thomas followed his gaze and saw nothing but the Downs. He frowned, then passed a hand before the Earl's eyes, and got no reaction.

The Earl stared into the empty air, fascinated by it.

He continued to stare, while other riders arrived in ones and twos: John Broad, Sir Robert, Jaggard's men . . . silently they dismounted, and stood looking about the blood-spattered plain, at a loss how to act.

Then came a sound that chilled them: a long wail of agony. And leaving the Earl to his private world, they gathered around the horse-master to watch him die. John Broad, his face grey, drew close to him and dropped to one knee. Fighting to master himself, he spoke.

'In God's name, Jonas Reed—'

'No!' the horse-master's cry was so loud that every man started in surprise. 'Not Reed . . .' He struggled to gain breath, then said: 'My name is Leach – Malachi Leach, the son of Jonas Leach, from Ormskirk in Lancashire, faithful servant to the one true God . . .' He raised his eyes in anguish. 'And now there is no priest to give the rites, and I shall burn in hell!'

The silence that fell was profound, broken only by the distant call of larks. Even the horses shied and began edging away. All eyes fixed on Reed – on Malachi Leach, as he groped feebly inside the neck of his doublet and finally drew forth a tiny silver crucifix that shone like a jewel. Grasping it in a trembling fist, he prepared to make his last confession.

'The Protestant Wind is a wind of ruin,' he said, so hoarse now that men bent their heads to hear him. 'It scattered our hopes . . . our hopes to see the true religion restored to this fetid pool of sin and wickedness . . . His Holiness on high above a Spanish king in his rightful place, and Cardinal Allen the new Archbishop . . .' He gave a croak that seemed to pass for laughter. 'And Malachi Leach, tired of living in a web of lies, vowed he would strike back: I am a hurricane of vengeance . . . *Vindex Reginae* . . . for ye have murdered my queen!' He grunted in pain and looked up at Jaggard. '*Perite scelesti* . . . you and all you savages, who fornicate like beasts and lie with scarlet whores, while my virtuous wife . . .' now a real sob came from his mouth, as the colour drained from his face, 'my true wife, that never harmed a soul, who asked for naught but to live by the grace of God, dies of the plague in this summer of evil . . . and my son!' He cried out in anguish: 'My golden-haired child, filled with grace, sickens and dies within a week of her – yes, they would pay! All of you would pay . . .'

Scarcely knowing what he did, Thomas came forward and dropped to the grass beside John Broad. 'The Dutch,' he said, his gorge rising. 'Those plain honest folk, who did you no harm—'

'No harm!' Leach turned a terrible eye upon him. 'When the laws of our land are overturned, and the sabbath defiled as it has not been since the Act of King Edward: "All Sundays in the year shall be kept for holy days, and it shall be lawful to all archbishops and bishops, and to all others having ecclesiastical or spiritual jurisdiction, to enquire of every person that shall offend . . ."' His voice rose to a feverish pitch: ' "And to punish every such offender!" '

There was silence as men on all sides stared uncomprehendingly.

Sir Robert stepped forward, gazing down at the dying man in

222

disgust. 'You dare to tell us that you took it upon yourself to do wilful murder – because of a change in the law?'

'The sabbath belongs to the Lord!' Leach cried. 'Those blaspheming Hollanders that care naught for holy days yet will leap to exploit the new law and labour on a Sunday . . . and behind them – yes, behind them, are the truly wicked . . . the corrupt rich men who take their money in return for protecting them . . . the unholy trinity of Wilkes and Brunning and that foul sinner, and his whoring wife!' He coughed and tried to raise a hand to point towards the still-seated Earl, but it fell weakly to his side. 'And no one cares,' Leach mumbled, his breath failing now as his senses clouded. 'No one would act, until the Lord charged me! So then, Malachi Leach would act, and not rest until all this wickedness was swept away . . .' He was mumbling now: 'This creeping canker, this slime that will engulf all Albion, turning our country away from godliness into evil . . .'

He choked then, as if his throat was full, as his voice was filled with bile. His eyes grew dull. 'Into thy hands, oh Lord,' he whispered, then swayed, and fell back.

Thomas got slowly to his feet, and walked off in the direction of the gliding falcons.

Eighteen

I t was Friday, the twenty-third day of September. Tomorrow morning, three weeks to the day since Thomas and his master had left Petbury, they would leave Barrowhill.

In the afternoon a Sergeant-at-Arms had arrived, a special envoy from the Privy Council, in prompt response to Sir Robert's message. The matter of illegal payments extracted from the Dutch community for their supposed protection was now becoming common knowledge; questions were being asked at the highest level. With the Sergeant was an escort of four soldiers. But after the man had been taken into the house, to the Countess's private chambers, he emerged alone; and after a brief conversation with Sir Robert, he and his men departed empty-handed.

Many watched them leave, but none were surprised, for the news had run through Barrowhill like stubble-fire: the Earl was but a living statue who sat in his Prospect Room all day, looking out towards the lake. He neither spoke nor responded to anyone, not even the Countess. For her part, the Countess had ceased to speak with anyone save her steward, who was now in sole charge of the management of Barrowhill. His first act was to put in motion the funeral arrangements for Henry Barnard and for Filbert, the Earl's fool. As for Malachi Leach, formerly known as Jonas Reed: word would be sent to his family, in the far-off North Country, and the body preserved until such time as someone came to claim it.

Thomas had spent the day with Will, tending the hawks. They spoke little, for all was now laid bare. It was as if a dark cloud had passed from Barrowhill, blown by the wind which came now from the south, bringing a scent of rain. Both men welcomed it as they walked on the Downs together for the last time, each with a bird on the wrist.

At suppertime, Sir Robert sent word to Thomas that he was free to pass the evening as he wished. So it was that, his heart heavy with a mixture of feelings he barely understood, he borrowed a horse from the stables and rode into Tadworth.

It was early, and the inn had not yet filled with drinkers. But as soon as the drawer saw Thomas enter, he came forward, his manner a deal more respectful than on the last occasion they had spoken. Instead of asking what he lacked, the man said that his instructions were to send Thomas through to the parlour, should he appear. Yes, mistress Moll had dined but she was still within; no, she was not alone . . .

They rose together from the supper table as he walked in: Moll in the same russet gown she wore when he had first seen her, her smile almost shy. Mannizzi, looking tired and dark about the eyes, met his gaze with a frankness that disarmed him. There were perfunctory greetings before Thomas took a stool and sat as he was bidden, accepting the cup of claret Moll poured him.

'You will go home, back to your daughter?' she asked.

He nodded. 'We leave early in the morning.'

Mannizzi spoke up. 'There is much talk of you, about the kitchens and halls of that . . . that *mausoleo* which is called Barrowhill. They say you have acted with courage.'

Thomas shook his head. 'Others did more. And as for courage –' he looked directly at Mannizzi – 'it takes many forms, I think.'

Moll glanced at Mannizzi too – briefly, but long enough for Thomas to gauge the magnitude of the feeling she had for him. He lowered his eyes and took a deep breath. When he raised them again, he saw they were both looking at him, Mannizzi with a mixture of respect and sympathy; Moll . . .

'I should go soon,' he said. 'I merely came to give you my good-bye.'

'But you will come back again?' Mannizzi asked. When Thomas did not reply, he added: 'I think you should, one day.'

Thomas rose to his feet and drained his cup. Mannizzi rose too, and came round the table to face him.

There was a moment, then: 'I hope you will come back,' Mannizzi said, with a sideways look at Moll. 'We both hope it.'

Moll had averted her face. Noting Thomas's look of concern, Mannizzi said at once: 'I will say my farewell here, signor falconer. Like we do in Italia – so.' And to Thomas's surprise the man clasped him in a tight embrace, and kissed him quickly on both cheeks.

'*Addio – fratello,*' he murmured, then moved abruptly away and went out of the room. The door closed softly behind him.

Now he and Moll were alone, he knew not what to say. He took a step towards her, and saw the tears in her eyes.

'Nay . . .' he began, but she reached out and took his hands in hers.

'I ask only for your blessing,' she said. 'For we have little time left together, he and I.'

He nodded. 'And after?'

'After?' She bit her lip. 'I will be here, as always. Every woman's friend, every man's favourite hostess. Where else should I go?'

'And if I did come back?' he asked.

'I have said – I will be here.'

She put a hand to his face, and when he bent his head, kissed him fiercely on the mouth. Then their hands fell from one another's, and she turned her back.

He went out then, and walked through the inn where the clink of cannikins sounded and voices rose. The Friday night crowd was gathering.

Outside, he untied the horse and climbed into the saddle. There was a shout, and he turned to see Ben Mallam riding up on King Philip.

'Jesu, whose jade is that?' the jingler asked, staring at the fine stallion from the Barrowhill stable.

Thomas sighed. 'He's not for sale.'

Mallam grinned, then saw his face. 'Troubles, my friend? Would a quart of ale not cure them?'

Thomas shook his head, and held out his hand. 'I'll wish you farewell, master horseman. I'm away back to Berkshire in the morning.'

Ben's grin faded. 'That's mighty uncivil, after all I've taught you. You have the makings of a first-rate jingler, did ye not know?'

Thomas managed a faint smile. 'I'll stick to my birds.'

Ben took his hand briefly, then let go. 'Look for me next horse fair, at Wantage. Mayhap we'll do business.' He brightened suddenly. 'Is the great steed still there, that they built by the lake? It was a most wondrous animal.'

Thomas shrugged, gripped the reins and rode off down the narrow street. When he reached the turn at the bottom of the village he looked back and saw Mallam sitting on his horse, his hand raised in farewell. Then he was lost to sight.

They stood in the stable yard in the damp chill of early morning, watching absently as Sir Robert's servant Simon tied up their packs. Will Holland and Thomas strapped the falcons' cage to the saddle of his horse and covered it with a cloth. Then the two falconers waited, awkwardly, searching for a few suitable words.

'What will you do?' Thomas asked at last.

Will looked about before lowering his voice. 'Master Broad says I may stay, but there is small need for a falconer now. No more hawking parties riding out on the Downs – indeed, no more revels at the house. They say her ladyship will be shunned at Court. And Lord Edmund is—' He broke off, shaking his head.

Thomas nodded. 'But is this not the chance you wanted – to seek work elsewhere?'

Will sighed. 'Doreth says we may marry, if I give up my hawks and become her father's journeyman. Picture that, Thomas. I'd be little more than a smith's 'prentice – a man of my years!'

Thomas frowned. 'That is cruel of her.'

Will said nothing. But Thomas gripped his arm and said: 'Let me speak to my master. He has many hawking friends – he might find you a place, as far away as you like. You may start again . . .'

'Without Doreth?' Will sighed. 'She would never leave here.'

Thomas placed a hand on his shoulder and turned away, for his master had emerged from the great entrance and was walking down the steps. With him was John Broad.

The farewells now were brief. Broad bowed to Sir Robert and wished him safely home, then turned to Thomas.

'There are some here that owe you much, falconer,' he said, 'though they have not rewarded you. Let me do so in my fashion.'

He held out his hand and proffered a small purse. Surprised, Thomas took it, murmuring his thanks.

'I believe you are the one who labours here without reward, master Broad,' he said. 'I do not envy you the remainder of your service.'

Broad gave a faint smile. 'You need have no concerns on my account. I have all I wish for.' He paused, and there was a faint gleam in his watery eye. 'Now, that is.'

Thomas's breath caught in his throat. A few yards away his master had mounted his horse and was ordering Simon to follow suit. When Thomas stared back at Broad, forgetting himself, the old steward said: 'It is the late Earl, Lord Richard Meeres, whom I still serve – as I have done from my youth. A true nobleman.' His smile widened as if at a fond memory. 'He used to say that I was the true spirit of the old manor, before a single brick of Barrowhill was laid. I believe now, that we may at last return to . . .' He trailed off, and gazed into the distance. 'Well; it may not be as it was, but it shall serve.'

Then, holding his staff of office erect, he raised his hand to Sir Robert.

Thomas mounted his horse, questions leaping to his mind. But when he glanced down at John Broad, the steward was walking away up the steps. In a moment he had disappeared inside the house.

Sir Robert and his two servants rode out of the gateway and into the park. There was no trumpet blast. Nor was there any shaft of sunlight to illuminate the splendid walls of Barrowhill. From the windows of the Prospect Room at the top of the south-west tower, no movement could be seen. In the distance, a skein of migrating geese drifted across the grey-white sky.

Then, as the three riders cleared the outer arch, Thomas heard a shout and saw a man running towards him. Falling back, he slowed his horse, and allowed Hugh Jaggard to catch him up.

'I heard you were sneaking out at dawn,' he said. 'Did you mean to give me the slip?'

He held his hand out, and Thomas took it, feeling once again the old soldier's hard skin, as worn as an ancient harness.

'I'm for Ireland,' Jaggard said. 'From what I hear, they're in dire need of men who can trail a pike over there.'

Thomas nodded. 'I believe I owe you my life,' he said quietly. 'If there is aught I can do in your service . . .'

Jaggard shook his head. 'Think of me when you're out with your birds, next time you get caught in a thunderstorm. 'Twill likely be me firing my damned culverin.'

He stood back and slapped Thomas's horse on the rump, so that it sprang forward. By the time Thomas had controlled the animal and glanced behind, the old soldier was gone.

They took the path across the Downs once again, turning north towards Epsom, and the wind rose, rippling the grey-green grass as the surface of a vast lake.

Thomas breathed in, a deep draught of clear air, and turned his thoughts to home.

Afterword

As many readers will have guessed, there was no Earl of Reigate, and Barrowhill never existed. Nevertheless there is little here that could not feasibly have taken place in Armada Year, 1588. Some details of the Barrowhill Pleasures were suggested by the Elvetham Entertainment in Hampshire, which Queen Elizabeth attended in 1591.

Nor was there, to my knowledge, a horse fair in Banstead. But since they were held in every county in England including, no doubt, Surrey, I thought perhaps there should be.

DUC   Ducker, Bruce.
           Bloodlines.

$25.00

DUC   Ducker, Bruce.
           Bloodlines.

$25.00

DATE	BORROWER'S NAME	

BLOODLINES

by

Bruce Ducker

THE PERMANENT PRESS
SAG HARBOR, NY 11963

Library of Congress Cataloging-in-Publication Data

Ducker, Bruce
      Bloodlines / by Bruce Ducker
        p. cm.
      ISBN 1-57962-060-4
      I. Title.
      PS3554.U267B58 2000
      813'.54--dc21   99-30774
                                           CIP

First printing: February, 2000
Second printing: March, 2000

THE PERMANENT PRESS
4170 Noyac Road
Sag Harbor, NY 1196

TO Jaren

By Bruce Ducker

BLOODLINES
LEAD US NOT INTO PENN STATION
MARITAL ASSETS
BANKROLL
FAILURE AT THE MISSION TRUST
RULE BY PROXY

FOREWORD

1940

THE LITTLE MAN CATALOGUED the reasons his friend might be late. First was the music. If Almo started playing, if someone were to seat him at a piano, he would not remember his appointment until his fingers tired. Then there was the endless fringe of cafés along his way, the tinkling inside a siren that lured him, from the conservatory as he walks to the bus stop, along the route that follows the Danube and crosses at Ezébet Bridge, and again where he departs, in Pest. Cafés frying sausage and onion, on their tables sat glasses that shone with schnapps of every color, amber beer. Almo could wander into any one and find there a pal or one who might become a pal, linger over a glass of bull's blood.

And, most likely, the women.

Three reasons.

Come now, he said to himself. Be realistic. Not three. Every fugue in the world, every new Bartók harmony is its own reason. Each café table is a reason. And how many women must I count? Those between six and sixty, merely those who might want to piss away minutes flirting with this student, so gaunt and tentative. While he examines his feet, his large hands, stammers and apologizes for his Hungarian. Although I happen to know his vocabulary, dreadful as it is, now covers quite completely, quite vividly, the female anatomy. Or apologizes for his country German, lisped and familiar. Not the guttural growl we are used to, but that soft, singsong voice that suits the whispers of poetry or the gentle phrases of seduction. Each of those women.

Perhaps I should affect that *Schweitzerdeutche* drawl. Perhaps I would have better luck. Affect that accent and become an artist. A short, serious pamphleteer, quite ordinary looking or worse, has little success with women. Perhaps I shall become an opal-eyed musician like him, six feet, dark and delicate as an oboe. My friend Almo may never arrive.

He smiled privately. After all, if it were not for Almo's fondness for women, I could set no trap for him. If he had never discovered that the women of Budapest are more liberal than those Calvinist dairy

5

maids he is used to, and, God help them, more easily charmed by his romantic bumbling, where would I be? Almo is the fly, and I am about to set in front of him a luscious drop of honey.

He allowed the smile to turn up the points of his mouth.

"Tell me the joke."

His friend had surprised him from the other way.

"There is none."

"Bullshit."

"None. I was simply letting the mood of the evening take me over."

Almo looked down at his friend's face. Moon-round, a cigarette stuck in the center of its lips like an apple stem, the mouth a figure-eight behind it. Eyes against the smoke, squinting angrily, an expression tortured by the tobacco habit of its owner.

"You are fibbing, Seggy. Your only pleasure comes from another's misfortune. Mood of the evening, my ass. You want me to believe you've become an aesthete." They had given each other private nicknames. Almo and Seggy, Almodozo and Segdugaz, the dreamer and the anal suppository. As unlike from each other as they appeared.

"You guessed my joke! That's it! I've been standing here thinking that if only I became an aesthete, I might more often get laid."

"Ah," and the student put his hand on the little man's shoulder, making them as they walked along appear like keeper and caged. "And forego all that talk of a better world? All those tedious meetings and the polemics of utopia and the earnest young women with bad complexions? Leave it for the flesh? Fuck the fascists, fuck the communists, you mean to say all that talk has been a dodge?"

Seggy shook off the hand and slapped the back of his own into his needler's stomach. "And your choice of words," Almo went on. "You might *more often* get laid? That contains the premise that you get laid at all. We both know that premise to be faulty. Seggy, you are becoming a master propagandist."

They walked away from the university.

"Bad complected, you think? Then you will not want to come with us tonight. I thought maybe, since Abbey is such a beauty, you would want to meet her. But apparently you think women with social principles are bad complected. Yes, perhaps you stay home and play with yourself. I'll leave you here. I will see to Abbey alone."

Along Kossuth Boulevard the restaurants were filled. It was the first evening of summer, and the city they walked through enjoyed a curious peace. The diners at the sidewalk tables could afford to ignore the political difficulties to the west. In the past months, since spring had begun, Germany had declared war on Denmark and Norway, had overrun Belgium, Luxembourg and the Netherlands. After some vacillation, the Hungarian government had made its pact with the Reich. When Hungary's regent, Admiral Horthy, dined aboard the Führer's liner *Patria* in Kiel Bay, Hitler had told him, "He who wants to sit at the table must at least help in the kitchen." Horthy had helped with the washing up of Czechoslovakia. Two years later, Horthy's country was enjoying the security that came from an alliance to so powerful a force. In the cafés that the two friends now passed, the joke was going around. What is the difference between Chamberlain and Hitler? Chamberlain takes his weekends in the country and Hitler takes his countries in the weekend.

They reached Rakpart Belgrád. It ran by the river, one could drive all the way to Rumania. On the far corner a young woman awaited them. She wore a dark navy skirt and a white cotton blouse open at the collar. Almo poked his friend's arm and pointed.

"That is she?"

"That is she."

"Why did we come down here? We'll just have to walk back up the hill to find a place for dinner."

"Dinner later," Seggy said. "We do a little business first. We have to go south to the suburbs. It won't take long."

"You invite me to meet this breathtaking woman and first you are off on some of your anarchist's bullshit? Seggy, why didn't you get the business done before dinner? What am I supposed to do in the meantime?"

"You'll come along. You'll find it interesting. And you'll enjoy meeting Abbey, believe me."

Almo did not have to extend his faith too far. The woman was remarkable to see. She could not have been more than seventeen. Her face was soft in its features, but made determined by her forehead, marked by a sharp widow's peak, and by her eyes of fierce black. Seggy introduced him, using his given name. Their nicknames were only for each other. She studied his face as if she were seeking some code, then replied formally but without distance. She wore no makeup or jewelry. They boarded the bus to the south, and took the rear seat, over the rumbling diesel.

The men sat on either side, Almo assuming Abbey would politely turn to him, the newcomer. But as soon as the bus rolled, she engaged Seggy excitedly about their business. Their disregard of Almo's presence allowed him to watch her, stare with such singularity that, had she not ignored him, had she turned in the dim light of the bus and caught his stare, he would have embarrassed himself. Almo paid little attention to what they said, though he sensed her command of the topic. They were considering, it seemed, some transaction involving a boat, its lease for hire, and clearly she was the expert on matters nautical and financial. Seggy sought out her opinion on tonnage, insurance, what crew might be needed and what papers they must have. Almo let the words wash over him. He had no experience in commerce, it bored him.

"You're following all this?" his friend asked ten minutes out. Seggy grinned. He could put his hand on the very spot where Almo's thoughts rested, though he'd get slapped for it.

Almo returned the smile, but directed it towards Abbey. "I am enjoying the ride and the scenery." Outside it was pitch black.

"And our talk interests you?" This time she used the familiar form of address.

"I know nothing of boats. I am Swiss, we are surrounded by land, and I can't tell port from starboard. Port from muskat, that's a different story, but not port from starboard." Abbey gave a nod that gently dismissed his background, his humor, indeed him, and they went back to their huddle.

This was not going well. Seggy had asked him along to meet the girl. The conversation should be his. Normally a patient man, especially with comrades, Almo thought to complain, but just as he was to speak the little man stood and walked forward to the driver. The bus squealed to a stop and the trio, by now the only passengers, stepped down.

They were in the middle of nowhere. The wharf district. Piers crowded with barges, moored tugs, the smells of bilge and coal and cargo stale from the farms. Up river, Almo could see the lights of Pest and the graceful silhouette of the Liberation Bridge. What in hell was he doing here? This young woman, beautiful as she was, admittedly worth all of Seggy's taunting and provocation if he could but catch her eye, had an interest only in davits, freightage, engine screws. He would miss an evening in town, and if they didn't get their business over with quickly, miss his supper altogether. Tomorrow started with an early class on the twelve-tone system. He would not be late for that.

He fell behind the couple as Seggy led the way. They picked a route through shabby lanes and arrived at a wooden shack perched among empty oil drums and cut fence wire. A bare bulb showed through the window. Seggy knocked, looked in, and waved his two companions through the door.

The office inside was surprisingly well fitted. In its center sat a large desk crowded with papers. The floor was covered with an emerald green rug that smelled slightly of mildew. Behind the desk stood a mammoth Jacobean cabinet. Its drawers had been removed, and files were housed in the cavities. Its top, however, was intact: between two turned posts was set a wooden door decorated in the Chinese style with careful inlay. The room seemed to be empty.

They heard the flush of a toilet. A corner door opened, and an enormous man, perhaps six-three and three hundred pounds, emerged. His belt was unhinged, its tongue lolled lubriciously. The man was unkempt, a greasy shirt, thick curls that hung over his ears and neck. He idly buttoned the fly on his trousers, and though Almo felt unease at having surprised him, he did not accelerate his pace or make any show at privacy.

"Well, well," he said heartily. "So you want to be sailors."

The three young visitors pulled up chairs and gathered on the far side of the desk. The man, whom they called rarely by name but when they did it was a short, ugly sound, Gül, was foreign. Almo guessed Turkish or Rumanian, but nothing more about him was offered. For most of the conversation he sat rubbing his crotch. His Hungarian was heavily accented, and Almo relied more on the reactions of his friends, both observed and in their speech, to make what little sense he could of the discussion. At unpredictable times during their talks, an uncaused hilarity would strike Gül and he would break into flesh-shaking laughter, while his proposed buyers — for it was clear Abbey and Seggy were to buy and the fat man to sell — sat patiently.

Almo stirs himself out of his moroseness by trying to follow what is going on. In the harsh light of the bulb, he gets his first view of Abbey and she is more striking than he thought. On the bus they established that while the girl was in charge, Seggy would do the talking. He does, putting the case. The fat man watches Abbey as Seggy gives the dimensions, capacity and days that are their specifications. A boat of such a size, leased with full crew for so long. All the while, the fat man watches her, his fascination, the license of his thoughts, Almo realizes in a flush of shame, not unlike Almo's own on the bus.

"Excellent," the fat man says. "Your search is over. I have precisely the ship for you. We will seal it with a drink."

"Is it seaworthy?" Seggy asks.

Gül feigns insult. "Seaworthy? Am I a murderer? I am a businessman."

"And the cost?"

"The cost is not inconsiderable. These are illegals you are shipping. There are risks."

"The cost?"

Gül turns in his oaken swivel chair. The metal joint yields the sound of a rabbit in a leg trap. He opens the door of the cabinet behind him and, without rising, withdraws a bottle and four small glasses. He inspects the appertif glasses, wipes one on his black seaman's shirt. Pours a transparent liquid to the brim of each, the slightest orange tint. Barrack, an apricot brandy. He pushes the glasses towards them.

"The cost?" Seggy asks again. Almo takes his glass, sips at the tiny mound the liquid makes at the rim. His eyes water — the stuff is vile. He puts it back on the desk. His friends' glasses, he realizes too late, have not been touched.

"Is ninety pounds sterling per passenger."

"For that cost," says the girl, "we can buy three tickets to Haifa, not one. And stay in first class cabins dining on roast lamb." They are the first words she says, and they reveal her passion.

"Then you should," Gül responds. "You should take your cattle first class and have them graze on roast leg of lamb and do their funny dances on the first class decks. But that is the price. I will refit my ship to carry eight hundred. I will not sail with fewer. They will be cramped, but then they are used to living that way. You may take it or leave it." He drinks off his brandy and his eyes twinkle as the fire hits his gut. Then, as if the liquor were a surprise, a punch line, he indulges a roaring laugh.

Almo is searching for a way to break in and even the score, but he has no entry. He knows from the talk on the bus that they must deal with this man. Whatever Seggy and the girl are transporting they have more coming, they have stores and stores in basements and hundreds more waiting to take their places. He realizes Seggy is dealing from weakness, that he has no alternative, but still Almo has begun to get angry. He has forgotten his lost evening in town. This man is clearly humiliating his friends.

Seggy looks to the girl. It is a mistake, even Almo sees this, his look is weakness and says we are getting nowhere, we need to concede, and the fat man notices.

"In addition," Gül says. "I am told that the British are running patrol boats to interdict illegal shipments. When they find them they impound the boat. I must insist that you deposit in my bank in Basle a sum equal to the value of the ship if she does not return. It is only good business. Your Jews would approve."

"Meaning? Your total?"

"You must pay ten thousand pounds down, here. The balance of ninety-two thousand to be deposited in the bank. Thirty thousand to be returned to you when the ship reaches any port on the Mediterranean."

The girl remains calm. It is why, Almo realizes, she has been chosen to lead. She explains the conditions, the children and disease. She tells him of the certain fate awaiting the refugees if they cannot get out. She tells him that Eichmann has said either you disappear or I will make you disappear. She tells him that her own cousin has come from Poland with tales of incredible excesses. It seems that the fat man may be moved. Her eyes shine in her stories and he drinks another glass of brandy. She goes further, tells him of a camp in which the announcement is repeatedly made, anyone who hangs himself tonight is asked to put a piece of paper in his mouth with his number on it, so that in the morning roll may be accurately called.

"Very orderly," the fat man said. "All the more reason that Germany will prevail. Very efficient. Listen, these are your problems, not mine. I have a ship. It is for hire, Jews, beets, lumber, I do not care."

In the silence he leans forward. He leers at the girl.

"You are one of them? Surely you should be willing to part with this money to help them out. And maybe you should part with a little more, too. I might be inclined to lower the cash portion a little, add it onto the bank deposit, for a night of *Rassenschande*."

Almo recognizes the term. Reich propaganda and Reich rules have been showing up in Hungary more and more since he came two years ago. The word means shaming the race, the crime of sex with a Jewish partner. Almo stands and pushes back his chair. It catches on the uneven carpet and tips over. Even he is startled by the noise it makes, the floor reverberates and legs of other chairs thump as their occupants turn. He finds himself reaching across the desk and pulling the giant ship merchant by his filthy woolen shirt. The man's bulk comes up slowly, he might be a great root being urged from the earth, and Almo hasn't thought of what he will do with him if somehow he budges him to his feet.

Seggy is talking in his ear to calm him. He releases the man, whose weight, when he falls back into the swivel chair, so jostles the floorboards that one of the glasses of Barrack tips and spills. Almo allows himself to be led out from the shack into the night.

His blood is racing and he can hear the tympani in his chest. He is no fighter, the scene is one he is glad to have behind him. He begins to fear for the girl, still in the shack, and for himself if Gül decides to come out. These matters are urgent, but he cannot seem to turn Seggy to them, Seggy making insistent and needless noises. Soon he doesn't need to — Abbey emerges, comes over and looks into his face as a mother might, takes him by the elbow and leads him back to the road. They ride the bus to town in silence. No one speaks. Abbey holds the trembling fingers of Almo's left hand, a flexible hand that can stretch over a piano the interval of an eleventh, holding those fingers between her cool palms. He has fallen in love with her.

He has no appetite, none of them do, and they decide not to go out to dinner. They see her to her house, and Seggy waits with him for the last bus across the river to the conservatory apartments where he lives.

"So this is what you do the nights you can't meet me," Almo says at last. His breath is shallow with excitement and fear. "Lead your political partisans into the cesspools of the city where they get propositioned."

"She knows what she is doing," Seggy says. "I was not leading."

"Thank God we pulled her away from there. That man is a pig. Worse."

"Worse."

"And why are you involved in this? How does this concern you?"

Seggy shrugs, pulls a pack of French cigarettes from his windbreaker and tears off the top to expose all twenty.

"I'm involved because I'm involved."

"For heaven's sake," Almo uses the other's Christian name. It is meant as a rebuke. "That man would have taken her to bed if we hadn't been there. All for a discounted price on some passage. I must tell you, you need to think more about the moral consequences of your actions."

Seggy looks deeply into the eyes of his friend. Even in the faint light of the bus shelter he can see how it is they appeal to women. The flecked colors move about with his moods, now the green shines in outrage. Up the street comes the headlights and faintly illuminated sign of Almo's bus, the last of the evening.

"I thought you understood. While you and I were outside she negotiated the final terms. She got him to take a lower price. Tomorrow she will return to deliver the cash portion, the down payment, and to deliver herself for the evening."

He spins the musician around and pushes him up the stairs of the waiting bus.

Almo missed the class on twelve-tone harmony. Or rather he went, but he soon wandered out without any idea of what was being discussed. He stayed close to campus that week and did not seek out Seggy or Abbey. Instead he read newspapers and taught himself a single Bach passacaglia on the organ at the local church.

When finally he found Seggy, in a usual café again beheading a pack of cigarettes, he told him of his decision. He knew very little about politics and he was not at all sure what he could do to help, but perhaps Seggy could find some use for him. And he was desperate to meet Abbey a second time.

In the next years, he did help. Seggy found him to be energetic if ignorant, hopelessly trustful despite how often he was deceived and of use for his fervor rather than his skills. To launch what would become the incident of the *Artemis*, ironically, he was of great help. The project could not have been done without him. But for all his involvement and in all that time, he never again saw the girl whose face had been so illuminated by her passion.

Three years and a day later Almo set sail on a boat he had not leased but had purchased for cash. In its life of a half-century, the *Artemis* had sailed under the flags of Greece, the United Kingdom, Liberia and Panama. Almo and Seggy negotiated its purchase from a Cypriot who had registered it in Bulgaria and moored it downriver in the Hungarian port of Tolna. Its papers were so crudely forged that the new owners, embarrassed at the amateur job, employed an engraver to forge different ones.

The night before its arrival the two friends stepped off the ship's dimensions on a football pitch in St. Stephan Park. They marked bow, stern and beam with white stones, and then lay themselves down to simulate sleeping spaces. It was important to assure that all 550 persons intended for the passage be able to fit comfortably, have a place for their bedroll and blanket. Their walk-through convinced them it was close quarters, and possible.

But the boat that docked that afternoon, tied up within view of the shack where, ages ago, they had met Gül, was significantly smaller than the one advertised. They had been told 180 tons, and that they could not disprove. A quick pacing, though, showed the dimensions were 53 feet by 20, half the advertised size. And that deception was one of several. The two engines turned out to be one: the housing of the second was intact, but the motor itself had been unbolted and carted away. The missing power did not trouble the men as it might have, since they had decided to stretch their insufficient budget for what was in fact a barge. The money they saved on engines would pay for towing if it were needed. The *Artemis* was fitted with one toilet, no kitchen, no wiring for food lockers or ice boxes. Whatever food they took on the voyage would have to keep.

That afternoon, Almo and Seggy worked with the hired crew to identify machinery not needed on board a passenger barge. Winches and hoists were dismantled and sold for salvage. Almo knew that, just like the purchase of the boat, these sales were to his disfavor, but he had no time to bargain. The ship's masters he dealt with teased him about the practices of those for whom he was working — you are making, they taunted, sharp trades for the sharp-noses — all the while taking every possible advantage of his urgency.

Bright the next morning, Almo's passengers came aboard. They included Poles, Czechs, a few Hungarians. Most were from Transnistria, that region of the Pale of Settlement that lies between the rivers Bug and Dniestr. Each family — for many traveled in three generations — found its paltry square of deck and laid out the blankets issued them. Almo handled the purchase and refitting of the ship, and Seggy scrounged parcels from the Red Cross. Among the crayons and books on elementary Spanish were blankets, the occasional food tin, even that most universal of currencies, tobacco. Seggy, terrified of the water and relieved to yield critical space, stayed behind. The *Artemis* pushed off before noon.

It was a lovely August day, the ship motoring slowly down the Danube. Had the passengers not carried the certitude from their past that the future also held travail, they might have enjoyed the pastoral

Hungarian *puszta* through which they floated. The weather was cool for summer, but not so chilly that sleeping on the open decks was uncomfortable. Almo and the boat leader, a man chosen by the passengers because he spoke the many languages of this ship of Babel, spent the afternoon organizing the food and water into rations for the journey. If they were careful and prompt, the supplies would last.

As the sun was setting in a rose quartz sky, the engine failed. The mechanic assured them it could be fixed. But by the next morning, they continued to drift. An easy wind moved them downriver, but as they neared the port of Tulisa, Almo decided that the mechanic's only skill was talk, and signaled a nearby ship for help. The engine was repaired. The cost of two million *lei* exhausted Almo's reserve.

That night Almo surrendered the single cabin, stuck aft of the wheelhouse like a paper construct for a grammar school project, to three infants and their mothers. He roamed the foredeck and slept intermittently. In the middle of the night he came across a little girl, crying softly into her rag pillow. He sat with her and talked. She was alone — the boat leader had assigned her to a family for purposes of the voyage, but she spoke German and they Rumanian — and her name was Suri. Almo produced a harmonica, courtesy of the International Red Cross, and improvised tunes. She made up four-note songs, and he played them for her as the boat drifted under a sky full of broken stars.

On the third day, the ship limped into view of the Bosporus straits. Through the narrow passage one could make out the bridges of Istanbul. The passengers sent up a cheer, and several muttered prayers of thanksgiving. Istanbul marked the passage into open sea, beyond was Palestine. It was only when the celebration ebbed that Almo noticed the silence. He turned to the captain, whose shrug confirmed it. The engine had quit again, this time for good. Charts were consulted — they had drifted sufficiently far into the harbor to drop anchor. Again the weather was in their favor. The cool had dissipated, it was hot and sultry, but there were no winds. A barge without a tow and without power in the choppy waters of the Bosporus could be endangered by the summer squalls that blow out of the Urals and down from the Black Sea. Ordinarily one would turn the bow into the wind and ride out the weather, but without the ability to navigate, the slightest sea could cause the ship to take water. Too, she had been allowed to drift close to shore for anchorage. These waters were calmer than those of the Black Sea to the north or the Marmara ahead.

They could wait here. Their predicament would be solved in a matter of days.

But it was not. The Turkish coastal authorities quickly placed the ship under quarantine and prevented Almo or any of its passengers from contacting the outside world. Almo argued with the harbor master, with the young lieutenant in charge of the cutter which hove to thirty yards off their bow, and with the sailors who detained his small dory as it tried to reach shore. A day passed and then a second. The weather held, but drinking water was low and provisions were giving out. A third day and a fourth. The crew rigged lines and the few fish they caught were carved into servings the size of a child's thumbnail.

Without the engine, the generator failed and the radio soon sputtered and died. The heat of a Turkish summer settled over the ship. At night the passengers could hear the sounds of the city. On the tenth day of what was to have been a voyage half as long from Budapest to Haifa, dysentery broke out. There were three doctors among the emigrants, and they warned Almo that chronic diarrhea leads to dehydration, and dehydration to death.

With that curse came a blessing. In that afternoon of leaden cirrus clouds, a motor launch set out from the wharves and made an unmistakable line for the hapless ship. Almo looked and could not believe his eyes. Hanging in the railed walk that topped the bowsprit was no carved mermaid but Seggy, squinting at him across the glare of the sea, cigarette centered in his face. Behind him on the foredeck were several official-looking men in dark business suits.

Were the circumstances not so dire, Almo would have told Seggy how comical the scene appeared. It looked to Almo that his old friend had privateered an entire cruiser of accountants. As it was, he had no chance. Seggy gave his news quickly. A political and propaganda battle was being waged over the *Artemis*. The ship had taken on some minor significance in the jousting for world opinion. The gentlemen on board the launch were Swiss, countrymen of Almo, and they had brought provisions from the Red Cross.

His speech made, Seggy was taken from his perch by an armed Turkish seaman, and the somber gentlemen in black suits began handing crates of supplies over the railings. On board the ship, the passengers formed a chain and the food, medicines, and five gallon water bottles were passed across. When the task was done, Seggy reappeared, rummaged in his shabby coat and tugged at something in its pocket. It wouldn't yield. The launch revved an engine and yawed to turn, just as Seggy freed his treasure and tossed it underhand to a speechless Almo. Almo caught it and stuck it in his own pocket.

The night again turned mercifully cool. The doctors assured Almo that while the weather favored them, the small children could not take too much longer in an open boat at sea. He walked among the passengers as dawn split the ancient skies over the straits. His dark-eyed Suri was waiting up for him. He played the harmonica softly and she sang the few notes as the sun rose on another day. Then he produced Seggy's gift. Carefully he peeled the orange as Suri watched, openmouthed. He removed every string and thumbed the meat into slender sections. She looked, he realized, like a tiny version of the young woman he had accompanied that night in Budapest. One by one he fed the perfect wedges to his friend.

That next day he made an announcement to the assembled passengers. From the launch that had visited them yesterday, Almo had learned that his colleagues on shore were making every effort on their behalf, reaching journalists who would publicize their plight, arranging for a mortgage on the very ship to pay for bribes, or for rail passage to Alexandretta and then a different ship to Haifa. He spoke in his low German, and his words were relayed in Polish, in Yiddish, Bulgarian, Rumanian. With the provisions, the water, and the unseasonably cool skies had come hope.

On the evening of the twenty-fifth day, the launch appeared again. This time there was no Seggy. A Turkish coast guard officer asked Almo to come aboard. In the cabin of the launch, glistening with brass and bright-work, the officer told him that his ship must get underway. Almo explained he would love nothing more, but as he had neither fuel nor motor oil — traded to their guard boats for supplies — nor engine nor food nor water, it was quite impossible.

"The harbor must be cleared," said the Turkish officer. "You must weigh anchor or stand ready to be fired upon. My boat will give you a tow."

Almo returned to the ship and informed the captain. The anchor was heaved up, and the mechanic and Almo made fast a line. The passengers were optimistic. They were underway. It had to be a good omen. The *Artemis* was towed for several hours. The launch stopped and her officer asked through a megaphone that Almo release the tow. Almo stood motionless with one foot propped on the capstan that secured the line. The officer addressed the ship's captain and made the same request, release the tow. The captain walked to Almo's side and said something in Rumanian. The Turk answered back and withdrew a pistol from his belt. The captain of the *Artemis* cleared his throat and spat into the water. The Turk gave an order and from his launch an end of the tow line fell into the water. The coast guard launch motored off. Through the passengers there rippled a murmur of speculation and fear.

The *Artemis* drifted along, three miles from the shore line. International waters. The night was again cool, pleasantly cool for mid-summer in the Marmara Sea, and a weak cold front was pushing across the Mediterranean. When the front passed through, a slight breeze moved the waters. Refreshing. Small waves lapped at the gunnels of the ship, and as the sea rose the *Artemis* took on a trickle of water. Overloaded to start, she settled further into the sea, imperceptibly further with each splash. The captain realized their plight and organized bailing parties. There were few suitable pails. The ship settled further down. Towards dawn the wind gave a final push, perhaps five knots. A breeze too light to fill a sail. It stirred up a wave, no higher than a foot, and that wave washed up and over the decks. The liquid ballast sloshed in the holds of the *Artemis* and she slid on her side. Like a sea turtle with a shell full of ball bearings, up on her side and, for a breathless acrobatic moment, still. Then she foundered and slipped under the sea.

1997

1

THE PIER SWAYED IN the fetid and fixed water. Beyond it the land swayed in tandem, a gentle illusion. But not a bad one, Peter thought, hanging over the ship's rail. The world moves and I'm stable. Beats reality. With a gull's screek, a winch at midships hoisted a net full of luggage from the hold. The arm swung its load over the ship's side and lowered it to the pier. The net was floored by a wooden palette, and a dock worker caught a corner of the wood and slipped loops from the derrick's hook so that the net spilled its catch. A half-dozen hands arranged the suitcases, trunks, and satchels indifferently in rows. Amid the hundreds of pieces Peter spotted his own, a large duffel of brown canvas. Not a duplicate — he could tell, for an extra ten bucks the store had stenciled his name on its side.

That was odd. The musicians had been told to stay on board for the turn. Two days of refueling and loading at Le Havre, then the sail back to Hoboken.

Peter hurried to his cabin and passed the assistant steward coming out. The man smiled and uttered a cordial, unintelligible word in German. Even without the language Peter knew it was trouble.

Marcus Collopy sat on the lower bunk, examining the marble-sized joints of his fingers. He wheezed as if the sea air was hard to get down his throat.

"Marcus, the steward. You were supposed to be at his office at eight o'clock."

"Eight o'clock? Man, look at that light." Marcus stuck his nose towards the bare porthole.

"Eight in the morning," Peter said. He'd reminded Marcus as they closed the last set, before Marcus left to tour the ship's several bars.

Marcus looked up at him from under a heavy eyelid, a deflated balloon. "You mean there's another eight o'clock?"

The old man snuck up on awake, irritable and reluctant. Sat on the edge of his bunk in his underwear, a patient who had failed his medical check-up, and stretched his face into today. "No problem, kid. Turns out I didn't need to be there."

"That's a relief." Peter needed this gig. Good money, a chance to work with Marcus, but mostly good money. "No need," Peter said, looking for the story.

"Yeah, seeing as how we're through anyway. Easier to let him come to us." Marcus nibbled at a ring-finger callus.

"What do you mean, through?"

"Through, done, caput," Marcus said between his fingers.

"Fired?"

"You got it. They want a more danceable sound."

Peter had to smile. That, and maybe a leader who led the band. Not one who led the pack at the unbanked turn of the first class lounge, running up whiskey bills for adoring Americans while he improvised stories of Diz and Getz and Bird, some of them true. Not one whose amusement was squeezing the desiccated asses of the sixtyish and occasionally delighted women passengers. Marcus got away with a lot. Of their impromptu quintet he had the name, he was somebody who had played with somebody. If you were a fan you knew that name, you could find it listed on the rhythm credits in the dollar ninety-nine LP bins. A long time ago. Rivers of booze had tinned his eyes, flooded his face, silted a permanent rash where the capillaries were too tired to close. Marcus had gotten this job for them, and now he had lost it.

"Fired," Peter said back. He had never been in Europe before, let alone broke. What would it cost to leave? "We get paid?"

Marcus shot a pained look. He had two sins on his list, stupidity and slipping the beat.

"Kid," he said wearily, "don't be a doofus hipster. Of course we get paid. We played the gig, we get paid. We're on file with the local. What we don't get is a ride back. So we figure something out. We scuffle around and figure something out."

Marcus dressed and they went to the ballroom to retrieve his bass. Peter helped him zip it cautiously into its cover. It was an old Kaye, yellow plywood, no one could tell from the way Marcus coddled it or the tone he coaxed from it just how cheap it was.

The other musicians already had the news. They had cashed out at the purser's window and had split a cab into town.

"Maybe we'll find something," said Marcus. "Europe, man. They love modern jazz here. Diz was very big here, Bud Powell. Very hip country, Europe."

They thumped down the gangplank among the passengers. The embarkation hall was gloomy, filled with the chaos of foreign languages. Peter felt a shortening of breath, stumbling onto the wrong stage. Customs inspectors in muddy blue uniforms moved through the crowd, ignoring baggage and blowing into their fists to fight the cold. November's blade swung across the English Channel.

A young ship's officer pushed through the crowd. Over an arm he carried a plastic basket filled with the mail that had arrived during the week at the steamship company's dock. He called out Anglo names in a thick accent, and when he got to Peter's, pronounced it with a pleased recognition. They smiled at each other, he handed Peter an envelope. Robin's egg blue, inscribed in Matey's mannish hand.

Peter moved into the gullet of the hall, long and low-roofed, slatted walls painted a dull green. Travelers waiting for connections stretched out on benches. He was looking for a corner of his own when Marcus caught up to him.

"I told you."

"Told me what?"

"Told you this is a hip town. The drummer may have something for us in Zurich."

"Zurich? That's not here. That's some other city."

Marcus shrugged indifference. He wore a stained gabardine great-coat, belted, floppy delta lapels of fake fur.

"Right. So you catch the subway. Drummer's gone ahead to sign it up. I've checked his kit and the bass. Meet me at the station tonight. Eight o'clock train."

"The eight train," Peter said.

"Fastest way to get to Harlem."

Marcus bumped his way through the mob. He moved heavily, no lighter on his feet for the absence of his instrument. The hall began to clear as passengers found taxis, tour leaders, their family to take them on. Peter claimed a bench at the far end of the building by a high window. He tucked his satchel and electric keyboard beneath his seat, took the envelope out of his pocket and thumbed open its flap. Inside was a single page. He examined it, looked dumbly at its blank back side. He had survived a shipwreck and now he was stripping the foil from a last bar of chocolate. Should he eat it in one sitting?

Peter dear Peter dear Peter
        Where to start? In the middle, I suppose. I've moved in with Christopher. He is talking about marriage. I'm not ready for that, but I do think I should get on with my life and he seems to represent getting on. You and I keep blundering

about, wander around, are we surveying a map of misunderstanding?

He is very sweet and represents owners of office
buildings about their leases. I can hear you saying Is that
anything for an adult to be doing, but you must understand,
it is. I want to take life less seriously, to see through it so it
doesn't hurt so much. With you it hurts. Really, without you,
which is the more common state of being. Christopher
doesn't exactly do that, take life less seriously, but he takes
the wrong things seriously and that amounts to pretty much
the same thing.

I don't know what else to say. Take care of yourself.

Paradoxically yours,
Matey

He was early to the railroad station. He ate a ham sandwich and a nut
roll. He had read Matey's letter a dozen times. Looked under the
stamp for a clue. He had a week's good wages and some extra the
cruise line had to throw in under the contract to fire them. It might be
ample, he couldn't tell.

Peter found a booth, read the instructions, placed a call. His
French got him to Boston information. They had four listings for
Christopher, residence, office phone, office fax, cell phone. Matey's
jumped from an itinerant pianist who doesn't own a dish towel to a
man with four lines in the directory. Hard to argue. He called the
apartment.

In the long electronic rings, a beat so familiar, his pulse steps up.
He sees the man dimly remembered from college days, wearing a
purple soccer shirt that laces at the neck, white cotton shorts.
Christopher is bouncing a ball from his forehead, ducking under it,
controlling its symmetrical bounces. The thumping is a metronome.

"Is Matey there?"

"No, she's not."

Peter said his name. Twice. Said he was calling from France. "I'd
like to speak to her."

"Well, she's gone out. It's just noon here. She had to run some
errands."

Peter felt his voice slip into a conventional tone, a tone he had
heard others use in movies.

"Listen, Christopher. I would really like to speak to her. There's no place she can call me back."

"Damn it, Steinmuller. I'm not a barbarian. If she were here I'd put her on."

Peter left no message. He sat unhappily imagining the report of his call. Christopher's lawyerly account, accurate and neutral, the soccer ball in perfect rhythm. How he had stammered. Christopher's command, equanimity even, Matey's face strong as a bolt. Why do I think of her mostly to miss her?

Marcus supervised the porter's loading of the drum kit. Everything was stored in hard cases, it would be safe in baggage. High hat, tom-tom, snare, kicking bass. Six or seven pieces. But the yellow Kaye he wouldn't let go. He carried it with him in second class propped against the opposite seat. Peter stowed keyboard and duffel in the rack overhead and sat by the window. The train pulled out ugging like a sound-effects tape.

"This'll do fine," Marcus said, settling his hat over his eyes. It was Russian-style, fur earflaps that tied on top in a bow. At the far end of the car a young couple was spreading cheese and sausage on a sheet of newspaper for their supper. A thick, greasy smell reached Peter and he could hear the purring sound of their intimacy but not what they were saying.

There was nothing to be seen through the black windows. Occasionally a platform, a stop, a few travelers moving on or off. Marcus looked up a first time.

"Zurich," he said. "That's Germany?"

"Switzerland."

"And we're coming from?"

"France. Le Havre is France."

He settled down again.

"My father came from Switzerland," Peter said quickly.

"That right?" Marcus asked from under his hat. "So you got people there we could stay with?"

"No. He came to the States as a little boy and he's long dead. My grandfather died in Switzerland after the war. There's no one left."

"Well," Marcus said, uninterested. "We all go."

"That's a comfort." Marcus scrunched down again and in minutes was asleep.

At the funeral for his father Peter sat dry-eyed and diffident while the doctor talked about an early call. As if they hadn't reckoned the difference in time zones. Death had come fast the man said, a massive coronary. Peter saw a jagged steel construct, a locomotive with a gauge too wide for the tunnels of flesh. Strokes are more fatal in one's early years, the man said, we don't know why.

A young age, hardly a full life. But Peter didn't think his father had been shortchanged. The man was always packed, ready to go. Nothing to leave behind. Peter was the same, except for his music. And music was simple, no motives or hopes. Or people, except for sidemen. The beat, the chords, the tune. Still, days on the road passed slowly.

He woke Marcus for the changes, once in Paris and again in Nancy. In the men's room while they waited for a train, Peter told him of his letter from Matey.

"*We're all an indigo hue*," Marcus said. It was a line from a song.

"'It's a Blue World.'"

"You got it, kid," Marcus said. They moved out to the main salon and found benches to lie on. Marcus hummed eight bars, something else. Closed his eyes, put his hat down over his brow.

Peter let the motion of the train take him home. Life without Matey, better or worse? He would miss being in love. A tune where notes are missing. The bridge, eight bars in the middle — the release, musicians called it — the bridge has washed out. But she was always at him. Why didn't he feel this or that, what did he feel? Just because I can't name it, it still may exist. Not what I mean, she would say. You can't name it because you're afraid of it. Find out what you feel, she'd say. Get in the car and take it for a drive. Her eyebrows would tilt inward, showing earnest.

"The heart as stone in the poetry of Peter Kurz Steinmuller," she announced. They were walking somewhere marshy. Water had seeped through his shoes and his feet were cold. Red-winged blackbirds scolded them from dry stalks. "It's a recurring theme, like a leitmotif. I'm considering it for my senior thesis."

"I don't write poetry," he said.

She looked at him aslant, shot him Bacall, up and sideways at the camera through wisps of hair.

"Perhaps. I figured that would be your defense."

They had met in college. He had noticed her from the start, a face serene in the midst of New England intensity, eyebrows inked across that face, the dashes of an editor's felt pen. The name, Mathilde, had been Matey forever. Her face was strong, igneous. Thick hair, brown with reddish tints in the sun, and eyebrows that were darker, and bushy like a man's. Her ancestry, she told him, was mongrel French, and her father was a doctor somewhere in the Los Angeles basin. The expression on her face was determined even when she was confused. She had a chin like a fist.

"Not bad, Steinmuller," she said. "You're getting the hang of this language business, English as a second tongue. Next week's lesson, I like you Matey. Simple declarative sentence with an appositive."

They first made love in the fall. His roommates were gone for Thanksgiving holiday. Too far to fly back to California for the weekend, she had stayed on campus and he stayed too. They lay in front of a fire on a black bear rug in a far dormitory corner. Afterwards they lingered, fingertips over each other's faces. The soft bristles of a Japanese paintbrush. It was the lingering Peter best recalled, wordless and inches apart, Ella singing *Body and Soul* over the speakers the way she sings, each note hit smack in its stomach.

"You got to give me the setting is romantic," he said at last. "The first snow of the season, a hearth, the pine logs. Maybe you'd prefer Rachmaninoff."

"Should I?" she said wide-eyed. "You think he does this better?"

That was the Matey he used to find sleep as his train bumped across France up tempo, the tough and soft and funny one.

He quit school midway in his second year. Developed a few tics. He would idly put his fingers to his face, touch the lower lip on its red plum. He rocked when he listened, slowly, a dance tempo. He grew the spare beard that he still wore, a scruff cover that didn't quite take, but he kept it. It made his appearance taller, thinner, ill at ease.

Dropping out of school was a manumission. He was freed. He had regularly earned pocket money playing occasionals, and now he took on established club dates. Backed on two CD's, got several solos. *Downbeat* reviewed one of the recordings and called him a young lion of the piano. But he moved away from that path, stuck to obscure bars. Recording jobs meant pursuit, you had to interview, rehearse, a lot of hassle. This way, no hanging around. The influence of events over his will comforted him. Winds were acting upon him, he needn't choose, he let himself be blown along.

Matey graduated from their college and moved to Boston to begin a career in advertising. He got a job playing keyboard for a rock group, wrote several tunes for their first CD and earned enough to last six months. He moved to Los Angeles, but a second record deal fell through. The Coast was a surplus of talent, stacked like cordwood, waiting to be selected. Pianists who cut him up and down, modulating everything through twelve keys. A guitarist he knew in Kansas City thought there might be something there.

Kansas City worked out. It was a singles disco, a DJ faked a black accent and played records when the band was off. Suits hustling secretaries, serious boozers. He found a rooming house by a park. There were rowboats on the lake. He took long walks in the afternoon and had an affair with a woman who played passable trombone.

Until her death Peter mailed his mother extra money. Not from charity, but to repay college expenses squandered on him. The money he sent made him feel better. Distant. He had in mind to set himself so free he could float.

There had been talk of money in the family, his Swiss grandfather. But the war changed everything, and his grandmother had arrived in the U.S., he knew, toting a baby and very little else. If there had once been wealth, only his grandmother would have the story, and she was long past recollecting and talking about it.

Between gigs he found his way to Boston for a joy fix. The first few times Matey took him in without dues. After Kansas City and the trombone, though, she was on him.

"You think this is some emotional flop house, Peter, you're wrong. You want to stay, I'm glad to have you. You want to sit and contemplate the predicament of man at the crossroads, no reliable information to help him along his existential way, include me out. I'm not at home for that."

He thought if he could stay near Matey he'd learn her passion. A summer theater on the Cape hired him, he and a drummer were the pit. Dark Monday and Tuesday. He bought a wheezing BMW motorbike the scrap side of antique. After Sunday night curtain, he snaked his bike through lines of returning beach traffic.

She pulled him, she and her delicate body. He visualized it like an Escher drawing, a *trompe l'oeil*. He saw her radiance, and a moment later saw the sex act as an interlude of risibility. The posture itself was the perfect analog for its dangers: consumption, expenditure, jeopardy. He was swallowed up, he had disappeared.

In Boston not far from Matey's apartment lived a man who had been their college classmate. Christopher pursued her, and the mention of him inflated Peter with anger and possessiveness. When Peter visited her in Boston he would scout the apartment for traces of Christopher's presence. Whether or not he found them, the search put him in a foul mood. Christopher had enrolled in law school, a course of conduct Peter described with some satisfaction as predictable. "Like typhus after a flood."

"Typhoid."

Peter considered this, his thumb to his lip. "Why doesn't he live across the river, where he belongs?"

"He means nothing, he's an escort," Matey would say, but Peter was not assuaged.

"Do you want me to send him away?" Matey asked one night across the serving bar in her apartment.

He looked away. "It's not for me to tell you what to do."

Matey was tossing a salad for their supper. It was a Saturday and they had been to the market for vegetables, striped bass, a particular and expensive wine. They were celebrating: a song of Peter's on the CD had won an award.

"If you want me to, just say the word."

Peter was leafing through a newspaper. "I do music, not words"

The thought of her body obsessed him. It was perfect, small, long and perfect thighs, a sculptor's creation, the back drawn with a single curve. The thought of someone else touching it filled him with animus. He was reading classifieds, he began to read one out loud, quoted the price of a Ford Taurus.

"Why do you get like this?" she asked.

"I don't *get* like this. I *am* like this."

The meal was excellent. She put out cloth napkins and set a full service. On the road, Peter often ate a can of something warmed on the motel radiator. He told her that some wit had said a man would rather his mistress be dead than unfaithful.

She looked at him as if he had uttered something clever. He regretted his words but they were out. She even smiled. When she spoke her voice was precise and low.

"Well, for one thing, I am not your mistress. Any more than you are mine. And for a second, I am not unfaithful. As a matter of fact, just the bloody opposite." She plucked the few capers from her plate singly and ate them.

"You and I happen to be two friends who fuck. Is that how you would like to see this? Nothing more, am I right? That's fine." And she lifted the plate and scaled it, with a practiced frisbee delivery, towards the kitchen. It scattered a contrail of onions and peas, the small, sweet kind. Most of the broiled fish had been eaten. The plate struck the splash board and broke neatly in half.

After a moment he rose and went around to her. He leaned over and kissed the top of her head. She began to cry.

"If you're going to do this regularly, I'll buy you a dog to eat the leavings."

She had her elbows propped on the raffia place mat and she leaned her brow on her fists. She cried for a long time and he stood behind her. He could not think what to say. His leg began to cramp. When she finally spoke he could not understand for the soft coughs that spotted her speech, the soft and sobbing coughs.

He bent his head down.

"I didn't hear."

She caught her breath and spent it on a single sentence. "Dogs don't eat vegetables."

He placed his palm between her shoulder blades and rubbed her back, her neck.

"Well," he said, trumped. "Then I'll buy you a pig."

Their lives connected and moved apart. A film of the braided trail of their passings would show as the chase scene in a silent movie, the car and the train pursuing each other, the road parallel to the tracks as passengers call out. Overpasses, severe turns where the routes part. Every so often an intersection, the possibility of violent coincidence.

Christopher, Peter's rival, had captained their college's soccer team. He liked to jog. Matey began to run with him, mornings on the iron-fenced asphalt trail by the Charles. They exchanged runners' gifts, fabric wallets and pedometers. Christopher graduated from law school and asked Matey to marry him. She said no. He joined a large Boston firm and took up the practice of real estate law. Peter too got a steady job — two months at a ski resort in Utah. Guitar and bass, his piano. Union scale, good conditions.

In the long separation from Peter, Matey had begun to sleep with Christopher. Christopher lived nearby, he was persistent and logical, and Matey had no indication from Peter that he would return.

A year later he signed on with a dance band, playing college proms in New England. He called and Matey invited him to stay with her. She had moved to a larger apartment with a view of the harbor. She was fit, jogging regularly, though for his visit she gave that up too. During the day while she was at work he looked for inscriptions in every book on the shelf. On the job he played authentic, carefully scored arrangements of the swing era. He found himself sleeping ten, eleven hours each night. Waking at noon, waiting for Matey to come home in the fading light, he watched television where people he didn't know told of their singular problems.

Matey continued to instruct him, and he resented it. Why do you know how I should live my life? Peter asked her. Because I love you. I love you, he said, but I don't tell you what to do. You don't know about love, she said. You think love and cruelty are antonyms, but they are not. A part of you makes love to me while another part hurts me.

There was serious music, much of it modern, that Peter did not understand. Its sound made him anxious. So with her words. Peter took a gig in a New Jersey saloon, cocktail franks in tomato sauce and cubes of yellow cheese. That is where Marcus happened on him. Two weeks later a bargain cruise ship was bearing him to France to find he didn't know what.

Peter slept the final leg to Zurich. Fretfully, amid elusive and inter-rupted dreams. Riffs came to him while he slept, snatches of a tune, but he could never bring them back. He opened his eyes to a thin grey bar that flashed code under the window shade. Marcus was gone. Missing, no sign of him, no hat, no greatcoat, no bass. Peter looked around. Most of the passengers looked new. Could Marcus have left the train while he slept? The young couple sat apart, dozing with their heads lolled back like corpses. At the far end opposite the water closet stood Marcus's instrument. And from inside, stool-high, Marcus's arm extended and his hand grasped the throat of the bass.

The train juddered into Zurich and with the city came the light. Came as a dim bulb, obscured by haze. Outside slept pleasant suburbs in ordered contentment. An old man with a limp moved down the aisle carrying a tray of white cardboard cups with rolled rims. He was selling biscuits and what looked like tea. Peter stopped him, paid for two cups.

Marcus returned from the toilet and Peter handed him a cup.

"You come into money?"

"Listen, Marcus. It's the dawn of a new day. We'll land ten weeks at some fancy spa, room, board and a Steinway grand. Besides, you don't get rich by keeping it. You get rich by giving it away. Reinvest. Didn't you tell me that?"

"Me? Do I look like I know about getting rich?"

The tea was strong and sweet. Peter rose and stretched. The train decelerated.

"Look at that sky," Peter said. "It's a good omen."

To the west the horizon was clear of clouds and in it hung a slender crescent moon.

"I thought omens were bad."

"Not all. Look, Marcus. How can that be a bad omen What does that moon make you think?"

Marcus peered out, sniffed. "Cuticles, man. Makes me think of a manicure."

Zurich. They retrieved the drum kit. Moving in shifts, they piled bags, bass, drum cases by an iron bench near the entrance to the Hauptbahnhof. Peter stationed himself over the luggage and propped his legs on the cases while Marcus went to phone the drummer. When Marcus did not come back Peter, restless to see Europe, ventured to the open entryway. People moved about with morning's purpose. Up the street he saw a park. The other way was the river, mud dark and hidden from the sun. But the city was lifting up to snag the low rays. It showed itself tan, weathered brick buildings with ocher roofs, spires from otherwise sensible cathedrals popping up Gothic as if dripped in sand.

When he turned back Marcus was sitting on the pile of cases, frowning.

"Listen, kid. I lose this bass *I'm* selling tea on the subway."

"You could do better. Steady work, no requests. So," Peter asked, "we got the gig?"

"Yes and no."

"Meaning?"

"Me yes you no. Turns out they had a piano from the start, alls they needed was rhythm behind."

Peter looked at him. "So much for the new era."

"Look. I got a leader's cut. Here," Marcus handed him some bills. "Here's a couple C's. See you through. Do like you said, reinvest."

Peter took the money, stuffed it into his pocket without looking. "Thanks. And for the advice. It's like having my own personal Louis Rukeyser."

"Don't know the cat. What's he play?"

They walked down the line to find a taxi large enough to carry the instruments and Marcus. An old black Citroen. Peter helped load dented drum cases into its trunk, the driver pushed back the seat and they maneuvered the bass, standing up, into the right front.

Marcus got in the rear seat. He scratched his cheek, high, where no stubble had grown. Peter handed him a last cymbal case through the window.

"So kid. You got to see the possibilities. Listen, we all got this. Women, dough. You hear what I'm saying? Trouble."

"Some more than others."

"I suppose. But it evens out. Women, dough, trouble. Let me tell you something. What's my chick's biggest problem? She's waiting for me to fall by, waiting and not waiting, and all these other cats are coming on to her. Man, I understand that. You got to understand that. So what is her problem? She's not in love. I'm on a bus I'm in Europe, she wants company, but she's not in love. There she is, sucking cock and she's not in love. So I want to say, look, Pearl. Be at ease. We're all cocksuckers. But I keep quiet. Do I want to ease her pain? To enjoy herself? I do not."

"Those are your closing words?"

"That's it," he said. "If you can't say anything real nice, Jackson, don't say nothing at all, that's my advice."

Peter laughed. "Yeah," he said and tapped the roof. The cab drove off.

Steinmuller was alone. On an enormous board overhead were posted times and destinations of trains. Vienna, Munich, Stuttgart. He had the beard and restless eyes of a scholar, an anarchist. He picked up his duffel and the Rhodes keyboard and crossed the street. Outside, workers were climbing scaffolds to steam the brick of the railroad station. He wore a black wool overcoat and a slouch cap in herringbone. His hands stuffed into gloves, he made himself warm against the day by hunching his shoulders and tucking his elbows in. He stopped at a newsstand, bought a map and a slender pamphlet about the city. Withdrew his wallet and opened its contents to the woman behind the window, like a pup turns belly up. She smiled, picked out two U.S. dollars, and made change in centimes.

Now the sun was warming the air and the color of the brick around him responded, deepened. He walked into the park and chose a bench looking east. He read about the founding of the guild halls. Maybe there's a musician's hall. Tucked in the pocket of his wallet was a yellow card, the famous New York local, 802. Maybe I'll check in, meet the brothers. Office workers passed him without notice. He looked about. The other benches had filled up. Down-and-outers catching a morning nap. Mostly young people, scruffy and gaunt. He put down his pamphlet, sat back in the new winter's sun and watched. A whispered exchange. There another. This was connection central, it must be Zurich's needle park. Commerce grew heavy as the morning wore on. The ones who stayed and dealt shot him hostile looks, but no one challenged him. A girl in army fatigues spread a blanket over the sidewalk and put out ski sweaters, reds, yellows. A young man in a scuffed leather jacket drove up on a motorcycle, rested it on its kickstand, and stuck a sign in its windshield. It was not unpleasant sitting there.

By his bench was a wire trash basket. He pulled out the newspaper at its top, the *Neue Züricher Zeitung*, refolded its sections. Perhaps there were ads for pianists. He could make a buck tuning, but he would need tools. Easier to pick up a casual date or two.

The classifieds, like the entire paper, were in German. In twenty-four hours I lose my job, my girl, and end up in some joint with three languages, none of them mine.

He started through the paper. The pages were yellow and stiff from exposure and smelled of the open air. Every so often he recognized an English phrase, the name of an American product. It encouraged him. The sports section had a photograph of Larry Bird.

He came to the last inside page. A single legal notice, taking up the entire space, with four columns of names. He turned to the back, the list went on.

And as he looked three words fell from the page. He held the paper high to bring them into focus, and the words fell from the page. They might have been written in slate, in mercury. Toward the bottom of the list, the print flashed at him and wavered, and three gravid words tumbled into his lap. His very name. Pietr Kurz Steinmuller.

CARS STOPPED AT TRAFFIC lights and started again on the green. Within the park, young users dozed on benches and on the wintering grass. Some went about their commerce in scowls. He was a minor figure in the Brueghel painting, the town tends to its business as Icarus drops into the sea.

Bold-faced type topped the notice, followed by a short paragraph. He could make no sense of it, what any of it said. He caught his breath. It was of course possible, even likely, that the ad had nothing to do with him. None of his three names was uncommon; the combination might be shared by others. He had been called after his father's father — he dimly remembered his mother telling him that, family history was spoken of rarely — and his grandfather had spelled his first name just as it here appeared. He would find out what he could.

The woman at the newsstand smiled to show she remembered him. She had a round face, red and full as fruit. One of her canine teeth was missing. Peter asked her to read the advertisement for him, placed the paper in the plastic money tray. Waited.

She picked up the folded page and wagged her eyebrows. Perhaps she couldn't read, perhaps she objected to what it said. But he persisted. He asked a second time, once in formal French, adding at the end, *bitte*. She smiled shyly and began to speak. It was tough going for her. And she read in German. He put up his hand, thanked her and retreated to the street.

At the entrance to the park the youth with the motorcycle sat on the curb. The bike was in sorry condition, a make Peter didn't recognize. A crayoned sign on its windscreen said 1050 SF.

"Forty thousand kilometers," the boy said eagerly to Peter. "The odometer just stopped working, and that is the truth."

"I don't want to buy it. I want you to translate something."

"I make you a good deal. Nine hundred francs, six hundred dollars. Extra fairings I throw in for twenty more. Francs, not dollars."

"Nice bike," Peter said. "Can you read this?" Peter handed him the newspaper. The boy was not out of his teens. He squinted down through the granny glasses at the end of his nose. Showed irregular teeth, striated in browns and yellows.

"I don't know," he said. "I need to sell my cycle."

"Here," Peter said. The boy took the five-dollar bill gingerly, by its corner. It might have been a summons. He placed a grimy finger on the headline and traced his surprisingly facile translation.

"Swiss Banks Begin Global Process To Identify Owners of World War Two Time Accounts.'" He looked up.

"Go on."

"The Swiss Bankers Association here publishes the second list of all sleeping,' there is a better word, *shluffen*."

"Dormant."

"Dormant, 'all dormant War Two time,' not exactly time," and looked at Peter expectantly.

"Era."

"Era. ' . . . World War Two-era dormant accounts. This initiative will be administered by the banks shown below under supervision of the Swiss Federal Banking Commission and the Independent Committee of . . . ' I don't have the word for this, famous, reliable." Peter motioned for him to go on. "' . . . reliable persons established to identify dormant accounts of Holocaust victims.'"

Peter held the boy by the arm. "What are you supposed to do, does it say?"

The boy scanned, read a list of toll-free numbers, dropped his finger to the last block of text at the bottom of the last page.

"'The process is clear and simple. Claims will be resolved as soon as possible. These banks are committed to use unclaimed funds for humanitarian or charitable purposes. Please come forward. You will receive prompt attention.'"

Peter's eye went to his name. Beside it was a dagger symbol, sending him to footnotes. He put his finger to it and looked at the boy questioningly.

"That relates to the specific bank you are to make claim at. This name," and here the broken nail sank to the last line of print on the page. "Löwenhoft Handelsbank."

"And this?"

"The address of the bank. Paradeplatz."

"Here? Zurich?" Peter yanked the paper back from the boy and looked around. He wanted directions.

"Yes, of course here. Zurich. Where else?"

"Where? How do I find it?"

"You follow Bahnhofstrasse. There. Ten, eleven blocks. That is pedestrian only, but the next street? The trolley takes you there. Towards the lake. It cannot pass you by."

"I can't miss it," Peter said. He was moving.

Must be a coincidence. His grandfather was not a Holocaust victim. Merely a sharing of names. Too many objects in the world, some must share. People were not presented with lost fortunes except in black-and-white TV shows that don't get rerun.

And although that is what he thought, the skepticism did not slow his feet. He reached Paradeplatz out of breath. His run down the wide pedestrian way, for it was downhill, a constant decline leading, he now saw, to the lake — there at the end of the street was the quay, the ferry pier, the lake glinting a soiled and begrudging pewter in the winter light — left him winded. His friend with the overpriced Italian cycle was right. It could not pass you by. The square was created by the intersection of five streets and was dominated by two massive buildings. Over the elaborate portico of one, the Hotel Savoy, flew the flags of several nations. The second, if the clues in its jaw-breaking name were accurate, was some sort of bank or clearing house. The density of so much respectability stayed Peter's headlong advance. He set his bag and keyboard case by his feet. He would take a moment to rest.

He took a window table at a café and ordered coffee. The architecture around him stood smug and secure. That of course was its purpose, to stay the timid and assure the powerful. He could sense his heartbeat. The idea of presenting himself as a claimant on lost property suddenly made him queasy. He unfolded the newspaper page and checked the address. Where to find a street number? He paid for his coffee and walked around the square. Several smaller buildings stood on the north side. On one, chest-high script on a modest brass plaque, were the words Löwenhoft Handelsbank.

The building went to four stories before the roof began its slope, then two more of gabled windows. Beamed corbels protruded just below the roofline. From a shingled cupola on top, a flagpole flew the Swiss flag and below it the blue and white banner of the canton. Peter shrugged. What the hell.

He struggled with the door, buttressing its weight against the luggage in his extended arm. An elderly guard walked over and held the door ajar for him.

"Thanks," Peter said. "*Dänke schoen.*"

"You will allow us to keep these here," said the man. He was over seventy, but he easily pried Peter's fingers from the handles of his baggage and took both pieces. "You will let me know when you are ready for them."

Peter nodded. He found himself in front of a blue-haired woman who sat in military posture behind a marble-topped desk. She asked if she could help.

Peter explained his visit. He had come from the U.S., Hoboken actually. He read from the notice, as best as he could remember the translation, improvising a sentence about interested parties that he realized was not included. The woman, the glasses on her chest hung from her neck by a bead and crystal string, smiled as he spoke and raised her telephone.

"May I have your name?"

When he told her the muscles at her eyelids winced almost imperceptibly, and she asked an odd question.

"Is that truly your name?"

"Truly."

She wrote on a pad and motioned to a bench. "Please wait. It will not be long."

It wasn't. Within minutes a runner brought her a brown manila envelope. She called Peter from his seat.

"Mister Steinmuller. These documents are necessary for you to complete. If you will do that and return them, they will be brought to the attention of the bank officer who remains in charge of this, Assistant Manager Durren."

The envelope held a thick packet of forms, perhaps thirty pages. He dropped his face into a slump of weariness, lower lip out. Wasn't there an easier way?

"I am afraid we must have you to complete these documents. The rules are the rules. Assistant Manager Durren will then review the documents."

"Does the name Kafka mean anything to you? Does he work here?"

The woman at the desk did not laugh, as Peter had intended, but someone standing behind him did. He turned to find a second woman, his age or a little older, perhaps mid-thirties, whose humor lingered in her eyes as she spoke to him.

"May I be of assistance?"

"You are?"

"Helene Durren." She said it softly, neglecting to pronounce the H. Peter found the elision provocative. She wore a banker's suit of a

38

grey darker and duller than her eyes, a gauzy white blouse and crimson bow, paisley print knotted askew, Chaplin style.

"Any relation to Assistant Manager Durren?" he asked.

Deadpan, she cocked her head, deciding whether to play. "We share the same flat."

"Lucky Assistant Manager Durren." Once more she let something show without changing expression, forward pass ignored at the line of scrimmage, and moved by him. He understood he was to follow. The task was not without its pleasures. Assistant Manager Durren strode off on unavoidable legs bound in white tights. Her skirt came to mid-thigh.

They walked at a purposeful pace across a large, open room. People spoke into the bone ends of telephones, spoke in small groups. Soft guttural words disappeared in the deep carpet, the spaces.

She showed him a chair and he sat. Across a glass-covered desk, Peter again explained his presence. This time he refrained from explaining the notice. It was fair to assume she knew its contents.

"You may be interested to learn, Mr. Steinmuller, we get very few responses from these postings. This and a prior list have been published for several weeks. Most claims come to us by post. None just walks into the bank. Until now. The account in what you say is your grandfather's name is under a power of attorney. In the nature of a trust."

She stopped to make sure he was following. "You are aware of the background of these accounts?"

Peter shrugged. "There's been something about it in the papers."

"Yes, you might say so. In response to criticism that originated in your country, the major banks of Switzerland have conducted inquiries into accounts where there has been no activity since World War Two. Their efforts have been Herculean. I can say this for I was assigned the job of ferreting them out. The computer work. Not that your press has acknowledged any of the effort. But it is there".

Peter turned his palms up.

"And when a claimant appears?"

"If a claimant appears and proves his title as beneficiary or heir, then of course the bank orders the money to be paid to him. Or in this case, the trustee to pay. The bank is not the trustee, you understand. We merely hold the deposits and the records."

The spear points at the corners of her eyes were very white. He listened to her words and watched those points, how the movement of her lids flexed their angle.

"Who is the trustee? Is he still alive? Perhaps he could help me figure out whether this is some relative of mine?"

Helene Durren folded and unfolded her fingers. Peter felt it a reasonable question.

"We cannot disclose that. Our banking laws put a great premium on privacy. We cannot give out that information since we do not know whether you have a proper claim."

"And I can't find out whether I have a proper claim unless I can get some information. Look at these forms." He slid an inch of paper out of the envelope. "They're in German."

Finally a smile he could take credit for. "Yes," she said. "So they are. I am sympathetic."

"Listen. I may have no connection with this. I don't mean I'm entitled to whatever money is here, but I did have a grandfather who lived in Switzerland and he had a name the same as mine. Almost the same. Except for spelling. Maybe there are thousands of Peter Kurz Steinmullers running around."

Helene Durren pushed back from the desk, crossed her legs. The whisper of movement disappeared in the high room. Peter wished he had seated himself further back, where he might see that knee perched upon the stockinged thigh. Her eyes held his.

"I think it more accurate to say you have the same name as he. And no, I think it not a common name. There are none in Zurich or in the major cities of our country, for example."

"You've checked."

She nodded. He wished she would not take on the role of the adversary.

"And you are not the trustee?"

"The bank is not the trustee. May I make a suggestion, Mr. Steinmuller?"

"Peter."

"These forms are somewhat technical." She wrote on a pad in precise strokes. She had slender fingers, nails clipped short. Was she a biter? There was something erotic in the thought.

"This is the name of a lawyer here in Zurich. Albert Frey. He does work with our bank. We know him to be reliable. It may be worth your while to seek his assistance in completing these forms. He will charge you for that but it may be worth your while."

Peter took the slip of paper.

"There is no way I can avoid the forms? Surely there's an exception in the rules for the illiterate, the mentally deficient?"

"I'm afraid not. The rules have been set by the Swiss Bankers Association and by our civil code."

"Every rule has exceptions. Maybe one for piano players? That would make your code truly civil."

She tucked in her lower lip, tasted it, crinkled her eyes. "Something you should know about us Swiss. We adore rules. More than anything. Many of us oppose joining the common market for that very reason. You see, the European Community has volumes of rules. And who would be the only ones to obey? The Swiss."

Peter got up slowly. He was hoping his pace would cause her to rise, walk him to the entrance. She had a full figure, seal brown hair cut in a mannish style, too short for his liking. But intelligent eyes and a wide forehead. She was nowhere as pretty as Matey. Given the Atlantic Ocean and the immutable existence on its other side of Christopher, that was a comparison he was prepared to overlook.

"Hey. It looks like I'm going to be in town for a while. Can you recommend a place to stay? Somewhere inexpensive, somewhere . . . " he thought to make her smile again, " . . . where they don't make you follow the rules."

She retrieved the slip of paper from him, wrote down a second address, handed it back without a word. When again she looked up at him with eyes grey as rain clouds, it was to signal she was through flirting. Peter retreated. The guard stood at the door holding Peter's satchel and keyboard. White hair to the collar, Captain Kangaroo moustache, but for the uniform and Sam Brown belt, he might have been an aging hipster. Peter took his gear and went out into the day

Albert Frey, lawyer and *notaire*, made clear that his fee did not depend on success. Half was due in advance. He could not estimate the time; much would depend upon the responsiveness of the United States consulate, at which venue Peter should know Frey had considerable yank — obliging respect was the term he used — but much would depend in turn upon their burden of work. The process was not difficult, merely comprehensive.

The lawyer officed in one of the low, whitewashed buildings overlooking the Limmat. It was difficult to tell from his desk whether his practice amounted to anything, but Helene Durren had given him sincere endorsement. Frey was a heavy man, dandruff speckling the black of his suit jacket. In a different time the surroundings might have suggested a wizard: the dusty light, walls lined with books, a few arcane and meaty volumes lying about in thoughtful disarray.

Peter told Frey what he could. The names of his grandfather, grandmother, father. No, he didn't know their cantons of origin, and he could only guess at dates of immigration. Yes, he believed both grandparents were Swiss citizens at the time, the one having died shortly after the war, some sort of accident, and the grandmother immigrating with her small child. That is the story he remembered. His own passport number, statistics. His grandmother's address in Florida. Would his grandmother be able to help? She spoke German?

Almost exclusively, said Peter. It had been years since he had seen her, before the nursing home. The old woman had fussed over him, asked him unintelligible questions about people who were long dead. Mistaken him for someone else. His own mother had died ten years after his father. The family history was chalk dust, clapped to the wind. If Peter had to justify his claim, he ought to give it up. Not at all, the lawyer assured him. There is a good chance to find this infor-mation. The Immigration Service of your country keeps records. That was where they would go to prove any claim.

Frey wrote down what Peter would need. Questions to ask the consulate, the procedure for confirmation of signatures and passport numbers, the name of the consular attaché for whom Peter was to ask. Most reverently and framed in a double rectangle that Frey had drawn for emphasis, the figures representing the fee. It amounted to most of the cash Peter was carrying. And Peter was carrying all the cash he owned.

He emptied his pockets on the scarred dresser top. Pieces of paper, strange coins, a few bills of florid design, more pieces of paper. His room, three flights up, facilities one down, had a narrow bed covered by a yellow tufted spread. The windows looked across low roofs. He was paying by the day, more expensive that way, but Frey had not been able to tell him how long this would take. Perhaps after he visited the consulate.

He inventoried the loose pile of paper. The notes from Helene Durren, forms to be filled out, railway timetable, the pawn ticket that now represented his keyboard. Just as good as the keyboard, said the man who ran the shop, a little man with Santa Claus glasses. Yeah, said Peter, but it's a bitch to practice on the ticket. Pawn shops were the same here as in the States: long on signet rings, tie tacks, trumpets. Don't tenor players ever run short? Ten days to redeem.

Here's how to make a new person. Put all the papers someone's collected into a shoe box. Insurance policy, letters from his squeeze, social security card. Then set out the box in a thunder storm and wait for a lightening strike, like Dr. Frankenstein. Boom, the immaculate conception. Peter had first emptied the shoe box. Now he was headed the other way.

He went for dinner to a basement café recommended by his land-lady. The special platter was nourishing — ham hocks, sauerkraut, beans. He washed it down with a glass of thick beer. When he returned, his landlady was waiting in the parlor. She snared him and seated him by a low table of tin-framed photographs and, with no effort at making him understand, spoke of her children's lives. He nodded, every so often asking something of her, which child was this?

Finally, safe in his room, he sat over the forms Frey had given him, their terms translated to English in Frey's sharp-pointed pencil over the Bank's official printing. The process was interminable, the same questions a dozen times. He gave the same answer — he didn't know. He was to include letters of credence and letters missive. What were they?

He simply did not know much about his family, and what he knew he preferred to disregard. The past has no application. All this crap is precisely what he had left behind. Don't step on me, man, Marcus would say. His way of telling the band to give him room, stay off the bass registers. Room was what Peter sought, even from himself. Room, not information. Whatever was inside was shrinking, receding further and further, so that it was harder to feel. A dried pea rattling around a box. In anger, in sex, in everything but music he found that he stood off to the side, looking at himself.

What if he could call his mother? He imagined the scene in a movie: the shabby little town, the closed mill where they'd manufac-tured shear blades until the steel business and everything that serviced it went overseas. The wide river valley humid and still in the summer, spotted this time of year with patchy snow. On his mother's street, hurricane fences marking unkempt lawns. Her house was a frame bungalow. Inside would shine the single light by her secretary desk, as she jotted in her lessons for the week, toted up who owed what. When the telephone rang it was rarely a new student, more likely a cancellation, someone dropping out. I don't think he has any real talent, Mrs. Steinmuller. I think we might as well give it up.

He saw her sitting at the Chickering, teaching. A drab and spiritless life. Oafish boys and polite, reluctant girls, hammering away at the Clementi sonatinas like rocks in a quarry.

He went back to finish the forms. She was unmoveable. When was the last time he had seen her high or low? She used to care about the music. Somewhere she lost it, and it was too bad. If you had the music, you could live there. A lot of musicians did just that, lived there, moved in and used isolation or dope or their instrument to lock the door. The music goes round and round and it comes out here. The inner ear has those lovely interlocking canals, those curls that shuffle on themselves. Once you get the sound in, you can move it from chamber to chamber, no one can snatch it away. The ear is a mollusk with its house stacked on its back. Bags packed, make my getaway. You can live there like a rooming house boarder. Cut loose, do without. He finished the last question after midnight and turned off the switch.

Morning brought a winter light quiet as moss. Peter drank a second cup of coffee in the kitchen and set off with his papers.

His rooming house was on the east side of the city and the route to the American Consulate was a twisting one. Zollikerstrasse was about two miles that way.

He walked for an hour. Finally he came upon the Romanesque portal of a building too large for its neighborhood. A single United States marine stood guard, wore woolen dress blues, held his rifle by its snout at parade rest. His face had been scraped clean and, in the cold, red splotches showed on his cheeks where they were beginning to chafe.

"This the American Consulate?" Peter asked for the hell of it.

"Yes sir."

"This a good job you got?"

"Yes sir."

Peter opened the door. Cat is standing out in the November wind, maybe twenty-five degrees. What's he going to say? Another soul who has pawned his keyboard.

After the requisite wait, he was assigned a junior officer named Jellicoe. She was a young woman who had invested effort into making herself drab. No makeup, hair cut garden-shear irregular off the shoulders, blue cardigan over knitted blue top. Curious dress code. Presenting an image to the world that the U.S. is immune to invasion and fashion.

To Peter's surprise, Miss Jellicoe was helpful. She reviewed his efforts and corrected entries, completed others with language Peter would not have thought of, issued letters of credence.

"They simply establish who you are," she told him. "You need to be recognized as a citizen of the United States."

"We all need recognition," he said, but she ignored him.

"What is your means of support?"

"I'm a musician." This did not satisfy her and she waited. He had encountered the problem before. "Really what I am is a tourist until I can resolve this. Then I intend to find a job to earn my passage back."

She pursed her lips. "I must warn you, Mr. Steinmuller, against accepting employment while in Switzerland. It would be difficult for you to obtain a work permit. Alien labor is a significant problem and the Swiss take it seriously."

"So shall I," Peter said. This place was an epidemic of rules and Officer Jellicoe had caught a dose. "Now, how many weeks will this take to clear up? I have to plan."

"Most of what is missing I can retrieve this afternoon. We're all connected, you see."

Peter looked mystified. It sounded like good news. Are we all connected as members of the vast human race? She indicated the computer screen behind her.

"If I can find the date of your grandmother's immigration, the other materials we need will follow. I can gateway into the files. That will allow us to be on line at INS, Immigration and Naturalization, and to the extent a manual search is needed, we can order that overnight."

"So you think . . . ?"

"Timing? I can't say. It should be within the week. Would you like me to call you with the results or simply forward these on to your address? You're staying in Zurich?"

Peter found the slip on which Helene Durren had written the address of his lodgings. He handed it over.

Miss Jellicoe riffled the pages on end to square them away. She fastened the note to the stack with a black alligator clip, then looked up surprised to find Peter still there. His face showed a pang of loss — he asked her to copy the address and give him back Helene's note.

A week, he thought. I never asked Marcus where they were playing.

"You don't happen to know the jazz spots in town, Miss Jellicoe."

Her eyes flinched. Had he asked something rude?

"I'm sorry. I do not. Perhaps the newspapers . . . "

Peter brought to mind his small room, the narrow bed. He had no training as an expatriate, and he was enjoying the ease of talking to an American. He had no plans.

"Where does one go? I mean, where do folks like us hang out?"

She regarded him. Looked down and held her finger under the entry where he had listed his college.

"You've had a good education."

It was not what he'd meant, folks like us. "Yeah. Well, I'm on the program. I'm a recovering educated."

She examined him again, substituting for distant curiosity a touch of reproof.

"You should see the Fraumünster. It dates to the Middle Ages and has stained-glass windows by Marc Chagall. The Kunsthaus galleries, the archives of Thomas Mann."

"Hey," he said, rising. "Thanks."

3

PETER IDLED AWAY THE first days, walked the streets. Nights he hunted the bars. No music, no sign of Marcus. He budgeted enough money for the cheapest non-sched ticket back to JFK. With his inheritance he would redeem the Rhodes and go back in style. Or stay. Perhaps stay. You're here, take your licks.

He settled into the routine of a tourist, content but for a growing anxiety. Not money, that was a condition of his life. His fingers. In a single week without practice one's touch became heavy, notes ran into each other. You had to keep flexible. He began to ask around. The Conservatory of Music, several churches said no. Then he stopped mentioning jazz. Sightseeing one afternoon he found a little church by the river. A lay attendant took his request to the innards of the building, the Wasserkirche it was called, and reappeared with a key. He led Peter down a narrow flight of stairs to a cool, dark room and left without a word, shutting the door behind him. The room was small and sealed. A dozen chairs lay folded against one wall, and against the other stood a cherrywood spinet. Robes the color of eggplant hung from a pipe rack. It was the choir rehearsal room, wonderful acoustics, soundproof.

Peter began gingerly, triplets, chord inversions. What little sacred music he could recall or fake. Then he played whatever came into his head. After three hours, his hands ached. He lowered the fall board and quietly shut the door. Passing through the chancel he slipped two francs into the poor box.

He returned to his rooms well after dark. His landlady had placed a note on his dresser. The hand was in thin black ink and, Peter could not say why, clearly Continental.

"Papers retty Miss Jellicoe."

He checked the pawn ticket. Five days left to redeem. This bet was starting to show daylight from the pack.

Next morning Peter rose while the house was silent. He showered, packed, went downstairs to the kitchen. He was looking for a skillet and coffee pot when the landlady entered in a bathrobe, and he helped her cook the breakfast. Fried bread on the pan, cracked and beat eggs, ground coffee in the wooden mill. He would be checking out, he told her. He wondered how her children would fare. Either Pietr Kurz Steinmuller was his grandfather, in which case he would treat himself to sumptuous digs, or he was not. In which case he had better think about feeding himself.

As promised, the consulate materials were waiting in a crisp white folder bearing the Great Seal of the United States. Christ, that ought to do it. He wrote out a note thanking Miss Jellicoe, saluted the marine, and began the hike cross-town to the Löwenhoft Handelsbank. Clouds hung evenly behind the city. Zurich shone in the sun, but in shade its ancient stones drank the spare light from the air. It was mid-morning when Peter arrived. The day's progress did not show in the glowering sky.

Helene Durren seemed pleased, genuinely pleased, as she strode to meet him. A man's handshake, a deep look. Intimate, that, the formal shake and the mind swab of her eyes grey as February rain. If her practiced manner were meant to beguile Peter from noticing her figure, her appeal, it did not succeed: today she dressed in blazer and black skirt, the jacket buttoned chastely over a lavender voile blouse. At her neck she wore a small piece of carved jade. Its glint, a sap green, influenced her eyes.

She brought him again to her desk and drew a chair beside him. They leaned over and reviewed the papers together, an outsider might have thought she was teaching him penmanship. Helene took him through his unknown history. INS and the State Department had been wondrously complete. His grandmother, the one now sunning on the sill of a Florida hothouse, had been born Marta Borsen, the daughter of a minister in Ettingen. Ettingen was, Helene explained, a small town to the north and west. Marta had married Pietr Kurz Steinmuller on the outskirts of Zurich, had given birth to two children. In 1946, months after her husband's death, she made application to immigrate with one son, Florian, age not specified. No mention was made of the other child.

"He must have died in infancy," Peter said. "That's the first I've heard of him."

"Dates are right. Marta emigrates with a child named Florian, and your father Florian turns up in the U. S."

"Can't be a coincidence," Peter said.

"Can't be," Helene agreed. She was beginning to use the rhythms of his speech. When musicians traded four or eight bar solos, they often borrowed the ending phrase of the last solo to get them started. Peter liked the inflection. They were trading off, not a duet quite yet.

She seemed pleased by the evidence.

"As you might suspect," she said, "the cases of legitimate claims to our notices are rare. We must make sure all the procedures are followed."

"Are you trying to tell me something?"

"No, no. Only that these documents are necessary and now it is required to be checked back against what we know about the history of the account. We have records there."

She left Peter by himself. He studied the room, chewed on the spice scent that she had left behind in the air. Are the waiting hours we spend the mortar for the few events that wall in our lives? It was a large open room covered in a carpet of deep blue pile. Islands of dark-stained desks, the rustle of suit cloth, of stockings, the click of trimmed nail on computer key, a busy sound. The lightest tympani. Helene had taken the bank's manila folder with most of his papers, leaving behind some of the documents he had brought from Frey's.

Odd. These old credentials brought back a curiosity in his father's past: the man had never been sure of the date or year of his birth. Of all the questions a person gets, you'd think that is one he could answer. Marta Borsen had been born as the first war began and had married as the second was ending. She was widowed and immigrated all within a few years. She had spent the rest of her life in a foreign country at odds with her daughter-in-law and distant son. That is how Peter remembered his father — stoic, cool, monachal. He couldn't bring up a picture of his father. When he tried the man took on the grandmother's face, resolute and set against impact.

Mother and child had immigrated and she had raised her child Florian by herself. Peter's father never spoke of them, but in the rare times Peter considered those years he imagined an earnest and disciplined upbringing. Pete's father had rid himself of any accent, for Peter remembered his few words as cleanly spoken. His job, Peter recalled dimly, was selling obscure machine parts. On the road, small mill towns of New England, metal stamping and fabricating shops. Peter saw a silent man in an armchair. Between trips he read his newspaper, smoked his pipe. Passed through their house so lightly that his early death had caused little disruption. A silent man sitting in wait, that chair might have been at a bus station.

Then had come the famous story of Peter's christening. It was one of their rare family jokes, how grandmother had gone haywire at the ceremony, had walked out and had for years refused to look at the child. Even afterwards, when she made tentative conversation with him, Peter remembered her as remote, a foreigner to comfort or love. Did I, he wondered, inherit?

If it was part genes, it was also part environment. Peter's mother had stopped enjoying herself when? — his father's death? The man got himself buried and forgotten in the same day. Once under the ground he was not a subject for conversation, like toilet habits and God.

In his one clear recollection, his father was packing for a trip. Peter was helping. A leather two-suiter lay open on the bed. Neatly bagged shoes nested together against the bottom of the suitcase. Then shirts. Peter learned to clock the trip, one shirt for each day. His father slid a shirt off its hanger, folded it carefully, palmed it into a plastic bag cadged from the supermarket. White shirts lined up in the suitcase with red letters spelling Fresh Produce across their breast. There's one place for everything, son, and one right way of doing things.

Underwear and socks around the sides. The curtain was drawn over that half, Peter got to turn the thumb screws to fasten it. Then the suits, placed on their collapsible hardware, folded into the second half. You see, son. A system. If you have a system for packing you always do it the same way. Peter understood his father meant to teach him something. He wasn't sure what it was. You'll remember this, he used to say about his aphorisms, you'll remember this Peter long after me. How had he known?

And one recollection of his absence. The embarrassment of the funeral, people asking how he was. Fact was he was not any way special, he was wishing he were home by himself. Someone said to him — was it his mother? no, someone else — it's all right to cry. They said it again, and he pinched the skin of his wrist to force a tear. Still nothing came.

In front of him now was the faxed copy of his grandmother's application to immigrate, the writing fearful, scrabbly as an old privet. Not unlike, he realized, the writing of his landlady. They might have been taught in the same schoolhouse. Beside the German responses, someone had printed English translations. Marital status: widow. Family: parents dead, one child. Occupation: none. Occupation of spouse: banker.

Peter smiled at the balance. Frey had interlined his answers with German, his grandmother's were decorated with someone's English. His grandfather had been a banker, that came as a surprise, and now Peter sat in a bank. Parallel walls with no connecting passages. It had a classical roundness to it, a Bach partita. So my grandfather was a banker. No wonder he left an estate.

It was close to noon when Helene returned. She took her own chair behind the desk and spread open the manila folder. It now contained two inches of paper. On top was a sealed white envelope clipped to yet another form. In its clear window Peter read his name.

"If you will merely sign this, Mr. Steinmuller . . . Peter, we can conclude."

"This?"

"This says you are aware of nothing that contradicts the documents submitted to us through your Department of State, and nothing that makes you believe you are not the sole lineal descendant to the man who set up the account, Pietr Kurz Steinmuller."

"There is his widow. My grandmother. She is still alive in Florida."

"She is not a descendant. Not in the line of his blood. The account was on a standard form. It states that any assets remaining are to pass to your grandfather's heirs. According to what we know, you alone are entitled to the proceeds."

Peter took the papers. The top copy was in German, the second in English. A third sheet set out in both languages that the documents had been represented to him as an exact translation of each other. He signed wherever Helene Durren indicated. Her nails were done to hard points, her index finger made a perfect arrow for Sign Here, live pink against the printed page. He handed the papers to her, and she in turn gave him the window envelope.

"This is . . . ?"

"The entire corpus remaining in the account. In Swiss franc, of course. We can convert that if you prefer to dollars."

Peter ripped open the corner. "When we do this at home, we have hand-held cameras. And Ed McMahon."

He withdrew a cashier's check. It was made payable to him, listed his full name. Three hundred and thirty-six francs, forty centimes. He looked up.

"This is it?"

"That is the full amount." She read the look in his face. "You see, Swiss banks pay interest at rates far lower than your country. Our banking system has attracted deposits for other reasons . . . "

He cut her off. "This is it? This is less than my deposit to the lawyer. I owe him again as much. Are you kidding?"

She pursed her lips. "We do not kid about money, Mr. Steinmuller. I regret if you have spent more in the pursuit of this matter than . . . "

"Regret? What the hell good does that do me? Why didn't you tell me there was only a couple of hundred bucks in there. I hocked my keyboard."

Helene looked around. Would she call for help? Would they throw him out? She leaned forward in a gesture of conciliation and control.

"I say again, Mr. Steinmuller. We regret if you have undertaken expenses. As you know we are not permitted to tell you the amount of the corpus until you have proven your claims."

"How can there be an account with three hundred francs in it after fifty years? How can that be? No one would screw around with an account that small."

She consulted the file. "The account was established in early 1945. At that time it was considerably larger. Since then, however, there have been distributions by the trustee."

"How can that be? My family never got any of this money."

Helene Durren had her banker's voice ready. "No, distributions were made at the discretion of the trustee. The account allowed for that."

"What are you talking about? You're saying the trustee took money out? Paid money to itself? How can that be? Some bank is taking my grandfather's money? Who *is* the trustee?"

"I am obliged not to reveal that information under our secrecy laws. All meant, as I have told you, for the protection of the depositor."

"Listen, lady. Your bank takes my money and it's for my protection? We have trustees like that, lady. They are all in the slammer, you understand? Warren Beattie, James Cagney." He made a gun with his hand and pointed it at her but his tone was threatening.

"This bank was not the trustee. The trustee was an individual. A highly respected individual. I can assure you this procedure is not unusual, perfectly permitted."

"That's permitted, but telling me the name of this crumbum is not. That's your story?"

"I regret how this is working out, Peter. I truly do."

Peter watched her, watched the concern dim her sky-clear eyes. Very convincing.

"Here he comes now," Peter said. "Let's ask him." Peter pointed over her shoulder and she turned to look. His chair slid over the thick carpet without a sound. He lifted the file from her desk, placed it under his arm, and walked quickly to the door. The guard was waiting with his gear.

He hit the street astonished. No bells, no dogs. A hill rose to his left, down there the Wasserkirche, his piano in its choir room. He walked instead towards the lake, the piers, the landing stage. At a pace just under a trot, he crossed the river where it flows into the Zürichsee and turned right again off the bridge. There sat a pleasant park. It was designed for the city traffic, for burghers from the shops, lenders from the many counting houses, for share speculators fresh from meetings at the bourse, to provide a quiet moment by the quay to contemplate the river.

Peter found a bench. It bordered a dry fountain. Leaves had gathered in the cement basin, pages of newsprint, cigarette butts, crumpled soft drink cans. They would clean it in spring. Peter turned up his collar against the day and stuck his hands into the rabbit's fur of his gloves. Take care of your hands. Cozied and alert, he opened the file of Helene Durren.

At its very back was the new account form, signed in January 1945. A single printed page with the name of the bank, the Löwenhoft, in typescript. Amid the compound German nouns Peter recognized the very address on Paradeplatz. And there, clearly listed as the trustee, the person with the power to spend the money, was the name Frederich Von Egger. Peter checked the reverse side. It bore three signatures: some supernumerary for the bank as depositary, his grandfather's as the creator of the trust, in a pen that might sketch Japanese watercolors, and last the legible and dramatic hand of one Frederich Von Egger.

Nowhere could Peter find amounts. There followed inventories and lists, tax computations. Investments, charts of foreign currencies, dividend histories, a blizzard of administration. Near the very top, for Peter had started at the bottom of the file with the oldest document and was working his way into the present, appeared court papers. Attached to one was a listing of securities from the New York Stock Exchange with share prices in January 1965, but nowhere a total of the values in trust.

Someone sat down beside him. Helene wore a dark green loden coat, in military cut. She held its lapels at her throat.

"We may get snow." She squinted into the sky.

"What is this?" he asked.

The light was flat, and she had only just come from the brightly lit interior of the bank. She narrowed her eyes to read the page he put before her.

"A petition for instructions. If we are unable to find persons with legitimate claims we petition a court for permission to distribute them. Then the international committee will see that they go to a fitting cause."

"This account has been dormant since 1945, and in all that time they've not been able to find me."

"They advertise, Peter. Here and in America."

"Look, lady. I found my grandmother's immigration papers in a week. Less. I know a vibes, he wanted me for ten days' studio work, he found me in Kansas City. They couldn't have been looking very hard."

"And what's all this?" Peter thumbed through an inch-high stack of court papers clipped to the manila.

She read over his shoulder, spoke first in German. "Over time the trustee asked the court for permission to expend moneys in charitable ways consistent with the wishes of the person who set up the account. Your grandfather."

"How much? What was in here?"

"I shouldn't be doing this, Peter. You must give this file back to me." She put her hand on his sleeve. "There are very strict laws about banking records. We would both be in heated water. Unauthorized inspection. Unauthorized removal from the premises."

He looked at her. He was prepared to trade the file for answers. She understood, went back to interpreting the court document.

"When the account was created, it contained one hundred twelve thousand Swiss franc. At the time of the first petition, there were one hundred fourteen thousand three hundred and twenty."

"That's almost ninety grand. Ninety thousand dollars, today's rate of exchange."

"A little more," Helene said. "I think it's a little over that."

"And the trustee, this Von Egger, spent that money which should have been my father's. Ninety grand. And the courts let him do it."

"The terms of the account allowed Mr. Von Egger to do just that. The terms of the printed form gave him great flexibility in using the assets."

Peter was unconvinced. He'd never seen that amount of money in one place.

"Where do I find him?"

For the first time since he had met her, Helene looked alarmed. Her eyes measured the distance between them. The answer to that question was not part of their bargain. He closed the file and handed it to her. Her shoulders sank in relief.

"Do you have any ideas? Where he lives, I mean? Where I can find him?"

She shook her head as if that would be impossible. "You cannot approach the trustee. It would be highly irregular. And you could not get admitted to see Herr Von Egger. There is nothing out of order here and you would only be wasting your time."

"He is in Zurich? You know him?"

She took a moment to study the lines of his face. The beard, his narrowed eyes made it difficult. "Frederich Von Egger is a highly respected businessman. Wealthy, I believe. He owns several different ventures. His investment firm has offices in the outskirts." She mentioned a company name, a suburban village.

"That's here? Zurich?"

"To the north. Maybe twenty kilometers, less. You say less or fewer?"

"Less," Peter said, rising. "Less will do."

He walked into the street and hailed a cab. She was seated. Her posture, gripping the file across her knees, was that of a little girl.

The driver looked up the firm in a directory he kept in the front seat. Would the gentleman prefer the autobahn? By the time we are on it, we are off it. Whatever works, said Peter, and to a Billy Joel tune on the Blaukpunt, they were off. He watched the woman in the loden coat recede through the back window.

It was under a half hour. Landscaped suburbs passed by and gave way to a modern office complex. Maybe the old boy will be off at lunch. Roast lamb and claret on my grandfather's nickel. God, it's like Dickens with pretty sets.

The severity of the three buildings brought Peter back. The complex sat in rolling berms, off the highway in the low hills. Each structure, connected by a vaulted passageway, was four stories, each turned inward to huddle around a formal garden. The cab stopped in front of the center building. There was no signage.

"This it?"

"Yes, yes. I wait?"

Peter paid the meter. "Tell you what. Run this," he added a ten-franc note, "against the clock. If I'm not out, you go on."

The lobby had a high, aerodrome feel. Through the tinted glass of the building's skin, he felt an illusive glow, golden and watery. A bronze of four children playing in a manufactured stream sat opposite the doors and a footbridge led Peter over the recycled flow. And plopped him at the reception desk.

A matronly woman greeted him in German.

"I'd like to see Mr. Von Egger."

The woman smiled, tongued the gold frame around a front tooth. Perhaps it was recently done.

"That is not possible. Mr. Von Egger is not here today."

Peter considered this. "His office is here?"

The woman nodded yes and repeated that he wasn't here. She looked like someone from his past. A grammar school teacher? He thought he knew her. Silvery, puffed-out hair, face rounded with understanding. Peter nodded in a mild lunacy, bounced his satchel in his hand. The elevators were over her shoulder. "Yeah, well." He turned and watched the metal children at play.

"I'll just take a look." He strode past the desk. His timing was perfect: the elevator's bell sounded as he got there.

But he didn't make it. Two guards, each cheerful as a cold-call salesman, had him by the arm at the very elevator door. They assured him in guttural words, steered him around.

"We can't allow people to sight-see," said the woman through a happy smile. "There really are no touristic sights. If you'd care to leave a note for Mr. Von Egger's personal staff, we could deliver it."

Peter's hands were tingling. The guards' grip had closed off the blood in his arms. Their uniforms were powder blue with red fascia piping, one must have been eighty and wore Tchaikovsky's moustache. How did Dorothy manage to get in to see the Wizard?

They seated him in the taxi. Please, not to come again, Herr Steinmuller, said the younger guard. Without an appointment.

Through the glass Peter saw the pleasant woman, smiling back at him. He determined not to wave and realized whom she looked like. Barbara Bush, down to the pop-pearl choker. A dead ringer.

The taxi turned around and pointed him towards Zurich. Once again in motion without a destination. Where am I going? If I am the arrow, who is the target? Who lives here that I know? A lawyer I owe, a stringy American foreign officer. A luscious banker who appears to be the enemy — she warned them, how else would the guard know my name? All the better, the more tantalizing. This arrow is still in the air.

Who else? Of course, his landlady. Spinner of domestic tales. He took a quick inventory of cash. No surprise. Still, more wiggle than he'd had before, especially if you forget what's owed to the lawyer Frey. Checked back into the boarding house, where the landlady made cheerful, clucking noises and signed him in. He tossed his satchel on the bed in the attic room. It was beginning to look like home.

He found an English newspaper listing Zurich's few night spots and, pencil in hand, killed the afternoon scouting work. No one was looking for a pianist, no one knew jazz or Marcus Collopy. The last hotel had an American-style sandwich board out front, eight by ten glossies of a grinning man behind a white piano. Rudi Plays Your Tunes. The manager unlocked the six-foot Yamaha and Peter played show tunes, light classical. Arpeggio stuff. He returned the key and complimented the piano.

"You play very nice. You have a tuxedo?"

"Yes," Peter said hopefully. "Yes I do."

"Leave us your telephone. If Rudi decides to leave, we call you."

"How long has Rudi been here?"

"Eleven years."

Back at the rooming house, he scoped the airlines. Tomorrow night he could stand by for a flight to Dulles. D.C. is a good town. He knew the union secretary there, also a tenor with a regular gig downtown. He might be able to get on.

He dozed. Was it possible that Von Egger, who had signed the new account application, had known his grandfather? He slept.

Was awakened by the landlady's call from the floor below. It took her a minute to climb the stairs and recover her breath.

"You have a visitor."

He slipped on his shoes and walked down slowly. The only name he could think of was Von Egger, and that had to be wrong.

Helen Durren had seated herself in the little parlor off the entry hall, by the table of photographs. Perched on the edge of the priory bench, she looked tentative and uncomfortable. She had unbuttoned her loden coat, and beneath it wore a different suit, brown tweed with a window box pattern. White leggings.

"How did you know where to find me?"

"It was I who recommended this pension to you. I asked the owner to let me know if you checked back in."

Helene struck him as a mixed bag. On the one hand, she had cost him a considerable sum by launching his chase for the impossible, and she certainly could have signaled him that the search wouldn't be worth its costs. She also tipped off Von Egger's office. None of that endeared her. On the other hand, the vee of her neck was deep and smooth, and the skin showed soft against the arc of a flat gold chain. This hand proved to be the upper one.

"If you're here peddling missing fortunes, I ain't buying."

"Listen, Peter. I am so sorry you spent your money." She moved to the very corner of the bench.

"Or selling taxi tours of the suburbs. I've just had one."

"That wasn't my fault. You took off before I could stop you."

They watched each other for a moment. Her face and posture had about it the ring of sincerity. Beware the ring of sincerity, Matey would say. Its center stone is a zircon. His eye followed the line of her jaw, followed where it rounded toward the ear in a strong angle, and where the flesh of her neck blinked with the pulse underneath. A conspicuous pulse. Peter was not good at petulance. Jealousy, yes, but petulance never lasted through the song.

"You interested in dinner with an ex-millionaire jazzbo?"

She laughed. Yes, she would go out with him, but only if he allowed her to be the host. She felt sorry about what had happened and she insisted on that as her apology. The choice was easy. Peter had had his fill of dining alone, of sausage and potato casseroles. Matey's letter, read as a daily lectionary, had laid a sturdy foundation for loneliness. He accepted.

She had parked her tiny sedan out front. The night air held the damp hint of snow, and Peter gave a noticeable shiver. "It will be warm inside," she said. They walked down the steps of the rooming house, and she handed him the keys.

"I don't know where I am."

"Never mind," she said. Her voice was low in the moist air. He hadn't yet decided whether her every statement was intentionally charged. "I'll show you."

Why would she have warned them of his visit and then come to fetch him for dinner? And who would be paying for the food? Did she get an expense account for these missions? Peter decided to trade his cynicism for a meal.

The restaurant fit the night. It was intimate, crisp cloths over twenty or so tables. Squares of laundered white linen, each illuminated by a centered white candle. Not, he thought, so expensive that he would worry about her. No tourists, just the kind of insider's place that Christopher would seek out if he were visiting Zurich on business. The owners, an older couple, knew Helene, together spoke to her and then, with unstated courtesy, switched to English. She and Peter sat at their table as if on an island in the dark. She recommended the blausée trout, and they both ordered that, with a white wine from St. Saphorin. The trout, she said, were from nearby, from Neuchatel and we want a wine that is their cousin but not their sister. Her voice was soft. He could barely hear her. A sister, he said, would be incest. Against the tottering flame of the candle the wine gave off a verdigris cast. He was content to leave the tulip glass before him on the edge of the table. The scent of pale grape was impermanent, and when he moved the glass he sensed her. The fish are prepared, she told him, by plunging them live into boiling water. Very special. They leaned forward to speak. Their words were whispered.

Also cruel? he asked. What is cruel for them, she said glancing down at her hands, is special for us.

He understood what they were doing. They were preparing to make love. They had already started.

"I am hoping this will make up for the hardship I have put to you," she said. She ate with gusto, she was putting the end of a buttery roll in her mouth. He watched it disappear.

"I am hoping this will too."

"That taxi ride was a chase of a goose. Is that the expression? I see it in the old movies on the television."

"Wild," he said.

"Exactly. A chase of a goose in the wild," she confirmed. "Von Egger is a very powerful man. Even had you found him in his office, where he is not, there is nothing to be done. I am quite sure of it."

Peter lay down his fork. "You know him?"

She shrugged, finished her bite. "I have met him. He is one of our bank directors. Occasionally he is in the bank for functions. He is also one of our owners, although that fact is not public."

"You know him? This guy who ripped off my grandfather's money?"

"Peter, I tell you. He did nothing wrong. The trust permits it. Mr. Von Egger is very successful, very wealthy. He would not have interest in your trust."

"Someone at the bank must have his address, know where he is."

She moved her head, raised her brow, to show that he was correct. "He has houses all over. One in your country. He holidays to play golf in Arizona, California somewhere like that."

"Could you find out for me? I'd like to meet him."

"Peter. We Swiss have certain virtues. We are orderly, industrious, patient. We pay respect to authority."

"And Americans do none of that and have brought to the world the United States Constitution, Saranwrap, rock and roll. Can you find out?"

She made an oval of her lips and dabbed them with the corner of her napkin. She had not said no.

"This restaurant is famous for its pastries. We will share lest they weigh us down later. Do you prefer chocolate or meringue?"

There was little coyness, no posturing. Their conversation, even the talk of money, had been a prelude. The food, the eating of it. When they returned to the car, she instructed him and he complied. The leader calls the tunes.

Her flat was modern and glassy. It overlooked the botanical gardens. In the distance, beyond the city, ferries lit fore and aft plied the darkened lake. Small pinholes of light flickered on the far shore, and beneath them traffic whirred by as if on tracks. They left the curtains undrawn. There was no one to see. It was noiseless.

In love she was forthright and strong. "Exercise," she said earnestly when he complimented her body. "The rowing machine and in the summer running." Their love-making was tender and refreshingly simple. She asked for no assurances, nothing he could not give. She was empirical, a finder of fact.

It occurred to him at the restaurant that she might have been setting him up, that she might be shielding her superior. But he left behind that suspicion, left behind for the moment his aloneness, his anger at Matey, all but a few words, left behind on the warmth of her breast, in the folds of her secrets, in the salt sweetness of herself.

They found themselves wide awake, exhausted but not sleepy. The city was dark.

"Tell me about jazz."

"There's nothing to tell."

She poked him. He could talk about dope, driving fast, even sex, though he rarely did. But jazz, what's to say?

"So this jazz you create, am I right? You make it up? Where does it come from?"

"It comes from your head. I know guys, they hear tunes all the time. I know this bass, guy I came over with. He wakes up, licks are in his head. He walks around, phrases."

"Not written down?"

"Not written down. It's the musician. Stuff that's scored sounds mostly the same. You take a story, it's written down. It doesn't matter who tells it."

Helene grunted. "You are wrong, my Peter. The story is in the teller, not the telling. Just like your music."

Peter thought on her words. But not for long. Words this night were swallowed in the dark, dissolved in the wine they had drunk and the soft wetness of her skin. He could hold on to words no better than to memory, and both slipped away unneeded in the flow of hours.

The day's glare awakened him, and when he peered out, Helene was dressed. Brightness surrounded him, let in through glassine curtains. It was as if he were in a different room. Everything looked new. She hurried him into his clothes and dropped him off at the boarding house. She was expected at the bank at nine, and romance, as she told him with the lightest kiss and a smile, should never impede orderly commerce. "That is the motto on the coat of arms of the Canton of Zurich," she said. "Our shield bears the Swiss franc rampant, not hearts or cupids or . . . ," and her eyes wrinkled with mischief, " . . . private parts."

The night had left him in need of sleep. He had, it seemed, only just lain down and closed his eyes when his landlady called him to the telephone. He waited for her to leave the parlor. It was Helene.

"Do you have a pencil?" she whispered. He pictured her in the large open room.

"God. You were right about the Swiss. Industrious."

"Pay attention. He usually winters in California. Some place he goes to play golf. They say it is a mirage. But there is more. I have this from the secretary to the chairman, who makes all arrangements for the entire board. She's a friend. Pay attention. As it happens, now Von Egger is to be found back in Switzerland. Over the weekend he is giving a large party for important bank customers. Our chairman is invited." She gave an address. Outside a town called Vincy. She spelled it for him.

"Sounds French."

"In the French sector. On the north shore of Geneva. Very posh. But listen, Peter. He is an unusual man, Von Egger. If you go there, take caution."

"Could be another goose in the wild."

"I mean that."

The landlady furnished a road map. Vincy, Helene had said. There it was, near the rail lines but not near enough. He would need transportation. He smiled: getting there would be half the fun.

"HOW MUCH?" HE ASKED and put his hand on the front fender.

"Eight hundred franc." If he recognized Peter from yesterday, the boy gave no sign.

The key was in the ignition. Peter straddled the bike, kicked it on, revved the engine. The rhythms were broken. Pre-ignition, the firing of the charge ahead of the spark. It could be carbon deposits or a cracked plug insulator. He revved it again. The engine sounded like a Cuban rhythm band.

"Tell you what," Peter said. "Cash. On the line. Clams, moolah. Four hundred, throw in the helmet and this," Peter touched the boy's jacket. Mottled leather, a gash on the left sleeve and the elbows whitened from spills.

"Bullshit, man. You think I am some country cousin? No way. Six fifty."

"Four thirty. All I can do." Peter opened his wallet as proof, they both looked inside and counted the bills.

"You have more. A little." His thumb twitched against his pant leg. He was sold.

"That little has to get me from here to Vincy, and then the States. Four thirty."

"No way," the boy said again, spat to the side. Then he stripped off the jacket and took the money from Peter's fingers.

Peter tried it on. A fit. The boy squatted on the ground, leaned on the day-glow purple helmet and began to complete a form. A Captain Marvel helmet, spangles and stars and a smoked visor, it yawned under the weight, and a split showed in back. Peter folded his over-coat, stuffed it into his satchel, and looked around for the names of streets.

"Can you hurry it?"

"These are, what I am doing, requirements. These are the law."

"Just my luck," Peter said coming around the rear wheel, scraping a flake of rust. "You're commissioner of motor vehicles."

"No," said the boy, straight. "A student at the university. Also I can sell you some very fine Bolivian hash. Now," he said handing the passport back to Peter. "I will send this in and they will issue a new certificate. You will need a motorcycle endorsement on your license."

"I'll need more than that," Peter said and hoisted a leg over the saddle. "Like the road to Geneva. Point me at it?"

The bike carried on small wheels and the duffel shifted on the fender like a corpse. Traveling the two-lane, he wobbled when he slowed for the roundabouts, found his balance on the straights. The two laws of Steinmuller thermodynamics: speed over stability, motion over destination.

Now on the autobahn he felt out the bike. For a while everyone passed him, rumbling trucks shuddering him from their sheer weight, he leaning to counter the wake they spread. Dead at sixty as at eighty, and he wrenched the throttle to its limit. The old Ducati backfired between his legs, wheezed threateningly and began to die. He came off the speed, screwed the handle down again. It was at its edge. Whether it was the compression or the configuration — he'd bungeed the bag so it sloughed over the fender like a pair of panniers — the bike would be urged no higher. Peter bulked down behind the windscreen. He was warm, content.

Play in the throttle increased as he drove on, and the cylinders popped off the beat. Something was wrong. He couldn't afford a break-down, he'd do the work himself. He turned off the highway to find lunch and a mechanic. A pushcart vendor in the town center sold him a wrapped sandwich and two bottles of beer, directed him to a garage that could help. Borrowing a screwdriver and wrench, he opened the cowling to have a look. An exhaust valve seat had worked loose and was dangling around the valve stem like a loose bracelet. He opened both beers, offered one to the mechanic, and they bolted down the seat.

Back on the road, the Ducati kicking along like a patient released from a hip cast. Ahead, the first blue sky Peter had seen since the New World. The engine sang now without belching. On the billboards and over the shops of the towns he passed, French words began to appear. The going would be easier.

During the trip, five hours on expressways, Peter hit on a plan to gain entry into Von Egger's house. He would need a specialty store. Outside Lausanne he left the autobahn and bedded down for the night. Vincy lay only twenty kilometers to the west.

The next morning he set about early. The props for the simple disguise he had in mind proved difficult to locate. A major city, everyone told him, he would find what he needed only in one of the major cities. The pawn shops carried only the usual electric pianos, horns, guitars. It was universal — musicians were the first to go broke.

Someone sent him put-putting up the hill to a violin repair shop. Peter left carrying a small leather case. The size of a burglar's kit, it was what he wanted. He snugged it to the rack of his bike.

He steered off the road at a sign announcing Vincy and drove north, upland. The countryside opened into vineyards, trimmed and tied for the winter. Vines pruned to the stalk. The houses became larger, the gates higher. At a fixed altitude, where the frost line began, farms replaced vineyards. The thin air a half mile above the shores of Lake Geneva could not coax sufficient sugar into the grape.

Roads turned to lanes, lanes to unpaved ways. Just as he decided he was lost, a postman's tiny Fiat rounded the narrow corner and slowed to pass. Of course he knew the way to the home of Monsieur Von Egger, what did Peter take him for? He instructed Peter brusquely and went on.

The private road was marked with neither name nor number, only a simple wrought iron fence. He pressed a button on the stantion and, to the noiseless push, a voice cracked over the cold air.

"*Oui*?"

"I've come to tune the piano," Peter said. "For the party."

A long, still pause while Peter's imagination set off searchlights and spring guns, followed by a click and the silent, even swinging of the gate.

Peter low-geared the bike down a driveway built of figured concrete and bound by a thick and landscaped wall. There was no house to be seen. Tiny electronic eyes blinked red amid the pfitzers.

By a final turn the hill flattened to a topographic bench. There the road divided, and he followed the wooden sign instructing service to the left. The bench was carpeted with a long lawn, improbably green in the damp winter. Looking down the extended landscaping, down the hill and over the town, Peter saw the mist that hid what must be Lake Geneva. Beyond, whitened by the near dew point and massive in their silhouette, the French Alps.

Now he made out the house. White too, it was stuck into the hill as if it had been dropped there when the mountains were made, white concrete contoured to the slope. The facade followed the land, not merely in elevation but across as well. The service road led to a concealed parking lot — there were three cars and several small panel trucks — and beyond, a subterranean entrance to the garage. Peter parked his bike by a low wall and looked about. A man, Gallic and dark, stood holding open a door and motioned him to it.

His greeter had a bovine look, pendulous cheeks, large brown eyes. He wore a knee-length green apron, its ties wrapped around his waist and fastened in front. He asked Peter something in accented French and, receiving no reply, "You are the piano tuner?"

Peter held out his case in answer. He followed the man through the kitchen quarters. Two women, his colleagues, were cleaning vegetables.

He was led through halls toward the front of the house. Lucky to be met by one of the help. They took the presence of a tuner for granted. If only he could slip off by himself. Perhaps he could snoop around, and find . . . what? He had thought of the hunt but not the treasure.

His guide stood at the entrance to a great room. He pointed. Peter passed him. There, centered on a Bokhara rug, sat a magnificent Bechstein. He had never played one. Concert length, a full nine feet, gleaming black. The instrument stood in front of a wall of important art. Its lid was raised to the full position, a magical insect readying for flight.

Peter placed his case by the bench, opened it self-consciously.

"This will suffice?" the man asked him.

"Oh yes, brother. This will suffice."

He struck a few central notes. A second piece of luck: the instrument was out of tune. Not extreme, but well within his capability. He removed two forks from his case and clamped them under his arm. While they were warming he lay strips of red felt to mute the outside strings of the center octave. He began off the one fork, sounding A 440, and went about setting the temperament. The first task was to set the key intervals: fourths, fifths, thirds, minor thirds. There are relative decisions to make. One tunes a piano as he might go about making a flower, from the inside out.

He moved to octaves. Listened until the beats, the differences in wave lengths, disappeared. It is an easier task. If the temperaments have been set properly the next step goes faster. It is work of precision and repetition, and Peter lost himself in the sounds. The task differed only a little from timing a motorcycle engine. The casing polished to a high gloss, the gilded harp of angels, the tuner's red crenelated felt stitched across the sounding board. Waves of sound beating in his ear while he listened, lowering and raising the frequency, twisting his wrench until the tone was right.

The work is hypnotic. The sounds, the inner spaces. He completes the lower octaves, withdraws, stretches. He has been transported and the voice startles him.

"It was badly in need?"

He looked about for its owner. "No," he said, finding no one. "No, merely a little flat. It should be played regularly."

Peter's apprehension rose as he searched for the speaker. Position, the advantage of the God of the Israelites on Sinai. As he looked a man stepped from behind a large bronze not ten feet away. How could he have concealed himself there? Anywhere? He was six-four, maybe taller, hair whitened beyond color, a tanned, raptor's face. The taut body of an athlete still holding on. Peter set down the tuning hammer.

The man stared at him without apology. Eyes glacially blue, watching a rabbit on the ground. There was no cover.

"Are you finding any problems?"

Peter was thankful for the question. "No, none. It is a magnificent piano. I've never seen a Bechstein."

"It ought to be played more," the man echoed. "When you are through, will you play some? It would give me pleasure."

Peter nodded. The man continued to watch him.

"There is one thing," Peter said. "Here. Someone has retied a string. It really should be replaced. That will go flat more quickly than the others. I don't happen to have that string in my case or I'd do it myself."

The man considered this. "Thank you. I appreciate the efforts you are making." Did the man smile? "The care you take." He gave a short bow from the shoulders and withdrew.

Peter finished up. He did the octaves, removed the felts and tuned the unisons. He paused and looked around. The room stretched forty, maybe fifty feet. To his left a wide, curving window interrupted by beams each of which had its own soffit, and within a select piece of sculpture. Against the far wall and the many perpendicular cubbies were hung a riot of color and shape. Art that was postmodern, pop, op, constructions of wood, wire, canvas. Stuck at random among the mostly modern stuff were singly lit canvasses. Small and, next to the explosions of expressionist color, sedate. Peter went over to inspect a familiar painting — he had owned that very Utrillo print, it had hung on the wall of his college dormitory room. This turned out not to be a print.

He returned to the piano and packed his tools. There was time to wander around. Instead, he adjusted the bench, sat down. He played Gershwin, Ellington, Monk. He played a Benny Golson tune and a piece he had written. Someone was listening, someone in the room or near, and he played the better for it.

At last he stood and pulled down the fall board to cover the keys. The tall man again appeared from behind a protruding wall.

"'Whisper Not,' is that not it?" He hummed the opening lines of the Golson tune.

"Wow. You like jazz?"

The man smiled, turning his lips inward. His face was set and the smile did not relieve it. "I do. But of course, I'm so old I remember Clifford."

It was an inside joke, the name of a second tune by the same composer. The man touched a panel on the wall and soft, indirect lights came on. They revealed lines on the man's neck that suggested more years than did his singular face. Years that could not be confirmed in the energies of his mien or the pale blue eyes.

"I ask you for a favor. If I presume, you will tell me." He had a courtly way to him, a considered speech that contemplated its effect. "I am giving a small party this evening. Forty or so friends, business associates. I wonder, would you be our pianist?"

Peter had all but forgotten his covert motive, and the invitation to play brought it back. It was an opportunity to hang around the house. He would also gain another few hours on this piano.

"Naturally I shall pay, in addition to the tuning. The going wage?"

"I'd love to."

"Very good. No need for you to go back to town. That is your luggage, is it not, on the motorcycle? You can change here. We have several rooms." He began to leave, then turned back in an afterthought. He saluted by inclining his head. "I should tell you. My name is Frederick Von Egger."

Peter bowed back at him in faint imitation. It seemed appropriate. "My name . . . " he began, even before he had decided what to say.

"Your name," the man interrupted, "is Peter Kurz Steinmuller." The man gave a brief and equally grim smile. "I suggest you bring your things in, change for the party and then join me. We can chat before the guests arrive."

The aproned houseman led Peter up the back stairs to a small room amid servants' quarters. On the connecting walls were hung masks and boat prows from some Pacific culture. Peter was taken to a room only slightly larger than its double bed, but fully appointed. Down to a cellophane-wrapped kit of toiletries — a comb, a fresh tube of toothpaste and a packaged brush — on the bathroom sink. The appointments continued the Polynesian motif. Spears and harpoons were racked on the far wall, and over the bed hung a primitive watercolor of a young pearl diver.

Peter hadn't worn the tuxedo since his last night on the ship. Field repairs, the tailor of the road musician. He pinned the cuffs of the trousers to a hanger and ran a hot shower so that steam erased the wrinkles. The new toothbrush made his a spare and he used it to rake lint from the shoulders of the jacket. At the bottom of his satchel he found a freshly laundered shirt in its plastic bag. He knew he should be strategizing about his confrontation with Von Egger, but it was easier to concentrate on the familiar. He tinkered with his clothes, a beard trim, jotted down titles as a repertoire for the evening. That Von Egger knew his name took his breath away. Had they checked in Lausanne? But Peter had paid cash for his purchases, his room. Showed no credit cards or identification. It was almost as if Von Egger had recognized him. Peter would remember if they had met before. The figure the man struck, its clarity, its intensity, would stick in the mind.

What the hell, he decided. Fake it, ear it out. Besides, Von Egger seemed to have created his own agenda. He didn't seem to mind Peter's impersonation, he was perfectly amiable. Peter had no answer.

Nor any when he came down the stairs and was led towards the front of the house and into a library. A somber room, burgundy walls, the two doors a dark oak stain. Books crammed the shelves and cubbies. A fire gave a yellow light and a computer screen on the burl desk glowed blue. Gerard, for that was the name of the man who was always his guide, flicked off the screen, turned on reading lamps at either end of the couch. Peter sat in response to Gerard's gesture and waited.

Behind him were books on art. Collections, a hundred of those, and theory as well, aesthetics, methods, history. On the lowest shelf, the bound catalogues of important gallery sales, many with paper slips showing from their tops. To Peter's right, the shelves held books on war. Armament, battles, military tactics. At eye level, displayed under a bright gallery bulb, a plaque of a figure. A man with the head and pronounced genitals of a bull, stretched parallel to the ground in mid-leap. Its ferocity, its sex made him start. Peter had a sudden sensation that the doors were locked. He reached for the sculpted handle of one, the door he had come in by, and as he put his fingers on the brass, warm as a hand, it moved and the door opened.

Von Egger regarded him. Was it the resuscitated tuxedo? He himself wore a double-breasted blazer, grey slacks, a blue shirt with a white pencil stripe and a tie of rich purple.

"The resemblance is quite strong," he said. "Quite remarkable. Your room is acceptable?"

"Oh, yes."

"I would suggest you stay the night. These roads are not to be driven by a novice in the dark. You will I hope be comfortable."

"Yes. Absolutely. Very kind."

"Not kindness. It is you who are kind. To allow me to entertain the grandson, am I right, grandson?, of a long-time colleague."

Peter quickened to the comment. Was he guest or prisoner?

"You knew my grandfather?"

Von Egger looked down at him, then put out his arm. He was pointing to the corner of the couch that Peter had first been assigned. Peter obeyed.

"A drink? Some whiskey? Do you drink?"

"Maybe a beer."

Von Egger pushed a white bell button wired to the desk. He traced his finger idly across the spines of a row of books and sat in an uphol-stered chair opposite. He waited to speak. Gerard opened the door and Von Egger gave him the order.

He turned to Peter. Again the avicular cock of the head the way owls turn their ear to the target.

"Do you believe in love?"

"I don't know. No," Peter said. Words spoken in that room had no echo. The bookshelves were covered in soft fabric. "I think I do not."

"Good. That will make our conversation more . . . " Von Egger looked about to see if the spidery word he sought was scurrying in the corners of the room " . . . direct."

"Your grandfather was a colleague of mine. At the bank. You bear, I am sure you have been told this, a remarkable resemblance."

"Actually, I haven't. You're the first person I've met who knew him. Besides my grandmother, of course, and she's long since . . . "

Peter let the end of his sentence die. Should he mention senility to this man, who might easily be her age?

Von Egger seemed to appreciate his sensibilities. "He was my senior at the bank. He taught me a great deal. He would have been eighty-six this year, I think. It was an irony, you see. And Pietr was so fond of paradox. Coming through the war, the travels and hazards, then to be killed in a car crash. You knew that?"

"I had heard."

"A drunken driver. An American G.I., of all things, one of the liberators of Europe." Their drinks arrived. Von Egger raised his glass of mineral water. "These are close roads. Another good reason for you to stay the night with us."

They sipped and Peter waited.

"You came here to ask about the account," Von Egger began. "Also to tune our piano, but to ask about the account. Your purpose and my sources should be no mystery. I am a director of the Löwenhoft, the staff there told me of your inquiry. It is proper that you should inquire. It is what your grandfather would have done, too."

"I would like to hear about him. And principally how it is the account disappeared."

"The account is very much in existence. It is the money that disappeared. And of course, it did not disappear, it was spent. By me. If we are to get on, Peter Kurz Steinmuller, you must try to be candid."

Peter considered the reprimand a transparent tactic to put him on the defensive.

"I'll be candid. I hope you will as well."

Von Egger nodded in gratification. "I will tell you about the trust. But first I must relate something about him, the man. And about the era. Unless of course your time is limited."

Peter motioned with his hand, a supplication.

"Your grandfather was an unusual man." Von Egger spoke softly, the only interruption was the occasional pop of the fire. "Self-made, isn't that the congratulatory phrase Americans so enjoy? I'm surprised your religious fundamentalists don't find it blasphemous. He had come from the country, from a family of school teachers and populists, and had determined to make something of himself. In Switzerland sixty years ago it was not so easy to rise above your origins. Now every European wants your classless system. There is a perception that freedom creates liberty, while of course every thinking man knows it is precisely the opposite." Von Egger looked at Peter to see whether his wit was appreciated. Peter registered the remark for his host to see.

"He taught himself business, finance. He saw great opportunity for the bank and, I say these things only in admiration, for himself.

"These were difficult years. I am not speaking about the war your country waged with Germany. I am speaking before. The New York stock market collapsed in 1929. There followed a devastating financial crisis. In the path of rampant inflation, deposits were withdrawn. First Germany, then Austria. England abandoned a gold-backed currency, the United States followed suit. These conditions affected the banks of Switzerland. By 1936 deposits in our banks from outside parties had declined by more than half.

"For a bank to yield its deposits is like the body to yield up its blood. It can do so intermittently and in moderation without effect; it can replenish the supply. But too great a demand can kill the corpus. Switzerland responded with a devaluation. The Swiss franc, proudest currency of the world. Devalued.

"This was the climate when your grandfather became an officer. The Löwenhoft left to fend for itself, at a time when larger banks, indeed larger Swiss banks, were failing. It was a bank of no importance. Where else, you might ask, would an inexperienced young man without connections find employment as an officer?"

Von Egger crossed his legs so that the top nested comfortably over the lower. His posture made him appear perched on a single prop. He held that position while he spoke, his hands easy on the heavy damask of the chair's arms.

"Your grandfather hit upon a bold plan. Europe was arming for war. We expected economic blockades and an increasing need for capital. Your grandfather proposed to the managing director that he be assigned to develop new countries to sell the bank's services.

"And then he traveled. Madrid, Brussels, Milan, Luxembourg, Bucharest. His Swiss passport gave him a wide berth. He hoped to arrange for payment and credit, textiles from Belgium to France, coal from Germany to Switzerland, foodstuffs from England to Italy. The threat of war meant high production, but the production could not occur without the flow of capital. Power plants, steel factories, entire new industries.

"His success came where there was less competition. Eastern Europe, considered by the larger institutions to be unfashionable.

Most bankers were snobs, you see. They avoided countries where cabbage is considered a delicacy. They still do.

"By the time the door closed, the Löwenhoft had become one of Switzerland's five largest banks. Lean years came for all of us. The war was a great hardship. In June 1941 the United States, certain that all neutrals existed to help Axis efforts, blocked continental European dollar balances. Trade was paralyzed by that act. No one could be sure of the availability of foreign exchange assets. But our bank was able to abide.

"I was by then an employee, fresh out of university. I worked for your grandfather. We were at lengths to defend Swiss financial interests in foreign countries. Contrary to all international law, we encountered discrimination against private property. The network he had created survived these times. He would regularly travel, irrespective of advancing fronts, to assure the integrity of the lines of commerce.

"This may sound boring. The English say cold potatoes? But private property is not merely certificates in a drawer. A folded tissue full of diamonds. These are people's livelihoods. Their safety. I will tell you what I mean."

Von Egger rose. He finished the charged water in his glass and Peter assumed from the way he stirred from his chair that he meant to ring for Gerard.

"I will tell you what I mean," Von Egger said. "But not tonight."

The interview was ending, and Peter rose in courtesy. He looked at the frieze of the man-bull and moved his hand as if to touch it.

"I would prefer," Von Egger spoke quickly, "you let it be."

"I've seen that before. The Minotaur of Knossos."

Von Egger smiled. "Very good. You've seen reproductions, sold at museum stores. That faience happens to be the original. I admire Mediterranean antiquities and have in another house a collection of some import. This is its centerpiece. It has become my amulet. I move it every year to Vincy and back to the United States."

The man pushed back his cuff and peered at his watch. He was a figure of elegance, slender and demanding. He looked outside at the fading light, white still through the mists of the lake.

"Now you will excuse me. I have duties to attend before the guests arrive. You shall play, I shall entertain, and tomorrow there will be time to talk. I held your grandfather in the highest regard. It is my hope that you will as well. You may stay here as long as you like."

Peter moved to put himself between the window and Von Egger.

In the glare Von Egger squinted. Still his eyes were the blue of noon, a lapidary color. In them were reflected the bowed rectangles of the window.

"I appreciate the offer. I want to find out about my grandfather." Peter kept his voice flat, to conceal the relief he felt. He needed to consider the odd turn his quest had taken.

"I am sure. And the trust. All in time." He turned to the door. "Events lose their consequence so quickly. Wildflowers. Tomorrow is far more important than yesterday."

"Still. I should like to know the truth."

A flicker sped over Von Egger's face. It might have been amusement. "The truth. Your Eskimo are said to have seventy-two words for snow. Just so we have many for truth. Not because we admire it, I think, but because we wish to be ready if it appears. And of all those names, one of the most common synonyms is falsehood."

Was he baiting Peter into debate. Peter rose to the lure. "Truth isn't so complicated as that. It's what happened. What's verifiable." Von Egger wince turned to a smile.

"You think so? What does it mean to say someone deceives us? Is it any more than he reveals to us one path? If a compass points north, then at the same time it points to the reciprocal. And if we know the reciprocal, can we not find our way?

"Now. I really must go."

He disappeared through the door. Peter stood at the window and watched the day ebb. He was resolute. Words would not decorate the facts. He was wary of words and costumes. Light percolated up from the mist on the lake. It was Friday. Earlier in Boston, by six or seven hours. Matey would be at lunch, considering the weekend, deciding whether to bring flowers home for the table.

He had played a hundred parties like it. The languages differed, the punch lines in French or German, but the rhythms were the same, solo and combo, the hush while the story was told and the guffaws of good fellowship that followed. Trays carried regimented *hors d'oeuvres* and gaily decorated toothpicks. White-jacketed staff passed among men in dark suits, women in silk and heavy gold. Peter enjoyed himself, testing the remarkable voices of the piano. It had great range. Milling guests passed through the angle the piano lid made with the gilded harp.

Mostly Peter watched Von Egger. Watched him move through the crowd like a horseman among cattle, so much taller was he than anyone else. His presence rearranged conversations, cut out groups, rounded up strays. Only once did he leave the herd, to lean against the far corner of the room, one hand cupping the elbow of the far arm, listening thoughtfully to a short, older man, the back of whose fuzzy head showed an Einstein silhouette. Von Egger's companion held a hand behind his back absently tapping his tailbone. Something in their postures held Peter's gaze until a guest interrupted, asked for an obscure Cole Porter tune. When Peter finished they had gone.

IN THE MORNING PETER dressed in a sweater and jeans. He took a ferocious appetite down to the kitchen, where one of the women fixed him a breakfast to match, sausage, eggs, bread thickly cut from a football-shaped loaf. Von Egger was nowhere to be seen. Peter asked for him, but they seemed not to know. He asked if he could roam about the house and raised only a perplexed look. He was, he chanced, a guest. The other possible roles on this lavish set, hired hand, hostage, suspect, undermined his confidence.

He began his exploration from the hall on the lee side of the kitchen. The house was built into the hill, in two levels, each with three ranks of room. The kitchen bordered a formal dining room. Off the dining room was the salon where he had performed, backed in turn by the library Von Egger had used for their chat. Everywhere art. Nothing quite so menacing as the Minotaur, priapic and feral. What he saw was cerebral. Giant constructions of wood and steel, watercolors of the English landscape, a sketch by Eakins and a gouache of Whistler's.

Beyond the salon were two small sitting rooms, decorated in traditional styles. In one the furniture was elaborate, lathed and embellished. Peter could not identify the period but he guessed that its origins were the Eighteenth Century. The decoration of the second was Chinoiserie, with lacquered cabinets, small chests. On the walls of both, art of the period, paintings of young, cultured gentlemen, Continental and Chinese according to the scheme, at ease in rooms of the sense and dimensions of those that housed them. In each painting was frozen a group in irenic conversation. It struck Peter: the rooms in the paintings were the very rooms in which he stood. Could Von Egger have commissioned the paintings to match his purchases? Or had he given the decorator these, oils in the one case, silk screen in the other, as his plan? Standing against the painted backgrounds gave Peter an odd sense. He peered closely — would he recognize the faces in the canvasses? Did they change as guests checked in? He was relieved to find that they were unfamiliar.

To the rear and above, staff kitchen and dining room, staff bedrooms and several guest suites, including his own. He had reached the end of the main house and was about to turn back to tour the far half when he heard the unmistakable chunking beat of the Count Basie band.

He opened one of two doors. It led to the underground garage. There, by a black and silver Daimler, his forlorn motorcycle leaned on its kickstand, a beggar on a crutch. He closed the door and tried the second one. It led him through a hall and into suffused light. He entered a vast, glass-enclosed room the length of the garage, facing south to the lake. At his feet and repeated in blue motif about the wall were mosaic lines of Greek fret, an angular design that fit within itself like a periwinkle shell. In the center of the room, the tiled floor, was sunk a long cobalt rectangle, a swimming pool. The stripe of water was perhaps five yards wide, thirty in length. And in it, in easy strokes carved in synchrony with the beat of Basie's "Girl Talk", swam Von Egger.

Peter stared. The form moved easily to the music. Von Egger wore nothing, though at first glance Peter was deceived. The swimmer's buttocks shone white in the outline of a tank suit. It was an eerie sight, the brightness of the sky captured under the glass panels, browned avian arms poling above the water. What held Peter's eye were the fish: dozens perhaps hundreds of fish in the pool's depths. Tiles of every color had been used to create a mosaic of a crowded sea bottom, and the motion of the water animated these ceramic schools as Von Egger glided over.

Peter watched. There was something sinister about his status, watching a private rite, the crooked falcon wing out of the water and down, then the second. Again, the rhythmic crawl, the turns, back arcing the water. Was he meant to find Von Egger in this chamber? Why, what should it mean to him? He withdrew.

He passed through the salon where Gerard caught up with him. Monsieur Von Egger asks whether he would enjoy a stroll after lunch. The question answered the one on Peter's mind — would he see his host again? Or would he have to track him through this complicated wilderness of civilization, hunt him down in his lair? Peter said that would be fine. In the meantime, Gerard said, Monsieur Von Egger thought the gentleman might be interested in this. He handed Peter a book, white slips marking several places. *Gallant Little Switzerland*. Peter took it and thanked Gerard. No, there was nothing he needed.

Peter found the library and settled into the couch corner. Over his shoulder leapt the stone Minotaur. The book was written by one Leonhard Maag-Reinhardt, whom the flap described as a distinguished journalist and author. It had been published in the sixties, originally in German but since in English, French and Italian, and had received some national award.

Gerard appeared. He assembled kindling and logs, lit a fire, withdrew. The latch clicked behind him. Peter flipped through and glanced at chapter headings: the contribution of the clergy, the International Red Cross, economic pressures. Towards the end, someone had inserted a long strip of paper. That is where he began to read.

As the war moved to its conclusion, the Allies turned again to matters economic. The United States communicated a diplomatic agenda. It included shipments of war materiel, Swiss-based assets belonging to enemies of the Allies, and use by the Axis of Swiss banks.

President Roosevelt appointed Lauchlin Currie, a veteran diplomat, to lead a mission to Berne. The prominent civil servant Walter Stucki was chosen to head the Swiss legation. He in turn chose advisors to accompany him, notably the experienced international banker Pietr Kurz Steinmüller, who served as deputy.

Negotiations began in Berne on February 12, 1945. The mood of the Americans was joyous. Their diplomats believed that they had entered into a lasting peace with the trusted Josef Stalin. The aims of the Allies were naive, but admirable. They wished to end the war as quickly as possible, and to prevent the Axis from ever again jeopardizing the peace of Europe. In their zeal to accomplish these aims, they were disposed to disregard the niceties of local law. Switzerland promptly agreed to all legitimate requests, such as prohibiting coal shipments from Germany to Italy through Switzerland's St. Gotthard pass.

One issue remained unreconciled. The Allies requested an unauthorized inspection of all Swiss banking records. They were interested in deposits made by persons who had perished during the war, and they claimed ownership of German assets, no matter where situate. The Swiss properly responded that this position was illegal, and resembled no more than the barbarian practice of claiming spoils of war.

Steinmuller and the Swiss legation argued that quarreling over deposits was unseemly, in light of the human tragedies wreaked by the war, and that the more quickly the question could be resolved, the earlier all nations could join wholeheartedly in the efforts to rebuild Europe.

There was a footnote to this second mention of his grandfather. Another strip of paper marked it. As Peter turned to it Gerard came in to announce lunch. "Yes, yes," he said. "I'll be right there."

P. K. Steinmüller was a successful young bank executive at the Löwenhoft during the war years. He pioneered transborder commerce during hazardous times. He was less known for having created the so-called Composer's Circle, a loose affiliation of agents who assisted the accomplishment of legitimate Swiss goals during the Second World War.

Peter had been set a place at the table in the pantry, a step up from his dinner last night among the staff. Nowhere was Von Egger to be seen. He was served a potato soup, fresh bread, a salad of endive and spinach, and he declined a glass of wine.

After lunch he returned to the salon and fooled with the piano. If there were others in the house, they were invisible. *Was* this man a mirage? Peter played a long improvisation on a circle of fourths. As he finished there was light applause, a single appreciation. He turned. Von Egger sat behind him on a love seat. Once again, his music seemed to conjure the man from air.

"Good afternoon."

Von Egger continued patting his hands. "This is the proper way to be heard. Not over the roar of several dozen plump businessmen chewing peeled shrimp. I enjoyed your playing last night, but this is the better way."

Peter turned on the bench. Would he be able to hold him long enough to find some answers?

"Gerald had mentioned a walk."

"Yes, yes," said Von Egger. "Shall we go?"

Peter retrieved the leather jacket he had bought in Zurich. With that and a scarf he was comfortable, for the climate around the lake was mild and there was no wind. Von Egger draped a thin shawl around his neck, put on a long shooting jacket with a high corduroy collar. Its distinctive shoulder patch showed wear. Peter followed his host through the rear of the house. A steep climb over flagstone led them to a second, higher bench. Here the dark soil was planted with trees no taller than Von Egger. They had been pruned back for the winter. The smell of fresh tar overlay that of the woods, the scent of decay. At the edge of the path was a piece of sculpture. Peter stopped to examine it. In a block of stone the size of a steamer trunk lay a human hand, palm up, in repose. Much of the stone had been left rough from the quarry, while that around the hand had been scored, almost at random.

"A remarkable piece." Von Egger was at his shoulder. "You have a good eye. As remarkable as the subject. Other mammals have evolved towards simplification: paws and hooves to support the weight, for transportation. The killing end of most of our cousins in the animal world is the mouth. But for us primates, it is here, in the palm of our hand."

He looked at Peter and quizzed him. "What is this hand doing?"

"It's resting," Peter replied. "It is getting ready."

"I agree. To give a blessing? To hold a baby, to pull a trigger? The human hand does all that."

Peter led the walk through the trees. They were planted in uniform rows. Under foot, the earth sank. Mulched leaves covered the ground. The air smelled of pitch and bark.

"An orchard?" Peter asked.

"Almonds and chestnuts here. Apples above." They heard a metallic sound. Von Egger crossed to a far row. A squirrel was rattling a wire trap. Von Egger lifted the trap by its handle and placed it gently in a barrow sitting by the road. Then he removed a large floral hand-kerchief from his coat pocket and covered the cage. The rustling stopped.

"We move them to the park. Free them there. They can be a real nuisance when the blossoms form."

They walked further up the hill. Peter had almost arranged his subject into words when Von Egger brought it up.

"You came to ask me about the trust."

"I did."

The man gave a satisfied grunt. "And you did your reading last night? *Gallant Little Switzerland*?"

"This morning, actually. Interesting. But I do not see how it explains the disappearance of several thousand francs."

"Of course you do not. There is no book to be read for that. That must come from personal witness." Von Egger stopped, placed his hands at the small of his back and stretched. Peter turned with him. Von Egger meant for him to notice the view, and he could not help but pause. Outlined against a sky the color of slate stood a chunk of the Savoy Alps. It was a sight for the fortunate.

"Mont Blanc you know. To the left, Mont Maudit. To the right Bionassay and in the foreground Mont Saléve. Bionassay is considerably higher. But she does not appear so. Things are not always how they appear."

"So I have learned."

Von Egger regarded him. Peter did not regret the tone of his reply, yet Von Egger's expression was that of the teacher who required of his student a certain simplicity.

"They give me faith. So far they are untrammeled, no billboards, no chalets made into condos. You have seen Davos? It was, you know, the setting of *The Magic Mountain*. Now it is a ski area. We are turning our world into an entertainment.

"It is the result of greed and stupidity. People without imagination become greedy. They are unable to hit upon any other form of amusement."

Was Von Egger merely another rich man who wanted to maintain the order that gave him advantage? Peter felt he must reply. "Perhaps those who desire money are merely people who don't have enough of it."

Behind them, the squirrel rattled the trap door. A single crow flapped across the grey, caught Von Egger's hunter eye.

"Just so," the man looked down at Peter. "You intend to reprimand me. I am indifferent, you mean to imply, because I am rich. I do not appreciate what it is to be poor. I tell you no. If a man desires money, it is a simple thing in this world to earn as much as he wishes. No, I think greed is the repetition of an exercise originally pleasurable that continues long after the joy. Have you not noticed how many of your friends continue to do something simply because they once enjoyed it?"

He strode forward before speaking again.

"But you asked me about the trust. I must tell you the story.

"Many people viewed Switzerland's neutrality during the war as moral indifference. The case is quite the opposite. It is too cynical to say that merely because she did not send armies she was apathetic or opportunistic. There are no doubt persons who profited, but no more in our country than in yours.

"Scores of Swiss leaders opposed the Nazi regime and undertook great peril. Some famous, but most were not. Your grandfather was among the quiet citizens.

"Your grandfather and I were very close. I had no family. He had a brother who had predeceased him, a brother with whom he had nothing in common, a simpleton. Briefly he had a wife who left him.

"You look surprised? Yes, who left him. She took a little boy and ran off to America. It was shameful, he a national hero, a prominent man of the government and she ran off. The rumors survived for years, rumors of the most pernicious kind . . . .

"He and I were closer than brothers, really. She wanted to leave and he did not stop her. Helped her, in fact, for she had nothing. He arranged passage for Marta. Gave her money for the child, a lot of money. She must have lived on it all these years. The divorce became final after she sailed for the United States.

"Pietr washed his hands of them. He changed his will. The automobile crash was only months away. It happened not far from here, on that road." Von Egger pointed down the hill. A square Mercedes truck was negotiating a turn on the serpentine below them. Peter shivered in a sudden chill. As if time meant nothing, as if he might see the crash now, reenacted, just as the painting captured the room it hung in.

"He left everything to me. I had a similar provision in my will, you see. I owed everything to him, and so it was logical for me. It was not unchivalrous. She had consented as part of the divorce.

"By that time Pietr was successful. The great fruits of his labor, building the bank, had not yet come to harvest, but he had money. When his son was born he put a sum aside, and gave me the power over it, named me as trustee. And frankly, he forgot about it. In the settlement with Marta, he was relieved of further obligation. He could have easily revoked the trust, for he had paid her amply. But he was busy with matters of state, and he overlooked it. The account survived his death."

Von Egger spoke in a flat voice. Now he paused and motioned down the hill. It was clear he had not finished. A light wind had risen and in the lower orchards he would avoid its bite. They walked again to the statue of the hand. Two rude stone chairs sat opposite, and Peter took one. The older man leaned against the sculpture. He spoke as if he were addressing someone beyond Peter, someone in the woods below.

"During all of this domestic squabbling, history was not on holiday. Your grandfather was an important person. The United States was pressuring the Swiss banking industry to bow to its prying eyes. In their fervor they felt they could dispense justice to all nations. The sanctity of Swiss laws, the concept of property all seemed paper constructs to the Allied leaders.

"Your grandfather had confronted these demands for what they were. Usurpation of rights by a military power. I had assisted him. After his death I took his place. My role was to defend our bank, and through it, the legitimate position of the Swiss government, its creditors, its citizens. Yet one could not be immune to the humanitarian concerns. Your grandfather's genius was to recognize the need for balance."

As he spoke Von Egger looked to the distance, as if this tale of some authority was carved on the rock of the Savoy Alps. Whatever the magic, Peter did not interrupt.

"Arguments were advanced for compensation. The State of Israel sought reparations on behalf of the victims of Nazi brutality. I knew that your grandfather would support those claims, that he would feel whatever the legal system could accomplish must be done.

"For the diplomatic negotiations, the Swiss government appropriated an insufficient sum for our delegation. I spent my own funds and those your grandfather had left me, to subsidize the Swiss delegation. We participated in regular sessions.

"The first step was taken at Paris, right after the war. It became known as the Paris Reparations Conference. Your grandfather, a pivotal player, lived to see the signing of the compact. After his death, there was more work to be done. The devastation was so vast. We all pitched in. It took seven years. How could we persuade any country, particularly one so devastated as Germany, so impoverished, to undertake voluntary payments? Is it possible to think that former enemies will treat each other in such a civilized way? But I tell you it came to pass.

"There was Swiss legislation in 1961. We coaxed our friends in Germany to comply. Payments were made in 1966. West Germany honored its obligations under the agreements to the last deutchmark."

Von Egger looked down. His eyes reflected the gathered snows across the lake.

"That is what became of the money in the trust. I am a wealthy man. I was wealthy at the time of your grandfather's accident. I had no need of those funds. In the scheme of things they were trivial. The trust was an aside, it was created on a standard form we used at the bank.

"I felt this was what your grandfather would have wanted. He had made his settlement with your grandmother, had paid what he was required to pay. No, *this* was the cause closest to his heart. Justice in post-war Europe. Many more Swiss francs than those were spent. Properly, I think. Your grandfather would have thought so as well."

There was no mistaking the sincerity in his voice. He put his hands into the pockets of his long coat and frowned. Behind him the stone hand gestured: there you have it. It might have been the hand of a saint, or merely the hand of the artist, the free hand that offered itself up as the nearest piece of anatomy for study.

They walked on. Von Egger did not respond to Peter's mumbled thanks.

"Did you know his brother? The one who died?"

Fallen limbs from the trees had been gathered in regular piles. They walked among them.

"I did."

"How did he die? Was it in the war?"

"During the war. Not in. The Swiss you remember were non-combatants. It was a shipwreck. A freak accident in the Bosporus. A passenger ship was overloaded." Von Egger bent to a neatly stacked pile of split wood and began filling a leather log carrier.

"May I give you a hand?"

"No need. At my age this is what passes for exercise."

Von Egger's tale had drawn in his guest. Charmed by its eloquence, flattered by the storyteller, by the teller's propinquity to family, Peter, who carried no anecdotes of his father's father — how that phrase rang — was marked by what he heard.

Peter kneeled and helped arrange the logs.

"I should get some exercise too. I didn't swim with the Count Basie band this morning."

They filled the carrier, a hemmed square of cowhide with rough rope handles, and Von Egger hefted it to his hip. There was a victory in his motion, a sense of ownership.

"You enjoyed the music? Please use the pool. I have found over the years several pieces of music with the right tempo. Count Basie, Woody Herman. You know him? Also Mozart, Messaien, Handel. Haydn has good tempos too, but he is boring even under water."

They continued down the path. Von Egger led the way, Peter behind. He watched with a new appreciation, as the old man bore the weight of the wood at his hip.

Peter opened doors and they delivered their load to the library. There Von Egger squatted before the grate and stacked twigs and five lengths of the fruit wood across the blackened andirons. He put a match to a single sheet of paper: the kindling blazed. A long-legged beetle white as ash fled the heat and paused near Von Egger's boot. He snatched it by a leg and flicked it into the flames. It disappeared with the briefest spit.

Von Egger spoke into the new fire. "Did you know that the Third Reich banned jazz? *Entartete*, degenerate music. There was also forbidden art, *entartete kunst*. The Nazis thought jazz symbolized mongrelization. Klezmer sounds, Negroid vitality. The basis of National Socialism, I am convinced, was sexual energies. The normal channels of sexuality were of no interest. They were all overloaded or celibate".

"You think political abusers are private abusers?"

"I do."

"And us?"

"We are capitalists, our conscience is the market place. We scourge not what offends but what remains in inventory."

Von Egger draped his coat and the small, fringed shawl, a muted pattern, over the back of a chair. Peter sat down.

"Tell me about the Composers' Circle."

Von Egger cocked his head. There was an unmistakable pleasure in his expression.

"You found that in the book, yes? We thought it so hush-hush at the time. When your grandfather saw the deteriorating situation in Europe, he moved to establish a network of financial agents in neighboring countries. The first was in Budapest. In an excess of drama, we determined to give each a code name, after a composer. We had a Mendelssohn, a Chopin, even for a boring, repetitious little man, a Haydn."

Von Egger studied Peter's eyes in the firelight.

"The Composers' Circle became a singular tool in allowing Switzerland to remain neutral and allowing its institutions to function. It also enabled many people to send assets ahead from their country and purchase their escape. Many agencies were working to extricate those endangered by the Third Reich. We were merely one."

He looked to the shelves on his left.

"Somewhere here I may have a second little book, there, that mentions these matters. If you are interested. Would you like to see it?"

"I would."

Von Egger scanned the shelves. The room was ringed by a waist-high brass rail. Attached to it, on noiseless wheels, were two stepladders that could be maneuvered to reach any shelf, and he rolled one around and climbed it. He withdrew a slim, grey volume.

"This book has an entry on your grandfather. You will be enlightened."

Gerard entered unsummoned, carrying a tray with glasses, a bottle of mineral water and one of dark beer. Or would they prefer something hot?

They took their drinks. Peter opened the book. It seemed to be short biographical sketches of several people.

They sipped at their glasses.

"One last question."

"Please."

"Your comment. The one about believing in love." He was not sure what to ask. Von Egger did not wait.

"Peter, I'm disappointed in you. One's view of the world depends upon where he stands on that issue. One is either sentimental or realistic, hard-headed or soft-hearted.

"That is not to say the realist cannot enjoy a sunset, the poetry of Heine, the thrill of infatuation and flesh. Quite the contrary. But I think until you settle where you stand on that question, the world can be a muddle. All artists, for example. Yes, I include jazz pianists by all means, all artists must be realists. They have no time for nonsense. They must understand the rules of their art. In your case, rhythms, tonality, harmonies. Rules that make the cosmos."

"Someone with talent pushes the rules," Peter offered. "Changes them."

"Exactly. But to play outside the lines you must know where they are. It is true of all human activity, even our humble efforts in commerce."

The fire gave out its last licks, and both men watched the dying light.

"So the rules of society don't apply to those who have the power to flaunt them. Isn't that facism?"

"I would say to those who understand the world. Those who see the world for what it is."

"You know what I think?" Von Egger looked up, his eyes ready to smile. "I think successful people come to think they're right. But you, you're not so sure."

Peter's host permitted himself a slight nod, walked to the hearth. He placed the toe of a boot against the bottom log and gave a deliberate kick. Embers brightened into bloom and the flames grew as the aerated stack took fire.

"The hard-headed, Peter, *are* right. I give you an illustration. Let us pretend that you have the magical power to ask a single question of every living soul. And that you will get a truthful answer.

"After consulting the great minds in science, medicine, theology, you frame your question. You decide to ask about the human heart. One simple question: tell me what you need. That is all. Tell me what you need.

"Now, before we examine the answers, let us put down some truths about the human condition. There are not many on which we can agree. Perhaps these." Von Egger held up a single finger.

"First, death. Second, free will. No arguments?" Peter shook his head.

"Three, life is aimless. Not that it is futile, but that literally it has no aim. We cannot claim, for all our ponderings, to have divined a purpose in our lives uncommon, say, to the clam on the sea floor. And last," and Von Egger raised a fourth finger, back of the hand to Peter, fingers skinny as gates pikes. "Finally, that we come to these discoveries and all others, alone. Now what will be the answer to your question? Many people will tell you the same thing. I need to be loved. I need my mother. I need to live forever. I need to see my father again for I never told him this, that . . . ." His voice rose in mimicry and trailed off.

"What are these people missing? The awareness of our few truths. Those who grasp these truths do not suffer the pain of the universe. A zebra does not anguish over the cruelty of the lion. He does not construct a metaphysic in which the lion can achieve immortality by renouncing cruelty. He avoids the lion. Zebras who do not, zebras who seek *rapprochement*, are disqualified by evolution. Which is to say, they are eaten."

He plucked a small box of matches from the mantle and held it in view as a magician would. Held it and let it fall.

"You see that? That is not the cruelty of the earth towards this object. That is how the galaxy is constructed."

"You leave no room for romance," Peter said. "For selflessness, for sacrifice, for being in love."

"On the contrary. I welcome it. I welcome enchantment, infatuation, romance. That is precisely why truth is deceit. I am an admirer of deception. It is a human artifact. *Self* deception I abhor."

Von Egger turned and frowned at the fire. The logs he had fetched were still green and they smoldered. Again he set his boot tip to them.

"You're saying," Peter ventured, "that the realist identifies what cannot be changed and is free to bend everything else. Morality, goodness . . . "

"All relative terms. All depend on the great What Else."

Peter finished the beer. Von Egger took the emptied glass as a cue.

"You must excuse me. I shall not see you at dinner but I trust you find everything you desire."

With that the tall man opened the door and left. His coat and scarf remained on the chair. Peter looked dumbly at the square box of matches on the brick floor of the hearth. It had hit with a wooden clack. Its magic was spent.

He walked to the shelf. Wary of his host's warning, he picked up the faience of the Minotaur. The living figure had been brought out from its background by a smooth glaze. The head and sex organs — those of a bull — were a darker umber. What was left of the beast to be human?

Peter set it back carefully and retrieved the slim book. The conversation had tired him. What had loosed that smirk off his host's lips? Had Peter's words touched a button, or was it merely his impertinence? Peter had little to guide him, he'd spent little energy on the human psyche.

He went up to his room and napped, a sleep stilled by the fresh air and longish walk. He awoke thinking of Von Egger's extended fingers and how the fire had lit them. Someone knocked. It was Gerard, inquiring about his preferences for dinner. Peter showered and went to dress. The soiled clothes had been removed from his satchel, ironed, and replaced. The tuxedo hung freshly pressed in the closet. He came down and thought to play the Bechstein again before the meal, but there were voices in the salon. It had not occurred to him, but evidently other guests were staying in the house and Von Egger was meeting with them. Peter left by a rear door, circled the house, and walked to the front lawn. Through the glass he could see the heads of several people sitting at divans in the salon, could occasionally sense their movement.

Amid the clipped green lawn sculpture sprouted like saplings. The pieces had no unifying theme or school or aesthetic, though most, Peter guessed, were contemporary. A stone fish, no more than the shape of a bar of soap in its last washings, swam frozen on an iron rod. Great chrome cubes mounted each other with precarious balance. It was an island of improbable beings, mummies without wrapping. Did they come alive one night a year, whisper their secrets to each other? Peter paused before a realistic grouping. Amid the other abstractions, the recognizable human form seemed out of place, and indeed this particular piece might have been a pastiche, a joke. It was a large bronze, life-sized, with a dark patina: a couple, nude, seated and with the gentlest touch of hand on arm, hand on thigh, frozen in a kiss. It was the pose of the famous Rodin piece, but with a queer difference. The young lovers were men.

What was to be made of Von Egger? Why had Helene warned him of Peter's arrival? When Von Egger first revealed that he knew Peter's name, Peter had felt a sure *frisson* of danger, as if the two were somehow in league. But with Von Egger's explanations, that seemed a false premonition. There was nothing Peter could do to this man, to either his person or his didactics. For a significant part of him was didactic, his beliefs as specific, epigrammatic, as his art works.

Was he to be believed? What was it Helene had said about who tells the tale? Surely she was wrong. Surely history was a chain of improvised solos, none longer than a chorus, each depending upon the virtuosity of whoever had the mike at the time. History was events, they happened. Is that, Peter wondered, soft-headed?

He took dinner in the kitchen. A perch from this very lake Gerard told him, and the wine Monsieur Von Egger had wanted him to try, an Yvorne from a grape grown on the far side of Montreux. Peter was indifferent to wines, though this was tasty, and he devoured the fish, the small cabbages and carrots, the noodle pudding. The day's paradoxes had given him a healthy appetite. The same meal, Gerard was saying, is served in the dining room.

"There are guests for dinner?"

"Gentlemen from the bank, I believe," Gerard said. "Also from the Confederation." The *Confederatio Helvetica*, the government of the country.

After dinner Peter went upstairs to stay out of the way. Yesterday's party seemed social, but the gathering tonight must be business since he was not invited to play. Curious that, if these persons were indeed Löwenhoft directors, Von Egger had not invited them to meet the grandson of a former personage. But perhaps not. His grandfather's era was now fifty years in the past. Who could be expected to remember?

He had thrown the book on the bed and now, in absence of anything else in the room, picked it up to read. Entitled *Thirty Who Cared*, it was inscribed by its author, the same man who had written *Gallant Little Switzerland*. "To Frederich Von Egger, with admiration."

The book was a collection of short biographies of Swiss who during the war had served humanitarian and national interests. The stories were inspiring.

The entry on his grandfather gave him little new information. It confirmed the date and place of his birth, the small town outside Zurich, the republican nature of his upbringing, by which Peter understood the writer to mean humble. His career in banking, his private diplomatic service. Two sentences on the Composers' Circle. He married, it said, in 1944 and was survived by one son. It omitted mention of his wife Marta and the other child, the one who, Peter assumed, died in infancy.

He was about to turn out his light. He glanced towards the book's close to find an index, perhaps there was more on Steinmuller. There was no index, but the last entry — they were arranged alphabetically — caught his eye.

Frederich von Egger

Among the many businessmen active in humanitarian causes during and after the war, none has worked more tirelessly than Frederich von Egger.

M. von Egger was born in 1920 in Arbon, Canton of Thurgau, the only child of a prominent local industrialist and his wife. He received his degree with highest honors in economics from the university of Zurich in 1941, and upon graduation became an officer with the Löwenhoft Handelsbank. That affiliation has lasted throughout his career. In business circles M. von Egger is known through his merchant banking successes. A recognized art connoisseur, he has assembled an important collection of Greek and Persian antiquities.

As a young banker, M. von Egger came under the tutelage of Pietr Steinmüller, *q.v.*, and assisted his mentor at the Currie Mission and the Paris Reparations Conference of 1945-46. M. von Egger subsequently was appointed to the Confederation commission charged with response to requests from the State of Israel, a duty which he discharged from 1954 through 1961. Article 8 of the so-called Final Act of the Paris Conference provided that nonmonetary gold found in Germany and millions derived from German assets in neutral countries were to be spent for the benefit of nonrepatriable victims of Nazi persecution and their families.

Article 8 required subsequent legislation and implementation, difficult and sensitive tasks given the need for consensus in the Swiss banking community. These tasks also involved the relationship of Switzerland to her long-standing allies, the United States and the United Kingdom. Strong and opposed views were pressed directly by diplomats and indirectly through the powerful lobbies of refugee and Zionist organizations throughout the world. M. von Egger succeeded in reconciling these various interests.

For his tireless and dedicated service to the cause of his country and the people of the world, he has received several honors, including the Order of the Eidgenosse from his own country, and the Citation for Merit awarded by Golda Meir, then Prime Minister, on behalf of the State of Israel.

Peter slept a comforted sleep. He had considered his past a trifle. The absence of any lineage had freed him of expectations. But even as he dismissed it, the hole was an irritation. Everyone had a history — why had he been left empty? Filling the void with a hero was winning the lottery.

He ate fried eggs for breakfast, cutting large slices from a loaf of coarse rye bread. The coffee he took in the local manner, half with milk that had been scalded in a separate pan. He was quite at home, at ease as the two women in service responded happily to his schoolboy French.

As he finished Gerard presented him with a white envelope. "Monsieur Von Egger has been called to the city on business. Then he goes abroad for the winter. He regretted not being able to say goodbye, and leaves you this. I am to assure it is satisfactory."

Inside were several hundred Swiss francs and a short letter. Von Egger gave an accounting, part for the tuning and the balance for his performance, both, Von Egger wrote, what he understood to be a usual amount, and a last paragraph.

"It gave me great pleasure to meet you and to be able to help inform you on the nobility of your forbearers. I must leave on business and do not expect to return in the near future. The Maag-Reinhardt book is yours, should you wish to keep it. Its excesses about me are embarrassing, and I am obliged to ask that you ignore them. Please use this as your home, so long as you remain in this country."

Von Egger had signed his initials only, an apt compromise, Peter felt, between the disparity of their positions and the intimacy that had in so short a time grown between them.

It took him only minutes to pack. He slipped the farewell note in the book as a mark, pocketed the money, thanked the kitchen staff. Gerard led him through the rear of the house to the huge garage and manipulated a series of switches to open the doors and the security gates through which Peter would pass. Peter primed some fuel into the cylinders, wrenched the throttle twice for luck and stomped down on the starter. The Ducati spluttered its fickle cough. A second and a third time. Finally, as if refreshed by the rest and made ambitious by the surroundings, the engine fired with the roar of its betters. He stuck on his helmet. Again the wind whistled past the plastic ear holes, played a raga of quarter notes. No fingers, only speed and direction plucked at the strings. He was off.

COUNTRYSIDE FLEW BY TO the sides, the motorway — concrete river bend, the Europa road — flowed underneath. He had space to give away. Arched bridges, towns, cathedrals. Money feathered his jeans, the motorcycle was resurrected, risen again, he was on wings. He listened. A topnote above the engine, from the coombs of the mountains came a choiring, a tuneless breeze that crossed the venturi throat of the hills and came to him green and singing. When you're in the clear, nothing can touch you, you can't be lost.

Running the engine flat out burned carbon off the points. The bike ran with a regular drumbeat. He pushed the needle to a hundred K, past on the downgrades. Speed was a high without lows. No wrong notes, no hangover, no Where is this relationship going. Only speed, and the kicky rush that it might end in an abrupt and unplanned stop. An improvisation.

The postcard landscape rolled out, still green from the temperate fall. It looked like the Berkshire foothills where he had spent hours, driving his motorbike and listening to the oboes of the wind.

Peter grew up in the valley flats. Not the field hockey and arugula Connecticut, his town was a grim and job-hungry place. The soil had been rich once, but generations had long ago plowed under fields of sweet laurel and bayberry to plant tobacco. When that gave out, they planted corn, and when that gave out potatoes. The long, slatted tobacco sheds lived a second life as cribs for the lesser crop, and a third and final life when they were torn down for firewood. By then the topsoil was leeched through and the land showed its trenched scars of traprock and mica.

Peter squinted ahead at the road. His lowland town would not fit here. On the main street there wasn't a car with four hubcaps. Rows of bungalows, wood barking through the watery paint. When he renailed a broken picket on his mother's fence, he tapped gently so as not to spring two tines for each one he fixed. Grass crept untrimmed around the gateposts and feldspar glistened in the hard-packed earth. His mother standing at the screen door, stolid, worn, set against the world's surprises.

After the farms went broke the town's wage earners worked at machinery. They did metal turning, they rolled and drew copper. Until it closed the main employer was a shear-blade shop that cut tool and die for the silverware factories in Wallingford to the south. Most of the townsfolk didn't consider Mrs. Steinmuller's piano lessons for their children. The few who did counted the dollars and saw no return on their investment. It's no wonder she braced herself against change, Peter thought. Most of her news, from her husband's death on, had been bad.

He had brought good news. Twice. At sixteen, he had won a state-wide high school competition for musical composition. That had surprised her, although not pleasantly. She thought the sounds he made — he had written the competition piano piece on the grand in their home — unmusical. Not to be taken seriously. But she came to the performance. She wore the corsage he had sent her though it made her eyes red, wore it to the concert and throughout the lemonade and ginger snap reception that followed.

The audience gave the piece a polite hand. Still, it took the prize. Peter gave his mother half the money and with the rest bought a keyboard and his first motorcycle. Riding on the prize came his second piece of fortune, a music scholarship at a college in a far corner of Massachusetts. A lovely place of the highest standards, the dearest tuition, the loftiest elms. He hadn't stayed long.

Midway into his trip, Peter steered off the autobahn to find a sandwich and a toilet. He followed a school bus through town. The kindergartners pressed their faces to the rear window, waving, giggling, trying to get him to respond. At a stoplight, Peter revved his engine and cut it, making a rude blat. They laughed, called for him to do it again. *Encore, encore le pet.* He shook his helmeted head slowly and they pleaded. Then as the light changed he raised the opaque visor to reveal an idiot's face with crossed eyes and distended tongue. Screams of delight, their laughter fluting over the cycle's noise.

He might have flown home from Geneva. The bike and his pay would afford him a non-sched. But he wanted to go back to Zurich. Why would have Helene called ahead? Could she know the hospitality Von Egger would extend him, know that this man was so close a friend of his family? If so, why the warnings?

Scoot through the Bernese Oberland, the Switzerland of calendars, castles, the valleys of Goethe. Drive into the deepening sky, an early dark that sprinkles a cold rain. Ring up Helene from a filling station outside Zurich. Her voice tuneful, how glad she was that he's returned, gets an immediate response. He blurts out his suspicion.

"But if you didn't tell him, how did he know?"

"You are no private eye. You make inquiries at the bank. First of the receptionist, then of the guard. I make inquiries for you, of the secretary who watches over the board. They have both worked at the bank for a generation. They are as old as Herr von Egger. And you marvel that he hears you are looking for him."

"What about at his office? The guards called me by name?"

"Peter, you carried your satchel."

"Yes?" He looks to the motorcycle. Even from the telephone booth he can see what she tells him. His name is written on the bag in black military stencil. They arrange to meet. Tonight, she says, and a sound beats in her throat. It is precisely the grace-note she makes when he touches her.

She came for him at the designated spot, an all-night car park. He left the motorcycle. Rain was falling in earnest and they would go back in the automobile. She was on time. They locked the satchel in the boot of her car and walked as lovers under a pink umbrella. Happened on a street fair. Musicians, jugglers, dancers undaunted by the drizzle. At a little flea market he bought her a plastic egg of Silly Putty, she insisting it was what she wanted. The cobblestones of the Old City streets shone wetly and their breath led them like speech balloons in the comics.

Helene chose a restaurant that was over a shop, quite small, white-washed walls and a beamed ceiling. She ordered for both. Roast goat, *Gegmesenbraten*, better to eat she said than to pronounce, tender and sealing off the cold. Aromas kindled their appetites as they waited. He told her everything he could remember, each piece of art, each peculiarity of Von Egger. As Peter talked the man became even more imposing than he had been in the setting he had so clearly designed. The waiter placed a bottle of sparkling water between them. Helene took the Silly Putty and rolled it in her hands; using the oyster fork, she formed a perfect rose of iridescent green on her butter dish. Leaves, a thorn.

"You are a sculptor," he said, astonished.

She smiled, did not look up, deprived him of her grey eyes. "A tinkerer."

Centered on the table was a small cachepot that held a flowering plant. "I cannot tell whether Von Egger is a sage or a madman. I have the feeling he is a little of both. He moves in important circles, yet he takes all this time with me. He disappears, but writes the most cordial note, the money . . . "

"Then what is bothering you?"

"Nothing, I suppose. He left so fast."

She had rolled the rose into a ball, was again doodling.

"He is a very important man," she said, her eyes on the plate where she worked the clay. She had tented the napkin behind the butter dish and Peter could not see her hands.

Peter watched her work. Her eyes were lidded, she worked the clay. It gave him an edge, like watching her through field glasses.

"I can tell you that much," she went on. "Important. The description in the book, it does not surprise me. He is very rich and very influential. Very private. But that he did not say goodbye, why should you be surprised? You do not think he means to adopt you?"

"No, no. I do not. There were just some things. For instance. He seemed to be running from me. Why would he? I'm down to my last centimes."

"So he is a busy man. You say yourself he spent time. Now he goes back on schedule."

"And another thing. He said how embarrassed he was about the book's description of him, yet he had several copies of it on the shelves."

She finished her sculpting. Now she turned the dish this way and that.

"Not surprising either. He probably has boxes. A bank director, an industrialist like Frederich Von Egger, if he liked it he might purchase many books. In several languages. Make it a best seller. And that he keeps them. So, we find he is not merely busy, not merely modest. He is also vain. That is not so unusual in a man."

She pushed the plant aside, removed the napkin to unveil her work. Lying in the plate and pointed at Peter, slightly serpentine, was a perfectly formed penis.

"Helene," Peter was shocked, looked around to see if anyone had noticed. He laughed with her. "This is Switzerland. For goodness sakes. Sober and industrious. And you a conservative banker."

"Now we see," she said laughing, "who is the conservative and who the bohemian. You Americans are so fond of your stereotypes."

The dinner was excellent. Simple, filling. The open ride had again driven his hunger. They took the food slowly. This first appetite would be slaked in an easy tempo, *andante ma non tropo,* what the fake books called swing.

Peter was tantalized, but he held back. For this, only their second night together, they could not rely on novelty alone. He was obliged to contribute, to deepen the expectancy, draw it across a long ballad line. A man thirsting for a drink will study his glass, place his hands palm down on either side before taking a sip. He presses on the anticipation, holds it from washing over him.

Over dinner they fell into a tacit pattern. She ordered, he asked for the same choices. She named a wine, he agreed. She looked to see whether he was mocking but he was doing the opposite, he was playing to her. His compliance aroused her, made her smile. He returned it. He had asked Matey, what do lovers bring to their bed? Do they tear down walls or put them up? Both, she said. First they take apart the maze of lust and curiosity. On the bare landscape, they build a new construct of impatience, or habit, of sympathy and loneliness and a need to be touched, to be there, not to be alone.

He paid the bill. Theirs was the only table. Still they sat over coffee until she was ready to leave. She set the time, and later she put him in the car for the ride back to her place and took him to her bed. She tasted of flavored vermouth and pepper. This night she would lead.

You learn, playing ensemble. Who leads, who follows. Opening in unison, a solo chorus for each, trading eights, trading fours. Then unison again, home and out. Constant the beat, the rhythm, the repetition. The words disappear first, they mean the least. Then the notes and the harmonies. After all is stripped away there remains the beat, the single rhythm. The single rhythm. The single rhythm.

Her morning persona was different. Full of purpose, brushes, coffee filters. He spoke to her naked back. "This is what a woman must feel like when she wakes up and the man has forgotten her name." She was doing her eyes at the bathroom mirror.

"You feel neglected," she said and stretched her cheeks and brow to see her work. "You are a spoiled child. The bedroom and the board room," she shook some sort of brush at him. "Don't mix."

He watched her make up her face. Then he dressed and they sat at a small table and took a breakfast of cinnamon rolls and coffee. He sliced a pear into thin crescents and ate them with his fingers.

"I'll take a ride with you downtown. Pick up my bike."

She bustled the dishes into the sink, looked through drawers. "Here," she said. "You'll need a key."

He had given no thought to the future. This life was not without its comforts. He could evidently stay with Helene. Perhaps he would see what kind of keyboard he could buy, see if there was a job to be had, and stay in Zurich. He might hook up with Marcus.

She dropped him off by the car park. Last night's rain lingered in the air, on the pavement. It was a bleak day, the first of February. Easy living. He had the day to himself, a little money in his pocket, room provided and board easy to scuffle up. If he couldn't find a reasonably priced instrument he would practice at the church.

It was a circular parking structure, Peter roving around its entire helix one time and then a second. He couldn't find the damn bike. On the third trip around, he saw the notice. Taped to the wall, the only point certain in a mad spiral. Never sure if you'd been here before.

Something about notices in German did not seem congratulatory. The parking attendant helped him through it. The motorcycle had been seized in order to satisfy the provisions of six or seven different ordinances. He could find out more by appearing at the main police station on Talstrasse. Which was, the attendant volunteered, only ten blocks away.

What the hell could it be? This great capitalist country seemed determined to prevent him from owning any private property.

Much of the morning he spent searching identical grey halls for the right bureau. The young sergeant behind the desk was soft-spoken and pleasant. His manner assured Peter nothing unjust could happen to him. For an hour he shared a bench with a woman whose Doberman had run off. It was not, she told him, the first time but it would be the last. She would have him put down as soon as she found him. Remind me not to take a gig as a Doberman.

Peter waited alone. Eventually the policeman located the paperwork and explained the problem.

"Your motorcycle was reported as sold, but we had no information on the buyer. It does not appear that the buyer has a motorcycle license in Switzerland, and he has no evidence of insurance."

"May I see?" asked Peter and the officer showed him the computer-generated report. He recognized only his name.

"*I* am the buyer," he said. "That's me."

This amused the officer. The system was working. "Well," he said. "There you are."

"And according to this pamphlet," Peter took out the weathered folder he had bought on first arriving in Zurich, "I need no special license or insurance. It says I can buy a green card for insurance, but I'm not required to."

"That is correct," said the officer.

"Well, then. May I have my motorcycle back."

"Of course. There are two other matters. The costs incurred in towing and storage must be paid. If you cannot, the machine will be sold for fair market value and any excess remitted to you. That is the law."

"Well, I can pay the costs. But it seems to me . . . ."

"There is a second matter." The policeman smiled. His face showed affability, no trace of beard. He was not interested in debate. "I have a note that you are to wait here until I am able to reach a Miss Jellicoe at the U. S. consulate."

He sat on the maple bench while the sergeant dialed. She was not in. Fifteen minutes later he dialed again.

"Perhaps after lunch," Peter said.

"Yes," said the young man, turned to the papers in front of him. "Perhaps."

Peter sat patiently. What possible business could the consulate have with him? Perhaps his grandmother's death? Would he go back for her funeral? Would the old woman like to know what became of the man she left so abruptly? If she hadn't died he would go visit her. He browsed notices in four languages, looked through pamphlets on the proper use of condoms, seat belts. A new policeman took the desk. Peter explained the matter and the man made another call.

"Miss Jellicoe will be in tomorrow," he reported.

"I'll come back."

The policeman said something in German. It sounded resolute and unpleasant. Peter guessed that he should be going, repeated his intentions, and cordially waived goodbye. He turned to find an enormous patrolman blocking his way. Red hair, beefy and cheerful face balanced on a frame the size of a stall shower in a cheap motel. "We will hold you here," said the voice behind him, "and release you to this Miss Jellicoe."

"But she's not in until . . . ." As he spoke a grip under his arm made his neck tingle. The message hit him at the same time.

"I'll come back," he started to say, but he was already moving toward a rear door. His protector wheeled him through like a dolly, he trying to use his heels, his voice to slow the pace. A second door, this barred, down a stairway with apple-green walls, a hallway, a row of cells.

It happened before his temper could kick over. He stood in a five-by-eight cell. There was no seat on the toilet. He gripped the bars in both hands, as he'd seen hundreds of TV convicts do. Nothing happened. He began to yell. A guard appeared, laconically heard him out, and walked away.

Hours later the same man served him dinner on a blue plastic tray, to be eaten with a flat wooden spoon. Only then did Peter accept he was not in some half-hour sitcom that would end with apologies and canned laughter. He sat on the bunk and took a spoonful of the hash on his plate. There was nothing to do. He stretched the meal some twenty minutes. The food was quite tasty. At nine o'clock the cell lights darkened, and the bare bulb in the corridor remained lit.

He slept. Early and briefly. He woke a dozen times. Each time it was to the sound of his own heart, up tempo, drowning out the other sounds. Was the weekend starting? Might Jellicoe be transferred, suffer an accident? By morning the place had him by the windpipe. That open toilet especially, he kept imagining himself falling in. He'd dreamed they'd chained him up. This was absurd, imprisoned for buying a bike he was allowed to own. The first person he saw served him breakfast. He spilled out his complaints, but the man shrugged and moved on. The second simply unlocked the door, led him gently upstairs past the sergeant's desk, into the light.

There an officer, equally taciturn, handed him an envelope with his watch and wallet. A good sign. They put him in the right front seat of an unmarked car, locked the doors and drove him away. It was only a few blocks, not enough time for Peter's new apprehension to find words. Miss Jellicoe saw him without delay.

"I'm afraid you're in a bit of a pickle," she said.

"A pickle? I've been in their goddamn lockup. They yank my bike by mistake, but I have to pay to get it out of hock. Then they refuse my money, and lock me up for the night. If you have the time I'll tell you about the plumbing."

She chastised him with a look.

"I know nothing of that, Mr. Steinmuller. This is more serious. It seems you have accepted paid employment without a work permit."

"Ma'am?"

"The household of one Frederich Von Egger filed a payroll tax report as required by Swiss law. It shows you as an entertainer, for which you have been paid two hundred francs, and a piano tuner, one hundred francs. They list you as a U. S. citizen. We have no record of an application for a work permit."

Peter shook his head. They had changed keys on him. "Lady, I'm a musician. I fixed someone's piano and I played show tunes on it."

Miss Jellicoe frowned. Von Egger's staff must have lifted his passport number when they laundered his clothes. Industrious and law-abiding, Helene had said. It made a hellish combination.

"The Swiss take their laws with the utmost seriousness. Particularly laws regarding immigrant labor. I seem to recall we discussed this. Switzerland is a highly desirable destination for all of Europe, many persons want to move here to get work."

"Look," he said. "This was a couple of hours. Cocktails, Jerome Kern, chicken livers wrapped in bacon. Three hundred francs, that's maybe two hundred bucks."

"Two hundred and three."

He looked as hapless as he knew how. "What can I say dear after I say I'm sorry?"

It was something Marcus would say. Jellicoe looked at him sternly. "All I mean is, I apologize. Who do I apologize to, whom?"

She consulted the papers on her desk. "That is not an option. The Swiss Immigration Office has filed a formal complaint. Our office must respond. They ask that you quit the country, immediately."

"They want me out of Dodge City?"

"The country. The city is Zurich. The country is Switzerland."

"On the next stage."

"Actually, they will need assurances that you are leaving. A one-way flight, tourist, to the United States costs six-hundred and thirty dollars."

"Look, lady. I don't have the money to fly home. If I did, I would. I could make the money if I had my keyboard and you would let me, but I don't and you won't. I'd leave on my bike, if I had my bike, but I don't. They do. You see what I'm saying?" His eyebrows bent to her cool look.

"I'm sorry, Mr. Steinmuller. I need to tell them something by close of business." She reached for the phone.

"Am I free to leave? Do I get busted again?"

"We need to tell them something."

He nodded, went into the street. Walked away. Helene would be wondering where he'd gone. Could he just leave, wash his hands of all this? Matey had told him he declined to care about anything, declined to love the people he loved. Leaving Switzerland — it was not as if there's anything here to lose. Helene would understand. As for Von Egger, he had spent only a few hours with the man. You could hardly consider him family.

He called. Helene was out, the secretary said. Gone to file storage. He described his troubles into her voice mail and headed to the police station. The humiliation, the fear of confinement welled back on him and a faint dew formed in the small of his back. The costs were not outrageous. He pulled the rest of Von Egger's cash from his pocket — even after their celebration last night he could redeem the bike.

In need of a plan. Immobile was worse than broke. He would bail out the bike and hit the road. Scuffle up a living. Head to a land where jazz is king. Or even the seven of spades.

The young police officer was pleased to see him. "Your problems have been solved."

"How so?"

"We had a bid for the fair market value of your machine. Here is the computation. Nine hundred and seventy Swiss franc. Deduct thirty for the towing, five for the storage and another five for the sale costs, nine hundred thirty Swiss franc." He handed Peter a small brown envelope, sealed at the end.

"For real?"

"These are all statutory costs, you see. All approved under the statute."

"Who would pay that kind of money for my bike?"

"All approved under the statute. Now, in light of your problem with our Bureau of Immigration, I must insist we know your plans."

Peter counted the bills inside. Just enough to make that one-way to Dulles, tourist. Coincidence or concert? Should everyone appear, an old teacher used to say, in class one day carrying umbrellas, the chance for conspiracy is inversely proportional to the chance for rain. He called Jellicoe from the station house and told her he would be on the plane that evening. She was gratified.

"Glad to make a pretty lady smile," he said, though odds on she wasn't smiling. Then again, she wasn't pretty.

"You can expect the authorities to check on you. They are serious about this case. If you fail to leave the country you are subject to arrest and prosecution. You are staying where?"

He gave her Helene's address. She said to expect Immigration well in advance of the flight time. "They will drive you to the airport, to see you on the plane."

Peter killed a last hour in the basement of the Wasserkirche. He did all the Bach he could remember, and where he came up short, he faked his way through. In the tradition, same changes, Bach would dig it. He checked his watch. His gear was packed to leave, no preparations to be made. He set off by foot to Helene's. As it was on his way, he stopped to see Albert Frey.

Inexplicably, the lawyer was expecting him. Frey knew much of what had happened, confirmed that the confiscation and sale of the motorcycle were procedurally correct. "From what you say, you got a good price. You should thank the police for their help."

"Yes I suppose so." He'd rather have the bike, especially with its repaired valve seat.

"In the United States you will find another motorcycle. That is the way to look at it."

"I still owe you half your fee."

Frye shrugged. "Given the urgency of your predicament, I am prepared to defer. When you are in funds you can send it to me."

Peter regarded him carefully. He didn't seem the deferring type.

"I have another matter to discuss with you, one that has happier circumstances."

The line in Peter's brow deepened. This day seemed fated to prove not necessarily how gallant Switzerland was, but how little.

"And that is?"

"I have received contact from one Frederich Von Egger. You are familiar with him, I believe?"

"Yes. I know him. How in the world do you . . . ?"

Frey dismissed his expression. "There is no mystery. As Miss Durren doubtless told you, I do some work for the Löwenhoft. Monsieur Von Egger is one of its directors. Indeed I too have been entertained at his house on the shore of Lake Geneva."

The lawyer delivered these words as a credential. How many of us, Peter wondered, has the man with glass-blue eyes romanced under the apple tree.

"Monsieur Von Egger wants me to express his regrets that your troubles with our Immigration Bureau arose because of forms his household were required to file. They had not thought that a friend of Monsieur Von Egger's would be inconvenienced. He called from abroad to tell me this. California, I believe. He goes there for the golf. He is quite fond of the golf."

"That was kind of him. Disturbed his day, I'm sure. Probably had to play through."

Frey ignored the jibe. "Monsieur von Egger also said that he had been contemplating the facts surrounding a certain trust corpus from your point of view. I do not know the details, but I do not need to. He said only that you must be particularly disappointed to think yourself an inheritor in one breath and to find in the next that you are not. Accordingly . . . ." Frey patted both hands about his desk. He found a piece of paper amid the clutter and held it at arm's length.

"Accordingly he has reconstituted the corpus of the account and is prepared to deposit it in a bank of your choosing."

"I beg your pardon?"

"He has reconstituted the corpus, as close as he could to the original. That was a difficult task without access to the rates of interest paid by the Löwenhoft in the intervening years. Reconstituted the corpus and is prepared to deposit it in a bank of your choosing."

"What does all this mean?"

Frey looked up. He showed no emotion at the hairpin turns of his client's fortunes. Peter still wasn't sure what this lawyer was saying. Frey looked carefully at his notes and resumed.

"He is prepared conditionally to wire to any United States bank you designate the sum of one hundred twenty-three thousand four hundred and thirty-one Swiss franc, or the equivalent in local currency. At contemporaneous exchange rates, I am sure. As your counselor, I suggest you choose a bank of stability."

"He is giving me one hundred and twenty-three thousand francs?"

"Conditionally. He is. Can you name such a bank for me?"

Frey's words fell like a blackjack hand where the dealer keeps turning cards. You're long since over and he keeps flipping cards.

"Can you give me an hour or so to get you a name? I don't have a bank in the States. I don't have a laundromat."

The lawyer's face showed no change of expression. His pen was poised to fill in a destination for wire transfer. He laid the pen down, and his shoulders twitched with the slightest tic of impatience. He had clearly hoped to complete the transaction.

"Yes, of course. When you establish a relationship, please inform me of wire instructions and routing. Your funds will be coming from the Löwenhoft, Zurich branch."

"I'll think of something. How much did you say?"

Frey repeated the number. There will be costs, he warned, and Peter froze. A fifteen-franc wire transfer fee. Net to you, Mr. Frey offered when he saw Peter struggling with the conversion, is a little over eighty-three thousand dollars.

The sum represented a considerable multiple of Peter's income of that last year. The news gave him great freedom, dizzying freedom. The world would provide him nachos and imported beer down through time.

"Conditionally. What is the condition?"

Frey looked at him flatly. "The condition has become irrelevant due to your difficulties with the authorities. He is concerned that you not be tempted to flout Swiss laws, and conditions it on your immediate return to the United States. But of course your difficulty already assures that."

Peter thought it over. He had nowhere else to go.

"He's made a deal. I'll get you a name. Can I write to thank him?" Frey assured him that a note addressed in care of Frey himself would be forwarded. Peter paid the lawyer the price of the D.C. flight that evening. The secretary made the arrangements, the ticket would be waiting for him at the airline desk, paid in full. The ticket was non-refundable, there was no turning back.

He walked the familiar route to Helene's, a long hour. His good fortune clicked around in his head. Ironies of circumstance linked together like a puzzle. But there was a perversity to it, the puzzle had to be solved in a mirror. When I need money, my job disappears. I get information instead, which I trade for a bike. That and the Rhodes, two favorite trinkets, are traded for money. Each time I pick the path, but each time it turns, veers to somewhere else. Now veering toward the Continental Flight 637 off Zurich 10:15 p.m arrives Dulles 5:25 a.m. two stops Frankfurt and Gatwick. Not a bad turn. All I have to do is pick a bank and eighty-grand shows up. Start here, finish there, do not cross a line or lift your pencil from the page, and collect the loot.

He reached Helene's before she did. Was he celebrating good luck or bad? How would Helene react, the Helene of no strings, no excuses? She was right — he was spoiled, and he liked his stereotypes. But she fit in none of them, and he liked her. So much he'd be sorry to leave her. Accommodating, hip, and a useful array of assets from financial savvy to breakfast. No demands.

This would end it for him. By half past five tomorrow morning he'd be home and out. Marcus used to call that to get out of the tune. You'd finish botching sixty-four bars, a solo that had no point to it, and you'd want to tell him how the chord structure lost you, you couldn't hear the bass line, you thought they were coming back in after thirty-two. Kid, he'd say, wearied and sad. Don't explain, don't complain. Home and out.

Peter wrote a short note to Von Egger. Tomorrow he would be in the States. D.C. was a good jazz town, there was that tenor and he knew a couple of club owners. He'd find something. Lots of piano bars, hotels. It's a singles town, men who tip to be big shots, women who tip to be friendly.

Helene burst in the door breathless. She tottered from her load, hurried to the kitchen and onto the kitchen table that served for meals dumped her purse, her sleek alligator attaché case, a brown grocery bag with leaves poking over the top.

"I have news," she spoke in agitation. Peter went over and took her hands.

"Want to have a contest?"

"I don't understand," she said. She wore a putty-tan suit with brass buttons.

"I have news too. I'm not sure I'll have time. They're coming to pick me up."

He kissed her bare neck, seated her at the table and poured her a drink. Kentucky sour mash, she took it neat with a splash of water. He uncapped a beer and drank from the bottle.

"I'd better go first."

He repeated the remarkable events since she'd left him yesterday morning at the public garage. The missing bike, the cell, the sale for costs.

Helene rose and went to the sink. She ran the tap over a bunch of celery.

"I've just come into a zillion bucks and you're going to wash vegetables?"

"I'm thinking," she said. "And starved. I've been at the archives all day. No lunch."

She broke off a few stalks, placed them on a butter dish, took one and chomped off a bite. "It sounds," she said at last, "like a fairy tale.

Ogres, peril and happy ending." Happy and, he found himself wanting to say, melancholy.

"So you see," Peter said. "I was wrong. Completely wrong to suspect Von Egger. I mean, what a gesture. I know it doesn't mean much to him, but he sure as hell didn't have to do anything like it. For one thing, his spending that money was legal. Just as you said. For another, the way he used the money. It was right in line with my grandfather's wishes."

"No no no," she said impatiently.

"Yes, that's what he would have done."

"Not what I mean," Helene said.

"You mean I was wrong to suspect him of ripping off my grandfather's account."

"No," she rushed to swallow. "I mean you are wrong now."

He began to argue, but she held up her hand, traffic cop style, palm out, and pulled her briefcase to the table. Unsnapped its latches. Files pushed up the lid. She removed a thick computer printout and an inch of old files and slid them across to him.

He looked without recognition.

"I did a computer search. I began thinking on what you said about him, Von Egger, a bank officer, the wealth. A good family, but bourgeois commercial, not wealthy. They owned a little plant that packs hams in St. Gallen. I checked. Not the kind of money that pays for Utrillo oils. His antiquities, he keeps them in the States, it is one of the world's most important private collections. How does someone make that kind of money? I ran his name first as a depositor. No luck. The computer had been blocked, access restricted, you can't search for depositors without several codes. I ran the search three ways. No information.

"So I took your notice from the paper. I searched names who were starred as powers of attorney or trustees. No one thought to encode the dead files on them. And the result," she tapped the print-out with the bitten-off celery stalk.

"The result? Frederich Von Egger is given power of attorney or designated trustee on three hundred and eighty-four of the dormant accounts. All opened between 1939 and 1945. And from what I have been able to retrieve, all on the same form."

She pulled the printout off the stack. Underneath were file jackets stamped *ABGESCHLOSSEN*. Closed. Sent to storage, where she had been this afternoon when he called.

"What are you saying?"

"I am saying that Herr Von Egger seems conveniently to have arranged to be the person who can sign on almost four hundred accounts opened at the same bank in six years where no one picked up the money. The printed form used on these accounts allowed the trustee to dispose of any unclaimed remainder. If they all had what your grandfather's trust had, 123,000 francs, then Herr Von Egger had access to over thirteen million francs. Over eight million dollars."

He looked at her, took a stalk of celery from the plate, studied it vacantly.

"I don't understand," he said, although he did.

"I think Herr Von Egger hopes to file you away, to place you in storage. Like these files. They are old, no one looks at them, there is nothing to be done."

"He said that the costs of the negotiations were enormous, that my grandfather's amount was a drop in the bucket."

"What bucket?"

"Just an expression. A trifle. Not nearly the whole cost." Peter chewed on the tender leaves at the top of the stalk, the palest green of new growth.

"A bucket means a trifle? Then a bucket is what he is paying you to go home. That is the real bucket."

"It makes no sense," Peter argued. "Clearly he spent a lot of his own money on these projects. The book, the citation from the State of Israel . . . ."

They both jumped at the sound of the buzzer. She went to the intercom and spoke in German.

"It is the Immigration Service. Two men. They have come to put you on the airplane."

Peter was on his feet. "What are these?" he said, grabbing a dozen or so slim files from the table.

"They were just pulled at random. I hardly had time to look at them. But here," she opened one in his hand. "Here is a way to get started. Only two cities. Vienna, Budapest. And the *notaire*, the notaries public, they too are often the same. See?" She pointed to an unreadable signature. Underneath, however, with a banker's precision, had been typed the name and address.

"It's a start," Helene went on. "We could look for the notaries. Do you want me . . . ."

The bell rang a third time and someone knocked. Peter called that

108

he was coming. "Listen," he whispered. "I hate to do this. Can you lend me some dough? Money? I'm stony broke."

"Of course. Here," she pulled several bills from her wallet. On a pad she wrote a lengthy name. "In Vienna. You can get a train there tonight. This is the bank where I will send to you." Again the knock, up-tempo. "I'll wire tomorrow."

"Vienna," he confirmed. "You're lending to a man who is walking away from eighty grand by missing an airplane. That give you pause?"

"That gives me flutters," she said. "In the heart. Vienna is one of the cities in the files. You can start your search."

He opened the door. Two men with identical moustaches stood and began to talk to him.

"Vienna it is. Assuming I can convince Butch and Sundance to put me on the night train."

She stuck the files into his duffel and zipped it closed. What had Helene told him that first day about Swiss laws? She had removed files from the premises, and in the company of two law enforcement officers he was packing them across borders. The inspectors waited, shifted from foot to foot.

"And, listen." He took her clumsily around the waist. The satchel was in the way. "Thanks." It was a rough kiss, a goodbye kiss, but it carried a remembered heat. Now, he was down the stairwell with his escorts, explaining to them the change in plans. There would be a new destination.

The authorization was difficult to get, since their office had closed for the day. But eventually they were permitted to take him to the station and to place him on any train so long as it left Switzerland and they saw him cross the border. Once out of the country, he was free. At the great Victorian banhof one of the officers, the one with English, bought tickets from a vending machine. He wished Peter luck.

Peter and the other officer boarded. The train pulled out almost immediately. Peter purposely set his satchel on the aisle seat beside him. The man was obliging; he sat across, propped his feet across to block Peter's exit and, having decided his charge was docile, lay back his head and closed his eyes.

Peter studied the files. Helene's theory must have a flaw, and if he could find it in the first hour he could still scurry to the airport. It wasn't even a theory. It was a circumstance. She was trying to recreate facts more than fifty years old. Time alone would warp their views, the way the atmosphere wrinkles news from distant stars. Helene started with a computer and the computer has an edge. It has no axe to grind, no point of view. I got no lock on de door, ain't no way to be.

The immigration officer looked up at Peter's singing. His eyes narrowed in thought. Peter raised the file jacket to his chest.

"Porgy und Bess," the man said.

Peter returned his smile. "Solid, brother." The man fell back to sleep.

Helene had mentioned a repetition of place and notary. Codes are broken by repetition, pattern. But the files Peter had grabbed at random were not uniform. They were bunched by city. In Vienna there had been two different *notaires*, in Budapest one, someone named Ishtvan Kulek. Odd diacritics — cedillas, dots, circles — embellished the Romany names like gingerbread. Peter wasn't sure he could pronounce them, how would he find who owned them?

He looked up to see an elderly man watching him from the next seat. The man smiled and nodded. Did they know each other? Swiss middle-class men, tended to dress alike. He could have been any one of a dozen with whom Peter had made eye contact in the past weeks.

They were at the border in two hours. The plane had departed. His companion made it clear that he would debark, and from the platform he would watch the train pull out for the East with Peter still on board. That would complete his duties. Peter thanked him for his courtesy, it seemed a Continental touch, and when the train halted the man stepped down from the car.

Peter was once again alone. In a short time he'd been stripped of his bike, arrested, jailed, and separated from a woman who took care of him cozily. More, he had been enriched and robbed by a master of paradox. Robbed because every time his anger perked with the first pin-bubbles of a boil, Von Egger turned down the heat.

Again alone. Only a handful of people knew where he stood on the planet, and none of them, including himself, knew where he was going. As the train labored to speed, he was shivered by that same feeling he'd had as he walked down the gangplank of the ship into a darkling horizon. A shallow bottom to the lung, a sense that the curtain was going up and he was in the house orchestra, down in the pit, the conductor was lifting his baton, and everyone but he had the score.

SHORTLY AFTER THE TRAIN pulled away Peter found the dining car. There was comfort in the rhythms as the train rocked through the night, comfort as well in the blackened windows smeared occasionally by lights. The ride suited him. Lights moved by too quickly to reveal whether they were a street lamp, a bulb burning in an empty hall, someone reading by a chair. The darkness made his journey all the more separate, and he was spared the views of monotonous and idyllic villages.

He seated himself at a table where only one setting had been laid. The flatware bore the monogram of the rail line, and a glass bud vase with a single rose stood at the cloth's fold. The scene gave a sense of repose. He glanced down the small menu card and ordered liver sausage and a bottle of Pilsner beer. He had meant to bring a book with him, but his only volume, *Thirty Who Cared,* he had left by the bedstead in Helene's apartment. He would retrieve it. He would see her again. He stirred with the thought, aroused and melancholy. He wished he were back in Zurich.

The beer arrives at his table, on a salver with a chilled, conical glass. The waiter pours precisely so it forms three fingers of head. He leans back in his chair, brings it close, sniffs its fragrance. It enforces his solitude. Does Helene replace Matey, the hole in his life that Matey leaves? Probably not. You get replacements for baby teeth, not emotions.

What had he been unwilling to give up to have her? Not these vagabond ways surely. He felt as if he'd fallen from a bridge onto a passing train. The events that put him in motion seemed remote.

Maybe it was hereditary. His father traveled for a living. Called on distributors, showed pictures of tooling parts from worn catalogues. The ailing black Plymouth, every week a different sector. His father leaning over the two-suiter like a scientist, fitting underwear, clean shirts, toilet kit into discrete spaces. He might have been constructing a bomb. Peter fetched shoe trees. His father spoke of routes, the motel shortage in Pittsfield, difficulties in the drive from Wilkes-Barre to Bethlehem. When Peter first heard the Christmas story he wondered if the wise men had run into that highway construction at Scranton.

He looked up and found, a second time, that his eyes met those of the elderly gentleman from the coach car. The man must have been sitting by himself at a table since Peter arrived, for his food was now being served. Again he nodded. With no more than a gesture of his hand he asked the waiter to stay and rose, approached Peter.

"You maybe would join me? Eh? Dining alone is the one regret of the solitary life."

Peter said yes, he would, and to his surprise he meant it. The waiter laid a second place and Peter seated himself. They introduced themselves. Doctor Gideon had ordered a plate of steamed vegetables and rice. Peter declined the offer to share the bottle of wine.

"Do you have an active practice?" Peter asked.

"No, no." The old man shook his head in amusement. "No, I am essentially retired. I travel, advising friends, taking on tasks where my years perhaps can help. Rare to find that one's years have some advantage. To others. They are only a nuisance to me."

Gideon had a large head that appeared more massive for his wealth of white hair. He was plainly but handsomely dressed in a dark business suit, midnight blue with a chalked stripe of cream, a tie of India blue, a shirt distinguished by the freshness of its laundering, even at this late hour. His face centered on thick glasses with scarred lines separating two, perhaps three lenses.

Gideon asked Peter about himself, why he was traveling, where he was going. Again offered the wine, wordlessly holding up the bottle, and now Peter accepted. They sat and talked. Peter was exhausted from a fretful sleep in the cell, and hungry for companionship. The man had a soft voice, thickly accented, all the S's palatized, and the manner of a waiter at a favorite restaurant. Peter relaxed. He found himself, voluble and tipsy, telling most of his European saga. A second bottle appeared. He shared his suspicion over Helene's discovery, that Von Egger had profited at the expense not only of his grandfather, arguably an excusable circumstance since his grandfather might have consented, but of others less prominent, less charitably inclined. Vienna might hold some answers.

"So, a quest, eh? You intend to go on?" Gideon asked him.

"I haven't thought that far. Ready, fire, aim. I suppose, if there is something to be found, I might. I have the time, and I may have the money. If enough to live on turns up when I get off this train."

"You don't trust this young woman who took you in?"

"Oh, no. I trust her. It's just that, everything else seems to have gone wrong, there's no reason to believe that won't also."

Peter's discretion was not so diluted by the drink that he mentioned names, the Löwenhoft, Von Egger, Helene. This stranger could not have cared, yet Peter was aware that Helene had used bank files. The Swiss took their laws soberly, there was no need to inflict discomfort on his accommodating dinner partner.

From the inside pocket of his suit jacket, Gideon removed a box of Turkish cigarettes, opened its lid and carefully turned back the foil, offered them across the table. Peter declined. Gideon removed one with satisfaction. It had an oval shape and a strong aroma.

"Do you mind?" Peter said he did not. In fact the smoke was welcome, a strong stimulant even as it curled around Dr. Gideon's head and hung in the air of the car.

"I would say the opposite. Everything seems to have gone right."

"How do you mean?"

"Simply this. You arrive in France without a job. Without contacts, without prospects. Without a past. You have no idea about your father's family.

"So? What happens? You discover the traces of your patronymic. Within one month, spent, eh?, enjoying the charms of a pretty young woman who has taken you in. Like a cat from the alley, you have that expression?"

"Alley cat, yes."

"Alley cat, and, I assume, my friend," Gideon allowed his eyelids the slightest elevation, "not one that has been altered. Eh? In one month you find a grandfather with a noble and recognized history, a patriot and a humanitarian. You make a new friend who appears to be a powerful businessman and offers you his house. You even find you have a choice. So. On the one hand you can collect a considerable sum to which, you admit, you have no claim of right. Or you can stay in Europe and indulge this curious if expensive sense of adventure. All because of a legal notice in a newspaper."

"You think I'm ungrateful?"

Gideon's face shrugged. "It is not a question of gratitude. It is a question of what you want to do. On the one hand, stay in Europe, another American misfit hanging on, until your lady sends you no more money. Or return to the United States. Pay her back, this kind woman who lends you for I do not know what. Get yourself established as a musician."

"I would like to know a little more about this," Peter said. "Just a little more about the past."

Gideon stubbed the butt of his cigarette into the ashtray. He might have been extinguishing a bug from the garden, his lips tightened in secret pleasure.

"You have a long future, eh? Leave the past to those of us who have little else."

"The future doesn't interest you?"

"The future interests me a great deal. It also, for the most part, excludes me."

The waiter brought two checks and the men paid separately. Peter tipped his wallet up so Gideon would not see the last of its bills depart.

Gideon led the way through the aisle. He moved steadily, a deliberate gait, pigeon-proud. "I'm afraid I bored you with my life story," Peter said as they moved back to the car.

"No, no. I enjoyed it. So. I have a sleeper reserved. It has a second berth, if you would care to."

"Thank you, no." Peter wondered if his response was not too hasty. But the old man made no comment on it.

"It is early for me," Gideon said. "I take less and less sleep. Would you like to sit up for a while?"

"Very much." They settled again in the first class car, this time on opposing seats. The train stopped and passengers departed. None came on. There were only a few other people in the car. An American student, three nuns in traditional habit, a young couple. Peter looked at the boy and girl. They dressed identically, wore black like the nuns. The girl had cut her straw white hair shorter than the boy's. She wore a small silver cube on the side of her nostril. Her companion's hair had a lime-green fringe. He too had pierced his body, a set of brass studs rimmed one ear. Casual, intense. Peter felt old.

He and Gideon sat silently. Their window looked out upon the ancient station sign. Peter read it aloud. Innsbruck.

"You're interested in the past? So, a little Innsbruck history," Gideon said, pointing to the sign. "In 1923 Hitler tried to foment a putsch. To begin his revolution. But the police routed him and his gang. He was arrested and tried for treason. Goering escaped and fled here, to Innsbruck. He was seriously wounded. A Jewish shopkeeper tended to him, his wife cleaned the wounds, they saved his life. It was a selfless and humanitarian act."

"So kindness gives birth to cruelty? That can't be right."

"A satisfying contradiction, eh? Someone has said we will find God not in Paradise but in paradox. To investigate both you must look at the human heart. In popular culture we believe kindness to be a product of love, cruelty a product of hate, eh? That is nonsense. These families we invent for our own delusion. If it were the case, then only those who hate would wage war. And we know that is not the case."

The train jostled out of its place and began to roll to the east.

"I don't understand war. I can't imagine how it gets started, when everyone seems to acknowledge its evil."

Gideon looked at him a full minute. He seemed to be deciding whether to let Peter in on some cabalistic secret. His right index finger played lightly with his lips. The car rocked its rhythm, its wheels clacked a complex beat. The sway was simple, four-four time. It was a setting for hypnosis.

At last Gideon spoke.

"So. You are right. And also wrong. We have wars, afterwards everyone bemoans them, victor and vanquished alike, and yet we continue to have them. Why?"

"Politics," Peter said with a shrug.

"I think war is beyond politics. What do we find when we look beyond politics? Only ourselves. War becomes not a reflection of who we are. It becomes, as it did for the Nazis, who we are.

"We like to separate the political from the individual, eh? That is another small deceit. And deceit, my friend, is at the heart of this. It is a deceit to think that war will benefit anyone. No one benefits, yet war continues. So? Deceit is necessary to war. More than armies, more than gunpowder or medals or parades.

"So. Why do I say this? The chain of command. What is the chain of command if not a refutation of individual responsibility? You do not think it was a general who pushed the bodies into the crematoria? The cloak of war allows us to obscure what we feel." Gideon pantomimed with both hands. "What am I doing? Not shoveling the ashes of incinerated corpses. I am merely keeping track of tonnage. So much nitrites, so much silicate. No one is shoveling. After a war you will find no one who manufactured gas. You find only chemical workers.

"So. An example. You know the name Henrik Himmler? The inventor of the *Geheimes Staatspolizei*, the Gestapo. In 1941, Himmler was sent to the Russian front, in command of the *Eisatzgruppen*, a touring brigade whose task was to roam the countryside executing anyone perceived to be helping the enemy. Men and women, often, since the entire household was rounded up, their children.

"Himmler attends his first execution. The condemned dig a large pit. Line up on its edge. The pleas, the nausea, the uncontrolled bowels. Some beg for mercy. Others pray. A junior officer, certainly not Himmler, gives the order. The soldiers fire. Himmler is surprised. There is no silence. Some are wounded, some not even hit. The soldiers fire again. Now they push the mass into the pit, hammering with the butts of rifles, shooting into the topmost layer. In the layers below some have not been wounded. They are merely trapped by the weight. And still no silence. The heap is covered with dirt. Air is trapped in pockets. The mound of earth continues to moan. It goes on for an hour, longer.

"Himmler is upset, eh? It is only natural. He has imagined something more elegant. Touched with compassion, he returns to Berlin to seek a solution. He commissions draftsmen to design a more efficient way to do this. He does not want his troops, the army of the Reich, to be submitted to these indignities.

"The draftsmen and engineers create a mobile gas chamber. It kills within the confines of the van. The soldiers are spared the sight.

"So. What is it we need to go to war? I have listed only the necessary conditions. A disregard for individuality, a yen to be deceived. Something else, eh? Deep within us. At our center, it lies between our legs, shrivels at the cold, leads us in ardor. Sex and war, sex and cruelty. They are connected.

"This is not a new thought. Most of us would concede the connection. We savor it to ourselves, it becomes a private vice like pornography. If we all have the capacity, are we all potential Himmlers? Is that why we fear opening the heart?"

Peter could hear the breath slipping through his lips.

"The heart. The defining muscle in the human connection. To achieve passion we must deploy it. But the heart may be open or shut, eh?, and if we fear its liquors we simply close down its spigot. That protects us. But that is the first deceit, the first dehumanization."

The train crunched slowly, stopped. A soft bump, as other cars were added or disjoined, punctuated the pause. Peter was tired and on the cusp of sleep, but the man's words were provocative. He spoke to lead Gideon further. "The libido as engine. But where is the diabolical machine going?"

The old man shook his head in thought. "The machine is neither diabolical nor angelic. It is just a machine. Yes? It drives us to poetry equally as to propaganda."

Gideon rose.

"I shall retire. So. I offer you the other berth. Rest assured, I am neither a pederast nor a chain-saw murderer from the films."

Peter shrugged embarrassment. Gideon had read his caution. "Thank you, no. But thank you for an excellent evening."

Gideon nodded briskly and walked in his pigeon prance down the aisle.

Some time during the night the running bulbs of the train car were dimmed, and Peter lay down on the seat using the leather jacket to cushion his head. He slept in snatches. During one waking period he became aware of a new and sustained beat, the unmistakable sounds of human coupling. Urgent, needful. The punk rockers two rows behind him. Later still, when he rose to go to the closet lavatory, he walked passed them. They slept unawares, entwined. The boy's arm lay over her chest. Wound about its biceps was a blue band of tattooed snakes.

In the morning the old man came through the car looking for him and suggested breakfast. Peter opened his palm, to begin to demur, but Gideon pushed it aside without a reference to finances. "You must be my guest." They were an hour from Vienna.

"I want to ask of your future," the old man began over coffee. "What are your plans here? First the Creditanstalt?" For Peter had told him the name of the bank Helene had written down for the transfer of funds.

Peter had not thought so far ahead.

"Yes," he said. "I suppose, first the bank." If the cash didn't come through, planning would be irrelevant.

"Once I've got walking around money, I figure I'd scuffle a little." Gideon looked at him to explain.

"Just hang out, see if I can pick up on these two names that notarized the Vienna documents."

"That was fifty years ago, my friend. Those are not uncommon names, eh? Your chances are slim."

"I'm sure you're right. But I can try Budapest."

"What are you looking for?"

"I don't know." As Peter said the words he realized he ought to have an answer. Still, there were chords he used that he could not define.

They watched the countryside fill up with houses. Gideon smoked a strong cigarette. Its first gulp made him cough, a sound like the sawing of wood. When he bent to cough Gideon disappeared behind his frizzy white hair. The train pulled into its station, gave a sigh of destination, shut down.

Gideon took the bill. "Until you come into your inheritance. Do you know anyone in these cities?" he asked Peter.

"No. No one."

"Here." He opened his suit jacket and removed a billfold from the inside pocket. For a panicky moment, Peter thought he would be offered money, began to frame his refusal. But the old man opened his wallet on the table. On one side was a note pad. Gideon wrote in black ink, leaning on the breakfast table. The waiter cleared the dishes while he worked.

"So," he said, tearing the page at its serrated edge. "Some telephone numbers. They can reach me. If you see a way that I may be of help, please call."

"Thank you," Peter said. "But I'm in very good health."

The doctor thought a second and then let go a pop of laughter. "No, no. I am not a medical doctor. No, my fields were political science, philosophy, economics. I am sure you are in very good health." Laughter, like a bakery's perfume, lingers in the memory, clings to fabric. Gideon's laugh hung in the air.

"You may want someone to talk to. They can reach me."

Peter looked. On a sheet of graph paper, the Doctor had printed Zurich, Vienna, Budapest, and beside each a telephone number. Peter reached across the table to shake the man's hand and thanked him for the offer.

The sound of that laughter triggered something. Was it taped in his past? His immediate past had been so transient, so insubstantial. And his distant history was an ocean away. Peter felt himself receding from it at an increasing velocity. People his age were spouses, parents, officers of responsible institutions. They kept calendars and spoke on the telephone as they walked down the street. What he was looking for, Gideon had asked him. Maybe he was, as shoppers say, just looking.

He stood in line at the Vienna traveler's aid desk. Ahead of him were three American girls in shirts naming a California college. Their voices, the twang of their language, sounded like a favorite tune. They too were looking for a cheap pension and were given a list. Peter was irritable from an uncomfortable night, his legs regularly dropping from the train seat.

"Ditto," he said to the woman behind the counter.

"Ditto?"

"I'll take the same list. C hotels." She gave him several sheets, one of which he was pleased to see showed distances from the Banhof. He was short of broke by one hard roll and a café au lait and had no prospects if the money didn't come in.

But it did. He found a small boarding house, bath down the hall. Access to a telephone in a guest parlor on the second floor. Checked in and called the Creditanstalt Bank.

And it had. A demand account, his name, Austrian schillings. He had the clerk tell him the number a third time.

"Wow," he responded, genuine and moved. That is a woman to count on. The advance would see him through Budapest and then some.

He showered, tried to nap on the soft and narrow bed. Too excited for sleep. He rose and took a cab to the bank to pick up his money. Back at the rooming house, he made arrangements with the landlord, an arch fellow perhaps five years his elder whose expression was meant to show that he dealt regularly with fools. Peter had several calls to make. He would use the telephone for the afternoon, but should one of the other guests wish, please let him know.

His enthusiasm flagged when he opened the telephone book. There were perhaps fifty, sixty Karl Brauns, one of the notary names, and hundreds of Schmidts. He began dialing.

An hour proved the task was hopeless. Half the numbers didn't answer. Of the others, only a fraction shared enough English or tolerance for his few words of German to entertain a conversation. And his inquiry seemed so remote, so absurd. I am looking for a man who was a notary public during the war. War, what war? During the Second World War. He was a notary in Vienna in 1943 and 1944. I have documents here that were signed by him, and I was wondering if you knew . . . .

Absurd. The enormity of it suddenly smacked him. He collected his lists, his files with the trust documents, and withdrew to his room.

Vienna had jazz everywhere. That night he found a club with a good combo. When they took a break he approached the pianist, a Swede, and asked to sit in. Peter pushed his solos, ventured out. One night on the boat Marcus had turned on Peter. "If this band was a gang of stickup men, we'd give you the gun." The drummer snickered.

"What is that supposed to mean?" Peter was smiling, ready to be complimented.

"We'd give you the gun. You're the safest, man, you take no chances. You'd hold the gun."

Ventured out, risky. Afterward the musicians exchanged quick, gratified looks. I could get on in this town. The Swede was relieved to get back his chair and Peter left smiling.

By the time he got into bed he was exhausted. The house had bought him beers beyond his capacity, and he had only dozed on the train. He looked forward to an untroubled sleep.

It was not to be. He was prodded by antic, erotic dreams. The girls from the Banhof appeared in one, the woman behind the counter in a second. Helene was on the phone. He could not make out her words through the hissing static. The grey morning brought a dream in which at last she was in his bed. It was a dream without sweetness. They were wrapped about each other in a braid. He sat frozen in the single upholstered chair, watching. A tattoo from one ran on to the skin of the other. It was Helene, and yes, he thought it was he with her, but there was no pleasure. The shapes twisted, the covers fell away. The bodies were sculpture, Kewpie-doll pink, and there was moaning and a soft *pot-pot*. Fleshless and plastic, the bodies wrestled in slick sweat. Each tried to turn the other towards the sound. Just as he succeeded, she would roll them around so his damp back shielded them. Squirming and still moaning, the bodies were tossed on a pile, never stopping, a pile of other bodies, then dirt, then other bodies and moaning and the constant and irregular *pot-pot* of gunfire.

He awoke staring at a colorless ceiling. It was dawn. The room had heated to tropical pressures and steam popped from the radiator valve. It was the sound track of his dreams. He rose and tried to lift the window. Jammed. He turned the radiator handle but to no consequence, and the steam popped on. He beat his fists on the top of the sill and tried the window again. This time it gave way and two inches of February air rushed in to save him.

Exhausted, he lay down and found an unrefreshing sleep.

Again the station, the unfamiliar currency, the too-familiar scenes. Had he not come this way before? If he found anyone, would they see him?

The train ran the track down the Danube. One could board in Vienna and travel its full length, Belgrade, Bucharest, and out at Constantine to the Black Sea. A route of ancient commerce, a route trod deep by profit and escape. Always pressing east, into the darkness of a morning the sun had left. Perhaps next time he would travel at sunrise, perhaps that would dispel the gloom that always seemed to descend from the iron winter sky.

Helene said these files were only part of the whole. Perhaps if he could get access to the storage vaults, perhaps he could find a regular contact that Von Egger had used. Just as likely, there was a good explanation for all this. What if, as Von Egger had volunteered, this was an accepted form of power of attorney, where he as a bank officer took on these responsibilities? What if these names of notaries were not secret confederates, looking to trick people out of their monies, but respected bank employees? Merely doing their job, at the request and with the full knowledge of the depositors? Is not that just as likely?

He decides: this will be the last leg of a journey of fools, he allows himself no more. The few Budapest files have the same name, Ishtvan Kulek. A firm signature, hectic and taut, close to the ground. Peter imagines the man as a bantamweight boxer, black curly hair, fierce eyes.

Peter seats himself by the train's window. He takes comfort that the same rail line connects to Zurich. Always keep the back door open. He can disembark at any stop, cross to the opposite platform and be heading towards Helene. On the river, moored beneath leafless trees, are punts with rotting planks. There are barges on the river, heaped with coal, some floating rail cars. An old woman boards and takes the seat across from Peter, even though the train is half empty. She falls asleep and snores. It is a musical sound.

Tunnels flit by, the closeness of the sides pressing in on him. Towns lie blue against the banks and in them no one stirs. Between the towns sit long, languorous farms, their hay cut and taken away. Tan and sleeping in the deep winter, the fields are orderly, all the stalks trimmed to the same length.

The names of the stations come from some old book of fairy tales, engravings of wicked elves, black-browed villains. Győr, Komáron, Esztergom. Gideon had told him that when the rail line brought doomed prisoners to Auschwitz, cattle cars with slatting so thin the cold came through and the prisoners could look out, Polish farmers working in the fields would stand and wave as the trains went by. They would joke with the passengers and wave, and occasionally one would draw his finger across his throat. The people inside were accustomed to gestures, to curses. They assumed they were being teased.

The old woman rocks with the motion of the train and Peter wonders what he will do if she topples over, falls on him. Her stockings are rolled to her ankles.

The train stops at Visegrád and takes on the morning's tourists, who have come to see the remains of the ancient city. The car is suddenly crowded. Peter purchases a booklet from a boy selling sandwiches and visitor guides. The boy carries a tray suspended by a strap around his neck, cracks wise in Hungarian, French, English. He keeps his currencies in tin cans that have their labels attached. Budapest, the pamphlet begins. City of contradictions.

The end of my search. If you're stuck in a maze, keep your right hand on the wall. Either you reach the exit or go mad. What next? Perhaps return to Vienna, pick up a job. Perhaps Zurich, the comfort of Helene. Perhaps home. Remind me. Where did I get the idea this was important?

A family across the aisle readied itself to leave. Retrieved books, pencils and pull-toys from under the seats, they had passengers two and three rows away looking around their ankles. A purple ball rolled the length of the car. The mother loaded an infant on her shoulder and the father carried a wicker valise. He attached a leash to the belt of his toddling daughter — she in turn pulled the string of a wooden duck that quacked as it rolled along. They left in line, several older children holding hands, the littlest girl on the leash, and last the duck. The father talked back to the duck.

Quack, said the duck. Bork, said the father. Quack. Bork bork. Quack. Bork bork bork. Everyone in the railroad car was laughing.

The train turns south at the Danube Bend. The river makes a right-angle turn, due east to due south, and the tracks follow. Everyone looks out the window and there is a buzz of appreciation. A tentative sun breaks through and lights the line of deep green hills in the distance.

Peter skims the booklet. He is recommended to see St. Stephen's crown in the National Gallery. The photograph of a rude headpiece, tinny and stuck with dull cabochons, looks like a prop in an amateur play.

Did he speak out loud? He looks up and the woman across the way is awake, staring at him.

The train slows. The pace is constant, stately; they might be towed by horses. Now he views the outskirts of Budapest. Unlike those suburbs he has seen from other train windows, these are dotted with onion domes, heavy Gothic imitation, tile and marble ornament. The sense of moving from one century to the last, from the domain of the west to that of Byzantium and the Orthodox church. With the sun, colors creep in: sorrels and reds, mortar buildings the grey of a skeleton topped with the tri-colored flag of Hungary. He looks up and the woman has disappeared.

In the Budapest phone book only one Ishtvan Kulek was listed. Peter's workday would be over with one call. The pamphlet suggested sights, and he folded down the corners of several pages. He watched the young woman ahead of him. Dial first, deposit the coins, push the plunger.

His turn came, and he dialed the number. The coins sank into their safebox with a clunk of finality. Just like the slots in Tahoe. They never paid off either. Someone picked up on the first ring — he was unprepared.

He said something irrelevant in English. Irrelevant and not understood by the woman who had answered. There was a pause. A man's voice came on, its tone bored.

"Hello, my name is Peter Steinmuller. I'm afraid I speak no Hungarian. I am looking for a man named Ishtvan Kulek, a man who signed a bunch of documents in the nineteen forties. For Löwenhoft Handelsbank."

It would be fruitless to ask if he was being understood. Just plod on. If they get it, they'll say so. In Vienna people had hung up on him as he spoke.

"I know this is an odd request, but do you have any information . . . "

"What?" the voice interrupted.

Peter repeated the intro slowly. "Do you have any information about that Ishtvan Kulek? By any chance." There was a second pause. Peter was converting his request to French, searching his conjugations for past tenses, when he heard the reply.

"Yes," the voice said. "It is I."

8

KULEK SUGGESTED THEY RENDEZVOUS at the lounge of the Gellêrt Hotel. Peter found the hotel in his guidebook. It and its gilded pools of mineral waters were an attraction not to be missed, and it was centered on the city map. The B rating was beyond his budget, but this remnant, once grand and now appealing to a touristic nostalgia, would celebrate his unlikely connection. He would take a room there.

Peter walked through a massive, nineteenth-century facade into a lobby cramped with travelers. Flush to the walls stood decorative Corinthian columns, and arrested in the fending point of each was a stone acanthus. Otherwise the appointments were drab. The insides had been stripped of elegance during the Communist regime. Slowly, its corridors were being redressed in velvets and crimson. The building was a concrete stump at the edge of the Danube. The Liberation Bridge passed its door and served as a main thoroughfare between the twin cities. The room faced the river and from his window he could see the university and the mooring for the hydrofoil across the way.

He unpacked his few things, sat on the bed and read the card that explained the use of the telephone. He called Helene. No answer. Left the name of the hotel on her answering machine. He was burning with the news of his find, who to call? The old man on the train had adopted him for two pleasant meals. First Marcus, then Von Egger, then Gideon. He didn't stay adopted long. He found the cleanly printed page and punched in the local number. The buttons fit loosely in the cover plate. A man answered. Of course, he could relay a message to Dr. Gideon. Peter told the man of Kulek, left the hotel's number.

He rang for the elevator. Quicker by the stairs, but the lumbering elevator suited his mood. Mirrored panels, terra cotta flutings, the extra weight of an earlier construction, the car descended in an arthritic creak. At the desk he asked for an English language newspaper. Yes, there was such a thing, but no, they did not have it. Yes, they could find one, although not today. An enterprising young man seated in the lobby introduced himself as a guide and asked if he could fetch a paper for Peter. No charge, simply an appreciation, the man said. That would be fine.

Peter strolled through the underground passages to find the baths. They were open to the public. The guide book noted their popularity in summer when the outdoor pool featured a wave machine. He followed signs in Hungarian and German through dank caverns, down a dungeon stairwell, coming finally upon the pools below. Turquoise and gold tiles around the walls like a Byzantine church. The smells of sulfur, chlorine, and sweat, juices of the flesh that cooked there. In the main section floated several dozen ample bodies, weightless, all white-capped. Other than the bathing suits, some of which stopped at the tumbling waists and others that covered the chest, there was no way to sex the bobbing inhabitants.

In the water's edge four men gathered around a makeshift pier that projected into the pool. On its top sat a chessboard. Peter watched the game. An old man waved him over as if to say, the water's fine. Peter shook his head. Every so often one of the players would push a piece down the file. With each move the perspective changed. The possibilities — what? increased, reduced? — Peter did not know enough about the game. There must come a time, as pieces disappear, when the choices dwindle. Black took a pawn and one of the kibitzers looked up at Peter and winked.

He went back to await his visitor. He walked outdoors to the front steps and looked to see his room. It perched on top of the first neon L in Gellêrt. Someone called to him from the foyer, and his heart kicked the bass pedal. It was merely the guide.

Peter went in, took the paper the man had fetched, and offered him two hundred-forint notes, the equivalent of two dollars. The man accepted. Peter was on the verge of asking whether that was sufficient when he heard his name behind him. A chubby, cheerless man was leaning over the desk, speaking to the clerk. The clerk pointed to Peter.

"You are Ishtvan Kulek?" Peter said, extending his hand. The man eyed him with palpable reserve. He wore his grey hair in a longish crew, it may have been close-cropped and allowed several seasons to return. Long seconds passed while Peter stood, embarrassed as if he were caught panhandling, the man studying his face.

Peter repeated the question. No answer. The man let out a reluctant breath, resigned himself to their meeting. "I am," he said and took Peter's hand without enthusiasm. Kulek seemed to know the surroundings and walked ahead towards the lounge.

The room was a large one — indeed there seemed no rooms of

graceful size in the building — used as an antechamber for diners. Within, tuxedo-coated staff clanged about their silver and glassware, laying the settings for dinner. Waiters avoided them. At last one was secured to serve them coffee. He came over in a grudging walk, his slump announced he had other things to do. But when he saw Kulek, his face lit up and he shook the man's hand. They had an animated conversation.

"You know him?"

"He recognizes me. In a modest way I enjoy a certain celebrity in this city."

"How so?" asked Peter. "You must forgive me for asking, perhaps I should know your name." It occurred to him that of course he did know Kulek's name, though little else about him.

"My writings. Scribblings over the years."

Their coffee came. A silver-plated pitcher, two cups and saucers on Lenz china, cream, sugar, and two glasses of clear liquid.

"Schnapps," said Kulek. "From the waiter. His hospitality, a little tribute."

Each glass was the size of a thumb and had been filled to a shimmering mound. Kulek raised the glass to his lips, sipped the hump of clear liquid from its rim, replaced it.

Peter followed suit. The brandy tapped a spring of tears. He choked off a cough.

"What scribblings?"

Kulek removed a tattered yellow newspaper from his coat pocket. "Political writing," he said and shook the paper. It must have been days old. "First, I am against the fascists, and that naturally gets me jailed. Then against the Arrow Cross, our little home-grown Nazis, jailed again. Then the Communists. A third time. Now I am against the Christian Democrats, but no one pays attention. Give them soup and they forget about justice. The Christian Democrats do not use jails, they use television commercials. They punish everyone alike. It is more Christian, more democratic."

Kulek was a short man, just over five feet. He might have been a model for a Botero sculpture. There was no sharp angle on him. The flesh that protruded from cuff and throat of the coat around his softly molded body looked flabby and unwell. Tiny hands with nails nibbled short, puffy wrists, white folds of a neck disappearing into the collar. A grey face, open and empty, unsuited and unused to expression. But behind his eyes, countersunk deep into their sockets, shone a serrated vitality. He might be someone who would pull a knife on you.

Peter unfolded the shaggy newspaper and looked at it. Its masthead, *Krokodile*, showed a toothy reptile whose clamped jaws dangled a square of cloth from its teeth. It appeared to be a caricature, but Peter sensed from the dense print that the newspaper's bent was not humor.

"You write for this paper?"

"Until one of us passes on. So far the pamphleteer has outlived most of the pamphlets."

He unfolded its pages and showed Peter a column. The name of Kulek alone was recognizable.

"'The Peaceable Radical', that is the best translation," Kulek said with his finger on the column's title.

"You bash the right?"

"The right is easy. That is like a hunter who shoots cows. They are stupid, slow, obvious. Like cows there are so many of them. They line up in stalls allowing their owners to milk them daily. I bash, as you say, the right. But also the left. Also," and here he waved his hand to show insignificance, ubiquity, "the center."

"That leaves you few friends."

"That leaves me few friends. I have only one mistress. Socialism. If I am unfaithful to her I could have many friends, but if I have many friends I will not have her. She is bereft, more so than I. And you know why?"

Peter said he did not. Was it possible that his one lucky call, last remaining lead, had produced a lunatic? Kulek went on.

"Because they have ruined her reputation. Because the know-nothing children who parade around in her name, saying they do her work, ruin her reputation. They would support her, but in their brutishness they slander her. The students of the left today have no intellectual roots. They worship movie stars, Che Guevara. These are wall posters. Do they read Georgi Plekhanov? Do they know Katusky, Leon Trotsky, George Bernard Shaw? They have never heard of them."

He smoked in fits. As they talked he pulled out an open pack, then a second from a different pocket, also opened, and withdrew a cigarette as if he were plucking a splinter. Caught the lip of its paper in his ragged nails and drew the cigarette out slowly. Relief. He would occasionally light a fresh one from the butt of another, then go a quarter of an hour without. The waiter attended to them in silence, and Kulek's ashtrays were constantly being replaced by ones newly cleaned.

"I once wrote that Jesus was the first socialist. For those views I was excommunicated from the Church, exactly one year after my first communion." Kulek had the habit of a slight shrug, a gesture of disbelief, that he gave at the end of every English sentence.

"Steinmuller is not buying my coffee to hear this," he said abruptly. "First, tell me what you are doing here." He pronounced Peter's name as Peter did, Anglicized.

"I came to see *you*. I'm trying to find out more about my grandfather. It seems he left some money with the power to sign given to someone named Frederich Von Egger, and Von Egger has used it up. What would have gone to my grandfather's heirs, to me, Von Egger spent. Von Egger seems a complicated character. I'm not sure what to believe about him. And I find that his name was on a dozen other accounts just like my grandfather's. It doesn't make any sense. He's a rich man, an art collector, he has everything he could want. It doesn't make any sense for him to be stealing."

Kulek showed nothing, spoke quickly as though he had the question framed before Peter had answered the last.

"Von Egger is still alive? You have met Von Egger?"

"I have. I spent a weekend with him outside Geneva. A very charming man."

"A very charming man, I am sure he is. That would not change."

"You knew him then?"

Kulek was watching Peter carefully. "His name is not unfamiliar."

Peter produced the Budapest files. He laid them on the table to permit Kulek to examine his signatures. Kulek's name had witnessed the execution of two different accounts on the same printed German form. To the lower left on each, Von Egger had signed also.

Kulek pointed. "That is my signature."

"I understand that," Peter said. "And you signed with Von Egger?" Kulek shook his head, moved a soiled finger over the page.

"You see, these were signed in Budapest. By the person making the trust and by me. Then they were accepted by Von Egger in Zurich. You read no German? Here. He is saying that he is designated to sign and the money will be kept in the Löwenhoft Handelsbank in Zurich."

Peter sagged. He had turned down another cul-de-sac.

"Perhaps," Kulek interrupted his thoughts, "you should tell me what you are looking for. Perhaps I can help you if I know more."

It was mid-afternoon. When they started, few people shared the lounge with them. At a nearby table a pretty woman in a hat sat before a glass of pale beer. By the wall, sitting alone, a very thin man snapped open a violin case. He wore a grey suit with wide lapels, black shoes that had never been shined, white socks. A cigarette stuck from his mouth and he blinked through its smoke. He lifted the violin from the case, held on end so its throat was to his ear, and began tuning.

Peter finished his tale. Kulek got up silently and walked away, leaving his host to guess, from the ragged coat on the back of the chair, from the two packs of cigarettes on the table, that he would be back.

He returned, checked his zipper, sat down.

"The bladder of an old man is like the mind of a young one, it holds onto nothing very long. If there really was a God, He would have done more work on both. If you have the time," he said. "I will tell you a story. It is not what you are seeking, but it may help, give you peace of mind."

"I don't need peace of mind," Peter said. "I simply want the truth."

Kulek turned his hands palm up. He had no more to offer.

"Of course I have the time. I'd like to hear it."

You are so young, almost the age I was at the time. Early in the advent of the Reich our Regent, Nicholas Horthy, made his deal with the devil. He chose Hitler and Hitler promised to feed him. When Germany devoured Czechoslovakia in 1938, it was like a farmer carving a huge goose. It served itself first, then threw to Hungary the fatty cuts, Ruthenia, the cuts it could not easily digest without vomiting. Hungary had established her price. She could be bought for the hindquarters. And so she was given northern Transylvania from Rumania in 1940 and the Baçka Basin from Yugoslavia the next year.

What is the consequence of living off another's leavings? Ask any house dog, any master. It is enslavement. The family which must rely on the state is a slave to the state. The country which must rely on the fascist state is a slave to the fascist.

Hitler tolerates Horthy until it suits him otherwise. I

write an article, "The Regent with One Ball," and receive my first jail term in time for my eighteenth birthday. Hitler appoints a minister under the Regent to report directly to the Reich.

Hungary is turned into a charnel house. The Arrow Cross, our local aspiring Nazis, wants to prove its dedication to the Reich. It observes that European Jews have been taking refuge in Hungary, since Hungary was a possible haven, friendly with Germany yet independent. That is an outrage. Their presence is described as a menace to the safety of German armament in the East. Adolph Eichmann and the *Sonderkommando* arrive. The menace disappears.

And our friend Horthy? He has not committed himself. He seeks an armistice with Russia. The Nazis kidnap his son, threaten to obliterate his family. Where are his principles? We have a saying, *mozom kezeim*. I wash my hands. Horthy's principles were so small to begin with, so puny, a pimple on the ass. He cannot find them. He returns, disavows the armistice. Of course he is too late. The Russians storm up the Danube and Tisza basins. They have no need to negotiate. Horthy has been jumping from one leg to another like a boy needing to piss. This man with no moral ground discovers now that he has no constituency.

I am boring you. Let me return.

Peter was not bored. He sat watching the black eyes dance while only the mouth moved. Nothing else in the face indicated involvement, life. Across the room the violinist was playing little snatches of song. Two men in ill-fitting suits had joined him. A small orchestra would play for the cocktail hour.

Kulek went on.

Before the war, the Jews of Hungary enjoyed a haven in Budapest. In the rest of Europe, particularly in the late Thirties, the situation was quite different. Hungary became a platform for emigration. The Danube leads to the sea. Perhaps if one could get there then one could get a boat.

Later people said, we didn't know, we didn't realize,

and my answer is Balls. We in the Vatican, in the White House, the members of the British parliament in their bespoke suits. Balls. We did not want to know. Why? It is unpleasant. Better to wash our hands. To know distracts us from our daily task of accumulating wealth, of taking our pastries, of pleasing our little dicks in the alleys.

The pretty woman had left. Where she'd sat now a middle-aged couple held hands. The liquid in their stemmed glasses was crimson. At other tables three or four men leaned into their talk.

Kulek returned. Peter felt they had been sitting there for hours.

"Am I keeping you?" Peter asked. "You have a wife?"

"Dead and gone," Kulek answered. "But not in that order." He settled into the bentwood chair, arranged cigarette packs and boxed matches in front of him, and continued.

The story you have waited for. You have a strong ass, my friend. You should consider running for National Assembly. That is what is needed, a wooden ass and a wooden heart.

In the 1930's, before the signs of this country's capitulation were visible, Budapest attracted a great many young people. She was a city of new trams and undergrounds, new music and poetry, boulevards sparkling with electric lights. To that city of 1938, a young Swiss music student adventures. He comes to study harmony at the conservatory, but too for the bohemian life, the life of the coffee houses.

This man is your uncle Hermann, the brother of your father. I met Hermann when I also was a young university student. Idealistic? Of course. Unrealistic? To a fault. Who else is there to be idealistic?

As Hermann arrived in Budapest, the Hungarian Duma passed a law restricting Jewish businesses. A year later, no trade licenses to Jews, no employment in newspapers. No entry into the professions. Hungarians did this. You thought persecution was the invention of Goebbels?

In other parts of Europe, things were worse. In Austria and Germany there had been imposed the *Reichsfluchsteuer*, a tax to leave the Reich. To go one must pay a large portion of his assets. At the same time, the Nazis made staying for some intolerable, and to the word intolerable they gave new meaning. It is a good business. These were not people with money. What they owned they ate from or wore on their backs. How to convert that to cash?

Still many fled. Budapest represented one of the routes out. Down the Danube, the Bosporous to Lebanon, and there to wait, to wait and hope that somehow one might gain entry to Palestine. The British, who controlled Palestine, signed treaties with Nazi Germany requiring that people be authorized to leave. The cattle must request permission of the abattoir to flee.

The greater the pressure the Nazis brought, the higher the traffic through Budapest. The higher the traffic, the greater the price of a ticket. An active commerce in misfortune breaks out. Assets must be converted to cash. Relatives must send funds. Permits must be bought. Refugee organizations raise money to buy ships, negotiate leases, single passages, the moving of whole families, villages. This is the industry of poverty and suffering. The victims remain victimized. We have a saying, drop a stone on an egg, woe for the egg. But drop an egg on a stone, woe for the egg.

I have been scribbling, scribbling, and my words have been noticed by some involved in these efforts. They seek me out. I am a young man, without funds. What could I do? I had only a pen, some paper, some friends. Aha, I said to myself. I have a friend, from the coffeehouses. He is Swiss. His brother is a banker. He himself has no interest in this, he is interested in Bach and women. My friend Hermann is what I could do.

And so I bring him to meet the world. He looked like you, thin, handsome. He comes to what he thinks is a social gathering to talk with beautiful women about aesthetics, and instead it is a debate. Next I take him to a secret meeting. We are searching for a ship. We go, we talk, we leave. I assumed Hermann was unaffected. But we had converted Hermann into a partisan. Whether it was the girl's courage or perhaps that Hermann liked her, her eyes were beads of the night sky, I don't know. We were younger even than you, the sweetness of the flesh. He is a naïf, long afterwards he realizes I lured him in. A good heart.

Hermann gave up his music classes. He still played the organ at St. Nicholas Church, he would sit for hours and play Bach and Buxtehude. But he had been converted.

In the next years he worked with a frenzy. He made several trips home to Zurich. He met a young Swiss woman and married. And still he continued to work for our cause. He convinced his brother, your grandfather, to become involved. That was enormously helpful at first.

What we were doing involved increasing danger. We worried about secrecy. He and I used private names for each other, they had meanings, derisive — you know how children are with those they love. Hermann hit upon the use of private code names for correspondence with his brother's bank. For himself he chose Buxtehude, one of his favorite composers. The music is thin, ethereal. Mystic. Like Hermann. It was simply a precaution, not anything from a spy movie. Afterwards, when his brother took his place, your grandfather, he liked that. Very covert, not like banking. Your grandfather used the name Brahms.

With our new contacts we were ready for a large project. The financing of the *Artemis*. You are familiar?

That is its own story. I take another piss. Then I come back. They want our table, you should order a drink. This good man can earn nothing on two coffees. Not for me. One of the benefits of prison life is hepatitis. It ruins your liver, so you save money on schnapps.

The orchestra was playing a fox trot and several middle-aged couples danced on the small wooden floor. A violin, an accordion, a viola, a stand-up bass. They flowed from one song to the next, Kern to Sigmund Romberg to Mixolydian gypsy tunes, without a break. The comradely waiter came by and again Kulek told Peter to order a drink. Peter asked for a beer. "And food," Kulek said and pointed to the table. "This man cannot earn a living on your talk. Food."

They were served two little meat pies, the thick crusts flecked with fat. Peter sampled his, decided to wait for dinner. Kulek finished both, washing them down with cold coffee. While he chewed they did not speak.

"You say my grandfather took over?"

"After Hermann's death. Your grandfather took over, in a manner of speaking. That is, you understand, all this is. A manner of speaking." Kulek shrugged.

"I want to hear more of my grandfather. And how Von Egger fits in. You were about to tell of a large project?"

The *Artemis*. How could you not know? The tragedies of the past get pushed aside. Another's ecstasies, another's tragedies. They are wildflowers, they bloom, they die and there will be others to see next season, eh?

Hermann now throws himself into the aid of those escaping the firestorm. He works his contacts in Switzerland, travels up and down the Danube valley, finding persons of like spirit. Szeged, Vukovar, Turnu all the way to the Black Sea. And up river, to Bratislava and Vienna. Tens, soon hundreds of thousands of refugees, impoverished and without food or papers. Ships leased for exorbitant sums.

Hermann decides to purchase a ship. He learns of an agency based in Paris that knows how, the World Refugee Committee, today it is in Washington. This man from land-locked Zurich decides he is going to start a passenger fleet. Except, one, he has no money, and two, he knows nothing about ships. I was his advisor and I had never been aboard a ship. I cannot swim. Without the bridges of Budapest I would still be on the eastern shore.

He raises a pitiable sum from his friends, begs a franc here, a mark there. On a bad day we tell our story and the door slams in our face. On a good day, we tell our story to a pauper. At least he has no door.

I was filing stories in newspapers. The editors would say, *mozom kezeim*, I wash my hands. Stories of suffering were commonplace. Budapest was interested in the Reich's continuing victories, and in the good life it had brought at home. They were doing the English waltz and the tango in the dancing halls on Margit Island. In the afternoons they sat in cafés among the chestnut trees. They drank peach brandy and bull's blood, was this a good Tokay or was that tastier? *Mozom kezeim*

Kulek began the story of the *Artemis*, and the waiter brought over a fresh pot of coffee. The room was chilled. Peter put his hands on its silver plate for the warmth. He listened openmouthed as the ship was purchased, as she coursed the turns of the Danube, sailed through the Black Sea, broke down outside Istanbul, as her radio gave off weak signals and died.

"Were there any survivors?" he asked after a long moment.

Kulek shook his head several times. Finally answered.

"One. A man named Fedderman. The others, the crew, the passengers, Hermann, all drowned."

Kulek stacked his cigarette packs in front of him. He studied them for a moment, put them in different pockets. His voice throughout had been even. Only from his eyes did Peter sense the heat of what he felt.

"The Turks arrested Fedderman at first because he had no papers, but they let him go. The World Refugee Committee intervened. Took pity on him. He had papers, they explained to the Turkish authorities. But he lost them when the five hundred others had drowned.

"So you see, my young friend. You have a great deal to be proud of in your past. *That* is what you need to know."

Kulek was suddenly agitated. Perhaps his bladder again. He stood, eager to be off. Peter shook his tiny hand and he disappeared towards the lobby.

Peter emerged from the hotel in time to see the last of the light in phosphorescent clouds yellow against the river. He walked by the avenue that followed the west bank. There were no paths for pedestrians and heavy traffic dared him to cross at every corner. Buses crammed with workers, trucks. An ambulance stood in his way. It had broken down, and two men in white smocks had jacked its rear wheel off the pavement. Still he walked, past the cable railway and across the Chain Bridge. The city was plum black against the sky, then in minutes night black. By the time he returned, ducking headlamps from insistent drivers, the city looked like any other.

He wished he had thanked Kulek more expansively. Despite the man's initial reluctance, Kulek had reached him. What had moved Peter so? The valor of his great-uncle, but valor was a knack, like a musical ear. It was more than that, more than courage — it was his decision. Hermann had planted his feet on the earth.

He would go back, draw a hot bath, call Helene and tell her of his conversation. They were on the same time. She would be home by six. Then, perhaps dinner, a good dinner. And early bed.

That was the plan. But the plan was delayed, then forgotten entirely.

Delayed for the reading of the two faxes the desk clerk handed him with his key. The original letters had been delivered to Helene and, he could see from the fax heading, she had sent them on only an hour ago.

My dear Mr. Steinmuller,

My offer to extend your debt was based on your representation to me that you were returning to the U. S. and would pay me from the fund available by doing so. Your continued presence in Europe revokes that offer. Failure to remit the balance in full will prompt me to use the courts to collect same.

Albert Frey

So much for the mood. The second communique was from the Court of First Instance, Canton of Zurich.

To the Defendant Peter Steinmuller:

Upon the petition of one Albert Frey this Court has entered judgment against you in the amount of 427 S. F. If this amount is not discharged in five days you are subject to attachment, fines and penalties, or to arrest and imprisonment, or both.

Peter stepped into his room. Maybe just a hamburger and a bottle of beer from room service. He idly flicked on the television set, and the image pushed him down on the edge of the bed. There on the screen was Marcus Collopy.

"YOU WANT TO KNOW how to walk a bass," Marcus was saying, his metabolism just this side of sleep, "watch a spider. Cat never moves, deep deep deep deep, gets those legs to carry him, no up and down. Deep deep deep."

The interview was in Hungarian, German, and when they included Marcus, English. It was a highbrow show, bare set and chrome stools, led by a condescending young man in rimless glasses who swung abruptly between his two guests. What about the validity of an American white playing music belonging to the Negroid tradition? Didn't Marcus think that was the equivalent of cultural slavery? No, Marcus did not. Marcus leaned over to the other guest, a wispy girl in black. Two fingers of his left hand did the spider on her knee and she laughed.

She was a local jazz singer, pale gamin face above the cowl of the turtleneck. The host asked her a question and she did two bars of scat, easy. Mentioned Ella. He turned to Marcus.

"What do you see for the future of your instrument?"

"Oh, I dunno," said Marcus. Any given sentence hard to tell whether he's there. "Maybe a new lacquer job." The host rotated a quarter turn and spoke to the singer. Shut Marcus out. They used one camera, focused on all three so Peter could see Marcus' eyes roaming the backdrops. Behind, Peter knew, riffs were going off. That's what Marcus did with quiet.

The young man swung back around. He wore a knit tie and over his frayed shirt a fully buttoned cardigan sweater. His tone knocked off Mike Wallace.

"Tell us, Marcus Collopy. What kind of music do you like?"

"I like all kinds of music."

"Do you like American country and western?"

Marcus looked through him. Perhaps he had missed the question. The young man repeated it. Still no response. Dead air. The host coughed, raised his voice, asked a third time.

"Do you like country and western?"

Marcus leaned across to talk to the singer. He jerked his head to point to the host.

"I think the cat's hard of hearing."

The interview ended. The host signed off in Hungarian, but Peter picked up the name of the club of Marcus' Budapest gig: the Amigo Drink Bar. Music from nine to one. Enough time to get a bite, catch the opening set.

He took a cab across the river and got off by the university. He entered a cafeteria. People furtively watched him eat. He tasted the stew, drank a glass of beer. To happen on Marcus playing in Budapest. Perhaps he would hook up with him, now that he had resolved his questions.

No one could challenge Kulek's credibility. There were too many details, and they poured out spontaneously, randomly. Hermann Steinmuller was a bona fide hero. Kulek was not impartial, he had a strong political slant, but what he said rang true.

It was only as Peter worked on the coffee, adding first milk, then sugar, then coffee, that he realized he never asked Kulek the important questions. What role had his grandfather played? Did Pietr expand the efforts of the younger brother after Hermann's death? Did he too live in Budapest and, as the Agent Brahms, continue to help the illegal immigration that saved lives? And what of Von Egger? His name was not unknown to Kulek, but had he also had a part in this? He must have, whatever deeds were recognized by the State of Israel. By his own account after Hermann's death Kulek was on the fringes. He might not even know of Von Egger's role at the close of the war, the Paris negotiations, the citation. He could check with Kulek in the morning.

Peter had wandered only a few blocks to find a place to eat, but the narrow lanes looked alike in the dark, and the occasional street signs were indecipherable. Peter could not translate them, could not recognize them when they appeared again. He was asking a group of mystified students when he saw the club's portal on the wrong side of the street, half a block down.

The band was well into the first set. Marcus' sidemen were the alto from the boat, a piano, guitar, and a flautist who doubled on tenor. The last three were all locals, each solo drew a cheer. The noise covered a gang of sins. The guitar amp hummed in a swarm of deer flies and the only time the piano hit an extended chord was by mistake. Marcus was two people. He flinched at every electric buzz and every stock progression like a man under the lash, but the pain of the whip vanished on his solos. The crowd revered him, an Apostle. There wasn't an ice cube to clatter, a lid to blink when he was on and the white spot, unfiltered and bolted to shine on him, floated him over the room.

The admiration watered his music and his solos flowered. He was good, parboiled in booze but cooking. Having fun — he called tough keys and fast tempos to push himself. In the major scale of D flat a bass has no open strings.

He came to Peter's table at the first break. Shook his hand hard.

"How you doing?" Peter asked him back.

"Without, kid. I am doing without. I got a piano player, I got nothing to do with him. My guitar, the doofus is going to get hisself electrocuted. But I'm getting by."

They talked. Peter told him of his odyssey, but Marcus was indifferent.

"So what do you say? You want a job?"

"Here?"

"Got to take the piano out and shoot him. Easy to do. It's not Storyville, and they pay you in this stuff as I understand it, one is worth about a penny, no shit. Their dollars, worth about a penny. But they love musicians here, man."

Two young men came up and asked Marcus to autograph a ten-inch record jacket. He pushed back from the table, sniffled, obliged.

"They love you Marcus. You recorded with Getz."

"I recorded with a lot of cats," he said. "Getz is dead. So is a lot more guys I don't even know about because you can't find out. You wouldn't believe it, they got newspapers here in Hungarian."

"That's not it," Peter said. "They love you 'cause you live for your music."

"I don't live *for* my music, man. I live *by* my music. That's all." Marcus looked around, uncomfortable. "So what do you think, kid? You in?"

Peter studied the room. The piano was an upright, but he could improve its sound if he could find the tools. That would help, and he could cut this pianist with mittens on.

Better to stay. He didn't want to pack. Each time he did he remembered his father bending over the suitcase, the way he put his clothes into each corner of the squared space, shirts into the middle. Time to practice, his mother would say, and he would have the piano. His father took off in the Dodge and he drove the Chickering. It took him into the frets, through the maze of secret signs and symbols, rests, sustinatos, tempo marks.

You were never lost. The printed music was a road map. It took you the same way, and you finished where Scarlatti or Mozart or Clementi wanted you to.

And then he discovered jazz. No map.

"Deal me in."

"Yeah," said Marcus. "I'll let him go after tonight. Tomorrow, nine o'clock. We'll talk money then. Maybe I can get us a little more, I tell the club owner we just signed one of Downbeat's young lions."

Peter caught the next set. Marcus called a tune the local piano didn't know.

"Just hang around B-flat," Marcus told him. "B-flat. Ear it out, man. You can't make a mistake." He caught Peter's eyes and rolled his heavenward for help.

Marcus told him, stay 'till we close, we'll get a drink, but Peter was tired. He went back to his room and a dreamless sleep. It would be good to move out of the hotel, into lesser digs. Start to play again. What possible difference what happened fifty years ago? You push yourself into caring, you still can't change it. He was not cut out to be an historian.

His morning call missed Helene, by then between apartment and office. Your life, Matey told him, puts you out of synch with the rest of the world, that's why you chose it. You are a reverse commuter, Peter. You don't get held up in other people's traffic or other people's emotions.

Breakfast was served in the main dining room, to patrons dressed below its furnishings. Filled water goblets, silver service laid out like armament, it might be for a duel. He was studying the menu, the left half printed in English, when he sensed someone standing by his side. He looked up. A man stood with his arm bent behind his back, the hand jiggling.

"So. It seems I am ever asking if I may join you at table," Dr. Gideon said. "At least this time we are on solid ground."

Peter was delighted to see him. For someone adrift in the midst of a foreign land, he was happening upon friends at a gratifying rate. He told Gideon of the great coincidences of Budapest. First he had found Kulek, then Marcus, now they had bumped into each other.

"Nothing of the sort," Gideon said. "You left word where you were staying, eh? I was headed to Budapest and checked in last night."

"Here? You're staying at the Gellêrt?"

"Of course. It is the old Budapest, before the Soviets, before the Nazis. I did not want to disturb you, so I asked the desk to let me know when you went in for breakfast. You see, coincidence has nothing to do with anything."

The waiter brought Peter's order. Gideon had already dined, but he sat patiently while Peter put away eggs, breakfast ham, a fried potato pancake topped with paprika.

Between bites Peter recited the remarkable tale of Ishtvan Kulek. Of the story of the young music student — did not the Doctor think that was astonishing, that his great uncle was also a musician? — and how Hermann had entered the world of refugees. Of the beginnings of the so-called Circle, with Buxtehude and Brahms. And finally, of the fact that this very man, no older than Gideon himself, had known Hermann. He'd discovered a missing family.

"I intend to see Kulek again," Peter told him.

Gideon studied him. "I advise against it, my friend. You found what you came for. And this man who plays jazz music has offered you a job. You have done enough."

"Yes," Peter agreed, "but you never get a chance like this. For explanations to fill in the past."

Gideon had not touched the a cup of coffee before him. Now he sipped from it, replaced it carefully in the saucer. Then he caught Peter's eye and smiled.

"Explanations. They never help, eh? Think of the lives we live. Whether we explain afterwards or before, it doesn't matter. Be satisfied. Nietzsche says the past is a thing so threatening that it must be forgotten."

As an afterthought Peter told Gideon of his troubles with the Swiss courts. "So. Even more reason to drop this foolish quest. You would not wish to return to Switzerland and wind up in debtor's prison."

Peter lay his fork down and waited. But the old man was through. He rose slowly, a morning stiffness, and placed the cloth napkin on the table by his coffee cup.

"You have that Budapest number. Do let me know if there is anything I can do to help. And if you take a job here, call also. I come to hear you play, eh?"

The man's words were sincere, Peter could tell. They shook hands and Gideon trudged through the lounge, where yesterday Peter had sat hypnotized by Kulek's tales. Was Peter being teased? Explanations don't matter? Gideon's smile seemed ironic, the indulgent expression of the play's director as he eavesdrops among the audience between acts.

Peter informed the desk this would be his last night. He would take a place near the club, where rents suited student budgets. Close by, no more getting lost. He tried Kulek, but reached only an intercept message that meant nothing to him. Telephones here were an iffy matter.

Peter had Kulek's address from the telephone book. Finding him would be its own adventure, a way to see the city. He boarded a bus bound for a street in a distant corner of Pest. Twenty forint at a newsstand bought him a blue ticket and another ten, the equivalent of a dime, a white transfer. The ticket marked him as a foreigner — there was no one on the bus to collect it. He alone among the passengers had paid to ride, the others seemed to know. He stuck his hand, holding the markers, into a pocket. Faces around him grinned at his distress.

The trip took most of the morning. A city of wide boulevards, stone the color of smoke, sooty back streets. He walked three long blocks, children staring at him, a conspicuous exotic. The house number had been marked on the door in grease pencil. The dusty building had a few names listed outside, none of them Kulek's, no central directory or mailboxes, no one to ask.

He knocked at the first floor apartment. The woman spoke no English. She recognized Kulek's name, spoke of him calmly, in Hungarian. A young girl was sitting on the front steps, singing the Ford truck commercial in English. Peter brought her in to translate.

"Herr Kulek is gone away, sir. He has moved."

"Last night, sir. Or perhaps this morning. She is not sure."

"No sir. She does not know."

"*Nem értem*. I don't understand."

Neither did Peter. Only that morning he had been assured that coincidence has nothing to do with the workings of the world. If that were true, then Peter was in the midst of a complicated script.

"Mysterious?" Gideon asked over the phone. "Why on earth mysterious?" Peter had reached him at the Budapest number he had written out that second day on the train.

"It's odd, is all, his suddenly moving after having spoken to me."

"You put cause and effect together when there may be none. That is illogical. Perhaps he moved before he spoke to you. There is no way for you to know. Perhaps he's planned to move for a month."

"He never mentioned it."

"Peter," Gideon answered patiently. "Did he mention his dentist's appointment, eh? His arthritis, his favorite recipe? You inquired, he told you the story. You got what you came for."

Peter was unconvinced. Finally Gideon said he would try to help. Then asked him to dinner. At Gündel, the famous restaurant in the city park. You must see it, Gideon argued, and the only inexpensive way to dine there is as a guest.

Peter declined. An elaborate dinner was not what he needed. Besides, Marcus' group was on at nine. Perhaps after he had found Kulek and put an end to his doubts, perhaps Gideon would still be in town. There was merit to what the Doctor had said, he had found what he came for.

He hung up, dialed Helene's apartment. Not home.In the Gellêrt's vast dining room, the small string ensemble, *tánchás*, Kulek had called them, was playing. They would soon break. It was just as well. Peter preferred quiet to think about what tunes to call. He went through changes, possible reharmonizing. He'd get to the bridge and be stuck: where does "Smoke Gets In Your Eyes" go? Maybe that's why they call it a bridge, because when you get there and it's out you drive into the river. When you lost your way in a tune, a wild panic set in your hands. Ear it out, the hands would remember.

To his room, picked up the leather jacket for the drizzle. You could get a month's wet waiting for the buses in this town. He was running late, but he would make one last try. The Zurich phone buzzed in waltz time.

"God, I'm glad I got you. I've got news for you."

"Peter," she shrieked. Her voice rang with urgency. His real concern subsided as she went on.

"Where are you? I cannot find you anywhere. I have the bankers in Vienna checking every hotel, every pension, I am thinking he has met another woman. That is his modus operandi."

"Helene, I found Kulek. Can you believe it? Vienna was a wash-out but I found Kulek on one shot. It was fantastic. What a story. And I've run into Marcus. I may work a gig. Look, you get any time off?

Can you make it to Budapest maybe for a weekend? I'm playing in a local saloon here. I'd like to tell you the story . . . ."

She interrupted him. She was almost shouting. The connection was weak. "Peter. I must talk to you. I have been at work on your questions. The computer, running batch sorts."

The static increased so they couldn't hear. Then a series of whoops, like an ambulance passing through the line, followed by clarity.

"Peter, I must tell you. Is that better? I shouldn't tell you by phone, but I must. You know I had those accounts with Von Egger's name on them?"

"Yes. I've been thinking about that. I may have the answer."

"Don't bother. That is no longer the difficult question. It occurred to me that those were the accounts with powers of attorney, the accounts in *trust*. Most people open ordinary accounts. You know the difference? Most people put their money in a bank so that *they* can draw it out, not a trustee.

"So I started to wonder, I went back at night. It's getting harder to gain access. They must suspect someone is inquiring. They have complicated the log-ins. I searched for accounts where Von Egger's name appeared, for any reason. It would not function. I had to rewrite the program.

"Peter? Are you there? So finally it computed. And this is what I found: four thousand, seven hundred and twenty-seven. Did you hear me? four thousand, seven hundred and twenty-seven accounts where Von Egger receipted for moneys deposited in the Löwenhoft Handelsbank."

The line was clear. No interference.

"For God's sake Peter, are you there?"

"Yes. I'm here."

"If your grandfather was being cheated, he was one of a very large number."

"But my grandfather was a special friend. Von Egger couldn't have made all that up. And listen to what he and his brother were doing."

Peter told the story of the *Artemis*, the desperate need for capital to save lives. Whatever else was muddled, it was clear that the brothers Steinmuller were working to save those imperiled by the Nazi onslaught. Could Van Egger have been pulling the wool over the eyes of his superior?

"Maybe," Peter speculated, "maybe Von Egger was simply accumulating money for their cause. That book he gave me? It cites him, mentions his work on behalf of refugees. Maybe that's where the money went. Do you have the book? I left it . . . ."

"I have it, yes, yes. That's another thing. The book led me to a second. You know how library shelves are a neighborhood? All the same subject? I found the opposite of those who cared, those who collaborated. Written by a Leftist, very much a polemic. He accuses the Swiss financial establishment of working both sides of the street. Says that the German High Command used the same lines to free funds as the refugees, that certain Swiss bankers were instrumental in setting it up. In wartime, it's a logical step. You never know what side will win.

"The pamphlet listed aliases. Names that known Nazis used to secrete funds in Argentina, Portugal, Panama. And especially Switzerland."

"And?"

"Of the four thousand accounts Von Egger brought in, I got three hundred and twenty matches. And of the matches, twenty-seven belonged to the single Nazi who was identified in this pamphlet. Testified at Nuremberg that he himself had used this alias, Max Heiliger, to set up accounts in safe places. One of them the Löwenhoft. It seems clear."

"Who? Who testified, who transferred?"

"Heinrich Himmler. The head of the SS."

When you come to a fork in the road, someone said, take it. When you're against a wall, what? Helene's news meant he had to keep going, but where? Information for Washington, D. C. He took A. T. & T. up on its offer to connect the call for an additional thirty-five cents. An intern-young voice answered.

"Shalom. World Refugee Committee. This is Natalie."

"I have an odd request, Natalie." Skip the intro, get to the tune. He explained about Shimon Fedderman. The Committee had helped him, the case had been newsworthy. Any information on where he could be found? The girl took down his hotel, its fax number.

"We'll see what we can do. Shalom."

"Shalom," Peter said.

Peter couldn't get into it, what Helene had told him blocked the notes out. He got dragged through the first set ten yards behind. Twice he heard the splat of a bass string snapped against the wooden neck, Marcus' peculiar way of summoning you back to the beat. On break Marcus cut him short.

"Look, kid. You want to quit jazz, quit. You hear what I'm saying? No need to murder it, some of us are pretty fond."

They sat at a long table in the hall by the bathrooms. People went by congratulating Marcus. Three fingers of whiskey the color of strong tea sat in front of him. They had secured a supply of American rye in his honor, one bottle per night.

"I don't know where you are, but I'd rather have the local kid. You both stink up the joint. At least he's one of them, they won't lynch him." Marcus unfolded a long-bladed knife and carefully shaved a callous on the heel of his left hand.

"Sorry. I got a lot on my mind." Peter began to tell him about the court order, but Marcus held up the knife pinched like a baton.

"Kid. It's a two-five world. That's all you need to know. Two-five. It'll get you out of most transpositions. Politics, alimony, you got a bad chick. Whatever it is, stick with that. Keep your mind free."

They went back. Marcus led with a hand in the air for the down-beat. In the air, thumb and two fingers extended. He called tunes no one had to reach.

He had picked up a young Hungarian who played trumpet, fast and angry. Whole choruses of up-tempo thirty-seconds, strings of them, eyes closed he would dot the sixteenths and hit the companion. When he traded fours he would play your last phrase — note for note, you couldn't leave him behind — then do his own on top.

"You got to come to New York," Marcus told him around the long table. "You'll get on. Know when Bird came back from L.A., he'd heard Chet Baker? In the late fifties? He said to Diz and Miles, 'Look out, there's a little white cat out west gonna eat you alive.' That's what I'll tell them about you. There's a little white kid from Estergom gonna eat you alive."

The trumpet grinned. He looked eighteen, nineteen. He knew everything they called, the usual jazz classics, but obscure stuff as well. His only English words were titles of tunes and key signatures. And for sentences, vocals from jazz ballads.

"This time the dream's on me," Marcus said to him and the kid sang the first two lines. You could tell he didn't know what the words meant. *"There may be many other nights like this,"* Marcus said, and the kid began to scat. Right on the middle F, where the next bar started. Perfect pitch. You could tell from how the kid sang the song where he had learned English. All off records, and you could tell from his phrasing whether the singer was Ella or Billie or Sinatra. Half the time the kid sounded black.

Peter's mind roamed on the edges. What was the Composers' Circle? Had Von Egger subverted his family's work into some economic engine that had no allegiance? Kulek had so plainly considered him, studied him. What was he deciding? What part of the story had he blue-lined? They closed at breakneck speed in F.

Afterwards they sat at the long table. "Can I tell you something?" Peter asked

"Sure, kid, sure." Next to Marcus' lowball sat a glass of water, a chaser, and he sipped from it and grimaced.

Peter spoke of who was telling the truth. Maybe Helene was the sandbag, what with her working for the bank and Von Egger a heavyweight there.

"So what do you think?"

The question surprised Marcus. "What do *I* think? Man, what do I know? I play bass."

"I just thought, I mean, I need some advice."

"No you don't, man. You doing fine. Ear it out, that's the way. Besides, I don't give advice. Not even to my own kids."

"You got kids, Marcus? I didn't know that."

"I don't even give them advice. Leave me out. I'm not your father, not a symbol."

"Not a symbol?"

"Don't want to be."

"Not even a high-hat?" Finally Marcus smiled, a broken, creaky split in the wood where the screen door had slammed shut once too often. The set was over, Peter rose and left.

A crisp rustle awakened him, close by, in the room. He was confused. The Frey letter and the menacing note from the court were by the bed where he'd let them fall. Perhaps they moved in his dream, he was sure he had heard the rustle of paper.

It was barely dawn. By the small entry hall lay a sheet. Someone had slipped it under the door. He fetched it and took a moment to orient himself to the letterhead of the World Refugee Committee. The fax was typed in caps, like a telegram.

SHIMON FEDDERMAN EMIGRATED TO ISRAEL IN 1946. THERE HE RECORDED HIS TESTIMONY IN A FILMED INTERVIEW, BUT WE HAVE LOST TRACK SINCE. HOPE THIS IS SOME HELP. NATALIE

He sat on his bed deciding. It took him not a minute. He made a quick call, packed, organized his passport and cash.

When he rang Dr. Gideon's room, the old man insisted he come around to say goodbye. Peter pushed the bell and Gideon opened his door wearing a wool challis bathrobe, black leather slippers. It was nine o'clock. Coffee and fruit had been brought to him on a tray; the table in his sitting room held what was left of his breakfast, newspapers in several languages.

Peter declined his offer of coffee. He had to be on his way.

"I wanted to thank you for listening. And for your advice."

"You need not thank me for something you decline." Gideon was not unfriendly. "So. What do you think you will find in Israel?"

"This man Fedderman, for one thing. He can confirm or deny the story Kulek has told. It's too elaborate not to have left traces. And if he confirms it, I'm still left with the question of whose side they were on." Peter added Von Egger's name for the first time. He mentioned the staggering number of bank accounts.

"What if he was in charge of generating new business? That does not seem so many accounts when you think of the span of time they cover."

Peter revealed the Heiliger accounts. "My friend Helene has it on computer. She hooked a group of them up with a known Nazi alias. Makes you wonder who Von Egger was working for, and whether he didn't cheat my grandfather after all."

Gideon took in this information and was either persuaded by it or resigned that he could not discourage Peter from his trip. "I would like to find out what you learn. You will keep me informed? You know of course the story of Theseus and the Minotaur on the Isle of Crete?"

Peter was impatient. On a long train ride this man's ramblings were an amusement but he had a flight to catch. He nodded.

"Then you remember how Theseus could not solve the problem of the maze by himself. You will need help. Where do you go from Tel Aviv?"

"I don't know. I haven't thought about it. It will depend on what I find there."

"Will it," Gideon said, but not as a question. "I must not understand. This tour of yours strikes me as an indulgence. You are on a quest that has no grail. How will this change your plans?"

Peter looked at him. He had no answer. The fact was, he had no plans.

On the telephone Marcus was diffident.

"Sorry, but I have to do this. You can get that local kid back."

"Israel," Marcus said. "Never been to Israel. Dizzy toured there, Diz was very big. They gave him one of those funny hats. Scuffle one up for me."

He sat on the airplane thinking of Gideon's words. A quest without the grail. Good band name, we could get satin jackets. The stewardess pointed to his tray table.

"You'll have to put that up for take-off."

He thought of Helene. He could use some support. Is that the first sign of need? First you need, then you want, then you love? Is it like a tune, you start with a riff, even before the chords or the rhythm? He hadn't a clue.

Steinmuller, Matey had told him, you haven't a clue. You'll know love the way you know great art. You don't wait for the critics. It hits you in the chest, once, undeniable and permanent. Was she right? Is there a single love, like one birth and one death, for each of us? Think of the timing you'd need, you couldn't be watching TV or practicing scales when she walked by. It can't work that way.

The plane waited at the hold line. He took the two letters from his pocket, from the court and Frey. Confinement was a secret terror, they had found his weakness. He folded the sheets into quarter size, lowered the tray table and carefully tore along the folds. Folded and tore twice again. Then across. What remained was a handful of confetti. He stuffed the bits into the ashtray and, just as the stewardess came at him with the frown of a meter maid, locked away the table for take-off.

10

SUN. THE FLIGHT LIFTED from the floor of an ocean of clouds and sharked through the grey. Broken beads of dew on the plastic of the porthole spread in running virgules, the clouds gave not a bump, not a rhythm to the climb. The airplane might have been a missile shot to the surface in some somber and stirred pond.

But the surface. That was birth itself, a forgotten blue, the eye of the sun. Airship hummed and rose, popped through the fuzzy surface and soared. Whatever water the silver skin carried from the depths to this new world atomized. Abracadabra.

He repeated the word. Was it Latin, did it mean something? An incantation meant more than words. Is that meaning, or is that music? A wonderful title for a tune, abracadabra. Perfect syncopation. He scored the five notes on the cocktail napkin that had come under his ginger ale, wrote five notes over a staff and flagged in their time values. It made a single, four-beat bar. Music was a puzzle, tempo the first clue.

He peered forward through the distorted edge of the porthole. They were flying the expanse of the Mediterranean, an opaque shell that was hard and polished. The sea continued to slip under him. He was served a plate of cucumbers and tomato, oyster crackers, a hard-boiled egg, and for dessert figs and coffee. The man next to him drank a muddy red wine and smoked a cigar.

Peter dozed, and when he next looked out there was landfall at last. His pulse moved. Endless shades of camel and tan, all scored with dense green in straight lines like typographic marks. Peter would not let it stand. Something inside had begun to flex, he felt engaged, nimble, and now as the plane curved toward earth he thought for the first time in his travels that perhaps the arc was describing a destination.

The airplane shed speed and altitude. It squared off in its pattern and banked to the east for final approach. The hydraulic effort that lowers the gear shuddered through the cabin. Passengers began their nervous picking up, their readying. Time to decide whether you are going home or leaving it. Abracadabra.

"I beg your pardon?" said the man next to him. He petulantly stubbed out his cigar at the steward's request.

"No," Peter replied. "I said nothing."

From the airport bus every building he saw was new. Had he missed a turn? Where was the land of the Bible? The city of Tel Aviv seemed to have been constructed entirely in the last few days, everywhere one looked the geometric and repetitive architecture of exigency. My father was a boy when the State of Israel was founded, three or four years old. There had always been some confusion over his date of birth, it was a rare family joke that he'd created the confusion to lower his age. All this has been built since then. Bone-white cement shimmered against the sky. How many sea shells were crushed to build this white city?

Everywhere flew the flag. From the roofs of Bauhaus apartment buildings, from short masts atop the repetitive two-story offices, in front of the government buildings and produce depots and petrol stations.

He settled on a C hotel in the center of the city. There was no sense wasting Helene's money on commodes and cable television. His room had a comfortable double bed, a radio, a clean bath with modern fixtures. It suggested how the city looked on the outside, no frills, just a cordoning of space. Utility.

Where to start? He pulled the telephone book from the night table. The front half, front to him, was in English. Hebrew read from right to left, so each language got the front half of the book. An agent's dream, equal billing. There were twenty-six Feddermans, but there was no Shimon. He recalled the thrill of finding Kulek on the first try, and happily punched in the first number.

By the fifteenth call his zeal sagged. Near the end he realized his mistake. There had been no other survivors. If Fedderman had close family, they would have perished aboard the *Artemis*. The family he hadn't taken with him may not have made it out. This was an unlikely expedition.

He went down the hall, dropped coins into a machine and returned to the room sipping a Dr. Pepper. Lay on the bed feeling alone. Nothing new, he'd long since grown used to loneliness, but this time it came with a soft melancholy at its center.

He rang Helene at the bank. He hadn't told her of this trip, she would think he was still in Budapest. Even if she were at a meeting he could leave word.

She picked up immediately.

"You sound upset."

"I can't talk to you now. Call me later."

"What's happened? What's the matter?"

"Peter, I can't talk to you. I've been fired. They found out about the records."

"God, Helene. I'm sorry." His words surprised him. He was sorry, and not for himself.

"Call me at home. I'm packing up my desk."

"I'll call you at home. Helene, I'm in Tel Aviv."

"Yes. I'm not surprised."

"Come. I have a nice room," he looked around, motioned to its walls. "I'll send you a ticket. Can you?"

"We'll see. Perhaps. Call me tonight."

Peter took a walk. He could try the four Feddermans where there had been no answer. He could try other cities, although most of the country's population was in Tel Aviv. The fax from Washington had mentioned testimony. Could there be some record? If so, perhaps it would be here.

The library's computer system had one set of terminals for English, a second for Hebrew. He ran the name through the quick search procedure, then the long search. No dice. Then he switched data bases: the public library system was only one of several he could access. Government records, the Universities at Jaffa and Tel Aviv, the medical school. On his first byway, the card appeared.

FEDDERMAN, SHIMON (1 of 1 entry)
HVT 632.23 video
av688fe
Cross-references:
REFUGEES
HOLOCAUST
IMMIGRATION, ILLEGAL
ALIYA BET
GLIWICE

Videotaped interview by Feuerstein, J. and Edgar, N. of Holocaust survivor S. FEDDERMAN. Archives of University of Tel Aviv, World Refugee Committee collection. Shimon Fedderman (1922-1986) recounts experiences growing up in Dobrzyn, training as bricklayer; imprisonment and escape; confinement in Gliwice and death march; travel to Bucharest in 1938, Budapest in 1941; starvation; booking passage; on the *Artemis* in 1943; passage to Palestine.

2 copies: master 3/4" and VHS 2"
Non-circulating. 56 min.
Yiddish.

Peter stared. Movement behind him — someone was waiting to use the machine. He jotted down the call number. The riddle was solved, and the solution was not a solution. Fedderman was dead. Fedderman had left a tape. The tape did not circulate, was in Yiddish. He could hire a translator, or he could use someone who spoke German.

On his walk he had passed an El Al sales office. Now he retraced his steps, went in, purchased a ticket for Helene on tomorrow morning's flight, open return, to be picked up at the desk in Zurich. She could always cancel.

He idled away the rest of the afternoon. Walked through the noisy streets, bought a pair of sunglasses against the glint that now smoked through the traffic's dust. This was his first visit, but something about the city clung to him. Not the conventional *deja vu*, it wasn't that he felt he had experienced this walk before, but a lesser sense, a sense he had seen these signs.

Was it the absence of a past? How does a city differ if it has no yesterday? How does a person? He knew a trombone who used to rail against the white race for infiltrating jazz. It's all the past we have and now you want to take it too. How can you steal someone's history?

Helene said yes. He was elated. She could be of help, translating the tape and thinking it through. There was more. His longing, something — was it the beating he was taking? — something was turning his solitude to heavy. He would sleep alone in a hotel room only one more night.

He spent a restless morning. The magazine in his room recommended sights he had no interest in. The distant Biblical Palestine, buildings that housed bureaus important to recent political events. From what he had seen, the past of this city had lost its fight. The past was not a contender. He found a popular novel in the hotel's gift shop, read it in his room between calls for the flight. The sex parts drove him wild and he skipped through them. They touched a finger to a hot and risen boil, a canker on the tip of his tongue that regularly caught and dragged across a tooth point. He was at the airport early. Heat rose in a surfing sea, and giant machines kicked up vortices in the dust as they descended. Each one was her plane, descending through the prismatic and sand-shimmered air. He caught his breath in short takes, the heat pressed down, he felt as if he'd been running. At last a 707 taxied toward his window. The sun flashed on its skin, across the set faces of the pilots and down the length of the vein-blue stripe that identifies the airplanes of El Al.

And she was walking through the causeway.

She wore a white sundress, the white tights. Her dress had loose sleeves cut above the elbow, a deep vee neck. He could see through the armholes where her breasts began. Around her throat she wore a slim gold chain from which hung a turquoise pendant. It might have been molten.

They said little in the cab. She had not been here before, had heard there was a nice resort in the south. He knew he should ask her about the job, whether she was in trouble for the risks she'd taken, but his mouth was dry. At the hotel room he gulped from a water glass. She took her few things from her bag, what she called a day case, and placed them carefully in the second drawer. He watched her with intense expectation. He could hear his breath. She patted down lingerie, fitted it into the corner. She might have been a mason. Peter walked to her while she stood at the bureau. He put his hands lightly on the tops of her hips and tugged their bodies together so they met. He held her in this posture he had selected, this posture of particular avail. He put his face into the softness of her hair, clean and smelling of the morning's shampoo, and inhaled.

"You like the back of my head," she said.

"That too."

They stood. He might have been breathing oxygen from a tank. Her buttocks leaned against him.

"God," he said. The voice surprised him. It was poor sound, hardly there, what the audio guys called bad fidelity, it came from underpowered, tinny speakers. "God, I need you." Rampant with the truth he spoke, he pressed against her.

Afterwards, he drank mineral water from a large bottle the hotel supplied, little points of carbonation. She watched from the bed, and he brought her a glass.

"Damn," he said suddenly. "The time."

What did it matter?

He tossed her clothes at her as he explained. The tape, the need to translate. Today is Friday. The town closes down an hour before sunset, everyone leaves for the Sabbath. If they hurried they could listen.

The librarian at the video cabinets was not pleased. She yielded the box with a second warning about closing time. Peter thanked her excessively, he was eager to start. Helene warned him they would likely have need of someone who spoke Yiddish. German was close, but it would only get her partway through. Partway, Peter guessed, would be enough. Corroboration of the *Artemis* story would dispose of the matter. It would prove what had happened.

In a small viewing booth, they loaded the video recorder and watched the ten-inch screen. Peter asked Helene to translate only what bore on Kulek's story.

On the television screen, a young man and woman, clearly university students, spoke with Fedderman. Only one camera was used. It swiveled from face to face at first, but as Fedderman talked, its operator seemed to forget. The result was one voice for a long time, trailing off, cued from just off-camera into another flat, reluctant soliloquy.

Helene said very little. In the early minutes, she spoke an occasional word, a gloss in the margin, so that Peter would know the subject. Childhood, she whispered. Parents. Games. Fedderman was a thin man, grey face and dull, inert eyes. He was someone you would avoid on the sidewalk, not shrink from, but someone you would rather not confront. There was a frailty in the bones of his face, in his eyes, and you felt he might not withstand the wake of your passing. Once Peter reached out to take her hand and she moved it away.

Fedderman spoke softly, with no traceable emotion. He seemed to be doing a favor for his interviewers, for the university they attended. Once he asked something of the camera operator and the students smiled and Helene did as well. Did they want him to pretend the camera operator was not there? It seemed a modest request, but he was not an actor. Helene started to explain, and as Fedderman began again, fell silent.

The man's hands sat folded in front of him. They never moved, not to emphasize, to explain, to importune. Not the hundred reasons hands move. Not to touch the face or check the button of a shirt. The table in front of him was bare except for an ashtray, a round black ashtray with the name around its rim of a famous New York restaurant. Often when Fedderman finished the students would sit for a moment, also still, before finding their next question. In those seconds, when only the whir of the tape drive could be heard like the breathing of another person in the room, Peter and Helene leaned towards the screen. They might have been prompters. Then it would start again.

It was an extraordinary sensation. Peter felt his chest move in rhythm. This was as close as one could get. Here is a film of a man now dead who tells you he sees these things. Or tells the interviewers. You eavesdrop. He tells the interviewers and they bring along a camera. Helene had said most important is who tells the tale.

On the small blue screen is a man in the last years of his life speaking softly, his hands piled on the table before him like two doves dead from scatter shot. One of the interviewers pushes on his chair and it squawks against the wooden floor.

Peter hears the word *Artemis*. Helene's fingers touch his arm. "The boat," she whispers when Fedderman pauses, but falls silent again. In the next minutes he hears the name Steinmuller several times. He looks to Helene, sees her listening, her mouth open the width of a sip. She puts up her hand to stop his question. Her eyes shine in the blue light of the screen. When it is over, Peter realizes she has been crying.

They returned the tape to the desk. The librarian had remained angry with them and their promptness did not win her over. They walked in silence towards the city. Small cars hurried by to beat the sun. At a traffic light, Helene turned to him.

"Why did you want me to see that?" Her voice was thick and harsh.

Peter put his arm around her waist and they walked on like young lovers. They walked in circles, went back to the hotel and showered, went into the soft evening. It was cool without the sun. They wore cotton sweaters.

The Sabbath had begun. Most places were closed. They found a Greek restaurant and ordered. Lamb, taramasalata. A resin wine that Peter didn't drink. Helene moved food around on the plate and nibbled on crumbs of white cheese.

"There was nothing," she said at last. "Nothing different from what you heard. The boat, the quarantine in Istanbul. It was all as you were told."

Peter waited. She looked at the plate as she spoke. "It was just . . . worse. The filth, the shit. People sick. What he went through. Before. His daughter . . . ."

She trailed off.

"He didn't care. He says that at the end. Of all those on board, he was the only survivor, and he had no reason to live. He thought again he was going to die, and yet it doesn't seem to happen to him. That is what he said at the end, it was his only joke. He looked up at them and said, perhaps of all people I, Shimon Fedderman, will live forever.

"Anyway," Helene let go a long breath from an imaginary cigarette. She opened a pack of saltines, put them down. "The story of the *Artemis* is just as Kulek said. Your grandfather's brother did all the organization, all the financing. He was on board trying to secure passage. Mr. Fedderman certainly looked up to him as a hero."

"So their stories are true. My grandfather, his brother, Von Egger. They were working to get these people out. For a while I thought what you found about the Nazi accounts, maybe Von Egger was profiteering. But it looks like they were genuine."

"Peter, what are you saying?"

"The Nazi names amid the new accounts. They could have been just mingled in. Von Egger was probably in charge of new accounts, took them as they came in the door. You got the list of them, all four thousand. It's not as if the Nazi names were a majority, there were only a few . . . ."

Helene looked at him in astonishment. "Did you hear me correctly?" she asked. "What I told you on the phone? When I ran Von Egger's name they were all accounts left dormant. Those were not simply new accounts. Those were new refugee accounts."

"Meaning?"

"Meaning Von Egger himself opened at the Löwenhoft more refugee accounts than had been advertised in the paper for *all* banks. Meaning he or his bank had use of that money all these years. Meaning who knows what use he's made of it in the meantime. If each account had a fourth what your grandfather's originally had, say thirty thousand francs, average, then over 120 million Swiss francs was abandoned at Löwenhoft."

"Over 120 million francs?"

"Over ninety million dollars." She narrowed her eyes to calculate. "Ninety-eight and some. At today's exchange."

"You think if he was ripping off my grandfather he was ripping off others? How do we find the amounts?"

Helene sat back. "I don't know. All I could retrieve by computer was the fact of the account, not the number. The amounts are probably gone. But before I got fired, I dumped whatever I could onto floppy disks. I have them at home, under the mattress."

They ordered coffee. Flecks from the cream floated on the cooling surface. The coffee had been brewed to bitter strength, then sweetened to overcome its bitterness. They sipped and grimaced.

"You don't think the Fedderman story . . . ."

"Proves that Hermann did what Kulek said he did? Yes I do. But you asked Kulek about *Pietr*. Why did he neglect to mention him? He told you mostly of Hermann. Did Kulek know Von Egger? 'His name is not unfamiliar' — isn't that what he told you? What does it mean?"

"There's still the Israeli citation. They don't give those out to Nazi collaborators." Peter heard the certainty in his words and added, "I wouldn't think."

Helene nodded. "We are in the place to find out. This is where the goose in the wild comes to nest. That will be tomorrow's project."

But tomorrow was Saturday and the library was closed until sundown. They would give themselves a holiday. They returned to the hotel and made arrangements for a rental car, retreated to their little room and fell dead asleep.

Peter awoke in the middle of night and studied her as she slept. What electrons moved behind those still lids, how could this woman be so efficient and yet so open to be moved? He put his lips to her shoulder, warmer than the air, and pulled the cotton blanket to cover her.

In the morning Helene drove them into the countryside. The landscape surprised Peter; he expected flat and unremitting desert, found instead long roads, easy curves carved through rock hills, colors that lay powdered and baked under stone.

"It's a curious thing," Peter said. He watched her watch the road. The beginnings of a double chin. "When we were listening to the tape? I don't understand any of the words, but the sound of the language, his speech. It was more like a horn. Like music. You don't understand music either, but you can sit and listen to the sounds. I started to feel I got what he was saying."

They rode a ribbon of highway. She drove fast.

"On the plane," Helene told him, "I asked the woman sitting next to me about the Hebrew alphabet. It all looks so mysterious. She said there were twenty-two letters. Some make a different sound when you dot them. She said that the ancient Israelites were always on the move, and this way they didn't have to carry around so many consonants."

They checked into a modest resort in the southernmost town of Elat and lay in the sun. The beaches were crowded and the walls of the room thin. They refreshed themselves easily, swam in the Red Sea, and made love as often as they could bear it. There was a bowl of fruit on their nightstand, dates and oranges from the Negev. Peter stood at the mirror in the disinfected bathroom, trimmed his beard, and shaved a slender crescent about the edges of his lips.

They drove back to the city. They crossed the desert as the sun went down, the landscape vivid in the glancing rays of light. Hues of apricot, rose, chestnut came out of the cliffs that had been dull dirt passed in the high morning heat. Were they tiring of each other? He knew what she was going to say and, he had so few words, she must as well. Surely that cannot be the test, he thought. What difference what someone says?

Helene needed to fly back the next day. So far her only penalty for the breach of secrecy was the loss of her job, mild, she told him, compared with what they might do. She intended full cooperation in her last two weeks. They had her cold on entering confidential files. This was a grave matter. She would need them to find another job.

Is it really that serious? Peter asked. After all, the people in these files, the depositors, and all the beneficiaries except Von Egger were long dead. It is not who has been injured, she told him. It is the rule. I need to get back.

But she had an idea where to go next. Peter had used the computerized index to search only one library. Many indexes were networked together. Through any one, the public library for instance, one might view doctoral theses or government records. Perhaps something on the enigmatic Von Egger would turn up.

Late Sunday afternoon they ran his name through various catalogues. Helene had shortcuts, even in a foreign system she moved quickly, saving steps that would have taken the search into days. They scanned likely places — graduate university records and historical files on foreign policy, diplomatic relations with Switzerland. Government publications. Government legislative history. An hour before closing, while they cruised government archives, an entry floated to the screen like a fresh corpse.

VON EGGER, FREDERICH
NA-RG591/Lot files Box 66/files 41, 42
Cross reference:
INTER-ALLIED REPARATION AGENCY (IARA)*
INTERGOVERNMENTAL COMMITTEE ON REFUGEES*
PARIS CONFERENCE ON REPARATION (1945)*
PARIS CONFERENCE ON REPARATION (1946)*
CITATION, STATE OF ISRAEL (1952)*

The librarian, the very same one they had offended two days before, did not conceal her delight in denying them the files. Restricted access, she explained in a kind, kindergarten voice. The "NA" stood for national archives. They are housed here at the university, but their category is available to government or university personnel only. The cross-referenced files are even further out of reach. They remain classified; security clearance would be needed.

Peter was about to protest as Helene thanked the woman cordially. She led him to the main floor, retrieved her lizard-skin briefcase from the cloakroom, and took out a sheet of paper. They found a coin-operated computer. Within minutes she handed him a letter, flawlessly typed on the stationery of the Löwenhoft Handelsbank, Zurich.

To whom it may concern:
This letter will serve to introduce Peter Steinmuller, an American scholar doing economic research on behalf of our bank. His research has the full support of the Swiss League of Bankers, and promises to contribute to the study of successful monetary policies in international trade. We appreciate any courtesies you show to him, and extend our gratitude in advance.

Yours faithfully,
Helene Durren,
Assistant Manager

Helene added a date, stale by a month, and signed her name. Peter asked whether the date was an error.

"I am no longer assistant manager. One cannot sign when one is not authorized." She added with a look of delicious sincerity, "That is the rule."

They left together the next morning. On the way to the airport, Helene's car dropped Peter at the university. He was back in the hunt.

Unfolding her letter, passing it across, he smiled at her skills — lover and forger — how she brought precision to the one task and abandon to the other. The chief research librarian was pleased to help. The library could not, Peter must understand, release the matters noted as confidential. The university had no authority to contradict classifications of government security. But they would certainly find the unrestricted files, Box 66, and let him browse there. A messenger was dispatched to retrieve it from storage. He was assigned a carrel on the third floor.

The box would be an hour in delivery. Peter found the cafeteria. He had not yet had breakfast. Cold toast, an orange uncertain about its color, weak coffee. A handsome young woman, perhaps twenty, followed him out of the line, sat opposite. She was, she said without a flicker, eager to practice her English.

"Am I so conspicuous?" he asked and she ignored his question.

"Tell me what you are doing here and where in the States you are from."

He was charmed, uninterested. She had Matey's straight brow, in a darker shade, quite black. Uneven complexion and a stern widow's peak. The strength of her eyes gave her the appearance of permanent resolve.

He told her about himself, explained the fictive research quoting Helene's letter of authority. Was it a crime in Israel to impersonate a scholar?

She asked about the subject and he mentioned the Swiss Bankers Association, the advertisements. Everyone knew the story. She shook her head.

"Does it strike you as ironic?" she asked.

"Does what?"

She leaned forward. Her hands made loose fists. "The reason we know so much about the horrors of those times is the Germanic bureaucracy. They followed all the rituals, all the niceties. We have their invoices, requests for bid, their orders. They kept double-entry books. No matter that they were invoicing the amount of calcium residue from a thousand bodies. No record went unwritten.

"And here we are, years later, doing the same thing. These events have lost historical significance. They have become an industry."

Peter protested softly. He was, after all, an imposter. He argued that interest alone would keep alive the moral dimension. She had heard this before and waved him off.

"We collect boxes, we cannot satisfy our curiosity. How is it any different from your American news? CNN. A shooting last night at a bar. Bodies on trolleys, red splotches. That is all it amounts to. I am offended by it. Enough."

She left. He placed the paper plate and peelings in the trash, the tableware in the dish pan, the white military mug half-filled on the conveyor belt. She had not dissuaded him from his purpose.

A single documents box had been delivered to the carrel and now sat upon the desk. Peter lowered it to the floor and thumbed its files. There were eleven in all, and nine he quickly determined clearly had nothing to do with his search. He withdrew files 41 and 42, the first a thick envelope, perhaps three inches, filled with random papers and clippings. File 42 was a thin, salmon folder. He glanced at its contents: a short memorandum, a copy of a government report, a brown envelope clipped but not sealed.

He began systematically to scan the larger file. Much of it was irrelevant. There was a great deal of correspondence that mentioned Von Egger. Most concerned where and when meetings would be held, what hotels were available. The papers confirmed nothing more than Von Egger himself had told Peter in their walk. Long negotiations had ensued after the war and, as Pietr Steinmuller's successor, Von Egger had participated in them.

Peter came across a memo on rough paper, pages stapled at the upper left. It bore a stenciled stamp on its upper margin, in blue ink the quality of an old tattoo: CONFIDENTIAL. It was a discussion draft prepared by a U.S. Foreign Service Officer. He pushed his chair back so that the light from the shaded window was to his back, and read.

Executive Summary of the Task Force
Heirless Assets/Middle East Desk
United States Department of State
April 5, 1950

This task force has been appointed to monitor the progress of the responsibilities of all signatory nations to the Final Act of the Paris Conference on Reparations. The Final Act states it was intended to aid the large numbers of persons who have "suffered heavily at the hands of the Nazis and now stand in dire need of aid to promote their rehabilitation but [are] unable to claim the assistance of any Government receiving reparations from Germany."

Article 8, Part I of the Final Act identified three sources for funds for refugee assistance. (1) so-called German external assets, (2) non-monetary gold, that is, loot seized or obtained under duress from political, racial or religious victims of the Nazi Government or its satellite governments, and (3) heirless assets, the focus of the efforts of this task force. The Final Act, Article 8(C), stated, "Governments of neutral countries shall be requested to make available [to aid resettlement] assets . . . of victims of Nazi action who have since died and left no heirs." This provision was agreed to in principle by all signatories, over the strong objections of parties who still block its way.

Little progress has been made. Participating nations have delegated implementation of the directive to teams of bankers and merchants. The humanitarian purposes of the Final Act have regularly been subordinated to questions of commercial nicety.

The principal location of heirless assets deposited in neutral countries is Switzerland. Amounts are very difficult to ascertain. The Swiss legation argues that depositors selected Swiss banks because of their safety and secrecy. The mere fact that these funds have been undisturbed, the argument continues, does not provide a reason to open the accounts to scrutiny and unwarranted distribution.

These arguments are not without merit. But they should not be allowed to prevail over every other interest. Refugees who could afford to, doubtless a small fraction of the numbers who perished, sent moneys on to "safe" countries. Many accounts were opened in the depositor's name. For those few depositors who used aliases, ownership could be solved by investigation. But only by a motivated party:

the Swiss government has delegated to the banks themselves responsibility for compliance with these accords.

This conflict is one of diplomatic volatility. We have negotiated with the Swiss Minister of Justice on this subject since 1946. The position of the influential banks remains that compliance with the directive of Article 88 is impossible. These banks have a disproportionate voice in advising the Swiss legation.

Peter's eye caught on a starred entry at the bottom of the page, circled in red. "The Minister of Justice has as his unpaid advisors a small band of businessmen who strenuously oppose compliance. Leading them is the prominent young banker Frederich Von Egger."

Clipped to the page was a note written in Hebrew except for a single English word, STEINMULLER, written across the top. As if it had been left for him. Peter slid off the paper clip, pocketed the note, and read on.

Until recently, we have been suggesting legislative solutions, thinking that time and world opinion were on the side of the Final Act. The task force now believes that these elements have turned against us. World opinion has tired of the plight of the refugee.

More urgent is the issue of time. The bankers have begun to solve the problem by bilateral agreements that avoid recompense.

The purpose of this memo is to request additional instruction. Those opposing compliance with the Final Act stand to benefit enormously. The longer this issue drags on, the more assets will fall through the cracks. Once converted into private funds, they will be impossible to trace.

Peter replaced the report in the file. He went quickly through clippings, English and Hebrew newspaper stories of the visit of Von Egger to receive his citation. Peter packed the materials neatly back into the envelope. A weariness had entered his joints. He stretched, twisted, rang out his hands. It would be good to find a piano.

He walked outside. Dust struck the whiteness of the sun, gave off the smell of cement. He went to the cafeteria and purchased vegetable soup that he ate with a stale roll. His zealous breakfast partner was nowhere to be seen and he ate alone. He was ineffably tired. How long had he been gone? It depends on where you place the starting point.

Enormous benefit. Impossible to trace. Kulek would be outraged. He seemed to think all in the Composers' Circle were heroes. Instead, Von Egger now appeared to be the chief engine in an apparatus to deny claims on heirless property. Is there any reason to think he had not similarly put his and his bank's interest before those of the Steinmullers?

He reentered the library. At a table by the stairs sat the widow-peaked girl. He stopped by her desk, wanting to tell her something. She looked up irritably.

"It *does* matter," he said instead.

"What matters?"

"All of this, what happened. We need to care."

"Oh," she said. "I agree. But not treat it like some amusement park attraction."

"That's a small price."

She considered this, frowned. "It turns people into spectators, though. They buy a ticket and observe."

"For every one who comes to observe, another becomes a doer. We need doers."

"I do not understand the idiom," she said ingenuously. "Dewar's. I thought it was a whisky."

He examined her face. She meant no joke.

"Can you translate this for me? It's Hebrew?" He handed her the purloined note.

"Yes, Hebrew. 'Close friend of so-and.-so, P. K. Steinmuller, who led the Swiss delegation in 1945. Steinmuller a secret *meshumod.*"

"What does that mean? *Meshumod*?"

"It does not translate."

"Try."

She pursed her lips. "It means one who assimilates. Worse. A Jew who disrespects his Jewishness. It is not flattering."

Peter thanked her and she nodded a grudging conciliation. He walked back to his carrel. Pietr Jewish? And me also? Does that explain this sense of revisiting? Of a book read a long ago, now falling open? If there is a cultural memory, perhaps it will speak up.

The library messenger was waiting for him. The gentleman is through with the files? Yes, Peter said. He was through. The young man put them back in the storage box, loaded the box onto his standing dolly. Not until Peter glanced down did he notice the salmon-colored fin of the single slim file.

With apologies, Peter unloaded the box from the dolly. Might as well see it all. He closed the door and withdrew the thin folder. It had three documents clipped to its right side, a brown envelope punched and clipped to its left. This was apparently a personnel file of the government, a repository of miscellaneous intelligence the Israelis kept on diplomats who crossed their path. The topmost sheet was a biography of Von Egger, no new information. The second entry was a photocopy of the few pages on Von Egger from *Thirty Who Cared*. At the very bottom were several loose sheets. They came from an early dry copier, on paper slick and shiny as a burn. Eight or nine pages, the middle of some ministry report, starting and ending mid-sentence. Peter scanned them. They were the center section of a strategic paper, addressing what position Israel should take about compliance with the Final Act. Negotiations were going on in Paris, and the author of this paper was advocating that his country bring its cause to the United States legation.

Two paragraphs toward the end caught Peter's eye:

> Yesterday Minister Stucki announced that henceforth the government's position would be represented by Frederich Von Egger. Von Egger is a young banker known for his hard-line view in these matters. Unlike the rest of the legation, he and his staff are housed at the *George Cinq*. We have advised US representatives of the vested interests of this group. Von Egger's staff includes two Ministry officers and his chief aide, the journalist Maag-Reinhardt, whom we believe to be in his private employ.

> Maag-Reinhardt let it be known unequivocally that any settlement (including distribution of any moneys what-soever from heirless assets under Section 8-C) must include a citation from either the United States or the State of Israel to Mr. Von Egger. The U.S. Deputy Secretary has stated that no system exists for alien decoration and that a letter of grat-itude might be possible. Von Egger has responded that this offer will not suffice.

Peter sat forward over the file. He read these paragraphs a second, a third time. He went again over the other pages, but found nothing more. The man was a fraud. He had gotten his citation, those files were not available, but clearly he had gotten what he wanted.

To open the envelope, Peter had to unclip it. The glue on the flap glistened. He slid out the contents, an eight by ten photograph, and felt to assure he had left nothing behind.

He looked at the print for a long time. There was no mistaking. The black of trees in leaf across the back, the dotting of Chinese lanterns, bulbs soft in the greys of the photo, three men sitting at a white tablecloth. Exquisite focus: the creases of fat showed on Kulek's neck and Peter could read the label on the Champagne — it was a Taittinger. A first course was before them, the restaurant photographer had caught them before the disarray of dining. Von Egger's eyes reflected the explosion of the flash. The light gave his smile a wicked gleam. Kulek showed no expression, he might be staring into the lens of a police camera. The third man's eyes had darted away for the instant — was it fifty, fifty-five years ago? — that would be frozen in silver paper for Peter to find. The eyes looked off, but his gaunt face was caught in deep chiaroscuro.

Peter pulled the front of his shirt from his trousers, slid the photo-graph against his chest white side out, clipped the emptied envelope back into the file. He stood to look for a reflection in the narrow window, but he had no chance against the sunlight outside. He cautiously walked to the men's room, examined himself. Satisfied, he repackaged the files, thanked the librarian, and strode, stiffly so as not to crease the print, out the building.

He stopped on the way back to the hotel for a can of shaving foam. There were new brands since he'd last bought one. For the little trim-ming and paring, he had used only bar soap.

Back at his room, he propped the photograph behind the taps and ran hot water into the sink. He lathered his face and began to shave. The beard resisted, there was a surprising amount of pull. The whiskers clogged the razor and there was as much tugging as cutting. When he was finished, he rinsed his face, looked deeply at the reflec-tion. And checked it against the photograph.

There in the mirror was the face of the third man. The face of Pietr Kurz Steinmuller.

11

"PETER, YOU MUST BE more subtle, and pay more attention." He had finished telling Helene the story. Von Egger's charade, the photo that proved the complicity of his grandfather and Kulek.

"Kulek never mentioned your grandfather or Von Egger. That is what you asked. Instead he told you the story of the good fairy, Hermann. That is what you wanted to hear."

Peter lay on his bed, reading a blank ceiling.

"Von Egger wasn't a collaborator, Peter. He was a businessman. A service for a fee."

"So you're saying Kulek couldn't have been a part of that?"

"I don't know."

"Listen," he plunked at the phone cord trying to get a sound. "Do you still have access to the bank's files?" He wished she were here. Doing on his own tired him.

"Of course not. That's why they fired me."

"Damn."

"Heirless assets," Helene said absently. It was a phrase without a human being in it. The words could have come out of a bank manual somewhere. People who didn't show up. Ever.

"Why?"

"I want to run another name against the accounts file."

"Oh," she said. "I could do that. I dumped the batch I was sorting onto a floppy. I have that here. It's not programmed but I could do that. All it will tell you is frequency."

"Meaning?"

"Whether the name appears. And how often. It's like an index to the hard data. We won't be able to look at the actual documents."

"Would you? Would you give it a try?"

Helene agreed. "What name?"

"My grandfather's. Pietr Kurz Steinmuller." There was a pause while Helen wrote it down. Peter told her his next destination: Budapest, to find Kulek.

"How? He has disappeared. How will you find him?"

He had an idea. They rang off.

It took several calls and patient minutes to find someone at Krokodile who spoke enough English to take down the advertisement.

In the best socialist tradition, the newspaper had no classified advertising, no rate card and had never received a request like this. Peter struck a price for two successive weeks, two columns wide by two inches. The man in Budapest suggested how his text could be fit in a smaller space, less money, but Peter insisted. The ad would run this Wednesday and next:

Buxtehude and Brahms
Urgent I speak to you, exchange photograph for more information on above subject. Same location, ten a.m. any day this week.

He called the Gellêrt to assure a room. The detective work had exhausted him. After dinner he pulled the thin cotton curtains across the windows and lay down on top of the bedspread. He fell asleep immediately and did not wake until sunrise of the next day.

Flights to Budapest were on alternate days, he had twenty-four hours to kill. He studied the photograph, turned it over. A slip of onionskin was pasted to the back. Typed, newspaper style, "(l to r: unidentified man, Frederich Von Egger, the Operative Brahms. Budapest, c. 1943)". Above the label, askew, a stamp from the U.S. State Department.

His face now threatened him from the mirror. He had unearthed a mummy in this land of cooperative housing and relics. When he walked past the metal detectors with this antiquity he would sound no alarm. He peered at the face. Its newness, freshly shaven, enabled him a critical judgement: the eyes were close together, the nose long, unrelieved. Youth but no freshness. The flesh of the lips was a vivid and unhealthy red.

How to spend the day? He had the rental car, he would take a drive. All this desert, maybe they had roads where you could let the engine out and see what it would do. He motored aimlessly from the city. Villages floated in the refracting air, tiny Venices of balconies, television aerials, flat roofs white against the water of desert. There was a blameless monotony, not to the landscape, but to his place in it. He was nowhere engaged, he was passing through. He veered from the road that led to Jerusalem and turned to the south. The Samarian plain. Everywhere road signs indicated historical reference. He had no destination or purpose, except to avoid destination and purpose. No sites or museums, no text. Lately Peter had a surfeit of meaning. He was a novice in this business of language, and it had been coming at him fast. Matey told him once, I have the title for the story of your life. Men Who Don't Talk and the Women Who Listen to Them.

Out the windscreen were endless cypress planted in a row and behind them groves of olive trees. The landscape reminded him of the girl in the cafeteria, industrious and earnest, and the memory put him in a mild melancholy. He stopped the car in a small town and entered a café. Several men sat drinking coffee from chipped cups. He ordered a beer, he did not care which, and the shopkeeper brought him the most expensive.

An Arab from the next table was talking to him. Would he like a guide to the religious sites? The Moslem section, the mosque? He would not. Very cheap, a special price. Down the highway was Beersheba. Peter got up to leave. His bottle was half full. Perhaps the gentleman would buy their coffee in the spirit of brotherhood. The new spirit.

He is afflicted by the solitude. The car tops out at 90 kilos, about 63, too slow to take his mind anywhere. He takes an arbitrary turn. In two or three miles, the road runs out, nipped off by the desert. He goes beyond — it looks as if the path might resume, as if it is merely interrupted. He brings the car to a stop amid exposed limestone and chunks of concrete. A thorny acacia tree stands where the road might have gone. He turns around. When he drives through the town, the men from the café stand on the sidewalk, pointing at him. Sure it is ridicule, he raises an angry finger at them, floors the pedal. His car chugs away and their shouts follow. He is desperate to leave.

That night he walked around Dizengoff Square and peered into clubs. The English newspaper advertised jazz at a half dozen locales, but he found a jumble of new wave and fusion. He fell asleep to a dream that repeated his afternoon's fantasy. A sandstorm of dry rain pelted against the glass on the window.

He rose at the first light, unrefreshed. The sounds of his dream had been real, for the streets shone wetly, the sky a heavy pearl. He dressed. There was a small restaurant around the corner from his hotel on Hayorken Street that opened early. He sat at a table so tiny his knees touched its chrome pillar. He ate a slice of melon, sour rolls with jam, red and filled with seeds, coffee. Asked for the second half of the melon. The coffee laced with cardamon gave reason to see out the day.

The menu listed Hebrew on the left side English on the right, running away from each other. He tried to decode the signs, oddly familiar. It hit him. They looked like music, tied notes, bulbs depending from bridged staffs.

A pale rain began again during the cab ride to Lod Airport. Misting, the air. He gulped in, his breath the first dose of antidote. He might get better. What was it about this land that stifled him? There was an excess of past, of future. Years were stacking layers of anthropological drama, residue on top of each other faster than excavations could peel them down. There was too much, it was too vast, here he might never be found. Budapest would be better. In Budapest, he had been recognized by a waiter, had played in a club, he knew the name of a single hotel.

Budapest was as good as home. There was an anxious moment at the airport as Immigration checked his passport against sheets of names, but, he reminded himself, he had done nothing wrong. At least in Hungary.

The Gellêrt put him in the same room, the staff was friendly and treated him with an incidental celebrity that added to his sense of welcome. He closed the drapes and slept until nine. Then he hailed a taxi to the Amigo Drink Bar. Marcus and the group were still booked and they were packing in crowds. Outside on a sandwich board someone had chalked the words U.S. Jazz.

"Hey, man. Change your mind?" Marcus did not seem to recall he had been away. "Love to have you. I'll take this kid outside and shoot him. Very keen to be an American. He'll think getting bumped off is hip."

Peter explained he had more to do. But if the piano player didn't mind, perhaps he could sit in.

In the first set Marcus called old bop tunes, fast, and the band ran for their lives. During the break they sat at the long table by the men's room. The alto was smoking a strong cigarette, Dr. Gideon's brand. Balkan Sobranie. Expensive, he told Peter, but he was doing well. This had turned into a regular gig.

The best cuts were last, Marcus deliberate and lyrical, chancy. Everyone comfortable. The lines cleared out Peter's head, as if someone had dragged the clefs through his ears and sinuses, just the lines on the page, and they had seined out the words. He stood the band a round after the last set. Told Marcus of his travels, of his Jewish ancestors.

"That's fine. Gershwin, man, Isaac Stern, Heifitz, the cat with crutches. Maybe you need to pick up on a violin."

When he returned to the hotel there was a message from Helene. The telephone operator had jotted it on note paper with the florid emblem of the Gellêrt at its top. "Pietr K. Steinmuller appears as originator on 3,661 accounts that have been forfeited. Cannot access files themselves."

Peter went upstairs and soaked his hands in hot water. They ached — he hadn't done three hours for a long time.

The next morning the advertisement ran in the *Krokodile*. He purchased a paper in town, but Kulek didn't show. He waited two more days. In the evenings he sat in with Marcus. The regular piano seemed delighted. Marcus had convinced him Peter was famous in the jazz world, and every night he brought a table of friends to see the American who cut him.

Peter sat over breakfast the fourth day reading the English newspaper. A concert was to be held at noon in the Matthias Church on Castle Hill, a concert of the music of Buxtehude. He set out in ample time and took the cable railway to the top. Cars were prohibited on the hill, they excepted only, in the new capitalist spirit, guests of the casino or the Hilton Hotel, which sat incongruously amid the great baroque facades. Peter walked the short mile to the church. He paid his few forints and seated himself to the rear.

It was his fancy that Kulek, seeing the concert announcement as well, would show up. They would exchange heated whispers and, amid the glory of apostolic monarchs, Kulek would break down and tell him the entire truth. He put the photograph in an envelope and took it along.

He arrived at noon and watched the small audience find their way among the pews. The concert was to begin promptly at 12:30. Some brought in a sack lunch and nibbled.

When he was little, his mother gave Bach recitals at the Congregational Church. The two of them would arrive, she settled him always in the last row, walked outside to the door to the loft and took her place. The organ had a mirror, so the organist could see the congregation, but his mother never used it. He would watch but she never looked up. Peter waited for the round and constant tone of the pipes. His mother played with her eyes closed and her chest rocking slightly. Blown by the mysterious wind from the pipes. She rocked, too, at home, where there was no wind, only the music tumbling out like water from a pump, her body the handle, the water flowing in rhythm to the pump, rapture's hand on that handle. If she were alive, could she help with his mystery? Or would she just keep rocking?

An old woman on a cane took the pew in front of him and slid to his right. She wore black, and around her shoulders lay a stole with two vixen heads flopping on her gibbous back. She withdrew a compact, opened it, inspected her face. Then daubed a muddy power to her face. The scent clouded the still air of the church, reached Peter's nostrils.

His mother's birthday. Peter took his nine dollars to Edwards Drug. Five of them from Christmas in brand new bills and four from the year before. Mr. Edwards leaned over, put his hand on Peter's head, said something Peter could not understand. Something about the funeral. Please, is he going to mention my father? Let him not. Let me just get out of here. When his father died, the kindergarten teacher asked Peter to stand and made a long speech to him. It was far harder to bear than the death. Perhaps Mr. Edwards was going to make him stand while he talked to him. Peter held out the nine bills for Mr. Edwards to see.

The money was only half of it, Mr. Edwards explained. You needed to pick something out. Something your mother would like. Mr. Edwards showed him about the drugstore. Note paper, toilet water, nothing he fancied. There in the glass case facing Peter was a magical box. It looked pink but when you moved it looked silver, and it was both. Mr. Edwards lifted it out and put it on the counter. "Would you like this, Peter? This is a little more but I'll sell this to you for your nine dollars."

Around the box was a maroon ribbon tied in a bow. What was the box for?

"Face powder. Here, I'll show you." Before Peter could protest, for he wanted nothing to disturb the bow, Mr. Edwards lifted the top. That clinched it. You could remove the top without untying the bow. It remained a perfect butterfly. Inside a snug cellophane shell, ochre powder and a white puff.

"You choose a card, Peter, and I'll ring this up." Mr. Edwards closed the magic box, took the bills and began to wrap the package.

Peter studied the cards. He wasn't sure what to do, there were dozens of cards on the rack and he read few words. He recognized a drawing. It must be what Mr. Edwards meant. He asked Mr. Edwards for a pencil and printed Peter S inside. Then he put it in its white envelope and licked it shut, and Mr. Edwards taped it to the gift wrapping. This was a special gift.

His mother was surprised to find a present sitting on the kitchen table when she came down for breakfast the next morning. Apprehensive. They sat together and Peter poured his cereal. She unwrapped Mr. Edwards' paper carefully, folding it along its creases. "It's a box in a box," his mother said. She sounded pleased. She didn't smile, so you had to listen to the voice to know. "A box in a box," Peter repeated as she lifted off the top.

"Oh, Peter," she said, and the voice went dead. "But I don't use face powder."

He sat silently. Perhaps the card would make up for it. The card must be a favorite of hers because he knew she had received several like it. She slid it open and looked at its bouquet of violets. Written on a velvet ribbon that curled through the flowers were the words In Deepest Sympathy. She put her head to the table, forearms flat, her elbow against the bowl of Cheerios, and began to cry.

A chord. Kulek had not appeared. Peter was not disappointed. The music that was played washed aside his purpose. This organ had a vast capacity, but the organist spent it as if the notes were his last coin. The church was dark and massive, and the sound traced a fault line through its foundation. The organist moved through each work with the inevitability of prayer. Yet the tone was not importunate. It was the opposite: self-contained, contradictory, an inner voice.

The music ended on a plum of silence, a physical object shaped by the cessation of air through the pipes. People in the audience gathered together their jackets and papers, whispered to each other. Walked out singly and in pairs. Peter waited and approached the altar. The organist was standing to the rear, deep within the choir. He was squaring away sheets of music.

"Excuse me," Peter said. He had foresworn expectations of who spoke English and who did not. The man turned.

"I wonder if I could speak with you a moment."

It was an ugly face, notable, almost startling, for just how ugly it was. A bulbous bone shaped the eye and brow. The cheeks melted to a soft, feminine mouth. The man looked at Peter as if he had been challenged.

"What do you want?" he said in a dark whisper.

Peter hesitated. "I merely wanted to tell you how I enjoyed your playing." He motioned towards the keyboard to fill the quiet.

The eyes lost none of their wildness. The man stared and Peter looked away.

"You are a musician?" he asked at last.

Peter said yes, he was. The man took a step back, swept his hand toward the bench, indicating Peter should sit.

"Oh, no. No, I won't play. But I wanted you to know how moved I was by the concert."

The man sniffled, looked down. "It is madness to care so much about music," he said. He was a person you would avoid, whose neighboring seat on the bus would remain empty. There was a sour smell about him. "It does not change things."

Peter shrugged, turned out his palms. "Nevertheless," he said weakly. The man picked up loose scores, making to leave.

"I wonder," Peter said, holding out the program. The man shrank, eyed the paper.

"I wonder if you could translate for me. The liner notes. I don't read Hungarian."

The man regarded Peter carefully. It could not have been an imposition, for the text was no more than a single paragraph. He took the program from Peter, read the words silently, preparing himself for the effort of translation.

He took a breath. "'Dietrich Buxtehude 1637-1707 was born in Hlasingborg, Sweden. For many years he held the post of organist at St. Mary's in Lübeck, where he gained fame as a composer of works for the keyboard. As a young man, Bach is said to have traveled two hundred miles to hear his work. Buxtehude remains important for his chorale preludes, and the use of polyphony in fugal types. He wrote of his music that it was an attempt to reconcile the godly and the satanic.'"

The organist handed the program to Peter, pinching it between thumb and forefinger. His displeasure was palpable. Peter thanked him and walked out.

The next day, Peter sat over coffee in the otherwise empty lounge of the Gellêrt reading a Buxtehude score he had purchased in town. He was humming the top fugal line. This was music he might play. One would need a certain strength, it was so forlorn. He looked up to speak to the waiter standing by his table, to ask for a fresh pot. The waiter was not there. Kulek was.

Peter had forgotten the man's size. Not five feet. He stood, slumped, as if waiting for his measure to be taken. He held his copy of the *Krokodile* rolled in his hand, it was a stick to beat back the wolves. He wore a leather outercoat, under it a grey suit from some other era, a dress shirt with no tie. The shirt hung loose around the neck. Peter indicated the chair, but Kulek had not decided to stay.

"What did my friend tell you?"

"Your friend?"

"Dösza. The organist. You quizzed him after the concert."

"You were there?" Kulek said nothing. "He told me about Buxtehude. The composer. His dates, what he wrote. You were there and you didn't speak?"

"What do you want?" asked Kulek peevishly. "Why are you having advertisements for me?"

Peter resolved not to lose the momentum. Outrage was to be his, not his opponent's.

"Now, listen. I sat here for three hours while you told me pretty stories. I traveled halfway to nowhere to find out about the *Artemis* and discover that Von Egger is a fraud, that his award from Israel, his biography are all set-ups. You never said one damned word. What I want is the truth." He regretted his last words as melodramatic, but they were out.

Kulek stood unmoving. "You travel across Europe and I travel across the city. Whose journey is further? My words come back and chase me out of my apartment, threats from the bullies I have known all my life."

"What are you talking about? No one can be threatening you. This was fifty years ago. I just want to know the truth, and you haven't given it to me."

A glint of scorn flashed from under Kulek's puffy eyelids. "The truth. A fool throws a pebble into the sea, but a thousand wise men cannot pull it out. A search for truth, only a young man would be so impertinent. Young and American. Make no more advertisements in the newspapers, my young American. I am through giving testimony. I am not on trial."

He turned to go. Peter pulled the photograph from its envelope and called after him. "It's a good thing. This would be exhibit A."

Kulek stopped, walked back. Took the print from Peter's hand.

He uttered a word in Hungarian. It might have been a curse. "The garden at Gündel's," he said. "You know, I went there once in my life. Marx was right about consorting with capitalists."

"You were consorting? It looks more like dinner. And a nice vintage to go with it."

Kulek put his newspaper on the table. Its ink had smudged where he had gripped it. He sat down.

"You too?" he asked. His brow dimpled slightly. "You are going to turn my past against me?" Kulek's lower lip had a slight and permanent swell in its corner. Where the cigarette wedged. It gave the side of his face a crooked and bogus smirk.

"I don't care about your past. I want to find out what my grandfather and you were doing with Von Egger in this picture. Why you told me a pack of lies. Why there were over ten thousand accounts opened with their names as representing the bank."

"One question at a time," Kulek said. "I told you no lies. I told you what happened. I have not told you all that happened, and I cannot. History is selective.

"That man you are pointing to is not your grandfather. Whoever typed this on the photograph is in error. It is your grandfather's brother. The agent Buxtehude. They resembled each other greatly. Indeed, clean-shaven you could be Hermann's grandchild."

Kulek had somehow ensnared the table cloth in his topcoat, and when he reached behind to remove it Peter's coffee splashed about. The waiter arrived in seconds to remove the soiled cloth, spread a fresh one, bring a full pot and two cups and saucers.

"You should order something else," Kulek said when the man was done. "He cannot live on the price of two coffees. He is supporting a family." His overcoat hung over the chair.

"I will," said Peter. "I will. He's been taking care of me every morning this week. While I waited for you."

"And when you pay your bill, not to sign for the tip. They hold that back, make the waiters beg for that money. Leave the tip in cash. American dollars if you have them."

Peter nodded.

Kulek appeared satisfied. He pulled at his shirt cuffs, folded his tiny hands in front of him. He might have been primping as a guest on a talk show, an incongruent posture given his appearance, careless, almost mendicant. That morning's shave, whether it was haste or inattention, had left patches of grey high on his cheek. The shirt, the color of mocha, had been worn thin by laundering. He thought for a moment, his eyes on the glossy print before him, and resumed the monotone that so compelled Peter that first time they had met.

All truth, if anyone can gauge truth. Hermann Steinmuller was my dear friend. What occurred later I am not proud of. But I will tell you, and then you will go away. I have no need for you in my life.

The *Artemis* was of course a disaster. Everyone lost at sea. The money lost, too. Even with his brother at the bottom of the sea, Pietr Steinmuller was not discouraged. He had made an investment. That sacrament of capitalism. This ship was to have collected fees for passage. For its price Pietr discovered a market for services he could provide.

To do the financing of the *Artemis*, Pietr had dispatched to Budapest his apprentice. A young aristocrat named Frederich Von Egger. You ask if I knew him. I met him several times. His ties were always knotted just so, he wore his arrogance sharp on the points of his pocket kerchief.

On this first trip he took us to Gündel's for an elegant dinner. The irony was thicker than the stew. We were negotiating passage for immigrants who had not the price of a turnip, and this hawk-faced imperial interrogated the waiter about a certain vintage. A bottle of wine that would have bought the freedom for three, four persons. We drank it. And then another.

There was a price on everything, a Tunisian visa, a ticket to Trieste, a passport in your own name without the stamp of the red J. Most in demand was a way to place sums in foreign banks. To enter England one needed to deposit a hundred pounds there. In all countries conquered by the Reich, Hungary too, it was treason to send capital out of the country. But the death penalty awaited these people anyway. *How* did one move money?, that was the issue.

In Zurich Pietr Steinmuller realized that his brother had created an entrepreneur's dream. His brother's acquaintances represented a sales force for the very service his bank could offer. He sent Von Egger the first time to propose to Hermann that they work together. Hermann would disclose the names of the organizations he worked with Bthey were, you understand, not listed in the telephone directory, just as I now will not be listed for people like you to call me outB and for those organizations, the Löwenhoft would render services.

These people needed help. And hope. I convinced Hermann. What difference that there may be a profit for their bank. Von Egger could not bear us. You have met him — imagine how he regarded our tatters and peasant manners. No less the hordes we were serving. To Von Egger it was a commodity. What difference, I said. We even consulted several refugee organizations. They studied in turn. These are civilized people. Before they save themselves their rabbis study. They concluded their Talmud permits ransom. It is a dirty business, but it is permitted.

Hermann was opposed. He argued that many of these people who are sending their little cache out of the country will never live to call for it. They are disappearing in Poland, in Austria, in Slovakia. Why not in Hungary? I said that was ridiculous. It is 1942. Hungary is not without its anti-Semitism, but the government will protect its people.

He declined Von Egger. Hermann said he didn't want his brother and Von Egger horning in. There would be no controlling them. Then he sailed on the *Artemis*.

After his death I was in charge. Our little organization was in pieces. What moneys Hermann and I had went down with the ship. Hermann's wife was expecting a child. She lived simply in Switzerland, her father was a minister and she lived with him while her husband was away. Hermann left them nothing.

It was for me to decide. Days after the sinking Von Egger appeared in Budapest. Like the devil to Faust. Yes, the sinking had been a tragedy, yes yes, it was sad about all those people, but what about the network? Isn't this a good time to consolidate? Could not Pietr Steinmuller and the bank help in the consolidation? Together we would be able to do some real good.

I hesitated. On the one hand, one must be pragmatic. On the other, Hermann had such strong feelings. Yet I was angry with him for dying on that ship. I could disobey his wishes, show him.

It turned out not to matter. I cannot tell you why, but I never had to decide. Without my intercession, they soon had everything. Names, telephones where they existed, who could find who. They must have broken through from the Swiss end.

So what happened? Hitler summoned our president, Horthy, to Schloss Klessheim for a meeting. The silly fellow was flattered and bragged to the newsreels about it. When he arrived he was locked up. In two days, Germany occupied Hungary. And by then, Von Egger had a dozen active contacts in Eastern Europe. People were sending moneys through him. Pitiful sums for the most part, ten, fifty Swiss francs. Sometimes a larger amount. The depositor would receive a bank statement, often signed by Von Egger or Steinmuller himself, acknowledging the receipt and stating the number. If they found that paper you could hang, so you memorized the account number and destroyed the paper.

They used printed forms. Some I notarized, that is how you traced me. In Hungarian, Rumanian, Yiddish. My landlord moved his pitiful savings to the Lowenhoft. He told only me.

You know how the story ends? Perhaps not. The occupation of Hungary by the Nazis began with an announcement that Hungary was to be treated no differently from any other inferior satellite. All her bending over so the Reich could bugger her would count for nothing. The Composers' Circle was so busy we could not close it down. It was channeling refugee and Reichstag dollar alike, for even party members were having second thoughts about who would win the war. You know? I will spare you. It is ancient history, horrors you have heard too often. The first time unspeakable. The second unspeakable, but also lurid. You understand me? Exciting.

Kulek raised his arm, fist clenched, to signify a lingam. He shook it at Peter, and to avoid misunderstanding, clamped his left palm onto his biceps. The slap brought looks from the few occupied tables. Kulek paid them no mind. In the center of his face burned a cigarette. He took it out and screwed it into the ashtray.

But the excitement dies. By the tenth time, you do not care. It is an exaggeration, it must be. Perhaps even a counterfeit. Perhaps it never happened. Perhaps, perhaps.

No, simply true. You said you wanted truth. You have probably changed your mind. Most people change their minds after a taste. They prefer falsehood.

The bank accounts that we helped gather the way you might gather bait fish in a shallow of the lake, then scoop them out with your hat, those accounts would sit and no one would come for them. As Hermann had predicted.

After Pietr died in a car crash, Von Egger took his place. He was offered shares in the Löwenhoft. How could they refuse him? He and Pietr had created a most profitable business. Give me your money, and for a small fee I'll give it back when you call. Oh yes, if you neglect to call because you have gone up in smoke like the Witch of the Forest, I will simply keep the money. That is a profitable business.

Then the diplomats. The Soviet press had a wonderful time, photographs of these earnest ministers discussing over the new asparagus whether gold teeth melted down in Poland should benefit Poles or Jews. Maybe a little for castrated priests, women from the experiments. Or perhaps build a statue. Yes, I think that's better, let's build a statue.

I need not exaggerate. Time stands on the side of the banks, I follow the story. The Communist press was as unreliable, as treacherous as its government, but it reports the foibles of the West in detail. And what happens to Kulek? That little man with the dirty mouth? He is in jail, out of jail, back in. He is imprisoned for his part in the 1954 Revolution, what they call the riots. It is a fucking joke.

The day he is released he starts a weekly mimeograph, to encourage the partisans. Another prison term. He scours newspapers for stories. He finds on a back page a story that Israel has asked for compliance with this agreement signed in Paris. This is the Sixties, you understand, this is a story of surprise and revelation, and it comes every ten years. We want to forget, so each time we are surprised. The Swiss appoint a commission to respond headed by Frederich Von Egger. Kulek writes about Von Egger's past. No one cares. Nothing happens.

Years go by. In the Seventies, under international pressure, a law is passed and Von Egger's commission agree to disclose all bank accounts of persecuted persons. I forgot to mention that although compliance with this law was mandatory, determining the accounts was up to the banks. Mr. Banker, if you have monies you do not want, please let us know, we will pick it up, the United States would like us to pick it up. And they will send it on, to buy clothing and soap for those smelly people who left here, you may remember, some decades ago. Good riddance to them. After a thorough investigation only a few accounts are found. Fewer than a thousand. So, you see, there was no need for concern. Refugees had not sought to squirrel their savings away, they had not been in danger. They likely had not even perished.

The story returns in the Nineties, the one you are familiar with. A U.S. industrialist, public outrage, this time the Swiss government means business. New work is done, accounts found. The matter is put to rest. Have they found all the accounts? What do you think, my friend? Have a few francs slipped through their net in the fifty years? A few million francs?

Kulek sat back. His body dragged the hands, dully crossed in front of him, to his lap, and just as it appeared he might nap, revived.

"Were the Steinmullers Jews?"

"Of course. You do not know? Their mother was. She raised them in the faith, although they had no interest. Later, when he joined with us, Hermann came back to it. He sewed the star on all his clothing. Pietr went the other way. Denied who he was, passed anti-Semitic remarks. It enraged Hermann. Once I heard him on the telephone, arguing with his brother. 'You and I have only one thing in common,' Hermann told him. 'We are both ashamed that you are a Jew.'"

"Yet he married a Christian?"

"Hermann was an artist. He married for love."

"And what became of her, and the baby?"

Kulek raised his shoulders. "I was not a tourist at the time. I traveled rarely to ski at Garmisch. I took my holidays in a Budapest cell."

"What did you know of her?"

"Only that Hermann loved her. He was not in it for chances, but for justice. They lived in a small town, near Zurich. I do not think I ever heard her name."

"The name of the town?" Again the raised shoulders. Kulek sat silently for a minute.

"Wadenswil," he said.

"What?"

"Wadenswil. Where they lived. Up the lake from Zurich."

"You are certain?"

Kulek stood up. Whatever vitality had been in his face had seeped out in the story, in the effort. "Mr. American, you are very young. You ask too much. First you want truth, now you want certainty. These are words I have put behind me. Sit in this seat for seventy-two years and see if you still use those words."

He took the cracked leather coat from the shoulders of the chair and slipped it on. Then he catalogued his cigarette packs, matches, stuffed the rolled newspaper in his outer pocket.

He shook a stubby finger at Peter. "Leave a nice tip. This man has one customer all morning."

Peter nodded. Kulek was strapping his belt through its cheap plastic buckle. He cinched it further, the next hole. It squeezed from him another burst of energy.

"Do not think, my friend, that you have won." Reproach charged his voice. He stepped closer as if he might strike. Peter looked in wonder. "Do not think, just because the corrupt system the Communists built over the years has collapsed, that you have won. This is not some football match, where it is resolved by a single goal in the overtime. All that dancing on the Berlin Wall. Your system continues to permit hatred and poverty and despair. Disregard them at your peril."

He turned and walked out.

It would be his last date, he told Marcus. He could sit in no more. He'd be leaving Budapest tomorrow. Perhaps Marcus would regroup in Zurich, was there any action in Zurich?

"Zurich is closed down, man. Unless you do marches. Hey," he remembered. "Zurich is Switzerland. They looking for you there?'

Peter shrugged.

"Watch yourself, man. You're on the most wanted list."

"No problem," said Peter. "Besides, it's nice to be wanted."

Back in the Gellêrt Peter sits at the kneehole desk and looks out at the river. The red light of the hotel sign burns just beneath the sill and tints the droplets on the glass. Hard to tell whether it was raining, but if you took a walk you were wet.

He asked her in Israel what he could give her as a present, once he was back in the money, and she said a letter. "In ink. That will pay the loan. And for interest, write me a song."

The words on the page are tactile, as if engraved and raised from vellum paper. He runs his fingers across the lines. Sometimes he'd show up for a job and the piano would have ivory keys. Like skin, like a woman's skin, the long curve of the back, the hollow above the hips. By four in the morning he has several pages front and back. The entire story. Writing it down has weakened him. He pushes up the window and looks at the wide boulevard below. "I'm through with this," his letter begins. "In the morning I'll fly to New York. I don't want debtor's prison in Zurich and I need to earn a living. As for this search, it's over. I wash my hands of it." The process has somehow freed him, the words have released him. Outside three cars sound their horns, talking to each other.

He rules off a musical staff and curls in the G clef. Wishes for a piano. It is an old wish. The child climbs onto his mother's piano bench. There the magical keyboard that charms his mother so. He knows that if you rock back and forth and press down, it makes music. He smacks the keys and ugly sounds come out. His mother slaps his hand. No pounding. There is some other way. He watches. The black keys are skinny and hard to hit. He avoids them. One day it comes to him — the black and white keys are built the way the hand is. His mother shows him scales. You can get the same sound starting anywhere on the board. But not quite the same, certain keys have their own flavor. He likes E-flat, the scale makes sense, the hand rolls around its changes.

Peter sits in this dark corner of a country knowing no one and it still works. He folds the music around him. Where do the notes come from, where are they housed? Tunes flit in the mind the way radio waves flit in the atmosphere.

He has written down the three notes of the car horns, unremarkable in themselves, but over a minor seventh chord unusual, reaching. They dangle in the lines of the staff. The three notes are the first word, and the second follows illogically, inevitably. Now a second word has extended the path of the first and is snared as well. Simplicity, two words that make a single phrase. Rhythms come with the idea, are the idea. The two words suggest the system. Next the structure, a recursion, a winding inward on the first words. The harmonics can be implied or they can surprise. Better if they surprise. Better to push away from equilibrium. Don't jump back — confront change, stretch for mystery. In the last moment, there is only the ear, what works.

Now Peter lies down, still clothed, on the bed covers. On the ceiling the hotel sign pops its glow. That is his last view, the intermittent color scarlet, and he sleeps without a dream.

12

IF YOU PLEASE MAKE reservations in advance, the hotel clerk scolded him, you would save money. Budapest, Frankfort, change at Gatwick, non-stop JFK. The man covered the telephone mouthpiece to keep this confidence from the airline. Peter mumbled something about urgency. He was thinking on his words, washing his hands. *Mozom kezeim.* What choice did he have? He had no weapon, no stone he could throw through Von Egger's window.

The clerk gave him an oversized envelope and he wrote out Helene's address and put in his letter, no salutation or date. Pasted on five stamps, engravings of mustachioed men from Hungary's past. The clerk dropped the envelope into a wire basket behind the desk.

Peter called from a house phone. Helene was out, job-hunting he guessed. To her usual taped message had been added a single sentence.

"Passengers arriving from Budapest should check in with the concierge."

She would have left a key for him. The prospect stirred him. She struck no obstacles to his coming or going, she accepted these rogue emotions as though she were a rooming house for them. This woman had not merely gambled her job for him, she'd lost the bet.

Peter's chest tightened, a foreign and unpleasant feeling. He'd been holding Helene at arm's length in his usual style. He looked at the wire mail basket, leaned over the counter and retrieved his letter. Tore open the seal, stuck the pages into his satchel, and tossed the empty envelope onto the counter.

"Sorry," Peter murmured. As the cabbie arrived to take him to the airport, the clerk was clipping free the uncancelled stamps.

He had his choice of several direct flights to Zurich and was pleased to find no penalty for switching from his New York flight. The pleasure didn't diminish his anxiety — he still had to face Immigration when he landed in Zurich.

He picked his inspector carefully and waited on a long line. The post-adolescent boy looked new, the checkerboard cap misplaced on his egg-shaped head. "Your purpose here in Switzerland?" The boy looked through Peter's passport — perhaps he'd been the wrong choice.

"Tourist. I'm a tourist." The lad stared at Peter's eyes with what the manual must suggest as a piercing look.

"Can you please open your bag." Peter complied. The inspector rummaged through, caught on the loose sheets of paper with scribbled tunes and chords.

"You are a musician?" He checked back at the passport. Peter, dry-mouthed, nodded.

"What instrument?"

"Keyboard."

"Ah," the lad said and pointed to his own chest. "Billy Joel, the Boss, rock and roll."

Peter held up a clenched fist. The magnetic catch on the gate opened and Peter passed through.

Helene appeared behind armfuls of brown sacks. Lovely stuff, green stalks, cream, fresh-cut flowers. She proposed to cook veal. To which, she said with a sly look, she objected politically, but was prepared to compromise just this once in the interest of pleasure. She wore a mannish blazer over a white blouse, black flannel skirt and the usual white stockings. She had been interviewing.

They stored the groceries, and she changed, a silk robe with small yellow roses. He sat on a stool by the kitchen range chopping and slicing at her instruction and telling of his discoveries. Of his newfound roots, "What do you say to that?"

"I don't know," and she shrugged, watching butter brown in a sauce pan. "*Mazel tov?*"

She pounded and rolled the thinly cut meat. The recipe was her great-grandmother's, she told him, a notorious witch of the turn of the century, and this veal was a proven aphrodisiac.

"That's what your witches do? What happened to boys into gingerbread?"

She was stirring wine over a blue gas flame, dissolving in the liquor tiny balls of flour, butter, and spice.

"The Swiss have many magic people. *Nixes* live under water and look like humans. Except they are fish from the waist down. The women dress up and go to market, but you can always recognize them because they are wet from the lakes. *Kobolds* are goblins and

Hinzelmännchen are good sprites. They do housework, sing songs you teach them."

"Do they cook veal scallopini?" He walked to her at the stove and caught her at the top of her hips.

"They do. They cook elegant food that no one can resist and they use their wiles — that is right? wiles? — to entrap young boys from the country." He put his nose in her hair and breathed in. "But not for gingerbread."

"I'm glad I have one of those witches." He pressed against her and moved his hands up the smooth robe to her breasts.

She sniffed the steam. "That, my young boy from the country, can wait. Veal and this wonderful Eppess I have opened cannot."

He moved off. Her pose was delicious, a flavor of the meal. Her availability, the timing of it. Timing in music, as in love, promised inevitability. He poured the wine and they sat down to dine.

She told him of her job search. A private investment fund in London had offered her a position. They delighted in her account of why she'd been fired, they were looking for someone with the very initiative she described. Rooting out forbidden information — as it happened, that was precisely the job. Quite a high salary, she told him the amount. What did Peter think?

He was surprised to be asked. "I've never been to London," he said without thinking. "It's supposed to be a great town." He knew no one who made that kind of money, not even Matey.

"It has a large jazz community."

"Does it?" he asked. It wasn't really a question, more of a convention, but not one that Helene played. "Yes," she said brightly and caught his eye. "Yes it does."

After dinner he fetched the letter. "I wrote this out," he said, then, taking a beat, "for my banker." She read intently. The opening passage, the clumsy thanks. Smiled when she came to the few bars of score at the end.

"Will you sing this for me?"

"It's more to play. The sense of it is in the harmony. I'll play it for you."

She nodded, please. "So the puzzle is solved. You have changed your mind and come to say goodbye in person, but you have come through the maze." She took a sip of wine.

"Helene, you know what I would like to do? I would like to visit Wadenswil. I can't tell you why, but it's where Hermann Steinmuller lived, where his widow lived. Maybe there's some trace."

"Yes of course. I have seen it on the autobahn signs. It is a little town, no more than forty kilometers. We will drive there tomorrow."

The London invitation, or rather Peter's discomfort with it, had perceptibly altered the mood. They spoke of their outing but the thought of the future, tentative and oblique, distracted him.

"Listen," he said as they loaded the dishwasher and poured the last of the wine. "About London."

She came and leaned against him. Stuck a finger in his glass, painted a stripe of wine on his cheek and licked it off. "I like this new look. The young ingenue, without the beard," she said. "I think I prefer this. London can wait."

She led him into her darkened room and seated him on the bed. The only light came from the glass of the window, the moving headlights of cars in the cold, street lamps reflecting asphalt. One by one she lit candles she had brought home this afternoon, candles in glasses, in hurricane lamps, in cut crystal holders. There must have been fifty, a hundred. The first, a plain white taper, she lit from a stick match that fizzed to break the dark. Then it was quiet, and she used the flamed taper to light the other candles in silence. Peter knew about silence, even had a vocabulary for expressing its lengths. Tension and release. But that was the silence around sound, as space is to sculpture, as whiteness to words. This night Helene molded the silence to set off their separation, silence that decorated not music but their *legato* touch.

Done with her lamping, she blew out the torching wick and laid it on the night table. Wax dripped and congealed in medallions. It gave off a thick, bodily scent. She kneeled across his lap and began to unbutton his shirt. He sat perfectly still, smelling her throat, her hair, the silk of the robe. He heard his breathing, the secrets of cloth, a hundred flames gulping air. The quietest notes. He was conspicuous, uncovered by the lack of sound. Conspicuous his need. He ached with the weight of his desire, and though he could not guess it, with the marbled density of his thoughts. It was only as he swarmed over her, as he buried himself deep within her, presence and consciousness, buried alive, he came to know that his act was one not of love but of aloneness.

They lay damp and spent. What is carried out on the tide of passion? In his humors was gritty and insoluble matter that did not dissolve or wash, it turned like sand in the tide but remained. Accumulating in long and shifting undersea banks. He awoke after love chilled and angry, unable to give a reason for his waking, unable to know what his anger forebode.

Wadenswil was an easy drive. The sun darted behind the dissipating nacre of a late winter sky. It might turn out to be a day of spring promise. They started after breakfast. Helene talked of the life she would have if she took this job. A steamer plied the lake as they drove, a harbinger more reliable than migratory birds that the earth was turning the quarter pole to spring, closing on its course.

The town was unexceptional. Brightly painted houses lined the streets, grocers filled their windows with produce, everywhere order and good sense. They stopped for a loaf of fresh-baked pear bread to bring home.

The Michelin Guide listed the town's church as the only point of interest. Helene translated from the book as they roamed its interior. It was an architectural disappointment, an Eighteenth Century building of the Reformation. God was to be housed sensibly, and the decoration was intended to remind Him and His visitors of sensible values, industry, sobriety, the transience of the flesh. Outside and to the rear was a small graveyard, and they wandered through its gate and among the tidy squares. Since the fixed acreage could not possibly serve a renewing population, it was stacked, with an instinctual economy, several levels deep.

Peter was reading off names and dates from the markers. In the Calvinist tradition, there was none of the sentiment that made other cemeteries so quaint. He had only just made this observation when Helene called to him.

He walked to her side. She opened her hand to the simple white stone marker, no larger than a brick, that was set flush to the ground at her feet. Before the grass had gone dormant for the winter, it had been trimmed to a neat margin, and the marker's face stood a crisp half-inch above the surface of the lawn. The stone read "Steinmuller *Kleinkind*. 27.11.45." The Steinmuller Infant.

For an hour it looked as though they would get no further answers. There was no one inside the church. The elderly woman at the adjacent parish house first determined not to understand Helene. At last she conceded that there were records but she was not authorized to show them. The sexton was needed. He was at work and could not be bothered. She didn't know where he worked, and when she remembered, she insisted the railway station could not be reached by telephone.

The sexton turned out to be a counterweight to the woman's stubbornness. He was, he told Helene, just taking a late lunch hour and would cycle up. They realized when he arrived that he was the old woman's spouse. He wore a heavy loden sweater and a knit cap, carried an unlit pipe in his mouth. He took them into the parish house, led them through a porch filled with air plants that he spoke to as he passed, and into a rear study. There shelves held ledger books containing entries for the church events. They browsed the book spines. The sexton stood happily, one hand folded behind his back, regularly tapping his spine. It was, Peter thought, an old man's pose. They found the page for the date marked on the stone.

"It has no new information," Helene said, tracing the line with her finger. Peter looked over her shoulder. By now, two months in Switzerland and Hungary, he had an exiguous German vocabulary. He pointed to the first word, which he did not know, and Helene gave it to him. Then he read the entry aloud.

"'Funeral service for the child of Marta Steinmuller of Ettingen, 27th November 1945.' Helene, that *is* new. My grandmother's name is Marta. The one in Florida? She was married to Pietr, not Hermann."

"Is it possible they both had wives with the same name?"

Peter held Helene tightly by the arm. First the gravestone, now looking down at this entry, set him to a vertiginous rocking. He yawed on the balls of his feet. Was Helene's explanation feasible?

Helene repeated her question. "These are not uncommon, Marta. That is the explanation."

Helene asked if there might be more, if there might be someone in town who remembered the event, but the man apologized and said no. He and his wife had held this post since moving here thirty years ago.

"The old sexton?" Peter asked. The man had a little English, seemed to understand. The man nodded encouragement.

Peter asked again, this time putting hope in his voice.

"The old sexton? Still alive?"

"No, no," he said sympathetically, took the pipe from his mouth. "Still dead."

Drag produced the void. A sense of falling into space blurred Peter's thoughts. Not falling into the earth but away from it, off its antipode. There were chunks of his life missing. Whether it was the effort to concentrate or some deeper problem, Peter fought a constriction in his gut. Facts were upside down. It was a puzzle, like his visit to Tel Aviv. The most modern of cities sat upon the most ancient of days. Which information did one choose? Does one use the past to explain the present, or is it the other way around?

He fought off dizziness as a dancer might in a spin — he concentrated on a single point. His father's funeral. Not in Wadenswil, Switzerland, but in the Housatonic Valley of Connecticut. It happened there, he saw a five-year old boy, in a cap and jacket, grey challis wool, the collar scratchy against his neck. No tears, he knows he did not cry, though he thought he should. It's all right to cry, the preacher had said. Peter meant to, but he didn't know how. He saw the empty church — was there truly no one there but his mother, his grandmother and himself? — heard the peremptory words and the thump of dirt on wood. He had stood in the wind of a false spring, his eyes so dry it hurt to blink. He saw the bare limbs of trees against the feather-grey sky. His eyes stung in the dry air.

"Peter," Helene spoke tentatively. It was not a characteristic voice. "I must ask you something. Why does all this matter? What your grandfather did, what his brother did. Who is buried where. What does all this matter?"

He had no answer. She pressed him. "Tell me whatever comes to your head."

"I need to know about my family. It is a question of blood. Who your family is, that's who you are."

Helene accepted his words.

They had neglected lunch and took an early dinner. He was morose, he said, and apologized for the funk. She needed no explanations. They chose a humble place, neither of them wanting to change from jeans. The waiter showed them a long wine card. Helene ordered a bottle. It disappeared quickly and they drank a second. Their moods seemed ever to be reflected over their meals, and tonight they moved quickly into a brooding drunk. Was the wine good? No one commented. They reached separately for the bottle, neglecting to pour the other's glass. "The last day of winter," Helene said. "Tomorrow is the equinox."

Peter looked stupidly at her. He had a disquieting moment when he could not remember her name. What was his scheme for Von Egger? His mind held nothing. Somewhere he'd seen a wooden bucket with all the staves shrunk so water poured from every seam. He was in a sauna, streams of water leaked over the stones. Torpor took the place of talk. Someone paid the bill and he leaned on her as they went down narrow stairs. They might have been strangers. Helene was helping him into the car. He was arguing. She let him go on.

They steered each other to her apartment. Peter sat in a club chair with a rough weave covering its arms, wishing he weren't drunk. A television set played. The corners of the room began to bank and dive. A grey towel twisted in his gut and wrung out soapy water. He was on the floor, leaning on the toilet. He pulled himself over and vomited up the meal. Wine was still in his blood.

He awoke in the middle of the night. Anxiety was pressing its steam iron on his brow, the hiss matched the whisper of breath through his nostrils. He was nude, erect, tense. She lay beside him. Her nightgown had ridden up to her thighs. In the night words were not needed. Words and stories, Helene had told him, mark us as human. Here in the night words served no function, they were parts of machinery that had long been discarded, had rusted out. Her breath made a slight noise. The kiss of an old record, a constant revolving whisper. He pushed against her shoulder and she slept on. He took her sleep as insouciance, as unconcern. He began to kiss at her flesh as an animal might, before it bit. There was no kindness to his love-making, and when she woke, it was in alarm, sensing his anger.

She moved to hold him. She spoke his name, and its sound brought him to the edge of awareness. Helene moved to meet him in the act, and her presence saved him. He clung to her and she pulled him along, she was the fish and she reeled in the fisherman, out of the razor-sharp air, off his legged stance, ungainly and unwet, into her world of water, her world of sleek and transporting time. No matter how desperate he was, how inclement and harsh his actions, they were with her transformed.

Afterwards he lingered on top of her, dead as meat. He rose to find the bathroom. It was dark, the door to the bedroom opened in and was ajar. Peter walked squarely into its edge and was knocked down. He saw a quick flash of white, and crumpled to the ground like a movie extra. For a second — longer? he could not tell — he lay unconscious.

Grey light came to him: his hand was held to the welt on his forehead, pushing down the pain. And he began to weep. He had not cried, he could not say, since a schoolyard ground ball had leapt up and struck him in the face. Now there were no classmates, no one to see, there was no reason to stop. He sat naked on the floor and wept, his lungs heaved in regular beats. She came to sit beside him. Still he wept, salt having started from his body would not stay, left in every flow, semen, sweat, tears.

HE WOKE BEFORE HELENE and prepared a large breakfast. She finally appeared, in her robe of the yellow roses. She had brushed her hair and wore a touch of incarnadine lipstick. He went over to her.

"It was either breakfast or a leap from the balcony. I am very ashamed and I apologize."

She pursed her lips. Brought him close. She looked to the swelling over the brow, placed on it the tips of her fingers still cool from the morning. The bruise within and the bruise visible, heat to heat.

"You should stay on beer," she said.

A tangible relief ran down his neck. His hangover crept like dust into small points, the eyelids, the coating of his teeth. "There is no need to apologize." Her words relieved him.

"Listen, I may be breaking up. Last night, I felt as though my rib cage might fall apart."

"That's good. You are simply feeling the flesh and blood, not so much the mannequin."

He nodded, to let her know that he would consider this wisdom. He was thinking about the pain in his head. Butter browned in a pan. She kissed him lightly on his chin. The squeak of her lips made him wince. She went to the stove and poured the bowl of beaten eggs into the skillet.

After the washing up, they decided on a day in the country.

"Have you thought any more about yesterday?" she asked. The first day of spring held promise not of warmth but of its possibility. She was taking him to a mountain tarn south of the city for a picnic. Again she drove.

In the car he closed his eyes, saw the stone marker. The nausea of the previous night welled in the back of his throat — perhaps he was still a little drunk. If the father dies as an infant, there is no son. Being and nothingness. If there is no son, there is no me to contemplate an answer. That may be why no answer appears. It was another puzzle, another Escher drawing where the figures migrate from positive to negative, substance to shadow. How can you have a maze with no exit? He opened his eyes as they came over a steep hill and the vertigo began.

Helene sensed his discomfort. She had been speeding and as the car crested the peak of the hill, it gave the sensation of leaving the highway. She braked. Behind them a close-following motorist honked, pulled out and flamed his Mercedes sedan past them.

The sound of the horn settled in Peter's ear, shivered the canals of balance. The horizon settled. The spin stopped.

"Why Ettingen?" he asked her.

She looked at him, not comprehending.

"In the church records," he explained. "It said, Marta Steinmuller of Ettingen. Why not Marta Steinmuller of Wadenswil?"

"Ah," she said. She was driving, her grey eyes fixed ahead. Peter could see the stripes on the asphalt blink in the windscreen.

"The northern Swiss are traditional. Ettingen would be the town of her birth. That is how she would be identified, no matter where she later lived or was buried."

"She might still be alive. Pietr's Marta is, she lives in Florida. Should we go to Ettingen?"

"We can. It's not far."

Peter was quiet another moment. "Ettingen. Why is that name familiar to me? Have we passed it?"

"No. It is a town to the west. By Basle."

Did I pass it on the Ducati? Pay attention. Hang around B flat, leave your hands in the right place, and the missing chords appear. The missing bridge plays itself.

"You asked me about it once before," Helene said, and it came to him. "Shall we go there? It's a two hour drive, I would guess."

"Home," said Peter. "Let's go home."

He zipped open his duffel and dumped its contents. Socks, the photograph of three young men in the Budapest restaurant, underwear, loose sheaves of staff paper, the slip Gideon had given him with telephone numbers, the shipboard letter from Matey. An interesting archeology. Helene's eyes touched on the feminine scroll on Matey's envelope, the word Personal. You put pieces of paper in a shoe box, leave it out in the lightning, and boom: you create a whole new person.

At the bottom of the bag was the crumpled fax copy from the U.S. State Department, responding to Peter's request to identify himself..

APPLICATION
BUREAU OF NATURALIZATION AND IMMIGRATION
NON-RESIDENT ALIEN

NAME: Marta Steinmuller
COUNTRY OF ORIGIN: Switzerland
Sex: F   DOB (m/d/y): 9/07/23
Marital status: D   Maiden name: Borsen
Place of birth: Ettingen, Canton of Basle

He smoothed out the paper, pushed it in front of Helene. Ettingen. That's where he'd seen it before.

They returned to the car. Helene knew a spot nearby, they could still salvage their picnic. There was nothing more to discover at the moment. A day in the freshening air would do him good, he agreed, and they walked out leaving the litter on the floor of the living room.

The Greifensee was a half-hour's drive, and they had to themselves a park overlooking the lake. They came back to the topic of their find. It was a wasp that buzzed them, could not be waved away.

"List the possibilities," said Helene. "That's what a good systems analyst would have us do. List all possibilities explaining the little white gravestone, and then we will use logic to decide which can be tested."

Peter began. "Two brothers, Pietr and Hermann, marry two women named Marta. Both from the same small town, Ettingen. Then there are two children. One immigrates with one Marta, a second gets buried in the Wadenswil cemetery."

"Or appears to."

"Or appears to. What happened to Hermann's Marta? Pietr's Marta tells the U.S. State Department she has two children, where's the other one? Is there only one Florian, and a bunch of stones in the grave?"

One Florian, Peter knows, someone had brought to the New World to begin the fragile line of American Steinmullers.

"It makes no sense."

Helene found an eyebrow pencil in her purse and drew a pattern of forks on the picnic napkin. In this chart the single answer sat on the left and bloomed into possibilities, meiosis halving each possibility and halving again into the next fork. They would force the circular riddle into a straight line.

"Let us go back to where we began," she said. "Not guess. Let us see whether there are facts we can find. The first — is the grave empty or not? Can we find that out?"

"Only by exhuming." She looked at him to explain.

"Dig up." Peter had a vision of a jumpy film, was it *Great Expectations*?, actors from the 'thirties in a dank London cemetery.

Helene dismissed that as impossible. "Exhume. Just like the Latin. *Ex humus*, out of the earth. We are not young enough to begin the procedures to exhume the grave." She had immediately adopted the word. "If we cannot exhume, we must answer the question another way."

Peter sensed he had held a clue in his hand, had absently put it down and now couldn't find it in the clutter. What did he need to remember? The undertaker, he suggested. The minister. Someone the sexton could identify. The newspaper account. Family of the deceased.

"Marta One had no family. Her husband Hermann died in 1943 when the ship went down."

"Pietr, my grandfather, would have been her brother-in-law. And her enemy."

"And we know Pietr died in 1946. Marta Two is your grand-mother in Florida."

"She's no help."

"There's Von Egger . . . ."

"And we have zero chance of getting to see him. Or even finding him. Didn't you tell me he had several houses and left Switzerland until the summer?"

The wind moved around to the north. They sat at a concrete table, pleasant in the calm, but as the air rose, scudding shadows slipped from the lake across their faces. Helene shivered, the day fled in the breeze.

They packed up and drove home. She had decided, she told him, to take the job in London. They wanted her there next week. It was time to begin closing up the flat, making arrangements. Peter listened. Should he give up this chase and follow Helene? There was no other lead. His grandmother hadn't talked to the family even before she turned senile. Perhaps by now she was gone. Still dead. When the tellers of tales die off, the tales change. He could be on a plane tomorrow.

Helene dropped him off. She had errands to run, needed to meet her landlord to negotiate an end to the lease. Her new firm had been generous about a moving allowance, she would use it to reach an amicable accord.

He put away the breakfast things, repacked the clothes from the floor and then sorted through the pieces of paper. Some, his guide pamphlets for Israel, a listing of Vienna rooms to let, he threw out. In his hand was the slip of graph paper on which Dr. Gideon had printed the names of cities and telephone numbers where he could be reached. Solid, in squared ink strokes that were unequivocal and black. Zurich, Budapest, Vienna. Gideon was a man who could be reached anywhere.

And it struck Peter at last.

The way the sexton held his hand, tapping behind his back. It was the posture of Dr. Gideon and the posture of the man at Von Egger's party who had commanded his host's ear that evening. The white hair, the crooked arm. Gideon was no coincidence.

He punched in the number so quickly he hit two keys at once. A close interval, sour and dissonant. He entered the sequence again, slowly. The woman who answered was professionally cheerful and alert.

"*Bonjour.*"

"*Bonjour.* Good day. I would like to speak with Dr. Gideon."

"Yes? Who is calling?"

"My name is Peter Steinmuller."

"I am sorry, Mr. Steinmuller. Dr. Gideon is not in today. May I convey a message."

"I need to see him. Is he in town? I'd like to meet with him today."

"I will convey the message, Mr. Steinmuller. You are in Zurich? You have a number where I can reach you?"

Peter gave the woman Helene's number. He would be here at least another day or two. It was very important to see him.

He hung up and turned on the television to watch news from Atlanta. He watched clips of revolution, Senate debate, economic resurgence. Should he have left that message with the secretary? Too callow, too energetic. The owlish Gideon might flee. Or worse.

His regrets were cut off by the ring of the telephone. It was the woman in Gideon's office. Dr. Gideon would meet him tomorrow at ten o'clock. She spoke slowly the numbers of an address which Peter knew to be in the financial district. Not far from Albert Frey. Yes, he would be able to find it.

Helene returned from her errands. He told her of the appointment over a light supper. Afterward Peter felt a great tiredness, went into bed and fell immediately to sleep.

It was midnight when she joined him. She slipped in beside him and quietly turned out her lamp. The gesture flooded him with tenderness, and he wanted to cover her with it. What is the weight of a body in free-fall? Weight has no dimension in a fall, it is measured at the stop. Or when you reached out and tried to grab on. He whispered to her. I have no energy. They lay holding on to each other. I can't move, he said. I have no muscles, no blood, only mass.

She spoke softly. In German we say you have *bettschwerre*. Germans think that a sin, indolence, but to the Swiss it is delicious. Bed heaviness, you are conscious but too heavy to leave the bed.

That is me, he said. You got it, lady. Too heavy to leave. Good word. You know some good words.

Good words, she said, are a present. I give you this word. After a minute, Peter was asleep.

Gideon's office was on the second floor of a renovated town house. Stones of an umber cast faced the street, a mansard roof, dark, cool hallways. The small reception room had no windows. Behind a single carved desk sat the woman Peter had spoken to yesterday. Her appearance, petite, complexion the colors of pressed flowers, matched her voice. She opened the door behind her and stood back for Peter to enter.

As if posing, the old man stood looking out at the window, holding his left arm behind his back. Its hand tapped absently. Proof positive, like a line-up. It was the photograph of the suspect Peter carried in his head.

Gideon turned. Peter could make out the spire of the Wasserkirche, where he had played scales, Gershwin. Perhaps later he would stop by.

"Peter," Gideon put a chime in his voice. "So. I'm glad you chose to look me up. Tell me what you have been about."

The room was lit only from the window, masking Gideon's expression in shadow. At his host's silent gesture, Peter sat in a leather side chair. He stared up at the silhouette.

"Do you mind," he asked, "if we close the drapes?"

Gideon made a broad, accommodating gesture. Peter walked around, let the stays fall from their hook. The room fell into darkness. As Peter walked back to seat himself, Gideon switched on two desk lamps.

"Better?"

Peter nodded. He could hear his pulse.

"Now, tell me of your adventures. When I saw you last you were off to Israel."

"I'm not here for that," Peter countered. His voice came out urgent. "I told you Helene's name at the hotel. That's what got her fired, isn't it?"

Gideon was immediate in his response. "Of course. That should not disappoint you, eh? We needed to learn who was entering our computer records. What she did is against the law. Once we knew we were obliged to put a stop to it. Only our regard for you has dissuaded us from pressing a criminal prosecution."

Peter sifted through the statement. Was it a warning? Was he being assured of the opposite? He was determined to look at last behind Gideon's words.

"And so all along, you have been working for the bank. For Von Egger."

"Not precisely. I am an advisor to the bank. I think I mentioned to you I have done some work in economics?"

"Philosophy, political science, economics, is what you told me. But I'm not sure what to believe."

"Peter." His tone chastised the younger man. Gone was the *gemutlichkeit* of the Viennese waiter. "You create your own labyrinth, eh?, and then complain when you find yourself trapped in it. You said you know the stories of Daedalus and Theseus?"

"More or less," Peter exaggerated.

"You might go back and read them. They are instructive. You strive to be both captive and captor. I assure you I told you nothing but the truth. Why would I not?"

Peter considered this. It was the same defense Kulek had raised. "But you never told me you were assigned to follow me."

Gideon lifted his face. "That would have been untrue. It was my idea, not that of Monsieur Von Egger, to travel along your route. I have no assignments. We thought you might need some guidance on your journey."

How to judge the old man's knowledge? Was he unaware that Peter had found out Von Egger's odious scheme? The likely source of Von Egger's fortune? His own grandfather's pivotal part in the drama?

"I found what I needed. My grandfather and Von Egger managed to secure thousands of accounts for their bank or for themselves, it doesn't matter. Moneys they got to keep. After a diplomatic wrestling match the banks won by default, the opposition simply got tired and went away. Even after some banks settled up, fortunes slipped through the cracks. I found that, and also that Von Egger's a fraud. That he secured himself an Israeli commendation so he could continue his masquerade as a citizen of the world."

"So. You've discovered a great deal. Then why were you eager to speak to me? At, I should add, risk to your personal freedom? Do not look surprised, you are still subject to arrest for debts, now that you are in the jurisdiction you would be quite easy to find."

Peter looked coolly across the space. He felt blinded by a kind of stage ignorance — he was in the spotlight and everyone else, those in the wings, those in the seats beyond the footlights, seemed to know the plot. The tragedy of Hamlet, Matey said, is not that he doesn't know he dies, but that he doesn't know the play ends. He had half-expected an apology, and Gideon had again disarmed him, this time by that most guileful tool of candor.

"I need to know about my family. About Hermann's widow and child, and how it is that Marta Steinmuller immigrated with a son named Florian after burying a son in Wadenswil."

Church bells struck at an interval of a fifth to mark the half hour. Through the heavy drapes they sounded far away. In the office a second set of chimes from a mantle clock went off as the distant ones finished.

Gideon studied him. "I cannot answer those personal questions. Why not tell me what you have discovered and perhaps I may recall some information that can help you."

"You cannot answer or you will not answer?"

"It makes little difference, since either way you must look else-where. But both are the case. I am not sure of the family history and, more, eh?, I am not authorized to discuss it with you."

"I thought you were not working for Von Egger."

"Steinmuller," Gideon's voice turned sharp and condescending, "do not quibble. I have offered to fill in the story you think you have found, but I have limits. Limits that I impose on myself, that emanate from a relationship I choose not to explain to you. You would not understand if I did. I've agreed to see you because we have shared a journey, because I like you, and because I am curious to see what you've made of your little deductions. But I do not have forever, and I have no intention of sitting here to receive your ill-considered, and I add, misdirected petulance."

The man is overreacting, I've touched a raw spot. Peter told Gideon what he and Helene had found and how they had done it. The batch and sort, the keyword searches, Kulek's confirmation of the scheme.

Gideon listened behind a steeple of fingers. Occasionally his eyes closed, but his fingertips continued to bounce in attention. At one point he removed a cigarette from a small silver case on his desk, offered the open box to Peter, and laid the single cigarette in front of him. When Peter was finished talking, he picked it up, tapped it on the red mahogany desk, and lit it with a stick match that flared to his eyebrows.

He dragged in a lungful of smoke and breathed out over Peter's head. The tobacco had a strong smell, not an unpleasant one, and Peter heard in the whistle of the exhaled smoke the old man's pleasure as the nicotine entered his bloodstream.

The cloud spent itself, and Gideon began to speak.

You have done a remarkable job of uncovering pieces of the puzzle in spite of no languages, no contacts, no training. You are to be commended, I am quite sincere.

But you must believe me as one who has studied history, eh? It is more like a skimpy paleantologic dig than the Rosetta Stone. Potsherds, do we share that word? bottle caps, pieces of flint. You cannot make a complete story on the basis of a few splinters of pottery.

You think you have heard the voice of history. But think again. You have spoken to humans. Humans with their petty foibles. Ishtvan Kulek too, he has his motives.

You are about to ask how I know Ishtvan Kulek. So. I know him better than you. How does not matter. You want to verify what is told to you rather than to understand it. No one lies to you, isn't that so? You should spend your efforts not on dates and places but on the human heart.

To understand what happened during the war you must understand before also. In the late 1930's Nazi money could be found as much in American banks as anywhere. President Roosevelt and his Treasury Secretary, Morganthau, saw the war coming. They wanted to find out who in America was doing business with the Axis nations.

The Axis powers quickly moved deposits from American banks to Swiss banks. In its paranoia Roosevelt's men, Morganthau especially, were convinced that Swiss banks were a facade for Nazi operations.

That was nonsense. You have an expression, eh? sitting on the sidelines. Switzerland was seated on the sidelines, front row to be sure, a seat with a view, but she was not a player in the match. The U. S. pressured Switzerland to reveal Nazi deposits and expected the Swiss to surrender. They hoped their paranoia to be contagious, and when it was not, they assumed that those not afflicted were part of the enemy. Swiss law forbade cooperation with American intelligence. Your Treasury officials were furious. In early 1941 they froze all Swiss assets in the United States.

Under international law, that is illegal. We were not at war with the United States. To the contrary, we considered ourselves her friend. But we were not going to be bullied into revoking our legal system. Morganthau, of course, was a Jew, and I have often wondered whether this fact did not color some of his judgments.

So. These arbitrary decisions of Washington worked real hardships. Many Swiss firms whose assets were frozen in New York vaults had never done business with the German war machinery. Many Swiss banks were hard hit.

Others were better prepared. The Löwenhoft, for instance. So. The fundamental rule of international law is *primum vivere,* first, to survive. We found new ways of doing business and managed record profits. Our small success was doubtless an annoyance to Mr. Morganthau. As the war closed, the United States decided to seize all the assets it could, and ignore issues of legality. The stated purpose was to prevent any resurgence of fascism. Have you ever heard a government state a purpose other than one of the highest nobility, regardless of the barbarism it proposes?

The blinds of the window were drawn shut, and pinholes of sunlight passed at their edge and formed perfect circles on the wall. Their track to Peter's right created a rude chronometer, and now beams struck the glass of a picture frame, reflected back in Peter's eyes. Gideon saw this, rose and pulled the corner of the drapes so the fringe of light was blocked. He sat down and lit a second cigarette. They were oval shaped, and he pursed his lips so that the cigarette perfectly fit the space.

That was the background for the Paris Agreement. In Switzerland there was sympathy for all of her conquered neighbors. But remember, *primum vivere*. One's first obligation is to survive. Do you think that the motives of the Allies to destroy Germany and control all these assets were altruistic? Controlling assets is controlling power. In much of U. S. policy were concealed Zionist motives.

Your grandfather, yes Von Egger too, represented the future of Switzerland. He agreed on her behalf to impound German bank balances, to halt electric current to Germany, to stop shipments of German gold. We thought the matter had been completed.

But the U.S. Treasury was relentless. It announced that there were billions in Nazi funds stored in Swiss vaults. Moneys belonging to those who perished in the ovens. The story had an enormous appeal to it — buried treasure. Not only buried, but available to the Americans. They had climbed the beanstalk, eh?, and had slain the giant Hitler. An appealing archetype. Who would not want to believe such a fairy tale?

The result was the so-called Final Act. The infamous Section 8 of the Paris negotiations. Switzerland I remind you was a *neutral*. So. The great military powers meet. They determine that Switzerland should abdicate her sovereignty to please them, she should invade the sanctity of her vaults to please them. I am not talking gold teeth. Those teeth, the piles of spectacles are dragged out always to sell newspapers. I am talking about assets which logic dictates should be taken over by creditors to pay for goods shipped into Germany. Goods never paid for, some during the war and some before. Is there a difference to the merchant who is out the money?

The Paris Conference ends, the Final Act is adopted. But time is on our side. In time the vengeful Morganthau is replaced by cooler heads. Britain and France are not interested in pressuring Swiss banks, they are interested in buying electric power. Principles are fine when making a speech, but later, you must keep warm. Your grandfather had said those very words. After his death, Herr Von Egger followed his words to the tee. To the tee, you say? A good choice, for Von Egger is an enthusiastic golfer.

That is the real story, eh? There were other pieces to it, of course. Israel began campaigns in the Zionist media to outrage the world. Once in the sixties, again in the seventies, and just last year. A good story, the heartless bankers against the impoverished refugees. But the procedural defects in this argument were obvious. Who was Israel, a sister state, to be making this claim? Israel had no more a claim than Britain would have a claim for all Anglicans. Israel proposed the unthinkable, allowing some outside organization access to records the institutions have undertaken to keep private. After all, this very secrecy had originally been enacted to protect persecuted minorities.

The weapon was time. Eight years after Israel presented its diplomatic note, the commission that Von Egger advised responded. By then no one cared. A second claim, a second commission. So. This last time the banks raised some funds, identified some accounts. Final reparations, the story is over.

Gideon's steepled fingers opened to signal the end. Open the doors, and let out the people. Smoke layered the air, and the circles of light, reborn as the sun had shifted its angle, lit up the tenuous lines. Peter blew out a deep breath and the lines dissipated.

"You can see," Gideon said, "that your grandfather did in fact render enormous service to his country. By helping to stabilize its economy, Pietr Steinmuller served all of western Europe. He was able to see the public good, even when private morality showed a popular but different course. We had a duty to operate for the public good."

"You're saying you needed to create a hierarchy in which appetite prevailed. Your sense of entitlement, security, order."

Gideon pulled himself up. "Take care, my friend. Think in your own life whether you ever chose the selfish course. Or indeed any other."

Peter understood the meeting to be finished. He rose.

"So. A lesson in Swiss history. Also you should pay attention to Swiss law. Body judgment means jail. We do not have your niceties of *habeas corpus*, you know. Should they jail you for non-payment of debts, you might not have any way to get out."

Peter took in the threat without comment.

"I appreciate your time. I assume that you will not tell me where I can find Von Egger?" Gideon's face tightened perceptibly, tiny muscles suppressing amusement. "Or that you have no authority to do so?"

"You have selected a better phrase, I think."

"You wash your hands?"

"Exactly. I wash my hands." The phrase on Gideon's lips made Peter smile, and the effect was to turn the old man sharp.

"I would advise you not to try to search for Herr Von Egger. We do not care to see you imprisoned, we merely want to be left in peace."

"And you cannot tell me any more about the other Marta? Hermann's widow? Where she might be and why it is there is a grave marker with the name Steinmuller in Wadenswil?"

Gideon's eyes widened. "Hermann's widow? I thought you understood. Of course. Hermann's widow married Pietr. She is the same woman living in Florida."

"She what? Married Pietr? How could that be? Hermann and Pietr were opposites. Why would she possibly marry him? And who is buried in Wadenswil? Is anyone?"

Gideon walked to the door and opened it. "That I cannot tell you. Herr Von Egger handled her emigration to the U.S. I was working on more important matters, it was the time of the meetings in Washington. 1946. But I can tell you she married Pietr. The year before, if I remember."

"Did they have any children?"

Gideon stood beside him. His voice had softened. "Children? Pietr by Hermann's widow? I would not think so. You are so naive, eh? Let me say this delicately, lest I upset you. Pietr and Von Egger were very close, the closest of friends. Sapphic, we say of women. When you were at Herr Von Egger's house in Vincy did you not notice something singular about the art?"

"Singular."

"About the art. Those pieces that express physical love."

Gideon's meaning flashed across his eyes like a struck match. The two men kissing.

Gideon had him by the elbow and was moving him through the reception room. His tone was again cordial, the voice of a solicitous relative. The efficient woman who had arranged the rendezvous had gone.

"So. Your ignorance suggests a new theory to me," Gideon said amicably. He continued to escort him towards the door. "You have heard the commonplace that blind people develop an acute sense of hearing to compensate for their loss? That one sense makes up for the other? My theory is the converse. I base it on you as my first and best example, you as a musician. It is that people with an acute sense of hearing develop blindness."

He moved Peter into the hall and closed the door between them. Peter stood looking at the blocked passageway and turned to the stairs.

A WALK OUT ON the high board of circumstance — Peter was dizzied by the drop. If Pietr had been gay, he had fathered neither of Marta's children. *If* there were two. Marta's application to Immigration says she had given birth to two. One lay buried in the tiny grave, and she had taken the second with her to the United States. Why would she have married her husband's brother? Why did she leave? To get away from the tragedy of her child's death? Most tantalizing, if both children were hers but neither descended from Cain, then they were both of Abel.

All this was undercut by Helene's question. What did it matter who his grandfather was? In the bungalow where he'd grown up, the past was hardly visible. There were no family keepsakes or souvenirs from journeys. Only one photograph, a wedding picture — or was it they? they looked so young. His father tentative, but alive, an energy in his eyes that Peter didn't remember from the man who ate silent meals, smoked his cigars as he walked around the block, packed and unpacked a suitcase. And his mother, her dress a lilac print, eager, vital. She turned gracefully towards her new husband and held his arm. It was like the faint impression of a distant star, an image viewed long after the fire had gone cold.

That photo had led him no further than the print of the three men at the Budapest restaurant. He couldn't connect his mother, frowning as her pupils pounded out scales a hundred times a week, to a vivid past. When Gideon's door had closed behind him, no others had opened.

Peter stopped in at the Wasserkirche. A new staff had come on, and the woman had no authority to open the practice room. Helene was out preparing for London. She had a long list of tasks and two short days before her flight. He needed to be getting on. He took Gideon's threat seriously. Besides, Helene's move would close down his place of residence. Eviction's a slam dunk when your domicile is the floor under your satchel.

He spent the day walking the streets. At the Credit Suisse office, he verified the balance left in the Vienna bank, withdrew it all in Swiss francs. Next to the bank was an airline office and he paid cash for a single ticket, non-stop, Geneva to JFK. And almost an afterthought, a single JFK-Miami. His grandmother could tell him nothing. Still, if he changed locations, perhaps he would find a way to put the tale together.

He asked Helene this last night to choose a place for dinner. As they drove away Helene pointed out a black Audi parked by the curb. The man behind the wheel looked away from her glance. Helene chose, oddly Peter thought, a humble Chinese restaurant in the north part of the city. The tables were covered in red oilcloth that shone wet in fluorescent light. Paper lanterns hung from string and travel posters had been stuck to the walls with masking tape. He fumbled with the chopsticks — she was expert — and asked about the new firm.

He began to tell her how he would repay her, he intended to, but she put her fingers inches from his mouth to stop him. I don't want to speak of debts and money, she said. I have foresworn being a banker. He took her fingers and kissed the rounded tips.

"I would like to know," she said, "how the story ends." It sounded like something Marcus would say, it was a line from a tune. The lick started in his head. This is how the story ends, she's gonna turn me down and say Can't we be friends.

"The story doesn't end until I find Von Egger. And even then I don't know what happens." Exposing him wasn't enough. No one cared about his reputation, the books about him, the Israeli medal. He was too rich to care about money. It needed to be something closer to the bone. "I have to find him first."

She glanced past him, avoided his eyes. "Perhaps I can help. My friend who is secretary to the board? Perhaps she will know." She turned a gristly spare rib in her fingers and decided against it.

"And if I discover this, where do I write to you? To your parents' house?"

"No, long dead."

"Boston then, the lady of your valise?"

The waiter brought small towels, dampened and hot. He took her hands. Her fingers were sticky with the fat of the ribs and he cleaned them one by one. Then he put them to his nose and inhaled. The scent of lemon.

"No, not the lady of the valise. She is the lady of the valise no more."

Peter called over their waiter. He was an Asian man, their age. Rimless glasses, thin face. Peter asked him for something to write with. He returned with a steno pad, both a pencil and a pen. Peter handed everything across the table.

"Put down your London address. When I get settled I'll write you." Neither believed what he said, and both let it pass. She watched his eyes a moment and smiled. Whatever she was looking for she hadn't found.

What am I doing? I could be satisfied with this woman, stay with her in London, loving her as best I can, she would bear me no grudge. Get on somewhere, lots of jazz there. Basie was very big in London, the Mayfair clubs. Bud Powell had lived for years in Paris, Dexter Gordon.

As they approached her apartment house the black Audi hadn't moved. Two men sat like crash mannequins in the front seat. She turned into the garage ramp and glanced over her shoulder.

"What?" he asked.

"Those two men, they're getting out."

"You suppose . . . ?"

"I don't know, they look like bailiffs. What do you think, Peter?"

"All the men in Zurich look like bailiffs."

The car was down the ramp and into the garage proper. Well-lit, no place to hide. Peter remembered Gideon's phrase. No *habeas corpus*, no way out.

"What now?"

"Peter, dump my purse on the front seat." He did, hoping he was not looking for a weapon. "Now place it on my head. And lie down."

The soft leather purse made a funky cloche, just a bit small. He lay his torso on the seat over the debris of her mirror, change pouch, lipstick. She circled to the exit ramp and drove slowly into the street.

"You see a lot of movies?" he asked as they zig-zagged their way and she checked the mirror to make sure no one followed.

"My share."

He recognized the street before she pulled the car to a halt. She checked him into the boarding house and talked *sotto voce* with the old woman who ran it.

"Listen, I don't care about bailiffs and debtor's prison. I don't want to spend my last night in Switzerland alone."

"There is no reason you should. You will stay here. So will I. I'll go for your valise in the morning without you."

He moved to put his arms about her. "This room, the bed. It's rather narrow."

"Well," she responded without embarrassment. Peter had whispered so the landlady wouldn't hear. "Well, my fugitive friend. We will think of something. It will be my job to keep you under cover."

He walked her to the gate. This way he could walk off before the flight was called, he would leave her. But she asked him to stay and he did. She kissed his cheek, then his lips. The briefest touch. "Better, I think," she said. The tip of her ring finger touched the corner of his mouth, traced its red swell. She closed her eyes again, to consider. "Without the beard, better I think."

She turned. Walked down the sterile causeway amid anxious people preparing to travel, tired people disembarking. There is a languor in airports as passengers rid themselves of energy, prepare to be carried, and she walked with none of that. He watched her disappear in the square tunnel, and free as a comet and cash in his pocket to the next gig, he could not guess how long, he wondered what he would do without her.

There was a movie on his flight and Peter watched it through. He had rented a headset but left it off. The faint mystery added to the tale. A woman seemed to have two lovers, perhaps two husbands. The woman was surprised when either man showed up, and much of the movie was spent moving the two husbands about so they didn't run into each other. Sally Field acted the woman. She played surprise broadly, with wide eyes and a mouth she stretched into a perfect circle. She could have been in the silents, this would have made a good silent. Without the sound track it was difficult but unimportant to tell why she found herself in this predicament, and evident how the story would turn out. One of the men, the one who wore a suit and spoke on the telephone, was destined to lose. His tie matched his pocket kerchief. He wore pajamas. The other man leaned against the wall when he talked, spoke through friendly eyes. Peter assumed it was a comedy — at one point a fuzzy dog the size of a calf ate a tray of *hors d'oeuvres* — yet the passenger in the seat next to him watched with a dead expression. Towards the middle, Peter got up to use the toilet and noticed the serious faces in every row. Perhaps it wasn't a comedy. Sally Field and her children chased the dog gleefully.

He knew the name of the nursing home in Ft. Lauderdale. It was run by Swiss. His mother had thought she would be comfortable there, even though she wasn't aware of her surroundings. Peter had not seen his grandmother since she was shipped off.

On the trip out of JFK he slept. Not sleep so much as a ribbed and tottering unconscious, dreams that slip from fingertips, slide beneath the surface, you lean across the water to watch them sink and cannot summon the will, the lack of will, to follow them over the side. In a brief passing Matey appeared, chatting with his grandmother on a sunny lawn. They sat in white Adirondack chairs, like the ones on sanitorium hillsides whenever George Sanders was in the movie. Wooden Adirondack chairs, seats slanting back. Peter couldn't detect their conversation and as he came close enough to hear they were speaking English, he was awakened by the pilot's professional voice over the public address. They would play a game. A mathematical game to calculate knots or nautical miles. Charleston, South Carolina was below on the far side of the plane.

He rode a bus to Ft. Lauderdale and checked into a motel. One fifty for the week, a hot plate for cooking. He unlocked his cubicle — the units looked as if they were sheet tin that had been bolted together, like metal shower stalls — revved the air conditioner to high and slept for twelve hours under the sound of churning freon. When he woke it was five in the morning, he was bright with rest. An icy breeze blew around the room and moved the glassine curtains. He turned on the television and watched a show about policemen in Los Angeles and a second about a couple whose washing machine overflowed. He flipped through the illustrated New Testament in the bureau drawer. Marta had been a minister's daughter, perhaps he would find an answer there, but he had no idea where to look.

At seven o'clock he went into the motel coffee shop and ordered a large breakfast. Homecoming had made him light and airy, no more wondering about dark sedans, court bailiffs, airport searches. The orange juice was in fact orange drink, and the maple syrup for the pancakes came in small plastic vials that might sell at a hardware store. The waitress sang a Jimmy Buffet tune. She had a miniature voice, like a doll's, and dead on. He ate everything she served, squeezed grape jam from crimped foil packets onto white toast.

The papers looked promising. There were three ads for pianists at clubs and two by groups seeking a keyboard. Just a start. Miami and

Lauderdale had lots of saloons, resort hotels. A loose union. He would get on.

At eight he called the nursing home. The manager was nervous, asked twice whether anything was wrong. Agreed to find Mrs. Steinmuller and make her presentable, would ten o'clock suit?

Peter felt the air in his lungs. He was shown to a common room off the entry hall. Inside the sounds of several television sets mumbled in competition. Somewhere the shuffle of a deck of cards. He saw a bag of knitting. By the wall where he entered, a bent person, he could not tell if it was a man or a woman, at an upright piano insistently hit the E above middle C. Morse, not music.

Residents sat in random patterns and stared into middle distance. One or two noticed him, called to him. He was a virgin in the prison cells, they would have a roll with his youth. Marta Steinmuller had been seated in a corner, at a card table covered in red. Its veneer had been stamped from heavy cardboard to look like leather. The matron asked if he would like her to stay. She had a soft, Swiss-German accent, not unlike Helene's. Peter said yes.

There was nothing in Marta Steinmuller's face to link her to the story Peter sought. No familiarity, no family resemblance, no light of recognition. He talked quietly to her. He used simple words. She paid him no mind.

The matron said it was time to go. He thanked her for helping.

"I'm sorry she was not talkative." The matron was unhappy at the performance. She wanted Peter to be pleased. "You must come again. She liked seeing you, I could tell that. We don't have many visitors."

Peter said of course he would. Did she ever speak? Sometimes, he was told. But to herself. Not anything you could understand.

He thanked the woman again for her time. Would she expect a tip? His hand fell lightly to his grandmother's shoulder. Through the fabric of her sweater he sensed bone, calcified and burled. He left and began his long walk downtown.

Nightclubs were staffing for the coming Easter vacation. The ads sought rock musicians, you didn't mention jazz if you hoped to get on. Peter auditioned at all three places and got two offers. One was a solo, he took the other. They'd booked an electric guitar, could he play with him? Could he. Close his eyes and coast. Three fifty a week, two weeks guaranteed.

He sat at the bar and drank a dollar cup of coffee. He'd been out of the country for months, didn't have any idea what tunes were popular and didn't keep track of them anyway. The owner wanted volume. Three chords, an uninterrupted power supply and speakers the size of a woodstove would see him through.

He toted up his funds. Money had skittered away faster than he'd realized. It was a jar of lightning bugs, open the screw lid and they flew off. Still, Marcus would say, you got to scuffle. He walked down the main drag, where doubtless the kids would hang out. It was the wrong place to buy a bike, but he needed transportation, his motel, the nursing home and the bar were miles from each other. At the first lot, he got them to halve the price of a '72 Yamaha stripped of everything but wheels. The pipes were gone, the kickstand, no rack. Its last paint job must have been the year of *Easy Rider* and rust was licking off the spangled stars. But it putted him about the city and he did not intend it for heavy lifting.

Gigs like this were nothing new. All decibels out, the drink of choice the long-neck beer. Unless you paid attention bills disappeared from the tips glass. Most of the patrons, happy not to have been carded, swarmed the bar, gnats in a summer meadow. Conspicuously male — tank shirts, tans, eager talk — and at the center of each swarm, usually a pair of girls, leaning against the bar, breasts pointed to the ceiling. The way movie cowpokes would hush the saloon by shooting off a couple of rounds. They puffed sex into the air like smoke rings, trying out their techniques. It was a young and immortal sex, not one that engaged Peter. He grew lonely.

The guitar was a sullen Hispanic who crowded his instrument, leaned over its neck trying to hide what he was doing, it might have been a stolen loaf of bread, and called tunes in an unintelligible grunt. Peter wasn't sure if it was Spanish or English. It didn't matter. He stayed close behind. The guitar hooked up to an amplifier out of Mission Control that drove massive speakers, and the sound glazed the eyes of the owner. It's the volume, he yelled to his band over the din. The volume will bring them in.

The sets were fifty-minutes, six to eleven. Midway they broke for half an hour and took supper in the kitchen — the tables outside were producing profits. The guitar never said a word, wolfed down his burger and onion rings, flooded catsup over everything, he must have heard that tomatoes spark genius. The saloons in town were cooperating to keep the kids in check so everyone closed at eleven. One night after they shut down, Peter stayed at the keyboard trying to recall the connection between what he had been doing and music. His fingers rested on keys, tight inversions playing ascending fifths. He looked up. The guitar took a line on top, knew his way around.

They passed an hour jamming, no words. One would start a tune and the other would comp through. Each would do thirty-two or sixty-four bars, a shout chorus and out. They fit together and drifted apart with a practiced ease. The Spanish kid, Marcus would say, the Spanish kid won't get lost. Gee but it's great to see you again.

He hit the nursing home same time the next day and ran through the same script. Again the matron had his grandmother waiting for him at the table, again he passed the gauntlet of false recognition, a call from one woman, Robert, Robert, that he in turn ignored. Again he told his story, softly, and again he put his hand on her shoulder as he rose to go. He willed himself to do that, he determined he would touch her, the rough weave of the blue sweater. This time he felt a tremor. The distinct and woody bones moved as if they might have been the antennae of thought. And when she spoke, the sound vibrated the joint and through his resting fingers.

He sat down. She spoke again. It was one phrase, repeated. Just below a mumble, perhaps one long word. The name Hermann. Peter thought of Kulek's comment, how he looked more like Hermann than Pietr. "Hermann," he said, and she repeated it. Did she think Hermann was here, come to take her away? What goes on in the brain? Science says discovery can more easily open memory than the heart, but science assumes a guide, assumes language. All the while she looked down at the table. Her hands were in her lap, below its lip.

He waited expectantly but nothing else came forth. If she had said anything, it was not in English. Her eyes looked up, avoided his face, flitted overhead.

The matron escorted him back to the vestibule. She had a practiced way to steer people by the arm. "I don't think you can expect anything. Even when she does speak, it's nonsense. Like that."

"The phrase you mean. It sounded like *toot beleed*. Over and over again."

"Nonsense phrases," the matron said. "That's a new one. But they all do that. They pick on a word or two and say it for days."

Peter went into the lot and fired up the Yamaha. He sat on the ground by the bike, used a nail file to adjust the carburetor, screwed in the mixture. It had been leaned out as if it had lived most of a happy life at a higher altitude, and now tuned, even by ear and by an amateur, it performed well enough for the money he'd paid for it. He looked back at the door of the home. The matron was watching. He shivered under her look.

The gig became routine. Five hours of blues and rock, the volume knob drilled out to full stop. Afterwards they hung out and jammed. The owner seemed indifferent, he sat by the register checking tapes, writing out inventory lists. Business looked good. Would Peter stay on another week, he asked. Maybe, Peter told him. If the follicles of my ears don't get fried. What else do I have going?

The guitar kept a tight silence. He seemed to understand English, everything that was said to him, but he had no words. "He's Cuban," the owner explained in his presence, talked of the man as if he were deaf.

"That's cool," Peter said, no other rejoinder. Later on over chili dogs and beer, to reciprocate, he told the guitar he was from Connecticut. The man nodded. Whatever Peter wanted was all right. They closed a third week, the crowds kept coming and the owner raised Peter's pay forty bucks. He bought a postcard, two crocodiles zonked in the Everglades mud. He wrote out the briefest message to Helene, scrounged the London address deep in the satchel and mailed off the card.

His visits to the nursing home were the same. He and the matron took the same chairs, he would repeat his story, softly, urgently. His grandmother would say her magic phrase, that phrase only. She never again said the name Hermann. The woman who had called him became more aggressive. Robert, Robert, I'm over here. I'm waiting for you. The matron went over to speak to her, and she quieted down. When Peter left, skulking out past the stares, he avoided her eyes.

In the fourth week, his grandmother fell silent. Whatever message she had for them had been sent, she would no longer tap out the signal in unknowable code. Peter called two days later. The matron told him his grandmother had gone to bed and wanted to stay there. They didn't force people, some places did, it made it easier on the staff. But they weren't like that. Peter asked if he might visit her in her rooms, and the matron checked with the superintendent. After an hour's wait he was taken upstairs. He set his eyes ahead, narrowed the lids against periphery. The halls smelled of strong soap, faintly soured milk, rubber sheets. He stood briefly at the foot of his grandmother's bed.

She lay with her eyes closed. Frail at the bed's center, she took up little room and her breathing sounded of a dry wind. A damp washcloth rested on her forehead.

Where would she keep a secret if she had one? Does she have a satchel like mine, at its bottom scraps of paper where she's written the missing words?

He didn't want to be a bother, Peter told the matron. Perhaps in the future he should call, rather than make the drive out. Was she in danger? It was a silly question, he knew. The matron assured him she was not.

When he returned to his motel that afternoon the manager had stuck a note through a hole in the screen door. See desk. He walked across the rolling asphalt. The manager was a huge woman with a mushroom-colored mole on her face. Her upper arms were the girth of a small child. The office was the sitting room of a trailer, carpeted in gold shag, cork board on the walls. There was a console TV playing, and on it a panel of six women discussed why they were bald by choice. The manager sat in a La-Z-Boy recliner, poured Sprite into a glass, added a spoonful of Grenadine syrup and stirred. Peter was ready to bolt.

"You got a letter," she said. "Over there."

It must have to do with the motorbike. He needed registration, new plates. Some of that was in the works. She didn't get up. She pointed him to stacks of paper, and he shuffled through. Ads for car washes and electrolysis, a series of laboratory tests whose details he avoided, magazines about Gerald and heart disease and Ivan.

"You sure?" he said. She was back into her program. "You're sure it's here?"

She rose, disquieted by his presence. The effort left her winded. He could feel the moisture around her body. She checked the same stacks of papers. Then she lifted a coffee cake that sat, half-eaten, by the sink. There were more letters under it. On the top, darkened by butter from the almond ring, was his.

He went back and lay on his bed. On the page in front of him Helene's hand curled tight, the letters coiled in a neat black line.

Dear Peter,

Thank you for your expansive note. They say we Swiss are reserved. I count sixteen words, not including the return address, although I should count that since it, and only it, causes me to speculate that you may wish to hear from me again.

You are either extremely reticent or extremely stupid. I choose the first explanation since it can be cured and will not be passed on to our children. If you miss me, say so. No harm will befall. I hope I have my conjugations right.

I assumed when you left me in Zurich, or as you pointed out, I left you, you were returning to the lady of the valise. If instead you are returning to the rootless life of a musician, decide whether that is what you want. Do not let yourself slip into some neutral place just so you can feel sorry for yourself. I was not raised to ignore matters that should be spoken of.

I liked the photograph on the postcard. Do you know the crocodile was the first beast to evolve a penis?

I will be in New York on business for the next two weeks, staying at the Carlyle Hotel. No news yet on your friend from Vincy.

Love,

Helene

He told the bar owner he was through after Sunday night. Too bad, said the man, a dapper fellow with a slick comb-over and bad skin. I was thinking maybe, keep those two on. They are starting to sound like something. Peter was pleased. He hadn't thought anyone was listening. He finished out the week, each night stronger. His solos grew lyrical, longer lines. The guitar followed. They played close together, infectious as the flu.

The guitar was surprised at the news he was moving on. Whether it was his leaving or his words — they rarely spoke, hadn't exchanged names — Peter couldn't tell.

Next morning he packed his duffel, bunged it floppily to his bike on a makeshift platform he'd rigged to the rear axle, and checked out. He called the matron.

"Of course. Come over before you go. I'll see if she wants to come down."

But she didn't. Peter made a second visit to her room and carried a pot of white chrysanthemums he'd bought at the Piggy Wiggly. He found her sitting up, staring, wordless.

"So," said the matron. "You will motorbike all the way to New York. Vroom room." She turned the crank of an imaginary throttle.

Peter smiled. "With any luck." They walked down the graceful stairway. There was a white Colonial balustrade on its inside, a metal rail against the wall.

"I really thought she might talk to me. At first, you know? When she kept saying that phrase over and over. *Toot beleed*? You know what I mean? I thought she was going to talk to me."

"Yes," said the matron. "You remember. You have a good ear, you could learn to speak. *Teut mir lied*. Nonsense." They stood in the vestibule. Peter had left his bike by the front door and two elderly ladies were trailing their fingers fondly over the chrome letters that spelled out Yamaha. Peter realized the matron had made something out of the phrase.

"Was that it? Were they words?"

"Oh yes. Eventually they all do it. I suppose we all will. End up that way, I mean. Nonsense phrases."

"Do they mean anything?"

"Not really. *Teut mir lied*. Literally, 'I'm sorry'. What does a woman her age have to be sorry about? Just words."

He slipped out of Lauderdale under gathering clouds. He would outrace the weather. With a splat he was northbound on the freeway. Sputtering relic of an engine beneath him, no map, no star, northbound running on a memory of geography, a sixth-grade recollection that Jacksonville was up there for a start and the sea off to the right, keep the sea to the right you'd get to New York. Helene's letter tucked into the back pocket of his jeans, there's no way they can hide Manhattan from him.

Twelve hundred miles. An easy three days if his legs didn't go to sleep, spread around the belching engine if they fell asleep you lose your balance. He stopped to drink coffee and walk them out. They tingled at the calves and then at the toes, but they came back. He'd make it four, sometimes four and a half hours, shut down, coffee up, kick on the heat and mount the horse again.

The bike beat over flat pavement. He left the interstate from boredom and fish-tailed down the ramp to the coast road. Couldn't get lost, someone designed the coast line to run right into the Lady with the Lamp, he was sure of it. South Carolina showed a face of rain, a pleasant warm splashing you could squint through at the start, but they turned up the hose and water leaked down his collar, all he could see was tears and headlights. A truck about ran up his back, oogahed its horn, and he dove his bike for the shoulder as it rumbled by. Went into a Stuckey's off the two-lane near Myrtle Beach for pecan pie washed over the falls with a hundred cups of coffee.

A pretty waitress chatted him up, told him he looked like a shepherd dog, the one the family abandoned by the seashore. He said it was because he couldn't be house trained, and she laughed too hard at what he said. She had a terrific figure, crooked teeth and green hazel eyes, he was partial to green hazel eyes, but around sunset it stopped raining and he went out into God's newest air, kicked on the bike and headed north. Rumbled most the night through the smell of wet asphalt and found a flimsy motel across the North Carolina border just where it ought to be.

Could you do this forever? Miles piled up behind him. If the engine held, could you just go north, past the crofts of New England — where better to bury a heart? — past Montreal and the tundra and the pole, come out the other side? Alone in a morning bed he knew he wouldn't, knew that he wanted to find Helene. Not the limitless pavement, but the destination. That was something new. An epiphany sweet and slight and sliding down easy as oysters.

The second day he slowed as the sun went down and found a place to stay. He fell asleep before dinner, wide awake at four and on the road before light. By the time the sun broke off to his right, a slow curve high and outside, he had done a hundred miles.

He crossed into Virginia. Spring lay soft in the hills, and blooming on the branches were thin lines of pink and yellow. A country that looked like cheap stationery. Forward in time but back in season. In another hundred miles the dogwood would not yet appear, the forsythia was shut down tight. An hour up the turnpike he saw a sign to the Chesapeake Bay Bridge. He swung his bike east and sped through county seats hardly awake. Road signs pointed to towns named Whaleyville, Grizzard, Isle of Wight, Princess Anne. In a town called Rescue he stopped for breakfast. A waitress with a gold square around a front tooth filled his coffee mug. He asked for the clams from the regular menu, and she said they didn't turn the fryer on 'till lunch, but if he wanted she'd nuke him up some of yesterday's. She did that all the time, not for breakfast, but it wouldn't matter they were real good done that way. Less grease if you put a paper towel around them.

He ate two full orders of clams with tartar sauce and catsup, coffee, orange juice and a corn muffin the size of a softball. He paid and took a toothpick from the roller.

"Guess you shouldn't eat fried foods," he said to her and he couldn't help but smile.

"Son," she said. She was maybe seventy. With the nail of her pinky she got whatever was bothering her between two back teeth. "Son, you gonna live forever."

The Bay Bridge was all he had hoped, more since he had no hopes. He left the Virginia shore amid cities and sprawl, soared over the water twenty miles, put its foot down on an island and slid, not a bounce, onto a narrow tip of saw grass and sand. The way you'd jump a stream, hoping to hit the small stone dead on and leaping from there to safety. His bike roared throttle full open and holding sixty-five, eighty when the road dipped, past Dover. At Wilmington he rejoined the interstate. He was back among crowds. From here on it would be transportation.

Traffic through Newark, every hour a rush hour, looked impass-able. He stopped at a service island. In the men's room mirror, he saw a face made urgent by the wind. He called the hotel. She had checked in. Without timing you got nothing. He left a progress report on her room's recording. "I'm on my way don't move. And, oh yeah, your conjugations? They're just fine." Took a bag of salsa chips to eat on the bike. The bag flew from his pinch as he broke into high gear.

Tension and release. The heart of music. All there is. It works the longest piece, it works the shortest phrase. That's what Marcus meant, it's a two-five world. Every dominant resolves into its tonic. Is it true of stories, too?

He crossed the city limits under the river in a tunnel that might be leaking, drops the size of plums hit his forehead. What if she's not alone, what if she travels with her own Christopher, a man of prop-erty? He should have called. Madison went one way against him and the street he came in on put him uptown from where he wanted to be. He couldn't miss it said a cabbie on Park, circle around and you can't miss it. He did. His brain had been dribbled over hundreds of miles of pavement, and now coursing with adrenalin, he flew past the corner, and turned to track back, wrong way against the traffic, his cycle hugging the cars parked on the Avenue.

A lit marquee and above it a tall building whose lights dot the New York air perhaps one of those lights hers. Now to ditch the bike but everywhere he looks they threaten to tow — he's had enough of the law. The doorman likes motorcycles, used to own a hog, he tells Peter, but they have three kids, the wife made him sell it, they have a Ford Escort now. Makes more sense, but he'd trade it all for the hog if they'd take the wife. They laugh. The man is dressed like an admiral in an operetta. You'll want to lock that up, you can chain it to the gate at the garbage dock. Get it out by noon or they'll saw it off and leave it in the streets and in fifteen minutes there won't be enough left to park. Not enough for the pigeons. Peter chains it taut to a heavy iron grill and runs in to use the house phone. Perhaps she's going to sleep, turning off her phone. Perhaps she's not back, perhaps she's not alone, not happy to see him.

She is.

THEY SLEEP IN THE dark of the morning, he in half-dream. He stands where two rivers come together. One is clear and the smaller muddy, the color of red clay. He has driven his first bike, a Triumph without fenders, out to the country to open it up. Driven to the edge of where the tobacco farms start, hot and moist land. It is a noon of late summer. The engine hums in perfect synch. Where the rivers meet he stops, pulls a sandwich from his pocket, begins to eat. A young girl in a yellow dress stands in a rowboat docked below him. Barefoot in a yellow dress. She hitches up her skirt to keep it from the ambient water. Her mother calls for her to come home. Peter is unnoticed, intensely happy. The girl leaps from the boat and climbs the path. Where the waters come together, they take on the clay color.

The ringing of the telephone woke him. It was the briefest chirp as Helene, dressed and seated at the Louis Catorze writing table, picked up on the short hop. He heard her thank the caller and explain it wasn't too early. That exhausted his German.

They walked down Fifth Avenue. Peter told her about spring in North Carolina as if it were something she might never get to see. A cool wind smelling of water blew at their backs and they held on to each other. She told him of her work. The streets were empty, it might have been a plague or the middle of the night. They turned back towards the hotel, on Madison and up the long hill, and stopped at a sidewalk table for steamed coffee. A red-haired man wearing a sweat-shirt that read Marblehead High was sweeping about their feet. Peter put his hand on hers and spoke too loudly.

"All I can think about is you, making love to you."

"Good for you, lad," the sweeper told him. Helene watched her coffee as if to blush, but when she looked up her eyes were bright and eager. "All I want to do is play music and make love to you."

"Surely not," she said through a fringe of hair, "at the same time."

Peter couldn't find his motorbike — thoughts of a lost bike shivered him — but when they got back to the hotel it was there, chained to the grate by the hotel's monumental stack of garbage. He squeezed it between two cars parked on the side street.

They entered her rooms excited as thieves. He was shy about asking for her body and she made him understand not to be. She wore a loose-fitting jersey, midnight blue, over jeans. He slid his hands up her sides to find the cool bands of her skin. All the while, even when he went over the top, he spoke sounds to her comprehending mouth.

It was not until noon that she asked what he found in Florida. He told about the nursing home and the old woman who had stopped speaking. She is taking so long to die, he said. Why is it that men die suddenly and women make little trips over and back, as if moving from a summer house?

"'*Teut mir lied.*' 'I'm sorry, Hermann.' I don't get it. About what, Helene? Why would she marry a man who had so twisted his brother's work? Why did she pretend that a son was dead when she was going to move him to the U. S.?"

"How do you find out? Do you go back to Von Egger?"

Peter shook his head. "I can't confront him unless I can find him, and we don't know where he is."

Helene rose, walked to the telephone table, retrieved a scrap of paper.

"But we do." She put the paper in front of him. It bore a single word. MIRAGE.

"I telephoned my friend. This morning, while you were sleeping. It was her call that woke you up. She said Von Egger is in Mirage."

"That he *is* a mirage or he's *in* Mirage?"

"He's in Mirage. She was definite."

Helene called the hall porter, asked him to send up a U.S. road atlas. Also, a bowl of fresh fruit, two liter bottles of Pelligrino, a pot of black tea, breakfast rolls and muffins. They had forgotten to eat.

The atlas produced no Mirage, in California or Arizona.

"He loves the sun," Peter said. "It must be some L. A. spot." He reached for the phone, considered whether it was a good idea, and to his surprise decided it was. Boston information gave him the number of Matey's ad agency. In seconds he heard her voice, notes from an old song.

"Peter," she shrieked and he was embarrassed. "How *are* you? *Where* are you?" Had she always spoken with exclamation points? Why hadn't it gotten on his nerves?

"Listen Matey, I don't have a lot of time. We're looking for some place in California, maybe a club or a spa. Southern California, I'm betting. You're the expert. A friend of ours goes there for golf. And all we know is the name Mirage. Have you ever heard of it?"

"*Rancho* Mirage," Matey said easily. "It's where they hold the Dinah Shore every year, it's just down the road from Palm Springs."

Peter searched the map, put his finger on the spot to show Helene.

"Wow. How'd you come up with that?"

"We've sold it. Feminine hygiene products, Virginia Slims cigarettes. High rate card."

Helene was nibbling a muffin. She put it down, looked over his shoulder, took the pencil from his fingers and drew a circle around the town.

"Matey, thanks. I knew you'd have it. How are you? And how is Christopher?"

"Oh fine." Her voice lost pitch. "I suppose less than fine at the moment. I've moved out, we're in one of those between times. At first Christopher was bereft, but he's been billing all those hours he used to have to spend with me. Net-net, as he would say, he's ahead."

"He doesn't really say that. Net-net?"

"He does."

"Sorry."

"Yeah. Well, we'll work it out. And you? You're with someone?"

"Yes, I am. I guess."

"Peter, don't guess. Do."

"Right," he said. "I will. Take care."

"You too." He waited a long second, then replaced the phone gently on its nest. She hadn't hung up.

Peter strung the facts along his uncertainty, and they gave him a single conclusion. It was, Marcus would say, a two-five change, inevitable. He needed to face down Von Egger. Where and to what end remained a mystery, but first find the man before he again disappeared.

Helene was ahead of him — she had opened the yellow pages to Airlines.

They spent what was left of the light on Peter's bike, gunning about Manhattan's fringes. Clouds hung low over the city. The air was cold and dense with exhaust. They crossed a bridge and watched ships in the Narrows. Why would Marta marry her dead husband's nemesis? How would that man sire a child? And on which limb of the family tree is Peter to hang?

"I have an odd request," he said. They were in the sitting room of her small suite. The ticket for the morning flight had arrived, and with it, again Helen's doing, dinner on a wheeled table, fresh daffodils and jonquils, two bottles of beer in an ice bucket. He sat on the floor, she above him on the sofa, a cinnabar davenport with velvet pillows. His head rested against her knee. He examined the long bones of her foot. Helene would know, she liked myths and stories.

"How intriguing. An indecent proposal." She slid the tip of her tongue across her upper lip. "And so early in the evening."

"No, no. At least, not yet. Gideon kept pointing me to the myth of Theseus. Theseus I can't place. Daedalus was the one who designed the wings of feathers and wax and his son fell into the sea."

"You have the right place," Helene answered, "but too soon. Theseus stumbles on the island of Crete. Daedalus has already been there, and built a maze to keep the Minotaur, a fierce beast. Theseus becomes trapped in the maze and kills the Minotaur. He eventually escapes and returns to take over his kingdom."

"So Theseus figures out the maze?"

"That gives him perhaps too much credit. A woman risks her life to get him out. A beautiful princess named Ariadne."

"How does it turn out?"

The plumpness of her fingertips rested on his eyes, his brow. She had soft, full fingers.

"No happy ending. Theseus stops off on the way home to camp on a beach. He eats something that makes him sleepy and neglectful."

"Bad dope."

"Bad dope. In the morning he forgets Ariadne and sails without her. He is supposed to signal his father on his return. Theseus' father was the King. White sails mean that his outing was successful, but he forgets that too. The King sees the black sails and, thinking the son is dead, kills himself. Theseus comes home an orphan and the new king."

Helene's fingers have moved to the bone that shelter's Peter's eye, have found the slight hollow where nest the nerves that hold the forehead tense. Have begun the gentlest pressure to release the tightness.

"And Ariadne?"

"The Princess Ariadne marries a *fuul* — ne'er-do-well, that is right? — she finds on the island. There is a constellation in the northern sky that is named after her."

"Not bad for second place."

"You think so? I say no. She knew what she wanted and she missed out. I say, better for the princess to get a bottle of cold beer and the boy of her choice."

Peter raised up on an elbow and pulled a bottle from the bucket. Screwed off the cap, licked the foam and put it to her lips.

"Done."

For twenty bucks the doorman agreed to look after the cycle. He loaded Peter's bag into the trunk and held open the rear door of the cab. "You just arrived," Helene said mournfully. "Every time we are saying goodbye."

He took her around the waist, smiled at the revision, sang back to her. "Every time we are saying goodbye I cry a little."

"So *vas is das*?"

"*Das is* Karl Porter. A Swiss songwriter."

They kissed deeply. She whispered a single word into his ear. Peter heard the driver's impatient grunt as the light he'd hoped to make turned against them.

In an hour he was in the air off La Guardia. The cabin was close, unstable, row upon itinerant row of university students back from Easter break. Peter changed in Phoenix for the short flight to Palm Springs.

He caught the van to town. The desert bloomed with glistening plastic banners taped to plate glass. Signs told of bargains in hospital beds and supplies, in pools and spas, pancakes, Oldsmobiles, perpetual care. Dropped on the strip, six bucks for the ride, Peter back-tracked fifty yards to a motel. A neon vacancy sign popping in the daylight advertised housekeeping units. The owner asked Peter what he did, and insisted on filling the white Styrofoam ice bucket, flicking on the television.

Peter sat on the marshy bed, the telephone coil snaking out of a hole in the headboard. Where was the plan? No different, kid. You do this for a living. Your solo is coming up and you have nothing to say. You'll think of something, the silence will launch you, just hang around B-flat.

The message he leaves with Gerald at the house in Switzerland is not an improvisation. It carries all the news that his quarry would need

— Peter's desire to see Von Egger and the name of his motel, the Cactus Rest.

He takes a walk, buys a book at a supermarket and reads it, a detective story riddled with coincidence, too much to swallow. He takes a second walk. Evening unhurried does not arrive, the pale sky lingers. The darkness drops at once.

U.S. Prime is across the four-lane, a glass-fronted box behind a window banner that reads Lunch: all the salad you can eat. He sits at the counter, drinks two Michelobs from the tap, and wolfs a New York strip everything on the potato. It is the perfect meal. The waitress who serves him looks like Lily Tomlin, did anyone ever tell you that? Makes her angry and Peter never gets an answer, the answer must be one too many.

In the morning he catches twenty minutes of the world's weather. Reads a second novel. The jacket said the story was informed by some post-modern quandary that is inexpressible, the times that are not communicable, and all we can do is evoke. He walks in the dry sun past the same stores and tosses the paperback into a dumpster. Von Egger might just as easily dispose of me, toss me into the same dumpster.

Back in his room he flicks on the television. On the screen is a foreign correspondent. He reports on the rape and mayhem that followed in the trail of a Serb march, like gulls after the garbage scow. Stories of horror and injury hanging in the air above the waves, flesh-pecking birds of stories, cawing and calling. The reporter tells several at a sitting without changing his tone. Brothels, mothers and their daughters, the fusillade of automatic weapons. The next feature is about four boys from a wealthy New Jersey suburb who avoided jail for abusing a mentally retarded classmate. They had entered her with objects, bottles and the handle of a broom. In both stories the dull silver of the mirror-back gleams through the glass of civilization, an ugly basil grey of bedrock, igneous. The acts on the screen are brother to chivvying the fat kid in class, hiding the books, smearing dogshit on the immigrant's door, they are hard cousin to the pogrom. A horn honks nearby and Peter turns up the sound.

Peter thinks to write down what he sees but there are already too many words. Trust and pity are test-market products of sophisticated cultures. Von Egger called it our tentative natures. They are hothouse flowers, they are the first to die when a window is left open.

The horn honked a third time. Peter had forgotten he was waiting on someone. He parted the curtains, looked out. A black sedan with a concours-class finish sat idling ten feet from his unit's door. Peter squinted, could see nothing through the tinted window. He pointed to his chest. As if that were the down button, the glass on the driver's side receded. A man sat at the wheel wearing pink reflector shades. The man made a pistol with his thumb and index finger, let the hammer fall. Bang. Got you.

He punched off the TV and walked out. Went to the front passenger door. As he reached for the handle, he felt himself pushed hard at the top of the spine. He caught himself on the hand-rubbed roof, and his driver, who had come noiselessly up from behind, patted him down, back, arms, inside thighs. Expertly, if Peter could judge from the cinema. The price we pay, he thought. Got in the right front seat. No word had been exchanged.

Peter had paid little attention to his surroundings. It wasn't until they were well outside the city, northbound from Palm Springs and Peter remembered the atlas at the Carlyle, Rancho Mirage was to the south, that he asked. This could be someone else's car, no one had held up an airport sign saying Welcome Mr. Steinmuller. Perhaps Peter was supposed to sit in the rear. The driver wore a laundered shirt and a black four-in-hand tie. He had a scarlet rash on his scalp behind the ear. Nerves maybe. Peter's asking annoyed him.

"To see Mr. Von Egger, that's where we're going." The man was about Peter's age. He tightened his lips to his teeth when he talked.

"I thought he was in Rancho Mirage. We're headed north."

"You want to see him, I take you there. You don't want to go, my instructions is, you don't need to go. Say the word, mister. I take you back. Which'll it be?"

"Let's go." The car was doing an easy ninety, had not slowed for their interchange. The driver loosed his grip on the wheel and held it lightly eight fingers on its top.

The dash was fitted in walnut. Peter let his head back on the padded rest, comforted by the speed. At least the car had the right owner.

"Where are we going?"

The driver took both hands from the wheel, turned their palms up. Two guns.

"Mister, just say the word."

Peter closed his eyes and listened to the pavement under the wheels. In a dim English movie, the victim is kidnaped in the trunk of the car. Later he leads Scotland Yard to the destination by listening — railroad tracks, gravel, factory whistles — Peter was impressed with the man's ear and admired the technique, but it didn't work for him. All he could hear was road.

They left the main highway on a feeder, took their first right. They gained a road among low hills, the landscape sandy, the brown of hen's-eggs, broken by palm and thinning pine. The car slowed. Between two large palm trees was a security gate. The driver inserted a card, and the striped barrier raised.

Their car circled up a long oval drive. Flagstone had been set to form rude walks through the sand to housekeeping cottages. Each cabin had a name written in Arabic, and under, in English: Devachan, Kamaloka, Radiance, Assamma. States of wellness from various theosophies, mostly Eastern. Had Von Egger converted, committed himself to some New Age lamasery that sought the palace of light? A young couple passed the car as it was parking. They were dressed identically, in loose cotton robes the color of wheat, white towels turbaned around their heads. On their feet woven scuffs. Peter sexed them by extras — his light beard, a diamond twinkling on her long-fingered hand.

The driver waited. "Now what?" Peter said. The man flashed his twin six-shooter sign again. His job was over.

Peter got out, closed the door gently. He walked toward the largest building, up a path scored by rounded boulders. All the structures had a single design, built of river stone and mortar, roofs of orange tile. One story, trefoil arches over doors and windows. He walked inside. Cool and as dark as a cave. His eyes focused slowly and while they sought to find a shape he heard the thin and unsettling quarter-tones of a sitar. It was, Marcus said, the hell they would find for him. A band with nothing but bagpipes and sitars, for eternity, where he's the only sideman, he'd get every gig.

From Peter's unseeing periphery, a robed girl appeared. Very pretty and close enough to touch. She said something in a foreign tongue and bowed. Then, "Are you with us for a long visit?"

Peter squinted. "I'm here to see Mr. Von Egger."

She bowed again, tenting her hands to her chin.

"Please," she said.

She shuffled through the room. Peter followed. "Are you a nun?" he asked. He asked only to stop her again and see the color of her eyes, her form. It worked. She turned, and was smiling. She was strikingly beautiful.

"No, actually I'm an actress. But this is an excellent venue until I catch on. Lots of people in the business come here."

She opened the rear door and the sun sent Peter back into blindness. He thought to reach out, but there was no easy handhold on the bogus sarong.

There were more cottages in the rear. They followed a cobbled path by a stream. Koi and gauze-finned goldfish swam lazily, rose to feed when Peter's shadow crossed the surface. The water spilled over architected falls, through small soaking pools strategically placed near individual cabins. In some, floating without self-consciousness or clothes, were tanned and slender bodies. Their hands occasionally fanned the waters.

They passed a circle of people, some wrapped in the house sarong, others nude, sitting on a lawn and breathing deeply. The harmonic minor of the sitar played softly through speakers concealed in the trees. Far beyond a swimming pool, empty, a square-cut aquamarine, lay three or four wooden troughs. But for a half-foot shelf built around the edge, the troughs might have been coffins. In one lay a man — rather, reclined, for his back was supported by a redwood board that held his head above the slick. The trough was filled with a creamy mocha mud, and the man's face had been carefully smeared to the hairline. White cotton balls sat on his closed lids. The guide spoke.

"Mr. Von Egger, the gentleman you were expecting is here."

A skinny brown hand appeared from the ooze, indicated the neighboring tub. Peter sat on the lid. In moments, the young woman fetched a rattan chair and placed it for Peter with its back to the sun.

"Thank you," he said.

In reply, she lowered her hood, shook out her hair as if they might be being filmed, flashed an unmistakably practiced smile. In case he was in the business. If not, she'd cut him a personal piece of cinema to take home.

The hand had submerged. The two cotton wads made Von Egger appear bug-eyed and blind. He lay silently while the woman padded off. She shuffled to keep the slippers on her feet, and the wire-brush riff faded out like the end of an old record.

"Peter Kurz Steinmuller. You are still looking for the truth?"

"I'd like to hear what you know about it all."

"A better answer." Von Egger spoke slowly. He may have been relaxed or, as likely, concerned that the mud would seep if he became animated. "Someone who does not believe in love surely should not believe in the truth."

"I may want to change my answer," Peter said.

"About which of these fictions? Love or truth?"

"Now look," Peter said. He sensed this was his last chance. "I've listened to deceits and I've had to track down secrets and I'm tired. I can't afford much more. I have to earn a living." The hand reappeared. Two of its fingers lifted the cotton ball from the eye socket nearest to Peter. The white lid opened, and the glacier-blue eye beneath locked on him.

"You've shaved your beard," he said slowly. "It emphasizes your . . . resemblance to . . . " Peter waited for the name of his grandfather. " . . . youth. Now, you must understand that a secret and a deceit are two quite different things. A secret is something one person knows. A deceit takes two, the one deceiving and the one deceived. Do you not agree?"

"I would like no more parables." Peter heard his voice. "I would like the story."

"Ah yes," Von Egger said in an imitation of one who needed reminding. "The story." He replaced the cotton puff, lifted himself slightly onto the reclining board. The tank had been cut for someone shorter and the caps of his knees mounded the surface of the muck. A man in white pants and shirt came over, removed a thermometer on a plastic lanyard in the corner of the tub, adjusted a dial.

"You will excuse me if I take my restorative bath while we chat. I'm not sure I believe in all this, karmic clays and coriander enemas, but I suppose it cannot hurt."

Peter thought the mask at the top of the tub smiled, a smile formed by the smallest muscles in the face, but he couldn't be sure. Von Egger shifted a last time and began to speak.

Gideon has told me your odyssey in search of this story. I cannot think why. It must be clear to you by now that you have no claim whatsoever, that what I offered to settle on you was purely voluntary and that you cannot complain either at law or in conscience. You have been treated fairly.

You made an error in losing the money when you stayed in Europe, and I will not make a second by renewing my generosity.

I assume your energies are driven by some need to know more about your family. I will tell you what I can. It will not answer all your questions, but it is what I can contribute.

The brothers Steinmuller were each remarkable in their own way, and in a third. It was this, their traits were exactly antithetic. Hermann was a gifted musician, an artist, he believed somehow that art could change the world. I did not know him well — my only meetings with him were at his brother's direction. When Hermann first got involved to save unsaveable minions fleeing eastern Europe, he turned to Pietr for help. Pietr thought his brother misguided. One cannot save a nation, a region, even a city. Can a bank prevent an earthquake? Catastrophes are part of history, some of natural history, others of human history. Hermann took offense and called his brother heartless. They quarreled.

But Pietr was a shrewd businessman. Wherever there is a strong demand, there is opportunity. Is that heartless? The question has no meaning. Events are neutral.

Hermann kept at it, finding passage for a handful of families at a time. By 1943 he was ready for something larger. He undertook to capitalize his venture as you might a proper business. Pietr sent me to Budapest to meet with him, to inquire about this investment he was seeking. I do not recall the terms now, but it seemed a foolish undertaking. I spoke to ship merchants in Budapest, in Athens and Piraeus, in Istanbul. They were being taken advantage of. Nevertheless, we agreed to help. We opened accounts for their passengers, told them what questions to ask, how to bargain. They were so eager to get underway, to spend money they did not have. Eventually the *Artemis* was purchased and the voyage began.

It was a complete loss. One can argue that these people, had they not have been lost in the Bosporus, would have perished at one of the many camps in the darkness of Europe, Nazi or Soviet. They were doomed. But there were many alternative homes for that kind of capital.

There was one bright spot. The mere arrival of the Löwenhoft in Budapest generated enormous interest. We devised several accounts, all fee-based. You may think that was heartless, again, but is it more compassionate to let people go on without hope? Are they less desolate because they pay a small fee to open a bank account? Absurd. Their lot is identical. It is only their state of mind we are discussing. And believe me, these were reasonable charges to buy hope. It was in short supply and great demand. Reasonable charges.

I returned to Budapest several times. I treated Hermann and Kulek to a three-star dinner at Gündel's, which I should tell you that little Bolshevik enjoyed enormously. He detested me, but he managed to eat his way through a pound of Beluga. I made other trips to Budapest to convince Hermann that his brother's bank could do the same good work, for the same reasonable fees, up and down the Danube. Hermann, you see, had the contacts. They were all in touch with each other, all scurrying around long in nobility and short in cash. It was the perfect marriage.

But Hermann said no. He desperately wanted capital, but he would accept only properly motivated capital. That is an idealist's luxury. Would you accept a life-saving operation from a doctor even though his beliefs clash with yours? Of course you would. Only an artist or a fool worries over motivation. To the merchant banker it is a simple matter, one question. Is the reward commensurate to the risk involved?

We were closed off. Our attempts to establish the Löwenhoft on our own were undercut by Hermann's resistance. We needed the imprimatur of approval from within.

Hermann never should have been aboard the *Artemis* in the first place. He had a poor, pregnant wife in Switzerland and he was the leader of the efforts in Budapest. It was typical of his judgment that he subordinated his responsibilities to his enthusiasm for the voyage. He went down, and I went back to Budapest to convince Kulek.

Kulek could not make up his mind. On the one hand, he saw the sense in turning over his contacts to Brahms, to Pietr but he knew of the brothers' hatred for each other and he worried that the ghost of his dear drowned friend would haunt him if he did. Time was running out. This was an opportunity that would expire. I wired Pietr of the man's indecision and he wired back that the answer was in Deuteronomy. It was a joke, I was sure. Pietr had no interest in religion. Knowledge, yes, but not interest. He was, you know, a brilliant mind. Not merely business, but art, diplomacy, history. It was he who . . .

The sky had not a single cloud. Peter thought the man was about to stray. He pushed back his chair. The legs made a deep rubbing sound on the stones, a bowed sound. It worked. Von Egger came back.

He was a man who appreciated the complexities of life, its paradoxes. He went to Wadenswil. He showed her the passage in Deuteronomy that instructs a man to marry his brother's widow, and instructs her to obey. It is our duty, he argued. Before God. She was a country *hausfrau*. Once they were married all Marta's property became Pietr's. Hermann had kept notebooks, in a simple cipher. I solved them in an afternoon. Names, addresses, enough detail about their operations so that Pietr could appear clothed in his brother's confidence.

Pietr had assured her that the marriage was for holy purposes, to care for her and her child Florian. There was to be no sex. Soon after the wedding, mother and child were to be given enough money to relocate and live. But Pietr had a love of irony, and a certain bitterness towards his brother. He also had enough bisexuality to realize a practical joke. On the wedding night, he took her. A messy event, I'm sure, he had no real appetite and she resisted, but a joke on his dead but no less sanctimonious brother.

Marta shut herself up in Wadenswil after that, awaiting her chance to emigrate. I arranged the paperwork for her and her child. The boy was a sickly thing. At the last moment I was told that she was pregnant with a second, Pietr's child. It was an administrative nightmare. Entry to the U.S., for that is where she wanted to go, did not permit a second child. We would have to start over.

But it worked out. One of the sons died. I do not know which. She took the survivor , under the papers I'd prepared. We were rid of her. Months later Pietr was dead.

Who can say? He might have enjoyed a son. The prospect is not so dreary as one ages.

No matter what you think, Pietr Steinmuller was a man of honor. Should you choose to share my view of him you will enjoy a happier recollection of your ancestors. You see how free will functions. You can decide how to order your reminiscence.

Von Egger raised a hand. Mud dripped down his long arm. The tanned skin was only a shade lighter, but the underside of his arm, like the belly of a reptile, showed meaty white. The attendant strode over. His rubber soles made no noise on the flagstone. Von Egger rose from the tub, hoisting himself by placing his arms on either side. The attendant opened two valves at the rear of the vat to start a hose, held the water to his elbow for temperature. As his guest stood, prehensile and dripping ooze onto the cedar duckboards, he let the gentle flow wash Von Egger's body. The interview was coming to an end. Von Egger's last words triggered Peter's thoughts.

"But *was* he my ancestor? Which child is in the Wadenswil grave?"

The attendant unfolded an oversize Turkish towel and handed it to Von Egger. Petals and bits of bark fell from its midst. The fragrance was faint, a woody smell, almonds. He dabbed himself dry, then wrapped himself in the folds, covering himself from shoulder to thigh. The lavender deepened the glint of his eyes.

"I cannot answer all your questions. I had completed the documents for her emigration. Only one son was to accompany her, one named Florian. Whether it was that one or the other who died I cannot say. I only know that there was a death and a rushed funeral in her town. At the appointed hour she took the papers, the tickets, and sailed for the U.S. with a child named Florian."

Peter looked at him. The attendant toweled down his legs, held out a wheat-colored robe. Von Egger let the towel slip from his shoulders and fall to his heels, allowed the robe to be looped over his outstretched hands. The armholes rested across his biceps. He shrugged it on, raised its cowl. He could not have been unaware of his Biblical appearance, six-feet three, dark as a moor, standing blue-eyed and hooded in that desert sun.

He slipped his feet into the clogs that had been laid out for him and began to shuffle back towards the main house. Peter followed.

"Do not be dejected by this. You know more about your father's family now than most do. You know the tree, you simply do not know," and here he paused, peered around the hood's folds, "from which branch the seed fell."

"But that is the central question."

"My dear young man. What possible difference could it make? One tried to divert the course of history and the other made his living from it. Do you really think it matters? A minor choice. Not a degree of difference in the outcome. Minutes perhaps, seconds. That is now ancient, forgotten.

"Have you not noticed? The evils of the Holocaust have already been transformed. That is what we do to control the dangerous and fearful. Why do you suppose the artists of Lascaux draw the dreaded beasts of the night? We draw our enemies to make them venal. What does our television set do? A serial killer sells his life story. A wife-murderer appears on a talk show with other spouse murderers. The one who performs best is asked to return next week for a special, the killers of various family members. It is mimesis, art makes our fears small enough to fit on the screen.

"No less the Holocaust. What could be a better subject? It is unthinkable to kill a child. A single child. A child and her brother? Unthinkable. An entire household? More of a story. Perhaps think-able. A freighter of Moslem pilgrims? A commonplace. That is daili-ness, back-page news. The Holocaust represents a cultural project. We make movies and books, even a museum to recreate a death camp. Now it is a folk tale, it is your famous Indian fighter, Davey Crockett. In and out of fashion. Put it out of your mind. It has nothing to do with you."

With that he swung open a door at the end of the path. Peter had paid no attention to where they were walking, and followed him into the darkness, keeping close behind the whispers of his robe.

Off to the left in the dim light he heard his name spoken. "Mr. Steinmuller?" He looked to see a form approaching him. At the far end of the room, a second door opened and in the renewed light he recognized the driver who had brought him. The supplicant tone was new.

"May I take you back now?"

Peter stood while his eyes adjusted. Details of the room assembled themselves: leather-covered furniture, rustic, a coffee table, a mantlepiece. Von Egger was gone. It had been his exit that had briefly admitted the light.

Face-up on his bed Peter listened to the breeze of passing traffic. Did one need to know to which side he connected? His chances stood at fifty-fifty, and everyone was prepared to leave them at that. Fifty-fifty. A riddle — two hunters are in a field. A bird flies up in front of them and simultaneously they shoot. The bird falls. Does it belong to either? He remembered the riddle but not the solution.

The last words of Von Egger beat a rhythm. This has nothing to do with me. Moral suasion cannot be inherited, our sorry history proves we don't do any better from generation to generation. Deeds don't pass through the genes. Does it matter if I carry Hermann or Pietr's?

It had early on. When there was nothing else to anchor him, pinning down his genealogy had seemed important. That energy had disappeared, he had spent it on Helene's body, whispered it down her throat. Why did he care now? He was witness to a heist, a fifty-year old heist. And he was the only one who could set it right. The other witnesses had either quit trying, like Kulek, or, like Gideon and Von Egger, had their fingerprints on the shotgun.

There was a telephone booth outside his motel. A giant neon saguaro cactus fizzed red in the noon haze. He left the simplest of messages on the hotel voice mail for Helene.

Von Egger had again proved impregnable. The man moved from castle to castle. It was so cool, so detached. He could not be touched because he didn't care. He had no heirs, only assets. It was a paradox the old bandit would enjoy — he is the owner of heirless assets.

No heirs.

Peter sat up and pounded a fist against the wall, harder than he intended. A man in the next room called out. He had it — the price Von Egger would pay. The price fell on him, like missing notes in a chord, and like those notes it was perfect, it fit his fingers. His next call went to the New York firm Helene had come to see. They retrieved her from a meeting.

"Peter!" she said. "Exactly right. But you cannot do this, it is a crime?"

"No, not if I get his consent. It would begin to square accounts. Here's what I need. Some of it, you'll have to do, and fast."

"Fast, yes."

Peter spent the rest of the day on his tasks. There were not many. He arranged for the car, the packaging store. A taxi took him to the row of pawn shops. The cabbie warned him they were on the rum side of town. That turned out to be his side, the side of the Cactus Rest. He saw what he needed in the window of the first shop.

"Just the case?" the man asked. "This instrument's playable, despite the crack."

"Just the case."

"Sure? I make you a good price on the cello. You can keep it with the case. They belong together."

"Just the case. And the key."

"O.K.," the man gave in. "You play?"

"No."

"Listen," the pawnbroker urged. "Throw in two hundred bucks and take the cello, you can always learn. We all have music in us."

One last piece to the puzzle. It wouldn't help to flush him out, Peter needed to corner him in his den. Telephone information didn't help, nor did the county treasurer's tax rolls. He borrowed a crippled Yellow Pages from the motel office. There were three golf clubs in Rancho Mirage.

"Has Frederich Von Egger booked our start tomorrow?"

"Yes sir," the answer came back. "He's off at ten-eighteen. It says here alone. Shall I make that a double?"

"No that's fine. Leave it as it is. I'll just show up. Who do I ask for? Will you be on the desk?"

"Yes sir. Just ask for Jimmy."

"I will, Jimmy."

"And your name sir?" Peter spelled it out.

He was done for the day. The sun, his abiding wish as he traveled in and out of Europe's root cellars, was too bright for a walk. He retired to his room, turned up the television so its volume overcame the air-conditioner's bass note. Selector in hand he stared at the set for two hours. In that time, through fast finger-and-thumb combination he watched all of twenty-three channels. MTV had two cartoon kids lighting a firecracker in a cat's anus, a man in black and white was building a raft out of coke bottles to leave an island, a bald young man with an earring was chopping celery, a bosomy woman in a paneled office was asking a hospital orderly about love. Moe and Curly were dressed as girls, a cartoon bird was removing the lid of a bulldog's head, four parochial school principals were addressing homosexuality in the locker rooms (you could call in your views on a 900 line), a diamond ring was offered for under a hundred dollars, a fat woman in a yellow plaid jumper won a trip to Cancun, a man was crying for, he told Oprah, the first time, Barbara Eden saved the day dressed in a diaphanous blouse and harem pants. It seemed to Peter a single show, it was a single show, different windows to look in. The electron had exploded time and space so that many scenes occupied the same place at the same time. There were no longer three dimensions, but ten, a dozen. With a channel clicker you could set the entire culture spinning in a vortex, sit back and watch it land.

Peter watched a cold front descend yet again from Alberta, hit the power button and went for a walk.

It was difficult to elect out of this language of shared experience. Marcus did it. Von Egger for sure. How? You must start with undiluted selfishness. No apology, no explanation, no complaint. Peter walked into the west. Sights on the road extended what he had seen on the television set. Pennants flapped yellow and red at a Geo dealer, a real estate office flashed a video of a ranch house with pool to the oncoming traffic, a clown stood outside the car wash, scooping drivers in.

The riddle of his grandmother was solved. When his parents had named him Peter, they were honoring the man listed on her immigration papers as Marta's husband. They didn't know of the two marriages and the humiliation that Marta had suffered. Peter's christening refreshed that humiliation, as her grandchild was given the one name she hated.

He must have gone five miles. Nothing on the landscape changed, not the pennants, the free cappuccino and hot dogs, the parking lots. Only the sun moved, descended — the landscape was suspended by its own lack of density, it would never sink. The sun bulged at an angle precisely to irritate Peter's eyes, precisely to flash off every scrap of metal in the California desert and into the back of his head. He turned and walked the other way.

16

A THIRST AWAKENED HIM at early light. He had turned off the air conditioner during the night, and the only sounds in his morning were the
hum of the giant neon cactus, alternating in a minor third, and the
whoosh of traffic. He got up and filled a glass from the tap. The water
was the temperature of the dank air and tasted of tin. He peered
through the curtains. The desert sun bobbed through the haze, scaling
the electric wires. A Federal Express truck was pulling away from the
motel office.

The knock sounded as he was buttoning his jeans.

"You're up early," he said to the manager. "I hope my delivery
didn't wake you."

"Not at all. I rise with the market."

"The market," Peter said dully.

"The stock market. Opening bell is six-thirty our time."

The man stood at the door, regarded Peter suspiciously, reached in
the breast pocket of his shirt to adjust a hearing aid. Peter waited for
him to speak.

"You some celebrity?"

Peter laughed. "No. I don't think so."

"Well," said the man. "You a musician and all. The car that came
for you. The Bentley? Wife noticed. We don't get many Bentleys. She
thought you might be somebody."

"No, I'm really not."

The man was unconvinced. He smiled and waited for Peter's
confession.

"This is Palm Springs," he explained. "Sometimes we get somebody. Not here, you understand. But a friend from Cedar Falls —
that's where we're from, Iowa? — runs a motel 'cross town got Robert
Stack. *The Untouchables*? Just walked in and signed the register."

"I'm really not," Peter said again. He liked the fellow, didn't want
to disappoint him.

"And then, this." The man had a practiced cross-examination. He
produced the colorful box from behind his back, the surprise exhibit,
"This. You gotta understand, mister. Nothing personal. Our guests
don't get Federal Express."

"I promise," Peter said, opening the screen door to take the box.
The man didn't want to give it up quite yet. He eyed Peter knowingly.

"I promise. As soon as I am somebody, I'll let you know."

"Soon as you are, you'll stay at Gene Autry's Hotel. With the movie stars. Or worse, at our friend's place cross town. That's what happens."

"I'll stay here. Promise."

The man relented and handed Peter the cardboard mailer. The return label showed Helene's hotel.

She had assembled everything he asked for. Tape, packing materials. Peter studied the two news stories, one in German one in English. Helene had outdone herself. They were set in print, broadsheet style, and in the center of the columns was a picture of Von Egger. A file portrait, the picture of probity.

Next, the auction house materials. Consignment forms, disbursement instructions. An irrevocable power of attorney and a short handwritten checklist from Helene. One item was underscored. Damn — he had overlooked it. But perhaps there was still time.

The Yellow Pages were no help. He got a name from the manager. Mr. Caruso did that sort of thing, the manager thought, he might be willing to go along. The manager turned down the TV volume — the Dow Jones was advancing, the announcer said — and made a call. Yes, Mr. Caruso would consider it, named a fee. Peter agreed. Caruso could not leave before ten. My appointment, Peter almost said tee time, my appointment is at ten-eighteen. We'll never make it. Best I can do is ten, said Mr. Caruso.

He returned to his room. He went through Helene's package to make sure he hadn't missed anything else. At the bottom of the stack was a single sheet of paper, with one sentence neatly typed and translated.

Hic quem creticus edidit Daedalus est labyrinthus e quo nullus vadere quivit ni Theseus nec hic ni Ariadnae stamine iutus amore.

This is the labyrinth which the Cretan Daedalus built, out of which no person can find his way except Theseus, nor he, unless helped by the thread of Ariadne, for love.

A late model Chevrolet, green with a lemon limousine sticker in its windshield, picked him up early. They waited in front of Desert Fruits and Vegetables, and at exactly ten o'clock Mr. Caruso appeared. He was a stubby man, teeth yellow as sand. The black crepe suit he wore fit tightly around his chest. They shook hands, Caruso asked him for the money, and Peter paid in cash.

Peter's blood ran warm and anxious as the car sped to his rendezvous with Von Egger. Traffic filled the center of Palm Springs. The driver caught Peter's eye in the mirror, turned to assure him. It is not your fate, the crease in his brow said. Traffic ensnares us all.

A hand-wrought birch sign marked the elegant subdivision that surrounded the golf club. They took a cobbled turn-in past chrysanthemums and cabbage plants, to a white gate-house with shingled roof. The driver let his window fall and Peter leaned forward and spoke to the guard.

"Mr. Steinmuller as Mr. Von Egger's guest. Call Jimmy at the pro shop."

The barrier raised and they wound their way through the ghetto of mansions. There was no movement. The cars were garaged, utilities buried, the people safely housed. They passed tennis courts, two with small galleries, luxuriantly grassed berms separating them from the vacant streets. Elaborate pools the colors of fantasy, houses that stretched out like aircraft carriers. The cab steered through a flotilla of the anonymous and heliotropic rich. The streets were empty but for a desultory sweeper and a Latino lining up trash cans on a balloon-wheeled cart.

Late. It was quarter to eleven. Jimmy confirmed that Mr. Von Egger was out on the course. Peter looked over the manicured expanse. Should he chase after him? It would be chasing him about in a circle — in golf you come out at the beginning.

"He won't be long," Jimmy was there to serve. "He only plays nine and he's by himself. Wait if you like."

A video was running on the television. Improve your short game. A golfer lofted balls into the air while a fluoroscope showed his spine on the screen. Every few minutes, a man in a yellow blazer came on and talked about a real estate development in Palm Desert. Peter preferred the breaks. The man was amiable and indelibly sincere. Several people who'd bought lots appeared and confirmed the truth of what he said, greying couples who stood with their arms stiffly around each other, pleased to be there. Over the announcer's shoulder, fully fleshed, the golfer who had given the pointers swung rhythmically at a line of balls. He would pop one up, take a step, pop up another. Balls flew like swallows, the same arc, hunting insects against the Kodachrome grass.

Peter had no idea how long it took to play nine holes. He sat on a leather and chrome chair and read a magazine, his courage slipping from its pages like a response card. He was thinking of the sound of the whirring club when he heard Von Egger's voice behind him.

"Our friend Gideon was right. You are indifferent to danger, economics, and good manners. A troublesome combination."

Peter rose and turned. Von Egger was looking down, scribbling on a card in his hand. His tone might have been the gloat of a man who spied his prey, or merely a self-satisfied, avuncular scold. Peter recalled what he had thought to be the hospitality of the man on the shore of Lake Geneva, and resolved to listen more carefully.

"Persistence and impertinence. Perhaps you should join the paparazzi."

"I would appreciate some time."

"And I some privacy." Von Egger pronounced this last word with a short *i*, in the English fashion.

"I have a business proposal for you. No questions, just a proposal." Don't repeat yourself, don't sound scared. Like Marcus' advice to a new man: just two things to remember, don't be nervous and don't screw up.

Von Egger studied him. The height of his stare was a weapon, the archer's parapet. The man always assumed a military advantage. He let his gaze drop and finished his scorecard.

"A proposal," he might be considering a joke whose punch line he didn't get. "From an itinerant musician. What might it be? Come."

"I have a car. Someone waiting."

"Jimmy will direct it to my house. It will meet us there. You'll come with me." Von Egger dropped the card and the stubbed pencil on the glass case by the desk and strode out. Peter went to his rented limo, assured Mr. Caruso, and retrieved the cello case. Then he hurried to catch his host.

"Are you going to serenade me? Let me guess, that is a tommy gun and this is a stick-up." Von Egger folded himself into a golf cart parked by the putting green. Peter ignored his questions and sat beside him.

Von Egger was dressed in gay colors that showed his skin darker, his eyes brighter. He steered down the asphalt path. Were they going to meet up with his bodyguards? to the tenth tee? The cart moved on noiseless wheels, pushed along in an electric whine.

They veered from the approach to a green and onto a dirt path. Through a windbreak of thin pine. A metal gate opened — Von Egger must have triggered it with a remote device that Peter hadn't seen. The gate gave access through a low stone fence. Behind, overlooking the fairway, lay a large, modern house built of river rock. The cart had entered Von Egger's grounds from the rear.

They drove around an oval filled with proportioned cactus in pastels, sage, cabbage, purple. At the turn stood a small fountain, water trickling over flat rocks, and behind it a bronze. The statue of a young man was Greek in inspiration but clearly modern in the rendering. The torso was hollow bronze, open like a hand puppet, the cut going from thigh to opposite rib. The youth leaned on a sill and gazed wistfully down the fairway.

Von Egger steered to a cement pad by the garage and got out. A middle-aged man, muscular neck, dressed in white shirt and black wash pants, came up and unstrapped the golf bag from the shelf at the rear of the cart.

"Edward, this is Mr. Steinmuller. He will be with us while I change for lunch, but he won't be joining us. I don't mean to be unsociable," turning to Peter, "but I haven't yet decided whether to have you arrested or simply thrown out. I have friends coming in an hour. What do you wish to tell me?"

Von Egger turned and strode over the patio. The mid-day sun might char sugar. He slid open a glass door and entered upon a large kitchen. Two women cooked and took no mind of them. Peter followed carrying the case, spoke to the length of his back.

"Before we talk . . . " Some licks you rehearse. "If you have a minute, I'd like to see your collection."

"You know of my little gathering?" Von Egger stopped and turned. They were in a wide hall leading to the living quarters. He had taken off his shirt, and held it in a loose ball in his hand.

"It's quite famous."

Von Egger received these words with undisguised pleasure, tipped his head in a shallow bow. "You flatter me. But it *is* worth seeing. The finest antiquities of each period, and its defining curiosity, all the pieces relate to war. Come."

He reversed course. Peter stepped back as he passed. He was lean and remarkably muscular for his age. They moved into a space with smoked skylights. It had been designed as a gallery, and the hush and controlled climate created a sanctuary. A pea-sized bulb blinked red on the wall. Von Egger punched a number into the keypad beneath, the light turned green, and he stepped down into a sunken center. Around the edges of the room were glass and chrome etagères, their gleaming shelves filled with small figures. Halogen spots illuminated each piece, netsuke in ivory and jade, small stone carvings. Beneath every one was a card carefully lettered and dated. On its own crystal pillar, lit from above, the faience of the Minotaur. His amulet, Peter recalled Von Egger's term. It travels with its captor. Von Egger ran his eye impatiently around several shelves, snatched up a piece, he might have just won it from a chessboard, and handed it to Peter.

Peter looked at the carving in his palm. "All bought," he said, "with the blood money of the Löwenhoft."

Von Egger pursed his lips, touched his fingers to them studiously before answering.

"It is popular to say that no one wants war, but it isn't true. If no one wanted it we would not have it. You suppose it persists because of negligence? Because it produces great technical advances, sulfa drugs, the reciprocating engine?

"You know of course that warriors bred the horse. First the Huns, then the Turks and Mongols. They bred for a strong back, to ride in a control position, not," and he tapped the piece in Peter's hand, "on the rear. Ninth Century B.C., I think you'll find. Assyrian.

"So the horse develops and is used for plowing and transport. Do you think those benefits were of any interest to the breeders? The breeders were interested in victory. Blood money is a charged term. All monies are touched by blood. To understand human nature is to be able to live amid its horrors, to feed off the carrion it inevitably leaves in its wake."

Peter studied the piece in his hand. It was green stone. A warrior with a drawn dagger sat astride the hindquarters of a horse. "Maybe so. And maybe some of us are overfed."

Von Egger looked carefully at his guest, deciding whether to take insult. He chose instead to be entertained.

"That is merely a question of disposition. Some of us are better at it than others, some of us more interested. You, for instance, you could learn quite easily. Yet if I offered you an apprenticeship you would decline. You are interested in music, not politics or commerce. Excuse me."

He spoke to one of the staff through an open door, disappeared down the hall. Peter looked about. Toy soldiers stood in poses of rest and attack. Directly in front of him a Persian officer carved in marble pushed his shield forward. Tiny as it was you could make out his brow and minatory frown. Take courage. When Peter next looked around, Von Egger was striding towards him completely unclothed. Peter shrank back as Von Egger reached for him. He took the horseman from Peter's hand, amusement showing in the flare of his nostrils, and replaced it on the shelf.

"Come. If you don't mind the sun."

The exigency of Von Egger's announcements was, Peter understood, part of the theater. As in any stage play once you saw the effort the scenes lost much of their effect.

Von Egger strode through the kitchen. Outside Edward had folded a white Turkish robe on a patio chair. On the table, under the shade from a royal blue umbrella, sat glasses of iced tea. Beads of frost, thickly sliced lemon and sprigs of green mint. Von Egger walked to the end of a pool, perhaps twenty-five meters in length, poised at its edge, and as the music started did a racing dive into the electric blue water.

Peter recognized the horn on the first notes. No one else played that way, Desmond's alto floating and easy. Desmond was a musician Peter admired, the way he found a line, just like walking out in the morning. Von Egger cut through the water, otarian, a leatherback come to land. Desmond blew on. *So I say to myself, get ahold of yourself.*

A short, Latin woman set the pitcher of tea on the table. In the middle of a tune, mid-phrase, the music stopped. It occurred to Peter — the music was a timer, to clock Von Egger's exercise. For a reason Peter couldn't name, the insight gave him confidence.

It was all a matter of confidence. How was he to persuade Von Egger? He hoped his arguments would move the man around, like a piece on a chessboard, until one of the squares opened its trap door.

Von Egger donned the robe and vigorously toweled his head. He combed back his silver hair. Then he rotated the umbrella so that his chair was in the sun. Drops of water fell to the hot slate around his chair and showed the colors of the stone. It was just noon.

"Moral choice is an illusion," Von Egger began. He held his guest in his eye. "Acts count, nothing else. Once you act, you crush the choice that came before. And so free will is both a necessity and an irrelevance. It is what we see in the rear-view mirror."

The man's features showed little sign of time. A tattoo of small tracings, red and purple, appeared in the pinpoint vessels about his nose.

"Bullshit," said Peter. "It takes energy to keep moral choices ahead of the acts, but people do it. People do it all the time. Hermann did."

Von Egger addressed him in bright voice.

"Hermann thought he could combat cruelty and sorrow in the world. That is like combating fog. The truly arrogant are those who believe they make a difference. They hide their arrogance in humility. They believe they are doing God's will, since God inflicts pain to test our faith. It is consummate arrogance. The rest of us merely play at God, but we realize it is a game."

Peter leaned forward. The move made Von Egger sit back.

"It's a *game*? Are you telling me that cruelty is make-believe?"

"Cruelty is quite real. But it is one of the two ways we humans act godly. We cannot be immortal, we cannot be everywhere, we cannot be invisible. But we can inflict pain without motive. That skill is peculiarly human."

"Two ways. The other is . . . ?"

"Sex, of course. Procreation, something from nothing. Sex and cruelty."

"And so some have sex to become godlike."

"To *play* at God. Only the deluded think they will become God. And others," here Peter thought the man blinked an eye, sent a flickering sign, "and others practice sex not to imitate God but to mock Him."

"So for the right stakes conscience can be overcome."

"Conscience is merely the absence of appetite. If our appetite for acting godly is satisfied then we indulge morality. If not . . . ." Von Egger shrugged, gave his head a brisk shake. He wore a noseclip on a pink rubber necklace around his neck. Peter only just noticed it.

Peter had his next argument ready. "To act as if there is nothing to be done about it avoids your choices. It says, I'll live my life on the sidelines and so I will have been right."

"When we try to change our predicament, then, we mock ourselves. An example. The Jewish people adopt the six-pointed star. The Magen David, literally the shield of David. But as it came to pass in Germany the shield protected no one. Quite the opposite."

"You speak as if you're not there. As if you're removed." Peter led him in. He had counted on Von Egger's taste for debate. You push one way, he pushes back.

"To act any other way would be hypocrisy. I *am* removed."

Put on your nose clips, buddy. You're about to dive in.

Von Egger raised his empty glass. Edward made to come forward, but Von Egger languidly put up his hand. Then he clinked his glass against Peter's in a dry toast.

"To making a difference. Now I must ask. Your proposal, sir." He pointed to the case Peter had carried with him. "Or your serenade."

Peter took a breath. "You are going to share your wealth with your heirs."

"I beg your pardon."

"You are a rich man. You have no children, no one you care about. Your wealth is ill-gotten and you yourself are a fraud. I am going to fill this instrument case with your carvings. You'll sign an irrevocable power of attorney allowing me to sell them and dispose of the proceeds as I see fit."

Von Egger let slip a laugh, a cat releasing a butterfly she can catch again.

"Preposterous. This is your proposal?

Peter nodded. His throat was dry.

"I am to do this because you suggest it?"

"You are to do it because it is doing right, and because you are at the end of your life."

The man raised an incredulous brow.

"You are calling upon me to do right?" he asked.

"I am."

A snort. "How very quaint."

Peter struck the wrought-iron table with his palm. The tea glasses jumped. In that still and dusty air the violence of the move startled them both, and made Von Egger wince.

"Listen to me. You've been living in a world of art and artifice. You've been living a lie. The show's about to start, it's time to buy your way back in."

Peter's anger seemed to bemuse the old man. "To buy my way back in. But my dear Steinmuller, you don't understand. I don't want back in. I've seen the coming attractions."

"Then you will do it for your own preservation. *Primum vivere.* You'll do it because if you don't, I will tell the story." Peter handed across the German version that Helene had written. Von Egger scanned it and looked up.

"That is how the story will look in the *Neue Züricher Zeitung*. I have the same release for New York and Geneva. We can even run it in Palm Springs. You'll be famous."

He handed across the English version. It included Von Egger's official bank portrait, the one used in the annual report. The face in the starched collar was stern and composed; the one in front of Peter showed the slightest line of doubt.

The man lay the paper on the table and stared. One hand went to the rubber necklace and fingered the prongs of the clip.

"These are allegations," he said, his eyes still lowered. He turned the nose clip over. "There is no proof."

Peter gave him the Kulek statement. It was of course a bluff. Helene had drafted it and forged the old socialist's signature.

Von Egger raised his head.

"One piece of paper. Signed by a lunatic, a Hungarian." Peter sat motionless. It was his turn to hold the target in the cross hairs. The old man changed his attack.

"Do you know what you are saying?" Von Egger's voice wavered with a new grace note. "You could take away millions of dollars in that ridiculous case. Millions in merely a few pieces. I have spent a lifetime collecting them."

"A lifetime of savings, gone. How fitting."

"I could have you jailed for this." Peter watched his prey carefully. "I could have you arrested for extortion. You have no corroboration. It's preposterous."

Peter delivered the next page. It was a summary of Fedderman's testimony, again doctored on Helene's computer to look official. The paper trembled in Von Egger's hand and he set it on the table. He looked up through narrowed eyes. In its fury, his voice raised a quarter-tone.

"Allegations, nothing more. The fables of some drowned Polish Jew."

Peter said nothing. Offered Von Egger the excerpt of the State Department report he'd dictated to Helene. The old man held this at arm's length. He made no move to conceal the shaking of the paper.

When he finished reading, he muttered to himself. "The medal."

"The medal," Peter echoed. And without taking his eyes from the man handed over the glossy print of an evening at Gündel's.

Von Egger's grip creased the photograph. He was squeezing the paper so hard, the tremor increased, his arm might be acting without him. Suddenly the arm shot forward and swept the little pile of sheets off the table, came back again and this time knocked off both tea glasses and the crystal pitcher. Glass splattered on the flagstone, cubes of ice and glass shards skittered across the patio.

Edward came running, and close behind the man who had been Peter's driver. They stopped when they saw the bent old man. They must have decided he was in no physical danger, and withdrew. When Edward reappeared he carried a broom and dust pan.

Von Egger raised his head at the sound of the sweeping. His voice was a whisper.

"No one would care," he said. The shiver in his eyes betrayed him. "It was so long ago."

Peter replied at once. "You think not? Perhaps you're right. Perhaps only in Israel. Or your Swiss neighbors, or perhaps merely the U. S. State Department. Or Sixty Minutes."

The man let the photograph slip from his fingers and fall to the ground. Peter took the gesture as surrender. He stood. He had one more argument to use.

"This completes the circle. You will release the moneys that have been frozen in these pieces of stone. It's what your children would want you to do."

Had Peter pushed him too far? The man stared up, his jaw hung slack. In the back of his eyes passed the quickest spasm, a crack in the glass. What had the man seen?

"Children?" The man grabbed Peter's shirt to hoist himself and pull him close.

"If you and Pietr had a son he would want you to do this."

Von Egger's face was inches away. Peter could feel his own breath bouncing off the man's cheek.

"A son?"

Again a silence. A long silence. Water in the pool scuppers made a rude rasp as it was sucked out and pumped to be cleansed.

Von Egger looked confused. Then he put his head back and let out a cracked laugh.

"A son. So the union of Frederich and Pietr produces a putative heir who robs their estate. Justice at her most ironic."

Peter would need to move quickly. Still he kneeled and picked up the photo.

"How do I know," Von Egger asked as Peter took up the cello case, "that you will not return to extort more?"

"You have my word. Like my namesake, I'm a man of honor."

In his robe Von Egger looked like a fighter whose corner would not let him out for the next round. He took his sleeve and blotted beads of sweat from his mouth. He gazed at Peter with a new recognition.

He spoke at last.

"The alarm is off."

Peter turned towards the house. "I'm not sure it will all fit in the case. If not, you'll need to tell me what is of value."

Von Egger glowered at him. "I'll do no such thing."

Peter checked for the steady green light. He lay the case on the floor and unsnapped it, removed the bubble wrap and tape. He started with the Minotaur, placing it cozily in the center of the case. Smaller pieces fit in the neck. The Assyrian horseman he set snugly into the box designed for resin and extra strings. The four snaps of the case latched with a satisfying chunk. He looked around at the empty shelves. White cards reflected back the halogen light. He was done.

When he returned to the pool deck, Von Egger had not moved.

"You'll need to sign these." He placed several pages in front of the robed man. Von Egger began to read.

"Mmmm," a grunt of satisfaction. The man was recovering. "You have named yourself as agent for the incoming commission, I see." Peter looked. Helene had filled in his name for the four percent finder's fee. "I am delighted that the burglar has some pocketbook stake in his burglary. He will not be so pious. He shows himself to be at least the moral heir of my Pietr. Also, in some perverse way my closest relative. As he perversely observes."

Von Egger read on. "Aha," he crowed. "Your little scheme is blocked. You have *not* thought of everything."

"What is it?" If he lingered to debate Von Egger, it wouldn't work.

"These forms. And the power of attorney. They require a notary. I am not leaving these grounds."

Peter turned and signaled the waiting servant.

"Edward. There is a green Chevy parked in front of the house. In the back seat a Mr. Caruso is waiting. Would you please tell him that he is on."

"On, sir?"

"On."

Peter turned back and tried to keep his smile from spreading. "My Kulek," he explained.

HE LAY SPREAD ON his bed in the peace of his triumph. There was a logic to it all, a progression that linked his past and Von Egger's to the pasts that had been lost. Dominant to tonic. No more travels, no more plans, he had crossed over. He called for an airline reservation, walked across to the little glass restaurant and ordered the same meal he had the night before. The New York strip, baked with the works, a bottle of the Heineken dark. Back in Manhattan he'd go see the union office. Introduce himself. Hang around the rehearsal hall for a day or two. He'd get on. Maybe cut a demo tape. If you want out of the saloons, you need to sell yourself.

He thought of calling Helene and decided against it. This news celebrates better in person.

It was a particular peace, and it sustained through the steak, the Thousand Island, through a second Heineken.

It might have sustained him through the night, but an hour before dawn a siren rattled his tinny room. Peter grabbed the packed case and rushed to the window. Had Von Egger changed his mind and turned him in? In his underwear he watched an orange and white ambulance stop in front of the apartment building across the street. What had Marcus said of their cruise? A land of the newly wed and the nearly dead. Palm Springs too. That ambulance driver has himself a steady gig.

He was wide awake and despite the premature alarm fully refreshed. There was no reason to wait for the later flight. He tossed his few things into the bag, called a cab. It flew to the terminal. The joy of a new day's air running by at seventy, eighty miles an hour. He would have driven it exactly the same, punched the same green holes into the same yellow lights. Down to the last of his borrowed funds, Peter scrounged a tenner for the tip.

There was a pre-dawn flight to Chicago, he wanted to be moving. He stood by and, too early for crowds, got a window seat. Pretty women in uniform smiled at him and he grinned back a mild, infectious lunacy. By running the concourses, the ticketing agent told him, he could get a nonstop from O'Hare to LGA. Too close for her to write it up that way, not a legal connection, but he could run, he looked young and fit. Be careful with that cello.

"I will," he promised.

A close connection. If he made it that would get him into La Guardia hours earlier. Helene would be downtown at her meetings. Bestockinged in white tights, working her financial witchcraft.

He snugged down in one of the aft-most seats. Virtue had its first reward and the door closed with the row all to himself. Going east the starboard side gave him a southerly prospect. They took off in darkness. He stuck his nose to the porthole. Amber bulbs lined the runway like potted sunflowers, sunk so that their thick lids were flush with the tarmac. Threshold lights pointed his way, night's arrow.

The airplane climbed out steeply and set its course to the north and east. A trickle of pink leaked through the sky. The pilot came on. His voice was fresh as coffee.

"To avoid reported turbulence, we'll first level off at twenty-one thousand, then climb to our cruising altitude. We'll be flying today almost to the height of the tropopause. That's the layer that separates the troposphere from the stratosphere. Visible weather occurs in the troposphere, clouds and moisture, and temperature declines there at the rate of two degrees Celsius for every thousand feet of gain. Breakfast will be served as soon as we hit cruise altitude. Our course this morning will take us over Lake Mead, northern Utah, the length of Wyoming and South Dakota, across Wisconsin and into O'Hare. We've got ourselves a quartering tail wind and we should arrive ahead of schedule."

Peter fetched a pencil from the stewardess and wrote the word on his boarding stub. Tropopause. He would bring it to Helene as a gift.

The aircraft dropped its nose and set itself straight and level. One note. Below, the landscape lay dark, black until you saw Lake Mead, blackest of all. The earth turned slowly and Peter's airplane, moved by the heart within it and impatient with its pace, raced towards the spreading stain of day.

Peter slipped the card with the new word into his pocket and closed his eyes. Felt the warm rush in his blood, the passion. Passion, she had said it in a voice that a child would use for a secret, a voice low and darksome, passion is all. He knew that to be true. You didn't need to know the tune or know the facts. Knowledge counts for very little. Knowledge does not drive life. Passion and connection. Those are the engines.

When he got back to town, he'd go down to the union office. His 802 card, the New York local, was still current and he probably knew a few people. He'd get a call.

Shadow and spot began to reveal the canyons of Utah. At their first altitude the colors were illuminated — melon and umber, seal grey, rufous, slate, buff. In the absence of sound, the colors flourished. The landscape of the desert revealed itself, legible as a book while the light spread over it. Not flickering, but rolling, luminous. Resolved in a single moment of clarity.

The aircraft tilted up for a second climb. As it rose, the geology below flattened out into unremitting prairie. Morning had arrived, and that slant of light that had lustered the ridges now yielded to direct sun. The earth lay faded and all but featureless. They flew above all visible weather.

Night's arrow, sprung from the bowstring, no digression, no losing the way. Arrow in flight, alone in physic and arc, ever on point. He would make the Chicago connection, arrive hours early. Helene would still be at work, he visualized her leaning across a conference table talking patiently, determined and eventually getting her way. It would be mid-afternoon, too early for her to be at the hotel. But perhaps he could conjure her home, he had her word in his pocket. He would think her back from the apogee of his journey and be there, be there she might.

The auction house made the transaction easy. They were pros, they did this all the time. Their New York office took delivery from Peter's hand with no visible dismay over the oddly packed valuables. Over the years, they had received diamonds secreted in books that had holes carved in their center pages, Flemish oils rolled into PVC pipe designed to carry sewage.

The arrival of a collection of museum-quality carvings in a chenille-lined cello case was unusual. "But," as the Director of Fine Art said as he oversaw the unsnapping of the case and personally removed each sheet of bubbled plastic, "it is not the wrapper that signifies, it's the popsicle." He uncovered all of the pieces and set them on the several maple library tables in his office. He plucked off his white gloves, turned to the two men from the mail room, and shrugged his head in a satisfied nod.

The two were dismissed — actually only one had been needed, the second was there for security, a regular procedure — and the Director pressed his intercom. Within minutes he was joined by two others, each a scholar of some renown. The staff documents expert went to work comparing the signature on the auction house form with the one they had on file. Frederich Von Egger had an active account, although until today he had always appeared on the buy side. At some point most customers change sides — it was not a peculiar pattern, accumulation and divestiture, even for the most devout collector. The markets, divorce, business reversals, and after all the pitfalls of economic life had been avoided, death.

"Perhaps," said the handwriting expert, frowning at the computer screen on which he had projected his analysis, "perhaps Mister Von Egger is running short of funds." The Director said nothing, intending his silence to disapprove the incommodious remark. A client's finances were never discussed in front of an outsider.

The second person was that outsider, despite all the time she had spent at this firm. She was the curator of the Greek and Persian collections at the Metropolitan Museum, only blocks away, and while her appearance at this unveiling might present a conflict of interest to the auction house, for indeed they hoped that the Met would be an active bidder for these very pieces, that conflict was a small price to pay for her judgment. There was no one like her for spotting a fraud, she had at least one eye, the Director liked to tell her, from the Fifth Century B. C. E.

"These signatures," said the man to his computer screen, "are a match. No doubt about it." The Director thanked him and excused him from the room. He didn't have to ask the curator, whose magnified stare was caressing a frieze of the Minotaur of Knossos. He could tell it was authentic from the expression on her face.

One month later to the day, Peter and Helene were in the office, to review a mock-up of the catalogue for the sale. The draft was missing certain information, the date and place of sale, the estimated prices. Its cover featured a photograph of the Minotaur. Many of the other pieces had their own full-page display, and each was accompanied by a scholarly description. No provenance was given nor was Von Egger's name mentioned, though the auction firm's antiquities expert had assured them that everyone in the field would know. The collection had a wide following.

"May we see a list of estimates?" Helene asked.

"Certainly," said the Director and handed her a sheet from his desk.

"These prices," Peter asked. "They seem very high."

"Those are approximations of sale levels," the Director told him. "We publish estimates merely to establish a framework, so bidders can decide whether they're interested. I think you'll find they will prove out to be low."

Helene scanned the list professionally, sharpened pencil in hand, and placed a neat checkmark by the auction house total. She dealt regularly with numbers in this neighborhood, but the figure made Peter gasp.

"What" he whispered drily to her, "what is four percent of that?"

She jotted the number, left to right. He reached over and squeezed her knee.

They'd already decided on what to do with the balance. The first check to Helene, to repay her several advances. A second to the Fort Lauderdale nursing home. The commission would bring an astonishing sum for Helene and him. Everything after the commission was to be remitted in a single distribution, anonymously and by bank draft, to the World Refugee Committee.

"There is one hitch," the Director said. "You'll notice we haven't filled in the venue for the sale. To draw the strongest bidders for these pieces we need to reach the Mideast collectors. They don't often cross the Atlantic. So we recommend our London gallery for the auction itself. Is that a problem?"

"Why would it be?" asked Helene.

"It has certain disadvantages," he explained solicitously. "It will be inconvenient for you to attend."

"No, by coincidence I'm on my way there," said Peter. "We'll be moving there."

"Also, if you wish to get same-day credit on your money, the funds will need to be deposited in a foreign bank. You could use London or Paris or, if you prefer, Switzerland."

Peter beat Helene to the question.

"Could we use the Löwenhoft?"

"Of course. One of the most respected Swiss banks."

The Director thought it odd that of all the good news he'd brought them — the quality of the collection, the demand for the pieces, the considerable fortune the sale would bring — it was this bit of information that made them giddy.

They turned from grinning at each other, and Peter spoke. "Switzerland, then. Switzerland will be fine. Better than fine. What's better than fine?"

The Director shrugged. "Ducky?" he offered.

"Exactly. Switzerland will be ducky."

Acknowledgments

This book and its characters are a fiction. To use historical fact I referred to several sources including *The Last Escape* by Aliav and Mann; *Safety in Numbers* by Nicholas Faith; *A Chorus of Stones* by Susan Griffith; Johr's *Swiss Credit Bank;* and *Escaping the Holocaust* by Dahlia Offer. Thanks also to Christopher Crowley, New York; Nell London, Denver; Fritz W. Meyer, Fechy, Switzerland; and Ruth R. Wisse, Cambridge.